MW01135401

The African Son

James C. Johnston Jr.

For Ann Marie
Best Wishes,
Jim Johnston

iUniverse, Inc.
Bloomington

The African Son

iUniverse books may be ordered through booksellers or by contacting:

iUniverse
1663 Liberty Drive
Bloomington, IN 47403
www.iuniverse.com
1-800-Authors (1-800-288-4677)

ISBN: 978-1-4502-8117-1 (pbk)
ISBN: 978-1-4502-8115-7 (cloth)
ISBN: 978-1-4502-8116-4 (ebk)

Printed in the United States of America

iUniverse rev. date: 3/2/2011

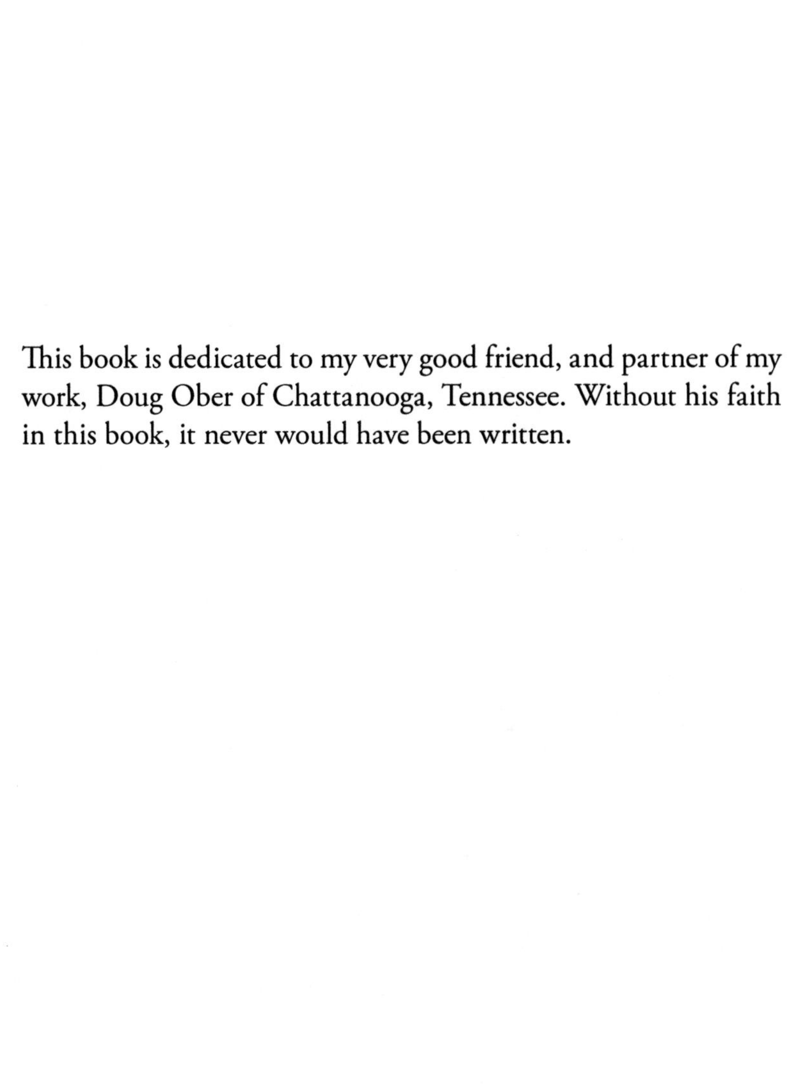

This book is dedicated to my very good friend, and partner of my work, Doug Ober of Chattanooga, Tennessee. Without his faith in this book, it never would have been written.

CHAPTER I

The cattle moved slowly as they grazed under the broiling African sun. They were fat and lazy with the satisfaction of their hunger. They were content to be chewing the sweet grasses that sprang from the rich grazing lands of the vast plains. The black rich loam, that supported the verdant splendor that surrounded the warrior tending the cattle, was the envy of all the people of the southern part of Africa. It was Atachawayo who was in charge of his father's cattle this day. His ancestors had seized these lands at the point of a spear. Atachawayo knew that his people were the mightiest warriors of all Africa. The Matabele were "The Chosen of Heaven". All of their subject peoples, including the Mashona knew this, submitted to their natural authority, and had survived as a result of their submission. The Matabele had ruled over these lands through the sheer force of their will and iron discipline. This discipline was key to their prowess in battle.

The Matabele had held sway over this vast expanse which was their empire since they had moved into the area sweeping all before them about 1652. The British had only now newly arrived to the south of the Matabele. They had landed in far away Cape Town, a hundred and sixty two years after both the Matabele and the Dutch had set their feet on this soil. The British knew that the Matabele were the masters of their empire as did the Dutch

Boers who had lived nearby in the countryside. Since the British victories in Europe, the Boers had unwillingly become subject to the rule of the island kingdom. These white men, of two different European nationalities, knew the value of the Matabele's territorial prize, but they had their own hands full with other problems and had not cast their greedy eyes upon it.

The British had to be ever watchful of the Boers, because these two European peoples hated one another. The old Dutch settlers were resentful that conditions in Europe, over which they had no control, had ended their rule in southern Africa. What these two white races had thought to be the end of a quarter century of warfare in Europe, with the fall and exile of Napoleon Bonaparte to Elba, had proven to be nothing more than a temporary delusion. A quarter century of bitter warfare had not come to an end as it was believed in 1814 when the pocket-sized emperor was demoted to rule over his tiny realm.

Now the European struggle was springing to life again, because this former Emperor of the French had fled his little island kingdom of Elba, which had been given to him almost as an insult as his sole domain after his fall from his position as the world's strongest and greatest monarch. The great Napoleon deeply resented the fact that he had been given this little piece of Europe to rule and on which to waste away amid the ruins of his imperial dreams. This tiny kingdom was an abominable mockery of his life, and he hated it. After months of confinement, the great Napoleon had embarked with his thousand men on fourteen ships for France, where he was welcomed by the very men who had fought and bled for him during his glory years. In this pocket sized warrior, the hopes of empire reawakened in France. The French were tired of the dreariness of the dull old Bourbon king thrust upon them. The rest of Europe, drained by twenty-five years of war trembled and girded itself once again for battle with this son of the revolution of '89.

To the young Matabele warrior, this war in far away Europe was nothing to concern him. Europe was very far away indeed.

Even the transplanted Europeans in the area dared not disturb the peace of the Matabele. Atachawayo's own world was wide and vast enough to hold all of his ambitions and dreams. The Matabele needed no more conquests, but they were always ready to defend that which was theirs. This Atachawayo also knew, and this fact made him proud. He knew almost from birth exactly what place he held in this world and what lofty positions awaited him.

He had heard his father and the other chief men of the Matabele nation talking about what occupied the minds of the white men in Cape Town now that the old bastions of reactionary rulership had risen up under the Autocrat of all the Russians, the Emperor of Austria, the Prussians, the English, and other frightened kings and princes of Europe who wanted to reclaim their power. The course of human progress had been betrayed and corrupted since the days of that bloody French Revolution of 1789 that had shaken the dozens of great and minor thrones of Europe with its convulsive violence. It was like a stone thrown into a pool radiating out rings that rippled all the way to the shore. Royal Europe had turned its face against the phantoms of liberty, equality, and fraternity, and Europe's royals were determined to grind those perverse ideals into dust as they turned back the clock of history to the world as it had existed before 1789.

The young Matabele watching his father's cattle today cared not a hair for Napoleon even though this distant white warrior was well known to him and greatly admired by him for his enthusiastic and successful practice of the art of war. Unlike most of his generation Atachawayo had been reading the newspapers at the missionary school for the last five years. He liked to read. Reading gave him almost as much power as his razor sharp assegai.

The news of the wars had interested him. He had read all about the European battles fought since 1810. But he was far away from Europe, and therefore, European wars were of no immediate consequence to Atachawayo except as an academic study mostly for his own pleasure. It also gave him pleasure that his king and the chiefs would stop him and ask him questions about what he had read about the wars. Even his contemporaries, who were not the scholar he was, were envious. However they dared not say anything to him about this matter or much of anything else. Such was his fierceness as a warrior and killer of lions and men that these others did not dare question him.

War was the business of the Matabele, and Atachawayo was chosen to be groomed as a leader of his people someday. But for now, only his father's cattle were an immediate reality as were the lions that roamed around the herds looking for an easy kill. The lions were always testing him to see if it was safe for them to make off with one of the beasts in his father's herd. These cows were his father's wealth. No remote doings of the far away white races mattered in the long run to Atachawayo when the cattle were to be protected.

For now the Matabele Nation was safe as it basked in the sunlight of the wealth of its rich empire, which had been wrested from the hands of the Mashona and other lesser African subject peoples. These lands were safe, dominated by the razor sharp spears of the mighty Matabele Zulu, and they were sacrosanct. Nobody, not even the Dutch sitting on their own vast land holdings or the British in Cape Town dared think about moving against The Chosen of Heaven. The Matabele were also exacting masters of all of their subject peoples. They tolerated no challenges to their absolute authority. The Matabele Ruler, from the time even before Shaka, was no less autocratic than the Czar and Autocrat of all the Russia's, Alexander himself. Nor was this Matabele king conflicted in his idealism when it came up against the reality of holding power as was that poor Czar Alexander. Unlike a true Matabele king, Czar Alexander's midnight dreams were haunted by the guilt of his passive involvement in that fatal patricide, the killing of his own father, which cleared his way to the imperial throne of Russia which he now fitfully occupied. The King of the Matabele did not know the foolish feeling of that special coward's guilt to which the European royal mind attaches itself when the odd murder of a king or czar is deemed a necessity to obtain or consolidate rulership. Matabele kings knew that kinsmen were expendable when their throne and security were in danger of being compromised even by ones closest relatives. The entire Matabele nation depended on the security of the throne, and on the unquestioned legitimacy and supreme authority of the king who sat upon it. And there was never any mistaking who that rightful king was. It was he that could hold the royal power in his strong hands until a stronger contender could take it from him. Nothing so unimportant as the lives of a few men, brothers, uncles, and fathers could be allowed to endanger a great people like the Matabele. The killing of a king or pretender was merely good Matabele survival policy if one were to be a strong king like the mighty Shaka.

The English did not transgress even now into these rich Matabele lands, nor did the Boers. Even for them with all of their guns, it would be too daunting a task. The other African peoples cowered before the might of the vast Matabele armies that were organized into the irresistible brigades or impis. These massed Zulu forces came on fiercely in battle. They were terrible in their unconquerable thousands, and they annihilated all those before them who dared resist their awesome power. The Matabele generals, operating at the direction of their paramount king, directed their impis with the same matchless skill of the best European field marshals. The Matabele warriors, whose unshod and tough feet could eat up a distance of fifty miles in a single day's march, were still fresh at the end of their daylong full runs. They were ready and eager for a battle even then. And that battle always ended with their enemy's annihilation. The Matabele Zulu seemed to draw power from some great reserve of energy unknown to other merely mortal men. Their slashing assegais were irresistible, and the only method of fighting they knew was to battle to the utter extermination of their enemies.

This inevitable victory that would follow would be the result of crushing their enemies between the horns of the great bull formation. These awful truths of Matabele invincibility were known to all the African people who had contested these Zulus and had fallen in defeat before them. In the end, all submitted to the fierce Matabele. The Mashona and other African people came to know by bitter encounters with the irresistible Matabele that, at the signal of the Matabele leader, those vast impis would transform themselves into the huge and almost magic formation of the terrible bull. That was the most deadly reality of all. When that irresistible army came upon a foe in the form of that mighty bull fully a mile wide, possessing powerful loins, and a deadly pair of huge slightly curving horns that would engulf its human prey in a huge pincer motion, these opposing warriors knew it was the end for them. The enemy would find itself drawn onto the bull's head, and then onto the horns of the beast.

The unfortunates who dared challenge the Matabele would find themselves surrounded by a sea of slashing and stabbing assegais wielded in unremitting fury by the mighty Matabele warriors who composed the horns and loins of that mighty bull formation. Now the unhappy enemy, surrounded by the blood drinking slashing assegais, would be unable to maneuver. The poor fools were then rendered incapable of defensive motion. The Matabele's enemy was crushed between the horns of the ravenous bull. These horns were composed of the best infantry the world had ever seen since the days of Alexander the Great.

The Matabele knew only victory, and their enemies knew only the pain and disgrace of defeat and subjugation. Who would dare encroach on these lands held by the most fierce and disciplined warrior people in all the world? In their wisdom, not even the English and the Boers were contemplating a move on the mighty Matabele. These were the happy thoughts of Atachawayo as he guarded the cattle while hoping to wet his assegai and gain glory in defense of the herd.

Even as the fifteen-year-old Matabele warrior watched the grazing cattle of his lordly father, he smugly smiled as he let his eyes drink in the sight of the huge herds languidly feeding on the lush green grass that grew under the African sun. Today this world seemed uniquely his own. Unlike most other Matabele boys of his age, he had some knowledge of the world beyond the lands of his father. His mighty king, and most exalted kinsman, had singled him out because of his obvious intellectual promise. His king had sent him to the English missionary school where he alone excelled. This school, that the King of the Matabele had suffered to exist under his royal patronage, existed only to serve his own purposes. The king had extended toleration to the missionaries so that the brightest of his young men could study the mind and teachings of these strange English lately arrived in their big ships armed with guns, civil servants, red-coated soldiers, and missionary teachers of writing and mathematics. The Boers never had any interest in educating the Matabele people just as they had no interest in fighting them. Then again, these Dutch had little interest in educating themselves or their own children beyond the teachings of their *Bible*.

The Matabele and the Dutch Boers had reached an informal, unwritten, but clearly understood accommodation a long time ago. The boundaries between these two peoples were well understood. A grudging mutual respect had evolved out of this meeting of the minds, but in the end, the Matabele found the Dutch to be brave and fierce but also a very dull race of men. The one value that the Matabele and the Dutch shared was their contempt for gold and their love of the land. However it was true that these new English might be a problem at some time in the future. This was the king's wise assessment. The Matabele King thought that knowing something of these English might be a good thing that would give him an insight into their thinking and maybe would allow him to sort out what kind of danger they potentially posed. The king knew that these red coated men from far over the ocean did not come to Cape Town to sit on the coast forever and only occasionally look into the lands beyond that self same coastline. The King of the Matabele recognized land hunger when he saw it and was on his guard against it.

The young warrior had learned to speak and read the language of the English very well. The others would learn only what they were forced to learn. Atachawayo wanted more. He had also listened to their religious philosophy with good-natured humor, and he studied their philosophy in their books deeply. He thought that the values of these white people were stupid insomuch as they lusted after mineral wealth that made very little sense to him. These English loved gold, which had little value beyond decoration and exciting an unhealthy envy among white men that could lead to real trouble someday.

The Matabele feared that their subject peoples might also be seized by this worship of the obnoxious gold metal. Atachawayo also found it curious that the white god of the English was a feeble and poor thing that seemed to value submission to his divine will as the chief virtue of his worshipers. Where was the proof of manhood reflected here? This meaningless flattery of the pale deity could never produce the proper fierceness required of a true god of battle who could excite his worshipers to military glory. Atachawayo also laughed at the stupidly exacting ritualistic behavior of the worship of these followers of this pale god of the Christians. This form of worship seemed to him to be of no purpose. How could this nonsense please any god of consequence? "What good is such a god to a great people?" he thought. "In the end, what can such a god do for them?"

There was always the foolish talk among these white men of someday looking inland for gold. When asked about gold, the Matabele always told them that such yellow metal was unknown. They told the whites that the little gold they had came from far over the great waters to the East. Why give white men an excuse to intrude with the obnoxious temptation of riches? What use was that yellow metal to a warrior nation when a truly great people like the Matabele had cattle without number, rich grasslands to graze the beasts upon, and thousands of the best warriors in the world to hold in perpetuity those vast lands against all those foolish enough to come against the mighty Matabele in arms.

Wealth was having and breeding a strong and energetic race of warrior people. This was the truth that the Matabele youth were taught and knew. Atachawayo was taught that to produce a race of such warriors, those warriors must save their seed and wait the passing of thirty-nine summers before any warrior could put his seed into their woman. By conserving their seed, the Matabele would and did become stronger than any other people, and as a result, they bred a race of giants. These warriors knew how to save their vital juices and thus extended their youth by not spilling this vital seed too early in their life making themselves weak by doing so. Matabele warriors would retain their youthful strength well into their sixtieth year as a result.

The young warrior knew that if he spent his seed before his thirty-ninth year, he and his entire family would be punished by being bound hand and foot and thrown down a mountainside to a certain death. This would become the law of Shaka and of all of the kings who would follow him. The Matabele also knew, that even if they were undiscovered in the satisfaction of their lustful desire to spill their seed before their time, that to spend that precious seed wantonly before one's time had come was to invite premature old age by sapping the body of its vital essence of life. A warrior's seed was the property of the king alone. No warrior of the Matabele Nation was free to spend his seed wantonly. Sons born to the wives of mature warriors, who had saved themselves for thirty-nine seasons, enjoyed the energy of youth until they were well over sixty summers. These children born to them would also grow to be big and mighty like their fathers.

The girls produced of these unions of mature and blooded healthy warriors and strong young Matabele women, would become worthy mates for the next generation of mighty warriors. And so all of the generations of the Matabele Zulu had evolved into their greatness in a well ordered cycle of life. These favored girls who would wed warriors in the fullness of time, who were also the blessed of Heaven, would become brides in the space of thirteen to fifteen summers. They would marry a class of men who had reached thirty-nine years and were youthful still. They would receive the seed of these mighty Matabele warriors and hopefully make sons. They would then give birth to children unlike any other children of their world. The Matabele were after all "The Chosen People of Heaven".

Atachawayo never doubted the wisdom of his elders for they had ruled these lands for more than two-dozen generations. The proof of their truth and their wisdom was all around him to see every day. The subject peoples of the Matabele, like the Mashona, trembled at the very act of having to pass near the physical presence of a mighty Matabele warrior. And this was just as it should be when the Mashona's mighty Matabele overlords passed by. Yet there were a few young bloods among the Mashona who did not always embrace the habit of servitude, which possessed their wiser elders who wore their shame of inferiority with resignation.

Once in a great while, a Mashona would make a fatal error. Once in a great while, these foolish ones might actually steal a Matabele cow, and when filled with some potentially fatal ambition for glory, they might even try to steal a Matabele man and take that captive warrior to the white coastal people in Mozambique to sell into slavery in exchange for trade goods or even for silver and gold. These places, to which they brought their captives, were the slave stations near the Portuguese towns to the northeast. These slave stations were walled and armed forts. The Portuguese would not heed or recognize the prohibitions that the English speaking peoples had imposed on the slave trade in 1807. It was here on the eastern coast that these foolish Mashona would endeavor to sell their captives for silver, gold, or goods. The Matabele were a rarity in the slave markets of Mozambique, and therefore the Matabele were valued at a much higher price than all other African peoples captured for the trade.

It was true that such rash foolishness was rare, and almost never crowned with success, but then Atachawayo reflected, the Mashona were a stupid people with a very small capacity of memory or for learning. So, these foolish ones might repeat their error in overestimating their power to take a Matabele warrior for the slave market. The Mashona were no more a match for the Matabele in battle than were other lesser peoples who had fallen before the bull's horns of the irresistible Zulu.

Atachawayo briefly reflected on this intrinsic tribal inferiority of the Mashona as he pondered all sorts of other philosophical questions as he guarded his father's herds. Then, in an unguarded moment of reverie, he heard the cows of his father making a strange commotion some little distance away. The cows acted as if they were in an utter state of panic. Atachawayo roused himself out of his daydreaming for action. Once again, with an excitement born out of the joy of an anticipated battle with either a man or beast, Atachawayo joyfully steeled himself to the contest. That this fight might be either with a human thief or a lion was of small consequence to him. In his warrior's heart, he knew that at the conclusion of the fight the result would be the same. He would dance in victory. His assegai, with its wide sharp blade and short handle, was at the ready to do his father's business. His blood was up. He thirsted for action in which to once again prove himself a true warrior to his father, king, and brothers. Atachawayo had killed his first thief at thirteen years of age, and he had cut the heart out of the man who was a Mashona of twenty something. It had been a proud day. For now he had become a truly blooded warrior. Other thieves had watered his blade since then.

Most of all now, he wished to prove himself once again to be worthy of the trust shown him by his father in his position of keeper and defender of the cattle. Atachawayo rushed silently into battle. He could move quickly over the land on sure feet and never make a sound. The young warrior was alert and sensitive to everything around him. Atachawayo ran silently over the savannah carefully avoiding the direction of the wind so that his foe would not discover him. At last, he came to the place that he sought. There before him was a lioness slashing into a cow with bloody claws. Having immobilized the poor beast, the lioness used her fangs to tear into her victim. Then she used her mouth to cover the better part of the cow's head stealing its breath finally smothering the animal.

The lioness never saw Atachawayo as she now clung to the cow with her claws sucking the life out of her victim. Swiftly the young warrior's feet ate up the distance between himself and the lioness. Too late did the lioness, now engaged in gorging itself in its hunger and greed, become aware of him as the youth's wide bladed weapon sliced into her flank and then found her heart. In a flash, it was over. The big cat was stretched out lifelessly beside the cow it would have dragged away to feed on along with its pride and perhaps it's young. "One lioness' robe for one cow was not a bad trade," said the youth to the cows who began to calm down and once again feed upon the grass.

This was most true when considering that his father had so many cows. This cow would furnish a feast of celebration for the killing of the lioness. The cow's flesh would not be wasted. The young warrior saw that the animal before him on the ground was a young female cat of respectable size. He could see pride in his father's face and the joy his mother would express when they saw this trophy of his skill and prowess. His father would exalt him for his bravery. This was one of those times when the young Matabele wished that he might have a woman to take pleasure with in his moment of the triumph of the hunt. He deeply desired a woman with whom he could share this moment of elation. This kill had excited him in a way that he had come to expect since he had become a full man three years past.

Quickly did he try to banish this carnal thought from his mind. Even to think such a thing might invite disaster. Atachawayo could not let his mind roam to that forbidden place of real danger. It was true that he had seen the maidens at their baths as they had frolicked naked in the river. He had felt the painful swelling in his groin as he watched the young girls cavorting there. He had felt the powerful surging in his loins of his seed seeking to escape. Atachawayo experienced a desire to wrap his strong loins about the young woman he had seen looking at him with desire in her luminous eyes. She was so beautiful as she had posed for him naked in the river. He had felt the desire to take her and then all of the so willing girls one by one. He could see himself naked in the stream with them, wrapping his arms about each of the beautiful girls in turn, and even spending his sacred seed as he enveloped them in the heat of his passion.

Quickly he shook his head again as he attempted to banish such thoughts from his mind, because he also saw in his mind's eye all the members of his clan bound hand and foot and then thrown headlong over the cliffs onto the sharp rocks below in punishment for his premature sexual transgressions, which were against the Matabele Zulu law. For surely this would be their punishment for his lapse into sexual temptation and unlawful desire expressed so many years before the lawful time of his marriage had arrived. Now Atachawayo wanted some physical action to help dispel the thoughts that enticed him. Those silly girls who had aroused and tempted him with their laughing taunts about his manhood would have done nicely. He thought much about them. His memory of them was still splendidly green just as it was as they played about in an obvious attempt of his seduction as they cavorted in the river just a few days ago. They seemed to have no care for their lives or his. But they were young and randy.

Yes, the young women had taken much notice of him over the last few years. They secretly, and then not so secretly, wanted this handsome, tall, and well built young man. Atachawayo too wanted to enjoy them every bit as much as the girls wanted to be with him regardless of their fates. Some of the elders noticed this dangerous behavior as well. They watched Atachawayo carefully to see if he could resist the blandishments of these maidens and continue to live to serve his king and fulfill the promise of his youth.

Soon these foolish girls would be wed to men who were old enough to be their fathers. Such was the foolishness of these young girls that they sought that which was forbidden so soon before they themselves would be initiated into married life lawfully. They thought of nothing else but their being randy with a warrior from the very beginning of the time that their own sexual awakening had arrived. These girls were born of proudly randy mothers who knew well their own sexual powers over the marriageable men who, in their time, had become their husbands. The young warrior knew that soon these girls, now newly come of age, would know the joy of being with their husbands after a huge and massive wedding to which the whole district would be invited. The guests would come to see the hundreds of warriors, of thirty-nine summers, married to hundreds of young and very anxious maidens hungry to fulfill their own sexual promise.

Soon now this whole class of warriors would be ready to take these young girls for their wives, and only too gladly would these girls go to these men even if they were old enough to be their fathers. For these men were still in their prime and very handsome in the eyes of the maidens. These men were very strong and eager for the marriage prize. Their thirty-nine years of fidelity to their king and to their nation was now about to be rewarded with the sexual joy, which would at last be theirs.

These girls were randy and had been made ever so ready for the adventure of their lives by the careful instruction of their mothers and grandmothers. These older women had initiated these all too willing girls into adulthood and had filled their minds with wise instruction as to how to best please their men. These older women had also filled the girl's heads with tales of pleasure that would take them to a place that they could not even imagine in their poor young maiden's minds. The young women of the Matabele had been bred for this one moment had they not? The very thought of their sexual awakening, and their long anticipated fulfillment of their dreams of following these warriors into the marriage kraals stimulated the imaginations of these young maids beyond all of what had passed for their capacity to reason or hold back their enthusiasm. Now they were almost mad with joy in anticipation of this most intimate side of marriage, and they could not wait for the day when they would dance.

The Matabele warriors knew that on their wedding day that these young women would seductively dance and sway in long lines before them. Each maiden would stand next to her sisters in an exalted state of excitement. These beautiful girls would dance with wild abandon, and facing opposite them would be the equally anxious warriors, who were now also dancing in wild anticipation of their sexual awakening and who would shortly be husbands to these randy and pretty young girls. Thirty-nine summers was a long time to hold ones seed. These next few hours would seem a long wait. Each girl would have a little assegai in her hand as a symbol of that first sexual penetration of fantastic painful delight. This would be the start of a long journey of pleasure that would truly climax the wedding day with the full revelation of the great life mystery. These greatly aroused passions burned in them. What would the reality of marriage actually be like that they had only tried to conjure up in their imaginations?

These maidens would dance and leap in an exotic frenzy swaying their hips in wild gyrations in their skimpy wedding costumes with their breasts firm and their nipples erect in anxious anticipation of the consummation of their respective unions with the warriors. The drummers kept up the tempo made even more frenzied with their wilder playing. This fantastic wedding music, fired with the frantic beating of the drums, was constantly further exciting the brides almost beyond their ability to restrain themselves until the moment their new husbands would take them into the marriage bed.

The warriors opposite the young brides matched them in leaping and dancing in equally wild anticipation of the prize for which they had saved themselves for what seemed a lifetime. The Matabele warrior's hunger for life's pleasures was no less than that of the women that they were about to deflower. The elders and guests would sit and howl out their own joy in anticipation of the unions that would ensure the continuity of their nation. And they would also watch the proceedings in nostalgic approval, smiling, and remembering their own nuptials. For some, that memory seemed very long ago, but after watching the dance many of them would return to their kraals to relive their own wedding nights. Those women who were now alone could only cry. For most of them were young enough for marriage still and randy yet, but their husbands who had been twenty-five years older now rested under the UmLahlankosi trees that marked their graves.

And the young girls who were watching everything, not yet old enough for marriage, would watch the wedding dance of their older sisters with joy. They would contribute their voices to the wedding songs while wishing for time to speed by quickly and take them quickly to their own day of marriage. Inside of all these young girls, not yet quite ready for complete womanhood, there was also now a new awakening fired by furtive imaginings and yearning for something deep in the well of their own unreachable carnal joy. The brides to be had shared with their younger sisters just what joys that they had anticipated in their marriage beds.

This same line of thought also had gone through Atachawayo's mind, and his own deep carnal yearnings, centered in his groin, did not help to calm the great crashing waves of sheer sexual desire that now washed over him. He had the body of a man, a tall well built man, with a strong man's desires to take a woman and have her for his pleasure. Even now he could feel his seed rising in him, and he feared that his seed would burst out from him in a heroic effort to escape. This had often happened in the stillness of his dreaming, and Atachawayo had awakened to find that his sacred juices had exploded from his body. He remembered the sublime pleasure he had enjoyed, and then the guilt came. Now he was in fear that this thing might happen now. At this moment he wanted either sex with a woman or at least to kill something to assuage these horrible torments.

Atachawayo looked about for something, even another lion, to kill. There were always at least a few other lions about if one lion could be seen. There had to be other large females. They were almost always in prides. Few lions were solitary beasts unless they were young males who themselves were denied the pleasure of mating. Atachawayo almost felt sorrow for these lone and despised beasts, for they were much like him. He would preferably like to take on a larger and more aggressive beast than that which he had just killed. He needed a life upon which to vent his pent up energy proceeding out of his utter sexual frustration. A large-maned male beast, the very king of lions, would be a choicer offering to his assegais' razor sharp blade as well as to his hunger for battle. Atachawayo's muscles seemed to swell matching the painful swelling in his groin. His body now dripped with sweat as he moved about in agitation in the full brutal heat of the sun at noonday.

Suddenly, he again heard the noise of another one of his father's cows in distress. This animal's call was not the same as that of the one that had fallen prey to the dead lion, but it didn't matter to Atachawayo. "Well," he thought, "The gods are good. That might be another and more important lion. Maybe it is the largest one ever seen about the district, perhaps it is a real prize. I will make this a most honorable kill."

The sound of the distress of the other cows standing nearer to him, now joined in a chorus with their fellow herd members. This thought excited him, and he sprang off in the direction of the first sound of bovine distress. On his long powerful legs, Atachawayo silently ran on. He was now leaping over the ground at a wild speed like an antelope. Atachawayo's feet ate up the distance as he bounded silently onward. He was like the wind, which he deemed to be his brother and to whom he confided his most secret dreams. While running at such great speeds, the world through which he passed was but a blurred image of something only slightly resembling what he knew to be reality. Atachawayo rushed onward to slay his unseen foe and to spend his raging sexual desire in a hot and lethal battle to the death and utter extermination of his yet unseen and unnamed enemy.

His seed had already burst through with the excitement of the run, and he didn't care. As the young warrior rounded a little hillock, he saw a fantastic sight. It was a lowly Mashona lashing a woven leather halter around a cow's neck for the purpose of taking her off from his father's herd. The Mashona youth seemed so occupied with his very act of stealing the cow that he did not even seem to notice that the young Matabele warrior was silently closing in on him with the single minded purpose of splitting his heart in two with one mighty sweeping motion of his razor sharp blade.

Then the Matabele's foot stepped on a small dried branch of a low bush rendering it in two with a slight snap. The Mashona looked up from what he was doing. His face became a mask of fear when he saw Atachawayo closing in on him with his deadly assegai. The Mashona screamed like a frightened woman, dropped the halter by which he had intended to lead the cow away, and fled across the fields with the young Matabele warrior in wild pursuit.

"What a fool it is, this thing who would rob my father's property," shouted the young warrior to his brother the wind. It was this very wind that would carry Atachawayo's words to this coward's ears and inspire great fear in him.

"Hear me Mashona dog! You might as well stop running, and give up your life to me now. Save yourself the trouble of a long death. Stop now you fool, and I will kill you quickly. You cannot outrun me you son of a jackal, and kinsman to the baboon, you thieving cur, and low stealer of cattle. You are nothing but a low thief like all of your mangy race," the Matabele youth cried after the fleeing thief.

The Mashona ran on as fast as he could in his state of abject terror. Because of that same fear, he never looked back. This accursed Mashona's speed was remarkable as were his long leaps over the grasslands as he sought to escape to some safe place beyond the young Matabele's horrible slashing assegai and the terrible death that must surely follow his capture. The young Matabele thought that the Mashona ran well even for a member of this hated tribe. The two youths ran onward for almost an hour, and then as they approached a low hill, the Mashona thief's speed seemed to slacken a bit.

As Atachawayo closed in, he sensed his enemy's energy flagging. Atachawayo whooped out more abuse and promises of a most gruesome death in unabashed glee. "Yes!" he thought. This was just the thing I need to fix me. To Atachawayo, the gods seemed in a generous mood this day. Atachawayo rejoiced in the anticipated triumph of yet another honorable kill. This time it was a Mashona thief! The young warrior ran even faster almost catching up to his prize. Atachawayo only regretted that he could not make a cloak out of the Mashona's hide. This run, for Atachawayo, had been merely an almost effortless exercise for his long legs and mighty body. Still this thief had run well for a lowly Mashona. The Mashona thief, now at the end of his strength, seemed to have used up the last of his energy. He ran over the low hill in a last desperate effort to save his life. "Could you run for an entire day Mashona dog? Could you run for a full day without stopping for a rest, and then fight a battle you lazy pig!" called the young warrior to the fleeing youthful stealer of cattle.

As the Mashona seemed to stumble over the crest of the hill, the young Matabele whooped again, "This is the place of your death dog! Why don't you just stop and wait for me, or better yet, turn and run onto my blade and end it all honorably and quickly instead of acting according to the customs of your cur breeding? Why do you not try to beg me for your life? That too would reflect your true breeding, the breeding of cowards and fools. To steal my father's cattle so near our kraal is stupidity! But then you are only a member of a foolish slave people."

With that, the Matabele warrior bounded over the hill after his prey. Now he prepared to impale his prize. His assegai, thirsty for the Mashona's blood, was poised for the fatal blow. A feeling of inner rage had displaced the sexual tensions that had been driving him mad. The swelling in his groin had abated with his run as well as with the dissipation of his seed. A fantastic and delicious rage was enveloping the young warrior's entire being. Atachawayo took pleasure in knowing that he would end the worthless life of this lowly thief, and that this deed would fill the hidden place inside of him where only a hollow and hopeless yearning had been housed only a short time before. Whereas Atachawayo had been suffering unrequited torment only an hour before, he now felt a special elation. The life's river of blood of this unworthy Mashona thief would wash away all the evils of his lustful yearning in its cleansing red flood.

Suddenly, his joy was compromised by his finding himself surrounded by a dozen Mashona all armed with spears, clubs, or nets. It suddenly came to him that this whole incident with the cattle had been only a well-planned exercise in duplicity. It was an elaborate trap set to lure him away from the security of his father's kraal and the proximity of his brothers. The Mashona thief was now smiling with his gaping mouth open and with widely opened eyes looking at his late pursuer with utter disrespect. The facial expression by the Mashona was a calculated insult. This face, which the Mashona youth now portrayed, proclaimed his disgust with the Matabele who had chased him to his own detriment as a witless fool. This insult could not be endured by the Matabele warrior.

As the supposed Mashona thief's friends began to encircle his former pursuer, the Matabele lowered his weapon almost in a gesture of surrender. Then without warning, Atachawayo sprang up into the air and swung the murderous assegai in a great arc that sliced through the neck of one of the Mashonas armed with a club then cut down another in the same motion. With another slashing arc, the Matabele then cut deeply into a defensively upraised arm of yet another man who then dropped his spear. Then the Matabele spun again landing directly in front of the Mashona thief who had lured him to this place of death and dishonor and who had dared to show him such profound disrespect. Now there would be a reckoning. In a flash, the Matabele's weapon swept upward and through the body of the pretended thief himself. The terrible point of the weapon was driven with the volcanic force of the Matabele's hate through his victim's spine. The look on the Mashona's face, as his spine was severed, was of shock and the most profound pain. Gone was the disrespect of just a few seconds ago. With a quick and violent motion the Matabele suddenly tore his well-blooded assegai out of the body of the man who had led him to this spot. The Mashona's body slumped like an obscenely articulated doll before Atachawayo in a broken heap.

Suddenly, in the midst of this uneven battle, a pain shot through the last consciousness of the young Matabele warrior. Then all around him was darkness. Within a little time, the story would go out that Atachawayo was missing. His brothers and friends would look for him for several days ranging all the way to the land of the Boers and the English. Their search would not be rewarded with success. For the captive Matabele warrior, it would not be long before a dream of horror entered his now dulled mind as he slowly came to himself through the fog of his almost fatal concussion. A horrible dream was now seizing his mind. He dreamed that he was trussed up and being carried with his body suspended from a pole like a gazelle or antelope brought back from a hunt. He became aware of swaying.

His wrists and ankles hurt him and felt as it they were on fire with a horrible burning and chafing sensation. His head throbbed as if there were drummers in his skull beating out a fierce tattoo on taut drum heads with their hands made red by their bloody effort. Even his eyes burned with the pain of the awful pressure that seemed to swell his brain against his skull inside of his head. Now his stomach churned as if it were on fire. And this fire moved up from the pit of his stomach to his throat. He dreamed that he vomited. There was a taste of blood in his mouth.

In this dream he tried to clear his throat by turning his head to the side. He coughed and tried to scream. Somehow he came to breath again, but his body was in pain. He tried to awake from this wicked sleep. He found that he could not. Atachawayo heard voices. Someone was yelling at some men who seemed to be placing him on the ground cutting at ropes at his wrists and ankles. But it was not a dream taking this African son far from his home. It was a loathsome reality. He discovered that he had in fact been carried bound hand and foot like some animal suspended from a pole. As he forced his eyes open through a crust of dried blood and mucus, he could taste the bitter vomit around his mouth. Had he been carried by men of the Mashona hunting party?

Had these Mashona really captured him? Slowly the reality of his situation was becoming clear. This horror was no dream. The young Matabele knew that this was the conclusion of his life. Somehow he knew that no more would he hear his name cried out by friend or family in greeting. He knew that he must be in something like this Christian Hell that he had been taught about in the missionary school. In his foggy brain, which burned with a fire inside of his head, some little voice seemed to tell him that from this day onward there would be no Atachawayo. That young Matabele warrior was dead now through his own folly. He was nobody. As he was dragged to a dark place and felt himself being shut in, he knew that some kind of death had overtaken him. Atachawayo was truly dead. He himself would never again speak that name out of his abject shame and pain.

CHAPTER II

Young Pompey polished the silver. He worked carefully looking over his shoulder to see if Old Caesar was spying on him, smiled to himself, and spat into the bowl of the large silver serving spoon and buffed the piece to a splendid sheen. In its burnished glory, Pompey could see his own face reflected. His dark wavy hair was combed to his mistress' taste, and his dark eyes focused on his reflection. He looked for all the world like a white man. Since he was six years old he had wondered how these white lords of the earth could hold him in bondage. He had even remarked on this bothersome question to Anna.

"I look like the white boys in the house don't I Anna?"

She had shushed him at once and said, "Chile don't you never say that again! I don't want's to lose you, but if old Miz Forrester hears you say such a thing there will be tarnation to pay fer sure. Now you minds what I sez to you boy." And that was the end of any conversation on that subject for a long while to come.

Pompey's well chiseled features, high cheekbones and less than full lips made his being cast in the role of a slave curious. These were also thoughts that crossed the minds of other people such as those people who infrequently visited the Forrester plantation from the North on business. Their intimacy with the slave world was at best superficial. Pompey served the members of the Forester household with assumed docility. The people looking at him in all of his brightness smiled if they were Georgians, for they knew the truth of the way things here. To blue nosed Yankees, such truth as miscegenation was an unmentionable abomination. To a southerner, it was just another way to acquire slaves and have a bit of pleasure in the process.

Pompey was always treated fairly well but still like the slave that he was. Mrs. Forrester, his mistress, had clearly shown him great favor since he had turned twelve and had grown taller. The fact that he had grown into a more handsome version of his white father over time did not seem to have impacted his life until just recently. Pompey was clearly a highly valued prize. He was in fact a highly valued piece of property. Even the elderly Miss Forrester, the master's sister and housekeeper, was not allowed to strike him as she freely did the other house servants with the exceptions of Anna, Caesar, and the silent and gravely important Samuel to whom she was forbidden even to speak.

Pompey set the large polished serving spoon on the table and picked up another. He applied the polishing mixture with a soft rag, which was made up for the job by Old Caesar, and carefully worked the concoction into the fine Georgian piece removing all of the tarnish. Again he spat into the bowl of the spoon, and smiled over his wanton act of rebellion. Pompey then buffed the piece with the polishing cloth. Once again, he looked around to see if Old Caesar was spying on him and spat into the spoon once more. It gave him great satisfaction knowing that the fastidious and nasty old white woman would be serving her damned family with a spoon polished with his slave spit.

He smiled more broadly as he admired his work as it caught the morning sunlight streaming into the butler's pantry. Pompey only smiled when he was alone. His moments of elation were reserved to himself alone. His feelings were private, because his feelings were the only thing he truly owned. He was happy that the summer day was not yet too steamy. The brutal Georgian sun would be high and without mercy by eleven o' clock, and it would grow worse in the coming haze of the afternoon. Pompey reflected on how almost happy and almost satisfied he was in the little space of this moment.

It had not really taken long for him to realize the benefits of his having escaped the fate of being one of the field hands so many years ago. He had a happy gift of luck that saved him from so much in the two decades of his life. He sometimes thought of those unfortunate contemporaries of his who had been hard at work since before dawn and were now slaving away. Now they were awash in their own sweat, under the unforgiving southern sun working on land that would never be theirs. But then the concept of Black men owning land was as strange to them as riding in carriages and dancing at cotillions.

Before Pompey had even arrived on the Forrester Plantation those many years ago, the cook and slave woman of all work, Anna, had asked Master Forrester if she could have a boy to help her in the house. Anna had wanted a boy that she could train from a youngster to adulthood to help her in the kitchen and with her many other duties. Pompey was assigned to her shortly after Master Forrester had won him in a game of cards more than eighteen years before. Pompey had grown tall and strong. There was no doubt that Anna had saved him from being marked for service in the fields. Here in the house, the handsome little light skinned slave boy could be dressed in livery and shown off like the bright domestic prize that he was. Mrs. Forrester fussed over him dressing him as if he were her own personal "play dolly". That was the phrase that Old Caesar had used to describe Pompey with utter contempt in his periods of jealous pique.

As Pompey rubbed away polishing the silver, he reflected on his relationship with Anna and the life lessons she had taught him regarding his basic survival since he had arrived in her kitchen all of those long years ago. He sadly reflected on just how much he had loved her in spite of the fact that he didn't want to love anybody. One thing was for certain, he knew that she was a selfless and dear old soul who had asked for nothing much in this life and expected to gain nothing from this world. But then, Anna had lofty expectations of something better later on in the next life when she would be gathered to her Christian God and placed somewhere in Heaven beyond the killing grind of her daily life here on earth and the brutality of the demands made on her by the old Miz Forrester. As cook and maid of all work, there was not a task that Miz Forrester would not set Anna to do for as long as twenty hours a day sometimes if there was to be a big "Do" at the Forrester house.

Old Miz Forrester was a dried up and driven old biddy who treated Anna as if she were an indestructible old mule who was something other than mere human flesh and bone. Miz Forrester was up at dawn and in the kitchen to oversee the breakfast. Anna had been up for two hours already building the fire in the new iron range and boiling water for her cooking in the fireplace. The brick oven was now almost never used except when the house was full of guests. The old biddy would walk about the large kitchen quickly, inspect all the pots, nod at Anna then go up to the dining room to join the family for breakfast. Anna would make a face at the old woman as soon as her back was turned. Then she would turn to Pompey and smile a quick and secret smile. That was Anna's rebellion. This whole morning routine had been acted out thousands of times over the years. It never varied, but to Pompey Anna's rebellion was a tonic that woke him up to unstated life possibilities each day.

In many ways, Anna was a force of nature. Her great fault was that she had compassion for all the folks on the place except for herself. She never flagged in doing what she took to be her duty. She never sought to escape the burden of her work by claiming illness. Above all, Anna deeply loved the funny bright little boy called Pompey. After he had come to her, she had lived just to see him each day. Because of him, Anna almost forgot the pain that too often wracked her whole being. Her huge heart melted when first she saw the little bright boy dressed in nothing but the long shirt that was the costume of all plantation slave children under seven years of age. The little boy's big brown eyes, seemed to ask the questions to which he almost never would give voice. Pompey also touched her unfulfilled maternal instincts deeply. The night that Caesar had first brought the boy to her kitchen was the night that Anna's world changed and lit up for her, as it never had before.

"You wants to stay working in the house don't you Honey?" Anna had asked the little fellow lovingly. "You gotta to be always needed Honey if you wants to stay, 'cause if you ain't needed in here, you is gonna end up in the fields by the time you is seven! You just listen to Old Anna now, and do like I tells you. If you ebber goes out to that old field, you'se gonna work from befo' the dawn to after the dark, and your back might gonna be blistered with either the whip, if you is sold off this place, or the sun, 'cus you's so dang near white. You is one bright little cuss ain't you! "She would laugh in an almost musical way. Her laughter was beautiful and sounded like birds singing when she said even this. Yet this lesson of being needed was imprinted on the boy's mind never to be forgotten.

"Old Anna" was perhaps thirty-nine years old when Pompey arrived at the big white house, and her heavy work load from "Can to Can't", that is from can't see before the dawn to can't see after nightfall which were the traditional hours of slavery, kept her laboring sometimes as long as sixteen hours each day without relief. She slaved away in ceaseless toil until she became prematurely old. At times Anna came very close to being broken by the weight of her work under the harshness of the master's demanding older sister who ran the house like a field marshal in her lofty position as housekeeper.

To Miz Forrester, this position of housekeeper on her brother's fine plantation was beyond what had been any realization of her own poor life's ambition. This position of power had outstripped all of the meager achievements of the first forty years of her own miserable life. Miz Forrester herself had been little better than a slave in domestic service in the chilly North. In Philadelphia, she had been only slightly better on than Anna before her brother's surprise summons south had reached her changing her own life forever.

Now in her desire to do all things well, Miz Forrester was driving Anna without mercy, and Anna was getting slowly used up from not only her duties as cook, but from lifting, toting, washing clothes, cleaning the kitchen, and doing all that needed to be done in the way of "helping out" in the big white house. The pains in her lungs and chest now came more frequently as the years passed and could not be dispelled so easily as just a few months ago.

Anna had told Pompey, when he asked about his own history, that he was about two or three years old, as near as anybody could tell, when he had arrived at the Forrester's. He had come from the Selby Plantation one night as an unnamed little bit of a thing. The records of his origins were a bit sketchy. Thus his age, like that of so many slaves could only be guessed. As it had happened, Anna had known his mother on the old Selby Plantation where they both had been held in slavery together before she herself was suddenly sold off to Forrester more than twenty years ago. She had told Pompey what she knew of his history and that his mother was younger than she was and was very pretty. Anna knew that Pompey's mother's father had also been a white man, and that Selby had purchased her in an estate sale when her former master had died. "Your granddaddy was white, and so was your pa. Now don't you ever tell nobody that old Anna ever tell you this. We ain't supposed to know about white folk's doin's. And we ain't to know that white men lay down with Black women. But I can tell you this about your ma Pompey darling. Like you Honey, she was bright. Maybe not so bright as you, but she was almost near enough bright to pass for white herself. She was powerful pretty."

The truth of the matter was that Old Col. Selby liked his whiskey, playing cards, and bedding his pretty young black slave girls. He liked them best if they were ten to fourteen years of age, but he would also bed any other slave woman if she was cursed by any sort of personal attractiveness. When he bid on slave women and girls, he always bid highest on the brightest and most beautiful. He was also known to have taken a few pretty and thin boys into his bed in his plantation office if the mood struck him. He wasn't too particular as to how he got his pleasure. But then a lot of the planters were like that out on those isolated plantations in the rural South.

It was common knowledge about the county for many years that a great many of Old Master Selby's slaves, born to his young slave girls, were high yellow or bright, and they all had old Roman names given to them by Selby himself. As the father of all these bright slave children, who would increase his wealth, he thought that the least he could do by way of a patrimonial gift was naming them himself before launching them into the world of slavery for which he had bred them. It was his primary article of faith that the slaves lived in his world only to do his bidding, supply pleasure, and increase his wealth. His part in their paternity was never a real issue for him. He considered it of no more consequence than breathing to supply himself with oxygen. Selby never had any emotional attachment for the children he created as a result of giving his seed so promiscuously to the women of his slave quarters. These girls were after all just attractive things that he happened to own.

These tiny bright beings, that resulted from his trysts, to him were never really his children. They were just fortunate and profitable dividends for his moments of sexual adventure and pleasure spent with his favored girls. Col. Selby had regretted that those pretty boys, that he had also bedded, could not breed. He often smiled to himself in the most angelic way when reflecting on his moments in the heaven of his hours passed in the slave quarters. He always congratulated himself on saving stud fees. In his way, Selby was an ambitious man. He did the weighty work of being the sire of his own little slaves and thus saving a lot of money and had bragging rights that be had bedded more women than any of his fellow planters. Such bragging was often uncomfortable table talk at Bucklands. Few planters would care to publicly contest or debate the point with the old man even here in their all male holy of holies that was their private retreat. This money Selby made from the sale of his young slaves most often ended up in the pockets of the sporting card playing James Forrester. Selby lost with some measure of grace. He paid his debts with dozens of slaves. He bragged that he would just have to go home and breed some more to make up his losses. Selby never seemed to mind that he regularly lost at cards to the amiable James Forrester.

One day, while reflecting on those strange Roman names, given to so many of the slaves on the Selby and Forrester plantations, Anna had asked Old Caesar, who was the butler and fountainhead of all plantation wisdom, "Where did all them old Romans come from in the first place that we is all named for?"

Old Caesar pondered this great question as Anna stood in awed silence watching the old butler's intellectual powers at work. Helena and a few of the other house slaves also watched this impressive cognitive process of Caesar's in action. In turn, Caesar gravely pondered as he puzzled out the obvious answer while stroking his chin as he had seen the master do while he was deep in thought. While thoughtfully stroking his chin in his own absent-minded manner, he coughed. This was the signal that Caesar always gave when he was about to pontificate on some grave issue or make a philosophical pronouncement on some great truth.

Caesar having issued this signal for attention and silence drew himself up to the full dignity of his six-foot height. He then announced in his rich and authoritative baritone, "Why them Old Romans," he paused again for the sake of the drama of the moment, and then continued, "Why them Old Romans, they all be coming from Atlanta," and the little assemblage nodded in appreciation of his superior wisdom in the ways of the world. That was the end of the discussion.

Little Pompey's young and pretty mother had died of childbirth after too much work in the field and too much ill usage by old Master Selby. All that the little unnamed slave child knew was that one night, some weeks after his mother's death, he had been taken to a strange place. Old Master Selby had gotten really drunk and lost once again at cards to Master Forrester. Little Pompey had the very good fortune to be part of his master's losses. When old Master Selby, still in his cups, arrived home, little Pompey, who was still without a name, because old Master Selby did not like to name slaves whose mother's had died in child birth, was gathered up from where he had been sleeping with the yellow hound bitch's pups. He had vaguely known that he was to get a little brother, but then death had taken his mother, and that was the end of that. He was taken by wagon in the night to the new home he had never before seen. The little boy with the wide eyes was deposited in the Forrester's plantation house. Master Forrester handed the little high yellow slave boy over to his butler and said, "Tell Anna that she can have this boy for the helper she's been wanting in the kitchen. She can train him as she likes. He doesn't seem to know much of anything right now. Old Selby runs a damned disorganized place. Maybe Anna can make something of him Caesar."

"Yes sir Master Forrester. I'll see to it, but sir, what is we all gonna call him?"

"That's a good question Caesar." Master Forrester thought for a moment then said,

"Why, we'll call him "Pompey" I think. We haven't had a Pompey on the place for ages now have we? "

"No sir," answered Caesar." The Old Pompey we used to have died seven years back as I

recalls sir."

"Well in that case, we might as well have a new one now. Maybe we'll have some luck

with this little yellow nigger."

Smiling at the little bright slave boy, who was looking up

at him with his huge brown eyes with a respectful detachment, Forrester exclaimed, "He's a funny little thing with those thin lips of his isn't he Caesar."

Caesar merely nodded. Master Forrester then had an epiphany of his own in a moment of recognition. He threw back his head and laughed, "Damn it Caesar, I knew this little fellow reminded me of somebody I knew. Now I know who it is! Damned if he don't look like his pa. He looks like Old Col. Selby himself, only I'll be damned if he's not an improved edition! That whoremaster Selby hates to pay stud fees. He likes to breed them himself!"

Caesar merely smiled in a tactful and noncommittal way. It wasn't his place to notice the white folk's doings. It was certainly not his place to comment on the sexual habits of his betters. He knew how to keep his place without outraging his master. Selby's reputation had been well known in the slave quarters for years, but no slave would be so unmindful of their place as to mention it. Being most tactful was how Caesar had achieved three score and ten years of age almost entirely physically unscathed. His dignity and decorum had also recommended him for training in his youth for his high position of butler. Now he was ensconced in the Forrester household where he intended to stay until he either died or was put out to a comfortable pasture as was the Forrester custom.

Master Forrester had turned back once again, looking at the handsome little yellow boy standing in that ragged sort of shirt and barefooted at Caesar's side. He smiled and laughed once more shaking his head while walking down the hall away from the direction of the kitchen on his nocturnal journey to the front of the house to share this joke of Selby's alley-catting in his own slave quarters with Mrs. Forrester. The mistress was still awake and waiting for her husband in her sitting room as was her habit when Mr. Forrester was out playing cards in the evening with the other gentlemen of the county. Mistress Forrester was never cross with her husband even on these nights when he was out, like tonight, 'till all hours. She was, like all well bred southern ladies, aware of her own place in the scheme of things, and there was always the reality that unlike herself, her husband was a totally free agent who was as much her master in matrimony as he was master of every slave on the place. That at least is what the position of what the law of the land was, but Mr. Forrester was a different sort of man. It was quite true that he took his pleasures wherever he wished, but James Forrester allowed his wife a free hand in all she wished to do herself. Most importantly, he considered her a real partner and friend with whom he shared both the gossip she craved and a small part of his substantial gambling winnings at the end of each of his gambling adventures.

Mr. Forrester always came back to his home sober, good-natured, loving, and best of all, he never lost at the card table. When he returned from his usual night out, he always pressed fifty dollars in gold coins into Mrs. Forrester's hand, gently folded her fingers over the coins, and followed this gift with a kiss. Mrs. Forrester waited demurely to hear about his good fortune, and she also looked forward to the rich treasure of gossip from the county that Mr. Forrester always seemed to gather. Most of all, she loved hearing the story of Old Selby tom-catting in his slave quarters and breeding more slaves to replace his losses at the gaming table. Now she was to become vaguely aware of one of those exotic little beings in her own kitchen. It would take a while for her to really notice Pompey, but when she realized the potential of the pretty little boy, she rejoiced at what an object of envy she could turn him into. The women of her circle would be pea green with jealousy, and that was just fine with her. Much to her delight, in time all of her plans for him came true. The bright high yellow little fellow matured into a most handsome young man. Pompey even made some of her friends gasp when he served them tea at her weekly afternoon gatherings.

To Mrs. Forrester, her James was the most perfect of husbands. He, in turn, thought her to be the best of wives. She was understanding, a good friend, and indifferent to his wanderings. Mrs. Forrester appreciated the good life, which Mr. Forrester had provided, and she had no objection to the sources of her good fortune. She rejoiced in her station. Mrs. Forrester never had a cross word for her James. She had not even minded his recreational visits to Miss Sally's. As far as she was concerned, she had done her conjugal duty by producing four children. Her two girls were her great joy, and her two sons were the everlasting crosses she had to endure. To Mrs. Forrester, men could be lovely, but boys were some sort of abomination and a punishment inflicted by an unloving God.

Miss Sally ran a clean house of pleasure of the very highest quality. It was a position of special status to be allowed entrance there, for it possessed all that any aristocrat could require in all of the best amenities that money and refined taste could offer. For this reason, Mrs. Forrester could pretend not to know of it and give tacit approval to her husband to visit that establishment. All of the best people in the county went there. In return, Mr. Forrester thought that his bride was the most open minded of women. He reflected on this as he smiled lovingly at the still handsome Mrs. Forrester as he fingered his substantial winnings of the night. His deep pockets, which were all but overflowing with gold and notes, always pleased his wife. Mrs. Forrester looked at her James and played with the ten coins, the five gold pieces in her hand that Mr. Forrester had so lovingly placed there.

And so it was that Pompey had arrived at the Forrester's plantation. Anna was glad to have him. When she had later discovered the little one's identity, she embraced her friend's child, and the child looked back at her in a most detached yet mildly curious way. The little boy seemed to have learned not to feel a single emotion of anything like affection. Somewhere in his mind he knew that to love was only eventually to lose.

This little boy did not smile, or come closer to Anna, nor did he try to push her away. Little Pompey just stood there with his bare toes curling against the coolness of the brick tiled floor of the kitchen. He just stared silently around him with his three year old's eyes and sort of evaluated what he saw. Maybe he was looking for some warm fat pups to bed down with. Nobody could read the child's mind. Pompey's inner workings hid behind that mask of indifference that was his face. It was as if he knew that he had to be here in this new place perhaps forever, or at least until he was sold off. But he also knew that he was not actually of this place or anywhere else. Somehow he knew that he had no real place in the world. Pompey always instinctively knew that there was no place that would ever be truly his own, and even this place could change at any moment. Pompey had a wonderful detachment born out of his early resignation to his lot in life as a person alone in this strange and ever changing world. He just wanted to live until the next day, and then he would consider his options until the next night fell.

Anna looked at him, and said, "Oh Honey, what has they done to you? Can't you love nobody? Has somebody taken all of the love out of you Sweetheart?"

He turned his large brown eyes on her with almost a half smile on his lips. To all the world, that was the total emotional limit that he would expose. The workings of his mind were his alone and not to be shared with anyone. In the years that followed, Anna trained him well to be the perfect house slave, waiter, and boy of all work. In this part of his education, Caesar also played a part. In his association with the boy, Caesar was at first only tolerant of Pompey and then grudgingly, he too grew fond of the bright little boy. Pompey was polite, clean, and was taught to serve in any capacity like polishing boots and generally making himself useful and quick, but he was always secretive. Such instinctive behavior was a basic survival technique for the slave who would succeed in this world of inequality.

Anna knew that Pompey was very smart. He was a quick study and learned to please his betters without fawning.

"Never let the white folks know what you is thinking Honey. Don't smile too much," counseled Anna.

Pompey didn't need to be told that. That wasn't too hard for him to understand on his own. He had always known it. After his mother had died in the childbirth of his stillborn brother, he was put out to sleep with the yellow pups in the barn to keep warm. He hadn't even questioned it. The mother he had almost never known was gone, and the pups were a living reality. All he knew was that in this life there was very little to make a slave smile. He also knew that as a slave he could never show how much he knew to anybody. A smart slave could find himself being whipped or even worse. As young as he was, the little slave knew this by instinct.

Anna kept drilling her own sort of wisdom into his head, "You want to be a house slave? It be hard work, but it ain't be so hard as being a common field hand. Now our Samuel is some different," she whispered.

The lordly Samuel dominated the world of slave life on the Forrester plantation like no other Black man ever could or ever had on any plantation. Even little Pompey was to come to know about this paragon Samuel within a very short time of his arrival. Pompey also knew that Samuel was a man never to be approached or spoken to without invitation. As Pompey grew older he hoped that someday Samuel would take notice of him and even favor him with a few words.

Samuel had also noticed Pompey from the time of his arrival on the Forrester Place. He observed the boy's quick intelligence, and he noticed Pompey's development and ability to quickly adapt to the Forrester plantation life in spite of his age. Slowly plans for the future of the little bright boy in the total scheme of things began to evolve in Samuel's mind as Pompey began to grow to maturity. Samuel's conversations with Anna, when he called on her in her kitchen, gave him the opportunity to see the boy and measure his progress. The boy and the overseer exchanged no words, but there was the recognition that something like a common sympathy and even a bond could develop in time. Pompey knew that this man was different from any man of color he had ever seen. This well built giant contrasted to advantage with Caesar, and Pompey suspected that he himself had been noticed by the big man when

Anna would send him off on some pretext or other out of the kitchen so that she could speak undisturbed to Samuel alone and without being heard.

All Anna would share about Samuel with Pompey was a little information such as, "Samuel ain't no field hand. I think that he wuz some kind of king or somthin' back in Africa. I know that he come right frum Africa a long time ago when he wuz young hisself. Samuel is a real man that even Master Forrester shows respect to. Ain't nobody ever seen such a thing as a white man showing no nigger respect before! Never has that ever happened I tells you boy, and that's fer sure. He's some kind of great man that Samuel is! Not even the master's own sister is allowed to talk to him or boss him. She tried once to tell Samuel what to do, and Samuel turned his back on her, and walked off to the master. A few minutes later, the master comes out of where he wuz, and called his sister into another room. I swear, I heard the master tell that Old Miz Forrester that she ain't never even to speak to Samuel no more, and Samuel is the boss man of what goes on outside of this house. Never before has no white man give that kind of power to no slave! Samuel's special all right. "

Anna would whisper many useful things to Pompey as he grew older in understanding. Pompey was to become Anna's closest confidant in the years to come. Whatever words went into the boy's ears, there they remained locked in his head no matter what sensitive information Anna imparted to him. A sixth sense seemed to dominate his thought process. It was the sense of silence. In turn, he spoke little, and Anna did not seem to mind. Her love for Pompey was unconditional. Just having this youngster to talk to and love was enough for her to make her life whole.

The one activity, outside of his work, that Pompey was allowed to indulge was playing with the Forrester boys, Douglas and James. They shared a strange sort of comradeship with Pompey for five years. For unlike Mrs. Forrester's daughters, they were not favored by their mother, and were treated by her like some species of subhuman life. The three boys got on very well together, because Pompey knew just how much to give of himself even to the Forrester boys, and then to give no more. He could have manipulated Douglas and James at will, but he was wise and passive in doing this even to a small degree. The Forrester boys liked him all the more for it. Strangely Mrs. Forrester also liked Pompey in the role of her sons' playfellow. She saw him as a civilizing influence, but then she despaired of any hope that Pompey's good manners and other virtues would ever rub off onto her Douglas and James. This special favor of family association Pompey was careful not to exploit. He was careful not to excite the jealousy of the Forrester sons.

Every so often, impelled by his curiosity, Pompey would ask Anna about Samuel when the time seemed right and they were quite alone.

"Now nobody ebber say that Samuel is no king back there in Africa or nuthin'," said Anna in a very quiet voice. "Nobody don't say that, but I knows it somehow. Don't nobody know nothing fer sure. But Samuel's some different. Master ain't never whipped him. And Samuel has always been head slave driver. He ain't never had to whip no slave either. The hands do what Samuel tells them to do. And I'll tell you one thing. Master ain't won him in no card game neither. No sir. Master talks to Samuel real nice, friendly, and respectful, and no white man's never done that to no slave I ever seen before. Samuel's real special, and nobody knows nothin' about him, nor does they axe him nothing about his self neither."

"Why is that Anna?" asked the wide eyed little yellow boy who for once betrayed his well-hidden and curious nature.

"They jist don't cuz they know his look. That Samuel jist looks at you like he could kill you with bolts of lightning comin' out frum those cold eyes of his. He's a man of respect. He gits respect from both the white man and the Black. Nobody knows how he do that, and ain't nobody never axed neither. Samuel is a wonderment. He's like some lord or prophet from the *Bible.*"

Even as a very young boy, Pompey knew that he would have to

know this African king who ran the field hands on the plantation without a whip and who sometimes was pleasant with him and had begun to show him a bit of attention when he had come up from the fields to visit with Anna and take a cup of cool buttermilk during the heat of day. Someday Pompey wanted to speak long and deeply to this man who was respected by his all-powerful white master. Unknown to Pompey, Samuel was aware of Pompey's every move. Nothing on the Forrester Plantation escaped Samuel's notice. He even knew of all the doings in the big house.

Anna would tell Pompey, "There be a lot of things I gots to learn you. First of all you don't talk to the white folks unless you is axed a question. Then you talks like me. And you don't say more than you has to. Don't never talk like the white folks, but you listens to what they says and hows they says it. They is gonna teach you more than what they knows. You might even learn to read the words in the books they got in that big dark room what they calls a library someday, and if you does, you don't never let on that you kin do it. If they find out you kin do this reading thing, they maybe gonna beat you real bad, and maybe they even kills you and even sends you to damnation. They be sure to kill you fer it maybe. It be a good thing to learn reading and figuring, but I seen a lot of niggers beaten and killed cuz they wuz too smart and uppity. Not on this place mind. Nobody here but ole Miz Forrester whips slaves on this place. We is lucky to be placed by Master Forrester beyond her hittin' us, but I seen real whippins back on the Selby place a long time ago and heard about it on other plantations. You got no marks on yo' back now, and if you want's to keep it that way, you take care that nobody knows that you is smart. No sir. No white man is gonna want no smart nigger on the place no how, cuz they knows that smart niggers is nothing but trouble. If they brings you here cuz you'se smart and be wantin' you that way, that be one thing. Anything is good if the white folks thinks it's their idea to want you to be such a way. They don't want no nigger on the place what has ideas of his own. Bein' smart for a nigger is doin' what he is told real quick and quiet like."

"But what of Samuel? He might be the smartest man in the whole world," answered Pompey.

"You hush up about that. You don't talk none about what don't concern you and you don't rightly know. You never mention Samuel to nobody but me, and then only when we is all alone. You are good about not talkin' too much Pompey. Keep it that way boy. That way you stays out of trouble," Anna said in a hushed voice.

The little bright boy listened and said nothing. Over the years that followed, Pompey learned how to stay alive and how never to give offense, and above all, Pompey learned the best of all lessons, and that was how to be invisible.

He learned not to trust mere humans, and he never forgot that to love was to lose. He never allowed himself to fully love Anna, or to respond to her affection beyond giving her a half smile. In the end, he did not even allow himself to mourn her when she was taken away by death. He knew all too well that a slave's life was a most temporary thing, and that a slave's own life was not something that a slave could ever own. If his mother could be abused and then taken from him at the moment of his brother's birth, anybody else he might love could also be taken away. He did not want to face that terrible pain of loss again with tearless eyes, and an unmoving and unreadable face. He did not wish to listen to that internal sad voice that told him that he had to keep the secret of his deepest sorrow in that awful silence of his most private and abject pain when death took somebody from him.

Over the next few years, Samuel slowly began to engage the boy in casual conversations more and more. He would ask the boy questions. Slowly over a long space of time, Samuel would draw Pompey out. Little by little, Samuel would encourage him to take walks with him about the plantation. As long as Pompey was with Samuel, no one, not ever the master, would question where Pompey was or what he was doing. Such was the personal authority of this Black man. One day Samuel commented to Pompey, "Son, you have a dignity far beyond your years. Now where does that come from do you suppose?"

"I don't know sir," the boy answered instinctively. "Maybe it comes from you."

"Don't you tell anyone else that, but then I'm sure that you have sense enough to know what to say and what to keep to yourself. You keep a lot to yourself, don't you boy?"

"Please sir, I don't like being called 'boy' except by Anna," Pompey said without a scintilla of fear of the big and all-powerful Samuel.

"I will never call you that word again, and someday no man will call you by that word either. It is a bad word meant to keep you in your place, and your place someday will be wherever you choose to make it. Now run along to Anna and see what she has for you to do. We will speak again later Pompey."

Anna never asked Pompey what he and Samuel talked about. She was just happy that the most powerful leader of the slave community had taken an almost paternal interest in her beloved Pompey. Anna knew in her heart that a time would come when she could no longer shield the boy from harm that might befall him in this delicate slave society. Anna knew that there are limits to all that is mortal. She had seen much and felt much and had grown to know this absolute reality of slave life one sad lesson at a time. Anna could also feel her own physical powers waning. On one hot Georgian spring day, when Pompey was about eighteen, Anna had finished the last of the washing. Pompey was polishing boots seated near the unlit hearth. On that very hot and steamy day, Anna was at the end of her strength. Her chest heaved as she panted while wringing out the last of the huge wash, and her lungs seemed to be straining to take in the humid Georgian air. The sweat flowed down her face in greater profusion than ever before, and the back of her dress was stained and darkened with the sweat. Even Pompey had taken note of her miserable condition.

“Let me take the basket into the yard for you Anna,” Pompey said.

“You stay where you are boy! And Anna, you get on with this wash. You don’t need that boy to help you tote that washing!” Miz Forrester was yelling in an effort to make Anna hurry up with her work.

“Boy, I told you to get back to blacking those boots. Anna don’t ask the boy to do the toting for you when he has his work to do! You are one lazy darkie!” snapped Miz Forrester.

The old white woman honked like some obscene goose in her anger, and her capacity for sheer meanness was never diminished by something so pedestrian as the furnace like heat blasting down from the unforgiving Georgian sun. No kindly human impulse ever seemed to emanate from that old harridan’s mouth, which was set in her prune like face. Pompey looked at the back of her head with hate and the feeling that he would like to cave in her skull for the pure feeling of joy it would give him. As she turned to look at him, Pompey resumed the look of total indifference as he polished the boots.

In response to the old woman’s bellowing, Anna had lifted the huge basket of wrung-out but still wet laundry, and she carried it out to the clothes lines in the drying yard as Pompey went on with his chores hating Miz Forrester for her meanness. As Anna struggled to carry the heavy wash out into the yard, she suddenly felt a sharp stabbing pain in her chest. Then the pain telegraphed down her arms and met in the middle of her back. Anna half stumbled, and then she dropped the basket. The freshly washed clothes went tumbling onto the beaten red earth of the clothes yard. Anna’s poor face contorted with pain. Her face ran with sweat as if she had been doused with a bucket of water. She grasped her ample bosom as she was again engulfed by a greater wave of a new and more horrible pain. Then Anna fell to her knees. She was now in obvious agony and at the point of vomiting.

The grouchy old white woman yelled out to her with her ugly honking, “Watch what you are doing you simpleton! That linen will have to be washed all over again. What are you thinking about anyway you foolish girl? You are a very stupid girl Anna. I have a great deal more for you to do today! We have no time to waste. Honestly Anna, you are a most lazy and thoughtless girl! I must say that I'm only sorry that my brother won't let me beat you slaves into anything like decent help. It would benefit you a great deal I suspect! You have no more care about wasting my time than that damned old tomcat you keep feeding good milk to!"

Anna managed to look up at Old Miz Forrester with her face contorted with pain, and she gasped out one last apologetic "Yes ma'am. I is sorry 'bout that."

With that, Anna dropped from the position where she had been supporting herself all the way to the red ground. Her face was convulsed with the awful pain that gripped her chest in its anaconda-like stranglehold. Anna writhed about in her last throes of agony for a few moments, and then it was over. The old white harridan stood over her shouting abuse and accusing her of faking illness to get out of her work, but Anna didn't move or hear her. Anna would never have to hear the vile honking of the old bitch again.

It was a very strange fact, but in death, Anna's lips seemed to form themselves into a smile as if she welcomed her own passing and the ultimate freedom from all care that came with it. Her face almost seemed to say in death the things that she had suppressed saying in life. Anna looked almost pretty, as her face seemed to relax. Even the deep furrows in her face seem to smooth themselves out a bit. For a moment Pompey, who had rushed out into the yard, thought that she looked a little bit like the girl she must have been so many years ago. Pompey studied Anna's kindly and beatific face in death. His heart broke, but nothing in his own face betrayed him or what he was fighting with all his might not to feel. Not a tear escaped his eyes as he stared unspeaking at the person he loved, as much as he allowed himself to love anyone in his life.

He silently looked on Anna as she lay in the red dust. Anna's silent lips seemed to say to him now what she had often said to Pompey when she had shared with him her contemplation of her own passing, "I'm over Jordan now, and I can lay my head down if I wants to, and there ain't a thing anybody can do about it. Hang your own old wet clothes out to dry Miz Forrester. I'm where you can't get at me no more. I kin see the face of my Lord, and he welcomes me to home in heaven."

Pompey stared at her with dry eyes even as his heart was breaking. Then he smiled when he thought that he could see a sort of triumph in Anna's face and in the relaxed attitude of her eyes and body. It was the face of a freed woman staring up at the sky who was now beyond the capacity of Miz Forrester's cursing and ability to inflict abuse on her anymore. The utter frustration of the old woman as she stood there helplessly screaming filled him with a sort of joy. Pompey thought to himself that Anna would have loved to see the old bitch's reaction to this, her escape from bondage and ultimate act of rebellion. When Miz Forrester sensed what the situation really was, she shook her head in aggravation. "Where in blazes are we going to get another cook?" she mumbled under her breath. Then away she went into the house to tell her brother that the old cook was dead in the drying yard.

In a moment, Samuel came along with the master. They had been in conversation together as was their habit. The master looked sadly down on Anna and removed his hat out of respect. Then Samuel knelt down by Anna's side and closed her eyes. Pompey marveled at this, and he never felt closer to the big man as he did then. Samuel arose and nodded at Pompey. Pompey sensed the meaning in this gesture of condolence. No words were needed as Samuel stood, brushed the red dust from his knees and ordered the plantation carpenter to come at once to the drying yard. The master put his hand on Samuel's shoulder and said, "I'll leave this all up to you. You know what to do."

"Yes Master James. I'll see to everything," answered the big man.

At last the carpenter arrived on the spot. He measured Anna

with a long piece of wood for her coffin. Then she was carried off to his workshop by two field hands. There a pine coffin was made up for her. On this day, the carpenter served in the office of undertaker to Anna as he had frequently done over the years for the many slaves who had passed over as part of his many duties on the place. The mourning period for Anna was neither long nor formal. Before the slaves went to bed that very night, and after the sun had retreated substantially to the west, Anna was carried to the slave graveyard in her raw pine coffin. There Anna was lowered into the hole which had been dug in the red Georgian clay to receive her earthly remains and covered with wild flowers tossed onto the coffin as it rested in the grave in an effort to lend some variety of color to the redness of the dust covered pine box as well as a measure of respect. After the job of filling in the grave was done, a rough wooden cross was stuck into the mounded red earth over Anna's body, which carried her name upon it and the words "Gone Home At Last".

Some of the house slaves cried softly. There was another poor little personal offering of wild flowers that were lovingly placed there over Anna by Mrs. Forrester's personal slave Helena, and the other slave girls that worked in the house wept softly as they returned to their quarters. These were the only flowers that actually decorated Anna's grave. There were no field hands here to mourn, except for those who had actually done the work of digging and filling in the grave, and they were wailing as if one of their own from the slave world of the field hands had been gathered up and taken away into an unknown eternity that might at least promise some freedom from the killing work of a slave's fourteen or fifteen hour work day.

Only Samuel was there officially representing that other division of labor on the Forrester plantation at Anna's funeral, besides the grave diggers. He said nothing, but the subtle glance he gave Pompey said much. The master watched the short service from his bedroom window far away from the slave graveyard. He could just see that part of the estate with his field glasses.

Something in James Forrester wanted to be there at Anna's service, but he knew that he was not supposed to know that any sort of service was taking place. The laws of Georgia had forbidden such things. And even he could be punished if they were discovered to have taken place if it was suspected that he knew of such forbidden activities.

There was a carefully crafted gulf that had been created between the house slaves and the field hands by the white folks over the centuries that slavery had existed in America. This gulf gave some degree of comfort to the white folks as a sort of insurance against rebellion by those who still remembered the night Nat Turner had disturbed the peace of every white planter's life. These two slave groups of house workers and field hands lived in parallel and separate worlds, which rarely if ever intersected. At Anna's impromptu service, Old Caesar had given a valedictory in imitation of what he thought to be a white man's religious funeral rite. His eulogy had its own kind of fundamental dignity. The whole ceremony was an illegal act, but it was tolerated. Master Forrester knew about this slave version of Christianity and its funerals, and like all slave masters, he thought it harmless and officially looked the other way even as he spied from a long way off with his field glasses.

After Anna was laid to rest, Pompey had walked back off toward the big house uncertain of himself and the mastery of his emotions for the first time in all of his years. Something in Anna's service had touched him. He stopped for a moment and looked on the last of the funeral goers who had lingered to say one more goodbye to their good friend then departed. Behind those expressionless eyes of his, there was an active mind working. Pompey truly grieved for the woman who he had dared not let himself fully love even as he knew he should have loved her very much. Pompey had steeled himself against the emotional investment in love of this remarkable woman in anticipation of the fatal day on which Anna would be taken away from him. Anna had been very religious in her way and a sort of Christian.

She spoke of crossing over Jordan in glory into that promised land of everlasting life and the freedom of Heaven when that day would come when she would die in the bosom of her Lord and in the comfort of her slave Christianity. At times, she even smiled in the contemplation of the anticipated heavenly reward, which would be afforded her by her simple faith when she had passed from this world. From far off, Pompey could still feel Samuel watching him, and this he found to be strangely comforting to him.

Pompey did not fully know that Samuel, who had said relatively little to him except during the few dozen walks that they had taken together, had watched him, the bright little slave boy, grow to early maturity. Samuel, who seemed to speak to none, and only a bit to Pompey, knew Pompey's whole history, but then, Samuel knew everything.

Pompey had studied Anna's kind and prematurely old face as she had spoken of her simple faith over the years of their close relationship. He had thought to himself, and had even spoken out loud into the darkness of a tortured and oven-like hot Georgian night, when he tossed about on his narrow cot unsleeping, "Let her have her dream of that better life over the river. What can it hurt?"

Then he thought some more on the subject, and came to the knowledge that her kind of simple faith in the God of the white man could do great harm in its way like a great many things that seem harmless at first blush. Pompey knew that this belief in the holy and Christian freedom of an afterlife would keep slaves docile and hopeful while they were toiling for their masters during their earthly suffering that passed for a life, and that is when he knew that this life of a slave could not be his life.

Unknown to him, his master and most of his plantation owning friends had thought the very same thing about the role of religion as the ultimate peace keeper in the slave quarters. They saw the simple slave religion as the restraining hand that might help avert a terrible slave uprising. This threat of a slave uprising was the great unspoken self-same fear that had been the greatest latent terror that slaveholders had all shared since the murderous rampage of Nat Turner back in '31. That is why these planters, in the red earth country of Georgia, turned a blind eye to almost all such slave religious services and impromptu Sunday meetings even though such religious practices were forbidden by law. The plantation masters knew that the dangers of denying all hope to slaves of a better life in the "next world". A slave world without hope of any sort might have horrific consequences in this one in which they lived with such great comfort. Nat Turner's Rebellion had been proof enough of that up in Southampton, Virginia. Sixty-seven whites had been slaughtered in their beds by slaves on a murderous rampage in a single night. That event gave the lie to the fiction of slave docility in a southern paternalistic slave society where the slave saw the master as father.

That great lie of happy docility was the official fiction of slavery. The reality of Nat Turner's Rebellion was something that filled the nightmares of every southern white man. None of them wanted that episode repeated, and that rebellion was a history that the planters wanted kept secret from all of their slaves. But the reality of slave life was that sooner or later all news travels from one place to another until it is known by almost everybody in bondage. Nat Turner's Rebellion was known by every slave over twelve years old. But none would speak of it. Even to know about it might mean death or at least a merciless beating.

All that the white folks were interested in was the work that slaves would do on this side of paradise. But Pompey would not think about that now. He felt an inner impatience growing in him, which he had always hidden under his carefully crafted mask of his feigned docility. This was a mask that he wore well. Pompey knew that changes must be coming in his situation. He would make those changes happen in their own good time, that is, if he could find a way. He would make plans to benefit from those changes. He wasn't sure of what form those changes might take, but there would be no long life of quiet resignation for him, as there had been for Anna, which would end in his crossing over

Jordan in a crude red dust covered wooden box into a heaven made for and by white men for fools who would allow themselves to be kept in bondage by its promise of rewards after a life of tortured slavery. He began to want those rewards now. As he thought of Samuel, standing at Anna's funeral in his neat black broadcloth suit with high stock and clean linen looking more lordly than Caesar, he began to feel some pride in himself as a Black man that grew out of his own tightly controlled integrity of spirit.

In the meantime, he would polish silver and exact his little undetected revenges against the white people who held onto the belief that they had the right to own him and his race body and soul as property. Pompey would continue to half smile, spit contempt into their silver vessels and food, and cheerfully feed them his clandestine hatred and contempt with a slight bow and an assumed air of profound respect. Above all, he resolved to know Samuel better. Samuel was a real man, an African man, who carried something of greatness with him, which was unlike any other man of color that Pompey had ever seen. He possessed a real dignity that even the master respected, and in the world of slavery, that was an unknown thing.

CHAPTER III

Now that Anna was gone, it became obvious to all that an era had passed. Anna actually had become missed if not mourned by almost everybody on the plantation, both black and white. Each mourned her for their own reasons. The Forresters were astounded to learn that it would take three girls and Pompey to replace Anna in performing her duties in the running of the household. Nothing seemed to go as smoothly as in the time before this black paragon's passing from the world. Even the testy Miz Forrester seemed to miss Anna. Even to her, time was measured in her little narrow world as, "The time before Anna died, and after Anna."

As Pompey had observed to himself, "The old bitch knows now just how much she needed Anna now." Pompey reflected on the idea that this dried up old maid must have been rejected by the white men of her youth of her own class whatever that might have been. There was an even better likelihood that old Miz Forrester never had entertained a beau. He observed to himself that the old biddy was essentially only tolerated in her family circle out of a sense of familial duty rather than loved. The truth was that she really didn't seem to fit in there with her unpretentious and rough manners. Here was another mystery that did not really interest him. Pompey only hoped that before her life was over that she would suffer some of the grief that she seemed delighted to heap on others over whom she had some small power to make miserable.

Pompey had been shaped in his childhood by Anna's wisdom and guidance and to a small degree by Caesar's instruction. But there was no doubt that Samuel had the greatest impact on the way Pompey now began to see himself as a man. By now, Pompey himself had won a certain degree of approval from the master and his family by the superior quality of his servitude. The Forresters knew that someday Pompey would step into the breech, which would be created by Caesar's passing. The master and mistress had even discussed Pompey's potential to make the transition to running the household when that time came. Pompey was the epitome of perfection in the execution of his tasks, and he even seemed to have the ability to anticipate the family's wants and needs.

The Forresters did not beat their slaves. Only the master's sister sometimes administered some form of corporal punishment on the serving girls in the big house who had not been exempted by her brother from her cruel attention. Samuel preserved order in the fields just as Caesar did in the house without recourse to physical punishments to enforce his authority. Samuel towered over every other slave on the plantation. His huge and hard muscled body only emphasized his natural domination by the silent force of his will. This was in and of itself most unusual in this time and place when physical chastisement was seen as the best way to establish the ultimate authority of the master or his agent on any well-run plantation. James Forrester was too preoccupied with his real life as a full time gentleman of leisure. Samuel was the real master of the Forrester Plantation who ensured the seamless running of the place. This was a situation that well suited these two strange partners.

There was no spirit of rebellion on the Forrester place. Among the people in the big house, only James Forrester seemed to care at all about the basic welfare of the plantation's people, and only his maiden sister, who betrayed the baser social roots of her own life far too frequently to please the mistress, seemed to have true meanness of soul. This brother and sister stood in stark contrast to one another in so many ways. James was sunny and fun loving. But the bitterness of an early life of poverty had crushed all pretensions of joy in his older sister. The rest of the Forrester women were obsessed with the pleasure of living their fantasy lives of great ladies from day to day. They were far removed from the reality of the mundane tasks of those who labored around them.

This work was the engine which provided the wealth that insured the continuity of that self same pleasure to all the Forresters. When alone and undisturbed by the rest of the plantation's people, Samuel and the master seemed to share a common history on a plane of something like equality. None would dare ask about their relationship out of fear of the overseer or out of basic indifference to whatever it might be. The master and Samuel would sometimes speak quietly together long into the night and share a drink and pipe in Samuel's cabin or plantation office like two old friends. They could be heard laughing as they talked and visited, and nobody could even guess what the subjects of these secret conversations might have been that went on deeply into the night. No white man ever saw this sort of relationship of something like friendship between master and slave, and the slaves who saw everything almost never spoke of it even among themselves.

The fact that Pompey had turned into a most handsome bright boy had never been lost on Mrs. Forrester who had watched him grow from a pretty boy into a handsome buck. She dressed him each year in new well-cut clothes. He became a sort of symbol of her superior status in the Georgian county slave owning society. When Pompey was fourteen, she had first told the master that she wanted her pet trained to drive the chaise, serve at table, and in short, to be prepared to replace Old Caesar himself when the time came. Until that time, there had been no other in-house candidate to replace the stately old man who Mrs. Forrester had guessed to be about seventy years of age. But then Caesar had seemed to be about seventy years of age for the better part of two decades.

"It's so hard to tell about these age things," Mrs. Forrester had said to her friends on the afternoon of her weekly "Drawing Room Reception" for the local women of quality. It was quite true that these rural Georgian women would never have been confused with the "women of quality" of the real Tidewater aristocracy of The Old Dominion, which was the gold standard for judging what was true aristocracy. The pretensions of these country Georgian plantation wives to the aristocracy of the more settled South amused visitors from well ordered plantations outside of Georgia. Aristocratic Virginia was not alone in the restrained contempt for this outlandish and less polished Georgian planter society.

"After all, Georgia was founded by a blue nosed do-gooder, a British general of narrow religious views, who didn't believe in card playing, dancing, or in the use of alcohol. He was an awful bore. His settlement in Georgia was made up of the former populations of English debtor's prisons who came to Georgia only in 1733! How could such creatures achieve any degree of real quality when measured against the better elements of our colonial gentry of the more established and settled South in only three or four generations!" said the wife of a business associate of the master who had traveled South with his bride from Maryland. She had spoken this opinion to her husband when they thought that they were alone one sunny spring afternoon on the Forrester veranda. This visiting Maryland lady had stated this while laughing softly in contempt in a voice that was hardly above a whisper. Her husband had snickered and signaled to her to be quiet. They had thought themselves to be alone. But every one of the Forrester house servants knew what had been said. And just as Pompey knew, even at fourteen, that with the factor of slave invisibility, no white man or woman was ever alone nor were their thoughts ever private.

These impressions of Georgian plantation culture were indeed the thoughts harbored by older southern society who had a century or more to forget about their own humble origins. These Tidewater aristocrats may have refined their own manners almost to the standard of British country gentry, but their roots were hardly more respectable than the Georgians if one looked far enough back to the days of the Wife Ship coming into old Jamestown with its own cargo of women of questionable virtue. Yet, Mrs. Forrester and her lady friends continued to imitate their betters who reigned over the tidewater plantations of Virginia who had that additional century to breed away their own questionable backgrounds, and an unspoken of ancestry of less than respectable roots. Many a proud Virginian matron, who presided over a glittering ball, was directly descended from a crimp girl from the slums of London and brought to Virginia on the *Wife Ship* of 1619 and sold off for barrels of tobacco to the women-deprived settlers of The Old Dominion. Virginia and most of the south had enjoyed the luxury of that extra span of time to polish their own rougher origins and forget.

A dozen ladies chattered away in the afternoon Georgian heat of the Forrester's best parlor with its high ceilings and great sweeping fans, passing to and fro overhead. These fans were powered by slave boys in crisp cotton whites. The slave boys were almost like part of the furniture which decorated the room, and therefore like all servants, they were invisible. The handsome furnishings in this salon, had been made in the industrial North of heavy carved black walnut, Honduras mahogany, and rosewood. Here in this room of thick and soft carpets from Persia and the gold leaf framed portraits of borrowed ancestors, were the mirrors, porcelain vases, cut lusters with their sparkling prismatic icicles, satin draperies, and crimson and gold cut velvet cushions all of which were calculated to impress these equally well upholstered women of Georgian county society who sat, gowned and equally well upholstered, perched on the edges of the balloon back black walnut chairs listening to the details of the intimate conversation of their hostess and fellow mistresses of gossip.

"Mr. Forrester bought this place from a family that was so lax about records and such, as well as with the inventories of their niggers, that it's hard to know how really old some of these slaves are even now that came along with the plantation. Why, it's worse than buying horses. You can't really tell much about most of these darkies by looking at their teeth! There is just no way to tell how old some of them truly are. Why one of our old darkies died just a little while back. She just dropped dead taking the wash out to dry on the clotheslines in the drying yard, and we don't even know how old she was. Can you just imagine that! I declare! This record keeping was just that bad and disorganized when we took over the place. Why that old Negress could have been fifty years old or even over seventy. She certainly looked it! She looked old enough to have come over here with General Oglethorpe himself." She laughed along with the polite tittering of the assembled ladies of her impromptu Athenaeum over her witticism.

Then she stopped, looked up and said, "It must be the heat getting to me ladies. Come to think of it, that old gal was one of the few slaves that we actually bought from Col. Selby." To this news the women laughed. Col. Selby's little foibles were known to the whole county, and fathering a woman of seventy was considered way beyond even his youngest efforts and precocious sexual powers.

"If she was as old as you say she was Mrs. Forrester, we know that the Colonel must have actually...," sputtered Mrs. Linus Poore.

"Mr. Forrester," gushed Mrs. Forrester cutting off her friend, "I declare, I had thought that he had won her in a game of cards from Col. Selby of Willows Farms many years ago. As a matter of fact, that is because Mr. Forrester won so many of Col. Selby's slaves in games of chance at Buckland's. Although," gushed Mrs. Forrester again, "As Mr. Forrester likes to point out to me so frequently, that with his gaming skills, card playing is no real game of chance at all. My Mr. Forrester is just so clever and witty! I declare, that foolish man just about has me in stitches all of the time. Life has been quite a merry journey these last twenty-three years with my Mr. Forrester," said the master's lady laughing behind her fan. She fairly rocked back and forth with mirth.

"Mr. Forrester does seem a most wonderful husband," exclaimed Miss Frances Spence of New High Grove Plantation wistfully.

The others in the room had severally expressed the opinion over the last several years that Miss Frances Spence was highly unlikely to ever enter the state of holy wedlock herself unless the groom was blind, very old, and past caring about much of anything concerning connubial bliss, or maybe just a well born imbecile. Even among these shallow daughters of the deepest South, Miss Spence was thought by all to have the unplumbed intellectual depth of a teacup. But there was little doubt that the women of Mrs. Forrester's circle did most decidedly share the mistress's admiration of the handsome and fun loving Mr. Forrester. They all agreed that he was a well-favored charmer. Men liked him for his sporting ways and lust for life and women admired him for some other qualities he also possessed.

Pompey, silver tray in hand, stood just outside of the door of the drawing room where he could see into the room but not be seen. His thoughts concerning the Spence woman were that even a blind man would shy away from that skinny female abomination that was this pale belle of the South. She was almost an albino of an unhealthy and deathly pallor. Miss Spence was not only a pasty pale redheaded and bucktoothed white girl, but she was too ugly and foolish to attract a beau of any sort. It was thought that southern gentlemen were supposed to favor that idealized pale simpering species of female. In that strange world of planters, that was supposed to worship women with ivory skins and beautiful heart shaped faces, this silly Spence creature was clearly bound for eternal spinsterhood. This romantic myth had been perpetuated by generations of southern women based on what the writers of cheap novels had been feeding them. Most southern gentlemen had more liberal standards for judging beauty. This was a fortunate fact for these women gathered here in the Forrester's best parlor.

Most of these women hardly fit the model of the albino, heart shaped faced, and gracefully shy maidens of romantic novels. Because they did not fit the stereotype, all but one of them had actually attracted husbands.

Pompey thought that it was no small wonder that so many white masters, and their sons, sought the dusky pleasures and carnal comforts of the slave quarters at night when faced with such horrible and ghostly pale alternatives as Miss Spence in their marriage beds. He recalled that the late Mrs. Col. Selby, who used to call at the Forresters in the afternoon to join these weekly gatherings had been one of those pale creatures. The fact that she had inherited all of her father's considerable wealth perhaps made her more attractive to the Colonel when he had wed her thirty years before. But Col. Selby was a man who appreciated the rich and dusky beauty of Africa, and preferred that beauty to the skinny, pasty, and pale daughters of the not-so-old Georgian South. The charms of the traditional southern belle had truly been lost on the Colonel who claimed, when deeply in his cups, to have fathered more than six score children by his pretty slave women. As lusty as the old man was, this claim was always a source of mirth at Buckland's. The county gentry would roll their eyeballs at his extravagant claims of paternity and wink their disbelief to each other.

Pompey was brought out of his musings and back to attention by a not too subtle cough. He turned to see old Caesar standing behind him glaring at him. The old butler motioned to him, noiselessly, to go into the parlor with the serving tray and see to his duties. Pompey entered the room and moved from lady to lady bowing slightly to each as he served them. Then he placed the tray on the center table just as he had done dozens of times before. He bowed again wordlessly to his mistress and exited the room.

"My, my Mrs. Forrester, that is one very fine looking boy you have there. Such good manners and so well trained. I declare they don't even have such fine looking serving boys in Atlanta. He looks more like one of those Spanish Dons than he does even a high yellow nigger. If ever he mates, I'd just love one of his offspring. Where ever did Mr. Forrester get him?" purred Mrs. Campbell with her eyes all aflutter and with her rouged lips fixed in a feline smile.

"I hate to admit it," said the mistress of the house laughing again," But Mr. Forrester also won Pompey in a card game some years ago from poor Col. Selby. Pompey was such a funny little thing then. He was only two or three years old at the time. The Colonel sent him over here wearing only some flower sack thing. If we weren't all such good friends here, I declare that I would just die telling you all this. It's almost a scandal the way Mr. Forrester always wins at cards. I can tell you that not less than three-dozen slaves on this place were won from Old Col. Selby alone. Can you just imagine what some northern gal would make of that?" she laughed.

"I wonder what those northern women would say if they knew how much the Colonel hated paying stud fees and how the old boy makes up his losses," said Mrs. Ambrose Merryman who had taken a large sherry instead of tea.

"Those northern gals have ice water in their veins I declare," said Mrs. Josephine Pettibone. "My Uncle Cyrus Clayborn married one of those northern gals after a trip up North to see the owners of some cotton mills in Providence, Rhode Island. She was such a prissy thing. But at the time he thought that she was a handsome woman, and went so far as to propose marriage to the foolish creature. She just about jumped at the chance to marry him. I held her to be nothing more than a hussy who was looking for a rich conquest. She always claimed that he just swept her off her poor feet, and we always said back at home that he must have used a pretty big broom."

"She wasn't one of those abolitionist persons was she?" sniffed Miss Eliza Fitzherbert.

"At the time we thought 'Lord no!' At least not one of those wretches anyway, but she did turn out nearly as bad. It seems that she would go down into the kitchen in the afternoon, sit at the table there and talk to the cook and the other house slaves just as if they had been white serving gals! Can you just imagine that! It was a scandal the way she behaved! Why she talked to them and gossiped along just like they were real people almost like you and me! She even invited them to take a rest and sit with her right there in the kitchen!"

"My stars, that is just scandalous. Do tell us more," gasped the ghostly pale redheaded Miss Frances Spence.

"She would even discuss intimate family matters and gossip with them just like they were real white folks of quality. She would laugh and invite pleasantries to be exchanged as well as gossip about their lives. Their lives! Can you just imagine such a thing! They laughed together right out loud, drank tea, and ate cakes too! When my uncle found out what was going on, race mixing right under his own roof from his maiden sister, who lived right there in the house, he went quite naturally into a rage. He told that Yankee wife of his that from that day on the duties of housekeeper would be his sister's and that she, as his wife, was to make friends in the district with other proper women of her own class and quality. She was told that any further pleasantries with the house niggers were to stop immediately. It would be bad enough if she was taking up with the wives of tradesmen, dirt farmers, mechanics, and shopkeepers but sharing intimacies with the house niggers was quite beyond the pale. Well I tell you, word of her strange behavior and actual race mixing began to get about the neighborhood, and I don't mind telling you that there was tarnation to pay."

"You know, now that you mention it, I kind of remember hearing something about that race mixing business being whispered about in the parlor one day when there was company at my mother's house back when I was a young girl. When I asked about what was being said, my mother just sent me outside to play and told me not to ask questions about grownup women's things again until I was grown up myself," gushed Miss Spence spraying her tea through the gaps between her teeth in a great show of enthusiasm.

Old Mrs. Washburn turned to her friend, Mrs. Cookingham, seated to her right, and while she was conveniently facing away from the company, said in a very low voice, "Don't you think that sending that Spence girl out to play right now while we grown-ups talk wouldn't be such a bad idea?"

"That's a very wicked thing to say my dear," giggled Mrs. Cookingham, "But of course you are quite right."

That little aside went unnoticed by the women as the story of race mixing unfolded and held them with its awful and horrific fascination.

"There must have been more to all those strange goings on than that. I mean your uncle just couldn't let her get away with that kind of behavior. He'd have become the laughing stock of the whole community, and the niggers would never respect him again," gasped Miss Spence now so excited by the conversation that she was all but spraying tea between the gaps of her splayed teeth like some obscene spouting and deformed whale. She had become totally carried away by the attention the revelation of her early and exciting childhood brush with these charged events of plantation history now under discussion was bringing to her in this adult company of which she had never felt herself to be a full member.

"Indeed he could not tolerate her behavior. My uncle had to be resolute. There had to be a price to pay so that this Yankee wife of his would understand the gravity of her offensive actions. So he took that nigger cook that his wife had befriended out to the slave quarters for all of the niggers to see. He called all the house slaves together along with the field hands to see what happens to an uppity nigger who dares befriend a white woman on a basis of something like equality. Never before had such a thing happened on the place or maybe even in the whole county. But there remained no doubt that a lesson had to be taught and an example made. He could not beat his wife, at least not in public.

So then he was forced to beat that nigger girl for mixing with her betters, that is to say that cook, whom he beat nearly to death. That girl was worth over nine hundred dollars, but the lesson had to be taught nevertheless. My uncle said that when a great moral issue was involved, we could not even consider the cost to us. Nothing more was said on the subject, but all the house servants knew why they had been gathered there to see the punishment and so did the field hands. They now knew their place in the natural order of things far better than my uncle's Yankee wife ever did. Let it be known that after that, not one of the slaves ever lingered in the company of his wife again. Now don't breathe a word of this, but that Yankee toffee nosed northern wife of his refused to sleep with him after he had administered that object lesson to that uppity slave girl. My poor uncle knew that the darkies were whispering in the halls and on the stairs about it. Some of those slaves were even taking her side against my uncle. They even looked defiant sometimes when they were doing their tasks. They looked just as if they could kill him and his dear sister."

The women, now totally absorbed by this tale of horror, sat in riveted attention. Miss Spence had even set down her tea, and Mrs. Merryman even set down her sherry.

"Now we never heard of any such thing like that happening before," continued Mrs. Pettibone, "My uncle's poor sister had to carry her riding crop with her most days just to get the darkies to move and do their tasks. Sometimes she had to carry a pistol as well. It was a cute little thing with a lot of silver fittings and mother of pearl grips that fit nicely into her apron pocket. Now then, that wayward Yankee woman so provoked my poor uncle that he even lost his temper and did something that no gentleman should ever be forced to do. He slapped her hard and told her that she had a week to educate herself in the duties of a proper southern woman, lady, and wife, and that his sister would see to her education. Failing that, she would have to go back to Providence in disgrace or to perdition! He said that the choice was clearly hers to make. She then so provoked him that he said that he really didn't care which she chose to do, but whatever her choice should be, she had a week to make it."

"He did just the right thing," said Mrs. Forrester, "I'm sure that your aunt learned the error of her ways then Mrs. Pettibone. Actually I think that your uncle was very understanding under the circumstances. Many Gentlemen would have locked a woman like that up and fed her on bread and water until she saw reason. It's bad business for a gentleman to marry outside of his class and region. One never knows what one will get when one marries an outsider. Most especially a Yankee! After all most of them are only shopkeepers."

"One would think so Mrs. Forrester. Indeed one would think that, but alas that was not the case. My uncle had the grave misfortune to fall under the spell of that northern wretch. She proved to be quite intractable about meeting his demands. She carried on something fierce about the way that the nigger cook was beaten. She took on like that cook was her very own dear sister, or close kin, or friend, or some such thing. She just wasn't natural about the situation. She treated the disciplinary incident just like the whipped girl was white or something! And I would like it clearly understood that this Yankee woman, for I could not call her a lady, was in no way kin to me except by marriage to my long suffering and unfortunate uncle. Let it be clearly understood that woman was not my aunt! Why she even nursed that nigger girl on the sly, and the servants covered for her. Now I tell you, that almost amounts to inciting a slave rebellion in my opinion. If slaves start feeling like equals, it could lead to something serious like that Nat Turner thing back in '31. It just makes shivers go up and down my spine thinking about her and those damned slaves conspiring together."

"Mrs. Pettibone, I do apologize for calling this Yankee creature your aunt. I can quite understand your sensibilities in this. Please forgive the presumption. I can see that her being called a close relative was a grave insult to you and your whole family. I was quite unjustified in my presumption by using that title."

Mrs. Pettibone clutched her bosom and sipped some tea to calm herself then said, "I know Mrs. Forrester that these revelations are shocking. Please take no offense. Maybe I should stop talking now. Maybe I've said too much. I would not wish to ruin your lovely afternoon gathering with your splendid tea and these superb cakes. Why if I did that, I never could forgive myself. Perhaps I should say no more about the awful business."

The women began to enthusiastically assure Mrs. Pettibone that she was not imposing on anyone's good nature, and that she was indeed merely telling them a morality tale for their personal edification and to please continue by all means. Knowing that she had everyone's total attention, Mrs. Pettibone continued her tale to an audience now on the verge of rapture.

"That low down Yankee woman bided her time. Why, she waited almost two months for everything to die down. My uncle, being a gentleman, after all, let the week he had imposed as a time limit for his wife to come to her senses slip by without comment. They lived apart but at peace. They took their meals together in silence, but in the end it was all a facade." Mrs. Pettibone then took a deep breath and asked for a glass of water.

"Would you rather have some sherry my dear?" offered Mrs. Drake.

Mrs. Pettibone politely shook her head, and Mrs. Drake fortified herself with another half glass of golden amber liquid in preparation for the rest of the horrible revelations to come. Mrs. Forrester poured the cool clear water into a cut glass tumbler and handed the glass to Mrs. Pettibone as if she were serving the Queen of England herself while the women sat on the edges of their seats in breathless anticipation of what was to come next in the narration.

"I thank you Mrs. Forrester. Now where was I? Oh yes, now I remember," Mrs. Pettibone said as she prepared to take up her story once again. "My uncle's wife proved to be a woman of cunning and deceit, and above all, she was certainly no lady. What she did from that time on was to take a few coins from my uncle's desk and from his clothing each day. The thieving went quite unnoticed. She actually stole a few dollars and a few gold coins here and there until she had accumulated quite a tidy sum of money for what would be a truly scandalous adventure. Then one night, when my uncle was away from the place in Atlanta on some business, she just took all of the household money she could lay her hands on along with her stolen cash and ran off to Providence, Rhode Island with that no account Negro cook, the very gal my uncle had beaten for trying to make friends with this Yankee whore!"

"That is shocking!" squealed Miss Spence spouting her tea again like some deranged fountain. "What ever did he do next? Did he chase her? Did he beat her?" Then screwing up her face and dropping her voice an octave Miss Spence asked, "Did he kill her? Did he call on his friends to track her down with hounds, and catch her, and whip her to death like she so richly deserved!"

"Miss Spence! Really. Do get a grip on yourself. I declare! You are an absolutely bloodthirsty girl! Pray continue Mrs. Pettibone. I am sure that Miss Spence will contain herself," pleaded Mrs. Augustus Jones who had herself just done all she could do to contain her own emotions up to this point under her ladylike facade while fanning herself with an unconscious enthusiasm.

"At first my uncle wanted to take the hounds and track them both down. Stealing a slave girl worth nearly nine hundred dollars is a serious crime after all, as was the taking of what amounted to almost six hundred dollars in pilfered cash as close as my poor uncle could guess. And then there was the real shame that it was his own wife who was the thief. The scandal would have been ever so much greater if the whole story had come out at the time. And going after her with all the dogs and armed men in the world would never restore his reputation if he were to make any great fuss. I'm afraid all that my poor uncle could do was track down every slave on the place who could have known anything about his wife and the slave girl's escape and beat the truth of their involvement out of them. One nigger boy of thirteen and a serving girl of sixteen even died under the force of the lash. It was their own fault. That is how stiff necked and uppity they had all gotten under the evil influence of that Yankee wife of his. That death of the boy and girl represented a substantial loss for my dear uncle seeing that that stubborn girl was going to have a child in six months time. Why, do you know that he had to chain most of his house slaves up and sell them off the place? Thank sweet Jesus that the field hands were beyond the corrupting influence of that damned Yankee bitch."

Mrs. Pettibone blushed as soon as she realized what she had just said, "Oh my dear Mrs. Forrester Please forgive my outburst. I really am so ashamed."

"Think nothing of it my dear. All of those damned Yankees, pardon my language," exclaimed Mrs. Forrester, "Oh, they just rile me up so. If my darling Caroline or Tilly ever brought one of those Yankee abolitionist creatures home to wed, I swear that I'd just die. Those people with their abolitionism just want to stir up nonsense and trouble where they have no business, and they will make no effort to ever understand us and our lives, culture, and traditions. They are just so unfair. All they care about is commerce and money. They just fill me with bile! The Devil take them all straight to perdition with their uppity free niggers too. They do give themselves such airs. They are just so hateful to us. How are we going to live our lives as we have done for more than a hundred years without the darkies? Tarnation, don't they know that it's impossible? White men can't work like the niggers do unless they are scrubs, dirt farmers, and such like trash. Southern gentlemen were not made to do lowly tasks. It just wouldn't be natural. Our men are noble. They are cavaliers. They were not made by God to serve as the lower races of this world were made to serve their betters."

"There is a very smart man by the name of Fitzhugh or Fitzherbert or Fitz something or other who wrote a book, my daddy said, that explains just how God made the niggers to be our slaves," chirped Miss Spence with a very knowing smile as if she had a secret. "It seems that God thought it was a good thing that the niggers serve us because they were so mean and deserved punishment."

"The Devil you say," exclaimed Mrs. Pettibone whose attention was now focused on the one individual in the room from whom no degree of enlightenment was ever expected.

"Yes ma'am. My daddy told me that when Noah and the *Ark* come to rest on dry land, that Noah got drunk and went to sleep all naked!" Miss Spence proclaimed with a smugness that comes from knowing something that the others in the room were totally unenlightened about.

"However did your father know that?" asked an agitated and titillated Mrs. Clayborn who blushed at the very thought of the father of all the surviving generations after The Flood laying there naked in her all too vivid imagination.

"He says that it's all in the *Bible*! He even showed me the place where it was written when I said that I doubted that a great man like Noah would ever lay around sleeping in the altogether."

"Land's sakes. I never read that anywhere in the *Bible*!" exclaimed Mrs. Roberts.

"Just the same my daddy says that it is there, and then he showed me just where it was, and then he let me read it right out loud for myself, and then he told me that reading it once was enough for a girl and never to read it again. I do not mind telling you that it was very shocking, but it's right there in the *Bible* all right. I saw it with my own eyes. And daddy then said that he hoped that I noted that one of Noah's sons, a boy named Ham, came right into his room where he was sleeping and laughed at him, right out loud too, because he was all naked and everything. God got real mad at Ham for laughing at his daddy and punished him by making him the father of all the niggers in the whole world. And during all the time in the world that was to come after the time of The Great Flood, the children of Ham were to be slaves. And that's where niggers come from to be our slaves. They all came right from that sinful Ham! I must admit right up to that point, I never did bother my head about where the niggers ever came from. My daddy just laughs at me and says that it's a good thing I'm a woman and can get married some day and don't have to bother my head about figuring out things. Then, he says, I will never have to think again. You know ladies, my daddy's words are always a comfort to me. Thinking always makes me powerful tired and sometimes I get downright dizzy."

"I can see where that notion would be comforting in your case my very dear Miss Spence. It's a good thing that you don't have to think very often. But to get back to what your daddy showed you about the niggers in the *Bible,* you mean to tell me that before The Flood there were no niggers at all in the whole wide world? Not even in Africa?" asked Mrs. Pettibone.

"That's the God's honest truth. There were no niggers in this whole world before that time. Ham's children must have been very busy making more little niggers after that my daddy said. My lands! How he makes me blush sometimes! My daddy, as I said before, even showed me the very place in the *Bible* just where the whole story of The Great Flood was and where that Ham business was that we talked about, and my daddy said that if it's in *The Bible,* it just must be so. It said right out on the page that the children of Ham would be the servants of servants. And daddy said that we white folks are the faithful servants of the Lord. So Ham's nigger children are supposed to serve us, who are God's most faithful servants. And that's why all the niggers even today are supposed to serve us as slaves. Daddy says that we should just accept the fact that niggers are slaves by the will of God almighty, and that's that. And my daddy says to question God's will is the most horrible of prideful sins. God even turned one gal into a pillar of salt for disobeying him way back there in *Bible* times, and that's a fact. That's in another part of the *Bible* about a fellow named Lot, but he said that I was too innocent to read that part before I get married. He said that there were too many naughty men getting up to no good with each other. Now that don't seem to make no sense at all does it?"

"I do not think that you had better spend too much of your energy thinking about that Dear Miss Spence," snickered Mrs. Augustus Jones.

"I just think that it is unfortunate that your daddy will not allow you to read that bit about Lot before you get yourself married Miss Spence," said Mrs. Pettibone.

"Now why is that?" asked Miss Spence in all of her innocence.

"It's just because if you have to wait until then, you might never get to see it. And by the way, did your daddy ever happen to mention just which of Noah's sons was the father of the Chinese? I understand that there are an awful lot of them in the world," said Mrs. Pettibone.

Miss Spence blissfully went on, "My daddy never got around to the Chinese. He says that those nasty Yankee abolitionists don't know more than the almighty does about the way things ought to be about slaves and their place in things in Georgia. I am sure that you will all agree that my daddy is right about that. Leastwise I don't think that they know about Mr. Ham being the daddy of all the niggers up there. Don't you think somebody should have told them by now and settled the whole thing?"

"Those Abolitionists, Congregationalists, Quakers, and some other Yankee preachers up North don't know a damned thing about us or *The Bible* either it seems. Most likely they are not as up on their *Bible* as our folks are down here in Georgia. Even Miss Spence's daddy seems to be in a position to teach those uppity northern preachers a thing or two. I mean with God condemning Ham, and all, for laughing at his daddy being naked, who could doubt the justice of it! After all, that was a very wicked thing for Ham to do since Noah was such a holy man and him saving the whole human race and all," interjected Mrs. Robinson who now spoke with an absolute air of authority now that she had just gotten her newfound knowledge of scripture.

As the conversation went on among the women of Mrs. Forrester's impromptu Athenaeum, Old Caesar came upon

Pompey standing once again in the hall just outside of the drawing room door listening to the women.

"What all are you doing boy?" he whispered harshly into Pompey's ear.

CHAPTER IV

"I'm listening to the white folks Caesar," whispered Pompey. "Can't you see that?"

"You is one bold cuss Pompey boy. You is one sneaking nigger. You come with me right now to the kitchen boy!" ordered Caesar invoking all of the grave authority he held as butler.

The women in the parlor were so involved in their conversation that the exchange between Caesar and Pompey in the hallway went totally unnoticed. Pompey returned to the kitchen followed by Caesar. When the door closed behind them, Pompey turned on the butler.

"Listen to me Caesar. I am no man's nigger and I'm not your 'boy'. I will never be

anybody's nigger, and I will not take it kindly if you ever call me by that name again. I am of age, and I am a man. I am not a boy. I am an African man who is as good as the best of white men, and I will suffer no disrespect from you or anybody else if I can help it."

"But Pompey you is a nigger," said the old man sadly. "And that is a fact. You might not be near as black as me. You might be the lightest high yellow bright boy in the whole county, but you is a nigger, and that's all you'll ever be. And if God gives you children, they is gonna be niggers too. I don't know where you is getting these high flying notions from, but you best stop it, or you are going to find yourself in a whole passel of trouble. If the master was to hear you saying things about you being as good as the white folks, or worse yet his sister, you is at least gonna git yourself whipped and maybe sold off the place. Now you know that the master don't hold with no whipping of his niggers most of the time, but he'll whip you fer sure if you go spouting off that nonsense. No nigger ain't never going to be the equal of no white man ever. And that is a fact!"

"Nigger," said Pompey, "Is one of their words Caesar. It means something to them. It means nothing to me. I am a man, a thinking man, a rational man. I am not, nor will I ever be, anybody's nigger. I can pretend to bow and scrape, and if by doing that, I know that I can stay alive. That is what I am doing now. I am just playing their game and nothing more. But being their nigger is not going to be my life. It is just what I do now to stay alive. Can you understand that?"

"Pompey, you don't sound like your own self. Why you talking white like that? You is almost talking fancy high white. That ain't right. That ain't right at all! If they hear you mocking them that a'way, they is gonna beat you fierce boy. Master Forrester ain't a bad man like most of them other masters on plantations here abouts, but he's gonna beat you fer sure if he hears you taking on so with high falooting talking. He ain't gonna allow no uppity niggers around here 'bouts. No sir, none of them white folks ain't. They is scared of niggers that don't act like proper, and that's a fact fer sure. They might even shoot you like a dog what's gone mad. They never goin' to put up with no nigger that thinks that he's as good as a white man!"

Mocking the old man, Pompey fixed him with his eyes, and said imitating Caesar's voice, "It ain't right old man, and you ain't never going to hear me talk like that again ebber. All you got's to do is not to disremember one thing. I ain't no damn nigger. I am a man as good as any white man and maybe even better than most."

"Master ain't going to like you taking on like this. You got notions boy. You got bad dangerous notions. And it's a big dangerous chance to take to having notions like that. I seen Black men like you killed for less. I seen them beat some poor niggers to death. You are a good boy. So why you taking on like this for? When I dies, you gonna take my job here over frum me. Ain't that enough? You gonna be all set for the rest of your life."

"Serving in Hell, even in the top position is no honor. Master ain't gonna find out about my notions Caesar, because if you tell him anything I ever say, I'll tell him that you are sparking Molly, stealing things, and fixing to run off with the bitch. That's what I'll tell him, and there is a little bit of the truth there as you well know, so they will believe at least a little bit of what I'll tell them."

"I ain't doing any such thing, and you knows it. I ain't never stole a thing in my whole life, and I ain't sparked nobody since my good woman died. I would not disgrace her memory like that. And besides that," the old man laughed, "I can't spark no girl anymore boy. I just ain't up to it."

"That don't mean a thing to them old man. That is just the point. You mean nothing to them except that you make life easier for them. Remember how they felt about Anna when she died. All they could say was how good she made their lives, and that it was too bad for them that she died before her time. I don't want to do you any harm. In fact I like you, but I will not allow nobody to get in my way! Nobody! And that means even you Caesar! In their world, if you are a nigger, all niggers steal, and that is their truth. If they beat you long enough, you'll confess to fucking that ugly mean old white woman that's Master Forrester's old maid sister that no man would have ever fucked even if he was dead blind drunk in his bed and paid a fortune to do it."

"That thought of doing that with that old biddy just abouts turns my stomach boy," said Caesar laughing. "What an idea Pompey Boy. Me having it on with that ugly old white bag of bones. How you makes me laugh with that one. Yes suh you does.

But how does you think Master gonna believe you over me if I tells him about you, which I ain't gonna do, but why you figure that a' way anyhow?"

"If you are a smart nigger, Nigger, you better not attempt to find out. I'll do what you tell me to do in my work because that is your job, but don't you ever tell me what to do when I decide to do something that don't concern you or the work of the house. When I want to listen to the white folks, just walk away an' don't see nothing. That's all. If I'm going to spy on the white folks, I will, and when I do, just you make tracks for some other place. Be somewhere where you won't catch any blame. I'm a man grown and will do what I want to do. Caesar, I don't hate you, but don't cross me up. I don't never want to hurt any Black man. But I will do what I have to do to get what I want out of life. You are an old man Caesar. You must be the oldest God damned Black man on this place. You didn't get that way by being stupid. Don't get stupid now. I have covered up for some stupid things you have done over the years that the white folks wouldn't like, because they would think you were getting too old to do your job. You weren't doing anything bad, and I don't think that you are stupid. You just forget things sometimes, but I covered up for you. We have to do that for each other. You are a Black man like me, and there isn't a white man worth a damn that I would get you or any one of us in trouble for. You have got to respect yourself Caesar. You have to respect yourself inside where those white bastards have no right to look. The inside of you belongs to yourself. Inside of yourself, you are the property of no man."

"I don't take no offense Pompey," said Caesar with a newfound respect and a bit of fear of the younger man. "But you is crazy. The white man, he is way over us. That is why he's where he's at, and we ain't. I'm an old man, and I know these things."

"That is what they want us to think Caesar, but I'm telling you that I have sneaked down to the field hand's quarters at night, and there is another world none of us up here in the house has hardly seen. I've met slaves who are just a couple of generations from

Africa! I hear them tell of the places far away from here back where our people are kings, and chiefs, and warriors. In Africa, some of our own people catch the people that they fight, hate, and defeat in battle. They then sell those other Africans to the slave traders, who in turn, sell them again to others. They sell them to white men in far away places run by the Portuguese called Mozambique, and they sell the captured Africans to masters of huge ships who bring those Africans over here to work on these plantations. This place right here, this plantation, is not the whole damn world Caesar. Your great granddaddy might have been a king of some big country in Africa. Caesar, just think of it, a king!"

"I'm sorry boy. I can't think no such foolish thoughts at my time of life. I just wants to get through it with no pain and suffering until the Lord takes me in his own good time. That will be enough for me to hope for. But now you is taking me back to when I was a little child and the old folks used to talk about old times in Africa. They used to talk in whispers like, 'cause the white folks don't like us to talk about such things. I sure loved to hear that Africa talk in the still of the dark of the night when all of us slaves were supposed to be asleep. Sometimes I wish I'd been a field hand so that I could learn all them old stories, but I also likes the fine clothes and the inside job that go with working in the house. Out in the field! Hell, I'd be dead now, like all them old niggers what came here with me back when my first master, that I can remember, come here and bought me from Virginia so long past and a far time ago. If you want's to listen to the white folks, I don't care as long as you don't get yourself caught and get me in no trouble. I is supposed to be in charge of you, and train you up to take over frum me someday. That is if I don't die first then you got to take over right away," the old man laughed.

"Caesar, you are going to live a long time. When I'm in the house, I'll talk like a nigger. I knows you is scared, and I won't cause you no harm. See, I kin do hit jus' fine as pie. But as stupid as those white women are, they are teaching me how to talk better. I can't ever let nobody ever hear me talk white. I knows that.

Like Old Anna told me when I was a little one, ' You can't never improve yourself unless the white folks thinks it's their idea to make you something so they can dress you up and show you off like a prize horse or something like that.' She had wisdom Caesar, and she knew what she was talking about."

"Pompey you thinks the farthest ahead of any soul I ever known black or white. God, I wishes I was like you. I'm too old now boy. But one thing's for sure you ain't like no nigger I ever known before except maybe Samuel. Wait a minute. You ain't gone and met with that devil Samuel has you? I mean, met up with him away from the house here?"

"Never you mind about my comings and goings. You don't want to know where I've been. I'm like a black cat, and nobody's going to see me. If I ever get caught, you won't want to know anything about it. If I get found out and discovered getting taught to read or something, you are not going to want any part of that Caesar. Sorry I have to be rough with you, but I will do what I have to do not to die on some damned old plantation like some damned son of Ham. I will kill first, if I'm forced to it. I am a man and so are you if you'll only admit it to yourself."

"Son of a ham? I don't know what in tarnation you is talking about. No Pompey boy. I got's to admit some new respect for you. I knows that Old Anna was a friend to Samuel, and she used to tell me that you two was alike. She wanted you two to meet up and be friends. I thought she was crazy, but I guess that old gal knew what she was talking about. You gotta be the man for both of us. My day of going off to glory will come all too soon enough, and I'll see the waters of Jordan or maybe Perdition's fire. Maybe I'll see Anna again and say hello to her for you. Either one's gotta be a relief in the end I figure. So Pompey boy, you go and be the man for both of us. I'm beat all to Hell now and got's to go and rest a spell. One thing about being head house nigger and so damned old, is that I get's to sit down every now and then. Master Forrester told me that was my right to sit down if'n I'm tuckered out. He told the old woman and Mistress Forrester too that I kin do that. Master Forrester really ain't a bad man Pompey. Believe me. I seen a lot worse than him in my day who would rip the hide off of a man or woman just for some low down no reason at all or just cuz they was feeling bad."

The old man then arose and left the pantry. Under his breath Pompey said, "Old man I have to get out of here."

CHAPTER V

The big man tossed on his narrow cot. Samuel's dreams of long ago filled his night. He was a prince of Africa. His heritage was that of a great warrior people who could run all day in the hot South African sun and then fight and win great battles. That Samuel was here in this strange place at all was the result of some prideful youthful foolishness. For he was a warrior of the Matabele Nation, son of a Zulu prince, and many a man had fallen before his assegai before he had reached his sixteenth summer. He was a cousin of Moselikatze who would be king of the Matabele. His eyes had seen the great Shaka, and his years sat lightly on him even as he slept this fitful nightmare. Samuel's back did not carry the scars of battle, but he had the white man's brand of slavery burned into his flesh on his shoulder and into his African soul. He had been no easy man to tame. In the end, he had not been tamed at all, but had entered into a bargain with a white devil, James Forrester. The partnership had given him a better future than any Black African man ever had who had been held in bondage, but he was still a slave, and that wounded his princely pride even though his slavery was a hiding place, and James Forrester was his partner in a criminal act. Fitfully he tossed as his story played out once again in his sleeping mind.

Together he and Forrester had stolen cash and himself from

the slave ship, which had brought him here to this strange country where white commoners could hold African royals in lowly slave bondage. As he lay there in his cabin, asleep in the hot darkness of the Georgian night, he knew even in his precocious mind and in his African Matabele soul that he was free to hate his fate and must be well resolved to reverse it when that special moment came by accident of fate or was crafted by his own ingenuity. He had never resigned himself to a life of slavery, but he did seize upon every advantage that came his way to make life more tolerable. Samuel had kept his unholy bargain struck with Forrester, and he had run this white man's plantation as his master and partner had wished. His master was a clever fellow who could trick the rustic gentlemen of the county out of their wealth at cards while also fooling the local gentry into believing that he was one of them. Even his wife of twenty-six years had no idea who James Forrester really was or how he had come to own so rich a property. Only Forrester's older sister knew the true background of her brother, and during her years of domestic service in Philadelphia, she too had learned to ape the manners of the wealthy ruling class and their patterns of speech when she chose to do so. She found it more difficult than he did to carry off the role he had assigned to her. She knew something of the special bond her brother had forged between himself as master and Samuel as partner of his work.

She had learned long ago that her condition in life was suddenly going to change one spring day when the post was delivered to her own Master's home by the letter carrier. As she had toiled in her employer's house in the heat of summer in Philadelphia, a letter had arrived addressed to her from a lawyer telling her to meet him in his office in Walnut Street in the city that very afternoon without fail. When she arrived at the law office, she found a letter from her younger brother awaiting her telling her that the lawyer would give her the sum of two hundred dollars and a ticket on a steamship bound for Charleston in two days time. She was told to come at once to a new life. And so she had quit Philadelphia for Charleston where she had been met by her beautifully turned out brother James and his well-dressed personal slave, Samuel. It was here that she was told something of the truth and became the respectable housekeeper of her brother's plantation. She also discovered that he was now engaged to the pretty daughter of a Georgia planter. Forrester and his sister spent a few days in Charleston buying her a new wardrobe and inventing a family history for both of them. James Forrester also bought some ancestral portraits to decorate the place and back up his own biography to give him true pride of place in his new world. Samuel was always nearby. He was a silent and stolid presence. He was young and handsome and always at his master's beck and call. Forrester's sister never fully understood the entire relationship between her brother and his bondsman, but neither did she question it. She was told that Samuel was not to be the subject of her authority and that she was never to question anything that this most special of slaves ever did. She was then forty something, and had been in a depressing domestic bondage of her own for almost thirty years as a maid of all work. Her natural manner was rough in her unguarded moments, and this roughness was something that she would have to try to mask. She was never to be fully comfortable in the role of a lady.

Samuel did not like the woman, and she did not like him. The two kept their distance from one another, and it rankled her to be told by Forrester that she had no authority over this Black man who was more of a partner of her brother's labors, such as they were, than she could ever be. The life that she was invited to live was unreal to her, but her life as a domestic in Philadelphia was so much less satisfactory a reality than the rich life of fiction that she was about to embrace. She now would have to swallow her misgivings and accept her new role in this strange new world. She had adapted reasonably well in time, and she was soon at home on the Georgian plantation of her brother. The only time that James Forrester and his sister ever clashed was when she would forget herself and issue an order to Samuel. James would then come down on his sister like an avalanche of rage. Eventually the master's sister gave up her attempt to dominate Samuel.

Samuel's agreement with Forrester had cost him much over the years. Yet his fate was far better than that of any slave held in that peculiar institution of the South. He had lost count of the days of his captivity from the time that he was captured by the Mashona people and sold to the Portuguese slave traders in the land dominated by The Mozambique Company. He had always believed in his heart that the Mashona were a little people who trembled in fear at the very thought of being face to face with such mighty Zulu warriors as the Matabele. The Mashona would run in a wild scramble to get away from his slashing assegai even when he was only twelve years old. These Mashona knew that there was never a safe place for them to retreat to if chased by one of the warriors of the mighty Matabele if they were caught stealing cattle or up to any other sort of mischief. But he, this prince and royal son of Africa, had been young and filled with foolish pride at the time of his capture, and he had paid an awful price for his prideful folly.

He had been tricked into chasing a lowborn Mashona stealer of cattle, because in his mind's eye he could only see the thief's blood dripping from his wide flat bladed assegai when he captured that unhappy thief. He thrilled to the chase as he dashed after the fleeing Mashona that he had discovered stealing a cow from his father's herd. He knew that this cowardly man running over the low hill was especially stupid because he was so near the kraal of his would be victim. The young Zulu could feel the delight of knowing that this thief would soon be impaled and then slashed open by his razor sharp weapon. This thief's death would be yet another reminder to the Mashona not to show such disrespect to a much nobler people than themselves by their feeble attempts to steal Matabele cattle. His nightmare continued to mirror his history.

In his dream, his feet met the ground with speed and power. His legs sprang under him eating up the ground across which the thief had sped wildly yet without hope of escape. In fact, the wretched thief seemed to be slowing in his flight from the certain fate that would be his coward's reward as he neared the low hill. Samuel tossed on his bed tearing at his bedclothes in a futile rage. No African warrior had the endurance of a Matabele Zulu. These, the most mighty of warriors could run all day and fight thousands to extermination. This repetition of thought increased Samuel's anger. This truth made his capture by an inferior people more repugnant to him. Samuel ran after the slowing Mashona over the hill and right into the ambush by a mob of Mashona armed, not to kill, but to capture him with clubs and nets.

As he dreamed, the man he had chased turned on him now mocking him, a prince of the Matabele Nation. Now backed up by a dozen of his own kind, the Mashona man showed his little store of courage and smiled and stared at him taunting him. That did not last long. The Matabele youth leaped into the air and cut down one warrior, nearly slashed the arm off of another, and then cut the man's spine in two who led him into the trap with one lightning fast slashing motion of his terrible wide bladed weapon. Turning with the speed of a leopard, he sliced into another man. Then in his dream he turned and caught another smartly under the ribs, and then he felt as if he had been struck by a mountain. All was darkness in his head.

The Mashona warriors did not kill this young prince. The Portuguese would pay well for the well-built boy of sixteen years. They would pay with with silver coins. The darkness in the young Matabele Zulu's head must have lasted a very long time. When he awoke, he attempted to move, but he discovered that he was bound both at his arms and feet. There was a horrible pain in his head, and because the bonds were so tight, there was pain in his limbs. The pain in his head throbbed like a war drum. As he grew more aware of himself, his body began to report back to him its full story of agony. His ribs ached from a bad kicking. But he discovered that none of his bones had been broken. Blood was dried about his face, and he could feel it caked and encrusted onto his skin as he tried to move his facial muscles. His body was badly bruised, and for the first time in his entire life, he felt real and unspecified fear. Now he tossed on his bed and moaned.

Why had he not been killed? What was this strange abduction all about? Then as he became more awake, within this dream, he became sensible to the fact that there were others there around and about him. There was the rank odor of confined humanity all about him. He could not tell how many people were there penned in with him, nor could he tell even if, like him, they were also bound. He did not know what peoples they might be. As he became more accustomed to the darkness, he could sense that there was some movement just outside the enclosure where he and the others lay bound in the darkness. This was the first time he saw Forrester through a space scratched out of the earth by efforts of some earlier hands under the door of the slave enclosure.

This scene in his clouded memory was unreal. The white man was trussed up over a huge log. He had been positioned there to be whipped. Forrester appeared to be frightened, yet bravely at the same time he was fighting back tears. Another voice rang out in English, which was a language of which the young Matabele had knowledge from his years of study at the missionary school.

"Steal my goods will you, you scurvy son of a sea cook! I'll have the hide off you me bucko."

"Only ten stripes Manning," called out a tall man of real authority who seemed to be in charge of the white gang here in this strange place.

"Yes Sir Captain Whitehouse. It don't seem right though that Forrester should get off so easy," replied the man with the whip who had some lesser authority than the man he had addressed. Another man stood by as well. He was a large and tall man with a badly scarred face. He was clearly not pleased by the prospect of seeing young Forrester trussed up to be beaten. When the first blow came, the man with the scarred face turned away. Samuel began to sweat even more as he thrashed about in his sleep.

"Damn his eyes, we are not many. Don't lay on so hard with

your whip Manning. We'll need him for the voyage home. Now give him two more and be done with it," bellowed the Captain. "And be quick about it. There is a lot to do yet."

The cowhide whip arose and fell twice more on the man's naked flesh with a lessened degree of ferocity than the first blows struck. But each time it fell, it was with an awful crack. The mate, Manning, knew his business, and he still exacted awful pain with each well directed but slightly less savage blows. Forrester had taken his punishment like a man thought the Matabele Zulu prince. The tears never came. That was to his credit the warrior thought. That was now a long time ago and a world away. It was strange to think that the master actually had the marks of the lash on his back whereas most of his slaves did not.

Samuel now tossed less fitfully on his bed. Other thoughts were now running through his mind taking him back to that hot and tortured night which was one of his last in Africa. Dark questions and old stories of people having been taken away by white strangers never to be seen again now ran through his young warrior's mind as he lay on the ground bound by his cords. Very few of the Matabele had so disappeared, but stories were told by the fires at night when the old men had sat in conversation and giving each in his turn a narration of their shared Matabele history. Thus the history of the Matabele people was passed on from one generation to the next. These stories of great battles, warrior heroes, and of great hunters and kings were to be told and retold for centuries. Such was the fierceness of the Matabele that they were least often the ones taken away by slave traders to that far away place from which nobody ever returned. For that reason, the Matabele men commanded a great price in the slave markets of Mozambique. He had heard of slaving parties of Africans who lived near the coast of the great ocean, where the white men were also living and trading in forts in their walled villages. They were trading for other African men, women, and children from tribes other than their own. The Portuguese, in turn, had forts and great ships there in which Africans were taken to places so far away that the end of the world must have been seen to be nearby.

This young warrior knew of the British in far away Cape Town. He had heard many stories of that place. His uncle and grandfather had even once gone to Cape Town, after the British came there, with their mighty Matabele king. To a fast moving people like the Zulu, it was not that far a place to travel to geographically, but in terms of culture, it was like a trip to the far side of the moon where no man had yet to see. These older warriors sitting around the fireside had been outside of the big British town by the great ocean once. They had told Samuel all about the distant city of Cape Town, when they had sat by the fires at night. It was at the time that the great king of the Matabele Zulus himself, Shaka, showed the white warriors at their very own settlement, what great feats of courage his Matabele warriors were capable of. The great Shaka had caused a fire to be set in the grasslands not far from where he stood with the British officials. He then turned to two of his regiments, his impis, and said, "Let not you men look upon my face until you have gone to that flaming place of burning grass and have eaten all of that fire." Samuel softly moaned again in his fitful sleep.

Thousands of Matabele warriors in those two impis had charged the flames and rolled the fire out to extinction with their bodies. Only then did they dare return to their dread king's presence. He had gained great face with the red-coated Englishmen. They had looked on him and his impis of warriors with wonder. The British were truly astonished by what they had seen. The English people had long since stopped the stealing of African men and women for slaves in their lands. But for those taken by the slave hunting tribesmen and sold to the Portuguese, there was no returning for those who had formerly been sent over the great waters as slaves. But not all white men who were English had given up this trade even though the price they would have to pay if caught slaving was death. The Portuguese had been at it for more than three hundred years, and the Arabs and the Americans were at it still in spite of the 1807 treaty which forbid the trade.

Samuel tossed again in his painful fits of sleep as he was revisited by his old dreams. Again he saw himself as the beaten warrior prince of the Matabele. His mind raced through the fog of his awful pain as it had for most of his life since he had been captured in his sixteenth year. He had seen the white man, Forrester, who had been lashed, freed and then allowed to stand. Forrester first stood erect in an effort to preserve what little remained of his pride. Then he had slumped to the ground. He then turned his face to the man who had beaten him. Forrester's face was a mask of hate. The man who held the whip, became known to the young warrior as the first mate of the ship. This was the same ship that would take him away from his homeland. Then Samuel looked on the man who had been whipped with some compassion as a fellow sufferer. Forrester looked back at him as if he understood this sympathy. Yes, there was sympathy in the face looking at Forrester from the wide space under the door of the slave pen. Here a connection was formed.

"Well Forrester, do you think that you've learned not to cheat your betters at cards? You are a scurvy thief. Get out of my sight lest I forget Captain Whitehouse's orders and do you like I should have in the first place. Get out of my sight you piece of filth, and don't let me see your ugly face, or I'll throw you to the sharks the next time we throw the dead niggers overboard."

"Yes sir, "said Forrester. That look of defiance had disappeared from his face but not from his eyes. The Matabele had seen that look before. He knew the trouble between the two was not over. Suddenly the awful pain seemed to split his skull again. With his exertions, he passed into darkness, and he did not see the sun until another day had passed. In this dark sleep, there was pain in remembering.

Even though another day had gone by, when he awoke in his dream, it seemed as if he had just closed his eyes and went off to some dark place. Again the young prince felt pain, a very sharp pain in his ribs. He discovered that he was not dreaming and that he was actually awake. He turned in his bed as he had so long ago in agony in a sort of half roll while dark skinned European men prodded and kicked the others who were around him. Their voices did not carry any sound of meaning to him except in an angry urgency. In his foggy mind, he knew that it was not Bantu, Zulu, or even English that was being spoken now. In truth, the fog had not lifted from his senses altogether. Yet there was that other language being spoken too, and it was something that he had heard before. Then he realized that it was the language of the coastal people. It was the language of the Portuguese, those dread slave trading Europeans who were from the seacoast towns, which were far to the east of Matabeleland in Mozambique. Yes, that was it. They were Portuguese. "These people would sell their mothers for profit if they could," he had heard the elders say when they were sitting around the fires at night. His mind was foggy with pain, and he had a very difficult time making his eyes focus. There was a sickness in his stomach, and he still suffered total disorientation with his concussion.

Samuel grew more fitful as he relived for yet another one of many hundreds of times the awful memories of his enslavement. He discovered that he was now aware of many others in the cramped space about him. They were moaning and crying. He too felt like crying because of a terrible sense of loss that he was beginning to feel with the realization that he may never see his home and family again if, as he had heard, he was among the coastal people who sold men into slavery. The deep fear he now felt had not been fully defined, but it was there nevertheless. He could not cry, because that was not the way of the Matabele warrior. He dragged himself to his feet at the prompting of the small dark men armed with clubs. He was very dizzy and weak. He also found to his disgust that he was covered in dried blood and filth, and that he was looking at his surroundings through badly swollen eyes. As his head began to clear a little, he tried to take some note of his condition. He had been stripped of everything except his loincloth, and this he must have soiled. The warrior recoiled from himself in this disgusting state, and he became more aware that he was painfully moving in a herd of fellow suffering humanity into the blinding sunlight.

In the awful heat of the Georgian night, Samuel lived it all again. Shouting continued around him, and the scores of Africans, who had also been driven out of what he now could see were nearby pens and sheds, were slowly joining the long and sad procession. He became acutely aware of the smell of the unwashed humanity around him even in the open air. Yet the air in the open was still better than that in the closed pent up place in which he had been held. He suddenly convulsed, fell to his knees, and vomited. One of the darker coastal Portuguese men advanced on him with a club raised as if to strike him. He saw this threat, but he could not muster even enough strength to raise his arm to ward off the awful blow that must now come.

"Belay that you stupid sot. That nigger is my personal property. If you kill him, he won't be worth a tinker's damn to me you idiot," shouted Captain Whitehouse.

The smaller dark man looked at the tall white man in tall black leather boots who was wearing an almost clean white shirt. The dark man with the club did not quite understand what was being said to him. He had a moment of confusion then looked back on the young Zulu warrior kneeling over his vomit. Then he raised the club again to strike. The tall white man who had shouted the order sprang over the railing that had separated him from the slave enclosure, seized the smaller dark man with the upraised club and threw him down into the vomit.

"When I give you an order, damn your eyes, obey it or I'll lay your brains out onto the sand you stupid sot!" bellowed the Captain.

"He don't understand you. He don't speak no English, but I think you make him understand now all the same," said a better dressed species of Portuguese slave trader.

He was an older and darker skinned slaver, and he had

addressed these words to the Englishman in heavily accented but understandable English. The Portuguese trader then expressed the Englishman's wishes to his countrymen in their own language and turned back to the Englishman.

"See Captain, everything is fine. I have explained that you want your cargo alive, fed, cleaned up, and loaded onto your ship. I have also told them not to kill any of the cargo or I would stake them out on the beach myself to be devoured by the crabs. After I actually did it to some idiot once, they know that I am indeed a very serious man," he laughed. "Everything you wish will all be done Captain, and there will be no loss of profit to you I assure you. Things can be so civilized if we are slow to anger and are always reasonable. You must not excite yourself my dear Captain. My nephew is young and very stupid, but my sister loves him, and I must be content to employ him for her sake. Business is difficult now that the English and Americans have ended the traffic in our product for these last eight years."

In Samuel's dream, the voice rang out for the thousandth time. "Those damned bastards had no business doing that. God damn them all and the Wilberforce *Bible* thumpers too! They could hang me and all the men that sail in my damn ship if so much as one of those black devils is found on my vessel alive or dead. This may be my last trip if I'm caught. That is, it may be my last trip with any expectation of reaching port."

"Holy Mother of God!" said the Portuguese trader mockingly as he crossed himself. "May all the saints in heaven watch over you my dear Captain Whitehouse, and may your cargo arrive with safety so that you may come back again to do business with me."

"I'm Church of England, but I thank you for your papist blessing all the same. If the Roman Church and the Pope himself can get me across the Atlantic to my friends in the Southern American states or Brazil with my cargo intact, I would be most grateful. Those black devils will fetch a pretty fair price that is if not too many of them decide to die in mid passage. Since my government and Mr. Jefferson's and now Mr. Madison's government have outlawed the trade in black ivory, I've been in a hard sort of way. It would kill me to have to be placed in the position where I would have to chain this lot to an anchor and throw them overboard to avoid swinging from a yardarm. And believe me, it's not the damned Yankees who trouble me. It's the fucking Royal Navy. Those bastards don't bring you back to The Old Bailey for a trial. They just convene a sort of court martial on shipboard, record the testimony, hand down the guilty verdict, and then hang you from a yardarm for a swing and dance in the air. It's not a pretty sight especially if you are the fellow swinging and doing the jig in the air."

"Look at it this way my friend," smiled the slave trader, "This little agreement of the Americans and British has taken care of a lot of your competition. The faint hearted will be weeded out of the trade, and they will have left the larger profits to us who are men of vision and courage. Besides that bastard Napoleon is keeping everyone pretty busy in Europe now since he has run away from Elba. So don't fret too much. As long as Bonaparte is loose in Europe, England will have a full plate of troubles to sort out. They will have no time for you my dear friend. And do not forget that the Americans are now quite busy with your English relatives in that stupid war of theirs right now. That is also good for you is it not my dear Captain?"

"Is that what you think Dom Pedro," laughed the Englishman. "I think that you esteem the European and American situations too lightly from the point of view of what we have to fear. But enough of that. Let's go down to the beach and see how the loading of the cargo is coming along. I want to see what I've got after I've cleaned the buggers up and have had a real look at them without all of that filth hiding any problems. The last time out, there were too many grandfathers in the lot. Too damn many of them died after we were at sea a while, and even with the great shortages of slaves in America and Brazil during the last four years, I had a hard time pleasing my investors. They don't fancy underwriting unprofitable enterprises. Too many old and dead niggers are not good for business Dom Pedro. And it's a hard business at that even when the cargo consists of prime material. This I don't mind telling you, and besides, your government don't give a good goddamn what you are up to unlike my people who are preoccupied with crawling up my arse with their Parliamentary acts to end the slave trade even as we speak. That they have had their hands full with Old Boney is true enough, and I don't think that they really give a damn about what The Mozambique Company, or its operatives who are trading in all sorts of goods are up to at the moment. Portugal is a British ally since the Peninsula War. But the time will come when they will put the Corsican corporal away or shoot him and turn their considerable attention on us. I don't think that day is far away my dear Dom Pedro."

"You do not have to trouble yourself on that score Captain, nor do you have to worry this time about the quality of what goods that you have gotten here. This is the most superb cargo I have ever assembled for you. We have been sending our people further inland you see. We even got some of the inland tribes to capture some heir own people as well as their neighbors. It's a friendly little cottage business out in Mashonaland and Matabeleland as well, that is if the buggers do not catch you at it. The Matabele caught some of my people a few years ago. They bound them hand and foot and threw them over a cliff one at a time. My poor fellows had a while to contemplate their fate before they took flight. The slave catchers we use don't mind the risk as long as they are the ones who do not get caught. They make some money and settle some old grudges of their own at the same time. I do not worry about any hard feelings they might stir up among themselves. My hands are clean to all observers, and I am not a greedy man. I share my profits with the authorities on the coast. I donate some money to the church to keep God satisfied, and therefore I will have no trouble there. Maybe you will make more voyages, maybe one perhaps two, and then we can both retire and get back to where we belong away from this stinking place. I would like a fine house in Lisbon and a villa in the country. How about you Captain Whitehouse? Would you like to be in Lisbon or London?"

In his deep sleep, Samuel listened once again to the Captain. Each word spoken had been etched into Samuel's brain and played out countless times. In his waking hours he never could have recalled the words, but when he dreamed of the time of his capture, everything returned to him in its totality. "I'd like to be somewhere quiet," the Captain had continued, "But with Bonaparte marching all over Europe, I'd like to see where my chances are in a few years. Who knows how that is all going to turn out? If Bonaparte wins, the war could go on for another twenty-five years. Right now the Royal Navy is busy with the French, as you so wisely pointed out, and the Portuguese royal family is still in Brazil. Why don't you plan to retire to a fine life there Dom Pedro? You can trade in all the bloody slaves you want and feel right at home at the same time. I've been there. It's like a garden, a new Eden on the South American coast. I hear that the Portuguese royals like it very well. Some even say that they have no intention of ever leaving the place and returning to Portugal."

"You make a good deal of sense Captain, but let us see about your cargo and finish our business before you invite me to dine at your fine villa in Rio," Dom Pedro replied.

As the two men walked along engaged in conversation, the cargo marched before them. In a bit, the beach came into view. The slaves marched down the path in the direction of the sea and then came to rest with those who had preceded them to the beach an hour earlier. Many of the slaves had already been washed down with seawater and fed from troughs. They were surrounded and guarded by the ship's crew and Dom Pedro's men. Their spirit was entirely broken as they sat there with no defense or retreat possible. The newly enslaved were frightened and ashamed of their reduced state. The young Matabele warrior was glad of the privacy of the water and an opportunity to slip out of his loincloth so that he could rinse it of its filth before he put it on again. He was not alone in attempting to restore some personal dignity to his shattered life. Many of these African men had owned cattle, had property, wives and children. Most of them were men of some substantial property or the children of men who were well to do and persons of respect. Some had even been great men in their own lands. Some of the women had followed their men into captivity willingly so that they would not be parted from them. Some even followed with their children. And this situation was to prove to be just more profit for the Portuguese slave trader. Maybe he could even increase his donation to the church, perhaps pay well for prayers for his soul.

The women who followed their men into captivity did not know that if they had another chance, they would not choose slavery if they could see what their future might hold. The longer they were with the men first captured, the more most of them had realized the horrible mistake that they had made. Here, in this situation, a Matabele warrior had an advantage. He would not have a wife following him into captivity, because he would not have been allowed to take a wife for another twenty-three years. A Matabele does not wed until he is thirty-nine years of age. The great Shaka had made this rule so that women would not sap men of their vitality. No crying woman would be following Samuel into this uncertain exile.

A hush had fallen over the newly enslaved Africans as they sat in the sun trying not to speak to each other. Inter tribal distrust still ruled the thought process of these people even now. Later on they would learn that for the most part they had shared very little language in common with the other Africans they traveled with. Here they were, sitting on the African shore, most of them not knowing exactly where they were. Most of them, from the interior country, had never seen the sea before and had no idea what, if anything was beyond the horizon. Maybe there was nothing and these big ships would just sail off the earth. In their small experience of the world, the sea may also have no end. Several of them, sensing that they would never see their homeland again, filled their mouths with sand in an attempt to eat some of their native soil. Others did it to kill themselves. A few succeeded in this in spite of the efforts of Dom Pedro's men and Captain Whitehouse's crew to stop them.

Samuel was now helpless in the private hell of his dreams when a knock came to his door. He sat up in a cold sweat relieved to be liberated from this nightly torture.

CHAPTER VI

A knock was heard at the door of Samuel's cabin, and the big man was stirred out of his dream. He swung his feet to the wooden floor of his cabin in gratitude that this private terror of his dreaming of his capture and baptism into slavery had been interrupted. Samuel simply said, "Who is there?"

"Pompey."

Noting that it was nine o'clock by the sudden soft striking of his wall clock Samuel realized that he had been sleeping only an hour. The big man slipped on his shoes and uncomfortably arose. He was now aware that his clothes were damp with his sweat. He called out, "Come in Pompey. What bribe did you bring me this time?"

"This is no bribe. This is a tribute for you Samuel."

"A tribute. I am pleased by that. You must want something young Pompey. What tempting prize do you have there?"

'Pompey opened his sack, unwrapped the food from its insulating towels and placed his offering on the table. This consisted of half of a roasted chicken, some baked yams, and half a blueberry pie. Everything was piping hot. Samuel inclined his head in approval, and said, "What is this feast going to cost me this time?"

Neither Samuel or Pompey spoke the Black idiomatic

language of slavery to each other when they were alone together. During this last year since Anna's death, Pompey and Samuel had bonded just as Anna had wished them to do all of those years ago when Pompey was deposited in her kitchen as a tiny boy. Samuel almost never spoke to anyone. He never spoke at all to the field hands except to issue an order or instruct them in their duties. Their inferior station placed them far beyond his interest except as workers. He had become wise in the ways of white men, through the lessons that he had gained through observation and reading Forrester's books. He learned to put his instinctive Zulu discipline and leadership to use. Forrester was amused to learn that Samuel had been taught to read by the British in missionary school so many years ago. It had been fortunate for Samuel that the leadership of the Matabele had wanted their best people to learn to read so that the secrets of the white man's world would not be closed to them. The Matabele had tolerated the missionaries when it was useful. Few converts were made among them to the Christian God.

Over the last quarter century, this Matabele Prince made himself most useful to his master and strange partner of his work. Forrester for his part had put Samuel in charge as overseer of the whole plantation as part of the agreement they had made long ago. Samuel was even empowered to negotiate the sale of the crops and was solely responsible for running the plantation office. Forrester was by nature a lazy man given to pleasure and card playing. Forrester had congratulated himself a hundred times over on the bargain that he had struck with Samuel when they had both escaped into the white world as slave and master. Samuel was used to commanding others and was a very quick study. Samuel at sixteen was a natural leader that mere ordinary men of forty would obey without question. Such was his natural habit of authority. He also had a skill for creating wealth. This left Forrester free to gamble and play at being the country squire while Samuel ran the plantation in every respect apart from the big house itself. Acquiring slaves was Forrester's domain. His fabulous luck at the card table did almost as much to bring an effective workforce to the plantation, as did his outright purchasing of slaves.

Even the white men, who had traded with Samuel when he conducted his master's business, never questioned his power to negotiate for Forrester. Nor did they question his integrity and open handedness. Nobody could have guessed just what the true relationship between James Forrester and his head slave driver really was. Sometimes there were speculations such as that they might have shared a common father. Such things were hardly rare events in plantation life. Everybody knew that Samuel actually ran the place but never in a manner to offer offense to the sensibilities of the prickly white southern aristocracy. More than once, a man would offer to buy Samuel, and each time Forrester would say that he could not afford to cut off his right arm for a mere fist full of gold. It was a strange partnership, which worked in the most practical way to the total satisfaction of both men.

When Forrester came to the slave quarters to see Samuel, it was always at night. All anyone knew was that the field hands belonged to Samuel in a strange sort of way, and he ruled over them with a fair but despotic sway. The plantation ran well, and that was all anyone ever knew. All that Forrester cared about were profits and a peaceful home. These were well provided for by Samuel. The culture of slavery was closed to all outsiders. Each plantation was an autonomous principality under the rule of a de facto absolute monarch, in the person of the plantation's master. Samuel was as complete an autocrat as any chancellor who had ever served his king in the ruling of a great nation.

On the Forrester Plantation, it was even more so. The field hands respected the giant Samuel who was more than willing to put stripes on their backs if they dared to challenge him in any way. The fact was, that he never used the whip. In Africa, to cross, disobey, or challenge Samuel would have had more fatal consequences rather than a mere lashing. The slaves were safe as long as they were compliant. Therefore, no slave was ever beaten. Here too on the plantation, Samuel was a sort of prince, and

Pompey had sensed it almost as soon as he had arrived here on the Forrester place long before he actually saw or met Samuel. Even the master's sister gave way before his quiet authority. The big man had taken to the little bright boy whom he had first seen in Anna's kitchen, and at her request had decided to make Pompey his pet.

Samuel had been amused when the little fellow first sneaked away from the big house and had came to him by night, begging to talk to him, and asking so many questions about Africa. Samuel was drawn to Pompey's intellect and willingness to be taught. There had evolved a friendship between the man and boy who were so much alike. Samuel became Pompey's teacher. The large and largely unread Forrester library was to provide the rest of Pompey's education. Under Samuel's almost tender tutelage, the boy grew in knowledge. He grew to love the big man, because there was a real strength in this giant that seemed to be proof against the awful threat of impermanence. Forrester knew all about Pompey's visits to Samuel and concluded that there was no harm in it if it amused his "Good Right Arm" to satisfy some paternalistic instinct. Pompey might even get the right sort of training to be almost as valuable to him as Samuel was himself in time was the thought that had evolved in the master's mind. Besides that, anything that amused or pleased Samuel was all right with James Forrester.

"Well Pompey, you do not disappoint. Once more you have brought a meal to me fit for a great king," said Samuel.

"A great warrior prince at least," said Pompey with devilish intent.

"Hush about that boy. You never know who might be hearing all of this even now. All these slaves have hearing so rare and sharp. They hear nothing most of the time, but at the same time they hear everything. They say much, but they also say little. Not one of you has seen Africa, yet Africa is there in them. It is just under the skin of each of their bodies. Africa cannot be whipped out of you or them or removed in any way. Even if your skin is fair like the snow of a northern winter Pompey, your soul is black and of the stuff of Africa. Each of us here in his heart has a bit of Africa in him. It is as his pride without even knowing it."

"I know it Samuel. I think I always knew it, but you have taught me to love it and respect myself for it and to be a man, an African man."

"That is a very dangerous idea for a Black man who is also a slave in this white man's land, but that makes this gift of pride rarer still and a treasure more to be valued than gold. Sometime in the future the day will come when you must get away from here Pompey."

"But what about you Samuel? I cannot leave you. You are my real father now."

The bond between the older and younger man had grown into more than that of mentor and disciple since Anna's death. Just as the wise old woman wished, the bond between Samuel and Pompey had truly evolved into that of father and son.

"Do you think that I do not know this thing? Pompey, you are not the son of my loins, but you are the true son of my heart. You know how to think. We shall wait for the right moment, and we shall tell no one what we dream. You know how to read the white man's ideas, and you even know how to get into his head. You can talk like him and ape his manners. You move like the leopard without noise. You have the manner of one who is obeyed in all things, and more than that, you can pass for a white man if you must. You have almost everything that is needful to make your way out of this accursed place. Someday you will do it."

"How do you know that Samuel?"

"Because the time will someday come for me to exact my revenge on the man who condemned me to a life of slavery so far from my home in Africa. To do that, I too must leave this place. I am getting older. You see, the Matabele Zulu cannot know women until they have passed thirty and nine seasons. To know a woman before that time is to invite death not only to yourself but also for your whole family. This is a royal decree issued by Shaka himself to keep the warriors of The People of Heaven vital. The warrior must not dissipate his power by having sexual congress with a woman before his time. It will sap his strength. The law was made, and the punishment is severe for those who would break this law. If a warrior of less than thirty-nine years would make love to a woman, if he would lay with her as a wife, and should he be discovered, this transgression would invite the punishment of death as I have told you. Both of the lovers would be bound hand and foot, along with their mothers, fathers, brothers, and sisters and thrown from a cliff onto the rocks below for breaking the Zulu law of breeding too soon without the king's consent."

"Why Samuel?"

"It is as I have said. To be strong, you must keep your powers in check so that you can run all day, fight a battle, and exterminate your king's enemies. To do this, you must keep your seed until the given time, and then all the warriors of thirty and nine seasons gather together at the king's kraal and enter into unions with strong young women who can give them strong children. Then they can have as many children as they have years left to live. The children will herd the cattle and become warriors or marry warriors. They will make you a rich man. They shall be warriors, the mothers of warriors, and the most important people in all of Africa. That is what it means to be a Matabele Zulu. Do you see me standing here? I am nearing my forty third year, yet I am stronger than any man on the place of any age. I have more endurance than any draft beast. That is not an accident Pompey. I cannot go to Bulawayo and dance the marriage dance before the kraal of the king and take my wife to make sons, because I am bound here in this red clayed Georgia. So I must do other things such as controlling my feelings and hunger. I will tell you when the time is right for us to make our moves toward freedom, and I will give you good notice of when we should go from here."

"I don't know if I am ready yet Samuel."

"No, that is true. You have learned the wisdom that is in the master's books that has given you a window into the history and culture of the white man. You have even tricked his stupid wife into thinking that she has taught you these things so that she can dress you in finery and parade you like some pretty trained ape to amuse her friends. You are fortunate that she finds you comely Pompey. She makes you her plaything. You were wise to have some foolish white man for your father who also had no luck at cards. You are now fortunate to have an indulgent master who has great luck at cards. If that were not so, you would be in the fields working on the old Selby place with your back broken by the whip and blistered by the sun."

"No Samuel, you are my father, and it is fortunate that our master has friends who like to drink strong drink when they play at cards. It is well that he is not caught cheating," said the young man laughing.

"What are you getting at young Pompey! Do you think that our noble master is less than honorable?"

The two men laughed and talked in low voices for another half hour. Then hours before the morning sun would arise over the red earth of Georgia, Pompey went back to the big house to his quarters, and Samuel went out into the night on his own ramblings. When Pompey arrived back at the big white house, nobody took notice of him. The Forrester boys had set out on one of their own adventures, and the Forrester ladies had long ago retired to their rooms. Slowly the household had settled into total quiet as the sweet aroma of the roses and the soft summer night slowly wafted in through the open windows and cooled the big house. Pompey drifted off into sleep.

CHAPTER VII

That night had been a beautiful soft Southern night. The moon was full. There was a light breeze, and the air was balmy. The thermometer set in the old hall barometer read a cool seventy-three degrees. James Forrester set out on his best saddle horse for his favorite haunt away from the all too confining world of his plantation as Pompey was just making his way to Samuel's cabin. Buckland's Tavern, where the county planters and wealthier members of the professional class gathered for refreshments and games of cards. This was the master's favorite haunt for recreation, that is, just after a visit to a certain cabin in his slave quarters where one of his latest winnings from another of his hapless neighbors, Anton Beauchamp Beauregard, rested her beautiful body down on her mahogany four poster bed. The master had so thoughtfully provided this luxury for her for the sole purpose of his pleasure.

For the time being, she would find favor with him, and there would be no work for her. There would be gifts of cheap jewelry, gaudy clothes, and candy, which would all be very grand for a slave girl of sixteen. When James Forrester had finished with her, there would be some little work for her to do but not too much. Master Forrester was always filled with gratitude for services skillfully rendered, and he knew well how to reward favored girls on his plantation. A word to Samuel would make a slave girl's life very comfortable indeed. There was also no telling when the master might decide to revisit her in the future. He was, after all, as he himself had remarked to his friends, still a young and randy man full of spirit and amorous ambitions.

Another of Forrester's favorite spots for recreation was Miss Sally Beer's Gentleman's Hotel. Here gentlemen of the wealthy planter class might seek activities other than those provided at other far more common country inns catering to the pleasures of men. Most of the planter's wives didn't mind a bit what their men were up to as long as they themselves were respected, and their husbands were discrete. The activities provided by Miss Sally kept their husbands satisfied and their all too often unwanted amorous attentions elsewhere. It was not that southern women objected to seeing to their conjugal duties, but it seems that these beastly men could not time the moment of their sexually adventuresome spirits for the convenience of a lady's calendar. Most wives were of the opinion that three or four children were quite enough sons and heirs and pretty daughters to satisfy any male ego. They raised their aristocratic noses at the farm folk to which families of ten or twelve offspring were all too common, but then those farmer folk were just very common folk after all. The fact that the men of privilege could seek a discrete and respectable place of release for their pent up sexual urges was a great relief to the more aristocratic matrons of Georgia.

James Forrester was no stranger to Miss Sally Beers and her ladies. Miss Sally did play the great lady well. In point of fact, she did so far better than most of the ladies of the county. She was well schooled in politics, literature, and the world. Miss Sally Beers was most satisfactory to the gentlemen of the county in every way. She had learned her trade to perfection in Paris. She had introduced most of the local gentry to unearthly and intoxicating pleasures that they had never imagined could exist. It was unfortunate that old Doctor Richards had overextended his physical energies with a beautiful high yellow girl from New Orleans on one fine night and died as a result of his enthusiasm for new games of pleasure. That night had been a very fine one very much like this night at Miss Sally's.

The good Doctor had spent the evening in the pleasure of the company of a highly skilled courtesan. For all of Miss Sally's ladies were just that. No lord or even a king in his palace had been so well served. These ladies of the night were not the average crib girls of the more sordid sort. These women could induce such pleasures that only the most imaginative of men could even aspire to. After the Doctor had passed from this mortal coil in the arms of a most lovely dusky vision of delight, he was carefully dressed back in the clothes he had worn on that most unfortunate evening. The good doctor was then taken home to respectably die again. This time he would meet death under more auspicious circumstances in his study reading "Revelations" which was a far more circumspect final venue for his untimely death. In the morning, the butler would find his master collapsed over his *Bible.* The doctor's good wife never knew the truth of the circumstances of her husband's passing which all attested to the kindness of the good doctor's friends and the great discretion of Miss Sally. It would not have done for this paragon of the community to have died under a sordid cloud. Most of all, it would have been most unseemly for him to have passed away at Miss Sally's in the bed of that high yellow beauty with whom the good doctor was so taken. Gentlemen, in the end, must protect other members of their class. After all, who might not be taken unawares one last time and be in need of such a favor themselves someday.

The minister did remark at the funeral of the good doctor that the smile on the good man's face, even in death, was quite angelic. Much the same thing had been said of Miss Sally's smile, when the doctor's death was discussed. The quality ladies of the county had heard vague rumors over the years about this bordello of distinction. One planter's wife had even asked her husband about Miss Sally's furnishings. It is said that her husband told her that his wife was not to ask such improper questions and restrain herself. He told her, quite frankly, that her interest in Miss Sally's place of business was unseemly.

James Forrester was quite the fair-haired boy at Buckland's. He was indeed famed as a good-humored fellow who was always ready to try his gaming luck with anyone at cards in a very open handed manner. His ready laugh made him popular among the planters over the last twenty some years along with his willingness to stand those with whom he played cards to drinks. He himself was a temperate man when it came to intoxicating spirits who would sip but one small tot of whiskey from the same modest glass all the night long as he played cards. James Forrester was a modest gentleman who never boasted of his winning at cards. He accepted his luck with grace. In point of fact, he did not always win at the start of the night. Somehow the cards did not favor him during the early evening. It was always about ten or ten thirty, by the tall case clock, that his luck began to change as the more alcoholically animated players lost their money to him. And to boot, he was generous in victory to a fault.

He would take a man's money and his slaves, in place of ready cash, like the true sportsman he was, but when it came to his winning his neighbor's land, even a plantation, he would always say, "Go home and sleep it off. I'll not take a man's birthright from him." Sometimes after returning the deed to the lucky man who had the good sense to lose his plantation to him and not one of the other gentlemen who might not be so liberal minded, Forrester would stand the entire company to a drink. It was common knowledge that Forrester was a good fellow who would never take unfair advantage of another gentleman.

As he entered the taproom on this well-favored evening, James Forrester waved expansively to all the local gentry assembled there. He was greeted warmly in return. Forrester walked over to the well polished bar and ordered his usual small whiskey. Another gentleman in tall boots, covered with a dusting of red clay, as were all the boots of gentlemen and laboring workers alike in that season of the year, bought a drink as well. This fellow had lost his plantation to Forrester twice within a fortnight and proposed to do it again that very evening. When informed of this, Forrester threw back his head and laughed.

"Why not give it a try old friend, it might be a good night for you. I'm tired and not feeling all that well. There is a very good chance that good fortune will not smile on me as it has been her habit."

"Just listen to the man. We had better be on guard tonight gentlemen or we shall be walking home in our small clothes. Well Forrester, you are a good fellow. Always willing to give a poor man a chance to best you by way of a little revenge. I have always supposed you to be the finest sport God ever made. In fact, I've got the deed to my place right here in my pocket. Let us see if you can take it three times before the moon sets."

"I know what your deed feels like. I've held it twice before Beauregard," laughed Forrester. "I do not think that you should pledge it again. My sons are to go to West Point one of these days, and if they do not do well there, I shall have to install them somewhere else or their mother will kill them both. I have some small affection for my Douglas and James. Your plantation would make a fine place to hide them away so that they could play at running a place of their own. So be warned my friend, and don't wager your plantation again. I would hate to turn you and your family out, but my Mrs. Forrester may insist on my own relocation if she has to have those two boys under foot for too many more years."

The room burst into laughter. Beauregard's friends counseled him to be careful. Forrester slapped his friend Beauregard on the back and asked loudly, "Now, do you know any other fellows who might want to hazard some of their earthly wealth tonight in a game of chance?"

Two other planters from the bar ambled over to the table where Forrester always played as they had done for years when those words were spoken. It was a clarion call to the red blooded gaming men of the county. A stranger also walked up to the table, bowed and asked, "Would you mind a lonely traveler in need of company sitting in on the game? I am looking for a bit of distraction. Might I join you gentlemen in a game of chance?"

Forrester sized up the man dressed in expensive and well-cut clothes and tall shining English riding boots. There was something oddly familiar and disturbing about this man. But that feeling of unease only lasted for an instant. Forrester smiled engagingly, as was his habit and said, "Sir, pull up a chair. You are most welcome at this table. My name is James Forrester. This is Beauregard, and these gentlemen are Carlton and O' Hara. And your name sir?"

"I'm Captain Peter Whitehouse sir," said the man in a fine clipped English accent. "Just call me Whitehouse or Captain, and that will be fine gentlemen."

Forrester looked down at his cards. He could not believe his ears. Suddenly the full horror of the moment was upon him. Even after a quarter of a century, the whole ugly period of his being in the slave trade came racing back, and filled him with fear and dread, but nothing in his manner or speech betrayed him or the awful sense of foreboding that every trapped animal feels just before the kill. He raced back through the years to his voyage on that slaver. His name then was also Forrester, and now his beard and mustache were long gone along with the mop of greasy hair and forty pounds of body fat. His manners had changed along with his size and manner of speaking. His soft and carefully cultivated drawl would not betray that rude northern voice with which he had spoken two and a half decades ago. He wondered if the Captain would remember him after so long a time.

"Well Mr. Goddamned Bloody Whitehouse, I'm an Irishman, and damn it all to Hell, I don't fancy sitting with a damned stinking Englishman!" said O' Hara in his unpretentious and unvarnished brogue that could be cut into thick slabs with a dull meat cleaver.

A hush fell over the room. The Englishman stiffened. His powerful body was like a coiled spring. His eyes narrowed. He was ready for action. The gentlemen in the room were no strangers to outbursts of violence and what may follow. All eyes were on Whitehouse and O'Hara. There was no telling what drama might be acted out between the two big men now. The gentry always enjoyed the distraction of unexpected mayhem.

"I take it that you sir are Mr. O' Hara. If that be the case, I just want to tell you that I am no longer an Englishman. I have resigned from that accursed race. Like your own unfortunate people, I too have had to leave my home because of the same sort of cursed stupidity that placed Ireland under the heel of England. That poor and English besotted accursed land has been made a pesthole by English misrule, and I hope whatever relations you may still have residing there will cut every throat of every thieving English landlord in the place. I drink sir," said Whitehouse, "To Ireland. May her people prosper, and her English enemies rot in bottomless bogs. May she someday be free of that accursed race of English land stealers and killers of poor mens' souls."

O' Hara stood stupefied by the Englishman's response. Then he spoke, "You sir may be the very first of your race I will sit and drink with. Very handsome of you too sir and very well said. You sir should stand for Parliament. Indeed you should sir."

"Mr. O'Hara, it is a pleasure to meet such a reasonable man as yourself. I count it my very good fortune to have met with such a fine gentleman as yourself. Now gentlemen, do you think that we might play cards?"

The entire taproom laughed at the conclusion of the little set-to and its quick and rational conclusion. Everyone then returned to the serious business of their drinking, conversations, and card playing. Some of the men in Buckland's, no doubt, reflected that a donnybrook between O'Hara and the Englishman might have been nice as a playful diversion, but they were all supposed to be gentlemen, and at least the same proprieties should be observed here as were observed at Miss Sally's. Anyone who caused a disturbance there would be ejected by two burly well dressed men, who would have been more at home up North in their native

Five Points. The quality of manners at Buckland's should at least measure up to the high standard of a first quality whorehouse.

Several hours passed in card playing. At first, Forrester lost several hands, and then his luck began to improve slowly as was his custom. This was unremarkable to all of the card players except for Whitehouse. Unlike the others, he did not talk during the play. Nor did he drink from the glass of whiskey he had carried to the table. He watched his cards and those of the others as well when they were dealt, called, or calling. After a while, the Captain seemed to focus his attention on Forrester alone. Forrester had the strange and uncomfortable feeling that he was being observed a bit too closely for comfort. When Forrester looked up from his cards, he saw Whitehouse making a study of his face. Somewhere in Forrester's memory there was emerging a vague tingle of an old and latent fear. The old long, twisted, and hidden scars from the mate's lash on his back began to ache again as they had so long ago. Forrester looked at the Englishman again. There was no mistaking it, the Captain was making a real study of him. Then Forrester looked back at his cards with an assumed good-natured shrug. Whitehouse could never confuse him, the refined man of property, with the stealing and cheating cur of a low sailor on a slave ship of so long ago. James Forrester still had a feeling of unease, but in a few moments, with his customary winning, his fear was gone.

The other players went on enjoying their customary little wins and greater losses with their good-natured chatter. They were oblivious to the strange rendezvous which fate had seemed to direct. O'Hara was the first to drop out of the game. For the first time in months, he was actually ten dollars ahead. But, he had been distracted by the arrival of an old friend with land to sell and a story to tell. "I hate to leave the table winning as I am, but Sean and I have some business and jawing to do. So begging your pardons gentlemen, I must leave for a bit of some personal business."

"Quite alright old fellow," said Whitehouse. "I'm sure that

Mr. Forrester will make up his losses without you. I'm really not feeling all that lucky tonight myself."

"That is Forrester's habit sir, and that's a fact to be sure. I'll not be far Mr. Whitehouse, and it would be my pleasure to stand you to a drink in a bit if you have no objections," said O'Hara with a flourish.

"That is very handsome of you Mr. O'Hara. It would be my honor sir to accept," replied the Captain.

O'Hara met his friend at the bar, and everyone's attention returned to the game. In fact, each time the gentlemen at the table had assembled for a game over the past few years, everyone had the good fortune to leave with a few dollars in winnings, on various nights, except Beauregard who seemed heroically stoical about his fate as the one constant loser. Carlton dropped out from the evening's contest next with a loss of two hundred dollars, and at last the hapless Beauregard left a hundred and fifty dollars poorer to join O'Hara and his friend at the bar with his glass of whiskey in his hand. He had wisely decided not betting the plantation that night. What would happen if by mischance the Englishman had won it? He reflected that he would have had a hard time explaining the fact of losing his home to his ever-patient wife. Beauregard decided that he would not care to relocate his family to some other living arrangements. His wife, who was not well pleased by his gambling at Buckland's in the first place, would most likely take a pistol from the desk and shoot him. Beauregard was willing to bet even money that his wife would be well sure of herself that she would not be hanged for it given the circumstances.

Now only Forrester and Whitehouse were left at the table. For the first time in the memory of the players, Forrester began to sweat. Whitehouse watched him like a hawk.

"I say Forrester, how would you like to double the stakes," asked the Captain with a devilish smile playing about his lips.

"Why not indeed," replied Forrester attempting to show no doubt in his ability to play at a higher level.

The unbelievable was now beginning to happen. Forrester was playing with someone who could go toe-to-toe with him and even best him at the card table. Whitehouse now smiled the smile of one who knew a secret, and Forrester's well-known good nature was slowly fading. Several hours passed. The clock struck one thirty, and Forrester was becoming more and more distracted. As the hours had passed his losses were now mounting to thousands of dollars.

Whitehouse consistently seemed to know when to hold and when to drop his cards. At first, Forrester's winnings were small and Whitehouse's slightly larger with each hand. Over the course of the next few hours, Forrester had lost tens of thousands of dollars. His eyes narrowed, and his mouth had become a mere slit in his face as he compressed them in his anxiety. Nobody who had known Forrester twenty or more years had ever seen him like this. His composure and bonhomie were gone. Whitehouse's smile began to turn into a sardonic jeering sneer. The men in the room began to grumble. They were turning on the Englishman. They did not like his manner. At last Forrester held a good hand and called Whitehouse. The Englishman folded his cards and dropped them on the table without raising the stakes. Forrester snapped, "Why the Hell did you do that damn it? Didn't you have a good hand? Why didn't you raise me damn you?" Gone was Forrester's veneer of civility and his caution. The onlookers were clearly perplexed.

"Do what Forrester? Fold my hand? Fold when I was holding three queens? It's tempting to stay in the game when one holds three queens securely under normal circumstances, but you my friend knew that I had three queens just as I knew that you held four fives," replied the Englishman between clenched teeth.

The room went silent. Planters and townsmen looked at each other agape. Only one thing could happen now. Forrester turned red with fury and began to speak just as Whitehouse's voice cracked through the fog and confusion of the moment. Here was the voice of a sea captain who was used to giving orders and being obeyed. It was the voice of one who had been a long time at sea and acted like the embodiment of a living god, both immortal and absolute. The master of a ship is essentially God on earth.

"Stop your infernal sputtering, and show these fine people, that you have no doubt been cheating for many years, your hand damn your eyes. Do it now!" bellowed the Captain as if he were speaking to an entire crew of mutineers from the quarterdeck of his own ship. Turning to the room, the Captain smiled, "Oh by the by, he holds a seven in addition to the four fives. It would have looked very badly for him if the cheater was holding a king or ace would it not?"

Forrester sat frozen. O'Hara reached over and seized the cards from Forrester's hand. Then he turned the cards over. There on the table were four fives and a seven of clubs. O'Hara turned to Whitehouse, and said, "Now, how the Devil would you be after knowing what the man held in his hand? Is it a magician you are Captain darling? Or is it a fortune telling tinker that you be?"

"Nothing so grand as that Mr. O'Hara. It's just that I've played cards all over this world and still alive to tell about all of the strange things that I've seen. Your Mr. Forrester was too clever by half, but I puzzled it out. Now, did you all not always play with cards first picked up by Forrester here? Now, I'm sure that you honest folk never questioned where they came from, I suggest."

"That it was. Indeed it was always Forrester himself that brought out the deck we were to use," finished O'Hara. "We've been after taking a thrashing from him for years. Are you telling us that we have been cheated out of thousands of dollars by a man with a crooked deck of cards? That would be a lot of shyte to swallow to be sure if it be true!"

Forrester regained something of his old composure. He was fighting now for his life,

"It's not me who is the cheat here. I am your friend. You have known me more than twenty years Daniel," Forrester protested to O'Hara. "You have never set eyes on this Englishman before this evening in your entire lives. He's the cheat. He's a cheating son of a whore," cried Forrester.

"Son of a whore? Are you casting judgments and aspersions on an honest woman's profession my good man? On the very character of she who was my own dear mother? She was an honest whore who gave value for cash paid. She never cheated or stole. She was, bless her, a much better soul than you boy-o. And in her way a rather grand lady. I'll tell you what is the correct thing to do right now. You should make all of your friend's losses to you over, say, the last five years good. If you've cheated them longer than that, and they were too slow and dimwitted to discover it, the more fool them. I intend no offense to anyone here, most especially my newest and dearest friend, Mr. O'Hara himself, but you must see my point. If you have permitted yourselves to be cheated for more than five years, more than that five-year recompense you have little right to expect. What say you all to this most fair proposition?"

"I say, and I think that I might be after speaking for us all," proclaimed O'Hara in his finest formal tone, "That Mr. Whitehouse, a fine former Englishman, God forgive him, and he is right in his assessment of the cheating situation. But apart from that, he has had no fault in that terrible fact of his birth, by the grace of God, and he has had the good sense to see the error of his ways and resign from the whole accursed race of bloody Englishmen. He has come up with a fair solution for Forrester here to restore to us our lost funds, which he has taken from us by cheating! It pains me to say it Forrester, but you should be after paying us the money you cheated us out of in a fortnight from this day right here, or we kills you. Now there be nothing of a personal nature in it. It's just the fair way it should be." O'Hara then turned to the assembly and said, "Do you accept that proposition friends?"

The score of cheated men cried out, "Aye! It is a fair solution!"

"Well there you have it," called out O'Hara. "Wake up old

Judge Bowen over there in the corner. He must have sobered up a bit by now, and tell him what we've decided in the matter of Forrester's cheating us at cards these five years past here. In two weeks time, we'll submit our claims to him for judgment. And that will be it."

"This isn't justice," cried Forrester. "Are you going to take the word of a self-confessed son of a whore or a gentleman of your own class that you have known for more than twenty years or more? I am one of your own for God's sake. Where is this bastard's proof that I am what he says I am?"

"If its proof you want, it is proof you shall have," said Whitehouse. "Would one of you gentlemen be so kind as to turn those cards face down on the table? Thank you Mr. Beauregard. Now I want you each to take a card and hold its back to me, and I'll tell you what card it is that you indeed hold. Very good gentlemen. Shall we now proceed with our experiment?"

Each man in the room took a card from the table and held it up, and in turn, each card was identified by Captain Whitehouse. Forrester cried out, "See! It is his deck! The devil has got rid of my cards and has substituted his own. They are of a common type. They can be found anywhere. I have heard of such things happening when cheats didn't want to pay their losses. Did this Whitehouse fellow not say that he had played cards all over the world? His experience is far greater than any man's here including my own. He has told us the truth of it out of his own mouth, and I say that he is the guilty man."

"Oh, I don't think so mate," said Whitehouse. "My dear Mr. O'Hara sir, would you be so kind as to arrange the deck in order, ace to deuce, and then in suits with clubs on top, followed by hearts, and diamonds, then spades."

"I'd be glad to do it your honor," replied the Irishman. After a few minutes, the task was done, and O'Hara said, "I see something, but it don't make any sense. Would you see what you can do with it Captain darling?"

"No, that's quite alright. I'll have a go at it with pleasure Mr.

O' Hara. I think that I know what our friend Mr. Forrester has done."

Whitehouse reversed the order of the suits, and with that, the initials "J. F. F." appeared along the edge of the deck. Turning to Forrester, Whitehouse said, "Now would those initials stand for James F. Forrester I suppose that these cards were precious to you, but, my dear fellow, to mark them with your initials Old Boy? That just was not very smart, but then your whole life has just gone overboard you might say." Turning to the room, Whitehouse called out, "Might we not say that gentlemen? Has Mr. James Forrester's life not just gone overboard?"

"You are finished here Forrester. Never enter this place again until you are summoned here to face justice and settle up with the men you have cheated over the last five years," barked Judge Bowen who was now as sober as the office he held. Then in his most somber and judicial voice the judge intoned, "And this court is adjourned for two weeks time when we shall reconvene right here at eleven in the forenoon. At that time Forrester, you shall make good on the claims of these gentlemen who shall submit a summary of their losses to you to this court for settlement, and you shall undertake to make them good."

"You convict me on the word of some English bastard none of you have ever seen before? Gentlemen, I must protest."

"Forrester, you have referred to the question of my parentage once too often. I loved my dear mother who had a very amorous nature, and knew many men of quality. On of these fine chaps was my father. He might even have been the late king by his own reputation as a sailor himself. But your jibes at my family honor causes me great sorrow Forrester. So now, I demand satisfaction," growled Whitehouse.

"What the Hell do you mean Whitehouse?" asked Forrester with some confusion.

"I am calling you out sir. Swords or pistols? The choice of weapons is yours. I am sure that these gentlemen here will agree that I have a right to call you out," Whitehouse coldly replied.

"Indeed you do your honor," smiled O'Hara in anticipation of some real and potentially deadly distraction and fun.

"Judge," screamed Forrester, "There is no dueling in this country. It is against the law damn it!"

"Forrester this is Georgian country, and as I am the law here about, I say if you don't answer when you are called out, you are no gentleman and indeed you must be considered a coward to be shunned by good county society as a duty to us all. You have insulted the man. Hell, you have insulted the man's mother whom I am beginning to like just from what the Captain here tells me of her high standards and honest character. You have given the man insult. Now you must answer for it."

The rest of the room agreed with the judge in a loud affirmative chorus. Captain Whitehouse glowered at the trembling Forrester. Then he smiled a mirthless smile, and said, "As a gentleman Forrester, do you need some further provocation? Does this suit you?"

With that Whitehouse smashed his rock like fist into Forrester's face crushing his nose. Forrester sailed down half the length of the long room. Tears came down his cheeks, and blood ran down his face. His former friends turned their backs on him in disgust as he struggled to gain his feet, and then he reeled out of the door of Buckland's forever. His life there as a gentleman of the county was over.

Whitehouse called after him, "I'll catch you up old man. Give some thought to your choice of weapons for our next meeting. It makes no difference to me. I can kill you with just about anything, that is, after you pay what you owe to these fine gentlemen here."

Forrester heard these taunting words from Whitehouse and the jeers from his former friends. The sense of loss Forrester felt now overwhelmed him as he stumbled out of Bucklands.

Whitehouse next turned to his new friends and said loudly, "My dear Mr. O'Hara would you do me the honor as acting as my second?"

"That would be my pleasure and honor, your honor," replied the big Irishman.

Whitehouse smiled to himself. He had paid back the thief who had robbed him of a substantial sum of gold and a prime Matabele slave buck. Forrester's friends shook Whitehouse's hand, and thanked the Captain profusely for restoring some of their losses. As the clock struck two, the men started for home, and Whitehouse went up to his room at Buckland's to change into dark travelling clothes.

CHAPTER VIII

James Francis Forrester had learned that in a society of unequals, there was always more than enough inequality to go around for everybody. Forrester was in a positive panic as a result of his ultimate unmasking as a cheat and something other than a gentleman. Horror compounded on horror in his poor and all but incapacitated mind. His fear of the Captain absorbed him. He had no idea if the man had truly recognized him or not after so many years. He also wondered exactly what had brought the fierce Whitehouse here. What did the Captain want? Did he want anything or was it a freak accident that he just happened to come to this county? Did the man remember the theft of the big slave and the money of more than twenty some years before in New Orleans?

James Francis Forrester had few options at hand as far as his own safety was concerned. He could honor his debts and repay those whom he had cheated over the past five years. By doing so, he would be making an open admission of everything with which Whitehouse had charged him, but that formerly well-hidden cat was well out of the bag even though he had never officially articulated to the charge of cheating in a public way. Forrester knew that he could never face the fierce sea Captain, who had beaten him at cards and at his own game, on anything like an equal basis in a duel with heavens knows what sort of weapons. He wondered again if Whitehouse indeed had remembered him.

Forrester wondered if Whitehouse might have seen him in other circumstances in the years since he had deserted from the slave ship in New Orleans with Samuel. He wondered if it had been the stolen money of more than twenty years ago that had excited the Captain's passion for revenge. Twenty seven thousand dollars of the Captain's personal wealth, his entire profit from his voyage, was indeed motive enough. Was it about his stealing of Samuel? Samuel was a prize of huge value and Whitehouse's personal investment. There was motive enough along with the fact that as a thief he had continued to prosper and was even respected. This must have been too much for Whitehouse. How did Whitehouse happen to come to Buckland's this very night? "Damn it all to Hell! I should have changed my name. I should have stopped making all those trips back to New Orleans for the gaming years ago," Forrester said aloud to himself in his near hysterical state.

His head rang with the awful punishment he had suffered at the Captain's hands. The old scars on his back fairly ached with the reawakened memory of the whipping he had endured so long ago at the hands of the mate under the Captain's eyes. That had also been for cheating at cards. What had been a long buried and ancient history was now the burning fact of his life reborn and more terrible. He thought again about his options. He could lay his hands on all of his ready cash and run to the ends of the earth, or he could blow his brains out. Those were the options open to a gentleman who had been exposed as a poser and a common cheat. He had now fallen from grace in that somewhat roughly aristocratic world of southern plantation life. By blowing his brains out, he could, in a small part, repair his honor.

Another option opened to him was that he could get very drunk and fade into an alcoholic stupor until he formulated some plan of escape. That solution seemed to have the greatest merit at the moment. When it came right down to it, Forrester knew that his honor was not of any great value. He had been living a lie for more than twenty years. His honor was a borrowed thing of little real value now that his very life may be in real danger. That thought of losing his carefully crafted place in society made him laugh. Then Forrester receded back into his gloom. He realized that he would have to tell Samuel about his fall. Maybe he would have to give his slave driver some money and invite him to make a run for it. Forrester even entertained the idea that he and Samuel ought to run off together with enough gold to start over somewhere else. Samuel deserved at least that consideration, and besides a big and strong body servant might provide some much needed protection. There were always the Mississippi steamers and the opportunities for large games with high stakes, but then New Orleans was a city well known to Whitehouse. In its way, the place was too small to hide out in for long. Clearly James Forrester would have to try his luck somewhere else. Suddenly the world seemed a much smaller place than it had been that morning.

Grasping his bleeding nose with his handkerchief, Forrester continued his ride homeward in the late night or early morning depending on the wounded man's frame of reference. Forrester once again began feeling more troubled than he had ever felt before in his life. He could not grasp the totality of just what had happened to him. Whatever it was, it had resulted in blowing his world apart. Just hours ago he had been master of his own private kingdom with unlimited prospects. He was the most popular man of his set. Now his world had come crashing down around him and crushing him as if he were some tiny insect. Slowly the awful truth dawned on him. There was no longer a place for him here in this storied world of plantation life. He was through. Worse than that, his wife would now also be a social outcast. Her afternoon teas would be shunned, and his children, who were almost of age, could not make good marriages anywhere in the county.

His daughters would be fortunate to marry the sons of common farmers with a dozen acres, a slave or two, and a serving girl about the place to help in the house. His sons could never aspire to appointments to West Point now, as he had intended, to start them on the pathway to becoming officers and gentlemen with the pride of place that goes with such educational achievements at the service academies. Where could he find a politician to nominate his boys for the academy now? With this scandal and the sure ruin of his family in front of him maybe there was only one honorable choice he could make after all. Forrester thought of what it would feel like to actually place the cold steel of the end of a pistol barrel to his temple or inside of his mouth and actually pull the trigger. What would it be like to end it all with some degree of pride? Then he shuddered at the thought of such a messy end to his life.

Forrester reached down into his saddlebag, and after groping around, he secured the flask for which he was looking. He took it from his saddlebag and released the top of the silver object, which had just caught the slight glimmer of the moonlight on its polished surface, and he drank a huge draft of the amber liqueur. It was the Napoleon 1809. It was his second favorite brandy. "Why could it not have been the best?" was the thought that skirted around the edges of his mind. If he was going to do the awful thing tonight not far from his door, should he not have the best brandy after all to see him on his last journey off this troublesome mortal coil?

Forrester had become a discriminating man of the world who would have nothing but the best, but now that was over too. "Thirty four year old brandy," Forrester thought to himself. He then reflected that it was a damned shame that he had been so mean to himself at the end. Yes, there was a fine seventy five year old French cognac sitting on the back of the dining room sideboard. He thought about this and damned himself for his judicious conservation of the rare old liqueur won from Old Judge Bowen. He wondered if the Judge remembered the night that he had lost that rare bottle to him at Buckland's as he was passing judgment on him. He laughed over this stray thought and drank again. Then he addressed the horse as the old friend that he was and the companion of more than a hundred adventures. "Just think. I could have had the '64. Old Caesar will most likely make off with it. Damn him. I hope the old black bastard does. Caesar is not a bad sort for a nigger. I like the old bastard. I hope that he has enough brains to enjoy the stuff. I hope that he drinks the whole damned thing and doesn't get caught at it by my sister."

Forrester drank more slowly now. As he sipped, the pain of his injuries began to melt out of his body a bit and his fallen pride seemed to be restored to a small degree. Even the ancient wounds on his back assumed the reality of their being healed by the passage of time. Again he spoke to the horse who listened as if he were truly an understanding beast. After all, Forrester had not been too demanding a master of either his horses or his slaves, and by the standards of his neighbors, he really was a decent sort. In point of fact, he seemed much less interested in the productivity of the place than was Samuel. But that was not so strange. That had been the arrangement after all. Samuel was the true partner of his labors such as Forrester's labors were. "You know, that black bastard Samuel is an odd stick. He looks at you as if he's some kind of a lord or something. Sometimes you'd think that you were talking to a white man. Samuel is a dependable fellow. He seldom speaks except when he has to, even in our relaxed discussions, and that can be a blessing let me tell you old friend. In many ways he is like you. He gives good service and does not ask for much except a sort of affection and respect."

The horse seemed to hang on to Forrester's every word. The master drank again. "Then there is Mrs. Forrester and those two bloody girls, and my darling old hag of a sister. They never shut their gobs. If I were a drinking man, they would drive me to whiskey," he declared. Then he looked at his flask, "Or brandy I suspect. Of course that would be if I was actually at home long enough to actually care. I don't think I'll miss them much at all. Damn it though, I shall miss the fleecing of the flock at Buckland's, the friendly thumps on the back, not to mention Sally's beauties. But it's finished. I'm finished. It's all finished now old friend. What a sad end to a perfect life. I shall take you with me of course, if I decide to run for it. I'll have one friend with me at least. Or perhaps two. By rights I should leave Samuel here to take care of my women and sons. My poor boys. I've been a horrible father to them and their mother hates them so."

Forrester lapsed into a state of melancholy. His chin sagged down to his chest, and he began to cry softly. He took another larger drink from the flask, and closed his eyes as if to block out the night. As the horse slowly trotted along, Forrester opened his eyes again and smiled as the alcohol warmed him and took the edge off of his sadness. "Oh well, can't be helped I suppose. And so, what the Hell. What about my sons and heirs. A sorry lot those two. Only thinking with their peckers. Well, looking at me as their father, I suppose that's not their fault. I never bothered with them, and except when they got into a little bit of trouble, they didn't bother me. I'm sorry for those two stupid bastards. Without a military education, they will be just two more drunken near do wells helling about the countryside. They are hated by their mother, and will be someday shot by a husband, brother, or father. Yes my good friend. They will whore around the countryside until some farmer, husband or brother shoots them I suppose if they do not get away from here. Their mother tried to make fops of them and failed. Good luck to her," he laughed.

The horse softly neighed and inclined its head to Forrester's plaintive speech. "I think that you understand a real gentleman's plight old friend. You are one very fine mount."

Forrester raised the flask and sipped more slowly, savoring the rich dark liquid. He closed his eyes and thought of the all of the pleasures he would have to leave behind. The women! The women, all pink, or yellow, or dusky brown, and mahogany too. His trips to Atlanta and even to far off New Orleans and the beauties he enjoyed there were now in his thoughts. His mind went back to that one special trip to St. Louis up river, but the best fun was always to be had down river in that grand old French city that lived for pleasure. There was no place like New Orleans in all the states of the union. The sound of it. The smell of it.

The food. The women. The gambling. The winning at the table. Once again Forrester addressed his mount, "The stupid thing is that I never needed to cheat. The thing is my friend, don't ever get greedy, and don't take more than one trick out of three. I have all this wisdom to give and none to give it too. It is really too sad now at the end of the day. My boys are such a waste. Pampered, neglected, and then spoiled in turn. Still I love them. Those poor buggers are just too much like the worst of me. The poor sots can't help themselves. Now their mother can't stand the sight or sound of them. God knows we neglected them most horribly. I didn't even teach them to play cards, and that is my only real talent. We dressed them well, threw money at them, ignored them, and let them go wild. They will be ruined. Oh well, that would have happened anyway."

He drank deeply as he thought of his two sons, James and Douglas. "Their mother has made some high-toned whoring high flyers out of those boys. Sometimes I think that she almost did it out of hate. Now she can't abide the sight of them. I wonder how well they will dress when I'm gone, dead, and disgraced, and left without a penny?" James Forrester almost sadly shook his head then laughed and threw his head back as if quite pleased with himself. "There will be no invitations to cotillions for those poor girls. How will they ever get on without money for their Paris gowns after the judge rapes the estate and their dear father cold and stiff in his grave by his own hand? What a monumental disgrace I shall be." He sipped again.

He was warmed by the idea of revenging himself on his ungrateful whelps by ending it all with a shot. He thought of his once beautiful but now slightly aging wife who still totally adored him and the gifts that he gave her. She had never wanted for anything. He had always shown her devotion if not fidelity in his love. She in turn had never complained of his back door romancing. On second thought, it really had been a very satisfactory arrangement for both of them in many ways. On reflection, Forrester considered that they had had a pretty good run of it as these marriages go, but now that the fiction of respectability was stripped away there would be no joy for her in the future. Maybe he did love her after all. In actuality she was still rather a good-looking woman.

"I'm sorry for poor Mrs. Forrester. She's a good old girl, and she knows where I have hidden most of the cash. It won't be too bad for her if she does what's smart and doesn't let on that she has this little nest egg. Alas, that has always been a problem for Mrs. Forrester. I wish that she loved James and Douglas just a little as she loves the girls. Why could she not love them as she has the girls? Damn! I wish that she could keep a secret. She has the devil's own time keeping her mouth shut! Too bad that. Oh well. What can I say," said Forrester now addressing these remarks to his distant but now slightly moonlit house, while lifting his flask once again. He pressed it to his lips and almost drained it.

This image of his home, caught in the fading moon's light and just visible in the distance through a break in the trees, gave him a small feeling of sad pleasure. It might have been the brandy too that inspired him to toast his bride once more. "Good-bye old girl. We had a pretty good run of it, and you were good to me. I wish that I could have been better to you. But my all too human nature being as it is..."

By now Forrester, who never had consumed so much brandy in one session as a professional caution against loss at the gaming tables, tossed down another gulp. He had consumed the better part of his quart flask, and he seemed well determined to drain it to the last. By now, he had passed into a state of deeper mellowness, which greatly contrasted with the reality of his situation. He welcomed the euphoria provided by the brandy. Forrester had hardly even realized that he had slipped off the back of his faithful steed and had landed on the ground. The fall had really been a sort of slow slide, and as he had landed, he never spilled a drop of liquor from his flask. His horse had returned and gently nuzzled him as if to see if he were well. Then the faithful mount stood by him nibbling at the odd blade of grass that might have poked its probing head out of the red earth to see if the sky would fall. Forrester just half rolled himself over to a tree to brace his back against the root system which rose above the ground to form a natural backrest against which he could recline.

Then having settled into some degree of comfort, Forrester's mind traveled back to Whitehouse and his strange and unanticipated resurrection from a long buried past which was the cause of all his new trouble. "Whitehouse. Whitehouse," he mused aloud to his horse as he passed into a deeper state of intoxication. Now laying down with his head pillowed against the great tree's roots with his body resting on the still warm red earth of Georgia on this still soft night, something began to stir in the dim memory of his long ago past.

"I was playing at cards on the boats going down to New Orleans even before I went slaving. Yes card playing was even then my trade. I was very young and just really learning. But I was damned good at it too. I should have stuck to the riverboats, but a' slaving I went. I was told that even a deck hand could make a good living at that trade. It was a very enticing idea and even more enticing after I lost a lot of money to this fellow one night on this riverboat and gave him a note on a plantation that I didn't own you see."

The horse inclined his head to the soft voice of his master and listened uncomprehendingly. "When and if he had discovered what I had done, that would be the end for me. He had a nasty reputation for killing men who didn't pay their debts. A trip to Africa would be timely to say the least. So a slaving I went, and a damned dirty business it was too. I hated every damned day of it. I took pains to look as lowly as I could. I let my hair grow and my face was half shaven. Lord was I fat then. I looked a proper sight with no trace of my days on the river about me."

The horse neighed and snorted in sympathy for his master, or so it seemed to Forrester who continued his tale. "Whitehouse's ship was down in New Orleans and shorthanded, just as I was told it was. So I applied to be taken aboard as a common hand,

and so I sailed in her to Africa." His horse seemed to listen to every word his master spoke. Forrester again began the one sided conversation, "You know I had to get away from that dangerous fellow on the boat that played cards with me. That's why I had to change the way I looked. He would never recognize me if he were to see me again. I had become the slovenly sailor not the dandy that he had been playing with and was hunting down to kill. And another thing old friend. He did not take losses well either. I heard that he was furious that I had cheated him by giving him that note on the plantation, I knew that he wouldn't be happy when he tried to sell that plantation. I tell you again, he would have cut my heart out for sure. That is why I had to get on Whitehouse's damned ship, and what a goddamned hell hole that turned out to be."

Again Forrester laughed when he thought of that game of so many years ago. "When I gave him the note, I though he might find me out, and I tried to make it look as if it were another player at the table, a Col. Sprague, a Yankee from Providence in Rhode Island going south to buy cotton, who had been deck stacking and cheating him all night up to the point that he had won. The damned fool fell for the trick and produced a pistol and threatened to shoot poor Sprague on the spot like a dog for cheating. I got away during that little typhoon."

Laughing all the way down to his belly Forrester continued, "The fellows on the boat threw Sprague over the side. Everybody on board thought Sprague was a doomed man. Sprague's friends said that it really didn't matter much, because he was a slave runner in the African trade as well as a cotton broker! That's how I had found out about Whitehouse. Sprague had told me during the night before how his friend was shorthanded and that there was a lot of money to be made in the slave trade. Now that's a tale to tell anyone that might want to hear it. Whitehouse is a slaver, and they can hang him for that!" exclaimed Forrester to his steed. All of a sudden an idea emerged from his alcohol-fogged brain. "That's how I can get the bastard. They can hang slavers and

Whitehouse is a slaver! At first light, we'll head back into town and talk to the sheriff. That will at least get him out of town, and if we are lucky even hanged."

"You are not a very clever fellow are you?" interrupted Whitehouse as he stepped out of the wooded darkness into the all but vanished moonlight. "You should not be so free talking to your equine friend here. You never know who might be listening to you old boy. Although he looks like he might be able to keep his mouth shut unlike your good lady wife. I followed you hoping you'd do the right thing and blow your brains out. Isn't that what your planter class is supposed to do when they are found out cheating at cards, buggering a boy, or shagging one of your sheep, or in some other dishonorable act like stealing my money and best slave? Although sheep shagging might be preferable to your lady by popular rumor in the county. So when are you going to do it? I mean blow your brains out, not bugger sheep. Soon I hope. I have some unfinished business tonight Forrester and time is fleeting. So don't be too long about it."

"What might that be to you Whitehouse?" Forrester attempted to draw himself up with some dignity, which was very hard to do when he was as deeply in his cups as he now was. "Are you a highwayman as well as a slave runner?" slurred Forrester now feeling both the warming incapacitation of drink and the courage inducing effects of his unaccustomed drunkenness that went with it.

"A slave runner? My Forrester, but you do have a fanciful imagination. But quite frankly, do you think that the locals are going to be outraged by that? Where are the local abolitionist societies? You are daft if you think anyone in Georgia gives a fig or will pull a hair about the immorality of the slave trade. They could not exist on their stinking plantations without their slaves. I don't suppose that they are about to pay wages to field hands like they do in the North of this backward country do you? Or do you think that like their northern cousin that they intend to labor in the fields themselves? You know as well as I do that slaves are not unlike cattle or your noble steed here to these fellows. Do get a grip. Goods are goods, chattel are chattel. They are all to be traded, bought, fucked, or sold at will. That is the nature of slave ownership in a free society such as yours. I think that they might still be more in sympathy with me seeing that you stole their money. You took money from me that I made working for almost two years of my life and that big buck who could have brought me thousands more. Where is he now? He can't be much more than forty odd and still must have considerable value."

"Slave running has been against the law for more than thirty years Whitehouse," said Forrester as he tried to rise from the ground.

Whitehouse pushed him back into his recumbent position on the red dirt under the old tree. Whitehouse planted the toe of his boot firmly on Forrester's chest. "Really Old Boy? What about desertion from my ship? What about stealing my slave? What about stealing my gold and the two years of my life that it took to earn it? What about getting an honest man thrown overboard for cheating at cards when he was just an innocent cotton and slave trader? Could I not also shoot you for helping yourself to my money alone? Now these are real crimes just like your cheating at cards, and these crimes are much more serious offenses to your good neighbors. What you have done over the years constitutes an impressive record of grand larceny Forrester. There are laws about those sorts of unlawful activities too. You didn't think that I would remember you, did you Old Boy? That is why I came looking for you Forrester. I never forget a slight or an injury. You stole two years of my life's work and my slave. I have looked for you whenever I was in New Orleans. You have become too well known my dear Forrester. You have cut a wide swath for yourself over these twenty years. There was word that you were doing quite well and were a wealthy planter here in Georgia. So I came looking for you. And here you are. You look different, but there is something in that voice of yours that I would not forget even with the changes that you have effected in refining your accent, and you have done quite a good job of it."

"And of course," continued Whitehouse, "I travel in gambling circles too when I'm in this country. And as I said, you are a rather famous man Forrester up and down the river and all the way to the coastal cities of South Carolina and Georgia. And as far as your voice is concerned, I've heard that voice without that cultivated accent. I'm only sorry that I didn't kill you in Africa years ago, but who would have thought such a lowly worm as you were capable of any sort of action that would have hurt me? So once more, what did you do with that big prime buck you stole from me in New Orleans? I paid a fortune for him. He was the prize in the lot. He was Matabele, and one does not capture or buy one of those fellows every day. Did you get a good price for the poor bugger? What did you promise him to get him to go with you? Freedom I suppose. You know Forrester, in point of fact, I don't forget much. I never forget a robbery, an insult, or a slight. Most of all, I don't forget it when a man steals the proceeds of two years of my life's work."

"You are not in Africa now Whitehouse, or are you now the lord and master of a ship. You are in my country you bastard, and I could have you hanged for what you do," snarled Forrester who seemed to have come back to something almost like sobriety and armed with the sort of courage that often comes to people in an intoxicated state.

"Do you think that your former friends, the men that you have fleeced for more years than most of them can remember, are going to give a damn for what you have to say now about me or anything else? Your own government doesn't seem to take the prohibition on the slave trade too seriously. When have they ever hanged some poor bugger for this high crime? When Americans catch the odd slaver, what do they do? Fine them perhaps and impounded the ship? They have done little else. You have shown yourself to be scum man. I hardly think that anyone would credit you at all or pull a hair for your fate. In point of fact, I'm the hero who exposed you for the cheater that you are. And above all you have committed the worst of crimes, and that is a breach of honor. You sir are no longer a gentleman. The rank to which you have pretended is stripped away from you. So you see Forrester, in your reduced circumstances you might as well blow your brains out and save a little of your assumed dignity."

Forrester blinked while trying vainly to string his thoughts together. Then he said, "They hang people for slaving Whitehouse, not for thirty year old rumors of some vague criminal activity in New Orleans! We are hundreds of miles from there."

"What rot. The damned English government joins with the Yanks to ban the slave trade. You fellows buy and sell slaves in every city and town in the southern part of this accursed country. Even here you buy, sell, and even breed them. You hire people's choice bucks to service your black wenches as studs. You rent bucks to service your slave women like horses when you are not up to servicing them yourselves. I understand that many of you fine gentlemen do that as well including the late Mr. Jefferson himself. You even keep studbooks! That is that some of you do, but I'm not here to hear your opinion about that. There was a second, just a moment back there when I thought that you might actually attempt to get me hanged. I guess that I was right to follow you home, you poor drunken sod. When I heard that you were still alive in New Orleans, I decided to run you to ground to get some of my own back. If not the money and my slave, then some measure of my own. It was a jolly good idea and a stimulating distraction."

"So what is that to you? Tomorrow, why Hell, it's tomorrow now. Everybody in the county is going to know who and what you are too Captain Fucking Whitehouse. And I just might as well try to get you strung up. The federals will be interested in what I have to say. Hell, it's worth a try. What do I have to lose Whitehouse? What indeed do I have to fucking lose now! Even that big buck I took. He was no good. The poor bastard died of fever," Forrester lied. "I had to leave him in the swamps when I was getting away. We were there for two weeks. I could not even bury the poor bastard. The alligators dined upon him I am sure. So don't even think that you can get a profit there."

"So you killed my nigger, and took my money. Now Forrester, just what might the charge against me be again?"

Forrester drew himself up now with great difficulty. "Being a slave trader. You may not hang because you have to be caught at sea with the goods, but you won't be the big bug in the town anymore either. You might even lose your ship. That must be worth at least twenty thousand to you. Slave traders are not exactly society are they? You fellows serve a need, but so do the brewer and the baker. They are not admitted into good society are they? You fellows don't get invited to dinner by the county gentry. Oh, you do us a service, but so does a blacksmith or an innkeeper."

"Do you think that I give a sweet fig about that? About society? My mother was a loving woman, and she was a whore of very high standards. That did not set me up as a duke did it? All I care about is making a good living and you threaten to take that away from me? You steal my money and my slave, and now you threaten me with this!" replied Whitehouse.

"You are on the wrong side of the law, and it's all the weapon I've got. So this small revenge will have to do won't it my dear Captain?" said Forrester warming to his threat.

"Have you gone in for becoming another fucking William God damned Wilberforce Forrester? Well my friend, don't you think you had better be getting on with what you were telling this noble steed you were about to do. Southern honor and all that. Blowing your brains out is the best course of action for you in the end is it not?"

"To Hell with honor. I've never had any honor Whitehouse. I can't afford it any more than you can. It's all a sham as you damn well know, but I've taken stock of things, and I have decided life is not quite as intolerable as all that. After I've told my tale to the sheriff, as well as to O'Hara, and the rest, I'll just quit this place. There is a bit of fun to be had in this world for me yet. I can go back to the river. I can make a fine living there, and there is something about a card playing man that draws the right kind of woman to my flame. In a way, you have emancipated me. I've tired of all this red dirt, and my God damned children, always wanting, and wanting, and wanting, and my good wife always nagging me with looks and unspoken words of recrimination, and my ugly and dried up sister who looks like she was weaned on a parson's pecker has been a trial to me long enough. Maybe I should thank you that I can still follow the life I was supposed to have had. I have decided to go home, get some essential things, and move on Whitehouse right after I have given my deposition to the sheriff and the Federal marshal. The world is full of Buckland's Taverns, riverboats, and Miss Sally's, and before I'm dead I'll have them all again. I am no gentleman as you very well know, and I thank God for it. I am equally happy not to be you my dear Captain Whitehouse. If they don't hang you as high as Haman, I'll at least make life harder and more miserable for you."

"Is that it then Forrester? That is your pitiful little plan for my undoing? Is that the best effort you can make? Don't you want to defend your honor? Don't you even want to swing a closed fist at me and try to at least knock me down? Are you totally devoid of any manhood Forrester?" said the Captain in a grimly firm voice and with his lips curled in a curious smile.

As Forrester attempted to mount his horse, he turned and replied, "Manhood is an expensive luxury Captain, and honor demands too much of a really civilized man. When I thought about it, I concluded that you are not worth the effort to do you any physical harm. And I don't give a damn for my manhood. As soon as I put finished and paid to you Whitehouse, I'll…"

With that Forrester swayed and fell from his half mounted position back onto the red soil of his own plantation. The effort he had put into reviving his dignity had exhausted his feeble reserves of energy.

"Too bad that," said Whitehouse shaking his head with mock sympathy.

"Too bad what? As the old saying goes, If at first you don't…"

With that, the Captain brought a rock down sharply on the side of Forrester's head. He had aimed it with skill at his victim's upwardly turned temple. "As I was saying Old Boy, too bad about that appalling fall from your nag. Must have had a tot too much of good cheer old fellow."

Whitehouse arranged the body of the fallen planter with the bloody rock located by Forrester's head nearby. He then picked up a fallen branch and brought it down smartly on Forrester's horse's rump while screaming out like a banshee for every living thing to hear in the stillness of the coming dawn, the horse was off like a shot and ran for the safety of it's stables.

There were none to see this drama in the road on the way to the big house but one set of African eyes from behind the shrubs that grew a short distance away. These hidden eyes had seen both of these men together in different times and under different circumstances many years before. Memories relived in nightmares were now the reality in the pre dawn lit night. The shocked hidden man's lips formed but one word, "Whitehouse."

CHAPTER IX

In the sober light of day, all of James Forrester's sins were forgotten for a time if not forgiven. The man was dead, and the judgment of the summary court, held by candlelight and fueled by whiskey at Buckland's on the night of Forrester's accident, was held to be hardly a true judicial proceeding or binding under the law. Judge Bowen had but a faint memory of the proceedings, and when he was faced with the sobering facts of the case, he clearly saw that he had exceeded the powers of his office. The Judge also knew that suing the dead man might be difficult most especially if the principal accuser, in the person of the stranger Captain Whitehouse, was nowhere to be found. These good gentlemen of Georgia also had no wish to expose themselves as fools who had been tricked out of fortunes by Forrester for almost two decades. Their pride was all they really had that truly mattered to them in the end.

Mrs. Forrester was outwardly a universal object of solicitude. In point of fact, she had loved the feckless Mr. James Forrester with her whole being even with all of his rumored faults. She shed no public tears, but in the seclusion of her room, she filled her pillow with her sorrow. The public Mistress Forrester would never show emotion. She had a position to defend, and she had to put on the best face she could on a situation that would damn her in the eyes of her class. She would never unbend in public in an undignified manner. Her daughters took their lead from their mother. James's sister lost control of herself when she heard of her younger brother's death and had to be sedated by the doctor. It was decided that she must not be seen by the county gentry and accounted as something less than a respectable member of the Forrester household. The word was put about that she was confined to her bed with a back sprain and therefore could not attend the services.

Mrs. Forrester's sense of loss was very real. The fear of an unwanted pregnancy dominated her thinking and had stolen away any sense of the pleasure she had once enjoyed with the handsome Mr. Forrester in her bed. His visits to Miss Sally's place of business was a cause of rejoicing to her, and her James was very comfortable in telling her the gossip of what he had seen there. They would both laugh at the stories he had brought back to her. "Better than lovers," she had thought, "We are such good friends."

One matron dared ask the incredible. Taking Miss Caroline Forrester aside, she began to relate gossip about the night of Mr. James Forrester's death and then asked about the truth of the rumors of the late Mr. Forrester's gambling activities. The dead man's daughter's eyes flashed an unspoken warning so terrible that the matron covered her face with her black fan, excused herself, and left the house. Needless to say, the subject was never again discussed by any outsider with the family.

Young Douglas and James Forrester, for the first and only time in their young adult lives, flanked their mother at the funeral and respectfully escorted her as dutiful sons. They were told to remain sober and gentlemanly during the hard days following James Forrester's death. Mistress Forrester had shown the boys her buggy whip, and told them that bad behavior would have physical consequences as well as the prospect of being disinherited. Mrs. Forrester had demonstrated within the last year with that very whip that she made no idle threats.

When the two boys had returned from their first binge of whoring and drinking at three o'clock in the morning, arousing the entire household and almost setting the place ablaze in the process, she had ordered the buggy whip brought to her. With Mr. Forrester being absent, she took it upon herself to enforce discipline in the house. Although no slave had ever tasted the whip on the Forrester place, those two boys were thoroughly blistered. They had then run off into the night crying and falling down in a drunken stupor as they fled terror stricken into the safety of the night. They had pulled each other to their feet after falling in turn, and they then made off for the deepest parts of the woods where they played not so long ago as children with Pompey. They moved as fast as they could amble in their besotted condition. The fear and respect for their mother's rage kept them away from the house until their father had returned the next day.

"Good enough for them mother," said Caroline from the landing of the great front staircase where she had been standing with Tilly when her mother had finished thrashing the drunken boys. "They were such awful brutes. They nearly burned down the house and scared us all half to death with their awful howling."

"Well I gave those scamps something to howl about. I don't think that they will return home in that disgraceful condition again. I'll have to speak to Mr. Forrester about it. Go to bed darlings," said Mistress Forrester. "Morning will be here soon enough." The girls had returned to their rooms. Mrs. Forrester went into Mr. Forrester's study, shut the door, and helped herself to the brandy.

When the boys arrived quietly back at the house the next day, James and Douglas Forrester had discovered that their father had returned and was on the veranda sipping coffee. "Your mother told me what you forced her to do to you last night boys. I suggest that you offer apologies to her. I have never seen her so angry. Believe me when I tell you that you had best stay away from here if you are ever in a condition like that again. If she decides to whip you again, I'm afraid that I'll not be able to save you."

The boys steeled themselves to the task at hand and entered the house to find their mother in her wrapper sipping coffee. When they had thrown themselves on her mercy and begged forgiveness, Mrs. Forrester looked at them for a full minute in silence staring at them with a new and intense fury. Then she said in a controlled voice as cold as ice, "If either one of you ever come into this house again in that state of intoxication, there is not a power on earth that will save you from me. I will have the hide off you in a minute's time, and just see if I don't. If you have to Hell around, don't do it in this county. I will not be held up to ridicule because of you and your whoring and drinking. Why don't you get yourselves together? If you are not careful, you will be nothing but useless drunkards for the rest of your lives, and your father and I will be done with you for good and all. I don't for the life of me understand why you cannot be respectable like your sisters. If you do not amend your lives, you will never get into West Point and become officers and gentlemen. Believe me my sons, this will be your last chance. I'll never forgive you for making me lose my temper like that. Next time, I'll not go so easy with you. Now get out of my sight until you have properly cleaned yourselves up."

As the boys made their way upstairs to their rooms to carry out their mother's orders, Douglas mumbled, "Go easy on us! Holy Christ! Next time she will kill us."

Mrs. Forrester had settled back into the comfort of her chair regretting that she had ever had sons. "They made me forget that I am a lady, and I just hate that. Making me lose my temper! It just makes my blood boil," she muttered to herself. For the next two years the boys had remained far from home when they were not presentable. Now they feared and hated their mother, but they never crossed her by disturbing the carefully crafted air of gentility that permeated the Forrester Mansion.

As soon as the whole story of the fatal night at Buckland's Tavern had become common gossip and was whispered about throughout the county, sympathy for the poor widow and her fatherless brood slowly came to an end. Outwardly, life on the Forrester Plantation seemed to drift along much as it always had done. But Samuel tightened up the running of the place. More than ever in its history, since the loss of James Forrester's gambling income, the crops of tobacco and the other products of the plantation became much more important as a source of real income. After she overcame her incapacitation caused by her brother's death, Old Miss Forrester attempted to take a more active role in the running of the plantation to the point of riding out to the fields in a buckboard and attempting to talk to Samuel about the day to day operations. In turn, Samuel had a word with Mrs. Forrester, and that brought an end to the old spinster's meddling in the affairs of the fields. As soon as the overseer spoke to Mrs. Forrester about her sister-in-law's interference, Mrs. Forrester put a stop to these visits. The widow Forrester had revived some of her old grit after the passing of her husband, and she knew in Samuel she had a protector as well as an able manager. She would allow nothing to interfere with that.

The big man kept everything in order. Everything ran smoothly under his control. When the crops were sold that year, they brought record prices. Mrs. Forrester, who had never done more than toy with the idea, decided that the hiring of a white overseer in an attempt to fill Mr. Forrester's role was a needless expense. In her heart, Mrs. Forrester had always known that Samuel, and not the late Mr. Forrester, was the real engine behind the plantation's productivity. From the point of actually running the place, James Forrester's death had no impact whatsoever on the actual running of the plantation.

Samuel was given even better living quarters, and the choice of any female slave on the estate was extended to him to fulfill his pleasure. He politely declined the offer of a woman of his or anybody else's choosing. Samuel oversaw the construction of his new house, which oddly resembled the Greek Revival splendor of the big house only in a more miniaturized form. Mrs. Forrester offered Samuel his freedom and the position of overseer as a free man if he would impregnate ten of the young female slaves on the plantation and agree to be sole manager of the place for at least ten years. He was also offered one percent of profits brought in by the sale of the crops for the following year if he would agree to the proposition offered by Mrs. Forrester who knew a good thing when she saw it. To this end, Samuel smiled and asked for five percent. He knew his true value and the value of the fruit of his seed.

"This is outrageous," sputtered the Old Miss Forrester. "That uppity nigger wants too much!"

The Forrester family was in an impossible situation. The boys were about to be sent off to West Point this very fall with the blessing of their congressman. Their aptitude for running a plantation, or doing anything else of value for anybody was nil. Mrs. Forrester, who always knew the reality of the plantation's life, insisted that every one of Samuel's conditions be agreed to. After all, what else could be done? Then came the final demand by the big black man. Everything must be put into writing including his manumission, and those papers had to be filed in the County Courthouse. To this, Mrs. Forrester agreed.

"What good will that do! You can't read a lick you black devil," snarled Miz Forrester, who was resentful of growing less important to the running of the place day by day.

Samuel then smiled and said to the old woman, "When I was in Africa, I was taught to write by English High Church Missionaries. Master Forrester allowed me the use of his library over the years, and I have read almost every book in it. I have managed this plantation's accounts for the last twelve years after Master Forrester fired the man who used to do that work for him, because he was stealing from you. I'm afraid that I can read Miss Forrester, and now that I'm a free man, that should not be a problem for anyone including you. Because I am a free man, I can read openly without fear of any man."

"Well for land's sakes! It's not lawful to teach a nigger to read or write a lick!" the old lady lashed out.

"It's quite alright Miz Forrester ma'am," said Samuel, "I was taught in Matabeleland not in Georgia. You are all quite safe you see, because I can say with all honesty that you never taught me a thing."

His accent was slightly English for the occasion mixed with a bit of singsong Gullah. Nothing about him betrayed the amount of amusement he was having at the expense of the old woman whom he regarded with the same contempt as the old Mashona witch he had defended back in Africa. He did not want her harmed, because she had made the Mashona so uneasy.

The contract was drawn up in short order. Samuel read it, pronounced it fair, and signed it. This was followed by the handing over to him his papers of manumission, which were also filed at the county courthouse. They had been duly signed and attested to by Mrs. Forrester and a befuddled Judge Bowen who just glowered as he signed what he considered to be the most impossible of documents. Freeing slaves and employing them at huge wages in a white man's job was against all nature as far as the judge was concerned. All sorts of rumors flew about the county. Over the next several months, the more respectable members of county society no longer came to the Forrester Plantation at all. But during the next two years, the growth of the Forrester Plantation's bank accounts well reflected the fruits of the efforts of the Forrester overseer, Samuel James, a free man.

Samuel had asked if he might take the late master's name for his own as a tribute to him. Old Miss Forrester had almost fainted at the very suggestion of sharing her surname with a "nigger", but Mrs. Forrester was really quite charmed by Samuel's sweet request. She stated that taking of the Forrester name was out of the question, but that her dear husband's first name, James, which had also been given to one of her unworthy sons, would be quite alright. Old Miss Forrester took to her bed after being revived from her swoon on hearing this news.

Old Miss Forrester did take to her bed for an entire week. This time it was nausea. She loudly declared that she may never eat again or show her face in public now that her dear and dead brother's name had been bestowed on Samuel as a surname. The scandal of meeting the other demands of a former slave was too much for her constitution she declared. This had all mattered not a whit since the outside world knew only a little something of the plantation doings. Old Miss Forrester was proven right in the end as salacious gossip about the "goings on" at the Forrester place spread over the countryside. Just what was so intrinsically "bad" could not be defined, but rumor had it that strange doings and stranger arrangements were taking place on the Forrester Plantation. As long as the money poured into the Forrester coffers, Mrs. Forrester did not give a damn what the county thought or indeed said.

Judge Bowen could not speak of it, but his clerks hinted of some very strange legal arrangements with the former slave-overseer at the Forrester place as they enjoyed brandy smashes at Buckland's. Gossip was the life's blood of the little planter society of the county gentry. And the gentlemen of the county swilled it down along with their whiskey and brandy.

Samuel was yet to have another laugh at the benefit of the Forresters. After the contract between himself and Mrs. Forrester was signed, and he had received his official manumission, Samuel called the two best looking and biggest young slave men on the place to his quarters and offered each of them two silver dollars to seduce and impregnate five of the prettiest girls of their choice on the plantation. The two big teenage boys looked at him in disbelief. Samuel had been their lord and master after only old Master Forrester himself. Now he was the master in fact. Such a command was a dream come true for these two randy young men now approaching their full manhood. Samuel laid down the conditions of the task for which he wanted to contract them. The girls must say that it was Samuel who had impregnated them, and the task of servicing the girls must be done within two months time. When each girl became pregnant, she would be given two store bought dresses, a new shawl, as well as extra food, a cabin of her own, and a silver dollar. Each woman would also receive seven months reprieve from work in the fields and very light duties after their children were born.

Each of the successful boys would be paid a bonus of five dollars for each live child born and have two days free to do whatever they wished within the bounds and the limitations of their slave condition. The proposition pleased all who participated in it. The pretty girls were chosen based on their willingness to be with these handsome boys. When the children were born, they were big and healthy. Mrs. Forrester was filled with pleasure when she saw each of them and congratulated herself in being so shrewd in her negotiations with the overseer.

When Pompey asked Samuel why he had not done the deed of impregnating the girls himself, Samuel said, "My seed is royal, and it is a sacred trust which I hold from all of my ancestors. It must not be given to such as these. These are lesser things. They are not Matabele, and I order you to reserve your seed to yourself for better times to come. It too must not be wasted on people who would be slaves. Someday you will be my son and a prince in my land. I look at you as my own true son of my heart. The time is coming for you to know my heart and the plans I have for you. Soon I will have enough gold to buy you for myself. The name I will give you will not be recorded in a white man's courthouse or in some plantation ledger. You will be a free man. Your name will be a name of a great Matabele Zulu warrior if you wish it. Someday you will warm yourself under the free sun of Africa in the land of my fathers. You will feel the softness of the grass under your unshod feet liberated from the white man's leather, and you will be free of these rags the white man wears so proudly that make him sweat and stink in this red earth dyed heat. You must read more books about the world and its politics."

Samuel had thought long and hard about his adoption of Pompey. The plan had been in his mind since he first took the boy under his wing twenty years ago. The reality of his dream would be the fulfillment of his ambition if he could carry it off. The overwhelming question was would the Matabele accept Pompey as one of their own when he had made his way back to Africa.

James Forrester's death had changed many things. This was an immutable truth. The supposed fortunate fall from his horse and his striking his head in that fatal collision with that rock had saved Forrester from the shameful death that must eventually have come at the hands of the much trusted Samuel. Samuel had planned to kill his old partner himself on that very night, because for Samuel's grand scheme of self-liberation to work, Forrester, who was always the pleasure loving fool and who was all too trusting of Samuel's apparent good will, was going to have to die. For that selfsame grand plan to work, Forrester could not be around to become an impediment. As long as Forrester was alive, there would be no freeing of the overseer or granting him the powers he now had. The awful truth was that a fatal accident had been planned for Forrester by Samuel for the very night that Whitehouse had killed him.

The fates had played into the big man's hands. Samuel could not believe his good luck as he watched Whitehouse strike the fatal blow in the oncoming light of dawn on the day that Whitehouse became the unwitting tool of Samuel's plan. It was a secret that the big man kept to himself alone. Another plan had also germinated in Samuel's mind now that he knew that Whitehouse was alive and active. It had always been a plan to put paid to the Captain of the ship who had taken him from Africa. Samuel had always planned to take a war party to Mozambique and burn out the dealers in slaves, and kill all of those who were still in that trade to wipe out the disgrace of his capture and sale. When Samuel had seen Whitehouse all the old fears and hate returned. He only regretted that he could not have killed the Captain then that night. The bigger issue had been that Samuel could not grow in power as long as the master was alive to stand in his way. Their own personal contract, struck so long ago, must now be ended. It just did not give Samuel enough power. Samuel bore Forrester no real personal ill will. In fact, he liked Forrester. Samuel liked that fact that he had told the slaver that he had died almost thirty years past. Forrester and Samuel had been mates for decades on an adventure of their own. But the feckless master was in the way of Samuel's great scheme of self-liberation which the advent of Pompey was making possible.

Unknown to Samuel at the time, Forrester's death had also had the benefit of saving his family from the disgrace to which he had brought on them. The many victims of Forrester's two decades of fleecing the gentry saw Forrester's brutal death as a judgment on him, and that event had opened the door of opportunity for this African son who now felt that he might spare the rest of the Forrester tribe from Forrester's fate and still get that which he had planned and worked for all along.

Pompey was a tall man standing well over six feet tall, but he clearly was not a Matabele. Samuel gave a great deal of thought as to how he could convince the elders of his nation to accept this almost white person as his son. He would have to show these great men who surrounded his king something tangible reflecting both his own and Pompey's worth. That something would have to be his own return from America and slavery into the world of the Matabele with Whitehouse as his captive in chains. With Pompey to play at being his white master, his escape was now a distinct possibility.

CHAPTER X

Pompey ran down from the big house to Samuel's cabin with some news that he thought might be of interest to his friend. In the world of the internal politics of slavery, it was plantation news of the most important kind. He arrived at Samuel's cabin door within only five minutes of his leaving the big house. Pompey carefully wiped his feet and knocked on the door.

"Come in young Pompey. I have been expecting you long before now," called Samuel from inside his well-appointed smaller version of the big house.

"How can you know what I'm going to tell you before I even say one word?" asked the footman and butler-in-training on entering Samuel's little mansion.

"It is very simple my boy. You have run all the way down here to tell me that Old Caesar is very sick have you not?" said Samuel with an all knowing smile on his lips.

"Yes. That is it exactly. How could you know that?"

"It is my place to know that fact and everything else that happens here on this plantation. My ears are everywhere. Nothing will ever happen here that I will not know about first. More than that, nobody will ever know how I know."

"The Forrester's are very upset. It's just as if they really loved

Caesar. They sent for the doctor, and he says that the old man might die," Pompey blurted out.

"No doubt they love Caesar the way they loved that old hound dog that Master Forrester used to feed under their dining room table. When that animal was gone, they cried like he had been a cherished member of their infernal tribe. But in the end, he was just a dog. There will be no difference with Caesar. He is, in the end, just another favorite hound. One who had served them. Already Mrs. Forrester is planning to adjust his coats to fit you for your new duties. She will have some new clothes made for you as well. I suspect that the family will even come to his funeral services. Some of the women and girls will even cry. They will cry for their favorite house hound and dear old pet all over again," said Samuel. He almost spat the words out with contempt.

"Why do you hate the Forrester's so much?" Pompey asked Samuel now that the two of them were alone in Samuel's cabin, which had added to Samuel's amusement, because his habitation had aped the Greek revival architecture of their big house so well.

"I do not hate them. They are not worthy of my hate, just my contempt, because they are weak and exist as a master race over us merely because they are white and we are black. You do not yet know what it is to be a Matabele warrior. We are the greatest warriors in all of the world. We are the chosen people of heaven. Even the English in Cape Town marvel at us and tremble in awesome fear before our might. We can run fifty miles in a day without hardship. Even men of the age of sixty can do this, because we save our seed and have iron wills and endurance. None can stand against us in battle. We are the master people of Africa, and these whites are without skills and thus are without merit in this world. If they were left to fend for themselves, they would die before the end of a single season. Yet I do not wish them harm. In fact, I have no intention of ever really harming them unless there is no other way to carry out my plans. Have you read Mr. Gibbon's *Rise and Fall of the Roman Empire* as I suggested Pompey?"

"Not as of yet."

"You should. At least read the first part of the work up to the date 476 AD. Master Forrester laughed when I asked to borrow it. In fact, he even carried all six volumes down here himself and gave them to me as a gift. They are sitting right over there in my bookcase bound in the finest red-tooled Moroccan leather. I was the first ever to read them although they sat in the library in the big house for well over half a century. Do you know why the whites love books? They love them because they dress up a room so well. He said that they would dry up and rot away in the bookcase of the big house before any of his brood would read them. He was always amused that I could read at all, and it pleased him to have so rare a treasure as myself to do all the work on the place including keeping his books. It left him more time to play, and it afforded me a chance to educate myself for a place in the world when the day shall come when I will go back to Africa. The big problem I faced almost thirty years ago was that I needed the skills and weapons to escape my fate here including Forrester's unwitting cooperation. His only talent was that he had some degree of charm and a gift with card playing. I was and am the real engine of work and leadership here. Forrester knew his limitations, and as youths of sixteen and twenty-one, we made our pact. I would do the actual work, and he would put a white face on our partnership. Part of that plan was that he would have to be my master. I hated him for that I think, but at the same time we were sort of friends who had to accommodate ourselves to this strange world in which neither one of us really belonged. We had to conform to the rules of the country and we made the best of it."

"Now I can see that your dream has a real chance of happening Samuel. I thought at one time that you were giving into some flight of fancy. Most of the slaves on the place think only of the Christian next life, because they have pretty much given up all hope of being free in this one," said Pompey.

"They are without imagination and ambition. Both of these

things are far too dangerous for a slave to possess and still be allowed to live. In order to keep slaves docile, this Christian belief promises the slave something better in the life that is to be his after death and a lifetime of service to the whites. It's that Christian next life that these poor fools believe in that does not exist. When they are dead, they just go into a hole in this damned red earth like any other beast of burden. There they can rest from a world that robbed them of their lives Pompey. Old Anna was a wonderful woman, but she had this borrowed white man's vision of some Christian Heaven in the sky and a life to come that would be filled by some sort of pleasure to reward her for the toil and misery of this earthly life spent in the service of her white master. They want us to believe that service had real virtue meriting some reward for being a good slave. But I saw her placed into that hole, and there were no angels on the wing to take her away in some sweet chariot gently swinging low to catch her and fetch her up to a heaven of anybody's making. Oh Pompey, this soft and hopeful faith is a white man's trap to make the Black man work for him and even to make the slave be content to do so with a promise of something better in a nether world. We will not be taken in so easily will we my son?"

"No Samuel. We will not. Is that why you are so contemptuous of them? Is that why you dislike the Forrester's the way you do?"

"They exist, and although they are a weak and troublesome lot who could not get along without the labor of even the oldest and weakest slave on the place, they have all the power over us. I resent that state of things. I am a free man, but that would mean nothing if Mistress Forrester should change her mind. Even now she has the same power that a Roman father held in the days of the republic and the empire two thousand years ago. The whites have the power of life and death over each Black man, woman, and child on this place just as if we were farm animals or idiot children, and that is why I hate them. She could whip us, sell us, starve us, torture us. Or do anything else she wanted with impunity. I hate them for what they are and not who they are.

The Forresters are not a cruel people as are so many whites, but they are masters still. We must get away from here as soon as it is practical to do so. We must go to England, the very homeland of Mr. Wilberforce. There we will be free, and safe, and from England we can make our way to Africa. We will need a great deal of money. I have saved quite a bit already, and I know just how to get more. The time is not so far off for us to begin our journey. We must plan for the perfect hour to get away. We are still not altogether ready my son. I want to buy you, then you will be my white man. That is, until I free you."

"Samuel, you are a wise man, but how can I be a white man?"

"Pompey, you are a white man. The next time you pass a mirror in the big house, study yourself. You look darkly handsome like a Spaniard or even a little like an even whiter version of the Portuguese slavers of Africa that I had known in another life a long time ago. Your hair is wavy like the white man, not tightly curly like my hair. I have seen how the white women look at you. They think you handsome. I can see that they even want you. That will be of great benefit to us when the right time comes. You are the very image of the very man I intend to kill some day. Do not fear that I will mistake you for an enemy then. My assegai thirsts for their blood, the blood of the men who make Africans into their slaves. Some day when we make our escape from this slave life, you will present yourself as my master. I shall be your manservant. To the American world, it will look right. You shall be from New Orleans. Maybe you will have a Portuguese or Spanish family name. As long as you have documents, you can be anyone you want to be in this country. They worship paper here. You are to be a white man for the needed time only. It will be a relief to you that this game will be of so short a duration. Listen to us Pompey. Do we not sound white?"

"Yes suh Mr. Samuel. That we duz alright suh."

"Yes, indeed, you do my son," laughed Samuel.

"You have made these Forrester's even richer than when old

master was alive," said Pompey," and I know that you have gotten richer yourself, but why do you still do it for them? I know now that you were planning something for the master the night he had his accident on the road near the big house. I could feel it when you sent me off."

"You will never say that again boy. Not even in a soft voice when we think we are alone, because we are never alone. These walls can hear, and what is heard can cause trouble. So come close by me, and I will tell you this one time of some things that you might find interesting, but I will whisper them in your ear so none but the souls in the spirit world will know what I have seen." Pompey moved closer to where Samuel sat.

"The Forrester man did not have an accident. You are right in thinking that somebody killed him, but that was not me. That night, I was going to kill him, but he was killed by another."

"Murdered?" asked Pompey softly but with surprise. "You mean to say that the master was truly murdered!"

"Yes. That is what I have been telling you. He was killed by this very man whom I hate above all other men on this earth, and I thought that he had been delivered into my hands by fate when I first saw him much earlier in the day. I thought that fate had done me a truly great service. It was this man who killed Forrester. When I went out that night to await Forrester by the road, I had thought to kill him and maybe his whole damned family. I had always thought that I would have to go to Africa to kill this other fellow, but fate brought him here to me. And fate removed him from my grasp. It was this man, Whitehouse by name, who had taken me into bondage. He is the man, the Captain of the slave ship, who stole me from my country as he has stolen thousands of other Africans from their nations and families to put the dirty money of the slave trade into his pockets. I would have killed Forrester just to get him out of my way had I not seen Forrester and this man meeting by the road. There was light enough to see all that was done there. Forrester was very drunk and he slid off his horse. Then he had a conversation with the beast. Can you fancy that?" said Samuel laughing. "And you should have heard the truths that came pouring out of his mouth made stupid with drink. As the Romans said, there is truth in wine."

Samuel then went on to relate the events of the half hour that followed between Forrester's fall and his death. He concluded with the murder of Forrester by Whitehouse. Pompey looked at Samuel in amazement while clinging to every detail. Samuel continued in a very low voice that could not be overheard, "I ran back here after I had seen what Whitehouse had done. I didn't want to be hanged for the murder of Master Forrester. As I have said, it is true that I had thought about it and planned to kill Forrester, but I have since decided that a better door has been opened for me. These Forrester women are helpless, and better yet, they are greedy. That was the very thing that will make my plan work. The mistress had known a little something of what the arrangements between the master and me had been. Some years ago, he had to take her into his confidence. It is true that she did not know everything. She thought that she had married an adventurer, not a cheat and former slaver. There were just too many things she could never understand. She knew with him gone that she would have to agree to expand the unwritten contract the master and I had made so many years ago into a written one. Never could she imagine in her life that a slave, newly made a free man, would want to leave this life. This situation created by Whitehouse is the key to the perfection of all our plans. These greedy whites even wanted my seed, my children. The children of my blood! Ten of them is what they demanded as if they were negotiating for cattle, and now they have them." Samuel laughed softly.

Then Samuel grimaced, "I have but one regret, and that was that I did not follow Whitehouse and crush the life out of him that very night. But I could not take the chance of being even thought of as a murderer of two white men in that early pre-dawn when the whole household must have been awakened by that scream on the forest road. It was not a chance I could reasonably take. I was rash when I gave into my rage when I was in Africa and chased that filthy Mashona that I had taken to be a cattle thief. That bit of impetuosity brought me here to America in chains. I had planned too well and too long to allow our chance for freedom to slip away for a moment of satisfaction, and that is all it would have been had I killed this Whitehouse. He had done me a service in killing Forrester. Had I killed Whitehouse and had been discovered then all my years of careful work might have been brought to nothing. The household had to have heard the scream just as Whitehouse had calculated. There would have been dozens of people about. So my regrets are mixed young Pompey. It is best if we do not speak of it again even in whispers. We must never forget where we are. This does not mean that the man Whitehouse is ever removed from my thoughts of revenge. In fact, I need this revenge against Whitehouse just as our crops need water."

"I will never say anything of this. I will put it out of my mind altogether," replied Pompey.

These Forresters, they are so stupid. In a short while, we will make a big change here, and all of those fine white folks will not be able to lift a finger to save themselves from what I plan to do. And Pompey, what is even better, they won't even want to save themselves. They will actually be happy to join in the plot against themselves."

"Are we going to kill them?" whispered Pompey.

"We, you say? Are you so ready to join me in the act of killing young Pompey? Are you ready to do murder at my bidding without question or hesitation? Are you so brave as that? Are you so foolish?"

"Yes Samuel. Indeed, I think that I am both brave and foolish. What do I have to lose? My life? As long as I belong to others, do I truly have a life? I have no questions of you Samuel. I will follow you without question wherever you may lead."

"Not even one question? Not even one doubt young Pompey?"

"No, I am ready to do whatever you ask. I trust you as no other."

"Then you are now ready to be a warrior of the very best sort. You are unafraid to believe in something and follow orders to achieve the intended goal." Then Samuel laughed again. He thought maybe Pompey was a bit of a Matabele after all.

Pompey wondered that so huge a man could laugh so fully and almost not make a sound. Then he heard Samuel say, "Do not be so bloodthirsty and bloody minded my son. We will not actually have to kill anybody if everything falls into place with my scheme. There are many ways to skin this cat, and we must never be messy about it. We shall advance our plan with deliberate speed. The people who happen on our artful work later on will not even know what has happened here until it is too late and we are well out of this place on the royal road to freedom. In fact, even then we will be safe, because the white man likes to save face and not to be thought to be a foolish dupe. They certainly will not wish to appear the fools of a Black man. No white man or woman is ever going to admit that they were fooled by one of us. These Forrester's will be left with more than enough wealth to get out of this country with some dignity to start over again somewhere else where they are not known. I know that they no longer love this place. Master Forrester has finished their old life here for them. Great wealth, in the end, will be all that will matter. And wealth is all I intend to leave them."

Samuel paused for a moment then went on, "I think for one white woman in particular it may be doubly needful to save her reputation. Now go back to the house. Maybe you will find that old Caesar is already dead, and that you are now head man in his place. It is a good thing that I convinced the mistress that I should teach you to read so that you would be better able to do your duties when the time arrives that Old Caesar does go on to his own heaven. She even thinks that this was her own idea by now. She is even convinced that when that time for you to step into the gap comes, that you would be a greater source of pride for her than ever. You are, after all Pompey, her pet and her pretty boy that she loves to dress like some play doll as Caesar was so used to saying."

"She is really such a simple creature at times. How does she come to think that I could learn to read and write so quickly Samuel? Does she think me a genius?" asked Pompey.

"She thinks that it was the good work of those English High Church missionaries in Africa of so long ago that made me so fine a teacher. And what makes you think that she takes notice of such things as the mere passing of time? She is a very shallow creature. It all comes of their primitive religious superstitions I think and their everlasting preoccupation with themselves."

"So you think they use their Christian God to keep people like poor old Anna simple and docile? Now that I consider it, I think that maybe you are right," Pompey said.

"Pompey, Old Anna was not so simple as you think. She was good to you, taught you, kept you in the house where you would be safe, and most of all she loved you like her own child. She knew why you were afraid to love her back. She knew that you were afraid to lose your mother all over again. She was unselfish, and the only simple thing about her was this faith in the white man's God. Maybe it made her life less of a burden for her, but it did not make her totally docile. Like you she rebelled in her way. Sometimes she would urinate in their soups and sauces."

"I cannot believe that! Not Anna."

"Yes Pompey. And she would say that the master's sister would screw up her ugly face and say, 'You put too much salt in the soup again you stupid girl.' Anna would say in return, ' I's sorry Miz Forrester. Hit won't happen again.' Then she would smile as she carried the empty tureen from the dining room back to the kitchen after dinner."

Samuel's use of the slave accent made Pompey laugh out loud. Then he clapped his hand over his mouth.

Now Samuel laughed right out loud, and said, "Ah never told you that you all cain't never laff did Ah?"

"Be careful Samuel, you are getting too good at talking like that."

"It's just a game Pompey. A game we play for the white folks up to the big house so that they can go on being so superior to us poor Black folks. Excuse me, 'Niggers', although the mistress always liked the fact that I sounded a little like an Englishman to her. She thought having an English sounding slave gave her some tone." Samuel's smile was now icy cold. "Now young Pompey, scat. I have work to do, and you have to go and find out if poor old Caesar is dead or if he just has the habit of looking that way. And if you are to be the new butler one of these days, it will put you into a wonderful position to be very useful to us in our escape from here. Believe me when I tell you that when we leave here, we will not be running through a swamp with a pack of dogs nipping at our heels followed by a gang of roughs making up a posse. When we leave here it will be through the front door walking to a coach like two gentlemen."

Three days passed, and the old man did at last die in the quiet of the surroundings in which he had spent the greater part of his life. Caesar just sat at the table in his pantry and quietly slumped over without making a sound, and without causing a bit of trouble, as was his habit. Old Caesar went to his rest in a plain pine box in a simple ceremony like Anna, but this time there was a profound difference. The Forrester women were there to see the old man they had known for so many years off to their version of a segregated Heaven. It was a certain belief to them that the races could not mix in Heaven.

It was as a certainty to them that the best part of Heaven was reserved for their own kind. God was a white deity after all. But in all justice, they also thought that a just God would have to make some accommodations for these lesser forms of human life that had served them so well. They knew this, because they also embraced the mythology that most slaves loved their masters and the security of slavery. There must be a heaven for slaves especially if the slaves were as well behaved and beloved as Old Caesar of whom the Forresters were very fond. Even Caroline, one of the silly Forrester girls, whispered to her equally silly sister Tilly, “Do you think our pups we’ve had over the years can go to Heaven if darkies can?”

“Well I should hope so. After all, it’s only fair,” replied Tilly Forrester.

CHAPTER XI

Pompey detected some degree of real sorrow in Mrs. Forrester's demeanor. Even the Forrester daughters were obviously saddened over the death of Old Caesar. He had been a material and loyal part of their lives for so long that he had seemed to be part of the very place forever. Caesar had been the classic house servant whose loyalty to the family was never to be questioned. Since the death of their father and the radical contraction in their circle of friends, Caroline and Tilly had come to depend on their house servants more and more for comfort and support. Even Mrs. Forrester seemed to talk to the house slaves as if she was speaking to real people, and for the first time she had begun asking them how they felt and what their thoughts were on various household topics. These were things which she would never have discussed with them in the time before her husband's and Old Caesar's deaths. She even took a domestic interest in their families and strictly forbid her sister-in-law from striking any of them in the future.

Slave families had existed as very fragile institutions within what passed for structure in slave society, but on the Forrester plantation, no slave had been sold off the place in more than twenty-five years. It was also growing obvious that although the plantation was flourishing under Samuel's hand, the Forrester family was becoming more isolated from polite county plantation society and were withdrawing into themselves. Fewer and fewer of Mrs. Forrester's old friends came to her afternoon teas, and the invitations to afternoon teas from other plantations had begun to dry up. Slowly the cheating scandal, although never openly discussed, was having a chilling effect on the Forrester's social life.

The flow of plantation life had been also deeply impacted by the year of mourning following the master's accident. The sorrow and pity that had been felt for the family following James Forrester's death by misadventure had turned to open resentment during the two years since his death. Forrester had siphoned off substantial amounts of cash from his neighbors' purses. Now his plantation flourished under his women folk and slaves while his neighbors were not faring nearly so well.

The Forrester place seemed to prosper even through the financial reverses of the country. Even Georgia was beset with the massive bank failures, which had begun during the later Jackson years. The Forresters held their wealth in gold, not in paper banknotes, which were increasingly of no value. Their bank was old and well established. This institution had not issued the millions of dollars in wildcat bank notes that so many failed banks had in the last decade. The contrast between the Forrester prosperity and the near financial ruin of the rest of the county was infuriating to their neighbors. The reason for this fury was that no restitution had ever been offered by the heirs of James Forrester for the gambling losses suffered by the gentry even though the dead man's family now were presumed to know that the luck enjoyed by the dead man at cards was all due to his many years of cheating at the gaming tables at Buckland's.

Even the Episcopal Church which was attended by the local landowners began to be a place of cold comfort for the Forrester family. The members of the congregation, who were once sympathetic to the family, were now distant, coldly correct, and then as time passed, not even coldly correct. The Forrester's were now shunned more than ever even as they prospered materially. They were, in fact, openly snubbed by the members of the congregation. The thought of attending any other church was not to even be considered. None but "The High Episcopal Church" would do for the Forrester women. The Baptist Church was for the farmers who owned few or no slaves. There could be no thought of going there with their rigid adhesion to the rule that alcohol was sinful and therefore had no place in the Christian life. A religion that did not even recognize the need for the comfort of a small sherry every now and then was not a place for civilized people. Rubbing shoulders with such rustics as the country people who attended the meeting houses of the lower orders of Christianity would be just too great a comedown in social standing for the Forresters. Each church had its own cachet, and even the slaves knew about this fact of religious social life. Both the Baptist and Methodist Churches were far beyond the pale of good taste for the Forrester women.

As for the Forrester boys, they had kept out of their mother's sight until it was time for them to go off to West Point. Their appointments had come through on the recommendation of their congressional representative. After their father's funeral, James and Douglas spent their time at Miss Sally's where the good madam had smiled on the wayward sons of her beloved Jimmy Forrester. When not at Miss Sally's, James and Douglas occupied themselves far away out in the countryside. Sometimes for days and even weeks at a time, they would ramble far from the restrictive life of the plantation and their mother's disapproving eye and whip. They could not stand the confinement of home, and they were not, as the sons of James Forrester, welcomed at Buckland's or in any other respectable part of the county where men of quality gathered. Even Miss Sally had to keep them apart from the rest of her patrons. They were caught between their wild natures and their unmanly fear of their mother's sharply enforced disapproval and threat of physical chastisement. They never had feared their father the same way they feared her. As long as they brought no trouble home to disturb the peace of the house, their mother tolerated them and provided them with the funds to Hell about as long as they did so far away from home.

At last, the day came when the boys were packed off to West Point. Mrs. Forrester had given them a substantial purse and allowed them each a maternal peck on the cheek as she sent them off with the admonition to study for once in their lives and to try to be gentlemen. Samuel, who seemed under normal circumstances to notice nothing of the social goings on of the little insular community of the gentry, saw it all, and rejoiced in his mistresses' social isolation. Even the church seemed to be playing into his hands. It too had contributed to the family's social isolation in a material way that was central to his grand design. And his grand design could not be working out any better for him than if he had engineered the whole Forrester social catastrophe himself.

A year passed. Then at last came a time when the family could no longer attend Sunday worship at all. The Forresters stayed home on Sunday as well as on other days. When things seemed to be able to get no worse, an official letter arrived at the Forrester plantation from The United States Military Academy at West Point's superintendent announcing that the Forrester sons had been expelled from the academy for conduct unbecoming officers and gentlemen. Just what that conduct was, was never fully known. The plantation community was small and the disgrace of the twin expulsions of James and Douglas Forrester was news all over the neighborhood and carried beyond those narrow precincts to all of Georgia. The story of the expulsions was eventually picked up by the newspapers and duly reported for weeks in the Carolinas and Florida.

A scandal of expulsions from the service academy was important news to be consumed and relished when the young men in question were from such a rich, prominent, and highly loathed family. It was even suggested that dealings with low women might be the cause of the lads' troubles at the academy. More likely a dalliance with innocent farm girls was the cause thought some.

Men thought that boys from a family that so lacked personal honor may have been caught cheating on their examinations. Speculation ran rampant throughout the county, but nobody was ever sure exactly what the Forrester boys' transgressions had been. Still the gentry talked of nothing else. Some wags even ventured to opine that the boys had really been caught cheating at cards. Some of the crowd at Buckland's had been reported laughing when Mr. O'Hara shouted out to Mr. Beaumont his thoughts on the subject, "The apple's not far from falling from the tree eh boys!"

Beauchamp's laughter was hollow. He was putting up a good front. His wife had left him and taken the children with her to Mississippi to live with her widowed mother and unmarried sister. It seems that Beauchamp wagered his plantation one time too many. This time it was not the charming James Forrester who won it. This time the deed had not been graciously returned with a nod and a smile. This time the man who beat him did not say, "Beauchamp, I could not take a man's home and birthright."

The county set gleefully rejoiced at the deeper fall of the once high and mighty Forresters. One day the boys came slinking back into the county and stealthily made their way back to the plantation. Mrs. Forrester was not pleased to receive them. James and Douglas made their way back to their respective rooms in the house and visited only with one another. At seven o'clock on the day they arrived home, Pompey was sent up to them with orders from their mother to wash, dress, and present themselves for dinner at eight. This they did, and dinner proved to be a silent affair. Tilly and Caroline spoke with their mother about trivial things. Old Miss Forrester sat eating silently in the isolation of her own profound gloom as she had done since her brother's death, and the two boys either looked at their plates or to each other for support and some small degree of comfort. When the last dishes had been cleared away by Helena, Mrs. Forrester commanded, "James, Douglas, I want to see you in the library now!"

Unspeaking, the two Forrester boys followed their mother

into the library and shut the door. Their mother turned to them and said, "Sit down, and listen to what I have to say, for I will only say this once. I do not expect either of you to take a bit of interest in the running of this place. You have no talent for running much of anything, not even your own lives. The fact that you got into West Point was amazing to me, almost beyond my understanding. It may have been your last chance to be gentlemen. Now all I can say is that I want you out of my sight, and I want to hear no reports of your helling around in the county anywhere near here. If you must misbehave, do it far away. If you cause me one bit of trouble I will not hesitate to lash the hide off the both of you and have Samuel drag you out into the road in your small clothes to make your own way in the world. I will give you each fifty dollars a month to do with as you please. You may come down to dinner dressed properly, but if you, either of you cause me one bit of trouble, I'll be done with you for good and all. Am I understood?"

The two Forrester boys looked at each other then said in unison, "Yes mother."

"Good. Here is a purse for each of you. From now on you will get your money from Samuel on the first of each month. Do not ask him for more. If you do, I will know of it, and then there will be no money at all. Now, we shall have coffee and cakes in the drawing room, and after that you may leave Tilly, Caroline and me for brandy and cigars on the veranda. Do not smoke in the house. Now be so kind as to get the door and follow me back to the dining room."

The two boys jumped to do their mother's bidding. The law had been imposed, and neither Douglas nor James had the courage to cross their mother in any way. The two Forrester sons now had a bond, which united them more closely than ever. They became each other's best friend, and seemed to move as one force backing each other up. As time passed and one season merged into another they became bolder in their exploits. That is, they became bolder away from their mother's noticing eyes far away from home.

James and Douglas seemed to have no need of male friendships or the support of the women of the family to whom they had never been close anyway. The Forrester women never had troubled to make time for the willful and wild Forrester boys who never conformed to the standards of good society at any level except in the area of snobbery and sporting the latest fashions. These were areas in which they truly excelled. They were all but unlovable to the women of the family in all things but their gift for fashion.

Women outside of the family however, found that they themselves had an endless passion for the wild and dangerous Forrester boys. The Forrester lads were actively pursued by women of all stations of life, who found them to be excessively romantic beings that were both handsome and sexually sophisticated. There was something seductive about young handsome rogues that one was always warned off if one happened to be a farm girl, young matron whose husband was frequently away on business or just an attractive girl.

Douglas and James were still fearful of their mother's wrath. They carefully helled around the countryside occasionally dipping into the pleasures offered at Miss Sally's Inn until the gentry tossed them out of this civilized sexual sanctuary of the planter upper class even during the off hours. After a while they no longer were told by their mother to keep their wanderings out of the county. She had concluded in the end that she didn't care what they did as long as they did not do it on the plantation. In spite of the fact that the Forrester lads were pointedly informed by a dozen of Miss Sally's most important and brawniest patrons that they no longer qualified as gentlemen and could not share in the pleasures of Miss Sally's or Buckland's along with men of quality, James and Douglas still managed visits on the sly.

The Forrester boys were hardly deemed worthy of the pleasures of Miss Sally's well-favored girls. But Miss Sally indulged her fondness for the handsome sons of her favorite lover when the place was not open to regular trade in secret. Their own father, whose memory was still special to Miss Sally, also opened her door and her heart to his sons for tea and chats. But she did not wish to lose any of her lucrative business, which after all, was the most successful income producing operation in the county after the Forrester plantation itself. Several of Miss Sally's friends had helped her invest her money in New York and New Orleans in bonds, stocks, and lucrative ventures. One of them, a banker, transferred substantial amounts of her funds to London to the Bank of England. She could well afford to indulge and even spoil the sons of her Jimmy Forrester. After they had taken their pleasure with their ladies, Miss Sally often went beyond tea and chatting. She frequently indulged them with supper and conversation. Here they were gentle and warmed to something like a sort of maternal love they had never received before from this most unexpected source.

Much to Samuel's joy, the wild Forrester boys had no interest in the running of the plantation, or working on it, or participating in its life such as it was. That would have meant real work for these two Hell raisers, and that sort of thing was not the province of young gentlemen about town even though they were more than ever outsiders and exiled from their own class and home as well. Their principal occupation of visiting low taverns, drinking, and gambling as far from the plantation as they could ride took them far away from any show of ambition in running a plantation. Low taverns had low women who were available to gentlemen who had been expelled from polite society. These wenches always abounded. As long as the Forrester boys remained in these less privileged areas of the county and beyond its precincts, there was no real problem to be had with the society of respectable people. Quite simply, their worlds never intersected. Here, among the lowly folks, the Forresters were kings, and together they were damned near invincible.

It was when they moved into the prim and proper world of the respectable church going middle class farmers, with whom they would never have mixed in the bygone days as county aristocrats, that the greater problems of their young lives began to arise. Douglas, the younger Forrester boy, dressed like the peacock that he was, had turned the head of a respectable farmer's daughter, seduced her, and deflowered her. Respectable girls were not supposed to be the objects of a casual dalliance even by the members of the planter class.

Fathers and older brothers of respectable young farm girls tended to see these depredations of the sons of the planter class as grave insults to be dealt with seriously. It was then that the real trouble began. When the girl's father learned of his daughter's fallen and sad condition, he put on his Sunday best, and in the company of his five grown sons, he rode out to the Forrester place to inquire as to when young Douglas Forrester was going to make an honest woman of his daughter through the proper institution of a good Baptist marriage. The unexpected meeting at the Forrester's which followed was an ugly event. The farmer and his sons marched into the drawing room of the big house wearing their big boots coated with red encrusted clay. Here they confronted Mrs. Forrester and the young Forrester men.

The Forrester girls were presumed to be far too innocent to hear the things which Mrs. Forrester knew would be said after she was informed of the reason for the surprise visit of the farmer and his sons. In her heart, she cursed the late Mr. Forrester for not being there to take care of this nasty business. Somehow she knew that such a day would come, but she was not quite ready for it. She wished that she had her whip in her hand and the offending Douglas before her in the stables so that she could administer the justice that she would have liked to mete out to her wayward cur of a son who once again had disturbed the peace of her house. She would have liked to turn him over to the men who were standing before her for the crime that she very well knew that Douglas had committed, but this she could not do. Mrs. Forrester could not allow the vulgar hands of these men to touch her son. There were issues of class to protect that were more highly esteemed by her than the justice that she really wanted to see done. But to inflict that justice she saw as her right alone, and it would not be inflicted before the eyes of dirt farmers.

In the place of the late James Forrester was Judge Bowen acting in his capacity as the family's lawyer. As luck would have it, his honor had a meeting with Mrs. Forrester on the very morning when the outraged clan of the deflowered girl chose to stride into the best parlor of the Forrester mansion. Mrs. Forrester summoned James and Douglas to the drawing room, and then she listened to the complaints. When the farmer stated his daughter's claim of young Douglas Forrester's paternity of his unborn grandchild, young Forrester denied all knowledge of the girl. His brother James said that he understood that the young lady's reputation was that of a trollop, and that if the truth be known, the father of her unborn child could have been any of a dozen young farmers in the area.

The outraged father and the girl's brothers were in no mood for the Forrester boys' parlor games or for the Forrester brother's trashing of their daughter and sister's reputation. Their rage was immediate and awful. Only the presence of the distinguished judge, Samuel, Pompey, and Mrs. Forrester prevented a massacre of the two offending boys from happening right then and there on the muddied oriental carpets gracing the floor of the grandly furnished Forrester salon.

The good farmer, with his face now deep purple, and with his veins bulging from his bull neck, spat out words to the effect that if the young Forresters were ever discovered off the Forrester place, it would not go well with them. In turn, the judge warned the farmer and his sons that no harm had better befall the young Forresters or there would be consequences to be paid in his court. The truth of the matter was, even though the Forresters were outcasts in their own class, that class of country gentry would still rise as one man to defend the prerogatives of their fellow members of the upper crust of planters in the face of the common agrarian middle class enemy. As bad as the Forresters may be, they had once been members of the gentry. Middle class intruders must never be allowed to think that they ever could judge their betters. Even a beating of the much-loathed Forrester boys would be the thin edge of the wedge. In a society of unequals, it was paramount that the upper class would always guard the gates of its privileged state.

Then the infuriated farmer stated that there were higher natural laws of God and sacred social traditions, which existed above and beyond written laws and the mere courts of men. The outraged father of the fifteen year old girl said that God might decide that a punishment be enforced in matters of a decent Christian girl being led astray by wicked men uttering false promises of matrimony. With that threat hanging in the air, the outraged father left the mansion with his sons in tow leaving a trail of slimy red Georgian clay to mark their passage into and out of the Forrester's aristocratic domain. As they left, each of the five sons looked back over their shoulders at the Forrester boys. They were not smiling. Their faces were filled with a grim tight-jawed awful resolution and the righteous holy anger of the plain and honest country folk of Georgia.

After the farmers had left her house, Mrs. Forrester turned to Douglas and slapped his face so hard that he fell backwards onto the floor. The old judge gasped in shock. Mrs. Forrester shot back, "Well what did you expect judge! The boy behaved very badly!" Then she turned to Douglas and spat, "If I see you within a fortnight, I'll strip the hide off of you myself. The only reason I am not flogging you now is that I know that I will kill you. Why didn't you stick to your whores? How could you deflower a fifteen-year-old girl and then say those awful things about her. You are not to leave this plantation, and you are to hide from me or there is no telling what I might do to you. Now stay out of my sight, eat in your room, or move to the stable where you belong with the other animals. Mark what I say. If you leave this plantation without my leave, keep right on going and never come back.

Both of the boys retreated without a word to seek out a hiding place. Their meeting with Superintendent Delafield at West point had not been half so terrifying as their mother's rage. Pompey almost felt sorry for them. No slave on the Forrester plantation had ever suffered the brutal treatment of those two boys at the hand of their mother. They had never had the maternal love that Pompey had received from Anna. The farmer and his sons were the sort of good "salt of the earth" people who would not stand by and let their innocent women be debauched by the privileged sons of the country gentry. They had studied the Forrester boys well, and they had fixed their images in their memories as they studied them through their narrowed steely blue eyes. This did not pass unnoticed by James and Douglas who could read the unspoken warning all too well flashed silently by these brothers. James and Douglas had seen it all before in the North just before they were asked to quit West Point when the father and brothers of a local farmer's daughter appeared at West Point equipped with two nooses, neatly tied, pistols, and two extra horses. The regular troops had to escort the farmers away from the academy. But later in the day the farmers returned with the mayor and sheriff of the neighboring town and asked to see the superintendent of the academy, General Delafield. After hearing what the farmer and the local officials had to say, the General called the Forrester brothers into his office to face their accusers. Within a day's time the Forrester boys were given a mounted escort off the campus to the train depot and sent South.

Three weeks passed after the visit of the outraged Georgian farmer and his five sons before the Forrester boys ventured out again into the night, and for those three weeks they lived in their rooms with only each other for company hiding from their mother. When at last they emerged into the world again, they rode far away from the places of their earlier debauches. Soon the news of their new adventures spread about the surrounding counties, and the Forrester boys became the stuff of legend and folk tales. They were much admired by some of the more impressionable young fools about the countryside and the wild set of mid and late teen-age sons of the gentry.

The Forrester boys were well provided with cash by their mother to whom they had become a greater burden than she could stand to carry in her soul from day to everlasting day. They still had respect for her buggy whip and were therefore never in their cups at home. Mrs. Forrester thought that giving the boys gold and sending them on their way to whatever it was they did was enough to keep them out of the way. She had changed her mind about keeping them on a short leash. She reasoned that indulging them in their wild depredations and their adventures was better than having to look at them at mealtime or to suffer them in the rare moments when they ventured into the drawing room for brandy. Here, after she had liberated them from their in house exile, they sprawled out on the sofas, relaxing in their new freedom. They became more obnoxious to her consternation just by living in her house.

These sons of James Forrester were investing their cash in all sorts of new trouble. Their flash and style was well appreciated in the low places where they bought food and drink for a set of low born hangers-ons and near-do-wells. As time passed, they seemed to be less and less guarded in their movements. Their easy celebrity was bought with hard cash earned by and paid out by Samuel. Samuel seemed to treat the boys in a paternal way as he doled out their monthly allowance. He winked at them and gave them extra funds. He knew that more money would mean more excess in all things and would keep them away from his world for greater periods of time. Each time he doled out the extra cash it was with the proviso that they not tell their mother. They laughed and promised not to compromise their friend Samuel in their little conspiracy. That earned him their gratitude and guaranteed that they would stay away from home longer.

That first flow of gold into the Forrester coffers from the increased profits had become a flood under Samuel's skilled management of the plantation. The boys became bolder, and they even returned and quietly invaded the precincts of Miss Sally's house unnoticed and unnoticeable by the aristocratic patrons of the place from time to time. By now, the Forrester boys were invisible to good society. Some of the planter's own wayward sons followed in the legions of Forrester boy's company of admirers. These sons of privilege liked the fast company that the Forrester boys provided. Many a young lad had a meeting in the barn with his outraged father and a buggy whip when it was discovered that they "had been running" with the Forrester boys. And many a lad sat uneasily after such an encounter with their pa.

Summer passed into autumn. The Forrester boys became bolder yet, and once again they grew more stupid and careless. They began again to pursue pleasures even nearer to their home than they had before. But by now they had grown so careless that they began to go their separate ways in search of any pleasure wherever they could find it. Some five months later, on a raw and windy night, a midnight storm blew up. The air was rent by lightning. Thunder followed in great claps like the roar of cannon. Douglas, the younger son of the dead master, rode like the wind down the same fatal road on which his father met his end. Douglas was excited by the storm and the memory of his night in the arms of a planter's lonely wife. The planter was in Atlanta arranging the sale of his late harvest and his young and pretty wife let young Forrester know that she was not above seeing him when her husband was absent. She was well favored, not yet thirty, and beautiful as the devil. It seems that not all aristocratic doors were shut to so handsome an outcast as young Douglas Forrester. After that exhilarating tryst, Douglas enjoyed the warm and lusting body of the beautiful serving girl at the Concordia Tavern. Sweet Betty's body was young and soft where it should be soft, and she was a delicious sixteen, and more than that, she was willing to please him for a dollar in any manner he could devise. He warmed to the memory of the evening with her, and he wished that his brother could have been along to share in the fruits of his conquest. Two delicious women in the space of five hours had been just another night's work for him of sublime pleasure. For pleasure was the only occupation of both Forrester boys. They were their father's sons. Miss Sally reflected that it was a shame that they did not have his charm.

Douglas contemplated the savory prospect of a return visit to the Concordia. Next time it would be with his brother. Even if the tariff became two dollars for the two of them together with the girl, the time spent in the company of so liberal minded a country beauty would yield a treasure in sexual profit beyond any mere cash spent. Yes, he thought, there must be a return visit. Then without warning, a shaft of lightning flashed nearby with such force that his horse reared up and nearly threw him to the ground. In those seconds, he could see the house as if by daylight. This was the very place where his father had fallen to his death from his horse. And in that same brilliant light and in that moment, Douglas could see the body of his brother James swinging from a lower branch of an oak tree not thirty feet away. James was held in space by a rope around his neck.

"O my God!" screamed young Forrester who looked at his brother with anguish and terror. "It's not fair. They thought that it was me."

Slowly the body of the twenty one year old James twisted in the wind. As the lifeless body slowly twisted at the rope's end, there was another flash of brilliant light followed by a cannon roar of thunder. Douglas could see that his brother's hands were tied behind his back. As he rode closer, the body twisted back to face him again. There in another burst of celestial light Douglas could clearly see that James's face was contorted in pain, and the front of his trousers was drenched in blood.

CHAPTER XII

Young James Forrester's funeral was a sad affair. The Forrester family was there, and his brother Douglas was even sober for this very short time. The ceremony did not last very long. There was no question of the funeral taking place in the Gothic splendor of the large stone Episcopal Church in town. The need to keep onlookers to a minimum number was of paramount importance to the Forresters. The details of the lynching and bloody mutilation were already too well known about the county. From the form of the crime there could be no mistaking the intent of those who lynched James Forrester. The awful truth of the wrong brother being hanged by persons unknown for an alleged fornication was also being spread about much to the consternation of the Forresters. It was not so much the crime that bothered the Forrester matriarch as that people actually had to know about it. The sheriff had questioned the farmer and his family as to where they had been at the time of the murder of James Forrester. They had said that they were at prayer at their home with the daughter of the house and their minister. The good Baptist preacher attested that this was indeed the case. Several friends of the family and the minister's wife also said that they had been at the farmhouse until quite late praying over their fallen sister.

As many people would have shown up for the Forrester

funeral in town as they would have for a hanging. But moving the services had not had the effect of making young Forrester's send off any less of a public spectacle. There were perhaps more people present at the last rites than if the funeral had been held in town. This had been a sad miscalculation on the part of Mrs. Forrester. James Forrester Jr. was not destined to go peacefully off into oblivion. His mother chafed at this fact as if it was one final calculated annoyance perpetrated by her older son in some sort of malice directed directly at her. To do this last thing with as little fuss as possible was just what the Forrester women wanted. But the circumstances of young Forrester's death militated against all hopes of privacy. His following had been a large one among the young set, and curious onlookers made up the rest of the throng.

The knowledge that his brother had died in his place would give young Douglas Forrester no peace. He wept openly during the service much to the disgust of the more stoic Forrester women who exhibited little or no outward emotion. Dignity in the face of adversity is what well bred southern people embraced as a major article of aristocratic faith. The Forrester women even moved a bit away from this last son of the family as he gave himself over to the open and unmanly sobbing for his much loved brother. His isolation began from this moment in this strange family. Douglas began to feel just how totally alone he had become. Douglas Forrester was now separated from all that had any meaning to him in his short, shallow, and useless life. The one person he had really loved and who had loved him for his entire lifetime had been taken from him. He was now inconsolable with the loss of James.

Few respectable planters and their families were in attendance. But the mob of onlookers who celebrated young James Forrester's legend of wild behavior made Mrs. Forrester want to flee, but she looked straight ahead as the minister droned on. How she wished that the man would hurry up the service. Instead he seemed to warm to his eulogy since he had been provided with such a large audience. His rich voice rose and fell significantly at the most dramatic moments. Mrs. Forrester thought to herself, "Oh God, if thou art just, smite down this windbag!"

Most of the boys who had come to the funeral had wished to be like what they saw as the dashing James. Others among them were there just to be there. The fact was that there were hundreds of young men and dozens of young women, most of them unescorted, with their faces covered, at the Forrester's private cemetery where a newly carved and huge ornate monument marked the passing of the former master of the Forrester Plantation. A much smaller marker simply marked "Brother" was on the ground nearby to mark the final resting place of young James Forrester who had been hanged for the sins of his brother and now was being lionized by the minister. Some of those in attendance thought that even if the unfortunate lad had not been hanged for the right crime, young James was paying the price for dozens of his other sins of commission. The stone selected for the boy to rest above his head for eternity was a pitiful little marker in the shape of a marble lamb. This was a great curiosity in itself. Later on Douglas was told that the grave marker was left over from a failed sale at the stonemasons, and had cost but five dollars. More than a few planters' wives, who had defied their husbands' injunctions to stay away from the funeral, had attended for the sake of the woman they had once befriended. There was something about losing a child that bonds women together even beyond their husbands' outrage over substantial losses of money at cards. And other women were there who had known the tender touch of James between the sheets of their beds. Miss Frances Spence stood with Mrs. Merryman, Mrs. Cookingham, Mrs. Pettibone, and a dozen other ladies who had shared tea and cakes in the Forrester drawing room. Douglas looked at them through tears then laughed a quiet little laugh to himself and his dead brother. He looked past his mother's disapproval and said to his brother under his breath, "Jimmy, don't you think that you are better off dead than married to that Spence girl?"

At a respectful distance, stood the real master of the plantation and the senior slaves and the household staff. These two slave factions of field and house slaves still seemed removed from each other, but now it was all for appearance's sake. There was a dynamic existing between them here unseen by the white folks. It was the power shift to Samuel away from the Forrester Family that was sensed by and totally absorbed the interest of the slaves now. Nothing of the kind could ever have been imagined by any of the slaves who had ever toiled on the plantation for any time and who had the virtues of blind obedience drummed into them from birth. But many things had changed in the last few years. Without being told a thing, the slaves knew this as a fact of their lives, just as they had always known when anything was afoot. Samuel and the others put on long faces as they watched their betters show a strange mixture of emotions at the passing of young James Forrester. Still, the two divisions of the curious and the admiring mourners now stood in almost respectful silence. Their curiosity now turned into real regret and sweet sadness with the realization that youth is not immortal, and young fun loving James had been funny and kind to most of the people gathered here. The outcast James Forrester had interacted with almost everyone at some primal level. James had made little distinction between the sons of yeoman farmers and the sons of the planters in his associations as a colorful rogue.

After the minister had intoned the final prayers, the respectable mourners were invited to join the family at the big house. The young bloods melted away. Only half of the respectable assembled party joined the family in repairing to the Forrester mansion. The unattended matrons made their excuses and moved off in the direction of the road, leading out of the plantation, where their coaches, carriages, and buggies awaited them attended by their drivers, some of whom dressed in mourning by way of livery that day. Pompey took note of one highly lacquered carriage, which was a bright red, and impossible to miss, positioned on a high knoll well above the site of the Forrester burial ground. It was there for all to see in its vulgar splendor. It was a brazen display of wealth and success by the one person who actually felt real sorrow over the young man's death besides his brother. Samuel smiled and leaned over to Pompey. Indicating the ruby red carriage he said, "Do you see that?"

"I didn't expect to see her here. That is quite a tribute to young master James." Pompey actually laughed quietly with his mouth appearing not to move. This was yet another trick in the arsenal of a born survivor captured in the fragile world of slavery. The lady could just barely be seen through the opened carriage door. Her black driver was in full livery as if he were arrayed to drive one of the aristocrats to a ball at some enchanted palace in one of the novels that Pompey had so frequently read to improve his understanding of good society, not of Europe, but of the type of households in which he lived and where the pretensions of a greater European world were the all absorbing theme. For those books were the only ones that the lady folks seemed to read in the American backwater of rural red clay Georgia. The Forrester men never read at all. This explained the wonderful condition of the largely neglected books in the old master's library as Samuel had so often said. The books' only enemy seemed to be dust and mildew.

Miss Sally looked out from her red lacquered coach genuinely saddened over the death of young James Forrester. Maybe she cared for him as deeply as she had cared for his father. Miss Sally was a handsome woman whose age could not be guessed. But her eyes were as old as civilization, but as beautiful and as warm as gemstones with just a latent hint of fire. Pompey had always thought that this was so when he saw her in the town when he traveled there with a pass from the plantation to do errands for the family. He had even once seen the beautiful red headed Miss Sally on the arm of young James Forrester walking under the shade trees. The looks that passed between them were of a genuine affection born out of friendship rather than love of a carnal kind. It was then that he knew that the boy was thumbing his nose at the whole planter community in the broad light of day while enjoying a moment of real pleasure in the company of a real flesh and blood honest woman who understood the world in all of its sometimes ugly reality. Proper society woman had looked at the young man with shock and also with a glint of delicious malice in their eye. Most of them could not wait to tell the others of their circle about this scandalous behavior they had witnessed. Pompey knew that James warmed in the radiant heat of this exotic woman's beauty and genuine kindness. At that moment, he actually liked the boy and felt some sorrow for him. Pompey had seen what life could be like when one was unloved.

Yet at the same time, Pompey also sensed that there was something deeper there in young James' friendship with Sally Beers. A sort of grasping in desperation for a feeling of something like maternal love on the part of young Forrester. Pompey reflected that James had seen little paternal or maternal love in his young life while he was growing into that wild young man who went off to West Point and had then returned in deep disgrace with his brother. All that Pompey could remember is that he had played for a short period of time with the younger sons of the house, and they had behaved with some degree of decency with him, as little boys of a similar age will. The three of them were united for a short time against the common enemy, which was made up of adults who would prevent them from doing what they wanted to do. The Forrester boys had enjoyed Pompey's company when they were children of five, six, and seven. Anna had used her wiles to remove Pompey from their company for his own sake, and that threw the Forrester boys back on their own small resources.

The plantation had held nothing else by way of love for either James or Douglas except for the real love they had for each other. Never had two boys of any class been so neglected and uneducated for their life. It was only in the area of their superficial social education, that they had not been failed by their parents. The full attention of the Forresters was focused on their daughters on whom they seemed to dote exclusively. James and Douglas had only a rudimentary education even by the shabby standards of the Deep South. But even this was a job delegated to old Caesar after they had been expelled by all the schools in the county. Pompey now wondered to himself what it would be like to have had an attractive woman on his arm like Miss Sally, or better yet, in his bed. Pompey had been thinking about that more and more lately. Then he remembered Samuel's injunction against being with a woman now until the right time came. Pompey doubted that he could wait until he was thirty-nine even if he were to be thrown down a mountainside for it.

Douglas, the last of the Forrester men, had been standing at the graveside during the service. The sweet-sour aroma of brandy was on his lips. Samuel saw the boy sway uncertainly, and Samuel had smelled the brandy too. Samuel smiled ever so slightly. There would be no challenge here to his authority from this young man. There was no support here in this community for the family among the planters. The slaves who were present at the rites had been warned by Samuel to show nothing but the deepest respect for the Forresters, and in turn the bondsmen knew that now they belonged to Samuel. In this, there was little challenge for the overseer. For such leadership behavior had been ingrained into Samuel from birth. None of these other slaves had had the experience of running over the Southern African veldt with the sun warmed grass under their feet, or ever had the chance to tend their own animals. They never had the knowledge that the blood of kings coursed through their veins. Once in a while, Samuel had felt that the burden of this knowledge was too great for him to carry, but carry it he must. And a great part of that burden, were the dreams that sometimes came like ancient furies to torment him in his sleep. It was his duty to himself and to all of those generations of warrior princes who had gone before him to keep himself whole. Samuel carried his authority with almost a regal grace that came very close to the smugness that was lurking just below the surface of his being. As he looked about him, he knew that the day of freedom was slowly drawing closer with each passing event.

Nobody noted Samuel's somewhat changed demeanor but Pompey on this day at young Forrester's funeral. Pompey himself was arrayed in his new livery as he stood next to Samuel. Samuel stood close at hand in his carefully brushed black broadcloth suit, smartly cut, with his feet shod in polished tall black leather boots. Those few planters who stood around the grave were aware of the economic miracle the freedman-overseer had brought to the Forrester Plantation, and to a man, they hated him for it as did their wives. Yet there was also a grudging respect for this Black man of impeccable behavior and dress. This was most true if they also employed him on the quiet as their own broker to the merchants of the North as so many of the planters at first so grudgingly did.

Few guests took part in the luncheon offered them after the funeral. After a polite interval of time, those who had actually returned to the Forrester home after the service also departed, and once again the family was alone. Young Douglas Forrester took a decanter of brandy from the dining room sideboard and went up to his room. He closed the door behind him and locked it. He removed his boots, coat, cravat, and vest. He then poured himself a water glass full of brandy, drained it, and stared out of his window in the direction of James' last resting place. He sighed, wiped tears from his eyes, and poured himself another tall glass of ancient brandy. He reflected that although his father had never been close to his sons, he at least had the good sense to lay in a stock of fine brandy.

The shadows of the oncoming night grew longer. Silently Douglas had drained the decanter and wept for the one member of the family he had deeply loved. He and James had shared a shallow existence of dissipated pleasure for most of their lives. Other shallow boys had aped them and worshiped them from a distance for their daring outrages and then later embraced them in a sort of worshipful friendship. It was a life given over to unhindered pleasure that only they had known or understood, because no other avenue of love was opened to them. In another hour's time, the glass fell onto the ingrain carpet next to the overturned decanter. In time, Pompey supervised the cleaning up of the mess the young man had made in his chamber, which he unlocked with his butler's passkey. Then Pompey undressed the boy and put him to bed almost tenderly. The Forrester women retired to their rooms for the night. The entire day had seemed like a bad dream from which nobody could seem to awaken. Young Douglas Forrester from that day forward would never leave his room.

In the weeks that followed young James' funeral, the young master kept to himself shunning all attempts to communicate with him not that there were very many. Only Pompey or the young house slave Marcus, who was under Pompey's direction as a footman, saw Douglas, and even that was out of necessity only. Once in a while, Pompey would order cold food taken up to the self-exiled boy on a tray.

The women kept their own society and never asked Pompey about Douglas. If the truth be known, they were glad to be rid of this last son and brother. Douglas was a reminder of all of the follies of all the weak men of the whole race of Forrester's who had heaped disgrace and social ruin on the family. It was now as if this boy did not exist, and that was fine with the Forrester women. Not one of them cared if Douglas lived or died. Now it was as if he had never lived at all. Douglas' room became a tomb, and in it he sat like a living corpse. He grew thinner and more filthy with each passing day. He drank, and he cried for his brother. Douglas sank deeper and deeper into abject depression. Still no member of the family came to see if he were still alive. They were content to have him where he was hidden away from their own reality.

The women passed their days as best they could. They stitched quilts, crocheted, embroidered, and did other needle work. In the afternoons, they would order the carriage and go for a drive. Only the master's old sister would stay behind to oversee the work in the house namely: the laundry, the kitchen workings, and the cleaning of the place. Only old Miss Forrester seemed to know about or care what was going on in the Forrester home itself. The other women were quite content to let the house slaves go on as they had done for decades. Somehow the dead master's sister had almost always regarded the house as her own. She would retire early to her room with a cup of hot chocolate brought to her by Minerva, the under cook, or Helena who was in charge of the washing up and sometimes waited on table at lunch or dinner. These slaves had been needed in the house to take up the slack years ago created by Anna's death. It had taken many hands to replace Anna, and these new servants had been there ever since. The other three Forrester women would play whist until ten then retire for the night. Few visitors ever came to see them in the weeks following the funeral, then none called in at all.

Pompey jumped to the old Miz Forrester's commands to humor her. She did not share her sister-in-law's confidence in Pompey as the new butler. She constantly complained that he had far too much freedom and authority in the management of the house. Old Miz Forrester had a great deal of fault to find with everything he did these days since the family had suffered its many losses of life and dignity in the community. The more she carped, the more the Forrester women chafed under her almost abusive criticism of Pompey, Samuel, as well as the other members of the house staff.

"But what can you expect when you make a bargain with that Devil, your precious Samuel," the old woman ranted at her sister-in-law! "You free a valuable slave like Samuel, and you pay him good money to run the place! It's just not right. It's not natural that a nigger like him is raised up so high. What ever would my dear brother have said?"

"What would you have us do sister dearest?" replied Mrs. Forrester with a thinly veiled and long suppressed rage lingering at the edge of her voice. "Who else could run the place, and so well as Samuel? Not that useless drunkard, that nephew of yours upstairs! I just thank the Lord that I never have to see him, that poor sot who is my son and my everlasting burden."

"Lord woman, we can't even show our face in good society," screamed the old lady verging on unaccustomed tears.

"And whose fault would that be dear sister if not that brother of yours, my darling James. There, I've actually said it. I have just surprised myself by doing it, but it's all the fault of my dear dead James! My dear whore-chasing, card cheating fool of a husband, James, your brother! God knows, I love him still, and I miss him beyond all the pain you can imagine. But we must face up to the facts. He is the author of all our problems my dear sister-in-law, and Samuel is the savior of our miserable situation."

"Margaret Forrester! For God's sakes woman! Don't you know what the whole county is saying about us? Don't you know that they are saying that Samuel is master here and maybe even your lover!"

"My lover. Oh that is rich. Apart from everything else, I declare that that man has ice flowing in his blood. Trust me. That man is nobody's lover. I count it a wonder that he fathered those ten little nigger babies. Though that is a great disappointment to me since only two of them will be anywhere as big as he is. I don't know what happened there. At least they were all born healthy, and we got six boys out of it. You can never tell about the breeding thing. I guess it is not as simple as horses. Now with horses you almost always know just what you are going to get."

Then Mrs. Forrester closed her eyes and returned back to her original thought. "But about the other matter, what do I care! Samuel makes this plantation pay as it never has, and I really do not care how he does it. On this plantation everything runs well, and now I don't have to worry what that drunken Hellion up in his room is up to either. There is more money coming into the place than ever before! If Samuel is master here, I don't give a damn about it. To damnation with the county and whatever stupid stuff and nonsense they have to say about us. In a few years, we can all quit this place and go where we please where nobody knows me, or my dear dead and cheating husband. Nor will they know of my sordid sons, or my poor and beautiful girls who have been robbed of the prospect of decent marriages, or even of you my dried up and sour as swill sister-in-law."

Mrs. Forrester shocked herself with this outburst. Then she smiled. "It is good to say this in the open at last. You have driven me to distraction for more than twenty years. Now shut your damned and stupid mouth and stop your infernal carping and interfering before you drive me mad. Why don't I just pay you off and send you back to Philadelphia where you belong! Now that I have actually said it, it seems a very sound idea."

"Margaret, how can you talk to me like that. I've given my life to this family. Has it been for nothing? Just think about it. They say that you are sleeping with him! With a nigger! With a former slave! Have you no pride at all?" Now for the first time since her brother's death, the old lady was weeping. "If you have no love and respect for me, at least have some for yourself and the love that my brother gave you. Maybe he was not perfect, but he was kind to you and provided for you decently as he did for all of us. Oh poor dear James, why did you have to drink and take that fall?" cried the old lady. It was the first time that anyone could remember seeing her with anything like a tender emotion. She covered her face, and then she ran upstairs to her room as quickly as her seventy years would allow.

"No, I have no pride," called Mrs. Forrester after her. "Thanks to your dear brother and his sons my pride is gone. One more word from you dear sister," Mrs. Forrester called in an even louder voice up the vast stairwell, "And I'll have you out of this house and placed out in the slave quarters, or the barns, or maybe in Hell. I own this place not you. You are just a poor relation. As of now, I am quite beyond caring what happens to you. Why don't you just go to the Devil and leave me in peace!"

These words were not whispered by Mrs. Forrester under her breath at the departed Miz Forrester, as had been the situation many times over the last two decades. They were bellowed out so loudly that even her dead husband could hear them without difficulty. Maybe Mrs. James Forrester could be browbeaten by the woman old enough to be her mother when she was a young wife, but that was not the case now. She was mistress of the plantation house now, and she felt that she alone would make the decisions. The dam had burst, and a quarter century of deeply felt resentment had raged out of the depths of her very being in a flood of self awakened rage that Margaret Forrester had found both most refreshing and liberating.

Margaret Forrester felt as if another huge weight had been lifted from her. Suddenly she just threw her head back and laughed as she had not laughed in years. Then she smiled. Years of pent up resentment of the bullying of old Miss Forrester were dispelled in a moment. The very next day, she fixed her sister-in-law with her eyes as if freed from the spell of some evil witch from the tales of the brothers Grimm. When Margaret Forrester caught the look of fear that her aged sister-in-law gave her in return, she snapped, "Well what are you thinking now? Do you have some other idiotic opinion to express? Have you packed your grips for Philadelphia yet? I'll have Samuel arrange for your transport to the railroad station whenever you are ready to get out dearest sister. Oh, don't worry about money. I'll pension you off. You can live in some respectable boarding house I suppose up in the North where you came from."

The old woman stared at Margaret Forrester in utter disbelief then cried out imploringly, "Why Margaret dear, I, I, I, "and with that she grasped her bosom, looked at her sister-in-law with shock filled eyes, and she gasped as the horrible pain grasped her in its iron grip, and suffering just as Anna had done, she fell to her knees. Then she looked up once more at the grim faced Mrs. Forrester who was looking down at her with a look of triumph. Old Miss Forrester saw not an ounce of pity or sorrow in Margaret Forrester's face. Then the old woman fell back onto the floor with her lifeless eyes staring at Pompey who had been standing in the doorway leading to the front hallway. He had been listening unobserved to the domestic play acted out before him. That spot had always been one of his favorite places to hide and observe the comings and goings of the white members of the household now that the reigns of power had slipped from Caesar's dead hands into his own.

"My God, can it be true? Anne, Anne?" Mistress Forrester exclaimed in mock astonishment. Then she smiled and called out," Pompey come quickly!" Margaret Forrester had not seen her butler standing in the hall.

Pompey had been just a few feet away. He had listened to the entire exchange just as he had always done since he could first appreciate the thrill of spying on the doings of the white folks as a small child. He waited but a moment then dashed into the room as if he had run the length of the entire house. One look confirmed his suspicions.

"Pompey, the doctor. Fetch him at once," said Mrs. Forrester in a flat and even voice.

"I'll fetch him ma'am, but it ain't gonna do no good cuz she is dead," Pompey said in the mocking language of slavery.

He had not stated anything that Mrs. Forrester had not known. She stood there feeling as if another great weight had been lifted from her shoulders. She smiled at her own manumission from the old lady's domination. She then thought of her last son upstairs drinking and alternately sleeping in a self-induced alcoholic coma in his room. "I have not had to look at him in months," she said quietly to herself. "Things are looking up I would say."

A day later, the women of the household, the minister, the house slaves, and Samuel saw the bitter old woman off to her reward. She died as she had lived, unloved and now unmourned. After the funeral, Pompey walked back to Samuel's cabin after he had seen to the needs of the three Forrester women. This time Margaret Forrester informed the minister that her departed sister-in-law insisted that there would be no eulogy and that the service be simple and brief.

At the end of the day of old Miz Forrester's burial, Pompey

said to the unofficial master of the Forrester Plantation, "You know Samuel, for more than twenty years that nasty old woman kept me afraid to love anybody. Because of her, I never allowed myself to love Anna, but I did love her in spite of that, and I do love you Samuel. Before I die, I have to tell somebody I care for that I love them. You are a father to me Samuel. I just didn't let myself know how to feel about the people who are important to me until today. I'll never forgive myself for that. I'll never forgive myself that I never told Anna that I loved her, and I'll never forgive that old bitch we saw planted in the ground today for stopping me from saying what I felt to Anna. That nasty old woman took too much away from me. I am glad that she died just like Anna did. I wonder if anybody really gives a damn that the old bitch is gone?"

"Everybody gives a damn that the old bitch is gone. They are happy! Now that's something isn't it? Don't worry boy," Samuel smiled, "Anna knew that you cared for her deeply. She knew that you loved her. In her heart she truly did, and she told me so. And someday you will meet a woman that will stir you up. You cannot use me as an example of how to live or love a woman. I am sometimes not even sure that I am human any more or can love a woman. I once could think of nothing else, but I think that part of me died a long time ago."

CHAPTER XIII

The sticky air, and the smell of uncollected garbage along with the smell of the discharged contents of numberless chamber pots thrown into the streets, combined to make The Five Points a very palpable Hell. As dusk came on, the women of the night appeared. Their well-armed pimps, protectors, and masters were not far off watching. The pimps were always watching their whores while they were busy fingering a pocket pistol, brass knuckles, or knives. The pimps were always ready to strike should they feel the need to do so. The police walked by "The Girls" in the twilight of the oncoming night. These guardians of the people and protectors of the peace were all bought and paid for right down to their blue uniforms and tinned badges. They looked through the pimps and the whores as if they were not even there. The whores walked the streets or waited on the corners for some man hungry for sexual congress to stop and chat with them. Not seeing, hearing or speaking of evil was exactly what the New York police were paid so well to do by the masters of the Five Points. They were paid to look through the criminal activities as if those happenings were panes of glass. The whole concept of uniformed police was a novelty here anyway. Some of the citizens of Five Points even thought that the police might even be disbanded. There were many who voiced the belief that the public was paying good money for nothing.

The masters of the Five Points lived and died by a series of shifting alliances negotiated with the craft of a Talleyrand. In fact Talleyrand had also walked these very streets a little over fifty years before, as a refugee from his native France. Talleyrand found New York to be a safer environment than his beloved Paris in the 1790's when so many fair heads, once worshiped by the mob, ended up severed from the necks and shoulders of those one time heroes of the people like Danton. "They had been shaved by the "National Razor." And there were at that time those who wanted to sever Talleyrand's head from his mortal body as well. It had been a good time to quit Paris for the Tontine Coffee House, taverns, and mansions of more friendly New Yorkers like Aaron Burr at Richmond Hill who had entertained the former Bishop and future First Minister to Napoleon Bonaparte. Now that neighborhood, once so fine, had degenerated into a vast slum.

The police showed their great capacity to be blind as they strutted through the Five Points brandishing their nightsticks. They delighted in sporting their badges of authority. The whole business was nothing more than an elaborate sham. The gangs of New York were multi-ethnic and delighted in spilling each other's blood, but they shared a common bond. They were all interested in money and power. They were also united in their hatred of outsiders. The police could overlook any prejudice to take bribes from any hand when they were offered them.

The Irish immigrant gangs clung to their strange and mystical Roman Catholic religion that was anathema to the somewhat more democratic but racist spirit of the Protestant Nativist gangs. These gangs had engaged in fatal meetings with one another in the full cry of battle in the streets of The Five Points for many years, and then after the bloody battles had been joined, the blood feast of slaughter commenced. The battles were fought, and the slaughter ended with the thrashing of one side or the other. Then the rival gangs melted away to lick their wounds, consolidate their victory, or recover from defeats, and then they paused for a decent space of time to mourn the deaths of their fallen brothers in arms. Votes were bought on election day with cash in each of New York City's municipal elections by greedy politicians from the gang overlords of the various ethnic blocks, and the Sons of Saint Tammany who, in turn, were ever watchful of any advantage to be had by hard and skillful negotiation to obtain support at the ballot box in this vast human sewer known as The Five Points.

The city of New York had spread out during the last two hundred and twenty odd years in a very random way. It had just grown in that haphazard way since the days of its having been founded by the Dutch. By some random design or happy accident, these famed five roads met at uneven angles here in Hell's Kitchen. This convergence marked the center of crime and defined the area soaked in the human bile of unalloyed evil. Thus was born the cesspool of Five Points as this little piece of urban geography was known in every dive and backwater all over the world. There was money here too. Money to invest in profitable ventures that traditional merchant bankers had shunned since Mr. Jefferson and the English outlawed the slave trade in '07.

Captain Peter Whitehouse walked to his appointment through Five Points in this darkening boiling cauldron of human filth to meet with an Irish gentleman who had some substantial capital to invest in an unusual trading venture in African black ivory. This gentleman had also backed Whitehouse's previous trading ventures. There was always capital for a venture of this sort in the soft underbelly of cities like New York and New Orleans. Where capital is raised by irregular means, it was always looking to be employed in conventional and unconventional ways, and ready cash was always to be had for a price. This would be a high price reflecting the element of risk. Once in a while, respectable capital also found its way into these dark streets and alleys. The ever busy agents of respectable people, and some highly placed officials in government and what passed for the halls of justice, came here to trade and make their fortunes in non-conventional ventures as well.

Whitehouse and his mate cut queer maritime figures here as they made their way to the appointed meeting place. Here, with a few dozen stout members of the ship's crew scattered about, Whitehouse was still not really sure that he would come out of this shabby place again. He never knew what sort of a reception he would get or what changes had occurred in the power structure since his last visit well over two years ago. Whitehouse was still a well-built man of the iron sort spawned by his hard-bitten career on the seas. He had been afloat for the better part of thirty-five years serving, as man and boy, before the mast. He was no stranger to the world of The Five Points. Compared to Hong Kong or Macao, it was an almost respectable place if one could actually turn a pair of blind eyes to the more obvious doings in the area and shut off one's olfactory senses.

"Five Points is a sewer," Whitehouse said to his mate, Mr. Starbuck, whose face was so crisscrossed with scars, that if it were not for a well shaped beard and mustache, he would hardly be recognizable as human, "Every fucking backwater of what passes for civilization in this filthy world has a Five Points. The neighborhoods of these cities are always filled with Irish, Lascars, Chinese, Irish, Portuguese, Spaniards, English, or whatever degenerate race spews out its dregs in greatest profusion. London, Paris, Macao, even bloody Hong Kong, as new as it is, has its bloody Five Points."

"Maybe Hong Kong is mostly Five Points from what I've seen Captain," said Starbuck. "After the next voyage, maybe we won't need to come into a sewer like this again for a long time if ever."

"And what are you going to do Starbuck? Retire to that damned little Nantucket Island of yours and raise and shag sheep? I don't think you'll find a white woman who would look twice at you. Not even a blind Quaker one. In fact you might be lucky if all the sheep do not flee as well."

"If I go back to my damned island, and build a fine house,

more than one pretty maid will look at me I think. Under their dresses all women are pretty much alike. I can put on the manners of good society if I've a mind to Captain. My dear mother taught me my manners, and I can remember her lessons as well. And as much as I respect you Captain, I'll hear no arguments reflecting anything less than respectful agreement on the score of my mother's virtues."

"The Devil you say Starbuck. I admire a man who has a mother who can tell her son just who his father is. I wish that my own dear mother could have done near so well."

"Well my mother did her best for me, and my sisters, and my brother Lloyd too. God rest her soul. I wish that I could have made her proud of my doings before she died. She tried the best she could with the raising of me she did, and I'm not so old that I have forgotten her teachings Captain. It's a damn shame that I didn't follow them, that's all."

"No, no old boy. I would never fault the lady. It's just that…," Whitehouse laughed, "It's just that I'm shocked that you actually had a mother!"

"I suppose that passes for humor Captain," then laughing himself Starbuck said, "I guess that is pretty rich at that, recalling my face in the glass the last time I trimmed my beard. It is a damned funny thing to contemplate I avow, but a mother I had until I was a lad of nine more than forty years a gone. Then she was took by God and by the flux, and I went to sea on a whaler when I could first get away from that little island. I was fifteen or sixteen then, and here I've been at sea from that day to this. And now I fail to see the romance in it that I thought that I would find. The sea I mean. I've been a cabin boy, a deck hand, and a mate, which is a damned queer circumstance, but then so is our trade. God forgive us. I do hate it so."

"Hush about that particular subject Starbuck. Belay. You don't know who's lurking about here in the dark. Hey, look there. That would be the place would it not?"

Whitehouse indicated a derelict old tavern that might have

been open for trade when the Dutch ran the place two hundred years before. With a slight gesture in the direction of the run down and ramshackle building the Captain said, “Our friend will be in there I think. You lads look lively, wait outside here, melt into the shadows, and keep alert as to who is about. Be ready for trouble and to come running with your weapons drawn if you hear the whistle.” The Captain then gestured to where he wanted his men posted. It was an old maneuver that these men had carried out in all the seedy ports of call all over the globe. Where these men found themselves, depended on what their cargo might have been. The seamen melted into the scene as if they had always lived here as the Captain fingered the silver in his pocket and walked along as if these streets were home to him.

These old salts knew what they were about. They had done this duty near a dozen times in every slimy port washed by three oceans. The slave trade paid well as did the trade in opiates. Whitehouse paid his men well. These were no ordinary sailors. They too had put money by in banks located on Cape Cod, Nantucket, New York, Martha’s Vineyard, and scores of other places in anticipation of swallowing the anchor someday after that eventual last voyage. It was no secret that Starbuck hated the trade, but he was held by the promise of profits, and to fulfill his plans he needed cash. His Quaker scruples, with the Quaker tradition of abolitionism, were stowed away far back in some dusty corner of his brain where he could pretend that they did not exist. Starbuck was obviously no abolitionist as his family had been. But as time passed he came to detest the business of slaving as a way of making a living.

The two big men entered the ancient tavern and advanced on the bar while half the people in the taproom stopped talking. The crowd watched the two stranger’s every move. Others watched the tanned sailors about the street who were the most obvious strangers here in spite of the sailors’ attempts to blend into the crowds. Maybe they were killers, or victims, or spies of a rival gang. Whatever they were, they were viewed with suspicion.

The bartender turned with deliberation toward the two bronze tanned seamen as Whitehouse asked, "Can I buy a silver cann of beer here mate?" The bartender looked at him full in the face, and said nothing. "Now would you be deaf mate? I asked if I could buy a silver cann of suds here." The man continued to polish the bar with his cloth as if no word had been spoken.

"Are you deaf or stupid?" growled Whitehouse.

"Now who would be after asking such a question as that of a poor man such as myself I'll be wanting to know," spoke a voice that would seem to be quite as at home in Dublin or Londonderry as it would be in Hell's Kitchen."

"It would be me, Captain Flask, who would be after asking you dolt," replied Whitehouse in a perfect imitation of the bartender's brogue.

"Well," said the bartender narrowing his eyes, "You are after being expected then Captain Flask. Would you be so kind as to follow me your high and mightiness darling? Sean, would ye be so kind as to be taking over for me behind the bar here? Now there's a good lad."

This remark had been addressed to a small red headed man in a dirty apron with almost as many scars as Starbuck across his face. He curtly inclined his head in the general direction of the bartender with a quick jerk and a tug of his forelock. Whitehouse and Starbuck followed the bartender through a rough and badly soiled curtain at the rear of the bar and then down a steeply inclined ramp into a sort of underground cavern. Here, in a dim light of a few lamps a man sat on a high clerk's stool looking rather like a dandy in a stylish black frock coat, yellow silk vest, red cravat, and fawn colored pantaloons. On his head sat a tall black beaver hat as slick as black satin. His linen was as white, crisp, and fresh as the driven snow, and with the exception of the fact that he had a very powerful body and exuded the air of a man born to be obeyed, he looked like a fish far removed from his native waters. There were dozens of other men around the dandy, members of the gang Whitehouse was to deal with beyond doubt. With an elegant gesture and an extravagant flourish the well-dressed fellow indicated an empty chair for Whitehouse to sit in which was somewhat lower than his own lofty perch.

Whitehouse sat, and Starbuck maneuvered himself into a position where everyone in the room was clearly within his line of vision. He also provided himself with the space in which he could maneuver if he had to. Only the throbbing vein that could be clearly seen on his forehead indicated that he was a bit unsettled by these hostile and dangerous surroundings.

"Oh do calm yourself Mr. Starbuck. If I wished to do you harm, or the Captain here, you would both have been dead half an hour ago together with your whole company of a dozen souls if I had wished it. Please accept the very fact that you are still alive as my consummate act of good faith and my intention to deal fairly with you as I always have."

"Well said sir," enjoined Whitehouse, "That is jolly well said. How is it that when you sighted a dozen of my men, you missed the other dozen? If our business goes well tonight, I do make my apologies for bringing my men here at all Mr. Ellis, but in my line of work, it pays to be prepared for any contingency."

"It is of little moment to me sir. A dozen men or an entire score and more besides matters not one whit to me. All I have to do is clear my throat and you are all dead men you see. In less than ten minutes, nothing at all will remain indicating that you ever had lived. Nothing happens within the Five Points that I do not wish to happen. The gangs here may well fight to exterminate each other, but they all understand wealth and those who can get it for them. You sir, are a most valued means to that end as am I. Shall we cut to the chase? Exactly what is it that you want from us this time?"

"Money for a venture that will yield at least fifty percent profit in say two years or less. If all goes according to my plans, the profits may be even larger."

"I like the sound of a hundred percent profit in less than eighteen months captain. After all, it is we who are taking the risks on your not so proven abilities of late. I mean your results have been rather spotty. Your plans do not always go according to your plans so to speak. *The Catalpa!* What a cock up that was. A total cock up at least old boy. Another incident like that, and everything will end very badly for you Old Son and all that sail with you as well," said the well dressed Mr. Ellis as his steely eyes fell on Starbuck.

His voice had an aristocratic silky quality with the subtle sharpness of a razor's edge. It sent chills up the back of Whitehouse's neck, but nothing in his demeanor betrayed him. His eyes were cool, and his chin jutted out with total confidence under his well-trimmed beard. The same could not be said of Starbuck, whose involuntary reflexes let him down, providing a clear insight into his thought process to the subtle mind of his host who missed nothing. Turning his gaze back from Starbuck to Whitehouse, the dandy asked, "So Captain, just what do you have in mind? What sort of arrangement exactly? And why do you need the princely sum that our mutual friend said that you would demand?"

"A voyage to Mozambique, and then a trip inland to pick up a cargo of four or five hundred prime Negro slaves costs money. Then a return voyage to New Orleans and maybe a few other southern ports in the dark of night, as needs be, to sell the cargo for a fine profit also runs into expense. I am not talking about capturing some ragtag lot of riffraff. I am talking of securing the best human trade goods available in all of Africa. I intend to capture slaves of a per capita value of fifteen hundred dollars or more value each. We will capture slaves from land just north of British holdings in Southern Africa in the area near Natal and a bit more inland beyond where some of the Boers have settled after '33 when that damned Wilberforce Act was passed by Parliament outlawing slavery. The Boers would have none of it as you may recall. So they trekked north to get out of the Cape Colony as the place is known."

"What is it to me where you get the niggers from. In the dark, all black cats are the same are they not Captain," quipped Ellis.

"We will capture Zulus. They are the most prized individuals in all Africa. We will treat this cargo like fine china, and then selectively unload the cargo and send it to auction if outright sale does not get rid of all of it at the right price. I have provided for everything. Black ivory of this quality is doing very well in the market now, as you know. There is a profound shortage of prime goods such as I propose obtaining. A good Zulu buck can fetch as much as fifteen hundred to three thousand dollars in the right market. All I would buy are the men. Their value is twice that of a woman, and the women would take up as much space for only half the return. And women on a ship of any sort are always trouble. That I know from my own experience. We are talking of something unheard of here. This has never been done before. Such a select cargo as this costs ever so much more, but the returns are also unimaginable. Imagine a single cargo valued at between two and four million dollars. Nothing like this has ever been attempted before in the history of the world."

"That is a live buck commands a large price Captain. A dead one is only shark food, which yields no return on hard cash at all. In fact," said the dandy with his eyes like two points of fire, "He is a dead loss. What sort of shrinkage of cargo do you expect during the middle passage through natural attrition Captain?"

"I would think not more than five percent with the quality cargo I intend to obtain. Maybe even less. With the stepped up activity of the British fleet, and even the token activity of the United States Navy, the prices of slaves are higher now than ever before and will even be more so for the foreseeable future. If I fill my ship with five hundred of the best slave stock that Africa has to offer, and even four hundred and fifty of the buggers survive, we should gross about two million, and if more than that number live, maybe even as much as three million dollars and maybe more. With the proper management, maybe there will be no loss of cargo at all Mr. Ellis. Nobody has ever tried reducing a ship's maximum capacity by ten percent to avoid crowding and treating and feeding the cargo better as well as providing a certified doctor to see to the buggers' needs."

"That does give us something to conjure on my dear Captain, but let's be realistic," growled the dandy. "Four hundred out of five hundred survival rate? Don't be daft man. You know as well as I do that half the cargo will be dumped over the side before you cross halfway across the Atlantic. The buggers will die, starve themselves to death, throw themselves overboard when they get the chance, or suffer some damned flux or plague that may get a whole damned bunch of them. It's just not as easy as all that."

"Not if we take better care of the slaves, buy only the best, give them more food, clean water, and provide bigger accommodations for the cargo, and a bigger crew to enforce order, and I am talking about professionals. We will even consider having a qualified doctor aboard Mr. Ellis. With the right handling, the survival rate will be much higher. We will buy only the most healthy stock. The doctor will examine every buck in the cargo. We will weed out and refuse to except any Blacks who are too old or have infirmities of any kind, and with careful attention to every contingency, the gross realized for the voyage might even top three million dollars. More than that, as I said we will buy only young and healthy male Negroes. We will buy no women or children to transport on this voyage. The dollar figures are not fast. There is almost no limit as to what profits could be made. But we must do this while we still can. One never knows when the slave trade will be shut down altogether. The slave trade was already outlawed in '07 and then there is this Wilberforce thing of '33 to consider. We have to look at how things are going in this insane world! How long will it be until the United States outlaws slavery altogether too? These abolitionists of yours outlawed it here in New York only in '28! We are fortunate that so many of our rivals have been driven out of the trade. Britain has outlawed it, and they own one bloody huge portion of the world and six hundred men of war to back up their policies. They are goddamned serious about the enforcement of their fucking policies as well you know. Mark me well, someday even The United States and Brazil may put an end to slavery. Where will we be then? If we do not strike soon, we will lose the opportunity of our lives. In a few years time, there may be no market for slaves in the west, and trust me, the Arabs pay precious little for their slave goods."

"Whitehouse, what you propose will cost almost double what the average slaving venture costs. The people whose investments and interests we represent are not patient men or fools. They expect a handsome return for their more risky investments. There is a great deal of abolitionist talk about. That is true enough, as you yourself know. Some damn fool named Garrison has been running a journal out of Boston for the better part of almost fifteen years on the subject. He has caused no end of trouble with his paper. His place was burned out twice, and that didn't stop him. Garrison has a fanatical following, and he has readers all over the North and even in the middle states some hang on his every utterance. His followers give him a great deal of hard cash for his inane crusade. In time, this stupid notion of destroying this great natural labor resource may even be debated in Congress more actively than it is now. By 1900, the peculiar institution of the South may well be swept away by law. What you say has a lot of merit."

"With all due respect sir," answered the Captain," It may very well happen long before that, and do you really expect to be alive in 1900? That is fifty some years away. Do you actually give a damn about the opinions of these radicals? If what you say is so, is that not all the more reason to act now? Can't you see? You are making my case for me very well. Well sir, I do not see myself as being alive in fifty or so years. I'll be damned lucky to survive another ten, and I'll be glad of that if I'm in the arms of a beautiful woman in some tropical villa when my end comes. What I need now is one hundred and sixty thousand dollars for this venture. Two hundred thousand would be better and assure absolute success. I will succeed best if I have more funding for the voyage, and I assure you that it will make us all very rich men. I am sure that your investors will not object to making a fortune will they?"

"Not to put too much of a fine point on it, but there is always that special Banquo's ghost at the feast creeping out of your recent history Captain Whitehouse. What about the *Catalpa?*"

"It wasn't the Americans that time. It was the damned British who cost me that cargo. The Royal Navy is a damned serious lot of hard arsed bastards on the subject of slave trading as you damned well know Ellis, and unlike the Americans, they don't muck about much or take too kindly to the trade. They hold a trial when they catch you right there on your own ship. Right there on the high seas, they try you, and it is a maritime court marshal at that. They appoint a court, put the questions, listen most politely to the evidence, record the testimony, find you guilty, and then place a rope around your neck. Then you stand there with a fine roll of the drums. Then there is a great thumping of dozens of feet down the deck. Then a dozen jack tars tug, and up you go almost to the yardarm. This is followed by a snap of your neck if you are lucky, and the job is neatly done. The Queen is satisfied. The gods of maritime justice do their duty to the satisfaction of all the Wilberforce folks, and I am dead, and that my fine friend would have been the end of the story had I not jettisoned the cargo of the unfortunate *Catalpa*. I would not be sitting here making you the offer of a lifetime had I done otherwise. In my life, I have had only to jettison a cargo once, so that I could live to trade another day."

Starbuck almost winced at the mention of the ship. He had shed tears that day in the privacy of his cabin with the memory of the little black children and the women going overboard into the sea all chained together to the anchor. Loudly and with much crying they went over the side to their deaths. Starbuck almost never saw the slaves during the actual voyage except if he absolutely had to. Starbuck made it his business exclusively to run the ship as mate without acting the part of supercargo. He always thought of Black Africans as people, and this feeling made his life almost intolerable. The stoic face he presented to the world almost hid the cloaked world of his inner soul.

That day when he had seen the sharks tearing into the living flesh of all of that humanity was burned into his memory, and the horrific images became his own private legion of furies which came to him in the night to torment his soul. All of his Quaker heritage had not been crushed out of him in spite of his grim determination to do just that. He was grateful that day for only one thing. When three hundred souls went overboard in chains secured to anchors and anvils, Starbuck was grateful that his mother could not see him or know his own deep suffering. Starbuck was always grateful for the sweat that coursed down his scarred face, hiding the tears that he could not hold back, in that oppressive heat that had also hidden the fact of his humanity overtaking his greed. He hid the shame of his humanity behind the ugly scars that seemed to sculpt his outward character.

Yet, Starbuck's resolve had almost given out altogether when he saw the last of the women, children, and young men chained to the ship's anchor then heaved overboard like so many linked sausages. That day, he had wished that the ship had been overtaken by the British, and they had all been hanged for the thoroughgoing bastards that they were. A sudden realization as to where he was here in the bowels of Five Points brought Starbuck back to the reality of the moment and out of the private Hell of his memory.

The natty gentleman fixed Whitehouse with his coal black eyes, and quietly said with clenched teeth, "You threw the whole fucking cargo into the deep. You sent a fortune down to Davy Jones' Locker. That showed a lack of purpose, courage, and support toward our former little enterprise. You might be sitting there a dead man already if it were not for my kindly intervention. The gentlemen who invested in that slaving venture are none too pleased yet. I have convinced them to leave the whole business with me. I shall determine if you will live or die or have another chance to redeem yourself and make good my investor's losses."

"Do you want a pound of flesh or a profit Mr. Ellis? In a business such as ours, there are acceptable risks that clearly must be taken. You fellows risk cash, and most of the time you make a fine profit. I risk my neck along with the necks of my men. If we lose, it's our lives. If you lose, it's only cash. With your whores and graft, you can make it all up in jig time. We have each but one life. You can come up with more cash. Can you grasp the argument?" replied Whitehouse as calmly as if he were asking about the state of the weather outside at that moment.

"I admire your sangfroid Captain. You toss three hundred niggers overboard and run for it, and all you can say is that you intend to make up for it in some way with another much larger cargo of prime niggers to be delivered intact, auctioned off, and then restitution made, and then you want 'Paid' put to your total lack of judgment. You are a cool one indeed. Yes sir, a cool one. My friend Slasher is waiting to cut your throat on the strength of a nod from me, yet you make direct eye contact with me, and dare suggest another venture. This is really too droll. You are a cool one Whitehouse, and make no mistake about it."

Captain Whitehouse paused for a moment at the end of Ellis' monologue to take a sip of brandy. Then he said, "I've always been impressed with your courage Mr. Ellis during our little business talks when you are sitting here with a few dozen of your friends about you all armed to the teeth. You are not really much of a man are you Ellis, but you know a straight proposition when you hear one. You are not really a stupid man. In fact, I'm really rather fond of your company. Maybe it's because you dress so damned well. Mr. Starbuck, take this man as your model and see your tailor while you are here in New York. You too could become a plate of the latest fashion. If I knew that I was bound for a long voyage, somewhere like Hell, for argument's sake, I think that I'd like to take you with me Mr. Ellis just for companionship. I am that fond of your company."

The two men sat with icy smiles on their faces, their eyes meeting in a steely gaze. "We are all going on that voyage some day or other my dear Captain Whitehouse," replied Ellis, "But I see no reason to make sail tonight. In point of fact, I have already discussed your proposition with all of my associates, and we are in substantial agreement with your plan, that is, with a few small alterations."

"Alterations? And what might these changes be Mr. Ellis?"

"First of all Captain, the profits on the first two hundred slaves will be for us alone. We are willing to accept some of the losses from the *Catalpa*. But we have no intentions of absorbing all of them. We will share profits on the customary terms for all the rest of the cargo delivered over the number of two hundred slaves. If what you say is true, there should still be a substantial reward for you and your men even after we have made up our losses on the *Catalpa*," said Ellis between clenched teeth.

"I'm afraid that I must protest Ellis. My crew can hardly be denied their wages for something I did. I'll sacrifice my own personal profits on the first two hundred slaves we bring in, but not on my mate's and crew's share. My men are not just common deck hands. They are sailors of the very highest order and tried and true veterans of the trade. They know how the business works and require no training. They are tough and smart, and as I have said, they are experienced in this trade. They have put their lives on the line in this business. Most of them have sailed with me many times past when we made your associates quite a tidy profit. To make such a sacrifice on your suggested number of two hundred is totally unacceptable."

"I'm not going to argue the point my dear Captain. You can accept the deal as I have outlined it on the basis of the two hundred slaves, or you can go to the Devil. Let your nobility of spirit dictate your own actions, but we gentlemen investors want our full share to make up for the loss that you have inflicted on us. You are lucky to be alive at all, and after all the losses we have suffered, we are only assessing you for the loss of the cargo not for the ship's stores as it is."

"Well if that is the long and the short of it, I guess that I'll be willing to agree to giving up profits on the first hundred parts of the cargo perhaps for me and my crew as well."

"Not acceptable," answered Ellis.

"Damn it man, I have just suggested that I am willing not to take any profits for myself or my men on the first hundred slaves that we capture and sell. I cannot possibly agree to allow you to take all the profits on the first two hundred. I'm getting a little short of patience here. You'll have to do something for my men and me, or I'll swallow the anchor, and we'll both retire to a warmer climate this very night. One more stupid remark from you Ellis and I'll be forced to lay you open from stem to stern even as you are covered by my dead body. I'm through temporizing with you, and it would be well if you would make an effort to best understand what I'm saying and compromise with me."

The tone of the Captain's voice had lost all pretense to civility. His hand was on the hilt of his sword cane and his mate had two pistols ready in his pocket. Without blinking Ellis said, "All right then. We will take all the profits on the first one hundred and fifty slaves then. Divide the other proceeds as you will Whitehouse. That is my compromise and the best deal you can hope to expect."

"Done," said the powerfully built Captain.

Whitehouse knew that Ellis was no coward. And he also knew that Ellis was as hard as flint under the mask of good breeding and fine soft clothes. He also knew that the mask was a borrowed one as was the accent and the studied air of refinement. Even his manhood was borrowed. Yet Ellis' artifice worked well for him.

"I am glad that we can still strike a bargain after all this time we have known each other, and I'm glad that you are fond of my company," the dandy smiled.

"Now why would that be?" said Whitehouse as he accepted a small glass of brandy from Ellis by way of sealing the deal.

"Because Old Fellow, I'm going with you. That is myself and my companion. We have learned a few things in the Five Points that might be useful even to you on a venture like this, and I'm always willing to share my experience."

CHAPTER XIV

Pompey softly knocked on young Forrester's door. A voice eventually answered from inside, and Pompey entered the hot and dark room. Young Douglas Forrester, unshaven and filthy, was sprawled on his bed wearing only thin cotton trousers like a field hand. Pompey set the bottle of brandy on the table next to the bed along with a clean tumbler.

"Shall I open a window sir and let some air in?"

"What?" answered the razor thin young man. Then reaching for a thought, Douglas brought himself up to a half sitting position to say, "No Pompey. No thank you. The sun hurts my eyes. I feel unwell. Pour me a drink. I need a drink. Is my mother still alive? Never mind. I don't really care. Everybody is most likely dead now. I do not believe that she liked poor Jim or me very much. My father, my brother, my aunt all dead," the boy sobbed. "But then I really don't care that my aunt is dead. No, that doesn't matter at all."

"Would you like something from the kitchen?" asked Pompey as if everything was quite normal.

"Heavens no! The thought of food makes me sick Pompey. Could you have Marcus take care of the slop pail? I think that I upset it in the night. At least I might have. I'm not sure. I don't remember very much about last night. I'm afraid I had too much brandy. What time is it?"

"It is past three in the afternoon Mr. Douglas," said Pompey.

"What day is it?"

Pompey's monotone was unchanging. "It is Tuesday."

"The date? What date is it?"

"July the fifth," replied Pompey.

"What is the year?"

"1844."

"Is it as late as that? 1844? How old am I?" asked young Forrester with a sob.

"You are twenty-one next month. Would you like a tub brought in and some hot water for a bath? It can be carried up from the kitchen. Would you like that?"

"No," said young Forrester. "I don't think that I'll need to bathe to go out today or any other day, or any day ever again. If I do, some damn fool or other will want to hang me, or better yet shoot me, or cut me. You know cut me there like James. Yes getting shot would be better than hanging and getting cut I think. I think that I'll stay in. Maybe I should be hanged? Do you think that I should be hanged Pompey? Send the boy to take care of this stinking mess. I may want another bottle of brandy later. Yes that's it. I'll need another bottle later. Now leave me, and close the draperies all of the way. I can see some bit of light there still. Close them tightly. The light makes my eyes hurt, and those damned farmers might see me."

Pompey closed the tiny openings between the draperies carefully avoiding the spilled contents of the slop pail on the floor. The stench of urine and fecal matter was horrible in the terrible heat of the closed room in the Georgian summer. The boy's all but naked and unwashed and wasted body was covered by a mass of bedsores. Pompey moved to the door with the dirty glasses on a tray. He wanted to escape the fetid air of that bedroom. The stench in his nostrils was overwhelming. He thought it smelled like death and putrefaction.

"Wait, one more thing," cried the boy now weeping to the point of convulsions. "What day is it?"

Pompey turned slowly and tested the boy, "Tuesday, July 7, 1844," he replied to young Douglas Forrester.

"Did you tell me that already or was it somebody else?"

"No sir. I did. You just asked me that a little time ago."

Pompey saw that young Douglas did not seem to notice that he had advanced the calendar by two days. The boy had clearly lost all sense of time.

"That's right. I just asked about the date didn't I? I'm a little confused. My brother died you know. They did something horrible to him. I think that somebody killed him. I can't think that he would do that to himself. Could you bring me some brandy? I think that I'm coming down with something. Maybe a fever, and could you send up the boy? I am so hot. Someone kicked over my slop pail, and I think that I must have stepped in it. I better have a footbath. My feet feel dirty. I can't have dirty feet you see. I'm a gentleman. I think that I must shave. I may shave today. Pompey, do you think I should shave? Oh Pompey, sometimes I think that you are my only friend. Is that so Pompey? Is that so?"

"Yes sir. I am your friend. Let's see if you can sleep now. I think that you must be very tired. And as for the rest, I'll see to it," said Pompey as if he had been asked to do some small thing in the course of an ordinary day.

"If anyone should call, I don't want to see them Pompey. I don't want to see anyone ever again, and I don't want them to see me. Oh look here Pompey! There is some brandy after all. I won't need any right away. Isn't that good Pompey? Can you send my brother to me? James will want to see me you know. Tell James that I'm not well. I want to see my brother so badly Pompey." The boy began to cry again. "They told me that I saw him hanging where pa died. Did I Pompey? I don't remember. It must be a bad dream. I have a lot of bad dreams. It can't really be true. Not James. Can you tell him to come to me."

"Yes sir. Very good sir. I'll see if Mr. James is about sir." Pompey took the distraction to make his escape. On his way to the kitchen, he encountered Marcus. Pompey told him to go up to the young master's room in an hour or two to clean up the mess. "You'll be safe then. He should be asleep. If he should awaken and ask for his brother, tell him that young Mr. James will be away for a while on personal business. Yes, that's it. Try to convince Mr. Douglas that Mr. James will be away for quite sometime."

The boy nodded. Marcus was thirteen, a good looking lad, and not too willing to be alone with the young master whose state of mind could be very confusing to so young a boy as Marcus not to mention the weird notions that young Douglas Forrester had adopted in his drunken stupor, but Marcus had enough guile to carry off relaying the message that Pompey had instructed him to deliver. Pompey thought that in the end, it wouldn't matter what young Forrester was told. He wouldn't remember it a few minutes later.

Even Marcus knew that if Douglas were ever let loose in the county, he might very well have been hanged and mutilated. The farmer's sons had been seen from time to time riding by on the beaten red clay road which ran through the plantation. These men knew enough not to stop. They had respect for the overseer and the pistol which he sometimes wore in his belt.

Although every slave on the place knew about Mr. Douglas' condition, they would never speak of it. They had stopped fearing the white folks for some time. But they never knew what Samuel might do if they ever showed any disrespect to the Forresters or got out of line in any way. They did not want to test Samuel's zeal and authority, which was the great unspoken force driving plantation life. No formal act had made Samuel total master officially, but nevertheless his de facto absolutism was clearly understood.

Young Douglas Forrester's mother was content to have the boy hidden away. She still never saw him, nor did she appear to want to. She liked the fact that he was entombed in his room, dead to her and the world for all practical purposes. Sometimes she even thought what a grace it would be if he followed the rest of the Forrester men to the family burial ground. The thought that he would shortly, which was the opinion of the doctor, had been a comfort to her.

No visitors at all crossed the threshold of the big house now. Not even the minister. From the day the old lady had her massive heart attack and died, no visitor but Samuel sat in that ornate drawing room of high fashion. Pompey thought to himself that he would never have expected to see such a day come when this isolated white woman and her daughters would sit and drink tea with a freed man of color here, even if he were the plantation overseer. Yet there Samuel sat drinking tea from the fine Dresden cups. He sat right there in Mrs. Forrester's drawing room in the large shell carved black walnut chair that had been the master's with its red velvet upholstery. Samuel behaved with an ease and grace that would suggest to even the most casual outsider that he had been born to his position as if he had been a white man of rank and of exceptional breeding.

In the last three years, it seemed that the whole world had turned upside down. The social death of the Forrester family, and the physical death of three of its members, the disgrace of the revelation of James Forrester's cheating at cards, the expulsion of the young Forresters from West Point, the disgrace and murder and castration of the young James Forrester, the physical ruin of Douglas Forrester through alcoholism, who was also guilty of so many sexual transgressions in the district that could not be spoken of, marked the sad end of the Forrester tribe's place in the social scheme of things. The fact that the Forrester boy languished upstairs in his family's mansion in his filth and in the darkness of his room, raving in drunken madness, and dead to all reality, if known throughout the county, would have been considered a divine judgment against the whole family. The Forrester's had truly suffered a sadly marked change in their social fortunes even as they had grown so much richer.

Douglas Forrester was close to starving himself to death. It was obvious to even young Marcus that Douglas Forrester could not last much longer. The family seemed to be waiting for the event as if they were waiting for the sun to set, or for a rainfall to end. There was never any thought given to calling in doctors again to see what could be done for the boy. Whatever the end would be, it would at least be the end of another chapter of pain. Few in the county felt any pity at all for the outcast Forresters, and none of the Forresters felt pity for Douglas. Even the young blades who had followed him had moved on with their own lives and put Douglas out of their minds. His legend had faded with the maturation of his erstwhile admirers, and his antics were no longer the stuff of romantic county mythology.

Mrs. Forrester and her two daughters, Caroline and Tilly, arose each day and lived out a routine that never changed. Breakfast, followed by a walk about the estate, needle work and chatting, lunch, then a ride in the carriage, or the coach if the weather was bad, followed by tea in the drawing room or in the garden, which in turn was followed by a rest period or reading, followed by dinner, then cards and more conversation, then to bed. Once a week, Mrs. Forrester would sit with Pompey in the ornate drawing room to discuss the workings of the house. In the late morning after her walk, she would meet with the cook to discuss the menus for the day's meals, and on Thursdays, Samuel would be invited to tea as overseer to discuss the business of the plantation. This pretense of activity had been a novel experience for Margaret Forrester, and she rather liked the sense of power that the process gave her even though she had abdicated all real power a long time ago. Old Miss Forrester used to do these things concerning the household. Now Mrs. Forrester could play at carrying out these tasks as mistress of her household. Thus were Mrs. Forrester's days filled with activity.

It was only on Sunday that slight variations were introduced into the routine of the day. After breakfast, there would be *Bible* readings in the drawing room, and after luncheon the women would read Dickens, or Thackeray, or the works of some American writers like James F. Cooper aloud. Once Miss Caroline read some of Mr. Poe's work, but it was decided that his stories were not suitable for reading on a Sunday afternoon. Poe remained a guilty and lurid pleasure for reading alone during the weekdays. This strange household had gone on its strange way for the past few seasons. The Forrester library which had been so long neglected, now became a vital part of the entertainment of the household. Samuel had even ordered new books to the delight of the Forrester girls. Still the Forresters grew richer and more isolated from their class.

Then one chilled and rainy day, with the wild wind of late autumn whipping around the windows of the house and making a mournful wailing sound, the last of the Forrester men died in his filth and raving against a God who had so twisted the world as to deny him a proper place in it. Douglas had cursed God for the loss of the companionship of his beloved brother. After the doctor had signed the death certificate and left the house, Samuel lifted the boy's body, that weighed nothing after he had wrapped him in his bedding as he was instructed to do by Mrs. Forrester, and deposited the body in the casket provided by the undertaker. Douglas Forrester was interred next to his father, aunt, and brother the very next day with just the family and minister to see him off. Samuel and Pompey were there of course acting in a most servile way for the minister to see. The high church service was blessedly short. Mrs. Forrester pressed a ten dollar gold piece into the hands of the man of God, thanked him for his lovely service and short collection of kind words, and set the man of God on his way with an air of absolute serenity.

She then walked back to the house with her daughters. Under her black veil of mourning, she smiled with a profound sense of relief that another ugly chapter of her life had been closed. All three women were dressed in mourning black for the service and for the minister to see as an expression of their grief. After lunch, they were again arrayed in their colorful finery from the Parisian House of Worth. With the prosperity of the plantation, nothing would do but to have the best dresses supplied to them that money could buy. Worth dressed the queens of France and England and now the Forresters of Georgia. An hour and a half only was given over to the mourning for Douglas Murdoch Forrester. There was no need to pretend sorrow any longer. There was nobody left to impress. The women chatted as if nothing of any consequence had happened that day in their drawing room in their sumptuous silk gowns.

That very afternoon, Mrs. Forrester called Pompey into the drawing room and asked him to have the ingrain carpets in Mr. Douglas' room taken up and burned far away from the house along with any clothes, the draperies, and furnishings which had been soiled and smelled foul. Then she said to Pompey, "Please make sure that the room is well scrubbed and aired. If needs be, also have it painted and the floors well polished. Take whatever you may find to be useful and clean for yourself Pompey along with any of Douglas' jewelry and money you may find there. Even though you are a Black boy, I wish that my son's had had but half of your grace and intelligence. You and Samuel have made life here most bearable, and that is all I will ever say on that subject. Now I thank you and set you to the tasks I have outlined."

That was all that any of the Forresters had to say on the subject of James and Douglas who were never spoken of again. The Forrester women saw nobody, but their ever-increasing considerable wealth allowed them to continue to buy all of the latest fashions from the shops of Atlanta. Their dresses and gowns continued to come from Paris' House of Charles Worth. All of their shopping was done through the mails by Samuel. They wore at least three changes of clothing each day and wondered how they could make time for all they did. Their formal routines, distractions, and clothes, and bathing made up the total fabric of their busy lives. Pompey ran the house like a well lubricated piece of machinery, and Samuel smiled to see the local slave masters so fallen and dependent on his management of their affairs as chief seller of their produce along with that of the Forrester Plantation. Samuel was a first class agent. He charged half the rates of competitive brokers. He had built up relationships with wholesalers up and down the eastern seaboard who bought all manner of crops that he had to sell for all of the plantations in the district that had sought out his talents in that area of commerce.

The people of the county did not even notice that the real power and control over the local economy had now passed into Samuel's hands alone as the authorized agent of the largest and most productive plantations in the whole area. Samuel alone seemed to get the northerners to pay the best prices for both the farmer's and planter's crops. The only condition he imposed on the planters whose crops he sold was that they were to tell everyone that they were selling their crops on their own. Every farmer and planter who did business with Samuel thought that his arrangement was unique. When some of the planters discovered that their arrangements were not unique, Samuel told them that confidentiality demanded the lie to protect his client's interests. He then would go on to say that if planters kept their mouth's shut, nobody would know. Besides, they were receiving the best money they had gotten in years. Such logic never failed to bring the prickly planters back to the reality of practical economics. As long as nobody would admit that a free Black man was making them wealthy, all was well.

Samuel accumulated a fortune even as the fiction of the white woman's authority over the Forrester Plantation seemed to be intact to the world outside. As the next few years slipped by, even the county gentry seemed to almost forget what was going on at the Forrester place. Samuel used white agents from the North to sell the crops in distant markets and to carry out the business of the plantations whose interests he secretly controlled. His role was shrouded in the deepest secrecy. Whenever clients came to the Forrester Plantation, he let it be known that the men were

Northern Forrester relatives come South for a little holiday. Mrs. Forrester and the girls thought it great fun to go along with the fiction and frankly had come to enjoy the company of these people from outside of their little world. Samuel knew well how the game was played in the larger world, and all he knew he carefully taught Pompey.

CHAPTER XV

Now that the autumn had come again, and all the crops had been harvested and sold along with the horses that had been bred for the Atlanta market, life on the plantation slowed just a bit. The laying hens had grown to become a larger part of the plantation's income than they had been in former days. Samuel supplied Miss Sally's and the local markets with eggs. Milk, cream, and cheese were also sold to the surrounding merchants and representatives from firms from closer cities like Atlanta. No facet of income went unexploited by Samuel. No slaves had been sold off the place since Samuel had come to power, nor had he used his whip on any man, woman, or child. His authority was unquestioned, and everything was done for the comfort of the white folks who continued to enjoy the ease of their fine and untroubled lives, and rivers of gold that seemed endless were pouring in like never before.

In fact, the Forrester women began to find themselves in an almost blissful mood each day, but why would they not? Life may have been unkind to them and taken a horrific toll on their men, but the prosperity of the place, and even the wine at dinner, seemed to produce a feeling of warmth and well-being unlike that which the women had ever known before. They were content and most satisfied with their lives. In fact they seemed to smile all of the time these days. Samuel had met with the house slaves a few weeks after the last of the Forrester men had died and told them that better days were coming for them. He then distributed to each of them ten silver dollars much to their total astonishment. He told them not to speak of the gift which came directly from him, and they took him at his word. Silence was something a slave could understand along with absolute secrecy.

At first, the slaves began to speculate about the general changes they had experienced without mentioning any of Samuel's gifts. Silver dollars came at more frequent intervals as time went on. The slaves followed Samuel's orders to hide the money and tell nobody about the gifts of cash. The slaves spoke quietly of some spiritual awakening and a migration to some new celestial plain of existence. Samuel quickly told them that no white man's God had anything to do with the good times that were coming, but that they were free to embrace whatever source of comfort they wanted as long as they kept quiet about it. Keeping secrets from white folks was something all slaves knew about. They had more than a hundred years of practice keeping things to themselves. Slave society was the most closed and secret society on earth. They also knew that crossing Samuel was dangerous and would have consequences that they dared not speculate about. They did not exactly know why Samuel inspired fear, but they just sensed that it would be an unprofitable enterprise to challenge any of his orders. Samuel told them that under no circumstances was the peace of the plantation to be disturbed, and that in time he would tell them more about when the good times were approaching. In the meantime each slave counted up his or her growing pile of silver.

One night Big Cyrus came to see Samuel. The big man held his cap in his hand as he knocked on Samuel's door. A few moments passed before the overseer answered the knock with, "Well what do you want here Cyrus? Come five o'clock tomorrow morning, you'll wish that you had slept some tonight," Samuel said this in a disarming way in anticipation of some vexing questions that he would really rather not have to answer. Samuel knew what courage it must have taken for Cyrus to have made this trip to seek out information from "The Boss".

"I ain't worried about that none," said the field hand. "I just got to trying to puzzle out what's going on on this here plantation Boss. Others are wondering about the same things I is. Nothing seems to rightly make no sense here. You are the boss and the white folks has died off, and them that ain't dead ain't been seen for a while. We is scared and concerned about what is gonna happen here. What's gonna to happen to us? We don't wants to get sold off the place and see our folks scattered all over never to be seen no more. During Master Forrester's time, ain't nobody been sold off and no families broken up. Now things seem really different. Times seem good but real different. It almost don't seem natural Boss. We is really scared Boss like it's all gonna end, and all Hell gonna break loose. I know that I got no right to axe you nuthin, but kin you just set my mind to rest?"

"Come in and sit a spell with me Cyrus. Now I just want to ask you something. What do you want most in the world?"

Cyrus sat thunderstruck. "What I wants most in the world? Why I don't know that Boss."

"Think hard," replied Samuel.

"I'm a'scared to think about that. I'm a' scared that I even come here at all to talk to you. Even when you was jus' Samuel 'afore you was even more high and mighty like you is now, I was scared to talk to you, but with all them white folks dead and the others so long gone from sight, we is all scared. We scared of what's gonna happen to us. Like we gonna go away some night, and our folks ain't never gonna see us no more. Something ain't right here. Something just ain't right, and somehow's we knows that."

"Everybody scared that way Cyrus? Everybody?"

"Yes Boss."

"How have things been for you all these past three years?"

"Real good Boss. Everybody's real good. We work, but it ain't as hard or as long. We gets rewards when things go good. We is savin' our dollars."

"Nobody hungry?"

"No Boss."

"Nobody getting whipped at all?"

"No Boss. Ain't nobody never been whipped."

"No girls getting visits from no master at night?"

"No, but ain't he dead?"

"That does seem the way of it Cyrus."

"It don't seem natural the way we is runnin' things here. Nobody thinks that it's natural. We never see anybody from the house, nigger or white, exceptin' Pompey who's down here all the time."

"Since when did any of you field hands see anybody from the house besides Pompey? You have nothing to do with them do you? You never did see the Master's women folks down here."

"No, not really, but we used to see them women folks from far away and sometimes at night."

"Everybody wants to know what is going on Cyrus. Is that right?"

"Yes Boss."

"Well I can't tell you what's going on right now, but I can tell you this. From this moment on, you are my man. You will tell me everything you see and hear in the slave quarters. You will tell the people nothing. I am going to give you two silver dollars each week to tell me what you find out. If you tell anybody what you are doing for me, I will have to kill you. I don't want to do that, but you know that I will. But I know that I can trust you Cyrus. Every week, I will put another two dollars away for you and when you come to see me, you can look at these big silver coins and count them if you wish for they will be yours to keep when the time comes. Keep thinking of what you want most in the world, and tell nobody but me your thoughts except if they ask you what you think about things here."

"And what does I say then Boss?"

"You just laugh and say,' We never have it so good as we has it now has we?' "

"And that's it?" Cyrus laughed. "And laughs like this?"

"You have it, and you do it right well. In time, you will learn more. Remember, you are my man and it's a secret. I like you Cyrus. I trust you. You are smart. I would truly hate to do you harm. Don't make me do anything that I would hate to do. Show me that I can trust you. I need you Cyrus. How do you feel about that?"

"I'm your man Boss. I ain't never known no black man like you. You is a real African. Some of us think you is one of them African kings or somethin' like that. All I wants you to tell me Boss, is we safe?"

"As long as I am in charge of things here, you are safe. There is nothing bad I will let happen to anybody on this place. You can tell anybody who asks you that is what you believe. And I promise you that I am going to be boss here for a long time."

"And Boss, I does believe it."

"Are you at peace with that now? You are not scared are you?"

"No Boss. Well maybe of you a little bit, but I knows that if I keep my mouth shut except for what you tells me to say, I'll be alright."

"Then I am happy, and you have no problems Cyrus. Trust me. I'm a free man, and someday you might be a free man too. And remember each year that passes, you will have more than a hundred silver dollars saved for you. Just remember right now I can protect us all. You are my man, my eyes and ears in the slave quarters, and someday I may give you a real job of real importance. Just show me that I can trust you."

Cyrus smiled his open smile and nodded his head. Samuel looked into the open face that beamed of hero worship. He had chosen his creature wisely. "Good night Cyrus. You can come to the field two hours late tomorrow. Make up something about being sick. I'll yell at you just for show, but we will know that it does not mean anything. It will just be a show for the others to see. Now run along."

"Yes Boss. Good night Boss."

"Good night Cyrus, and take care to keep everything to yourself," said Samuel.

Away Cyrus went. Samuel watched after him wondering how this would play out. He hoped it would be a good beginning for the second part of his grand scheme.

CHAPTER XVI

The Forrester women were now in a perpetual state of euphoria. Their every need was seen to as they passed from hazy day to hazy day in a delightful state of giddy pleasure. By now, the house servants were all a part of the planned coup, and were becoming more comfortable with the new arrangements of the household. Pompey had delegated his duties to Helena. She had served in the Forrester mansion for six years. She had spent most of those years loathing the old spinster sister of the late Master who had boxed her ears as a young girl and had made her deaf in one of them. She had exhibited no sorrow on the passing of any of the three Forrester men or the nasty old bitch that had beaten her. She blamed Old Miz Forrester for the death of the much loved Anna as well as for the general misery of the household during most of the time she had served there as housekeeper. The three surviving Forrester women had treated Helena neither unkindly nor kindly. And that was a good thing. Indifference, after all, was most healthy for a slave. And the Forrester women were always at least civil.

The slave's unofficial code was to go through life unnoticed. Being unnoticed saved a slave a great deal of unwanted trouble. Helena had been in service in the house like some kind of automaton. She succeeded in never showing any emotion. The

Forrester's had hardly ever thought of her as human or indeed at all, and now Helena thought of the Forrester's as a group of interesting animated dolls. To her they were just silly puppets in some grotesque puppet show run by Samuel and Pompey. Helena had loved Anna who was like a mother to her from the time that she had come to the Forrester plantation just a year before Anna died. As she dressed the Forrester women's hair, Helena had begun to think of them as almost hateful objects. They seemed strangely less aware of themselves each day. They smiled at some point beyond their reality quite satisfied with life. She felt contempt for the white women's weakness, and thought to herself that if she had wished, she could beat them all, tie them up, and take whatever she wished for herself. She caught herself thinking of this revenge and looked around. Then she caught herself and scowled, "What do I care. Pompey ain't goin' to read my mind," then she stopped. She looked around and saw Samuel standing there. She choked up and said, "Afternoon Mr. Samuel."

Samuel just looked at her through narrowed eyes, shook his head as in a warning, smiled coldly, then walked away down the hallway to exit by the front door. Helena almost fainted. She was still sure that Pompey could not read her mind, but she was not at all sure about Samuel. Still Samuel made Helena feel safe as long as she behaved herself. She had no fear of what might happen if the true nature of what was going on in the big house was discovered by the outside world. She knew that Samuel could fix it some way or another. The social isolation of the family had been an established fact of life since the death of the master, and this isolation made discovery of the Forrester's real and strange new condition seem less and less of a problem. She knew, that after what she had seen, that nobody would be surprised as to what the Forrester's had become as a result of the unfortunate things that had happened to them over the last half decade. They would not be the first members of that class of southern gentry to turn to drink and laudanum to cure their social ills and give themselves solace from the outrages of unfriendly society. In view of the ostracism the Forresters had suffered at the hands of their own class, nothing would be a surprise to the community should anyone find out about the reality of their condition.

Helena had been made a part of the plot a year ago. Her loyalty to Samuel was sealed by the fact that she knew well that if she crossed him in any way, she would disappear into a swampy bog never to be seen again. After all, that is what Samuel had told her after he had enlisted her in his game. With all her heart, Helena believed him.

1844 had passed to 1845, and then to 1846, and at last life on the plantation advanced onward to 1847. From time to time, the three Forrester women could be seen riding together in their landau in the afternoons of balmy and beautiful days but always at a distance. Time had seemed to have no meaning for them. They didn't even know that a war was raging in Mexico. Once in a great while, an old and former acquaintance would come within nodding range of the three women, but the silent salutation was never returned as they passed on in the extreme comfort of their well-appointed carriage. On those very rare occasions, they just smiled and looked beyond the faces turned to them. It was supposed that the Forrester women held all the county in deepest contempt. Only their huge wealth protected them. Even the good High Church pastor was turned away at the Forrester's door by Pompey who was always the very model of dignified and correct civility as he apologized that the Forresters were not receiving any guests at that time. On some other occasions, Pompey told the pastor with embarrassment that Mrs. Forrester told him to tell whoever was at the door that she was not at home.

Such a calculated rebuff stung the man of God to the quick, and from then on he avoided the Forrester Plantation like the plague. The pastor's unexpressed thoughts on the whole tribe of Forresters was most unchristian on the last occasion of his riding away from the plantation. Only tradesmen and their delivery people ever went out to the Forrester Plantation during the time after the family's fall from grace and their multiple losses. Here all accounts were paid in full on delivery in hard cash by Samuel who always invited the merchants into his office to, "Have a little something." Such hospitality built the freed man's reputation as a fine open handed sort of fellow. This payment for goods in hard cash in a timely manner by any of the county gentry was in itself a novelty. In private away from the eyes of the world, the tradesmen almost thought of Samuel as being a white man. They liked the fact that even though he controlled great wealth, "He knew his place and didn't get uppity." Samuel always treated them as patrons of total superiority intoning words of great respect while commanding respect for himself in the most subtle way of being proper at all times as well as quick to pay all monies owed. This all the tradesmen said almost to a man. More than a few members of the county gentry shared the opinion that it was a shame that Samuel's late and unlamented master did not share his quality of integrity in his dealings with them.

By the end of 1847, the general consensus of all of the local planter and merchant class was that Samuel was an honorable man and the author of their sharply improved fortunes through his consummate skill as a broker for all of their crops. They also enjoyed the unstinting hospitality of the man. No tradesman ever left the Forrester Plantation without at least a drink on the sly. Samuel even served lunch from time to time in the butler's pantry. When the tradesmen and merchants heard the rumors that the Forrester's were high-hatting the citizens of the county, the tradesmen defended them as the souls of friendly liberality as represented by their man Samuel. Nothing could warm the heart of a tradesman more than prompt payment for goods.

True southern aristocracy was always months if not years behind in settling their debts with the tradesmen who were accustomed to living off of ancient and hard collected receipts of their patron's parents and grandparents. Some debts of the old planters were not settled until long after death took them, and afterward it became a matter for the probate courts or future generations of the debtor. Many a tradesman had failed because their upper class clients were very careless about paying their bills. Some tradesmen were forced to settle for fractions of what they were owed.

The Forrester property taxes were also always paid on time. In fact, the county collector of taxes always noted that the first annual returns were always from the Forrester Plantation. Samuel's man Cyrus, now quietly dressed in the clothes and boots of a sub-overseer, always delivered these payments in advance of due dates. Cyrus was noted for the economy of his conversation, which most often consisted of, "Yes Suh," or "No Suh." There was always speculation about the strange way slaves were trusted by the Forrester women to carry about large sums of money, but that was all the talk there ever was regarding the Forrester slaves outside of the fact that they were very industrious. This in itself was amazing in the absence of a white overseer.

One fine evening, Samuel and Pompey were taking their ease in the parlor of the overseer's house. Pompey had brewed coffee, which tasted so very good with just a drop of the late Mr. Forrester's best brandy, to ward off the chill of the early December air. Years of planning had led to this moment when Samuel's grand and crazy idea now seemed possible. Pompey was now a polished man of the world who had learned French, Spanish and Portuguese from well-paid native speakers who posed as Forrester relations visiting the plantation from far away Virginia.

Pompey's manumission papers were drawn and signed by Mrs. Forrester herself who had sent word to her new lawyer, Judge Jarrod Darby of Atlanta to take care of all the details. She had ordered these documents drawn up as part of a communication delivered to him through the mails. Mrs. Forrester had been most explicit about having this business done with dispatch. She had wished these manumission papers drawn up and then filed at the county courthouse with all due haste. That Judge Bowen was past it, was what she wrote to her new attorney, and therefore he no longer served as the Forrester attorney. Mrs. Forrester complained that Judge Bowen repeated too much about the plantation affairs about the community to be continued in his capacity of the trusted Forrester family lawyer any longer. Judge Darby had been the Forrester lawyer for four years now, and he called at the Forrester Plantation in person to deliver the papers only to find Mrs. Forrester alone in the drawing room. For the first time, he heard that the Forrester girls had made a trip to Saratoga to take the waters, then had gone on to New York to spend the spring and summer in the cool northern climate visiting relatives who had taken a place in the Hamptons for a season. It was all very natural to this man of affairs that these cosmopolitan women should make such journeys.

"Oh no my dear Judge Darby," said Mrs. Forrester during Darby's most recent visit to the Forrester place, "Feeling as weak as I do, I of course could not make the journey with the girls, but my dear cousin Amanda has undertaken to introduce the girls into good northern society far away from all of the unpleasantness here. It is so difficult you know. People are quite horrible and my Pompey and Samuel have helped me so. I do thank you for coming out here. I appreciate the hardships that you endure for me dear Judge Darby. Truly I do," she had said taking his hand and patting it like an old and trusted friend."

As Darby left, he thought that the "otherworldly" quality of Mrs. Forrester's vague demeanor quite remarkable and almost attractive, but he supposed, given the trials that the poor woman had suffered since the death of her husband and the other three members of her family in such close succession that her present condition was quite understandable. He was amazed at Mrs. Forrester's serenity in the face of the nature of her husband's fall from grace and the fatal accident which he had suffered. To him, her strange behavior was almost wonderful given the circumstances of all the losses she had suffered.

He pondered on this and other questions as he rode away. He too had been paid promptly and handsomely for his efforts including generous traveling expenses. Most of all, he had been deeply touched by Mrs. Forrester taking him by the hand in such a friendly and intimate way. On his arrival home, Mrs. Darby, anxious for fresh gossip about life on the Forrester Plantation, asked her husband a thousand questions, or so it seemed to him. "What was Mrs. Forrester like? How did the house appear?" she had gushed hoping to hear that the reports of dire gloom which she had learned through county gossip which had reached all the way to Atlanta.

"Good God woman! Listen to yourself. Mrs. Forrester was as calm as could be. She was quite self-possessed, and the house was as well ordered and every bit as beautiful as it ever was. Now that is quite enough woman. The poor lady has suffered so many losses, and this county has treated her shamefully for things over which she had no control. Now I will hear no more about it. The confidences of Mrs. Forrester will not be betrayed by me, you, or anyone else in my household, and if I ever hear that you have participated in any slander against that great lady, there will be Hell to pay madam, and now I shall hear no more about it. Is that quite clearly understood?"

Mrs. Darby just stood in complete shock at the almost savage rebuke she had received and looked at her masterful husband with newfound respect. She replied, "Of course dear. That is the way it should be of course." Her look was now strangely adoring. She loved it when the Judge was so masterful. It nearly made her faint with admiration.

After Darby had left the Forrester Plantation, Mrs. Forrester turned to Pompey and asked,

"Did I do well? Do you think he knows that I've gone quite mad?"

"No ma'am. You did very well today. Very well indeed. Samuel and I will protect the family. Nobody will ever know your horrible secret. Nobody must ever find out that you are sometimes a little confused these days and have difficulty remembering things. After all you have been through Dear Madam, it is all very understandable," cooed Pompey to his mistress who adored him.

"Did I look well? Pretty? Nice?" asked the woman of her butler and protector hoping for his approval of her appearance as well as her attempt to appear sane.

"You looked like just what you are Mrs. Forrester, a beautiful woman who owns the most beautiful plantation in the whole of the county. Now I think that you should have some of your nerve medicine. The doctor gave it to you especially to let you sleep and forget all of the unhappy times you have suffered. We all here appreciate the awful strain on your nerves of these last years," replied Pompey who epitomized kindness itself.

"Yes you are quite right Pompey. I must sleep. I must rest, and I am ever so happy. Shall I see the girls tonight, or are they really in New York? I can't remember Pompey. It's really so hard I'm afraid that I'm confused again. You are so good to me Pompey. So very good."

"Helena will take you to your room for your nap now Mrs. Forrester. She will see to your medicine too."

Mrs. Forrester, now at the end of her strength, leaned on Helena's arm and made her way to her room where she would sleep until the next morning when she would then rise again with a headache and call out for her medicine.

CHAPTER XVII

The Forrester fortune had grown to huge dimensions, and the time was coming for Samuel and Pompey to move on. Samuel's agents in New York had made arrangements with Miss Sally Beers to have her brother secure a ship for the purpose of transporting one Don Raphael De Ruiz and his servant on a voyage to England, the land of William Wilberforce, which had outlawed slavery once and for all in 1833. Captain John Beers was in charge of the outfitting of the vessel and the hiring of a ship's crew. Captain Beers knew his business well and had sailed before the mast these twenty-three years as both man and boy. He had gone to sea leaving no family behind him save his sister. As far as he knew his sister was a beauty who had made a very good living at her fashionable resort in rural Georgia.

Although Miss Sally Beers traveled North to visit her brother in his schools when he was growing up, she had never invited him to visit her in Georgia. As he was frequently absent at sea for a year or two at a time, avoiding him was not really a difficult problem. Captain Beers never knew the nature of her enterprise except that she was a very fine businesswoman and knew how to both make and hang onto money. Miss Sally also seemed to have a gift for investing money. One of her northern banker friends got here into excellent shares, and in spite of the panics of the thirties, she had done very well.

Although he understood that Miss Sally had done well in operating her upper class country inn for tired gentlemen, the affairs of business were dragging her into a sad state of depression. Not only that, but the deaths of all three Forrester men had made her sad. She had really cared for them and in her way loved all of them. For her, Georgia was losing its charm, and she had been drawn in friendship to the big freedman who ran the Forrester Plantation which supplied her establishment from his bountiful acres. Their platonic relationship was based on the fact that they were both intelligent business people who were impressed by their own mutual honesty.

Neither Miss Sally nor her younger brother was a friend of slavery. Nor did Miss Sally care for what passed for gentry in this Georgian backwater. What she had liked about James Forrester was that he was an honest rogue. The local aristocrats were merely sheep for her skills as a shearer. The locals simply were nothing like the lively and uninhibited folks of her adopted New Orleans or the cosmopolitan cities of the North, that is to say, the men of the cosmopolitan cities of the North. The women of society were always the same everywhere, but it was not the women of society that Miss Sally Beers encountered socially or in business. When asked what she thought about the women of society, or women in general, she always had the same answer, "I do not like them, nor do I trust the sex. They are all liars and talk too damned much. And besides that, they cannot focus their brain on a conversation on a single serious topic for more than a second or two."

Miss Sally had many virtues. She was a woman of business, and she knew how to get things done. She was as good as her word in her dealings, did not suffer from Christian prejudice against Jews, Blacks or atheists as far as that went, nor did she do needless injury to anyone. Miss Sally never betrayed a confidence nor did she go back on a bargain once made. Her honesty was legendary, and her connections reached all over the country through her many friendships both professional and otherwise. She could even obtain Congressional help for hopeless young lads wanting to get into West Point just as she had done for James and Douglas Forrester. Samuel, who respected no woman, respected the integrity he found in the Madam. It was largely through her and her brother that Samuel's grand plan was to be executed. The friendship that had developed between Miss Sally and Samuel over the last four years was genuine and was based on their relationship of being honest brokers and possessing a true mutual respect for one another. Miss Sally had discovered a real friend in Samuel. She liked the fact that Samuel had no interest in her as a woman. She also liked the fact that he enjoyed the complexity of her mind on a basis of total equality.

The genius of the whole enterprise was that white society believed that people of color and women did not possess the intellectual capacity to carry out any real intrigues. It was thought that because most slaves spoke only the patois of slavery that they were of very low intelligence. Samuel and Pompey always found this prevailing attitude useful.

The majority of Black slaves in the South had all the initiative beaten out of them over the course of more than two hundred years. But there was always more than a few active and intelligent minds at work in the slave quarters and in the big houses of the South planning for their own day of liberation from bondage. There had been that business with Nat Turner, and there were a lot of free men of color in the North who also wrote books and lectured on the subject of abolitionism. But nobody in the South was enlightening slaves about these people who had shown a great deal of initiative by the bucketful. Not every slave spirit had been broken. There were dozens of special cases of real great men and women who emerged as natural leaders in the Black slave and free community all over the nation.

The name of Harriet Tubman was on the lips of the planter class all over the South. Even slaves had heard of her as a latter day Moses leading runaway slaves over the underground railroad to places in the free states and even further north to Canada. Canada like England was William Wilberforce country. Tubman was giving hope to people who would never even lay eyes on her in her lifetime. Even after generations of slaves had been beaten into submission and deprived of every shred of human dignity, there were still a considerable number who would dare to run, escape, and be free. Harriet Tubman was known as Miz Moses, and Miz Moses certainly was more than a light of hope. She was a stark reality. To the planters, she was the Devil incarnate with a high price on her little head. Miz Moses was a tiny thing with a very big gun and a commanding presence who had guided more than five hundred men, women, and children to freedom. To the planters, she was a rogue to be killed on sight who had stolen more than a million dollars worth of property from them. They wanted her dead. "To Hell with her initiative," would have been their thought on that subject had they bothered to do much deep thinking at all.

And Samuel was not just any man, and Miss Sally knew it. He was a prince of the Matabele Zulus and a warrior of the fiercest nation on the planet. Pompey was well schooled to play his part in the plot to steal themselves. The Forresters would also unwittingly play their role. When he had first heard of Harriet Tubman, Samuel threw his head back with a full-bellied laugh and announced, "That little Lady must be a Matabele!"

His conversation and talk then returned to the massive planned exodus from the Forrester Plantation of its Black population. "By the time we are in New York, Mrs. Forrester and her daughters will wonder where they have been for the better part of the last four or five years. I hope that they won't be too unhappy to find out," said Samuel to Pompey. "At least they will be very rich. Maybe all that money I'm going to leave them will buy us forgiveness. What do you think Pompey? What is the price of forgiveness these days?"

"I think that they will keep their peace if we leave them rich enough. And that Samuel, you will have done. They should be the richest landowners in the whole county," answered Pompey. "Even without a single slave on the place, they will be richer than any other planter for a hundred miles around.

"Nor will they want the truth known. The disgrace of their being in a state drunk on Laudanum for four and a half years would be far too heavy for them to bear. They still have more than enough pride to want to protect themselves and will go along with any fiction we choose to fabricate. And we all know how this wretched class feels about saving face. Now let's speak some Portuguese Senor Ruiz. Practice makes perfect. You never know when that might be useful since it is for at least a little while to be your native tongue."

Pompey answered in the perfectly accented aristocratic dialect of Lisbon. "My dear Cabral, how do you like being in my service as a manservant? After all, I don't beat you all that frequently do I? And I am often kind."

"It suits me well master. Are not your clothes kept in good order and your shoes shined my most handsome young lord?" replied Samuel in the most unaccustomed tone of total servile submission.

"Do curry my horse Cabral for I would ride to the races this afternoon and parade myself for the young ladies who stroll with their maids in the plaza by the fountain. I live in expectation that one of the beauties there will drop her fan so that I can retrieve it for her and gain her favor by returning it to her in her own drawing room."

"Your reading serves you well. If I did not know better, I would think you a grandee of Portugal myself my dear Ruiz, I mean Sir. I mean Pompey."

"Master will do Cabral. Yes it will do very well indeed. And I will confess a weakness for reading Camoens' *Lusiads.* Please do order my coach so that I may call on the lady of my last delicious encounter. I understand that her father is away, her mother dead, and her brother has gone to the wars. I must go to her and comfort that most beautiful daughter of a noble house. Maybe her sister too."

"Both of them at once my lord? You are pushing the Fates Senor Ruiz. I much admire your courage."

"Hello boys. I see that the lessons are going well. I even thought that I caught a word or two here and there," laughed Miss Sally as she breezed into Pompey's pantry.

Pompey switched to French, "Ah, Miss Sally, it is as you say, always a great pleasure to share your company. To what do I and my most humble servant owe the pleasure?"

"Why Pompey love, you do just sweep me quite off my poor little girlish feet with such gallantry!" gushed Miss Sally in her best Creole French.

"What news do you bring us Miss Sally?" asked Samuel in a more businesslike tone.

"My brother will meet you on the twenty-second of next month at Charleston. He has a fine ship, and a crew many of whom have served under him before he informs me. There will be no slip-ups or mistakes I assure you Samuel. I will get a good carriage to take you there. I have arranged for it to meet us twenty miles north of here. There we will make the change. The driver of both carriages is an actor, a very good friend of mine, and an abolitionist. You will even swear by his accent hat he had never set foot in the North when you hear him speak. In fact, he is a distant relative of Mr. William Lloyd Garrison himself and shares our sentiments. In point of fact, he has already given half of the payment you have made to him to the Massachusetts Abolitionist Society. He really is a good man Samuel. I think that you may depend on him as you do yourself."

"That your brother trusts him is good enough for Pompey and me. Here is another ten thousand dollars to cover your expenses Miss Sally. Maybe you will free your coachman when you return to New Orleans to settle there," said Samuel.

"The Hell I will Mr. Samuel sir! I don't ever intend to free that beautiful man. And I'm not going to settle in New Orleans either. I'm just sending all of my girls there with manumissions of their own and money enough to set up a 'House for Fatigued Businessmen and Country Gentry' who want to go to the city, kick up their heels, and have some fun damn it! I bought the girls a house as a little going away gift for them. Those gals are going into business for themselves, and they are going to do right well and share and share alike. They have a lot of talent, and they should do well with those sorts of high-toned fellows one finds in that big and easy town. Me and my 'slave' are going to retire to Merry Old England where I stashed away half a million pounds in The Old Lady on Thread Needle Street my sweet Samuel. I will buy an estate in the countryside in the Westmorland's. There my slave and I will be very happy, and you and Mr. Ruiz here will come and be my guests."

"Do you mean to tell me that you have two and a half million dollars in the Bank of England," gasped Pompey, "That makes you richer than Queen Victoria!"

"Well honey, I have made a few investments in real estate in New York, Boston, Providence, and Philadelphia with the help of a good banker friend, and I have also invested with my dear brother in the China trade. I even staked a few local gold miners here in Georgia and in North Carolina. I'm even in with a fellow named Betchler who minted much of my gold into hard money. Some of my investments have been in mines not very far from where we are. I have even had some of the bullion mined turned into coin right in Dahlonega at the federal mint. I've moved most of my funds equally to New York and London, and I even have some small amount in New Orleans just in case I had to leave the county quickly. Then the bankers do the rest. They just moved a lot of it off to The Bank of England. Bankers make bad lovers, but they surely do know how to move money."

"You are a wonder Miss Sally," said Pompey with a sweeping bow, "But what are you going to do with your coachman in England? They do not allow slavery there."

Miss Sally just raised her eyebrows and smiled.

Samuel cleared his throat and said, "Darby delivered the manumission papers for the house slaves this afternoon. He was a little puzzled, but when he was paid his full fee and expenses in cash and was allowed a few minutes with Mrs. Forrester, who was careful to explain that she was not quite herself today, he patted her hand and wished her well. On my instructions, he did not discuss business, because Mrs. Forrester just found it so taxing in her present state of health. The good judge understood."

Samuel continued, "I have also the funds for the freed slaves and have arranged for their passage North to Canada by steamer thre weeks from next Tuesday. They will depart from Charleston. I ha e arranged it to look like I'm selling the lot down the river if ar yone should question the movement of so many slaves. The captain and crew are abolitionists. It will be in the dead of night when they steam north. Miss Sally, it truly was so kind of you to take care of the harbormaster and the sheriff. Besides his huge fees, which I have overpaid him, even Darby might start to ask questions that he really does not want to ask now. The white mans' greed is a beautiful wonderment, but I am sure that the good judge would have no taste for a plot on so grand a scale as this. He likes money as much as the next greedy lawyer, but he does not want to be hanged."

"I have had more news from my brother Samuel. He thinks it best if you do not sail to New York. He thinks it best if you make straight to England. There is no need to pretend anything once we're out at sea, and he thinks that a direct route is the safest," said Miss Sally.

Samuel thought for a moment then said, 'Those are my thoughts as well. Please tell him that I also think it best.

CHAPTER XVIII

The polished chaise rolled off on its way in the direction of the Charleston docks with a handsome dark haired swarthy dandy resting languidly against the polished leather of its deeply upholstered seats. His large well built manservant sat next to the driver. The handsome young aristocrat alighted at the dock and drew the attention of half a dozen belles about to embark on a nearby ship bound for New York. The steamer was sooty, and some sparks flew through the air as the stokers in the bowels of the ship piled coal from her bunkers into the infernos that powered the massive engines that were to turn the huge paddle wheels. Her boilers were being fired up to get up a large enough head of steam to take the ship out of the harbor once the pilot had done his job and the new harbor tugboat put back to shore.

"I'll never get used to those infernal fire buckets and their smoke pot engines. They create filth, stench, and soot enough to cover the ocean from here to Lands End," expostulated Captain Beers to his Mate.

"Say what you will Captain, but the steamer is here to stay," replied the first officer. "Look at how much better steam engines are now than they were a decade ago. We live in an amazing time. It's all progress now sir. Look at what has happened in just the last few years. You can take the steam cars to New York at twenty-five miles an hour and beat sail by days. One can travel three times faster by steam trains than by coach. You can telegraph Philadelphia in minutes whereas it might take weeks, or months to communicate by post. Someday we'll be able to send messages by wire all over the world with this new telegraph thing. People can lay on gas and light up their homes better than they ever did with candles and smelly whale oil. No sir, you must face the facts of change. We will see nothing but iron ships someday with four, or five, or even a dozen times our tonnage and capacity. The times are changing sir. There is no doubt of it," said the mate carefully twisting his captain's tail and exacting every ounce of joy from the experience.

"Mr. Foss, I should have left you in Hancock, Maine where I found you. Steam! That is blasphemy! And telegraphs! Do you know that some damned fool said, 'Now Maine can talk to Florida,' and our Mr. Emerson said, "But does Maine have anything to say to Florida?' Now you must admit that Emerson is not only a clever devil, but he's on to something there."

"Leaving me up in Maine there! That might have been a pretty good idea at that sir, excepting that then I wouldn't get to see any of these new steamships now would I? That is had you left me on the dock up north where you bought this fine vessel," laughed the mate.

"Now that would have been sad," sneered the Captain with a decidedly ironic tone in his crisp Yankee voice.

The mate, well pleased with himself in the full wisdom of his twenty five years, merely smiled indicating that he was having a good time of it by winding up his captain on their favorite topic of sail vs. steam just as Samuel and Pompey came into view. Samuel and Pompey drew up to the gangplank of *The Neptune* now freshly tricked out in her new paint and looking very sleek.

"Well lookie here will you. Did you ever see such a duded up swell all rigged out like that before in your life? And he's got his colored manservant with him too. You don't see anything like that in Portland Captain, and you are damn sure not to see anything like that over to Hancock," laughed first mate Almas Foss.

"Mind your manners Mr. Foss. That fellow is some kind of Portuguese aristocrat who has hired the whole of our ship except for one other cabin. I'm told that he had to leave the sunny South pretty damn quick. Something to do with a lady, or maybe it was a bunch of them, mostly the pretty wives of planters and several daughters. But any way, the story goes that he had to shoot somebody's husband over some scandal. These upper class European types like to keep to themselves while on shipboard if there are no women about I've been told. Show him every mark of respect. I understand that the young fellow there has killed more than a few men in duels and such," warned Captain Beers. "I would not twist his tail if I were you Mr. Foss over steam or any other subject. You might not find that to be a profitable venture. There is not too much even a ship's captain can do if some grandee decides that he has been insulted and takes a notion to shoot you. After all, he's the customer so to speak, and therefore, he must be right. There is nothing I could do until he actually spilled your entrails on the deck. And as good a fellow that you are, it would all come down to about what he would be willing to pay to hush it up so his father would not find out about his troubles. I understand that the old man has threatened to cut this young fellow off without a cent if he does not get to London in a fortnight."

"Hot blooded bunch these Portuguese ain't they," stated the mate as he looked at Pompey and Samuel with a mixture of new respect and still some residual curiosity.

Samuel, as the manservant Cabral, carried the pigskin bags and saw to the trunks carried by sailors under special orders of Captain Beers. First Mate Almas Foss then took over and saw to the luggage, which was being carried to the two reserved first class cabins. He had banished all thoughts of asking any questions of these two men. Whoever they were, suddenly no longer fascinated First Mate Almas Foss. His thoughts had already moved on to the other ship's passenger who was a very attractive lady. She also had a tall and handsome black manservant with her as well as a very attractive maid. The Captain told the crew that the foreign gentleman, who was incognito, would be the only passenger besides a widow lady and her maid and manservant on the voyage, and under no circumstance were these persons to be disturbed or approached during the voyage by any member of the crew.

Captain Beers then went on to tell his officers that he had standing orders to alert the gentleman personally if any irate planters came looking for him. First Mate Almas Foss had been more interested in the pretty lady who arrived at the ship with her pretty maid and manservant. It did not take the Captain long to take note of the young mate's attention to the lady passenger. It also did not take long for the Captain to inform his mate that the lady and her party were off limits to all but himself and the stewards. About this, Mr. Foss was absolutely certain, because the Captain had expressed his wishes in this matter with unusual force.

By five o'clock that afternoon, the tugboat had carried away the pilot, and the steward had delivered a light meal to the cabin of Senor Ruiz and his manservant Cabral per Cabral's instructions given directly to the cook. When the meal was concluded, Pompey suggested a turn on the deck. Samuel agreed and, in turn, suggested that this would afford them an opportunity to practice Portuguese. The public roles the two played as master and servant seemed less strange with each passing day.

Samuel played the compliant role of manservant well, and because of the roughness of the planter aristocracy of rural Georgia, there had been very few role models either in and out of the Forrester plantation over the years to shape Pompey's view of a proper aristocrat. In many ways Old Caesar had carried himself with more dignity than the vast majority of the white men Pompey had seen. But he had read extensively and had cultivated that insouciant air of the true European aristocrat. What he had learned best from the county gentry was how to carry with him an air of intrinsic superiority that went along with being a member of a class used to commanding and holding domination over others.

Even the sordid sons of the ill-starred Forrester Family had been useful models in this respect. Along with the books of Jane Austen and other writers who inhabited the shelves of the largely unread Forrester library, Pompey became a finished gentleman of quiet refinement as well as of assumed command. He was more the gentleman than any man who had entered the doors of the Forrester Mansion or who had hunted on the plantation with the possible exception of Old Caesar himself who had seemed weaned on the abstract concept of "Dignity."

Pompey seemed not to notice the glances he got from the crew and mates. The looks he received from the women he had encountered on his journey to the ship needed no interpretation nor did the angry glances and glares he also received from the men who were with those self same women. The ship was bound for Southampton, and there was no telling exactly what surprises the sea would hold in the fall season. The air took on a distinct chill as the vessel made its way across the wide Atlantic.

Each day, in all kinds of weather, Samuel and Pompey walked the distance of four turns around the deck from prow to taffrail and back to their cabins where they enjoyed their splendid state of isolation. The lady and her two servants also walked the decks, and only nodded politely, or at best, exchanged but few pleasantries with the Portuguese grandee when she encountered these two other passengers on the ship. From time to time, Pompey thought about those beautiful white women who had stared at him on his journey to the ship with a sort of longing in their eyes for the exotic dark and handsome stranger, and then he would remember how he would watch them vanish behind their carriage doors and into hotels and shops located on the streets of the towns and cities through which they had traveled. He had clung to the code which Samuel had instilled and resisted all temptation. As for Samuel, he had chosen to be celibate until the day when he would return to the People of Heaven and take a proper Matabele wife and produce sons to carry on his name.

Samuel had some duties that took him out onto the deck for his master's comfort. Three times during the trip from the plantation to the port to begin their voyage, some pretty young thing would press a note, and a coin, into Samuel's hands. It was clearly understood that he was to keep the coin and that the note was to be delivered to his master. The sweet things would then rush back to their hotel rooms after looking to see if she had been observed by anyone of consequence. On returning to the coach or lodgings, Samuel would give Pompey the notes about which they would share a laugh knowing that they had passed yet another test, and that the impossible ruse was working. Then Pompey would ponder what it may have been like to have met with the pretty and young girls who had desired a tryst under a different set of circumstances when such a thing might have been possible. He was not immune to the healthy urges of his young and much suppressed manhood.

Samuel also got the odd indecent proposal from ladies' maids, a middle-aged woman of some beauty, and a strange young thin manservant. He was amused by all but the last. That was not the case with Pompey who seemed most amused by the homoerotic advance. That was very new to his experience of the world. For one of the few times in his recent history, Samuel was made uncomfortable by this young man's advance.

Samuel grunted his disapproval when he read this note. He crushed it , and he sent it to the floor where Pompey retrieved it and read it later at his leisure. Then confronted with the discarded scrap of paper, Samuel convulsed into laughter along with Pompey. He was laughing at Pompey's unworldly view of the situation as much as anything else. Soon one moon lighted night a few days later, as a softer breeze indicated the approach of the warmer waters of the Gulf Stream, Samuel turned to Pompey and asked, "What do you think of life at sea. This is all new to you."

"It's less isolated than the place we came from in its own

strange fashion Samuel. At least we are moving somewhere where I will have some idea as to where we are in the scheme of things. Here you can see for miles. It is funny how the appearance of another ship can bring one a sense of joy. Only now things are upside down. As the old slaves would say, 'Bottom rail on top'. "

"That's a very good way of stating it," said Samuel. "You are so high and mighty that no man or woman that you have met on the way to this ship, with the exception of the Captain himself and his sister, could even presume to talk to you. One would wonder just who is the prince here. But soon I will have my own place back again among my people. It will really seem strange, and getting from here, that is back to my own country of the Matabele Zulu, will be an adventure. I really can't even think of going there until I have settled a debt long overdue with Whitehouse. I will have to settle it fairly soon as I swore that I would return to my home before I was an old man. After all, I must hurry to father at least half a dozen children. This I owe my posterity. Somehow I knew that it could be done, this escape of ours. From the time I was taken off of that slave ship in New Orleans by James Forrester, I knew that I would have to find a way, and I knew that I would have to transform and educate myself to do it. It is good that I learned English from those High Church missionaries, and a little Portuguese from the coast people, as well as to read. I never knew how I was going to make my way even this far. Before you came Pompey, it really was not possible to carry out any workable plan. It is strange to think that a white man being your father has made the whole scheme work so well."

"And a white man being my grandfather as well Samuel?"

"That was the most vital part of it no doubt. Not to mention my beautiful Black brains Master," said Samuel with a laugh.

"And my devilish good looks, my good man Cabral."

"We have almost done it. It will not be long now. The ship I came to America in did not sink young Pompey. The last time I crossed this accursed ocean, I wished that it had sunk so many dozens of times. But it swam well and true to New Orleans where I made my bargain with Forrester. There are nights that I still wake up with the stench of that voyage in my nostrils. The smell of unwashed bodies, the smell of urine, and moved bowels of men and women, both living and dead, sometimes seem to be all about me still. Yes, the awful stench is still in my nostrils sometimes at night when I toss on my bed. It is the bitter fruit of my memory. It is the memory of the screams of the slaves followed by more lashings, and the blows of clubs, and belaying pins, and the rough commands of the slave drivers to the slaves to silence themselves even in the midst of this horror. These orders were followed in turn by the curses of the sailors, and softer sobbing of children, and women, and even some of the men. Then there was the moaning, and then the awful silence of the slaves many of them now dead. The next day their bodies would feed the sharks, but they at least would feel nothing. In thousands of dreams, it all haunts me still. I still feel everything. The silence that came as exhaustion consumed us made us fall into a tortured sleep. Even I, a prince of the Matabele, found myself crying softly to myself like a girl or some small abandoned child. I was a man of sixteen years and a blooded warrior, yet I wept. Well let me tell you, I have not wept since. There is but one piece of my work undone before I can see Africa again. There is one man I must punish to wipe out my shame, and that man is Whitehouse."

Samuel never looked so sad as he did in that unguarded moment. Then he suddenly was himself again. "Did you know that back on that slave ship, when they dragged us up onto the deck each morning to take out the dead and throw them overboard into the sea, that there were sharks following the ship waiting to be fed. Yes, from what I have told you, you must have known that. There in the ocean near the ship the sharks were always waiting for the bodies. The sharks seemed to know the ship, and they waited for their morning feeding. They never went hungry. There was among those of us who had been captured, a pretty Matabele girl who had married a warrior of thirty-nine years. She may have been eighteen or thereabouts. She was really something to look at even though she had been so abused by the lusty crew and mates. That is all the men but one. He seemed more a sailor than a person interested in taking the girls for his pleasure. He was a very odd man in that randy bunch of white men."

"You have never spoken of this before. Why should you now Samuel?"

"I have to speak of it now so that you will know why I will do the things that I will do and must do. Now just listen to me for a while. That girl had a baby with her. He was a boy of one year. She held him close to her as if she could protect him by clasping him tightly to her body. She was a true Matabele mother. In fact, she and her child were the only other Matabeles on that ship. You see, her man had died and been thrown to the sharks. She was very pretty. There was a mate on that ship who wanted her and would take her for his pleasure as something less than some low whore. He would have used her like an animal. His name was Manning. He was the same man who had discovered Forrester cheating and had beaten him for it back in Africa before the voyage to America. That Matabele girl clung to her son and resisted the Mate Manning. That white man tore that baby from her arms and dashed his brains out against a beam and threw the little corpse overboard. The Matabele girl screamed like a lioness and attacked Manning with all the fury of a savage animal with her fingernails and teeth and no other weapon.

The fool had unchained her in order to have his way with her. He pulled out his sheath knife to defend himself from her sudden attack and cut her badly, but that did not stop her. She gouged him with her fingernails and tore out one of his eyes. The mate fell on the deck screaming. She fell on him in a frenzy, bit off half his ear, and she tore at the veins in his neck until there was an explosion of red blood as she bit deeply into his neck. Men came running with whips and guns. They beat her to the deck. She lay there for a while not moving as her life's blood oozed out of her body and onto the wooden deck.

The white men did not seem to notice her as they looked after the all but dead mate attempting to stop his bleeding which was like a fountain. The sailors were in shock. The Captain, that is Whitehouse, came down below deck where the slaves were with a cutlass in his hand. He looked around at the scene, surmised what had happened, and grumbled that the filthy mate Manning had been served his just deserts. Then the woman suddenly bounded up from where she had been on the deck. She was all bloody and now armed with the mate's sheath knife. I could see that she had been very badly cut and could not last very long with all the blood draining from her body. I still wondered that she could move as she did. Hatred can give strength to an almost dead man, or woman too. She slashed out at the man nearest to her cutting him deeply with the fallen mate's knife. As the man fell back, she scrambled up the stairs topside. From above, on the deck, she screamed out a curse then cried, 'I shall be sister to the shark before I serve any white man.' With that, she jumped overboard. That was the end of her, but she had made her passing costly to the slavers. The man she had sliced with Manning's knife also died."

The two men stood at the rail and watched the sea as it receded mile after mile behind them. Neither man now spoke to profane the memories of that voyage of so long ago. There was nothing to be said. The night just swallowed them up.

CHAPTER XIX

Mrs. Forrester was aware of feeling sicker and sicker still. After some long and undefined time, she seemed to come out of a sort of fog located in dank mists inside of her head. As reality became clearer and clearer, she called out for Helena, but nobody came. Hours passed and at last, she seemed to be getting a bit better. The world became less misty and more real and familiar as the fog in her head began to subside and lift. At last, she seemed to gather a bit of her old strength. She also became acutely aware that the feeling of calm and joy she had been enjoying for years had ebbed away. It was replaced by paranoia and confusion. With a great deal of effort, she dragged herself from her bed. This she found to be not at all an easy thing to do. She got as far as her washstand and slop pot when she vomited. She vomited and vomited again with a violence that doubled her thin body like a horseshoe. It was the violence of the vomiting that made her pass out of consciousness back into the unreal dream world which she had seemed to occupy for an age.

When she awoke from her faint sometime later and came to something like her old self, Margaret Forrester could hardly move. She called out again for Helena with a feeble voice. She was surprised to hear only herself saying, "Where is everyone? Caroline? Tilly? Helena? Marcus? Pompey? Is anyone there? I need help. I need you. Where are all of you? Where have you all gone?"

Her voice seemed strange to her as if it belonged to somebody else. Then from down the hallway came two equally feeble cries of, "Mother, mother."

Dragging herself to her feet once again, Mrs. Forrester clung first to a black walnut chair, which was standing nearby and then to another. Then she stood for a full minute beside the chair to steady herself while the distant cries for help continued in a feeble way. Mrs. Forrester looked into the mirror hanging over a chest of drawers across the room. There she saw the face of an old haggard stranger staring back at her. The hair of this bedraggled creature was matted, streaked with gray, and dirty. She looked like some old engraving of a woman of the Left Bank in the French Revolutionary period. She seemed like a wraith hardly looking female at all. In fact, her own image was difficult for her to make out and identify. Mrs. Forrester had no sense of herself as herself at all. She thought she saw a vision of some primal form of human life that must have appeared in *Harper's* from time to time in some article about early man drawn from fossils lately discovered in Germany.

Slowly she realized that the primitive creature in the looking glass was indeed herself. Her dirty greasy hair was all about her face. Her clothes hung away from her once buxom body. The mirror reflected an old apelike woman with sunken eyes. She stood transfixed with horror at what she saw. Then the full horror of what she saw came crashing in on her again when she realized that the image was her own. Then slowly she became aware that she was again being called by her daughters. Her mother's instincts awaken by her daughters' cries for help, long dormant, seemed to motivate her to push on.

She walked along an invisible path that separated her from the door of her room and the spot where she had been leaning against the chair. Somehow she found herself making her way toward the bedroom door slowly grasping and clinging to each piece of furniture standing between her and the door of her chamber. Slowly Margaret Forrester managed to walk out of her bedroom and slowly make her way down the hallway, which seemed to have grown impossibly longer than she had remembered it being. As she clung to the wall, and then moved on, she seemed to need the support of every piece of furniture and woodwork she could grasp. Foot by foot she made a very slow but deliberate progress down the hallway. It seemed to be taking her an eternity.

Helena still did not answer the calls coming from the girls' rooms. "Helena! Where is that girl?" Mrs. Forrester called out to nobody in particular. Her mind was still far from clear. She felt that she was still in a dream or a nightmare, which was itself inside of yet another dream. She wished that Caesar or the long dead Anna were still there to answer the summons to help her. Mrs. Forrester knew that Anna and Caesar would have helped her if they could. "Pompey, where in blazes are you!" she tried to call out in a forceful tone.

After what seemed an age, she at last reached Caroline's room. What greeted her eyes in that chamber was horrible chaos. Her mind was a little clearer now. Caroline was on her bed still dressed in her day gown and looking as if she had been ill all over herself. At least she seemed to be moving and making some speech like noises. Something like reality was awakening in Margaret Forrester. All of the drawers of every chest were open or turned upside down on the floor. What had been the neatly folded contents were a series of piles of clothing mixed with books and various ornaments and glittering bits of jewelry. Muddy boot prints covered the carpet in red clay. Mrs. Forrester looked down the hallway from which she had come. It too was covered with the red hue of the vulgar clay.

"What in tarnation has happened here?" she heard her disembodied voice ask. Her mind tried to embrace it all, or at least some part of what she began to see as a new reality. Dimly she was aware that her daughter was speaking to her.

"Oh mother, I don't know. I don't even know where I've been.

I am an absolute wreck. My hair is filthy. Oh my God mother! What has become of you! You are a fright!" cried Caroline.

Then she began to weakly laugh like some demented hysteric while she attempted to point her finger at her mother. Caroline had awoken to so many bad dreams of death and damnation with the four deaths in the house of the past half-decade dominating her dreams, and now she seemed to awaken from her own death. It had seemed like years had passed until this resurrection, but she could not tell how many. There had been no sense of time, just a deadly sense of the unknown and unknowable dread. The girl began to cry on her filthy sheets. From horrible dreams she had now moved on to the disgusting living nightmares of the horrible reality in which she now found herself.

Mrs. Forrester, now more in charge of herself, looked into the cheval glass, and there she saw herself in a full-length view for the first time.

"My God, you are right. I am a horror." She sat on the edge of her daughter's bed and asked, "Where have we been? I can't seem to remember very much. In fact I don't seem to know anything except that I feel very sick."

"So do I. I wish that I could remember something mother. Was there a party? I can remember a lot of laughing, and people, and they were moving about and even dancing. I think that you, Tilly, and I were dancing. I can remember people having fun, but who were they? Were you there? Of course you were. You were dancing a reel, but I can't seem to remember who was there. I think that it was here in the house, but I just don't know. I think that Tilly was there dancing with Pompey. Is that even possible? Was I dancing with young Marcus and then some field hand?" asked Caroline as she tried to make sense out of the jumble of half memories racing now through her fevered brain.

"I don't know. Dancing with Pompey? Who would even come to a party here? We have no friends in the county now, but yes, I think that there was something like that, but I think that someone slapped me. Who could have slapped me? Who would slap my face?" asked Margaret Forrester.

"You have a dark mark on your left cheek mother as if you were struck." Caroline then suddenly seemed to recall something. "Was it Helena?"

"My God I think it was Helena who hit me! What would she be doing at a party here in my house? Why the very idea of it! Wait. I think. No that can't be, but that's what it was. Then I think that she took something, but I just can't remember."

"Mother! Look at your dress!"

"It's torn at the neck! Look. I'm scratched. My brooch! My diamond and ruby brooch that your father gave me! It is gone! Helena slapped me, and then she gave me more medicine, and then I don't remember. I have to lie down. I'm so tired, so tired, so very tired. I have to sleep. But I can't sleep. I can't sleep again. What if I do not wake up?"

Mrs. Forrester, at the end of her strength, collapsed onto Caroline's bed, and there she slept another dozen hours on the filthy bedding. It could have been a week or a year as far as she was concerned. As she slept, she had a series of epiphanies. The cards. The wine. The dancing. The female house servants all dancing in the Forrester women's Parisian finery. Such dreams! They came and went. So foolish. How could this ever be? The houseboys, Samuel, Pompey, Marcus, and all the male house servants dressed like obscene beaus in their dead masters' clothes as if walking for a cake. They had been strutting in the bright and gaudy clothes with brightly lacquered canes in their hands. It's really too funny she thought. Slowly sunlight filled the room, and the two Forrester women slowly roused themselves. It was daylight again after another night of oppressive blackness and heat. Their heads pounded as if they had drank too much wine. But they hadn't, had they? No, no that was not it. There had been but a little wine. But the wine was wonderful. It was strangely different. At first it was bitter. Then it was magic. It had made them so happy. Then there was music. The music of a fiddle. There was dancing and a sort of riot. Black people were dancing in finery. Things were broken. The Forrester women had been given more medicine, and everything was fine again. Mrs. Forrester didn't seem to mind suffering the indignity of Helena slapping and robbing her. They all had more fun all dancing together. Then someone put her to bed. How kind that was. "Oh my God! How long ago was that?" cried Margaret Forrester.

Mrs. Forrester raised herself up to a sitting position on Caroline's bed, rubbed her eyes, and found her legs. She discovered that she could stand and walk a good deal better if she took her time. Slowly she put one foot ahead of the other until she reached the door to the hallway. She labored her way to the head of the stairs, and then slowly taking the banister firmly in her hands, she descended to the landing. She could see more clearly now.

Then suddenly she became aware that the tall case clock on the wide landing had stopped. "I must speak to Pompey about that," she said aloud to the vast emptiness of the hallway. Something was not right. Her head throbbed, but her mind seemed to be clearer now as she at last almost reached the lower hall. It was very quiet. That was not right. Then from the landing, she saw a chicken crossing the hall and heading into the drawing room. "Who is there? Pompey! Samuel! Helena! Marcus! Where are you God Damn It!" she bellowed. Then she sat down on the stairs having shocked herself with her last outburst. Then she heard a hen clucking from the drawing room.

The sun was now streaming through the fanlight over the entry as well as through the acid etched windows on either side of the great mahogany door, which to her amazement stood wide open. "My Lord in Heaven! What is that boy thinking? Pompey must have taken leave of his mind," she said to nobody for nobody was there to hear her voice of feeble outrage. Once again the hen clucked her satisfaction with her own new living arrangements.

The sound of her own voice had startled Mrs. Forrester. She stood, then stopped for a moment and steadied herself. The demands that she had made on her body by making the trip down the staircase had weakened her and sapped her of most of her vitality. Mrs. Forrester plopped down again on a wide and deeply carpeted stair to rest a moment. She looked where she was sitting in disgust. The red clay actually made a crunching sound even as she sat there. After five minutes had passed, she arose again grasping the handrail. Then she lurched forward and made her way to the last step gaining the floor of the hallway. She went forward again, but had to grasp the edge of the ornate marble top center table. Margaret Forrester seemed to be more aware of the things around her as her mind began to clear a bit more. She became aware of the bright Georgian sun streaming through the open door. Its warmth felt good on her aching body as she moved toward the center of the entry hallway. Next she gathered her strength for a minute and stood in the center of the hall viewing the ruins about her of shards of broken Dresden china, Parian statues, and Sevres vases. Margaret Forrester had never shed a single tear for her departed sons, but now her eyes welled up with tears for these lost pieces of imported porcelain.

After a minute spent in mourning for her china, she collected her energy for another effort. She was remembering things more clearly now. She stood erect, and without thinking about it, smoothed the torn collar of her dress where her diamond and ruby brooch had been. Suddenly she missed the jewelry again, and then she felt the torn fabric where the brooch had been reconfirming that it was in fact now not there. She then fell back but kept herself from falling further to the floor by catching the edge of the center table again. "I cannot fall," she said. "I can't fall. If I fall I'll shatter into a thousand pieces like my dear china."

Mrs. Forrester pushed her body off from the table where she had balanced herself as if she was pushing a skiff into a millpond for a quiet row about the little waterway between the green meadow and the woods that bordered the plantation to the west. She launched herself in the direction of the drawing room then entered.

Before her was a scene of total ruin. The great gilt mirror

over the mantelpiece was smashed. Mr. Forrester's portrait, or what had been his portrait, hung from its frame in long tatters of canvas. The carved walnut furniture with its wonderful upholstery was broken and the parts of these precious pieces were thrown all about the room. The Meissen figures were resting in a hundred pieces all over the hearth. The rosewood Belter center table with its marble turtle top had been thrown through the French doors onto the wide veranda. The beautiful polished marble was smashed like the porcelain. Slowly the lights went on in Mrs. Forrester's brain. "Oh God! It's real! It's True! They are all gone! Damn you Samuel! Damn you all to Hell!"

The little hen watched Mrs. Forrester from her freshly constructed nest filled with eggs in the niche, which formally held a large Dresden vase. That priceless vase now lay on the floor in a hundred little pieces. The little hen seemed content in her splendid new world, which she viewed from her nest in the niche in the wall.

CHAPTER XX

Whitehouse paced the quarterdeck of the *Sea Hound*. The ocean was much rougher than it had been in the morning. It was clearly making weather as the ship neared the Cape of Good Hope. He thought about going further south in his attempt to stay out of the conventional sea-lanes. This was his fourth slaving voyage with his partners from Five Points. He was not entirely comfortable with them as his backers, but until now Whitehouse had few options. His investors were not as interested in backing ventures of this kind with the climate in the country shifting away from the pro slavery forces. His third venture with the Five Points crowd had cleared the *Catalpa* account and even netted him a decent profit. This voyage, and third joint venture would be even more profitable as he was following his new formula for investment.

The third joint venture had proven the wisdom of the efforts made at a better treatment of the cargo with a capital reward of double the returns expected. His partners in Five Points had been quite pleased with the success of the voyage and this led to the easy financing for this next venture. Backing was obtained without any trouble whatsoever. Ellis once again came along as supercargo. This fact of life was the principal fly in the ointment for Captain Whitehouse.

The man irked the Captain beyond all belief. Ellis was the

constant reminder that the Captain was not the master of the situation in the absolute way he was used to. Whitehouse looked up at the skysails billowing overhead. He fancied that the ship was making at least fourteen knots. To race before the wind always exhilarated him and reminded him of just why he had fallen in love with the sea in the first place. The Captain reflected on the red sky of that morning and then looked at the heavy storm clouds in the west. In his mind's eye, he knew that as surely as the sun sets, that there was going to be a great storm blowing up. This sort of thing was not uncommon in these latitudes at this time of year. "It's nothing like The Horn," he thought. "There at the end of the earth the storms are something to see. How awesome and grand even if we are broken and doomed for it. God! How I love it."

Cape Horne was the death scene of countless hundreds of ships. Even great mariners like Captain William Bligh had to turn back after he had attempted to beat it around the Horne for an entire month reflected Whitehouse who knew the nautical history of the world as well as any Oxford don knew the campaigns of Caesar.

"What's that you say Captain?"

Turning, Whitehouse noted the coming of the supercargo with a nod. "Oh, nothing Ellis. I'm just muttering to myself. That's something we old-time salts do," muttered the Captain to the supercargo.

Ellis' dress did not diminish in its glamour even on this second voyage with Whitehouse. All of a sudden, salt spray drenched the deck. Much to his disgust, the Captain had concluded that Ellis dressed to impress nobody but himself. The big man even had a black freedman to keep his clothes clean, pressed and in good order on the voyage. This servant was a handsome young man of delicate good looks, which seemed to beg the question of exactly what other services he rendered his master to whom he seemed all too devoted. Ellis was as tough as nails in spite of his appearance, and he handled the Portuguese slave traders roughly and beat down their prices for prime stock with a mixture of finesse and brutality which Whitehouse admired as unmatched in his almost forty years of slaving.

Yet Whitehouse did not like the man. Ellis was an itch under his skin that he could not scratch.

"My dear Captain, there seems to be a storm blowing out there in the west. How severe will it be do you think? Are we in any danger?"

"Well Mr. Ellis, I would say that we are in for one Hell of a blow. A full-fledged gale at least. It might even rip the canvas all to Hell and blow us all to damnation under our bare poles. Now would you see that as being in danger? I've seen storms like this rip every shred of sail from the yardarms and drive a ship over onto its side then right her again with a third of its crew washed overboard to be shark food before a boat could put over for them. No boats can be launched in such seas you see. When the ocean wants its way with you, it has it. Then the sea just takes you and eats you up, or spits you onto some reef to break your back. The sea is a vengeful bitch you see!" Whitehouse said this knowing that Ellis, who was brave in taking on any two men in a brawl, was an abject coward in a storm. Brawlers Ellis could control, a storm was something that he could not beat into submission. During the last three and a half years, he had only seen Ellis break a sweat when confronted with the savage elements while afloat. If the truth be known, Ellis hated the sea, but he was the only partner and supercargo that the backers in Five Points would trust with their substantial investment.

Attempting to put a good face on his fears, Ellis asked, "How rough do you think it's going to be really?"

"Looking aloft there to the west, I'd say that we could be in for the storm of a lifetime. A full blow of Hell from old Neptune's lungs right into your face. There is always a good chance the ship will go down. I'll do the best I can to save you, but fate being what it is, who knows what may happen. In my time, I've seen ships split in two, or with their backs broken in a troth as a result of hogging, and I've seen them run aground and broken to pieces on uncharted reefs, but I always lived to tell the tale, that is, so far. You never know just when your luck will run out Mr. Ellis. I have a feeling that this might be the very day. So, I wouldn't worry about it Mr. Ellis. There is nothing, not a goddamned thing you can do. In fact, I think that you should stay topside this time so you'll have a tale to tell when you go back to see your friends in Five Points, that is, if you do ever get back. I am sure that they would want to hear every goddamned word of your narration of what could be the worst storm of the century," said Whitehouse with a fiendish look on his face.

"I think that Ajax and I will keep to our cabin through this one Whitehouse if it's all the same to you. The boy's nerves are delicate, and its better that he doesn't see how bad it really is. And by the way, I have a habit of never relating tales of any of my adventures. Life is kept simpler that way."

"I'm a sailor Mr. Ellis, and tales are what we sailors like to tell. I can imagine that a handsome big fellow like you has many a fine tale to relate of your conquests of women for example. You got a lot of women in your life do you Mr. Ellis? That is when you are ashore? You look like a real lady-killer to me. Aye, that you do. Let me tell you a tale of the time when I was a lad during the last days of the Great Nelson when I was a cabin boy of eight or nine years of age in the merchant service."

"The sea has been mother to me ever since I can remember," continued Whitehouse.

"Every once in a while a mother can get agitated with her youngsters. The sea is a great deal like that you know. She thinks that you might be bad or getting too big for your breeches. Then she feels that she has to impose some discipline on the children who sail on her. She goes in for punishing them you see. I do believe that our oceanic mother is about to take us to task for our sins Mr. Ellis. She'll help us on our way all at the same time, and she'll help us evade the British Navy. Unlike the Americans, the good men of the Royal Navy do not hesitate to hang good honest slavers like ourselves, but never mind that. Let me get back to my tale."

Whitehouse cleared his throat and winked at Starbuck who had just come topside onto the deck. Starbuck covered his mouth to stifle a laugh, because he knew what was coming.

"Mr. Ellis, back when I was a lad of eight, I went to sea to make my fortune under the loving care of Captain Bully Douglas of the good ship *Oberon.* She was a Frenchman taken as a prize by one of Nelson's frigates sometime after the Battle of Copenhagen. Now Captain Douglas had command of her from her owners who had bought the prize from The Admiralty in auction. He was a hard man, but a fair one as long as you followed orders and kept order 'tween decks' and attended to duty. One day, I was on my way to the Captain bringing him a bumper of hot buttered rum to take down against the awful cold, and what do you suppose I saw?"

"I haven't the slightest idea Whitehouse. What ever did you see?"

"Well sir, I saw a sailor of the ship's company. We called him "The Big Swede". Well Mr. Ellis, the Big Swede came reeling down the deck a bit worse for having taken a dram too much of Christian comfort."

"How remarkable," Ellis sneered showing the obvious sarcasm to cover his growing and transparent fear of the great tempest, which was forecast to erupt upon the ship by Whitehouse.

"Yes sir, the Big Swede was feeling no pain whatsoever. He was in fact quite intoxicated. Except he suddenly was taken sick at the same time and reeled over to the rail to heave up his innards. As he leaned over the side letting go of his cargo into the sea, the ship took a big wave, and the Big Swede went overboard right smartly."

With that Whitehouse just stood with a smirk on his face and waited Ellis' reaction. After a few seconds of realization that the Captain would not go on without prodding, Ellis feigned disinterest, but then human nature got the better of him, and he asked, "What happened then?"

"Well sir! I did my duty! I ran down the deck to the Captain crying out, 'Man overboard, Man overboard.' I ran all the way up to the Captain, handed him his hot buttered rum, not spilling a drop mind you. I didn't want to get my ears boxed. And I says again, 'Captain the Big Swede's fallen overboard sir.' "

"The Captain looked down on me and asked, 'What the bloody Hell are you going on about boy?' "

"Begging your pardon sir," said I, "Please sir, the Big Swede has gone over the side!"

"The Swede eh? What the bloody Hell do you expect me to do about it young Whitehouse?" I was taken by surprise that he actually knew my name you see."

Again the Captain stopped his tale, and Starbuck turned his back so that Ellis could not see him laughing. Whitehouse looked up at the top sails, and Ellis impatiently asked, "Well what happened next to the Big Swede?"

"Oh yes. Sorry about that. Where was I now? Oh yes. Well Captain Douglas asked me what I thought we ought to do about the Big Swede you see, and I said that we should put about for him and pick him up in a boat."

"'Put about! Are you daft boy?' he replied, "Put about for the Swede? The damned fool was most likely drunk again like the majority of that sodden alcoholic race! If I put about for him, I shall be behind my time for the better part of two hours and maybe more. By then he will have drown himself and gone to Davy Jones' Locker and Hell most likely. The bloody fellow couldn't swim a stroke to save his life, and by now some shark has had him for his supper."

And then the Captain drained his noggin as calm as you please and walked on down the deck with never another thought about the Big Swede. Very smart was Captain Douglas. So Mr. Ellis, make damned sure that you don't fall overboard, because I know that you will be dead before I can put about to pick you up. And I don't have two hours to waste any more than my old Captain did. Captain Douglas taught me a great deal about the value of keeping to a schedule at sea."

"Trust me on that score Captain. Staying with the ship is my very plan. Now if you will excuse me, I'll go below to check the cargo and my man Ajax."

"Take care Mr. Ellis. We have kept most of them alive. Only nine deaths so far actually, but they will have spent the last few hours puking a lot with the weather making up and all. Don't slip, or you will ruin your pretty costume. Your darkie will have one Hell of a time cleaning it up for you. There is a lot of piss, vomit, and shyte down below. We haven't cleaned it away yet today."

Ellis exited below to his cabin with as much dignity as he could muster seeing that Whitehouse's psychology was having the desired effect on Ellis' delicate digestive function. Starbuck turned to the Captain and said, "You were pretty rough on the duded up nob sir, but it was nice and gentlemanly of you to warn him off inspecting the cargo."

"I don't give a damn about Mr. Ellis' sensibilities Starbuck, nor do I give a tinker's damn about the sodding Mr. Ellis himself. The Royal fucking Navy is not going to take notice of us for at least the week that this bloody storm will take to run its course. It's going to be one great Hell of a big blow of four to seven days duration if my life on these seas for all these years has given me the judgment with which I credit myself as a sailor. We are going to reef the skysails and set the mains. We are bound for an alternative destination rather than making for New Orleans on the return voyage, and I have no intention of clearing my decision with our good friend Mr. Ellis Mr. Starbuck. That destination will be one that our supercargo has no awareness of. We are bound for Rio de Janeiro in that most civilized country, the Empire of Brazil. There slavery is fashionable and the slaves of the quality we have here with us shall bring a very good price. A much better price than they will in New Orleans."

"Excuse me Captain. We are going to take the cargo and sell

it in Rio? What about the Five Points mob? Ain't they going to be the slightest bit resentful of this change of plans?"

"To answer your question Mr. Starbuck, the gentlemen of the Five Points are no longer in the picture. In point of fact, this little change in plans will make every man on this ship thousands of dollars richer. Your own share my dear Mr. Starbuck should make you much richer than you ever imagined possible. It all depends on how many of the African buggers we can deliver alive and reasonably sound. Now we have a very good chance of doing that if we can survive this big blow. I was not far off my mark I'm guessing when I told Ellis what to expect the next several days to be like. But I also know the merits of my ship, my men, and my first officer. Mr. Starbuck, we will do just fine. Did you not tell me that you wanted to spend the rest of your days on the Island of Nantucket and reign supreme as a selectman of the town or something of the sort?"

"I'd not say no to that Captain sir. It always gives me the creeps to go so far on land as to go to that fucking cellar in Five Points where all of those rats meet together. I know that it's really only a short distance away from the shore, but it seems so far from anything I know to be safe. I feel safer here on this deck with five hundred savages in chains below sailing into a gale than I do standing on the sodding earth with those Five Point's cutthroats around me. It's the same as being on a good ship when I'm on Nantucket. I feel safe there. It's like I said. It's like being on a big ship at sea with water all around on all sides. Nantucket always felt safe like a ship to me even though she's not sailing anywhere. Now feeling safe and at home is what I crave. I just guess that I feel like I'm getting too old for this trade."

"I know what you mean Mr. Starbuck. I cannot do what we have to do without you and your support, and I thank you for your interest in our future welfare. Be assured that I'll thank you in a very material way when this voyage is done and our business transacted in Brazil. What would you say to a fortune that will secure every dream you ever had as well as whatever property that fancy man Ellis may possess in his cabin as your reward? Should the unfortunate Ellis find himself swept overboard during the next few days, all of his rubbish can be yours."

"I'd say thank you very much Captain! We have been through a lot over these years we have been together sir. I don't like the slave trade as you know, but I would follow you to Hell sir should the situation demand it. As much as I hate the trade, the one thing I can count on is that you will never let me down or betray my trust. If you want Mr. Ellis to have an accident, I'll see to it as soon as a proper situation presents itself."

"I knew that you would agree with my plan, and in fact, I counted on that. Now about Mr. Ellis."

"Don't give Mr. Ellis a thought sir. I fancy that gold watch of his that plays tunes. And I'm bloody sick and tired of his superior ways. I think that a fine swim on a day like today would be good for Mr. Ellis and good for us as well."

"I think that watch would look very well on your honest Yankee black broadcloth vest when you preside over those meetings of the board of selectmen on Nantucket. And about the little Black fairy cake Ajax. I rather fancy him myself if you don't mind. And when I'm done with him, he'll fetch a pretty price in Rio. You are a good and loyal man Starbuck. A few things such as Ellis might have is small reward enough for all the service you have given me over our long association. I thank you for your willingness to toss Mr. Ellis overboard. Your kindness touches my heart my dear Starbuck. Trust me it really does," said Whitehouse as he turned and climbed down the companionway to his cabin.

CHAPTER XXI

Miss Sally Beers had used some of her considerable wealth to purchase a fine manor house in a lovely shire in the rolling country of East Anglia. It was splendid in the very best taste of the Georgian period of ninety years earlier. The house was built of warm red brick, and it had been designed by the Brothers Adam. Its crowning glory was that it had large formal gardens. The whole estate was supported by many tenant farms, which produced a rich income for the new landlady. The fine stables, and well-stocked streams and ponds also appealed to Mistress Sally Beers whose curious hobby was that she liked to fish. It was a habit of her country Tomboy youth spent in company with her little brother on whom she had doted. Her Black American factor/coachman, Daniel, was a fine man of business who now lived in the gatehouse which in and of itself would have rivaled many an important American dwelling house in terms of its intrinsic grace and elegance.

Miss Sally had grown tired of her factor as a lover, and she decided to truly emancipate him, give him a good income, and hire him as the guardian of the cash resources of the estate as well as in the position of estate supervisor. Daniel, in turn, had found a girl in the village who had discovered him to be as handsome and as pleasing as his former mistress had during the time she had found herself captivated by his charm.

Although Daniel and Miss Sally were no longer formal lovers, they were still friends and each others close confidant. Miss Sally was quite happy with her former lover's new arrangement, and the village girl moved into the gatehouse as the estate manager's housekeeper. With the advent of the couples' first child, the vicar was summoned in to preside over a wedding. Then there was a high Anglican baptism of the child itself. The village liked a party, and all went swimmingly. Most of the district showed up, "To wet the baby's head."

Miss Sally danced into the night to the music of the village fiddle players with the rural farmers and their sons. The down to earth yet exotic mistress of the manor had captured the imagination of the shire, which at the same time did not know what to make of her. She was strangely democratic and at the same time the undoubted mistress of all she owned, and above all, Mistress Sally was a lady. This exercise of mastery over village life had quickly won the loyalty of all who lived on her lands.

Miss Sally had not done anything in the area of entertainment since she had taken up residence at the manor. The first people to whom she would open her doors were guests lately arrived from America as the story went about the shire. Old friends from America in those parts were also an exotic curiosity to excite the imaginations of both the gentry and the farmers. One guest was her sea captain brother and the other a Portuguese aristocrat and his manservant who had spent some time in the rural South in the American republic. All the gentle folk of the shire wanted to know what the great, wealthy, and secretive American lady was up to. After all, she was rather newly arrived herself and had purchased Hatton Hall from the ancient family whose members included an officer who had served Queen Elizabeth herself as captain of her royal guards. Rumors had spread about the neighborhood that the supposed American lady was really an exiled royal who had mastered the American southern idiom of speech. There was not a landowner, or a near-do-well, in the district who did not wish to entertain the lady in an effort to enliven life in this dull backwater.

"My land agent, Mr. Smyth-Jones, tells me about everything that happens in the neighborhood," Miss Sally told Pompey and Samuel. "He says that people are beside themselves wanting to know just what is going on over here. I think that I will play the role of a simpering belle of Louisiana up to the hilt and just keep all of these fine folks guessing about me. I think that I will be a woman of mystery and of such deep discretion that I just won't ever have to say a thing about my past to anyone. What do you think Senor Ruiz and Cabral?"

"I think that you have chosen to play your part quite well Miss Sally. Have you decided to buy a title?" asked Pompey.

"That idea has lost its charm along with entering into marriage with my dear friend and coachman Daniel. He loves living at the gatehouse, and he is very taken with his country girl-wife who is no better than she ought to be. He tells me that he is very happy with her, and that he tells his doxy that he is from a fine family in the south of Italy. None of her people have been south of anywhere so it just doesn't matter what he says. They think that he's a rich Italian expatriate driven from his home in some uprising back last year. So her parents are content with the prospect of dark Italian grandchildren in their future. Of course they loved the wedding. The whole thing is quite on the up and up. Daniel has made an honest girl of their daughter. That's rather rare in this land where even royal bastards abound. Now boys, I don't mind telling you that this whole trip has been a curious first for me isn't it? Now what have you boys been doing in London these ten months past?"

"We have been attempting to find information about an old friend that Samuel once went to sea with," said Pompey.

"Now Samuel, when were you ever at sea?" asked Miss Sally playfully.

Samuel looked rather solemn, "Only once before our last voyage."

"Oh. I see," said the lady who then let the entire matter drop.

"Someday I'll tell you more if you really want to know more about that voyage. It is not a pretty story," said Samuel.

"Someday will be fine Samuel," said Miss Sally who returned to her own narrative. "It just adds to the adventure of what we all have been up to, don't you know. I think that it is a good idea that I remain a woman of mystery. I have been to a few social events, mostly lawn parties and one ball, and I have discovered that a lot of these English lords and gentlemen have very bad teeth. And the smell of their breath is hideous. In fact I heard a story that just about made my legs buckle."

"Pray tell what was that your Ladyship?" quipped Pompey.

"It seems that some of these English are just so damned lazy that they make Georgian planters look ambitious."

"I find that hard to believe," said Samuel.

"Listen to this story and then say that. It seems that one of these English lords had this valet in his service for more than fifty years. This man did everything for him. He even dressed him! It seems that he was even in the habit of placing tooth powder on his lordship's toothbrush every evening and morning. One day the valet just upped and died. Well! His lordship was very put out. He could not even organize his trousers, and worse than that, he could not even make his tooth brush work. He came down the stairs after absentmindedly ringing for his dead valet as he was most frustrated when the man failed to present himself. Now he was at the foot of the stairs ranting and raving about being abandoned and left alone. The servants called his wife from her chamber to see what she could do about his lordship. The distraught wife tried to calm him and discover exactly what was wrong. It seems that his lordship flourished the offending toothbrush in her face, and then he screamed out, "The damned thing won't foam!"

"It seems difficult for me to understand how this nearly

imbecilic nation can actually be taking over most of the planet considering the state of the ruling class here," said Samuel.

Miss sally laughed again, "Not only that, but in these big country houses they have screened off areas in their dining rooms where guests go during dinner to relieve themselves in commode chairs! Can you just feature such a thing back in the States? I declare! I have been told that even the Queen has that arrangement in her palaces. The servants told me that it has been that way for as long as they can remember. The locals were very anxious to know what I was up to when I put a stop to that ancient custom, and I had an inside water closet commode installed in a little anteroom just outside of the dining room with running water to take the waste away and provide for hand washing. I had to get plumbers down from London to install the fixtures. They are all painted and look like fine china. I understand that they are manufactured by a Mr. Crapper. Now that is a curious name, and wouldn't you know it but he has his name on each piece of that pretty chamber set!"

"I like a man who takes pride in his accomplishments," said Pompey with a laugh.

"And there's another thing about these English gentlemen! The horror of their breath and sometimes their persons! And I'll tell you, I won't have a man with bad teeth. None of these so called gentry work either, and I have no interest in a man that does not work and trouble to manage his affairs. And by the way, I did tell you that my former coachman, Daniel, is just wonderful with figures? I knew that he was smart, but I had no idea as to just how damned intelligent he was. If I showed him anything about bookkeeping, he just learned it at once. He is just wonderful with the accounts. And with what I'm paying him, he'll be loyal to me until the day that foolish girl he's taken up with kills him with loving! About the time she has him sire her twelfth brat he'll be about done for and ready to be laid to rest by the church. May God help poor Daniel, and besides that, I can't have the darling bastard die! I really need him damn it."

"My dear sister, could you be in the market for a husband?" asked Captain Beers.

"My dear brother, I do believe that I am. But be so good as to please remember. I have very high standards. I am very fussy. Any husband of mine has got to be a man of ambition who likes to work the land and a man that I can actually like and respect in and out of my bed. He must be a man that I really do admire. I don't think that I will find a fellow like that amid the fops that come down from London for the season when there is no London season. I cannot tolerate the dullards at these house parties. Hell! If I close my eyes, I might even think that I'm back home with the terminally stupid sons of old Georgia. These people are dull and unread. In fact, I don't think that I shall accept any more invitations from these local people of quality. In point of fact, I find their quality sadly lacking. I am afraid that the Englishman I would marry does not attend the social events that make up this class of county near-do-well's principal entertainments. Any man who could be a husband to me might be a country squire who is interested in the land and livestock. And I would not object to a man who reads books and was interested in the world no matter where he came from. As I said, most of these fellows I have met remind me of home in Georgia, and home is just what I wanted to forget."

"That might be wise my dear Miss Sally," Samuel said in a fair imitation of an English gentleman.

"I am of the opinion that if this society cannot know you, that they may esteem you all the more. At least they will be consumed with curiosity. This will allow you to nod with a smile when you ride by them in your carriage. It will drive them to distraction. In time, lightning might strike you and you might even find that lion you are looking for among these boars," said Captain Beers.

"John, I haven't seen any lions at the few parties I've attended," said Miss Sally as she fanned herself in her very best Southern belle style. "Hell, there wasn't even a decent pussycat to be found."

"Well you are going to meet two well reputed young political lions of a different sort who are 'on the make' tomorrow," said Captain Beers who had not joined Samuel and Pompey on their journey to his sister's home, but had come by locomotive.

The Captain was only able to visit his sister due to a favorable break in his professional commitments in Southampton, and then he still had commitments in London. Captain Beers continued, "In fact, both of these fellows are quite infatuated with the sea in spite of their being professional politicians. I fell into conversation with them on the cars on my way here. As it happens, they are guests at Lady Harrison's for one of her husband's political weekends. They seem to be interested in the same things that you are my dear, and their roots are in the upper middle class. They are fascinated by the fact that we are Americans, and they are absorbed with the war that the United States has on with Mexico at the moment. The fact that the United States is spreading its territory all the way across the Continent to the Pacific, to them is an awesome prospect. They can see that this new nation of ours is well on the way to becoming an empire potentially greater than any in Europe or even Russia. After all, Britain is in a fair way to becoming the vastest empire that the world has ever seen, and they want to see what the future competition looks like I think. Neither one of them is a candidate for your hand Sally, but they are amusing company.

Captain Beers stopped to take another puff of his pipe then continued, "One of these fellows is opposed to imperial growth as England's future, while the other embraces it. They are both members of Parliament and the Conservative Party. It seems that they have both heard of you, and that you are a sort of celebrity as well as an heiress and an American of exotic curiosity. They have even heard about you in London Sally. Best of all, from their point of view, is our being members of this exotic race of Americans now in England. They have been consumed with a desire to meet you. I told them that your poor husband was immensely rich and left you very well provided for. I also took the liberty of telling them that he died in an affair of honor and that you never wanted it spoken of under any circumstances. Everybody in Europe thinks that southern gentlemen fight duels all of the time you see. In fact, I made their not speaking of his death or even of him a condition of their visit."

"Good lord! What has possessed you to that?" laughed Miss Sally. "You are just so clever. They will just be dying to know, but never can ask. It is the most perfect cover. Brother Dearest, you are a genius. It is no wonder that I love you John."

"Come along, I thought that you would need some diversion in this dull palace of yours. And I will warn you that one of them is a charmer with a reputation of being something of a lady's man who has been sniffing around the wealthy widow of a late literary friend of his who was also Governor General of India or some place or other, or it might have been a relative. It seems that the lady's late husband wrote a rather well known novella. It was even one I had actually heard of, and I know that you have read it. Let me see, what was it called? Oh yes I remember it now, *The Last Days of Pompeii*."

"I do hope that it wasn't about me," laughed Pompey.

"Aren't we full of ourselves Senor Ruiz," teased Miss Sally.

"Young men about town are supposed to be full of themselves," rejoined Captain Beers.

"Tell me Captain Beers," asked Pompey while warming to the idea of entertaining two men who actually had ideas and interests beyond the narrow society of his hostess' neighbors and Georgian gentlemen, "Are they Wilberforce types?"

"Most decidedly. I can say that without reservation," replied the Captain.

"Just what are young English political lions like these days? Will they amuse Samuel and me?" asked Miss Sally.

"Well, one looks like a parson weaned on a dill pickle, and the other is a flashy sort of fellow. Somebody told me that he was a Jew whose father had all of his children baptized into the Church of England so that they could get ahead someday," replied Captain Beers. "He was the one I warned you about. He also writes novels.

I was quite surprised that he was in Parliament. I had no idea that Jews sat in Parliament. It's something new in English politics and a rather healthy thing if you ask me. I think that you will like him. He smiles as if he has a secret and isn't telling anyone what it is."

"Oh, I think that he'll tell me if I ask in just the right way," said Miss Sally. "This really is too good. Do these political paragons have names by any chance?"

"It is strange that you would ask that. I don't quite recall what they were off the top of my head, but I remember seeing them in the newspaper this morning," replied the Captain. The paper was retrieved from the breakfast room by the parlor maid and handed to Miss Sally, who in turn, handed it to her brother.

He scanned it for a moment then said, "Ah yes. Here they are."

"And their names dear brother?"

"Their names appear to be a Mr. William E. Gladstone, he's the one who looks like a parson, and a Mr. Benjamin Disraeli. He looks like the fox just out of the hen house that has just had a good meal on the sly and has fooled the hound charged with guarding the hencoop. They are both M.P.'s, and as I told you, they are visiting with the Harrison's."

"Ah," said Pompey, "He is indeed a Jew this member of Parliament, for is his name not Benjamin of the Israelites?"

"You are the scholar Pompey, not me," said Samuel.

"I've read a book he wrote a few years ago. He is a romantic and something of a reformer. Quite a few people don't seem to like him in his own Conservative Party because of his reformer sentiments. In fact I've read in *Punch* that he is thought of as a fop and was booed in Parliament during his first speech. In fact, I also read that he was a real dandy who draped himself in gold chains which seems to be the thing if one is a young man of fashion but of no taste these days."

"Gold chains indeed. I would never have allowed any of my

ladies working in my," stopping to smile at her brother, "My restaurant and hotel to dress with as much flash as that."

Miss Sally's brother smiled, "I am sure that only dishes of truly rare delight were ever good enough to be served by you my dear."

Everyone had come to accept the open secret of the origins of this exotic lady's wealth.

Miss Sally's brother made it quite clear, that considering the course of their lives, both of them had done quite well and even enriched the lives of others. Brother and sister had a real understanding of each other and the need to conform to the conventions of good society when it was in their interest to do so. In fact, it became the great central joke and the essential bond of their lives.

"You know something Samuel" said Miss Sally, "I have great respect for you, but I must confess to you at the same time that I really loved those Forrester boys, both James and Douglas. Oh, they had their faults. Many, many faults. They had an insouciant lack of consideration when dealing with young girls who were pretty and susceptible to their masculine charms, and that was unforgivable. But they could be quite sweet. All those poor boys were looking for was love. I think I really knew Jimmy Forrester Senior. He was a gambler, a cheat, and whoremaster, but in many ways he was the most honest man I ever met, and Jimmy, unlike his sons, was a man of supreme kindness and consideration. He never stripped a man of his plantation even when he had the chance to do so many times. And believe me when I tell you this Samuel. He thought the world of you and that was as a man not a slave, and that is one of the reasons that I respect you so much."

"That's all very fine Miss Sally, but he had the damnedest way of showing it. But never mind all that. I'm going to do him a favor by killing the man who killed him."

"What are you saying Samuel? He fell from his horse. People even heard him when he fell after that bolt of lightning struck.

There was that rock where he hit his head that had his blood on it," said Miss Sally sadly.

"That may be so, but I was there. I saw a slaver named Whitehouse kill Master Forrester. And believe me, I have known James Forrester since I was almost sixteen years of age back in Africa, and now is the time for me to tell you the whole story."

For the next hour, Samuel held the Beers spellbound.

CHAPTER XXII

Mrs. James Forrester and her two daughters were registered at The Grand Hotel. Paris was beautiful, and everything Mrs. Forrester thought that it would be. The Opera, the avenues, the Louvre, and The House of Worth had been a fantastic tonic to all that had been toxic in Georgia. There was absolutely no doubt that the Forrester women were happy to be far away from the red earth of Georgia. They were happy to leave the United States behind them along with all of their troubles. Years of their lives had been lost, but the loss of all of the men in their family did not seem to weigh heavily on them here in this wonderful new world where wealth could isolate anyone from ugly reality.

When they had recovered from their drug induced coma, the Forresters were shocked to discover that it was1847. The lawyers had told the women that all their slaves had been freed through their emancipation of them by the Forresters themselves or by sale to owners who later freed them. As a result of the supposed slave sales, which Samuel financed himself and was the chief and only buyer, and the sales of the crops, and the plantation's profits, Samuel had banked a fortune for the estate during his tenure as manager. Mrs. Forrester had almost three hundred thousand dollars on deposit in gold in Atlanta. The sale of the plantation had netted her another seventy thousand. Margaret Forrester was a very wealthy woman by any standard.

After the sale at auction of all of the mansion's furnishings and fixtures and the farming tools and stock, Mrs. Forrester, Caroline, and Tilly made their escape from the county. Mrs. Forrester had also become at forty-seven, a very old woman in her views if not in her person. In fact, with the addition of twenty pounds of weight and a good rest, she appeared to be quite a pretty matron once again. In her worth day gowns she drew the admiring glances of all the men of fashion who were in the habit of strolling the boulevards.

As Violet, Mrs. Forrester's new and capable English lady's maid left the room, Margaret Forrester turned to her daughters and said, "What a pleasure to have a white girl to wait on you, dress your hair, and fetch and such. And that Violet is just so attentive and intelligent that I swear that I'll never have a colored servant girl again. A person is just not safe with them. Those people have no gratitude. I treated Helena so well, and she," her hand went involuntarily to the place where her brooch had been, "And Helena just took my, Oh, I just can't say it," and then she let her hand fall for a moment.

A few second's later her hand absently went back again to her neck and the place where the diamond and ruby brooch had been. She looked out of the window at the beautiful park setting beyond the balustrade that framed the lower portion of her window. She had never seen anything like the well manicured grass of the great parks before or the likes of the wonderful tree lined boulevards of Paris. All thoughts of the missing brooch were forgotten in that moment.

"Look at this girls. Atlanta never looked at all like this did it? Don't it seem exciting just to be here? Just look at how wide the streets are. Isn't it wonderful just to be in Paris? Isn't it wonderful to be away from that stupid God forsaken Georgia and all of those shallow people with their gossip and meaningless lives? God how I hated all that red dust!"

For just a moment, in the sunlit window, Margaret Forrester almost looked young again as her enthusiastic love of the French capital gave her a bit of color. "I wish that your dear father was here to share this moment with us. He had traveled quite a great deal in his youth. He told me about Africa and all that, but I'm sure that he never saw Paris. He would have loved it poor angel."

"Yes mama," replied Caroline who was looking over an English language guide book of Paris, and having just read some astounding facts, she looked up suddenly, and said, "Mama, do you know why these roads in the city are so wide?"

"No dear, I guess the French just like the way they look. They are so pretty. I think that these streets, pardon me, boulevards, are so majestic. Yes, I do think that the correct word would have to be majestic."

"No mama, that's not the reason at all. It seems that two revolutions began in Paris in less than sixty years, because of the oppression of the poor people, and when the people get upset with their king, they blocked off the streets and did a lot of shooting at the king's soldiers from behind barricades. They killed a goodly number of the king's men back in 1789, and they even chopped off the head of the king himself. He was named Louis XVI, and that was way back in 1789."

"Why child, that is shocking. Where did you ever get such a book?"

"I found it in the library back at home. It came all the way to England from Georgia, and now it is here with us in France. Now isn't that interesting? I brought it along, because I thought that it might come in handy since we were coming to Paris and all."

"Good heavens child, when did you ever begin reading such horrible stuff and nonsense. Believe me, your brothers never did any such thing as reading such shocking books!" Turning to her younger daughter, Mrs. Forrester asked, "Tilly, do you ever read books like that!"

Tilly marveled that her late brothers were now invested by their mother with any virtues at all. Then she thought that time and distance does heal after all. "Why of course I do. When a girl has nothing better to do, I guess she must read or go right out of her mind. I got tired of Mr. Dickens and those other serious folks. I began to read books about the real world of years ago just in case we ever got off that God forsaken old plantation. Personally, I'll always be grateful to Samuel and Pompey. Otherwise we would still be stuck there I declare. And say what you may with all we went through, but they left us rich. Now Caroline, what else has that old book got to say about this place," asked Tilly with glee.

"Tilly! I am shocked. How could you ever forgive those two monsters," moaned Mrs. Forrester.

"Wake up mother. If it wasn't for Samuel and Pompey, we'd be rusting away back in dreary old Georgia now instead of being in this beautiful city. Those missing years of our lives weren't that bad considering what might have happened to us in the hands of men who were not so fastidiously careful in the treatment of defenseless women held in their total subjugation. We didn't even know where we were for the most part, and when we got over the effects of the soothing syrup in two months time, it was just like having had a really bad cold with stomach upset. I was mad just like you, but when we found out that Samuel left us really rich, and that we could get out of Georgia, I was never so happy in my life," said Caroline. "Mother the thought of that dirty place with all of that awful heat, and red dirt all over the place, and having people around us as slaves, and those poor Black people hating us, and the county looking down their noses at us was awful. To stay in that place for the rest of our lives with nobody to visit or talk to was Hell mother."

"Why Caroline. Your language just surprises me so. And so do your feelings, but of course you are quite right my dear. I just didn't have the courage to see it that way. Did you feel like that too Tilly?"

"All I am going to say Mother is that I guess I did, but Caroline puts it so well. It's nice to have it said right out in the open. For the first time in my life I sort of feel free to say things myself I hardly ever dared to think before. I think that if I ever see Samuel and Pompey again, I am going to thank him for freeing us to come to Paris and letting us meet so many new people. Now Caroline, what is in that book that you haven't shared with me?" asked Tilly.

"Well, let's see. Oh here it is. Not only did those revolutionaries cut off the king's head, they cut off the queen's head too and the heads of about twenty thousand other people as well, because they were aristocrats or friends of aristocrats and were considered to be in cahoots with the king."

"Tilly! Caroline! After the revolution we went through back in Georgia, don't tell me anything else about these awful French," cried Mrs. Forrester. "I just couldn't abide another revolution of any kind."

"Did you know that they had another revolution over here almost eighteen years ago? That's when the king they have got now came to the throne. Yes, it says so right here. King Louis Philippe. That's his name, and he came right in 1830 to be the new king in what they call The July Revolution. They called it that because it happened in July I suppose."

"Whose head got chopped off then Caroline?" enthused Tilly warming up to the subject.

"Oh my God girls, no more please. My nerves are just raw. Where is my soothing medicine?" moaned Mrs. Forrester again.

"Oh mother, you don't need that. It seems that the King was driven out in 1830, a Mr. Charles the Tenth. In fact, it seems that he still lives in England. That is, unless he died since this book was written. But isn't that romantic? A king dying in exile! Or if he's still alive, we might get to meet him when we go to England. Now wouldn't that be something!"

"I don't think that we are going to meet any French kings in England or even in France," Mrs. Forrester opined.

"Oh don't say that mother. We might get to see one especially if there is another revolution and we can help him to escape getting his head cut off," purred Tilly with a dreamy far away look in her eyes.

"Tilly, don't say 'Getting his head cut off.' You are supposed to say de-cap-pit-ta-tion," corrected Caroline.

"No Caroline, You say it altogether like this, 'decapitation'. All the sounds get run together. Now doesn't that sound better?"

"Girls, please. There is nothing that can sound good about anybody getting their head chopped off, and I do think that after all of this foolish talk that I need my soothing syrup."

"Oh mother," said Tilly, "We are just having a little fun. Now let me see the book here Caroline dear. Ah yes, it seems that Charles X was the youngest brother of the King who was decapitated in 1792 and a cousin of the man who is King now. This Mr. Louis Philippe, the King's daddy, sided with the folks who cut off his kin, Louis XVI's head, but later he had his head cut off too. Now this is funny. They call the machine that actually cuts off all the heads, 'The National Razor '. Now isn't that just the funniest thing you ever heard?"

"Give me that book at once Tilly. These horrid French! Cutting off everybody's head! The very idea. They wouldn't do that sort of thing in England!" cried Mrs. Forrester.

Tilly half laughed, "I'm sorry mother, but I got ever so bored. I read a book about English history while Caroline was reading this one. It seems that they chopped off King Charles' head way back in the 1600's sometime, and Good Queen Bess before that cut off King Charles' granny's head. She was Mary Queen of Scots, and when they cut her head clean off, well after a lot of chops actually, the ax man picked it up by the hair so he could say right out loud, "Behold the head of a traitor," you know, like they do and all, and he picked up her head by the hair, and guess what?"

"What, what, what!" Caroline cried.

"Her head fell right out of the red wig she had been wearing right onto the floor, and her real hair was all thin and white just like an old lady, and her little dog crawled right out from under her skirt! That brave and loyal little lap dog followed his mistress right down to her last moment on earth. What devotion! You know, when she had her head hacked off so brutal like. Now isn't that romantic? I wish that I had a loyal little dog like that one," said Tilly with that dreamy eyed look of a romantic once again in her eyes.

Then returning to her subject and newfound knowledge of English history, Tilly said, "And that's not all. Other English kings died too. Edward the Second was killed by his wife and her lover, a man named Mortimer I think, or maybe it wasn't but no matter. This time they killed Edward II by sticking a red-hot poker up King Edward's bum and into his heart. Of course there are those who say that it was not a poker. Some say it was a very long marrowbone. By the way, do you know how the English say 'bum' instead of 'behind' so it don't sound common? Why they also say 'fundament' when they are talking about bums when they are being extra specially refined. Can you just fancy some high toned folks saying, 'There she is sitting on her fundament,' Now, I never thought that was very nice or romantic, but it is kind of funny. The English are a very funny people, but they have been around a long time and have a big empire. So it must be alright to talk funny the way they do."

"Tilly, I find this whole conversation to be both rude and shocking! I would not want Violet or anyone hearing us talking in such a vulgar way about our English cousins," moaned Mrs. Forrester.

Tilly in all her enthusiasm continued as if her mother had never spoken at all. "And Richard the Second was killed by his cousin who became King Henry the Fourth, and Mr. Shakespeare and his friend, Mr. Johnson, wrote plays about that too. Evil King Richard the Third killed his little nephew, Edward the Fifth, in that nasty old Tower of London. That was in Mr. Shakespeare's play about that bad old king Richard the Third. So mama, a lot of English kings and one Scottish queen got themselves killed by the ax man or some other way, that is if you don't count the two queens that were just wives of a king, Mr. Henry the Eighth, who were decapitated by their husband. Henry the Eighth was a bad king, but like I say they weren't real queens, the ones he killed I mean. They were just queen consorts, which means that they didn't get to rule or even chop off any heads of their own unless they could get their husband to go along with it too. That would be like when Queen Anne Boleyn got King Henry VIII to chop off Sir Thomas More's head, because Sir Thomas just didn't like her. Now I don't think that would be as much fun as being able to have heads chopped off whenever you wanted them to be done to people that you don't like, would it mama?" said Tilly now more animated as she thought of a catalog of candidates for decapitation.

"You young ladies are going to be the death of me. Proper young ladies don't waste much time reading books like that about people getting all chopped up and such. You should have better things to do with you time like needlework," replied Mrs. Forrester sternly.

"Well for land's sakes," squealed Caroline with some exasperation, "With daddy disgracing the family by cheating all the best folks in the county at cards, and the boys getting thrown out of West Point and getting young girls in trouble, and all that scandal about those years when we were God knows where, what would you have us do? Reading was all we had. We couldn't sew or play cards all the time. And now we kind of enjoy it. In fact, once you can sound out all the hard words, it's really sort of fun to read about all of those strange people who lived a long time ago and live now too. You can imagine it all like a play and see the people all acting out their parts in your head. In fact we kind of like reading when you can get the right sort of books to read that is. You know, the exciting kind! Isn't that right Tilly?"

Tilly nodded her head and added, "Now that you know about all of those revolts in Paris you can understand why these roads are so wide mama, and besides Mr. Balcome says that all our misfortunes were caused by the fact that we had slaves. He told Caroline and me that owning slaves was a big sin, almost the biggest sin there is, and that we are all going to be punished for it if we do not see the light and repent. He said that we were very fortunate to get out of Georgia and let most of our slaves go, even though I don't rightly know exactly when we did that. But he said that we did it just in time before the judgment of the lord was visited on us and the whole state too."

Mrs. Forrester fell back into her chair, "Where ever did you hear such foolish talk young lady. I demand to know and know now!"

"It's nothing of the sort mama. I am twenty-seven years of age and Tilly is twenty-six. We certainly have the right to form our own opinions. Isn't that right Tilly?"

"Well Caroline I should say we do and so does Mr. Balcome," said Tilly with an air of certitude that had passed unnoticed before by the thoroughly befuddled Mrs. Forrester who found that she could not keep up with all the changes in her new and confused life.

Mrs. Forrester drew herself up, pulled her shattered sensibilities together, and asked, "Just who the Devil is this Mr. Balcome person whose opinions are so highly regarded?"

"You might as well know it now mother. Tilly and I met the Balcomes on the ship coming over here. That was mostly when you were so sick in your cabin with the *mal de mer.* They asked us to dine with them at their table. Their whole family is along on a grand European tour. It's the third time for Mr. Balcome's parents and aunt and the second time for the younger Balcome's and their cousins. You know mother. They speak French and German. They are ever so smart and know everybody worth knowing in New England and even in New York and Philadelphia too. All of the Balcome men were graduated from Harvard! They even invited us all to their estates when we return to Boston. By the way, Tilly and I intend to settle in Boston. We have met ever so many nice people of the better sort on the voyage over here. I am so pleased that Judge Darby told us to go to Boston and then go by packet to Europe from a northern port. Otherwise we could not have grown to know this fine family and form such warm friendships. They are so fascinated by the fact that we freed all of our slaves and decided to move North. They even said that there was hope for us. Now isn't it just the limit mother!" Caroline enthused with delight.

Mrs. Forrester turned quite pale. "No daughters of my flesh are going to be with Yankees. Please God, not abolitionist Yankees," Mrs. Forrester almost cried.

"Why mother, he is the Rev. Mr. Balcome of Boston. He is a highly respected member of the best of Boston society, and a graduate of Harvard College, and he is traveling over here with his whole very wealthy family, a fact that I will never mention again, because to do so would be in the very worst taste and reflect very poor breeding. Now Caroline and I have not decided which one of us is going to marry him, but I suppose it should be Caroline, because she is older after all. Time is running out for you dear," said Tilly almost sadly.

Caroline nodded her head with an almost sweet and angelic smile playing about her lips. Then Tilly went on, "And I can always get one of the Balcome cousins I suppose. Perhaps one of the Phillips, or Cabots, or even a Lodge. They are all handsome, well spoken, very rich too, and ever so well connected. They are the cream of real Boston society. And don't forget that Boston was settled one hundred and three years before Georgia. And Boston was not founded by a bunch of low convicts who owed people a lot of money either."

"You would degrade yourself and marry a Yankee!" shrieked Mrs. Forrester, "An Abolitionist!"

"Mother please. In the North, all of the best people are Congregationalists, Episcopalians, or Unitarians. They are all abolitionists, and if we want to fit in, we must be abolitionists as well. It's a very good thing that Caroline and I kept our looks through our horrible experience. That experience which makes us unmarriageable in Georgia makes us most desirable in Boston. I am happy to say that we are very desirable in the North. Let us face the facts mama dearest this is the best that we can hope for a good marriage unless you would rather marry us off to a couple of Georgian dirt farmers, because that is what we have been reduced to. These gentlemen offer a decent way out of the whole marriage dilemma. So, you had better make up your mind to go along with it. In a few days, we shall have these fine society men as gentlemen callers, Yankee gentlemen callers, and you will behave mama, and be everything good that a real southern lady of quality should be for your sake as well as ours. Just remember we can a tale tell that you do not want told. And rest assured that we are firm in this. We intend to be good Yankee wives even if we have to become abolitionists as well. All the best people in Boston are abolitionists. Caroline and I have made up our minds to do this, and there is no turning us around. So learn to accept our wishes. We are of age mama and can wed as we please. It is, after all is said and done, the only road to real respectability," said Tilly in a voice reflecting her newly discovered will.

For the first time in her life, Margaret Forrester saw her daughters as they were with wills of iron much like her own and possessed of the grit of true survivors. She felt a sort of pride in her girls and sadness that her sons James and Douglas had not shared that grit. In fact, it was the first time that Margaret Forrester felt any sadness for Douglas and James. It would take some getting used to, but Caroline and Tilly did seem to make as much sense in their thinking as anything had during the last six years. In fact, for the first time in the years since Mr. Forrester had been exposed as a cheat, something less than a gentleman, and taken from her, Mrs. Forrester felt some relief. She looked at the girls with resignation, and said, "That's right my darlings. You decide what is best. I trust that you will do the smart thing in the end. Mother must rest now. I hope and believe that you can make very good marriages. Of course we can never go back to the South again. I will do my best to be charming to your Yankee gentlemen. Georgia is gone forever."

"That mother dear," said Tilly, "Will be no loss to us at all.

Mr. Balcome has a fine yacht, and he likes to sail to Bermuda. He said that beautiful island would put most of the South to shame."

"Shall we help you to your room mother, or should we have Violet take you in to rest?" asked Caroline.

"Yes, call Violet. I can sleep well now. Kiss me darlings. You are really very clever girls you know. I think that your father would have been proud of you. I wish that your brothers had half of your salt. Poor James, poor Douglas. I just know everything is going to be alright from now on. But, Oh my God. Yankees! That is going to take some getting used to. Now you did say that they were at least rich and in society?"

"Yes mother. And they are very handsome besides. Please don't mention money again. As the French say, 'It's just so de classy,' or something French like that," lectured Caroline.

Ten minutes later, Mrs. Forrester was settled into her bed, "Violet dear, fluff up the pillows and bring me that book that my daughters were reading. Ask them if I can borrow it. Now that's a dear."

The English maid was taken aback by the familiar little American pleasantries, but she was beginning to warm to them, "Yes mum," she said and went out to do her mistress's bidding. "And tomorrow I'm going to find out about living in the country." To Hell with Paris and the bloodthirsty revolutionary riffraff," thought Mrs. Forrester. Then she smiled to herself and fell to sleep before she had a chance to read a word of the book that Violet had gone to fetch for her.

CHAPTER XXIII

The ship was about on its beam-ends with its sails ripped away and making heavy seas under bare poles. "I've not seen it rougher Captain," bellowed Starbuck to Whitehouse, "Should we cut down the masts sir?"

"If we do that Mr. Starbuck, we may not be able to keep her from being turned and crushed by the waves. Get the new mains aloft, and keep her headed into the wind. Make sure that the hatches are not leaking, and set every man you have to the pumps."

"Aye, aye sir."

Starbuck was a good man in a fight, be it with thugs, and wharf rats, or the sea itself. For the next three days, the ship fought for her life. No man slept. The slaves in the hold alternately cried softly, vomited, set up a mournful howl, or made no noise at all. This storm was another phase of their own personal Hell as they headed even further away from Africa on their journey to the slave hungry Americas. Their waste accumulated as every hand was engaged in the working of the ship. They were hardly fed. The dignity they had formerly enjoyed in their villages had been stripped from them, as had the very essence of their humanity by their enslavement. Now their lives were threatened by a force they had never dreamed of. None of them ever had experienced a storm at sea of any kind. This grandfather of all typhoons was a baptism of fire. The slaves could see nothing of the great fingers of the ocean that were tossing them about as they were confined cheek by jowl in the black pit of what had become their own private Hell in the belly of the ship taking them to a life of damnation. The ship tossed them like dolls, and jerked them roughly in their chains.

But by the sheer force of the Captain's will and superb handling of the ship, the canvas was kept aloft this time, and the voyage continued. After what seemed an age rather than days, the winds abated. At last at the coming of a blessed dawn, the seas became flat, and all remaining on the deck could see a sun filled morning under a blue sky and with a fair sea. Captain Whitehouse looked skyward, then checked the compass in its binnacle, and called Starbuck to the quarterdeck, "As soon as you are able Mr. Starbuck, I want a damage report."

"Right now Captain, I can tell you that the men are pretty beaten up and dead on their feet sir. I think that two were lost overboard, one killed by a falling spar, and we have two with broken arms."

"How many fit for duty Starbuck?"

"We were lucky there. I think about thirty seven men more or less."

"Make up a first watch of the fittest. Get new canvas aloft. Feed the rest, and send them to their bunks. We are making sail for Rio. I want all the rest in their bunks resting as long as possible. Tell the cook to fire up the galley and to make as much porridge as it will take to fill this crew's hunger for something hot. See if Mr. Ellis is in his cabin, and bring him to me as soon as you can."

"Aye, aye sir. As you wish sir."

"And Mr. Starbuck. Take five of the strongest men and see to the cargo. Feed those bastards. We will want to get them on deck as soon as we can, and clean their quarters and themselves. I want no boils or festering sores on their skin. Take care of any serious cases of illness now. Now see to it Mr. Starbuck."

"Aye, aye sir," said the mate. Starbuck went on down the deck giving orders in quick succession. The men of the first watch jumped to, and the rest went to their bunks. A few minutes passed, and the ship's boy approached Whitehouse with a noggin of grog. "Pardon me sir. Cook said that this would have to do until the fires are lighted. He says that I was to tell you that the galley has to be put right, and that he and myself will work without rest until it's in order and working sir."

"Thank you boy and give my best regards to the cook. Tell him that I appreciate both of your efforts."

"Aye sir," said the boy pleased that the Captain had been so agreeable with him. Away he padded back to the galley on his sea washed bare feet."

The Captain looked back at the boy walking away with that rolling gait that sailors develop just to stay upright on a moving ship. He tried to remember what life aboard ship had been like for him in that long time ago when he was but twelve years old and a cabin boy at sea for the first time. It was getting harder to remember. It wasn't on a slave ship that he had spent those early years until he was eighteen and a bearded man of the world. By the time he was twenty-one, he was a captain. Whitehouse reflected that he liked the lad and resolved to place the orphaned boy on a merchant vessel in an American, British, or Brazilian port as soon as he was able.

Whitehouse then laughed at himself thinking about this impulse to do something decent for a change like giving this cabin boy a new start in life. He shook his head because of the warm feeling that doing something good gave him. "I must be going soft in my old age," he quietly remarked to himself. Whitehouse was growing tired of the trade, and after this horrific storm, he knew that his age was overtaking him. He knew that he was an excellent sailor. He also knew that he was a dead man on his feet after these four days of fighting the storm. All he knew is that now he wanted to swallow the anchor and enjoy time ashore while there was yet some time left. A clomping of footsteps brought Whitehouse out of his musings along with a plaintive voice that went with the footsteps.

"Your mate dragged me from the comfort of my cabin. What in damnation do you want to see me for now? Can't you see I'm sick as Hell? I cannot begin to tell you how much I want to be off this damned ship!" cried Ellis in a plaintive roar.

"My dear Mr. Ellis, it is with the greatest pleasure that I oblige you," said Whitehouse with a voice of assumed civility. With a movement so fast, the Captain grabbed Ellis around his knees, lifted him into the air and threw him overboard. The whole action was of less than a second's duration. The only man to see the supercargo go overboard was Starbuck who was just coming up the gangway at that moment to update the Captain on what had been done to set the ship right again. The look of shock on Starbuck's scar crossed face spoke volumes about what was going on in his head at the sight of the Captain's action. The Captain looked upon Starbuck's reaction to Ellis' abrupt departure from the ship.

Whitehouse smiled and said, "Mr. Starbuck, when I enter the events of the storm into the log, I'll have to amend your report. It now seems that three men were lost overboard in the storm including the poor brave Mr. Ellis. I can now honestly report that you yourself saw him swept over the side by the irresistible force of the waves."

"Aye sir," said the mate. "Not that I was looking for the job mind, but didn't you want me to see to Mr. Ellis myself Captain?"

"Thank you Mr. Starbuck. That is very kind of you. I did want you to take care of that little task for me, but sometimes I just get a notion to do something to remind me that I'm not yet too old to see to a few small personal details myself. And as it happened, I just had an urge to toss the sodding bastard overboard. The sound of his voice was grating on my nerves, and after that blast of weather we went through, I had just had enough of Mr. Ellis. I hope that you forgive the impulse. I know that you were looking forward to doing the job yourself. By the by Mr. Starbuck, as the poor fellow went overboard he told me that he wanted you to have his watch and anything else of his property that he may have left in his cabin that you might fancy. Come to think of it Mr. Starbuck, you are about the same size as our late friend. Maybe you should take the man's clothes and see that some use is gotten out of them. I know that as a good Quaker that you hate to see waste. All I want of Mr. Ellis' belongings is that little serving man of his for myself. Send him to me so that I can inform him of his new duties."

"Aye sir," replied Starbuck. "He'll be along shortly sir." .

"And Mr. Starbuck, did you check the cargo as I instructed, and make sure that it is secure. And see that our 387 guests below decks are calmed down? See the cook and make sure that the cargo is fed as soon as things permit. Muster some men from the watch and see that the cargo area is cleaned up as well as it can be done until a better job can be made of it tomorrow. You are in charge of the deck Mr. Starbuck. I must go below for a bit. I will try to relieve you as soon as I can, but I will confess to you that I am spent."

"Aye aye Captain," replied the mate as the Captain left the deck.

Captain Whitehouse knew that he could not sleep for more than a few hours no matter how long he had been awake. The time would pass too quickly and his mind would continue to work the ship even in his sleep. But he would think of his beautiful new life and home in Rio that would be his new reality after he had quit this horrible business as well. Then having done a good job of work according to his lights, Whitehouse went down to his cabin and fell onto his bunk. He fell to sleep with no more thought to the men and women chained together not a few feet from where he slept. Only the actual working of the ship now intruded into his dreams. It was well that the ship swam safely after its great trial. The Captain's sleep lasted two hours only. He was awakened by the general activity of the ship. Whitehouse stretched and yawned. As he looked around the cabin his eye fell on the person of a young man of color sleeping on the upholstered seat that ran along the shelf under the stern windows. Whitehouse looked to make sure that he was seeing what he was seeing. The little man was quite naked.

"What the Hell are you doing there boy!" roared the Captain. "Stand up damn your eyes! Who the blazes are you?"

The little fellow bounded to his feet and stood almost at attention. He was about five feet tall and of such proportion as to look as if he was made by a manufacturer of elfin garden fixtures. He seemed afraid to speak. It was clear to see that he had never been whipped or abused in any way that left any scarring. "Well who the deuce are you boy," asked Whitehouse in a gentler tone.

The boy's eyes fluttered, and he replied, "I am Ajax. I was the free man in service to Mr. Ellis. Your Mr. Starbuck told me to come here and serve you as I did Mr. Ellis."

It was all coming back to Whitehouse now as his sleep fogged brain cleared. "I thought that you looked after Mr. Ellis' things and kept his clothes in order. Why in Hell are you naked boy," asked the Captain smiling to himself.

The pretty little doll-like man smiled timidly and replied, "Mr. Ellis liked me to work this way."

"Why in Hell does that not surprise me? What else did you do for the late Mr. Ellis Ajax, that is when you were finished with your other chores?"

"Ajax smiled and lowered his eyes, and said, "Other things. Things I could do for you Captain if you would like me to," replied the little man.

"Well why don't you just show me what you can do that might be all that interesting. Come on over here and just do what you do," replied Whitehouse reclining back on his pillows in his bunk.

Ajax went to the Captain's bunk and obliged him. After the passage of some hours of distraction, the Captain leaned back onto his pillows again quite relaxed and smiled. "That was different Ajax. Now would you be so kind as to put on something and go fetch me some hot coffee from the galley. I want it black and strong."

"Yes my Captain. It will be strong just like you," said the little man as he pulled on his trousers, and went off to do Whitehouse's bidding gently shutting the door behind him.

Whitehouse lit a cigar and puffed mightily thinking it would be hard to sell the pretty little fellow unless he got a huge price for him, and then a thought came to him, "Why do I have to sell him at all? With Ellis dead and little Ajax willing to curl up his body next to anyone who was kind to him and who could protect him there was no reason to sell him at all.

Five minutes later, Whitehouse heard the patter of Ajax's feet as he approached the cabin door. There was a soft knock, then the door was opened by the little man with a mug of steaming coffee. Whitehouse took it and sipped gingerly. Ajax began removing his trousers when Whitehouse ordered, "Ajax, fetch Mr. Starbuck, and be so kind as to put on your shirt as well. We don't want to shock the poor Quaker. Tell him that I want to see him as quickly as it is practical for him to come here. Now be off with you boy, and report back."

"Yes my Captain," said the smiling Ajax as he slipped into his shirt and went off in search of Starbuck.

The Captain pulled a blanket about his naked body and paced the decking of his large cabin as he stroked his beard. He noticed that his clothes that he had thrown onto the deck when he first turned in were drying over a rack, and the rest of his things had been brushed and carefully put away. Then he shook his head and returned to his deeper thoughts. At last Ajax returned to the cabin, "Mr. Starbuck sends his compliments and says that he will come as soon as he can in a little while. He apologizes that the ship demands his attention."

"Very good Ajax. Now I want you to be a good fellow and inform the doctor who is in the cabin next to this one that you are now working for me, and I would take it kindly if he would take Mr. Ellis' cabin, because you are moving in to his to take up your new duties here. Is that understood Ajax?" ordered Whitehouse with a knowing smile.

"Your orders are my pleasure my Captain," said Ajax with a smile.

"Then be off with you lad, and take your time in moving the doctor and your own things, and for God's sake put on your boots. You don't want to do yourself an injury boy."

"My Captain is very thoughtful of his humble servant," cooed Ajax.

At that moment Starbuck knocked at the door. Ajax opened it, "It is Mr. Starbuck Sir."

"Very good Ajax," said the Captain adjusting his blanket, "Now run along and take care of those matters."

Starbuck looked at Whitehouse and smiled, "I am sorry I was delayed. Does your new servant please you sir?"

"Yes Mr. Starbuck. He does very much. It's not quite like a woman, but near enough I assure you. You can see for yourself if you wish, but I'm not sharing him with anyone else."

"He's all yours sir. He is of no interest to me in any capacity of that kind. In the absence of a white woman for this year past, I understand your needs in this, but it is not to my taste sir. I thank you all the same."

"You should have been a diplomat Starbuck. How well you decline a buggering of a very soft and pretty piece. How do you feel about returning to Nantucket as I suggested before?"

"I would like it well, but I do not have what I calculated as enough saved yet Captain."

"Mr. Starbuck, there are 387 bucks on this ship in first class condition because of the practices we have put into operation. Their value in Brazil is at least seven hundred thousand to nine hundred thousand dollars. Along with what we have banked most of that could be ours. Only the doctor and Ajax are from the northern part of the United States. Most of my crew is southern or English with a smattering of Europeans from a dozen or more places. It is highly unlikely that the Five Points crowd would encounter any of them if I leave them rich in Brazil. And the sodding New York bastards won't see you tucked away on your island."

"What are you getting at Captain?" asked Starbuck as he too felt some degree of excitement.

"What would you say if I told you that our dear ship, *The Sea Hound* was lost during one of the worst storms in history, in spite of my magnificent handling of the ship. Let us say that it was lost with all hands save one, and that one fellow is yourself?" smiled Whitehouse like the fox that he was.

"Go on sir. Your plan is drawing me in. I would like to hear more," said the mate in a tone not unfriendly to the idea.

"Well it's like this. The poor doctor, who likes to drink too much, is going to have a fatal fall down the companionway as soon as I no longer need him. That will give us more money and keep the good doctor from going home and telling tales. I know your scruples Mr. Starbuck, and I can arrange that small accident myself. You will in no way be involved in his misadventure. We will set you adrift as the lone survivor at the right time. I can pay you off with what I have on the ship. There is seventy two thousand dollars I have held back from Ellis as well as the funds that Ellis was holding. And there is money that I have hoarded myself over the years. Most of it is in twenty pound notes issued by the Bank of England. These, as you know, are negotiable anywhere. I also have eighteen thousand dollars in gold. All of it will be for you."

"That will be most handsome of you sir," replied the mate.

Whitehouse held up his hand and said, "I'll drop you somewhere in a sizable port to do your banking. Then it's back to the sea-lanes with you. In a few days you will be rescued and you will tell of being afloat as the only survivor of the unfortunate *Sea*

Hound. You'll have empty tins of boat stores about you from the boat's stores, and you will tell how you fell into a boat and struck your head when the boat broke away from the ship during the storm. Then you will say that you were rendered senseless by a blow to the head. I see even from here that you have such a lump now on your head. No doubt a souvenir of the late storm. You can expand the story as needs be. There will be none to contradict you."

"You seem to have thought of everything Captain," said Starbuck.

"Not altogether. It was a sort of inspiration. I'll keep Ajax for myself for good luck I think. Now the rest of the crew will not be a problem. Ajax will never return to New York. I'll pay off the men in Rio. They can either return to England or wherever the Hell they came from. There will be those who might choose a life in Brazil. Those who don't choose to take the money and keep their mouths shut, will join Mr. Ellis and the doctor. Now what do you say to that Mr. Starbuck?"

Starbuck held out his hand, which Whitehouse shook with a mighty stock of goodwill by way of an answer. Ajax came into the cabin.

"I apologize my Captain for not knocking. Shall I go back to my work sir? Is there anything I can do for you?" smiled the little man.

"Thank you Mr. Starbuck. I'll take the deck in three hours time. Please see that I am not disturbed by anything."

"Aye Captain," saluted Starbuck with an exaggerated air and left smiling closing the door behind him.

Ajax was already naked and anxious to please. Whitehouse reclined on his bunk took the little man in his arms and rolled him over onto his side. The little fellow lay with his back tightly pressed against the Captain's chest happy that the Captain only wished to sleep. Whitehouse thought as he wrapped his arms around the little man, "When he's like this, he's just like a woman."

CHAPTER XXIV

The gentlemen who Captain Beers had met on the cars had let him know that they were staying at the estate of Sir Richard Harrison of Harrison Hall. Two days later the Harrison carriage made its way up the long drive to Hatton Hall. This sixteenth century pile of fabulous Elizabethan stone had been altered some sixty years ago into something resembling a fine Georgian manor house. Miss Sally Beers had chosen the place because it reminded her of so many of the stately homes she had admired in her youth. At last the carriage pulled in under the porte cochere where Captain Beer's guests alighted. The Captain greeted them himself and led them into the house where the butler took their hats, which he then deposited on the center hall table. Captain Beers then whisked the gentlemen into the drawing room and introduced the M.P.'s, who had been his train mates into the Westmorland country, to his sister and her guest Don Raphael de Ruiz. Don Raphael's serving man, Samuel as Cabral, stood behind his chair as Don Raphael resumed his seat and smiled at the two very British gentlemen who sat as members in the House of Commons. Mr. Gladstone had inclined his large and increasingly well known head over the dainty hand of Miss Sally on his arrival and expressed his pleasure for being invited to afternoon tea. Mr. Gladstone had been caricatured in *Punch* since his maiden speech in the House of Commons. His face and the large head to which it was attached was often an object of fierce political satire. Mr. Disraeli had smiled a smile not unlike that of the Mona Lisa as he inclined his handsome and inscrutable face over that self same tiny hand.

"I am pleased that you gentlemen can join us on this lovely afternoon," said Miss Sally in response to the gestures. "My brother has told me that you are in the government here. As an American, I find that most fascinating, that is meeting with gentlemen who are at the center of things in the most powerful nation on earth. Now that must be a pretty heady experience for the both of you."

"Well we are not quite as exalted as that ma'am," intoned Mr. Gladstone as if he were addressing a rally of voters or the congregation of a Baptist meeting. "We are rather the party workhorses and mere members of the Commons. We are but one step above backbenchers actually. I find it refreshing that a young woman like yourself is interested in the sometimes sordid world of politics."

"I tell you Mr. Gladstone that all things are interesting to me not the least of which is literature. I find the novels of Mr. Disraeli most fascinating. They deal with the real lives of ordinary people not just the doings of the rich. They speak of the trials they face in making a living and in fact staying alive. In many ways, your books compare most favorably with those of Mr. Charles Dickens. I understand that even the Queen reads your books Mr. Disraeli. Now I do find that mighty interesting."

"I am most flattered Miss Beers that you have read my efforts and that they seem to meet with your approval. What do you think about the poverty in your own country Miss Beers?"

"Why Mr. Disraeli, it is true that there are some poor people in my country, but most people can farm and eat on a regular basis as a result of working the land or seeking regular employment. If they have ambition, they can travel to the west and open new lands to farming. In other words they can become landowners themselves. Many men and even some women open businesses of various sorts. As you know American ships sail all the world's oceans in trade with Europe and China chiefly. My country is growing, and we need a workforce. People tend not to go hungry unless the harvests are awfully poor or they are very lazy. There is some poverty in the northern cities where people tend to work in mills and a lot of immigrants have made landing without providing for their futures in advance of their arrivals, but that is not so bad as more new and younger people, as I said, tend to farm in the West if they have the drive. In the near future, I should think that even millions of settlers will build a civilization over the waters of the Mississippi and go on even to California. As this war with Mexico progresses it would seem to be the way of things. And as I said, there are many merchants who do quite well, and shipping of goods is a source of wealth. And as I suggested, we are opening the western lands to more settlement. After this war is over, there will be millions of acres open to settlement. We have a very big country sir with room for a great many people. We have a great deal of room to grow in without reaching deeply into Asia or Africa over the seas in order to build an empire."

"Well answered," nodded Mr. Gladstone with profound approval and admiration for this woman who seemed to understand the human condition and her native country so well. "But are your cities not centers of vice? I have heard that such industrial centers as Providence in Rhode Island and Boston in Massachusetts sadly have many houses of ill repute and women who freely walk the streets selling themselves."

"Please excuse my friend, Mr. Gladstone. He is inflicted with that most horrible condition namely 'World Saving Ambition'. He really should have been a missionary minister," laughed Mr. Disraeli.

"My sister is hardly shocked by Mr. Gladstone's frankness Mr. Disraeli. She is a wise woman who knows the human condition well. She has, after all, read your books," said Captain Beers.

"Well said brother,' laughed Sally. "We women are not immune to the knowledge of the shortcomings of the world, and although we may deplore some of the evils that exist there, we are realists after all. Have we not ruled you men since Eve?"

"Miss Beers, I find your conversation most refreshing. You are nothing like any other American woman I have ever met, or any English women either," replied Disraeli.

"I think that it is unfortunate that a woman of your intelligence and fine sensibilities must even know of such beastly things This only shows how depraved the world has become when a virginal vessel of womanly virtue such as yourself Miss Beers must hear such stuff in your very own drawing room. Many a lady of your obvious refinement would swoon to hear such talk," expounded Gladstone.

"Mr. Gladstone, have you read Gibbons or Suetonius?" asked Miss Sally. "Depravity is something that has always been with us since ancient times. I do not like the hypocrisy that we of the fair sex are innocent of knowledge of the world. Actually when you think of it, wouldn't that just make women stupid to know nothing? That which we view with moral outrage, the Romans would but smile at. Then they would have turned images of their debauchery into a wall mural for one of their principal rooms. Isn't that what they are discovering now in Italy with the diggings at Pompeii? There is nothing new about depravity at all. Each generation thinks of itself as more wicked than the last, because wickedness is personally discovered by each new generation in its turn you see. As Shakespeare says, there is nothing new under the sun. The *Bible* tale of Sodom and Gomorrah also attests that the ancients were thinking about depravity in all of its infinite variety almost all the time even when they were writing the *Bible*. And as you may recall, in that part of the *Bible* there are quite a lot of various kinds of depravity that I had to have my daddy explain to me. Now when he tried to answer my questions, he blushed, and he suggested that the pastor of our church should tell me what I wanted to know, and when the pastor failed me, I discovered that the best scholar on the subject was my cook. Now she knew a lot about the *Bible*," said Miss Sally.

"I really don't know what to say. You astound me," said Gladstone.

"Why Mr. Gladstone, I was just amazed to discover that men could have so much fun together like that back in Sodom, and that Lot had offered his very own virgin daughters to that mob so that they would not rape the angels, I was just shocked! And just think of it. Lot was the only good man that could be found in not one but two cities. It really makes one think now doesn't it? Whether these *Biblical* figures actually existed or not as real historical beings, we don't know. And as for urban centers as centers of vice and depravity, your own London scandalizes Paris. It is said almost everywhere that nine out of every ten births in London are born to women who are unwed. Is that not so sir? Now maybe you can tell me something Mr. Gladstone since you know so much about the *Bible,* after Lot's wife turned into a pillar of salt, and his two daughters got him drunk and had sexual congress with him do you suppose that…"

"I think that you should ask your spiritual adviser about that Miss Beers," said Gladstone quickly as his face turned even redder.

Pompey saved him by asking, "What about London's great rate of illegitimacy?"

"It is true that many fallen women do live in the capital, but I do not think us a modern Sodom and Gomorrah. One thing is true, and that is that we must never question whether these cities existed or not. On that point, I must protest sir because the *Holy Bible* is the incontrovertible truth and word of God. We mortals cannot challenge it," Gladstone expounded with some force.

With his most insouciant smile playing about his lips, Disraeli said, "I'm afraid that my good friend Mr. Gladstone takes the *Old Testament* quite literally. Your ideas in the area of theology are too radically modern, and advanced for his taste."

The fact that Disraeli was enjoying his friend's discomfort

was not lost on Miss Sally. As she raised her cup of tea to her lips, Mr. Gladstone expounded, "My dear Mr. Disraeli, the truth of the *Bible* is not a subject of light speculation. The holy word is what the holy word is, is it not? Is it not the inspired word of The Almighty himself?"

"My Dear Mr. Gladstone, is it not true sir that the original sin of Sodom and Gomorrah which was being punished was that of sexual abomination of a homoerotic nature? Is this sin not to this day called sodomy? And is it not true that the Greeks, in all of their advanced city-states, practiced homoerotic love without guilt? Why then did God not destroy all of the Greeks who practiced homoerotic love at once instead of allowing them to exist for thousands of years down to the present day?" asked Pompey still playing the part of Senor Ruiz.

"God's ways are strange, and he does not have to answer to us for what he does," replied Gladstone. "And besides that," Gladstone added, "For almost four centuries the Greeks were under the heel of the Turks. Now isn't that punishment enough for any sinning nation?"

"Yes, but as you will no doubt recall from your school days, the Turks came into Constantinople on May 29, 1453. That was a long time after the Socratic Greeks were taking their pleasure with young boys Gladstone. But do not let anything so mundane as factual events get in the way of a good Biblical story," quipped Disraeli much to the consternation of Gladstone.

"Do not reproach God Benjamin. That is sacrilege!" snapped Gladstone.

"I would say that God has a great deal to answer for. He seems to discriminate against the poor Sodomites while leaving the Greeks and the Romans to their fun and games. And about the question of slavery, how could any rational God worth his salt allow human slavery to exist in this modern age of Christian enlightenment? Not only that, but he even justifies it by his punishment of Ham and his children. And not only that, but in Miss Beer's United States, where I have been a guest, slavery abounds. And they claim to be a Christian nation. Even now, the United States is fighting a war, which they have provoked with their neighbor Mexico for the express purpose of stealing the northern portion of their neighbor's country to extend slavery to places where it does now not exist. Do you not feel that slavery will in time be extended to those newly conquered areas with the blessing of law? Not to think so would be rather naive. So Mr. Gladstone, why isn't God doing something about that?" said Pompey in a flat and emotionless voice as if he had asked if rain were expected in the afternoon.

"I do not think that I would have missed this discussion for all the world and the riches in it," said Disraeli whose smile was now far from insouciant. "My dear Gladstone, as God's greatest spokesman on earth, how do you answer that well stated charge as presented against The Almighty?"

"For God's sake Disraeli, don't encourage this blatant disrespect for the Lord. Do you really wish a bolt of lightning to come crashing down on the house of our hostess? Maybe we should all change the discussion and avoid the retribution visited on poor old Sodom and Gomorrah," said Gladstone with something of a twinkle in his own eye. "In fact, does anyone feel a tremor underfoot?"

"Maybe I'm having a good influence on you after all," said Disraeli to his friend. "I find your answer almost funny."

"My poor Disraeli, I am afraid that you are beyond hope of any redemption. In fact, I am quite sure that you will either die upon the gallows or of some loathsome disease, and frankly sir these are two fates I would really like not to share with you," rejoined Gladstone.

"My fate all depends sir," retorted Disraeli, "As to whether I embrace your politics or your mistress."

"Now that is what I call real interesting political discourse gentlemen. You seem to understand the human condition far better than most of the men I have met on either side of the Atlantic," laughed Miss Sally.

"Miss Beers you do amaze me. I hope that this will not be the last time I may call on you for such enlightened discussion," enthused Disraeli.

"All of you gentlemen provide such a refreshing change of pace from my poor humdrum life here in the country. All we seem to talk about is crops and the seasonal patterns of the weather. I am so happy that my brother met you on the cars, and that you asked to visit us here for an honest to God discussion of some real ideas."

"Is that what you call the train in America? The cars?" asked Gladstone.

"Well there is the locomotive thing which pulls the cars in which we ride, that is when they don't catch on fire from cinders landing on the roof and not quite extinguished. And that does not happen so often as it once did I am happy to report," she replied.

"When I was in London," said Captain Beers, "I went into a bookshop and saw a rather amusing print. I do not exactly recall the name of the fellow who engraved it, but I think that it was called 'Hyde Park as it Will Be'. It pictured a lot of people riding little locomotive engines all over the place like horses. I think that someday something of its like might just be possible."

"The author of that print is a fellow called Leech I believe. And trust me, something like that certainly will be possible in time," said Disraeli.

"But is it desirable?" Gladstone intoned. "I think that people are too fond of luxury and speed now. People travel far too fast as it is, and do we need all the filth that these engines will emit?"

"Maybe people of our class travel at an accelerated rate of speed my dear William, but a man, or woman for that matter, who works ten or twelve hours or more a day in some industrial manufactury might not agree with you. Farm laborers pulling their forelocks to their 'betters' may not agree with you either. I think that working people know very little of luxury William. And what is wrong with a laboring man taking himself and his family on a little weekend journey to say Brighton to look upon the sea or even to venture to bathe in it?" asked Disraeli.

"Do you gentlemen know what hours that slaves work in the United States?" asked Pompey.

"Exactly what are those hours Mr. Ruiz?" asked Disraeli.

"They work from can to can't."

"And just how long would that be?" asked Gladstone.

"That would be from can to can't see. That is before sunrise until after sunset. Those are the hours of slavery in America. In the torrid heat of a day in Georgia in the summertime, that day is very long indeed. It is in fact fifteen to sixteen hours in length. The rest of the time, slaves are allowed to see to the making of their own meals, the bedding down of their children who have been in the care of an old slave woman who feeds them like pigs, using a troth, and beats them when they cry or just when she feels like beating them. She may set them to doing any tasks that she thinks that they should have to undertake. At the age of seven, the children go to the fields even if it's to do nothing more than picking up little stones just to get the feel and habit of being there to labor during those hours of a slave's workday. Gradually these little ones find themselves working too. It's a wonderful life for a child is it not? And the rewards are not low wages, for they get nothing at all in the way of money, but often beatings. They have even been known to be worked to death."

"That is truly a sad tale," said Disraeli.

"Ha! But that's just it you see. It's not merely a sad tale Mr. Disraeli. It is a horrible truth. It is a gross reality," said Pompey.

"Well said," replied Disraeli, "But here in England, we have workhouses and factories where thousands of little children toil long hours six days a week from dawn to dusk. Is that so different from slavery in America Mr. Ruiz?"

"Indeed it is. They will not be beaten or shot if they elect to leave at some time. And be it ever so little, they are paid for their work. And either they, or at least their parents, choose for them to work there. These are places of shame for you as they should be, and the people there have little economic choice but to work there, but they need not return the next day if they do not wish to once they are of age. In point of fact, one of your greatest and richest writers worked in such a place as you describe when he was only a child. Yes, Mr. Charles Dickens himself worked in a horrible ink factory. Look at him now. He is a very celebrated, wealthy, and satisfied citizen of a free country with the rights to which all Englishmen are entitled to by British Constitutional reforms dating from the days of Henry II in the twelfth century. Trial by jury and Habeas corpus and all that. Could a slave do what Mr. Dickens did? In the United States, it is a crime often punishable by death to even teach a slave to read or write. There are very few Negro writers in America today although there is genius enough to go around within the community of slaves to provide more than several I am sure. In America slavery lasts a lifetime. A slave works until death without any choice in the matter," replied Pompey.

"I understand that one Frederick Douglass both writes books and is a well known young Negro public speaker. He was a slave who quit slavery by stealing himself and making his way to the northern part of your country Miss Beers. Is that like our Mr. Dickens?" asked Disraeli.

"I have been in the South of the United States, and I can assure you that almost no slave has had Mr. Douglass' good fortune," said Miss Sally.

"For a Portuguese gentleman, Mr. Ruiz, you have a real understanding and compassion for those who suffer in human bondage. You sir are possessed of truly noble sentiments and sympathies. "Noble!" exclaimed Gladstone as he pounded his knee in approval. "I hope to live to see the day that the horrible institution of that abomination that is slavery is removed from this planet." It took most of Mr. Wilberforce's lifetime for him to see the end of human slavery in the colonies and mother country. He died the year his bill was passed by Parliament ending slavery. But his spirit lives on in the heart of every decent Englishman."

"Thank you Mr. Gladstone. I do apologize to you for making sport of your beliefs. That is not my habit, but I do love irony and an argument. It is a terrible character flaw to which I freely admit. I am pleased that you share my view of slavery," replied Pompey.

"How about your own people sir? The Portuguese? Do they not wink the eye at slave trading in Mozambique still? Is Brazil not flourishing with its own institution of slavery well in place?" asked Disraeli.

"And that is the great curse of my life sir. I am ashamed to say that they do. With your permission I would ask if my man Cabral could take a chair and tell you his tale. His knowledge of the subject is far deeper than my own. His story is one that should be told in the courts, clubs, universities, Parliaments, and Congresses of the entire world."

"That's very liberal of you sir," said Gladstone. "More gentlemen should be so liberal in the sharing of their ideas with their servants."

"I would like to note that Cabral is not only my trusted servant, he is my friend. I would like him to tell you how he came to be a slave at the time of his capture in Africa and about his voyage to America. That is if he would consent to so favor us," said Pompey.

"Cabral?" asked Miss Sally, "Would you be so kind to take tea with us, and take a seat, and share your story with my guests? I would be so pleased if you would."

Samuel took the offered chair, and during the next hour, he told the story of his growing up a warrior prince in Africa, about his capture, and the story of the horrible voyage to America. Gladstone and Disraeli listened. They were both appalled by Samuel's story, and in turn, also fascinated by the tale. When Cabral concluded with his arrival in America, the Englishmen urged him to go on.

"I cannot," he replied, "Mr. Ruiz has done things for me which could get him hanged should he ever have to return to America or is taken there by force. I can tell you no more than I have without putting him in the greatest danger," Samuel replied.

"I can assure you Cabral that you and your master are quite safe in England," said Gladstone with some force. "I am sure that even the American minister is not friendly with the interests of slavery."

"That was true of Mr. Everett, the former American Minister to Great Britain, but now I'm not so sure sir," replied Ruiz. "There are low men who would take us by night out of this kingdom if they could, and they would put us on a ship in the dark of night and return us to America for the farce that passes for justice there." Pompey then added, "The very fact that my man is speaking to you at all on this subject is truly remarkable."

"I assure you that such an action, as your being forcibly removed from this country would start a war sir! Indeed it would. Just as in the days of Jenkins's ear. A crime against one individual that violates British Law or justice is a crime against the whole British Nation. We fought Spain over that bit of nonsense, and we beat them too. And we have waged war to defend our individual rights all over the world," boomed Gladstone. "And in my opinion defending the democratic rights of Englishmen is the only reason for this nation ever to go to war. I do not support wars to expand the empire."

"Now that sort of passion is not quite like you is it old man?" asked Disraeli with a smile of amusement with Gladstone's passionate outburst.

"Quite right Benjamin. That is quite uncharacteristic of me. Forgive me again Miss Beers. I have once again forgotten myself," Gladstone apologized with a nod of his head.

"It's alright with me as long as you gentlemen don't have a stroke and promise to return with your passion intact on your next visit," she replied in her best southern belle manner.

"How do you think this war you are fighting with Mexico is going to end Captain Beers?" asked Disraeli.

"The United States will win sir. Our weapons are better. Our ships command the waters. Our armies are better led by people like General Scott and General Taylor. Our motives are strong to fulfill our destiny to rule all of America from the Atlantic to the Pacific and to fill up the continent with towns, farms, and cities. That motive is far stronger than the extension of slavery from any new territories and is supported throughout the nation. We are building a great American Republican Empire, and some say that it is our manifest destiny to rule from sea to sea. It may take four or five hundred years to settle and civilize the vast expanse of the continent, but it will mean that there will be endless room to grow into. That land is now all but empty," the Captain replied.

"I understand Captain Beers that there is some opposition to the war with Mexico in New England on moral grounds of it being an illegal and an immoral expansion of your nation," said Gladstone.

"There is that sentiment in America. Former President Adams is opposed to the war on moral grounds as is a young congressman from Illinois named Lincoln who is in the press from time to time, but I think it has more to do with slavery. Mr. Adams hates slavery. He has been rather quiet about his views on the subject until just a few years ago, but now his opposition is well known. He has even defended slaves who took over a slave ship before the Supreme Court of the United States and won. Slavery, and the Northern fear of the spreading of it, seems to shade every political consideration and argument. I'm afraid that someday a real split will come in the nation that might even lead to disunion or to a civil war," answered Captain Beers.

"There is something going on in Europe too. The mercantile classes are becoming more and more educated. They will not allow themselves to be ruled by the absolutism of monarchs whose minds are mired in the past and in absolutism too much longer. We saw liberal revolutions sweeping all over Europe back in '30. I think that we will see such revolutions again soon in Austria, Russia, the Germanies, Italy, and in France as well. The whiff of revolution is in the air," said Disraeli. "I can almost smell the gunpowder. Enlightened people will not allow the medieval institutions of absolute governance by a single ruler to survive into a modern world. We have evolved a constitutional monarchy over the centuries here in England, and the day cannot be far off when the days of absolutism will be merely a subject for historical study and not a fact of European political life."

"I thank God on my knees that the Channel stands between us and Europe," exclaimed Gladstone.

"Yes William, I'm sure that you do," purred Disraeli, "I am sure that your prayers include divine thanks for the world's greatest fleet of warships which is in it."

CHAPTER XXV

There was little joy in Five Points when word arrived that Ellis and the slave ship had sunk in a horrible gale in the South Atlantic not far past the Cape of Good Hope along with Captain Whitehouse and all but one of his entire crew. A steamer had reported the *Sea Hound's* loss at Cape Town, and the news of the sinking made it back to New York. It was reported in the popular press that the ship carried exotic woods and ivory, and gold valued at five hundred thousand dollars. It was also reported that Captain Whitehouse had gone down with his ship from which nobody was rescued from except the first mate, a Mr. Starbuck, of Nantucket Island who was found in a boat floating in the sea-lanes without oars on the edge of starvation with a large lump on the side of his head received when he and the ship's boat were swept overboard. It was noted that it was fortunate for the *Sea Hound's* only survivor that the boat was provisioned with tinned foods. It was further stated that he had been rendered unconscious during the storm and had awakened in the well-provisioned boat not quite remembering how he had gotten there in the first place. Starbuck said that he remembered falling during the storm then waking long after it was over in this boat and that was all. He had not even seen the ship go down, but was sure that it had been lost all the same.

It was also reported, according to the captain of the rescuing steamer, that as a consequence of his escape from death Mr. Starbuck had decided to swallow the anchor and retire to his native island of Nantucket to enjoy the rest of his days on his property newly acquired there. Almost four years had passed between this voyage and the loss of the *Catalpa's* cargo. The gentlemen who had invested in the most recent voyage had been gravely disappointed. But after the first loss, the second adventure to Mozambique had made up for the loss of the *Catalpa* quite well. Greater anticipated profit from Whitehouse's next voyage in the *Sea Hound* had turned out to be a dead loss. Only the value of the ship could be recovered through insurance. It seemed that without the manifest, the insurance brokers were not inclined to pay damages on the reported cargo. Nothing was therefore paid out to the investors for the supposed rare woods, gold, and ivory. And to be certain, no manifest for the cargo of the fatal voyage would ever be found. The late Mr. Ellis, had failed his friends by not furnishing insurance forms properly signed and notarized on the phantom cargo. His friends in the Five Points did not remember Mr. Ellis with any amount of charity after the loss of the *Sea Hound*.

It took many months for the story of the sinking to be told in the world press. As it happened, the news traveled from Cape Town to various British colonies and then back to England. From London, the news traveled throughout the United Kingdom, and from there, it was carried throughout Europe, and then to the United States. The investors in the voyage of the *Sea Hound* proved to be very skeptical. They were determined to find out what had happened to their investment on Whitehouse's last fatal voyage.

These men of business in Five Points did not like taking losses, and one investor suggested that this Mr. Starbuck, who by some act of Divine Providence had been saved, should be invited to New York to furnish an explanation of the *Sea Hound's* loss at sea. They also wanted to know the story of how he alone survived the sinking of the ship with its exotic cargo. The newspaper accounts did not satisfy the Five Points investors.

For that purpose a small delegation was to travel to Massachusetts to extend an invitation to Mr. Starbuck to attend the proposed investor's meeting back in New York. Mr. Starbuck's help would be appreciated when the investors finally looked into the matter.

The Shipping News of London also carried the story of the loss of Whitehouse and his ship, and the fact that only the first officer, a Mr. Starbuck, had survived that tragic event and was now returned to his island home of Nantucket. That island was well known to British sailors. Many were fascinated by this story of Starbuck's miracle rescue when all of his shipmates had perished in what had been termed the worse storm of the decade in the South Atlantic. Like so many items of human interest, the article was reprinted in newspapers all over the English-speaking world. Eventually word of Starbuck's amazing salvation reached far off Rio de Janeiro where it was duly reported in the Brazilian press and read by the late Captain Whitehouse whose reaction consisted of jumping up from his table and screaming, "Damnation! Why did that bloody fool ever open his mouth to the press?"

Whitehouse paced up and down the length of his room as Ajax stood looking at him. The impassive face of the little serving man did not betray his active mind, which was reassessing his own position in the Captain's household, which might afford him an opportunity for a dramatic change in his life. Ajax's face did not betray the thoughts he entertained about his own prospect of self-emancipation and greatly increased wealth.

"My Captain," said Ajax. "I do not believe that Mr. Starbuck is the author of this statement. It is not in his character to meet with people like these scribblers. I would wager that it was the captain of the English steamboat who rescued him who gave out this story. I know something of these Five Points people in New York. They are very serious people my Captain, and they will not believe this story in the newspapers for a moment."

"Really Dear Ajax, and why is that?" asked Whitehouse.

"I was close to Ellis since I was a boy of nine. And I saw everything he did for these Five Points people. Trust me my Dear Peter, "Ajax said soothingly as he moved over to the Captain and began massaging Whitehouse's shoulders, "They will send some people to Nantucket and bring Starbuck to New York. They will do things to him, horrible things, and trust me, even a strong man like Mr. Starbuck will break and talk. These men know how to extract information. It is well that Mr. Ellis is no longer with us. He was very skilled in getting information from those who possessed a great reluctance to speak, but his henchmen are alive and share his talent for extracting information from those people who are reluctant to speak. If they secure Mr. Starbuck, he will tell them that you are here. And they will come for us. They are not forgiving men."

"You are one smart little piece Ajax. Do you fancy a voyage?" asked Whitehouse.

"This is Brazil. New York must know this news by now. I would say the sooner we are out of this place the better my dearest Peter. And I would never consent to be left behind without you. I could never stand to be away from you. There is one more thing to consider. When Mr. Starbuck reads this in the American papers, as he must eventually, he will assume that it was you who may have told the press these things for reasons of your own. I know that the idea lacks logic, but we must consider the man's suspicious mind."

Whitehouse bounded from bed and paced the floor thinking about what he had just read, and what Ajax had told him. As time passed, Whitehouse for the first time in his life had found someone who could talk to him and show him something like devotion. He also was pleased to discover the little man's perceptiveness and intelligence. As he paced the floor, plans quickly formed in his mind, as was his habit.

Whitehouse's next move was to calculate just when the news might have reached New York and if there was any reason to sail his own ship to Nantucket to see what fate might have befallen Starbuck. Then, based on what Ajax had suggested, he began to speculate as to why the story had been spread to the journals of the world. He knew that newspapers were so desperate for printable material that the same stories might often be circulated for years to come if they had some smack of truth about them and held the power to fascinate. There was nothing like the story of the loss of a ship at sea to stimulate the reading public in the English-speaking world. Details of the sinking were sketchy, but it seems that the steamer captain, who had picked Starbuck up floating in the ocean, had told the press of Starbuck's amazing rescue, and then he related the story which Starbuck had told him which had been concocted by Whitehouse and agreed to by Starbuck. Whitehouse knew that this tissue of lies could easily come apart overnight.

Whitehouse, following Ajax's line of thought, also speculated that the captain of the ship which had rescued Starbuck, or some of his officers, may also have actually sailed to New York after Cape Town, which had the world's freest press. The press was always hungry for old news, particularly a story like Starbuck's, which had a romantic twist. Many editors knew that such stories would appeal to the sensation loving American news market for months to come. Thus there was more than a good chance that the story might have been reported there, and eventually all over the world even to Mozambique.

Whitehouse's whole neat package of lies and the faking of the loss of his ship might now become undone if anybody actually were to get to Starbuck and make him talk about what had really happened during the three day gale. The mate had not liked telling a story in which he was the principal actor. Whitehouse knew that Starbuck was not an accomplished liar and that his Quaker scruples might get the better of him. "Good God! The damned fool might even be tricked into speaking to *Harper's* and that would tear it," Whitehouse said aloud to Ajax. Since none of his servants except Ajax spoke English, it really didn't matter if they heard him or not. Ajax was loyal and was content to return to slavery in Brazil in exchange for the position of butler in the Whitehouse establishment and in fact being the master's lover. Ajax rather liked his new arrangement with the Captain, especially after he was allowed to buy a pretty yellow houseboy inclined to his own way of things. Whitehouse had also enjoyed the company of the lad just as he had loved his newly found decadence and his new fully crewed yacht which his new fortune had also bought him. He hated the thought of putting out to sea so far from his new life.

But Whitehouse also knew that if Starbuck talked, that he would have to sleep with one eye open for the rest of his life which might not be so long if the New York crowd had its way and reached out a very long arm to exact a little justice of its own in South America. Whitehouse ordered his carriage, and when it arrived at his door, he made for the harbor where his newly purchased vessel was at anchor. She was trim and very fast. His coachman lashed the horses making them dash as fast as they could fly over the late evening streets of Rio now all but empty of their usual traffic. After the fifteen-minute drive, the carriage came to a halt next to Whitehouse's ship. Whitehouse bounded out of the carriage, and in less than a blink of an eye, he was up the gangway, and running into the main cabin where his crew would be gathered for their nightly entertainments.

Whitehouse burst into the cabin and roared, "Get rid of these women! There is something afoot! Do it now!"

In a flash a dozen men were on their feet, and a dozen women, in various stages of undress, were dismissed and hurried off the ship with vague promises of better things to come the following night. The dozen sailors, all of them veterans of many voyages with the Captain, returned to the cabin tugging on their own clothing such as it was on this hot tropical night. The effect of rum had been largely shed in the heat of the Captain's sobering state of near fury.

To the first mate he bellowed, "Mr. Wright, this ship is to be provisioned and armed as best we can arm it and made ready to sail on tomorrow evening's tide. We shall be gone for at least three month's sail. Gather up the rest of the crew from ashore! No questions asked. Those who do not report at once by sailing time shall be left in port. That is all."

With that, the Captain returned to his carriage as his men, long practiced in their Captain's ways, jumped to and began all the needful preparations. The women were all but forgotten. There was one thing for certain. This flight would be no slaving voyage. This wasn't the right ship for that business, but that could be taken care of with a judicial sale of this ship and the purchase of a more substantial craft. This fine craft could be sold in any civilized port in the world. That would be no matter at all. Providing for another ship would never be a problem for Whitehouse now that he was rich. A sinking ship can yield a profit under the right circumstances thought the Captain. This was doubly so when it was repainted and renamed. But now what occupied him was the idea that Starbuck knew where he was, and that subjected to torture, Starbuck may be forced to give information about the Captain's new home.

The story concerning Starbuck's amazing rescue at sea was also to be found in the rural papers of England. The news even reached the sleepy shire about Westmorland. Starbuck's story was tucked away on page three of *The Westmorland Gazette* where it caught the attention of Don Raphael de Ruiz at his breakfast. He arose from his bed almost knocking his breakfast tray onto the floor. He then pulled on his dressing gown and ran across his bedroom and knocked on the door separating his own room from Samuel's. The big man came to the door and opened it. Pompey handed him the newspaper indicating the article he had been reading that very instant. Samuel read it with satisfaction. A sardonic smile wreathed his lips.

Looking up from the journal Samuel said, "I wanted to kill that bastard myself. Now that damned Whitehouse is claimed by the sea on which he made his foul living! I tell you, I don't believe it. It does not smell right to this old lion hunter. I do not believe that the devil is dead. It's all too easy to just disappear like that Pompey. Something does not smell right as I said. It is all too neat and tidy. I am sure that this Starbuck must know something. Perhaps we should sail to Boston and then to this Nantucket and interview Mr. Starbuck ourselves. I am sure that he knows a great deal more than he is letting on."

"Trust me Samuel. The man is not dead. He only wants his enemies to think he is. I am in total agreement with you. I too am sure that this man Starbuck knows the truth, and as I am your friend, I will see that you shall have your justice. I am very sure that Captain Beers is well acquainted with Nantucket. We will meet him in Boston, and when he has come, we shall go and see this Starbuck for ourselves."

"Wait Pompey. Let me think. I believe that I remember this Starbuck fellow. Yes, he is the one I told you of. As I remember, he was second mate of the ship that took me from Africa. He was a very large young man with scars on his face. He was very fierce, but I think that the work of that trade disgusted him, and when the girl killed the first mate on the slave ship, this man Starbuck was placed in charge of the crew in his place. On a little ship like that, one did not miss much. Starbuck and Whitehouse were very close after all that happened on that voyage. I am sure that you are right. But you cannot go back to America. If you are caught, it's death, or at least a good beating, or at best you will be returned to a life of slavery."

"Without you Samuel, my life would still be that of a slave. The life I have belongs to you, as do the lives of my children when they come. As a white man, I can move about as no man of color alone ever could."

"Pompey my son, I think that this will be an adventure that neither one of us would begrudge our selves."

Back in Brazil, as Whitehouse cleared port, only one thought ran through his mind. And that thought was that he had made a great mistake and miscalculation in choosing the path he had taken in allowing Starbuck to live. In fact it was Ajax, who had first made the observation that the mate should have followed the doctor into the deep where the sharks are not so discriminating about their diet. Whitehouse missed the little man who was nowhere to be found at the time of departure. Clearly Ajax had betrayed his master after leading Whitehouse into a zone of comfort. The mysterious departure of Ajax only compounded Whitehouse's anger over the fact that he now had to abandon so much of his accumulated wealth in Rio. He despised the fact that his beautiful mansion would sit undisturbed only until his servants and slaves felt comfortable in looting its magnificent furnishings. Worst of all, Whitehouse knew that he would have to make another voyage to Mozambique to invest the money he had managed to keep. He would invest everything he had in one last slaving voyage. There could be no storms, British warships, or acts of God to ruin his success this time, because he knew it was his very last chance.

CHAPTER XXVI

The great Nantucket fire of 1846 had opened up a lot of opportunities for buying good property on the island. Although rebuilding had been going on for some time, there were still good buildable lots on the market where earlier structures had stood. Starbuck thought that this would be a good opportunity to make investments in the very potential of his town, and he intended to make the most of the considerable fortune he had saved and had recently been increased by such a staggering amount. Most of all he wanted to create something he had not enjoyed since he was a big and lusty lad of fifteen. Starbuck wanted the world of his childhood and the respect of his old friends as well as a home.

Starbuck reflected on all the money he had made with Whitehouse. That association had ended many months ago, and now the smartly turned out Starbuck entered the town hall on his native Nantucket his beard and mustache were barbered perfection. He really felt that he had come home again in real style. Whitehouse was dead to him. Starbuck never wanted to think of him again unless it was prompted by the news that the murderous old sodomite Captain was truly dead. That morning Starbuck had walked down from the Popsaquatchet Hills looking about for some purchasable real estate. He even entertained a pleasant fantasy about buying the whole island one property at a time. Starbuck even considered making an offer on Tuckernuck or Muskeget. Owning whole islands appealed to him no matter how small, sandy, and uninhabited they might be.

In the meantime, Starbuck had bought a square Greek Revival mansion that had once belonged to his grandfather, Gosnold Starbuck, in the center of the town that contrasted well with even those grand federal homes of some of his Barnard, Mayhew, Coffin, and Swayne neighbors. These men had looked at Starbuck who had been gone from the island for thirty years with some suspicion now that he had returned and especially because he had returned so damn rich. The overwhelming public opinion was that Starbuck thought himself to be "The cock of the walk". In truth, Starbuck thought that his new wealth had entitled him to some position here in his native place. He swaggered without taking notice of how he was moving. This only irritated the surviving generations of sea captains who openly resented him. The island was overpopulated with ancient ship's officers, and somehow Starbuck just didn't fit. Where had he been? Why had he not been seen in trading ports all over the world where respectable Yankee ships trade? Just who was this strange son of Nantucket anyway? What trading would have removed him from the familiar ports where Yankees go habitually? And why did he dress like a dude?

There were many rumors about the county. There were stories of Starbuck's likely involvement with every sort of low dealing from piracy in the Pacific to slave trading. There was also a great deal of speculation about the origins of Tristan Ballard Starbuck's great wealth. It was known that he had paid hard cash for his grandfather's old family homestead. His cousin Solomon had accepted the seven thousand five hundred dollars which Starbuck had offered for the house and all the land that went with it. Starbuck had hired a decorating crew from Boston to repair and paint the place in a record two weeks after they had landed on the island. He had bribed the workmen, threatened them, and inflicted a few well-placed blows and kicks, mixed with hundreds of inventive and most profane oaths to hasten the work along. In spite of Starbuck's interference, the work was done in a fortnight, and cash bonuses had well plastered any physical wounds inflicted by Starbuck.

The gaudy furniture for the Greek revival mansion had been ordered through Lloyd Coffin's mercantile establishment and had cost almost half as much as the house. Starbuck's new furnishings arrived on the island a month after the decorators had left for Boston. Hollis Swayne reported to his friends at the Post Office that Starbuck had deposited forty thousand dollars in gold in his bank. This made Starbuck the bank's, and thus the island's, largest depositor. Swayne asked each of the score of people he spoke to keep the information he told them under their hats. Of course each in his turn told others the secret with the same request for secrecy. Starbuck had even hinted to the banker, who was a distant cousin, that there was a good deal more gold hidden away which might find its way to the bank's vaults over time. Starbuck knew that saying this to his cousin would result in the whole island's knowing what a success he had become in the world and increase esteem for him among his fellow islanders.

The town's board of selectmen had also learned that Starbuck was interested in running for one of their seats in the next election. This did not sit well with Starbuck's cousin Thomas Starbuck, and his fellow selectmen Jacob Barnard, Hezekiah Mayhew, Jonathan Coffin, and Seaborn Swayne who had no intention of giving up their seats on the board until called home to their God in much the same way as the men who had preceded them in that position. Once elected, the venerable town fathers intended to hold the position of town leadership for life. The native Nantucketers also held, as a foregone conclusion, that unless the selectmen were proved to be unworthy, life tenure is what they could expect. The only other reason for removal from power would be some act indicating that they were damned fools.

The women of the island, unattached or otherwise, did not seem to warm up to the flashy and well turned out Starbuck quite as he had wished or expected. The pretty girls who had looked at him with admiration when he had shipped out on a whaler so many years ago were now married matrons, waiting for their husbands to return from the oceans of the world, or much older looking widows. When he had left Nantucket as a six-foot tall boy in the handsome glory of his mid-teens, the girls of the island had shown him favor. But that was a long time ago. Somehow the memory of those pretty girls in his mind had rested there fixed in time untransformed by time. The sad reality of the present time proved disappointing to Starbuck. Those pretty maids, living by the sea, hadn't aged any better than he had. Only the thrice-widowed Melanie Pruitt seemed to show an interest in the newly returned Starbuck and his wealth which was by now rumored to be quite considerable. In spite of her best efforts, and several of her best apple pies, there was no hiding the fact that Mrs. Pruitt was well over forty and of absolutely no interest to Starbuck whatsoever. Mrs. Pruitt was bound to disappointment and was forced to redirect her efforts to the Congregational Deacon, Mr. Erasmus Brewer, whose wife had passed on during the previous winter. That poor soul had died of the flux.

The town did not favor Starbuck in the role of the long lost son come back from some heroic odyssey as Starbuck thought they would. There had been the vexing and difficult questions about the nature of his career at sea about which he had always answered in a vague sort of way that never satisfied the islanders and only led to a worsening opinion of the sailor now come home. Even the old friends of his childhood had failed to drop in for a visit. After a while, tired of the snubs that he received at Church, the Quaker meetinghouse held no charm for him either. Starbuck also gave up trying to impress and win the town over with good will. He discovered that he was not very good at the game of being charming. Starbuck's life at sea had not educated him in the social graces he so sorely lacked. Slowly he did begin to learn that overdressing was almost always in poor taste.

Instead of seeking approval and public office, Starbuck

concentrated on his own revenge on the place of his nativity, which had chosen to shun him. He thought to do this by buying up all of the Nantucket land that came on the market. "Maybe this would impress the islanders in quite another way," he thought as he tried to figure out just what it would take to buy them all out and chase them off of their own island. Such had the man's ego become that he wanted to share his disappointment and anger with his fellow Nantucketers who he blamed for the failure of his dream of a glorious return home and the recapture of the halcyon days of his youth. All this did he think as he mounted the steps of the Town Hall.

The impression that Starbuck had made about the island was not the one he had initially attempted to make. The reception he received was not the one he had anticipated. Now when the natives saw him coming down the street, no matter if they dwelt in a whale house or mansion, they turned their backs on him and walked away. For all of his finery and his great gold watch with all of its seals and massive chain, Starbuck had not the respect of even one islander with the possible exception of Mrs. Pruitt who never abandoned hope of a romantic union with him even as her pursuit of the Congregational Deacon Brewer was meeting with some success. Compared to Starbuck, the Deacon seemed a poor catch, but he was an obtainable catch nevertheless. Still, Mrs. Pruitt kept her options open. In spite of her three trips to the altar, she remained the eternal optimist in anticipation of a fourth. Starbuck even had to go off island to find domestic help to run his big house. Nobody on the island wanted to work for him "keeping house" or in any other capacity. It was through his agents in Boston that he had secured a couple named Maycock as cook and man of all work.

As Starbuck entered the island's town hall, people moved away from him. He advanced on the office of the town clerk and knocked on the closed door. The door to the little office was opened by an older island woman who had been cleaning that selfsame office. "Where is Lewis, the town clerk?" demanded

Starbuck in the highly uncivil tone he had come to use when addressing Nantucketers lately.

"Now how would I know that?" responded the cleaning woman roughly in the same manner that Starbuck had posed the question in the first place.

"What hours does he keep woman?" demanded Starbuck.

"He don't keep regular hours mister. Cousin Richard be a busy man. And I'll thank you not to call me 'woman'. I got a name, and, to my friends it's Miranda. To others it's Mrs. Brewer, so you call me Mrs. Brewer, because we are no friends," she snapped out giving as good as she got.

Ignoring the comment, Starbuck continued, "When does he get any town business done?"

"What kind of business did you have in mind mister?" demanded the cleaning woman.

"Town clerking business I suppose! Seeing that this is the town hall, and this is where the town records are, not to mention the town clerk's office. I even had supposed that a citizen might be able to find the town clerk in the Town Clerk's Office as strange as that might seem," snapped Starbuck.

"Well why the devil didn't you say that in the first place mister," replied the woman with a sneer.

"What do I have to do to check out land records and such then?"

"You have to talk to Richard Lewis. He's the town clerk you know."

"I am aware that he is the town clerk. Now how do I catch him and make him do his damned job? Just how in blazes do I do that?"

"Well, first clean up your language when talking to a lady, and then I suppose that you could look him in the face then flap your jaws much in the same way as you are doing now. You seem to be pretty good at flapping your jaws mister even as rude a fellow as you seem to be."

Starbuck, fighting all of his savage instincts to kill this annoying female, barked out,

"Well how the Hell do I go about having a meeting with the absent Mr. Lewis?"

"Nice language to use to a lady I declare!" said the cousin as well as office cleaning lady of the Nantucket Island's town clerk. Miranda Brewer then slammed the door in Starbuck's face and continued her work.

As he turned to leave, Starbuck could not help but notice a little knot of townsmen nearby snickering at the very short shrift he had just been given by yet another one of the island's undoubtedly favorite characters. He turned on his heel and walked out of the town hall into the street. He looked about for a small boy who would most likely give up the information he needed for a penny or two. At last he saw a likely lad walking down the street in bare feet kicking the dust of the street halfway up his legs with some measure of joyfulness in his ability to get so splendidly dirty. "Here is a lad to whom two cents will look really good," Starbuck muttered to himself. "You boy. Come here."

The boy looked around, and then turned to Starbuck and said, "Are you talking to me mister? I ain't used to being called no boy."

Starbuck inhaled deeply and calmed himself. "Yes lad, I'm talking to you. Do you know the town clerk Mr. Lewis?"

"Well that would all depend."

"Depend on what?"

"Depends on who might want to know."

"How about a man who wants to know and will part with two nice shiny red pennies in exchange for the information," said Starbuck as he tried to smile benignly.

The boy looked at him and said, "I guess that feller would be a person who didn't want to know too much about where the other feller was, or leastwise that's the way it looks to me."

"How much would it take for a man who really wanted to know a lot just where the town clerk is?"

"A lot more than two cents mister. I can't hardly remember where I live for that kind of money."

"How about half a dime?" The boy just stood mute. Starbuck waited while the boy's stare grew more surly. Then the old mate barked, "How about half a dollar?"

The boy with a look of wisdom well beyond his ten years just smiled back at Starbuck and said, "A dollar mister. That's my price. Take it or leave it."

"A dollar!" Starbuck gasped, "Many a man would be glad of a dollar for a whole day's wages for hard work! A dollar indeed. I ought to…"

"My pa is twice as big as you mister, and he says that he don't like you too much. But then nobody around here does. They all say that you are trying to be a big bug or something. It would be a mistake for you to think about hitting me. My father is the law around here, and you would end up in court, and maybe even get yourself locked up. If you want to know what you want to know, then you have to give me a dollar mister. In silver or gold. It don't matter to me how you pay me the dollar. I don't take no paper money nohow. It's got to be silver or gold."

"Alright boy," said Starbuck. "Now for God's sake, tell me where this Lewis character is."

"First the dollar mister. Just toss it over here," said the boy looking like a clerk in a counting house.

Starbuck took out his purse, opened it, and tossed the boy a silver cartwheel. The lad took it, turned on his heel and ran about fifteen paces down the street to get a head start, then wheeled around. "He's over there running the post office in that store right where the sign is hanging that says 'Lewis'. You've been talking to him for months. He's my pa, and he's a runt half your size. I guess what they are all saying about you is right! You sure are addle brained mister!"

The boy ran off down the street laughing all the way. So were the half a dozen men, surely old sea captains, sitting in front of the store on the long benches reserved for their use. Starbuck knew that the store served as a post office for the island and as a gathering spot for retired seamen of all ranks. Another local character had just made his reputation at Starbuck's expense. Glumly, he vowed revenge of some unspecified sort on the vicious scamp. Starbuck grumbled this to himself as he stepped up on to the porch of the island's principal mercantile establishment. He walked into the store where a little man with steel rimmed eyeglasses was sorting the mail behind his counter, which passed for the local post office.

Starbuck cleared his throat, and the little man looked up and said briskly, "Well what do you want? I don't have all day you know! You'll be wanting some of these newfangled postage stamps I suppose? Damned things taste like something left on the bottom of a tar bucket when you lick the backs of them, And licking them is what you have to do when you have to stick them on an infernal letter. It was better the way they had it before I tell you. Progress I guess. Here we are in 1848. So we have to have progress, and that I suppose it takes on the devilish form of these damned postage stamps. Look at the damned things. Did you ever see a hundred copies of such an ugly little picture of George Washington? Each one is ten cents, and they are black! Well what is it that you want? I suppose it's some of those infernal stamps. How many stamps do you want? If you want the ugly brown five cent ones with Ben Franklin on 'em, I ain't got any. Just buy some of these ten cent ones and cut them in half, and they will do just fine to send your mail to where you want it to go for the half dime rate. Hell, the damned thing might even get there with a little bit of luck. What's the difference? You have to cut the dang things apart any way. If you want five-cent stamps, just cut the ten cent ones in half. It might make Washington look only half as ugly," said the postmaster taking up his scissors and a sheet of the black ten cent stamps. "Well, well how many do you want? Like I told you before, I ain't got all day," repeated the little man. "Come on, I'm pretty busy here."

"I don't want any stamps thank you very much," replied

Starbuck thinking that there must be something about living one's whole life on this damned island that drives people just a bit nasty and more than a little mad.

"Well why did you say that you wanted stamps then?" fumed the little man.

Finding it easier to disregard the fact that he had never asked for stamps, Starbuck pressed on. "Am I to understand that you are the town clerk and postmaster as well?" asked Starbuck.

"Now that all depends who gets elected this year as president. I'm a Jackson-Democrat man you see, and so Mr. Polk, who is also a Jackson man, gave me this job as postmaster. I am the president's man," said the postmaster with his chest puffed up with pride."

Then he continued, "But I understand that Mr. Polk don't want to run for president again. So some other feller might get in, like, if it's a Whig that gets elected you know, then I'm out. So I'm postmaster now, but if a Democrat don't get elected in November, Moses Tiddet will get the job, because he's a Whig, and I'll work for him as his assistant. Now that I've got the job, Moses works for me when he chooses to. Leastwise he gets paid to. It's a pretty good arrangement on account we are cousins. Now come November, somebody is going to be elected, and then come March fourth of next year..."

"Enough! Please enough. I have to talk to you in your capacity as town clerk," said Starbuck.

"Well alright. Keep your shirt on mister, and don't soil yourself. Sit down over here, and we can talk. Want some cider?"

"Yes. That would be nice. Thank you."

Lewis indicated a seat for Starbuck to sit in. The big man sat down thinking that this offer of cider had been the first act of kindness that he had been shown for many weeks by any islander, that is, if one did not count the gift of the widow's pies. The thought of the widow Pruitt made Starbuck shudder and grimace. Lewis returned and placed a horn tumbler of cider in front of Starbuck, and as Starbuck reached for it Lewis announced, "That will be five cents."

Starbuck laughed to himself as he once again took out his change purse, unclasped it, and handed over the little half dime silver coin with Miss Liberty seated like a queen of the people on it, and placed it in the hand of the shopkeeper. "At least it wasn't a dollar," Starbuck said softly as he raised the horn vessel to his lips.

"A dollar! For a horn of cider! I should say not. Even if you were dying of thirst on a desert island, and I had the only life giving liquid in sight, could I charge you a dollar? I should say not. All I'd charge would be the five cents."

"Well should I ever be stranded on a desert island, I hope it is with you I'll have to deal and not your son," smiled Starbuck.

"My son? What's that rotten little scalawag got to do with it I'd like to know? What's he been up to anyway?"

"It's just that I met him outside just a little while ago. He's very sharp and born to make his fortune I think. He even charged me a dollar to let me know that you are the town clerk. He might even bring back piracy someday in a big way."

"That lad is too sharp by half if you ask me. His mother spoils him rotten and she let's him run about like a wild Indian. I feel like I ought to give him a taste of the razor strop every night just in case he's put one over on me or been up to something I don't know about during the day. Steer clear of that one. You were lucky to get off just losing a dollar. I ought to take him out to the woodshed and give him what for. His mother would raise Hell about it of course. I just hope that someday he'll just run off to sea and won't come back before he's the death of me. After him, I wanted nothing to do with no more children. Well, what were you so all fired up to see me about? I've got the mail to sort yet. We wasted a pile of my time already. You know that you talk too damned much mister."

"As the town clerk, do you know when property comes up for foreclosure sale for non payment of taxes?" asked Starbuck.

"No, not as town clerk I don't, but as town treasurer and collector I do, but what's that to you? And by the way, that's not a 'foreclosure'. That's a 'taking for non-payment of taxes'. Foreclosure is when the bank does it for non payment of the mortgage, and that's when I act in my high office as the sheriff and hold an auction around here."

"I may want to buy some parcels of land as they come up for sale. I really don't care how the land comes on the market. I just want to buy as much as I can, and I have the money to do it. Now when could I begin to do that?"

"You can do that when the parcels come up for sale."

"Well, when would that be?"

"That would be when the sheriff holds an auction or sale for the town or the bank. I ain't too particular as to who is paying my commission as long as it is paid."

"Who would decide when this would happen?"

"The sheriff. You do ask an infernal lot of questions mister, and I'm pretty busy with the mail and all."

"And you are the sheriff ain't you Lewis?"

"Right you are there. I'm the sheriff. Didn't I tell you that before? You did ask me. No need for me to be sheriff unless I have to serve papers on you, or lock you up for something, or do the auction of seized lands. So what was that you wanted to know again?"

"I want to know what properties are going to be up for sale for any reason so that I can buy them."

"Well let me see. I got a list hereabouts." Lewis moved over to an ancient walnut fall front desk and extricated a thick pile of folded papers. "These are deeds of property that the town owns outright, and should have been sold over the last three years. They are mostly abandoned parcels of land on which nobody wanted to pay taxes no more, because they were thought to be worthless. The whole stack can't be much more than a hundred dollars."

"Could you sell them to me now?"

"No, I'd have to hold an auction. Any damned fool ought to be able to see that. It's got to be fair. Everybody has got to have a chance to bid on those parcels. So I can't sell no land lessen I hold an auction."

"When could you do that?"

"Just about anytime I damn well please Mr. Starbuck. All I have to do is post a notice on the town notice board over to the town hall and then put the notice in the paper. So that would make it in about two weeks."

"So you know my name?"

"Ain't backward. Everybody knows who you are. The island ain't all that infernal big you know. And besides I'm the sheriff. I know everybody's name. That's my business to know that."

"Well, will you hold an auction?" asked Starbuck.

"Sure enough. In fact, I can see if the bank has anything they might want to dispose of in the way of property, and maybe some other folks too. And as long as I'm at it, it might make a good day outing for the whole town just like a good old fashioned hanging. Or we can have a big fish fry just like at a good old time sheep shearing. As they say around these parts, "t'is tew I can, t'is tew I can't."

"Oh my word. I had almost forgotten those old lines. I used to see them painted on the carts all over the island at sheep shearing. It does take me back."

"Take you back where? They still do that. Things out here don't change all that much less'en you have some big fire like we did in '46. Oh but that's right Mr. Starbuck. With your big city ways, I almost forgot that you were born here on the island."

Sadly Starbuck thought back to the days of swimming with his friends and brother back at the cove. He looked sadly and said, "Things change. All you have to do is go away, and it all changes in a little time."

CHAPTER XXVII

For the next several months, parcel after parcel of land came on the market on the island of Nantucket. The first auction was a holiday just like a sheep shearing as Lewis had predicted. And a shearing it was. The auction was very well attended, and bidding was spirited, more so than ever before in the history of the place. The natives turned out dressed to the nines, and they bid like madmen. Auctioneer, Sheriff Lewis, cried the auction of real estate interspersed with remarks like, "Bid high folks, the good Lord ain't making no more land, and the sea is ripping away the little what we got. Here's your chance to get some good buys on very choice parcels. Land like this don't come on the market every day."

Starbuck was astonished that there was so much money on the island. Whole blocks of New York City could have been bought for less money it seemed than for the little parcels that were offered that he won. He was truly amazed at what all the available real estate was costing him, and the parcels of land were less than prime. In spite of the spirited bidding running up the prices he was forced to pay, Starbuck won every lot. At last, a light dawned on him in the dim recesses of his mind. He came to the conclusion that the Nantucketers were having him for breakfast along with his wealth for parcels of worthless sandy land with a few good lots thrown in here and there just to keep the whole game interesting.

After the third land auction, Starbuck faced Sheriff Lewis in his store and post office with the grave charge of corruption. Lewis was very short with him. "Judge Haemon Sewell was standing right there in front bigger than life at all of them auctions. Let me tell you mister, the judge would take a mighty dim view of some outsider questioning the integrity of any legally constituted sale at an open land auction with all free to bid or not with him standing right there big as life and twice as…well never mind the rest. You might be rich, and you may be a big bug where you come from, but don't be going around here expecting any special favors. We might not be as rich as you, but we are hard working God fearing folks here with no shady past to hide or be running away from."

For the first time Starbuck's composure cracked. His big ham like fists clenched and unclenched. He stared an icy stare at the man of all civic offices and fixed him with his steel blue eyes. For the first time the sheriff, postmaster, town clerk, town treasurer, auctioneer, and storekeeper did not make a nasty retort. The fury on Starbuck's face only lasted a second, but it was enough. For the first time since he cut into a cake, baked by his wife for the cake contest at the county fair before it could be presented to the judges, the Nantucket man of all civil offices knew real fear. Cold, all numbing, nameless fear that almost made him faint. Lewis staggered back as if he had been actually struck by that huge ham-like fist belonging to the furious giant standing before him. Then Lewis regained his composure a little.

"Well, that is, all I was saying Mr. Starbuck was that I was a little hurt that you seem to think that there was something wrong with the bidding and all. We just try to do things right here just like on the mainland you see and…"

"Mr. Lewis," said Starbuck cutting him off in mid-squirm, "All I was about to say is that I will not be accepting delivery on those miserable parcels of land that I bought at the last auction.

I spent the day yesterday looking at them. Most of them have been half under seawater since those deeds were drawn up over a hundred and fifty years ago. And the rest ain't good enough for beach grass."

"No Mr. Starbuck. You see it's final. All sales final and…"

Starbuck delivered a kick of such force to a full fifty-five gallon barrel of hardtack that the whole room was filled with a blizzard of staves, hoops, and fragments of crumbs. It would almost have appeared that a barrel of gunpowder had exploded. He then lifted the sheriff up off the floor by his vest and held him aloft for a second or two then dropped him. "Do you see my way of it? If you give me an iota of trouble over this, I'll take you out to sea, open you up like a cod, stuff you with rocks, and send you off without a trace to the bottom of the channel never to be seen again by your misses or your whelp. Do you get and understand my clearly stated intentions here Mr. Lewis!"

"Yes," the man choked out.

"Are we going to have any trouble over those bids on those trashy lots?"

"No Mr. Starbuck sir. Your bids are canceled as you wish," squealed the little man in a plaintive voice close to tears.

"And until further notice Mr. Lewis, you will discount my purchases at your emporium here by half," growled Starbuck between clenched teeth or there will be Hell to pay making this little episode here look like a child playing.

Lewis nodded weakly. Now the anger returned with a new thought, and Starbuck's steely blue eyes were all but popping from his head as he continued in a quieter and more menacing voice, "And speaking of child's play, tell that dear little son of yours that there had better be a silver dollar delivered to my door by noon tomorrow, or I'll have his hide hanging on my gate post by one in the afternoon, and not even the high sheriff or his sweet mother can save him."

"Yes. I'll tell him that," croaked Lewis.

Starbuck tipped his tall beaver hat to Lewis and left the scene of ruin that had once been the village's center of commerce.

"Oh my God," said Lewis to the broken barrel and wreck of his store in the softest of voices he could manage. "What ever has little Dickie done to that man?"

Starbuck walked briskly back to his grand Greek revival house. He smiled and hummed a tune that he could not identify by name. He had heard it somewhere in some happier time. He was pleased with himself. He had just had a little justice for the first time in many months. After a brisk walk, Starbuck turner, unlatched his gate, and sauntered up his walk to his fine house gleaming with its fresh paint.

The old gloom returned to him as he turned the key in the lock of his grandfather Gosnold Starbuck's big paneled front door with its bull's eye panes of glass set in a row above the wooden lintel. Each pane had an almost perfectly centered pontile mark in the center. In spite of its renewed grandeur, that house was a place of cold comfort. Starbuck had not been received back into the bosom of his own extended family on the island. Not even Lloyd Starbuck stopped by to visit. The friends of his youth shunned him. All of the generations of his parents were dead, and the rest of his family did not want to know him. His contemporaries seemed neither to have remembered him fondly or at all. He was seen as a threat to the island's political structure, and that had frozen him out. Worst of all, the community had conspired to bring him down, cheat him by using his own greed against him, and making him a figure of fun. It had suddenly come on him like an epiphany. He had no real home or real interest here. It came to him as an awful and unbidden painful truth. He remembered his mother's kindly face looking at him just as she had when she had nursed him through childhood illnesses. The memory of her was the only thing that warmed his heart at all, and that was far from enough. All that remained of this saint who had been his loving mother now lay under a stone raised to her memory in the town's cemetery. It was clearly time for him to go away from Nantucket even though he had only been one season in the place.

The married couple Starbuck had hired from Boston to run his house seemed to be as cold and correct as people at the top of the serving class in the big city houses were supposed to be. They kept a polite distance from him as their employer, as custom and usage would direct. Since they had arrived to take up their duties, the house had run like a well-oiled machine. They kept to themselves when not cleaning, cooking, tending the grounds, or doing the other things to make the big house work. In a way, Starbuck felt that this big cold place was really more theirs than his.

He walked into his big and showy house by the front door, then entered his office and sat down at his great polished mahogany desk. That very late afternoon he thought of writing to his Boston lawyer ordering him to sell all of his property on the island for whatever it would fetch. Starbuck sat heavily in his well-upholstered chair and put pen to paper. He further ordered his attorneys to retain the receipts from the sales of the properties until he could come to the city to claim them at some unspecified time. He also instructed his lawyer to pay the hired couple to stay on at the island house and look after the place until it was sold. He also instructed the lawyer to pay the couple a bit more money to cover their living expenses for three months past the time of the sale and a generous hundred dollars more by way of severance pay.

That having been done, Starbuck walked into the hall and turned the brass key in the polished box lock on the front door locking up for the night. No doubt, he was the only man on the island to do so. People on this island had never locked their doors at night against would be robbers. But then when the islanders engaged in larceny, it was in the full light of day under the guise of doing business.

Then Starbuck did something he had never done before. He walked back to the kitchen where his two servants, the Maycocks, sat on either side of the fireplace warming themselves against the evening dampness and chill while rocking away the cares of another long day's work. Mrs. Maycock was knitting mittens for the winter, and Mr. Maycock was reading *The Island Gazette*. Starbuck knocked at the door and said, "Pardon me folks, but I'll be going away on a long trip off island shortly. You will be getting your wages for the next three months from my man in Boston by post."

Starbuck stopped for a moment as the two unspeaking people looked at him with some puzzlement. "I would like you to mind the place while I'm gone. Here's seventy-five dollars for food and any other expenses. Mr. Lewis has kindly offered to reduce the price of his goods for this house by fifty percent out of gratitude for all the business I've given him. Should he forget about the fifty percent discount, just remind him that I'll be around to remind him of it in a few weeks time. You can also tell him that I'll not be quite so understanding and gentle next time should he forget his pledge. If I'm gone longer than a fortnight, my lawyer in Boston will send you whatever you need to cover expenses and take care of your wages."

The Maycocks, long experienced in service, were uncomfortable with the master's informal manner. They stood but were motioned back to their seats by Starbuck.

"How long are you to be away sir?" asked Maycock.

"I don't rightly know how long this business will take, but it will be a while. At least two weeks. Maybe longer. If you need to contact me, write to my lawyer in Boston. He is Judge Jonathan Jones, and his offices are in Court Square. Here I've written the address down for you," Starbuck said as he handed the quarter sheet of folded foolscap to Maycock who, in turn, placed it on the mantelpiece where it would be safe and where he could remember placing it.

The Maycocks were correct in every way, and therefore asked no questions but merely indicated that they understood the master's wishes. Mr. Maycock did venture to remark, "Excuse me sir, but has anyone told you that there was a story printed about you in this week's island newspaper? It is an old story I'm guessing, but I was kind of surprised to read that you were the only survivor of a ship's foundering almost a year past in the South Atlantic in a bad storm not far from Cape Town. I thought it was pretty exciting, but I can understand your not wanting to talk about it with all of your mates lost at sea and all. Mrs. Maycock and I would just like to say that we are sorry for your loss Mr. Starbuck."

Starbuck was stunned and grabbed the sheet from Maycock's hand. He scanned the page until he found the place. He found the article and read. To his horror he discovered the story in print on the very island on which he lived. He wrongly presumed that Whitehouse had planted this fiction of his escape from the sinking of the *Sea Hound*. "Why did he do that?" he said out loud.

And now here it was, that cursed story having found its way into the island press. How soon would it be before the word got out that he was on the island? How long would it take before the word reached New York? The Maycocks looked at him strangely, and after a minute or two Mr. Maycock ventured to ask, "Are you all right sir?"

Starbuck jerked his head up and attempted a smile, "Yes Maycock, just some very bad memories coming back you know. Floating about after a shipwreck in that boat all alone. Losing all my mates. It's sometimes hard to deal with. I was out of my head most of the time. Oh well. Life has a habit of going on with us or without us. Best make the best of it. That's what I say."

"Yes, I can understand that being the case. Almost going down with the ship in a big storm like that with everybody else drowning must be a disturbing memory. Why I find it hard to even imagine such a thing. We are very sorry for your trouble."

This was the first real expression of kindness Starbuck had experienced during his whole stay on this damned island.

"Thank you folks. That's very nice of you. Have you any tea left in that pot over there?"

"Why Mr. Starbuck, there is quite a bit of tea yet and some apple pie if you have a mind to try some," said Mrs. Maycock with real warmth. It was the first time in the many months that the trio had spoken together in a way other than as master and servants. The conversation lasted for another hour or two. The trio finished the pie amid laughter and stories. Then Starbuck said goodnight and went to his room. From the back of the closet, he dragged out a chest that he had brought onto the island with him. It was of the type that a ship's captain would have taken to sea. He removed four leather bags each containing one hundred and fifty ten dollar gold pieces. He wrapped the bags in some clothing, and placed the two bags into a small leather traveling case. He then repeated the process with another bag. These he could carry. There were twelve more leather bags in the bottom of the chest, which would have to be left behind. He remembered the day when the teamsters he had hired to take his goods from the boat that he had chartered up to his house. They had strained with the cases including five chests which were marked "BOOKS".

"What are these here books made out of mister? Lead?" the workmen had asked as they moved the chest from the wagon and carried it up the stairs to Starbuck's room.

"No, it's just a lot of heavy reading. Mostly books on religion. God damn it if I am not a lunatic on the subject of salvation! Amen." Starbuck had replied.

The treasure had arrived with the help of four strong men. The problem now in Starbuck's mind was where to hide the balance of his gold. He had already buried twenty five thousand dollars in gold coins five feet below ground near his beach at a stone breakwater in the littoral zone. He had buried it at low tide in the dark of night on the shore where he had played as a child where nobody would find it. After his land purchases, which included this bit of beach, he had seven thousand five hundred and fifty dollars left in the bank from the funds which he had deposited there. That sum would have to stay to avoid any suspicion that he had taken flight. Starbuck then padded back to the kitchen to see if the Maycocks had gone to sleep in their chamber at the rear of the house. He listened with care and heard the man and wife softly snoring. He stopped for a moment and spoke softly out loud to the night, "I doubt if either one of them even thought about the snoring the other makes." He felt a sense of loss for just a brief moment, but then his task at hand brought him back to reality.

Taking a whale oil lamp from the mantelpiece, Strarbuck struck a Lucifer, which popped to life with the first scratch. He lit both burners of the lamp and went down to the cellar. Starbuck moved a stack of logs, and proceeded to dig with a spade. The soil was not too compact near that particular wall. The work went quietly and quickly. Starbuck then went back up to his room wearing carpet slippers and removed the rest of the gold from the great chest to which he had transferred it after the men who had delivered it in the form of books had left. He then carried the gold to the cellar. He placed the treasure into the hole, which he had just dug in the soft earth and then proceeded to fill it in. Then Starbuck piled the logs back into place over the gold exactly where the pile had been. He then smoothed the earthen floor. After looking his work over, he spent the next fifteen minutes walking all over the floor reflecting a logical pattern of the activities typical of use of the space. He retraced his steps dropping small bits of wood scraps and twigs as he went. Then he walked over these bits forcing them into the earth as if they had been there on the floor for a long time. Nobody would be able to detect what he had done here this night.

"Nobody will find anything here," said Starbuck to himself in a reassuring whisper. Then he laughed softy to himself. "You have been on your own too long talking to yourself all the time Mr. Starbuck. People will say you're going soft in the head. Well maybe I am. Maybe I better make a few maps in case I forget where I've stashed everything. Poor Old Starbuck, you're going soft in the head old son. But with everybody else being so goddamned daft on this bloody island, who the Hell would notice the difference?"

He padded upstairs to his room, poured water into the

washbowl, stripped off his shirt, and cleaned himself thoroughly. He changed into respectable traveling clothes, seized his two traveling cases and divided the contents of a bag of gold between them, and walked down into the front hall. Starbuck placed the big brass key into the well-oiled box lock. It unlocked the door, which swung open quite easily. He then took up his cases, and went out into the night.

It took him half an hour to walk down to the shore to a whale house at the end of the little lane with the pretentious name of "Broadway". Here was the cottage named *Land's End.* There were a lot of these funny little places all along the shore with names like *Auld Lang Syne, Heart's Content, Captain's Rest,* and lastly that of the only man on the island more of an outcast than himself, Captain Fuller Weston. Starbuck knocked on the door of *Land's End.* A few minutes later a scruffy character opened the creaky door and appeared in his stockings and nightshirt scratching himself and demanding to know why he was being rousted out of his bed at such an ungodly hour. Through his whiskey blurred eyes he began to focus on the person standing in his doorway.

"Well blow me down! If it ain't almighty fat arsed Mr. Bloody fucking Starbuck his self." Changing his mood to an even blacker one, Weston continued, "What the Hell do you want here your worship?"

"I want to give you twenty five dollars in gold," replied Starbuck looking down on the thin troll like man."

"I'm much obliged your worship for all of your kindness. Who the Hell do I have to kill for it?"

"Nobody. Just take me to the mainland. If you get me there by early afternoon, I'll give you another ten."

"Well, that be a bloody fortune ain't it though. You must want to go there real bad. It will cost you fifty in advance, in silver or gold, and we'll go right this very minute."

"You seem to have the advantage of me Captain. I'll give you the money when I set foot on your boat. I want to make sure the damned thing floats," replied Starbuck with a sneer.

CHAPTER XXVIII

Starbuck and Weston sat under the billowing sail as the little boat scudded before the wind on its way to Falmouth. Captain Weston hummed some tune half to himself and half to the wind, "Fare well and adieu you ladies of Spain," he droned on in his gruff, raspy, and tone deaf voice.

In the east, there was the hint of a sunrise just beyond the horizon. The wind cut Starbuck to the bone with its early morning chill. With the wind blowing up, there was at least one benefit. He could not smell the foul master of the little craft as he sailed in the direction of the far distant Falmouth shore.

"It's a God damned expensive and miserable voyage we're taking Weston," snarled Starbuck now both cold and hungry. He was freezing as the boat cut its way through the chilled sea. The cold air now seemed to cut keener like a knife across his scarred face.

Weston clamped his jaws together smartly in disapproval of Starbuck's carping and came about in a flash. "If it's too fucking expensive for you, Mr. Starbuck almighty sir, maybe we'll just go back. Let's see how expensive that will be your lordship!"

Weston began sailing, tacking against the wind, and turning back in the direction of Nantucket.

"What the Hell are you doing you damned old fool!" bellowed

Starbuck whose pain and hunger had already made the trip thus far in the cold air a horrible trial.

"If you don't like the tariff over to the mainland, you sure in Hell ain't going to like the fare for the trip back to Nantucket none. Since you spoke to me so damned disrespectful like, it'll cost you another fifty dollars," laughed the all but toothless old mariner.

"Are you out of your mind? Come about at once, and head back to Falmouth."

"I think you're forgettin' whose captain here. Since I put about, Mr. fucking Starbuck sir, the fare is another fifty dollars. Payable now."

"For fifty dollars, I'll cut your throat and throw your carcass overboard you miserable bag of bones, and sail this God damned bum boat myself you stinking old cod! Set a course for Falmouth now and be quick about it or by the Lord Jesus Jumping Christ, I'll do you in a trice!" bellowed Starbuck.

"Try it matey, and I'll dice up your bloated carcass and boil you down for oil. You ought to yield three barrels at least you fat bag of dung."

Starbuck pulled out his sheath knife whose blade caught the rising sun. "Don't you think that I can sail this sorry bum boat myself you sorry fucking piece of scum? I don't need you any more than a toad needs another wart on its arse. I could open you up and dump you into the deep Weston, and none would be the wiser, and fewer than none would care."

In a flash, Weston produced an ancient pistol from the depths of the rags he wore by way of clothing. "Not so fast there matey. Them fellers from New York tells me that they want you alive. They must have something special planned for you. But you see, I suspects that you must have a lot more gold on you or in those pretty new leather cases you've got tossed over there. It don't matter too much to me just how I gets paid as long as I gets paid. Maybe if I plays my cards right, I gets paid twice," he said flashing a grim smile that showed every decaying tooth still remaining in his mouth. "But I'm betting what you got in them cases there be a whole lot more than them New Yorkers will be paying for you. So maybe I just shoots you and sails off with your treasure after I sends you to see your old friends in the deep."

Weston now sat at the tiller, which was held under his arm, and he rested his body against the stern boards. He pulled back the flintlock mechanism of his pistol. He continued to smile as he spoke, "As I said, it don't matter to me nohow how I makes me day's pay. Lookie here. Nice dry powder, all primed, and double shotted just in case you should want to give me an argument on the score so to speak. You are just like most of the high toned fellers I've knowed that like to come out to the island now and then, and looks down their noses at the likes of poor old Captain Weston. You folks are all so high and mighty thinking that you be better than poor old Captain Fuller Weston."

"I'm no swell you stupid squid. I was born on that island!" growled Starbuck.

"That be no matter to me one way or 'tother matey. What cods they be, those swelled up dudes. A few of them over the years was short with me when they wanted the lease of my craft. They was a toffee nosed lot to be sure and abused me good nature. And guess what? They was all high and mighty, and today there ain't nothing left of them but bones on the bottom of the Atlantic just a few dozen fathoms under us. They had gold in their pockets, but not half so much as you got I'm thinking. Who the Hell would miss you? Maybe I disgust you, but all of the rest of you high toned people who been here for two hundred years or more been making me sicker still for longer than I can remember. You all think that you be captains and lords and such. You ain't, and they ain't. Down deep Captains Doane, Folger, Mayhew, and the whole goddamned race of ever lasting Starbucks ain't so good or smart as me."

"Is that so Captain Fuller shyte Weston sir?" asked Starbuck with mocking feigned tone of awe in his deep throated voice.

"Laugh at me if you like, but in the end, they all have to

come to me when they want something dirty done. There just ain't anybody else but me who could do the job they need done you see. Those New York fellers told me that you did something to them that they didn't like too much, and whatever it was, it weren't none of my business to worry myself about they says. And I tells them that is fine with me as long as they pays the freight. They just told me that they want to get their hands on you, and then you would come to me out of the blue like, because, most likely, I be the only one who could help you. It was all too good to be true thinks I. Of course it weren't really out of the blue. They got me to take some letter to *The Nantucket Inquirer* to get you into the mood of asking me for transport to the mainland. Must be something important says I to myself."

"I can see that you are no fool Weston," sneered Starbuck.

The comment passed unnoticed as Weston pressed on. "They tells me that they want to get their hands on you, and that you would walk up to me, just as nice as pie, to get to the mainland, because you will want yer little voyage to be a secret. They tells me to signal with a lantern when I take you close to the shore, because they want it to be dark by the time we get there. We'll need the light you see. That was the only hard part in the whole thing, that is the timing of the thing, but now that you know about it, ain't no problem at all. First I figured that it would be better if I killed you and just take the gold that I supposed that you might have had on you, because you must have stolen it from them to make them so mad in the first place, and I knew that you would have to take it with you when you had to run. Then I thinks, I'll wait and just see what happens. Now it's all confused up again. How can I get paid by them fellers and get your gold? And them damn fools wants you alive and kicking. You sees my problem don't you?"

"You are pretty smart at that Weston. You must be smart enough to know that if I have a lot of gold with me now, and if those men came all the way from New York to get it, that I must have a lot more back on the island well hid away, maybe somewhere in the ground. Those men are not coming all this way for whatever I can carry in those two little leather cases there. That don't seem too logical to you does it?"

Weston's attention was now much focused on what his prisoner had to say, and he thought that he might have heard an opportunity there.

"Just what might you be hinting at there matey?" asked the old shark with a greedy cast to his black eyes.

"Maybe I'm hinting of splitting as much as a hundred thousand dollars in gold with you to save my life. I may not be anything to other people, but my life means something to me, and I'm ready to bargain with you. Half a loaf is better than being dead, and it's such a big loaf Weston being as I said a hundred thousand dollars in gold and all that. Only I know where it is. That's why these men came all the way from New York to get their hands on me. It's their money, and you can be damned sure that they have no intention of letting you have a dime of it. In fact I'll wager that they intend to kill you rather than pay you for your trouble here. After all, you'll know too much. And as you yourself said, they want me alive. What the Hell will they want you for? After all you are hardly in a position to stop them from doing what they damned well please. Do you think that they are so fond of you that they are going to let you live one day longer than they will need you? You are a smart fellow. I'm sure that you can figure out the answer to that. As soon as you turn me over to them, it's all over with you too. I wouldn't mind seeing you getting your throat cut you see, but I don't want to spend eternity with your rotting carcass next to me either should they change their mind about me or force me to talk too soon."

"Wait a minute there Starbuck. Nobody has a hundred thousand dollars in gold in all of Nantucket town. They may have land, and they may have ships and paper, but not gold. How can you have so much?"

"Now who mentioned that figure? Are you fishing Weston? No, come to think of it, I think that I must have let that cat out of the bag myself. You have me that frightened Captain. It is the God's honest truth that there is on that island," said Starbuck pointing to the southern horizon to Nantucket, "More gold than any hundred islanders will ever see in their whole lifetimes."

"You just made mention of that figure and well you know it. And how did you come into money like that?"

"I was into slaving."

"You mean to tell me that you were into selling niggers down South ways? You mean to tell me that you were going all the way to Africa to get ships full of niggers?" asked Weston with his eyes wide open and slack mouth agape.

"And to Brazil as well. Slaving is not even against the law there, slaving is a going business in Brazil all right. Brazil has more slaves than you can even think about, and they want even more. There is no end of money to be made there. And no white man can do the work that they want done in the Amazon region. White men drop like flies even if they don't work all that hard there."

"Well I'll be damned," said Weston laughing, "You're a real black hearted rogue ain't you Mr. Starbucks, and I think that you are telling me the truth ain't you? Yes sir, I can see it in your eyes. You are telling me the truth, and you wants to buy your life real bad too don't you Mister Starbuck?"

"Tell me again partner. Just how did those New York boys know that I was going to want to leave the island? I know that you told me once. I just want it straight and real clear in my head," said Starbuck in a voice that he hoped was ingratiating and confidential.

Beaming at the word "Partner", Weston narrowed his eyes and confided, "They came to me and told me to make up to you and let you know that my craft was available if you was wanting to leave the island for the mainland anytime soon. This I did, if you recollect. That is why I stopped you away back down by the shore. If you recall, I did nothing about the making up to you part, because it's against my nature to make up to swabs like, but I did tell you that if you ever had to leave the island real quick like,

I'd be your man. Then they give me this envelope to bring to the paper. They said that there was a story in it that would make you want to leave for the mainland soon. They said that it would be more than likely that you would want to make port for Falmouth. They went on to tell me that all hands would be watching out for my signal with the lantern here. Then they said fer me to flash the light every twenty minutes as we got near to the port after nightfall. They said that they would hang two lanterns where they was so I'd know where to make my landing. It's just like that Paul Revere feller in those old stories over to Boston. When it gets dark, all we'll have to do is look over to the northwest yonder ways, and we'll see them lanterns. So all we have to do is wait out the day after we come off shore until dark. Then there will be no trouble seeing them lanterns, that is, if I don't turn back, and you take me to all that pretty gold."

The two men talked the rest of the day as the boat made its way slowly and circuitously toward the Falmouth landfall. Exactly what had to be done if anything was yet to be decided by the two as they attempted to make an unholy pact. Weston was so animated and carried away by his dreams of shared wealth that hunger and thirst seemed to mean nothing to him. Visions of wealth dominated his discourse with his passenger, half partner, and prisoner. Starbuck nibbled on a few stingy bits of hardtack that Weston had doled out to him and sipped from a flask of water. Starbuck studied Weston through hooded eyes, contemplated the New Yorkers who seemed to be three in number, according to the seedy captain, and slowly Starbuck hatched out a plan of his own.

With the onset of dusk, Starbuck strained his eyes to make out two points of light like two distant stars low in the sky and so close together that they looked like one light if one didn't know what one was looking for. Starbuck turned to Weston, and said, "Well what do you say? There are your two lights over yonder ways. Are you going to kill me, turn me over to them, or throw in with me? Which is it going to be?"

"I'll throw in with you Starbuck. I really didn't like the cut of them three fellers anyway. They was a pack of Irish Whores' Sons."

"Were they big men?" asked Starbuck.

"Only one of them was a big feller. The other two was on the average to small size, but they all had knives and pistols and such. They be loaded for bear, and let there be no mistake about it."

"Are they now? That's very interesting Weston. I think that you are the most clever man on the island of Nantucket to take note of all that. That is the very sort of information we need to take the measure of the enemy. All I can say is that, I'm proud to partner up with you. When one gets to know you, you ain't such a bad sort Captain Fuller Weston."

"Why thank you matey. It's good of you to say so," beamed Weston radiating in his newly found fortune and friendship.

"More than that, you are the only man who has been straight with me here of all the islanders I've met so far in all the months I've been on that bloody island. I've made some maps of where my treasure is. Do you want to see them in case something happens to me when we mix it up with those New York boys?" purred Starbuck.

"That I would. I'd be proud to," said the Captain leaning forward. He never saw Starbuck's hand move as the former mate drew another sheath knife from its hiding place under his jacket. Then in a flash, Starbuck brought it up smartly under Weston's sternum and then drove it up and into Weston's heart. The whole motion did not take more than half a second of mortal time. Weston turned an even more sickly white. His eyes were staring like a dead mackerel, and his face was a mask of pain, betrayal, and total surprise. Blood welled up into his mouth as he tried to mouth the words, "Oh, matey."

Starbuck pushed him back to avoid contact with the streaming blood. The last glimmer of thought that the dying Weston had was, "Damn it! That's what I had planned for you."

CHAPTER XXIX

Starbuck took the pistol from Weston's dead hand, carefully covered the flash pan, and lowered the flintlock. He then placed the weapon inside of his own coat where it would be kept dry and at the ready. With any amount of luck, Starbuck would not have to test its utility. He then ripped the rags from Weston's body and let the blood settle in the lower part of the corpse. Then Starbuck began a search of the body for anything useful for his purposes. Then taking all that was useful from the many pockets of the dead man's coat, he found the gold, which he had paid the Captain for his ill-fated passage, and the advance money which the old rascal must have received from the Five Points crowd. Starbuck's best find however was an excellent compass of German manufacture.

"I wonder how that miserable old fool came by that." Starbuck asked out loud.

Then he laughed into the night air as he recalled Weston's hints at what had become of his other sea going client's that he must have killed and sent to Davy Jones. Starbuck mused that Weston must have robbed them all of whatever they may have had with them at the time. Starbuck felt good about ridding the world of at least one of the human maggots who had infested the place.

This act of killing this bit of human lice relieved Starbuck of a great deal of the tension from which he had been suffering. He felt alive and useful again. Looking down at his knife, he shook his head at the blood on the blade. Taking note of the possibility of rust, Starbuck calmly wiped the blade with the rags, which had lately been some of the unfortunate Captain Weston's wardrobe. Now Starbuck sat back to rest from the strain of his exertions. After all, he had a busy night ahead of him. He studied the two points of light as he slowly drew closer to the shore.

At last he roused himself to needful action. He shifted Weston's body just a bit so that it faced directly up with its opened dead eyes seemingly observing the stars. Starbuck smiled sardonically as he observed Weston's fishy eyes looking up to the sky. "No hope there you poor bastard," laughed Starbuck at his own little joke as he sliced into the body cavity of the unbleeding corpse. Starbuck felt nothing more emotional than if he were gutting a large mackerel. He filled the body cavity of the corpse with stones, which Weston had so thoughtfully put aboard the craft in anticipation of perhaps sinking a corpse of his own making at some future time. Using every rag, and bit of twine, and rope on the craft, he bound up the unprotesting and still staring corpse.

"I'm not going to close your eyes matey. I want you to see the crabs and fish that will nibble you away to nothing but your old bones you rotting bastard," remarked Starbuck almost sweetly to the corpse. Having done this, he scanned the horizon. There was nothing to be seen but the bobbing boats tied up for the night in the far distance near the Falmouth shore. He and Weston were alone on the sea. They were far enough off shore as to look like night fishermen if they were noted at all. With skill born of practice, Starbuck rolled Weston over the side into the sea. The old man barely made a noise as he slipped, open eyed over the side of his own boat. Starbuck watched Weston's body descend down into the deep until it was lost in the darkness of the water. As Starbuck had heard Whitehouse say dozens of times when the bodies of black slaves, who died during the dread middle passage, were thrown into the sea, Starbuck recited the only Latin phrase he had ever known, "Sic transit gloria mundi," as if it were some kind of prayer for the dead.

When he was mate, Starbuck had asked Captain Whitehouse just what the phrase meant. Whitehouse had replied, "It's too bad that your glorious arse isn't in this mortal world anymore." Then the Captain would laugh at his own joke as he walked away from the rail saying, "Let's just call that a liberal translation of the original Starbuck, and let it go like that."

Somehow it seemed appropriate to speak these familiar words, but at the same time, he doubted the precise quality of Whitehouse's translation. His former Captain confessed to translating the holy Latin screed rather loosely. Starbuck was not sure that the Almighty really had such a crude sense of humor. Weston's body had been properly weighted and had sunk well out of sight rather nicely. Starbuck knew very well that Fuller Weston would not be having a private resurrection anytime soon. Starbuck then added to the eulogy, "All the fish will dine well tonight and leave not a trace. Peace to your ashes you murderous old sonofabitch."

He then looked about the craft noting what work had to be done to receive his three guests from New York in their proper turn. At least these three fellows were not unexpected guests. Starbuck scrubbed away the few spots of blood that had made their way to the decking with a bit of a rag, and he congratulated himself on his neatness. Then he made the craft shipshape. He folded the extra sail and made a makeshift cot to lie on. Then Starbuck set the course away from the distant pair of lights and tied off the tiller. He then pulled the sail down, and let it lay loose on the deck. This allowed the boat to slowly drift. Starbuck then took a bit of sail and rope and fashioned a sort of sea anchor to slow the drifting. Observing the clear and cloudless sky overhead, which was starlit as if for his convenience, Starbuck decided that the weather would be fine for the foreseeable future. In fact, it had even warmed a bit. Starbuck decided that it was best not to arrive near the rendezvous point with the New Yorkers before he could put together a good plan of action for the following night.

Starbuck wanted time to get ready for his company from what he supposed to be the Five Points. After all, if they had gone through such a great ordeal of trouble to meet and chat with him, the least he could do was arrange a proper reception he thought. Suddenly he felt weak, hungry, and tired. He decided to eat something and rest. Starbuck ate half a water soaked piece of hardtack. As he lay on his improvised cot, he covered himself with a scrap of sail. Starbuck's eyes grew heavy, and he slowly slipped off into sleep. How long that sleep lasted, Starbuck did not know. The next mortal event of which he became aware was when somebody tugged at his sleeve and softly said, "Avast matey. Art thou dead?"

Starbuck awoke with a start. He shook his head and looked into the plain face of an honest Quaker fisherman from the island. "No, I don't think so. In fact, every pain in my old back tells me that I am not," he laughed. Then Starbuck turned to the fisherman and said, "Thank thee for asking all the same. T'is good of thee to take an interest brother."

The fisherman laughed and asked, "Art thou a brother then?"

"No mate. Not any more, but most of my family were Quakers in the old days, and some of them may be yet. They were Starbucks, you know, of Nantucket Island. I have not lived there since I was a lad gone off to sea more than thirty years ago."

Almost sadly, the good man turned his eyes to the heavens and said, "I regret to see that thou art not one of us now, but well, t'is no great matter."

"Please friend and brother, I am not making sport of thee. My people were Quakers for some two hundred years or more, and t'is easy for me to fall into that manner of speech from the old days, and it gives me comfort to talk to thee such. For that is the manner of speech I heard from my mother and the elders during my childhood on the island. In fact, it is comforting for me to hear thee speak. The old way of talking does fall sweetly on the ear. Nothing has made me feel near so well as talking with thee in more years than I can remember."

"I thought that thou might be hurt brother, and that is why I intruded in on thee. I am happy that thou art not. But I do take note that thou hast been badly burned by the sun. Take care that thou does not fall gravely ill, blister, and take fever."

"No friend. Thee cannot burn a burn, or," Starbuck smiled indicating his face, "Scar a scar. This old tanned hide has seen the sun burn down on all the seas of this wide world for too many years on both the seas and the lands far from these shores. I've been to Africa, and Brazil, to the islands of the Pacific, to far China, and the shores of California in my time. This mortal flesh has been burned on all the seven seas and great oceans of the world for the better part of most the years of my life as both man and boy. I have taken some rest this night past, and now I must make sail and land at Falmouth this night to meet some friends who are keen to see me again. I have the whole day before we are to meet, and I shall enjoy this fine clear day. Now fare thee well my good friend, and pray for me, a poor sinning sailor, who long ago lost his way."

"Dost thee need provisions friend, for I have more than enough for the both of us brother," asked the Quaker with real kindness reflected in his old gray eyes.

"I would be glad to buy what you could spare in all truth friend," said Starbuck. "I will confess to thee that I am better provided with cash than with bread."

"There is not enough gold to buy what I can give thee for naught. Take some bread and cheese that my good wife has made with her own loving hands and also a goodly portion of roasted chicken too. I shall place the foodstuffs in this linen drawstring bag for thee, and then I must be off. The fish do not wait upon us," replied the Quaker.

"You are kind indeed brother. May I not give thee something?" said Starbuck feeling a warming to the kindness of the man that he had not experienced since childhood in the arms of his mother.

"Go to meeting some Sabbath, and think of me sometime. Maybe you will even see me and my good wife there. Open yourself to the loving forgiveness of God, and remember that the best of us is only a poor sinner. Do kindness in the world. That will be enough reward for me brother," replied the Quaker. "Now I shall be shoving off to fish, and I shall pray for thee this morning while I attend to the business that the Lord has given unto my hands to do this day in the deep. Fare thee well friend."

Starbuck was glad of the unexpected rest he had gotten and the food he had received, as well as for the unexpected kindness from this unknown Quaker fisherman. His rummage about the boat had revealed only some little hardtack, whiskey, and water. Starbuck had thought to make do with the hardtack and water alone, and to reserve the whiskey for his reward when his job was done in Falmouth that night. Now Starbuck fell on the freshly baked bread, roast chicken, and cheese like a wolf. It was the best meal he could remember eating in an age. After satisfying his private wolf of hunger, Starbuck decided to save the rest of the Quaker's food for later. He rigged a sort of awning out of a sail over the deck and remade his makeshift cot. Without the sail up, he hoped that from a distance the boat would look just like another fishing dory.

Ashore the New Yorkers were waiting for their man. They had expected him yesterday.

"What do you suppose happened to Weston and that Starbuck feller?" asked O'Flaherty.

"These things always take time. Don't be in such a hurry for the man Michael. We don't know if the boss' plan will work. Maybe this fellow don't choose to run yet. I remember him from some meeting with Ellis some years back in the cellar. He seemed a deliberate sort who moved guided by his own inside compass. Maybe he don't understand what the whole thing means. Maybe he's figured it out, or maybe he's just got no fear. Or maybe he's too dumb to be afraid. Maybe he's still on the island, and we'll have to pay a call on him, at some little time in the future. For now we'll wait and see boys."

"Ryan, me lad, he'll run. He'll know how bad we want that shyte Whitehouse in our grasp. He has also known our Mr. Ellis. I'm sure that he's after knowing that we are damned serious people. He must also surmise that the boss won't be taking the loss of two ships and his pal Mr. Ellis none too well, and he knows that Whitehouse scum ain't dead neither. And he knows that the ship in question ain't sunk. It does nobody's reputation no good if the word gets around that we can get taken like that. The Boss don't want to end up no joke. That would be very bad for business. It could be the end of us in Five Points if the word comes 'round that we can be taken in by a Limey swindler like Whitehouse. We'll rest up today and be on the alert tonight. Michael O' Brien you keep a look out, and wake us at dusk. Don't fall asleep! Understand!"

"Yeh, yeh. I understands just fine."

"Make sure that those two lamps got oil in them. They burned all last night. I don't want no foul ups. Have you got that?"

As evening came on, Starbuck began to make Weston's craft look as if it were making its way back to Nantucket. He took down his improvised awning and raised sail and started heading into the wind. Starbuck took his readings carefully, and when night fell he changed his course again. This time he was headed for Falmouth and the two lights that had been relighted on the shore to mark the place of his rendezvous with the three men of Five Points.

He lighted one of the lucifers he had taken from his plundering of Weston's pockets. It sputtered to life in a fine flame as he had struck it against the inside of the boat. He then sheltered the fragile flame with his hand, lit his lantern, and then covered the light with its tin shielding shutter. A few seconds later, he opened the shutter and flashed a signal lasting a second or two then covered the flame of his lamp again with the tin shield. He had flashed the light so fast that the men ashore may not have seen it. Fifteen minutes later he flashed the light again for just a moment longer. For the next three hours, he repeated the procedure while planning his attack on the three men as he slowly worked his way to the shoreline to make landfall.

He had rehearsed himself through the plan of attack over and over again in his mind until it almost seemed as if he had actually carried out his plan of slaughter a dozen times over. If all worked out well, the whole deadly exercise should last only a few seconds. In many ways, Starbuck reflected that his whole life had been a rehearsal for this specific moment. He wrapped himself in Weston's old oilskins. The forlorn looking foul weather garment looked as if it were old enough to have gone around Cape Horn with Captain Cook eighty odd years before. The years of accumulated stench was all but intolerable to Starbuck's senses. He pulled the great old greasy wide brimmed hat down over his face and tied it under his chin by its cords. Starbuck correctly fancied that the oilskin slicker would hide his huge frame and muscular bulk under its filthy expanse.

As the boat drew closer to the shore and the waiting men of Five Points, Starbuck braced himself. His blood was up, and he was ready for the fight of his life. In fact, he was now looking forward to the confrontation. All the hate he felt for Whitehouse and the taunting islanders was looking for some further release. He remembered those thugs well from the cellar meeting in Five Points and the smell of their very attitude seemed to be cutting through the air. He knew the depth of their ruthlessness. Starbuck was eager for the fight that he knew would come. A desire to strike out at everyone who had offered him insults over the last year overwhelmed him, and the kindness that he had recently encountered from the Quaker only fed his desire for revenge on all those who had offered him only contempt and insults.

He flexed his muscles under the hot oilskins. He was working himself up into a state of readiness. He felt like some caged animal with the scent of a fine prospective kill in his nostrils. Starbuck was ready to spring as soon as the door of his cage was opened and he was unleashed.

As the last hour passed and the signals from the shore were returned, Starbuck's heart had warmed to the contest to come. It would not be long before his blood lust was to be satisfied. His muscles were like steel springs ready to uncoil on command. At last, someone of the three New Yorkers called out as he neared the shore, "Hello the boat!"

"Belay that noise you damned fool! Do you want the law on us!" Starbuck said in his best Weston style. The men stopped talking and just awaited the arrival of their quarry. Their anticipation made them keen, and their excitement grew as the boat came closer to the shore. Starbuck, once again in imitation of Weston's voice, in tones both very low and gravelly, said, "Belay that noise ye cods! Your man be all nicely trussed up under this here tarp. He'll not be goin' nowhere, and damned your eyes, he be alive just like you wanted. So take your own sweet time gents. He'll not be goin' nowheres." Then Starbuck half cackled as he laughed in perfect imitation of Captain Weston.

The big Irishman stormed with a muffled snort, "Well you took your own sweet time getting him here. Where the Hell have you been these days past?"

"Never you mind where I've been. This damned fool got a mind of his own. He didn't want to come along as quick as I thought he would. He ain't too easy to make cooperative like. He's a big feller you might remember. Have you got my money? I want to get back to the island by first light before anyone knows I've slipped me moorings."

"Don't worry your head about it Weston. You'll get everything that's coming to you soon enough," replied the big Irishman. "You'll be off before you know it."

The three men relaxed and then slowly advanced on the boat to get their prize thinking that they would dispose of Weston who was their dupe and who had so nicely delivered their quarry. The big Irishman came on board first saying, "Let's get a good look at the big ugly bastard with all his scars."

He was the first to crowd into the boat followed by the other two. Now the three men were like so many sardines all packed together in a tin. "So much the better," mumbled Starbuck with his body all bent over under his oilskins in an effort to make himself look smaller. At the same time, he was all tensed and ready to uncoil and spring.

As the big man bent over to rip the tarp off of what he took to be the trussed up Starbuck, the old slaver neatly and deeply slit his throat with one deft motion that was totally undetected in the dark. The Irishman barely made a gurgling sound as he appeared to trip over the body under the tarp and fall onto the lump that was supposed to be Starbuck. The second man laughed into the pitch blackness of the night, "What a foolish ape you're after being. Can't you stand up more than two minuets at a time without falling all over your own big feet Shamus?"

A second later he too was falling down on top of the big man. "You are a race of clumsy oxen. Can't you get up?" cried Starbuck.

As the third fellow wondered at the comic spectacle, he smiled broadly. As he leaned forward, he felt the hot and fast thrust of Starbuck's knife going up under his sternum and into his heart. It was all over in less than twenty seconds. Starbuck almost fainted, not with the horror of his deed, but from sheer animal fatigue resulting from the explosion of energy he had expended in the killing of the three men. His last reserve of strength had been spent in his murderous attack. He sat in the stern of the boat looking at what he had done and smiled. As the minutes passed, his heart stopped racing and his breathing became more regular. "Old Starbuck's not the man he used to be. No siree, he's not. You're old and fat and not on top of your game," he heard himself saying to the night. Then he smiled, "Still not so bad for an old fat man."

For several more minutes he just sat surrounded by the victims of his spent fury. At last, his energy returned, and he exposed his lantern light just long enough to look at his watch. Starbuck noted that there were still hours of blessed darkness left until sunrise. He would have to act fast. Gathering all of his strength, he forced himself to heave ahead, and he waded to the shore. Starbuck then selected some large rocks and deposited them into the boat along with anything that could be used for bindings. With his bloody cargo aboard, he shoved off heading out to sea and the island.

Starbuck, taking advantage of the land breeze, raised the sail, and made for the open sea. By the time he had sailed off shore some two miles, he knew that less than two and a half hours remained before the dory men including his Quaker friend would be on the waves in search of their livings. He turned his attention to his ghastly cargo. Having placed each of the bodies face up, he let the blood nicely settle to the lower part of the corpses. As he stripped and then opened up each man to load him with stones, there was little blood to contend with. One by one he trussed up each corpse and heaved them overboard, one after the other. They sank to the sandy bottom of the seabed never to be seen again.

Next he placed the oilskins, which had protected his clothes as well as all bits of his victim's clothing into the bloody spatted tarp along with the rest of the rocks. Then Starbuck tied it all up, and tossed this final package into the sea as well. Now he was alone without company neither living, anticipated, or dead, for the first time in a day and a half. Being alone felt really good to Starbuck who was now finding his own company more congenial than ever.

As he hoisted the sail again, he sailed away from the scene of his grisly activity, Starbuck knew that he would have to get rid of the boat. Weston's craft was too well known by the locals. The last thing he needed was anyone asking about the late Captain Weston although it was hard to imagine anyone caring about the fate of the old degenerate. Starbuck knew that nobody on Nantucket would find it strange if old Weston had just sailed off in this old tub and had foundered far out at sea. This night, he had bought himself the gift of time. Starbuck set a course for Nantucket, and he thought about the rest of the things he would have to do before he could return to his fine white house in the center of the town. He would have to sink the boat of course and bury all of the rest of his gold in some safe place that he could remember easily. So much to do, thought Starbuck as he slipped off to sleep with the tiller tucked under his arm dragging the sea anchor that would keep him from sailing too far.

CHAPTER XXX

Samuel and Pompey had booked passage on a Cunard steamer bound for Boston four days after reading of Starbuck's rescue at sea. The news story was growing old, but they had to act on it nevertheless. They raced down to London by coach, and two days later they were at sea as first class passengers aboard the *Unicorn.* Now there was nothing to do but play their parts as a traveling gentleman and his valet. Samuel's role was never too closely defined as this led to a certain adaptability. He was a sort of gentleman's gentleman of all work as various situations presented themselves and were subject to some modification. This game was no longer new to Pompey and Samuel. Years of close observation of their "Betters" was paying large dividends. They lived their roles of a Portuguese gentleman and servant with a casual air of grace. Pretty ladies aboard the ship were always seeking peeks at the handsome Pompey who stood half a head taller than most of the men in the saloon or the main cabin. Samuel also drew attention, being fully as tall as Pompey, and as the paragon of the perfect manservant, Samuel was always at his master's elbow.

The two men could be seen walking the deck in fair weather. Pompey seemed both aristocratic and distant. He was rumored to be an exiled Carlist from the Spain of Isabella II. It was rumored that he was a Prince under the sentence of death for high treason. This surrounded him with an air of romance. His fellow passengers found Pompey to be charming and polite to a fault. He was thought to be shy by the female population of the first class, but he always did them the favor of accepting invitations to sit at table with the social climbing Americans who were just discovering European aristocracy and thought that Mr. James Charles, as he now called himself, epitomized the best of that self same aristocracy. Everyone assumed that this name was an alias covering a great mystery. Even the sole other titled passenger, a handsome middle-aged English baronet traveling with his wife, attempted to discover who this stranger was without success. Pompey never actually defined himself or offered any self-narrative during this voyage, which was perfect for his persona as the ultimate man of mystery.

One evening at dinner, the baronet asked about the personal interests of the young man sitting opposite him. Pompey had answered him, "I enjoy the usual run of recreation I suppose: fencing, riding, shooting, and sport in general", said Mr. Charles who knew well that English aristocrats were mad for sport.

"What fencing style do you prefer? The French, Spanish, or Italian?" asked Sir Ambrose, Baronet of Malke.

"I am a student of the Spanish school. My fencing master was educated in Madrid. He came from a very long line of distinguished swordsmen. I believe that he was of Castilian ancestry Sir Ambrose."

"I prefer the French style myself Mr. Charles. So precise and intellectually demanding. In fact it is the only intellectual exercise a gentleman should expend his efforts on."

"Oh Ambrose! You are so English," laughed Lady Anne who was the intellectual in the family Pompey thought.

"I say! Should we have a bit of fun? How would you like to test our schools and our skills on the deck tomorrow? This voyage has been one of unrelieved boredom. I could do with a bit of excitement and sport eh what! I think that it is a capital idea, don't you?" asked Sir Ambrose.

"Well really Ambrose! You are the limit. Doesn't the Oxford crowd ever grow up? I cannot understand your obsession with sport and games," interjected the handsome Lady Anne.

"You spent years at the university and never took a degree. What the Devil did you fellows do down there? You certainly didn't spend any time with the dons or do much reading."

"Good heavens Anne. When a fellow goes down to Oxford, it's to meet with other fellows of one's own sort. People who actually go to those damned boring lectures and sit examinations are really not gentlemen you know. They all become civil servants, parsons, and such awfully dull middle class twits. Gentlemen have better things to do with their time than read and listen to a lot of rot about Shakespeare, Caesar, and that sort of thing. What ever are you thinking woman! It is a proven fact that reading dulls the mind. Talk to any of those silly twits who take degrees, and I'll show you a real dullard. They can't ride or shoot worth a damn either I tell you. In their undergraduate days, they were no good on the playing fields, and later on they were no good in war either. That is where real gentlemen prove their worth!"

"Quite right," said Pompey with his best "Mr. Charles" smile, "I understand Sir Ambrose's love of sport. After all, he is an Englishman, and are not all of your nation's victories in battle just the results of what you have learned on the playing fields of Eaton and your other great schools?"

"Right you are Mr. Charles. What do you say to a bit of good fun eh what?" said Sir Ambrose.

"As they say in America, you are on sir," replied Pompey with uplifted glass which Sir Ambrose met with a proper clink of his own glass in true bonhomie.

Samuel, properly standing behind his master's chair looked on with a hint of disapproval that went quite unnoticed by the company except for Lady Anne. She tapped Pompey on the arm playfully with her fan and said, "I don't think that your man approves of your contest of tomorrow Mr. Charles."

"He doesn't Lady Anne. He's rather a prude and sees fencing as a rather silly use of my time. He will insist that I read and improve myself. I sometimes think that he fancies me as his juvenile charge and sees himself rather in the the capacity of a nanny."

"Oh Mr. Charles," laughed Lady Anne, "I wish that I could find somebody like that for dear Ambrose. He is a terrible little boy who needs taking in hand. Now, I do like your man. Should you ever feel the need to let him go, please let me know. I shall engage him at once for very good wages. There is not another quite like him in all of England I am sure."

When Pompey retired for the night after brandy and cigars, Samuel shut the door of the cabin, turned to Pompey, and asked, "What do you think that you are up to? Fencing with that British aristocrat? Pompey, you have to remember what we are doing here. You cannot put us in harm's way."

"Why did I spend all of those hours in the garden back on the Forrester Plantation with Senor Sandoval if it was not for moments like this? Do you want me to appear to be some sort of fraud? Gentlemen play with swords. This is what people of my class do in Europe, or even in the South as far as that goes. Sir Ambrose is a large child, and he want's to play knights or something like it. That is what we aristocrats do. We play. We do not go down to Oxford to do anything so prosaic as reading or attending lectures. Didn't you hear?"

"What if you lose? What then?"

"I suspect that he will like me better than if I win. As long as I put up a good show, it does not matter if I actually best him. And should I win, well, he will respect me more. Either way we win as long as I can put on a good show. Trust me. It is not a fight to the death. It is just a bit of fun. I have to put on a good show, and that is the extent of the game. That is all I need to do," said Pompey.

"Well I suppose you had better practice. All you have right now is your sword cane."

"There is no point practicing really. I will have to parry and thrust and see what he's up to tomorrow. That's all there is to it I think. After all, I haven't the damnedest idea of what the French style is. I suspect that fencing is fencing after you have taken your stance. I guess that I'll find out tomorrow," Pompey said as he undressed for bed. Then he turned to Samuel and said, "I think that I can recall one technical difference between the Spanish and French styles. The Spanish don't mind stabbing in the head area, because it is most unexpected and the head is therefore most vulnerable. Everybody else thinks that such a maneuver is very unsporting. In a serious contest, the Spanish simply think that it is just best to win and stay alive. To disregard the niceties just makes good sense to them."

The next day was a fair one. The sea was like glass. The Captain was called to oversee the contest of skill. Pompey stood with Samuel waiting on the deck with the collar of his shirt open at the neck and his coat unbuttoned. Sir Ambrose strode onto the deck some ten minutes late. His valet carried the sword case containing a fine pair of epees. The case was first offered to Pompey who looked at the weapons carefully testing each for balance.

"Well Sir Ambrose, these are Toledo blades. They are Spanish, and I think that these are the best in all of Europe. They are both very fine. Perfect actually. I'll select this one," said Pompey taking the nearest blade from the case.

Sir Ambrose smiled and replied, "I didn't say that I did not admire the best swords made in Europe even if the best just happen to be Spanish. I just admire the French school of fencing. For a Saber, a Wilkinson blade will do well as a Solingen, but for an epee or rapier, only a Toledo blade will serve."

"I quite agree. Either of these fine weapons is quite acceptable to me Sir Ambrose."

Lady Anne came up onto the deck followed by a steward with a silver bucket containing a bottle of Champagne. "With this as a reward to be shared by both sides, no matter who wins, at least the rest of us will have something civilized with which to celebrate along with you, and in the end that is all that really counts. I think that we'll agree that the French are the only ones who have real style gentlemen."

"How un-English of you my dear," replied Sir Ambrose.

"With that, I shall agree Lady Anne. Shall we let the games begin?" said Pompey with an uncharacteristic flourish of exaggerated bravado.

The men took their places, while the Captain intoned, "Are we ready? Gentlemen begin."

Lady Anne added, "Now don't you little boys hurt yourselves. Samuel and I will be very cross with you if you do!"

The blades moved with slow deliberation while each man took the others measure, then Sir Ambrose began an attack with a series of deft thrusts, which Pompey parried with a less than practiced smoothness. Sir Ambrose then saluted, and the two faced off again with Pompey beating back the next attack with a much better show of skill. Again they saluted, and Sir Ambrose commenced a third attack which Pompey beat back with an even better show of mastery. By now, each man had taken the measure of the other.

Now it was Pompey's turn to attack. It was in the style of the masters of Madrid. Sir Ambrose beat Pompey back with real skill. The group watching the contest was respectfully silent as the two fencers moved around each other in what might have been, in another time and place, a dance of death. At last, after a half hour had passed, Sir Ambrose said, "Enough! Age must give way to youth. You are a fine man with a blade sir. Shall we indulge in some of my good lady wife's Champagne my young Cid?"

"Thank you. Could we invite my valet to join us? He really does not approve of such frivolous sport, and so it would give me pleasure for him to recognize the hard work we have put into developing our skills. I assure you Sir Ambrose that you will really like the experience of helping me bring that lesson home to him, and we can enjoy watching him exhibiting his puritanical displeasure, which will compel him to show disdain. That is with the permission of your good lady."

"Quite right Mr. Charles. I think that would be good fun, but I fear that your man is rather a more mature gentleman than either of you. What do you say my dear?" answered Lady Anne.

"Seems like a good fellow. Not a slave or anything like that is he Charles eh what?" asked Sir Ambrose.

"My dear Malke! A slave! Now really. You are the limit." laughed Pompey.

"Well I was for Wilberforce and all that. Don't approve of the slavery thing eh what! Wouldn't do. You really seem like a good chap. Glad to see you don't go in for the slavery business. Just not right you know," said the baronet.

"You are a good fellow Sir Ambrose. I pay my man well and take rashers of abuse from him for all my missteps social and otherwise. He has the good grace to dress me down in private I assure you," replied Pompey.

"Well then. I'll be happy to drink with your man then. Come along then. Will you give us the pleasure of your company then? I understand from your master that you are a good and decent fellow. Do us the honor of drinking with us," said Sir Ambrose to Samuel who nodded his head and took a glass from the hand of Lady Anne, and drank a toast to the contest of the afternoon.

Among the passengers milling about the deck was a southern planter and his wife. They watched the whole proceeding quite aghast, and then stormed off to their cabin loudly muttering that the world was going mad with people who were supposed to be of the "Better Sort" engaging in race mixing.

Lady Anne was both youngish and still quite pretty. She was still absolutely beautiful when she smiled as she did now and said, "I think that what we are doing is a civilized ending to the event with honor being satisfied on all sides. It's nice to know that we ladies have you fierce gentlemen to protect us from footpads of all sorts my dear Ambrose." Turning to Pompey, she said, "Those two, the couple who just walked off to their cabin in such a huff, are they not from the South of the United States?"

"I gather that they are Lady Anne," replied Pompey.

"They seem rather primitive, even more so than you are my dear Ambrose. I wish that I could steal that Black gentleman to be your gentleman's gentleman. Lord knows you could still use some instruction in private."

"Anne, really. You are the limit, but somehow I cannot help loving you darling girl. Besides you seem to fill that niche rather well," replied Sir Ambrose with a loving smile.

"Let's drink then to a fine friendship. When you return to England, you must visit us at Truxton Hall down in Kent. I rather think that you would like it there. Bring your man there. I rather like the fellow. Maybe I could steal him from you yet for my dear Ambrose. He really needs a nanny, and your man would set him a good example of what a gentleman should be."

"Thank you Sir Ambrose and Lady Anne. I think that I would like that very much," replied Pompey.

"You know something Charles. It would be quite a scandal if it got around, but Anne is almost as good with a blade as I am. She is rather a dark horse. Aren't you my love?"

"Ambrose you are a ridiculous fellow! Dark horse indeed. For a romantic, you can be down right stupid about your use of analogies. And there is nothing wrong with lady's liking a bit of sport as well as your lot as long as it does not become an obsession."

CHAPTER XXXI

The voyage back to America had passed quickly and without incident, and Samuel was gratified that Pompey had passed yet another test. Pompey was glad that his education had stood up to the tests to which it was now subject. Samuel and Pompey had always known that money alone would never buy acceptance in the social circles that they would have to travel in to get where they needed to go. Within three weeks, they had found themselves in Boston. It truly was the "City Founded On A Hill" by John Winthrop almost two hundred and thirty years before. Boston was the national hotbed of abolitionism and home to the most influential people who were fighting to end slavery in the United States.

Mr. Charles and Mr. James checked into Dunham's. This was one the finest hotels in the city. It was just the sort of hostelry that should accommodate a gentleman of Pompey's assumed breeding along with his servant. After they had established themselves in their rooms, Samuel and Pompey took themselves to the offices of *The Liberator*. This journal was owned, edited, and published by America's greatest champion of the abolitionist movement William Lloyd Garrison. The walk to Garrison's office allowed Samuel and Pompey to study the city by daylight in all of its manifold variety. They discovered that no place in Boston was too far from any other place of note in the city which had the compact feeling of a vast village in spite of the fact that its streets were so convoluted in their arrangement. At last Pompey spotted the sign over *The Liberator's* offices marking their destination. As they opened the door to the office, a bell rang out, and a man approached them. He was tall and thin with steel framed glasses perched on his nose. Their thick lenses made the young man who wore them seem much older than his twenty-some years and rather like an owl.

"May I help you gentlemen?" asked the young fellow.

"Yes, could you inform Mr. Garrison that we are here to see him on a serious matter," answered Pompey in a tone of almost detached gravity.

"May I tell Mr. Garrison who is calling on him sir?" answered the thin young man.

"Simply inform him that two friends of the cause are here and that we shall explain our business to him if he would be so gracious as to receive us," replied Pompey with an implied and subtle air of superiority that impressed the young man.

"I shall do as you ask sir. Would you please take a seat? I shall return at once," said the young fellow indicating two armchairs.

Samuel and Pompey did not have to wait long. Shortly after Mr. Garrison was informed that a man and his African manservant wished to see him on a matter of some urgency, Samuel and Pompey were ushered down a short hallway and into the dimly lit office of the great abolitionist publisher himself.

Garrison was a little taken aback. People who wanted to see him, as a rule, did not do so with their black menservants. Having had his offices burned out on several occasions, as well as his presses smashed, Garrison was a bit uneasy when any exotic stranger was in the neighborhood. Still he had told his young printer's assistant to admit the two strangers to his private inner office. As usual his intellectual curiosity overcame his caution. As Pompey and Samuel were ushered into the room, and before a word could be exchanged, Pompey asked, "Might we shut the door Mr. Garrison? Our business here is both delicate and confidential."

Garrison's natural caution was now totally overcome by his insatiable curiosity. "Close the door, and take a seat gentlemen. What can I do for you?" asked the man who published the most important abolitionist newspaper in the country.

"Mr. Garrison, when I was held in bondage as a slave, I was known as Pompey, and this is Samuel, who was kidnapped some thirty five years ago by slave traders from his home in Africa. Today we are known as Mr. James Charles and Samuel James. We are both manumitted former slaves once held in bondage in Georgia."

"Mr. Charles, I would have taken you for a white man. Please gentlemen be seated."

"Mr. Garrison, it is because I look white that I am free to travel as I do. My father was a white man as was my grandfather. This fact of my birth and racial heritage is no matter to me, for I consider Samuel to be my father. My mother was a slave woman whose mother was an African taken from Angola. She was a woman still possessed of beauty when my father took her to his bed. She died of overwork, and physical abuse, in childbirth only eighteen months after I was born. At three, my white father and master lost me at a game of cards, and that great good fortune brought me to the plantation where Samuel was head slave driver and the real master. More information than that, only Samuel can tell you, for only he has the right to relate the rest of the story."

"Well, you have answered a lot of my unasked questions Mr. Charles. How can I be of service to you?"

"First of all Mr. Garrison," said Samuel, "We would deem it a great favor if you do not publish anything we tell you or repeat any of our conversation to anyone without consulting us first. If you cannot do this, we must leave your office at once. I have been told in England that you are a man of your word who can always be trusted. This was told to us by friends of the late Mr. William

Wilberforce who greatly admire the work you are doing here. I am right in this am I not that you are a man of honor?"

"I would like to think I am. I thank you for your kind words regarding that great man, Mr. Wilberforce. I shall respect your wishes for privacy of course. Trust me, slavery has no greater enemy in America than William Lloyd Garrison unless it is Miss Sojourner Truth. Whatever you relate to me will never pass beyond the walls of this room. And here is my hand on that gentlemen."

After shaking hands with Samuel and Pompey, Garrison said, "Mr. James, your story is one that I would very much like to hear."

"I thank you for your kind words Mr. Garrison," said Samuel.

"Will you pardon me for just a moment gentlemen? I wish to make sure that we are not disturbed." Garrison got up from his seat and opened the door. "Harry, come here please," he said in a low voice to the thin man in the steel rimmed spectacles.

The tall young man came running to the door of the office, inclined his head as he no doubt had done a hundred times or more before, and listened to Garrison's quietly given instructions. When Harry had left, Garrison shut the door and returned to his seat. Turning to his guests he said, "I told Harry to say that I was out if anyone were to ask for me. I told him not to disturb us for any reason. My people are used to this sort of thing. Not only are they dedicated abolitionists, but I think that a lot of them like the tension and excitement of being involved in the abolitionist crusade for its own sake and would work here for no wages just to be near the action if they could afford to. I trust each and every one of them for they believe in the cause. They risk everything they have or ever want to have by just working here each day. These presses have been attacked, and the offices have been burned several times. But we soldier on. Working here is not just an occupation for them. It is a philosophical commitment and a statement of deepest faith and belief in the cause of human freedom. Besides that, Harry is a good man. He could persuade the Devil that I was already in Heaven two days after I had missed my appointment in Hell."

"I am pleased to hear that Mr. Garrison. I would hope that Pompey, excuse me, Mr. Charles would do the same for me. My appointment in the Christian Hell has already been experienced when I was rudely introduced into slavery more than thirty years ago by some people who were very good Christians no doubt," said Samuel.

"If I can presume to call you familiar, Samuel, I would be pleased to hear your story in total confidence," said Garrison.

For the next two hours, Samuel held Garrison transfixed with his story from the day of his capture down to his entry into the office of *The Liberator* itself. He did so discreetly leaving out of his narrative the part of drugging the Forrester women as much as a courtesy to them as well as for protecting his and Pompey's reputations with Garrison and his friends.

Garrison, in turn, listened to the narrative with total rapt attention. At the conclusion of the story, Garrison said, "Samuel, my friend, you leave me in a total state of awe. Your genius is absolute. May I have the pleasure of shaking your hand again? For now I have a better understanding of the esteem in which I should properly hold you sir? Whatever you shall need, I shall endeavor to provide if it is within my power to do so, and please call me William."

"That is most appreciated William. Thank you. Trust that we will take you up on your kind offer of help, for help of a sort is just what we need. I will tell you this. We have more than ample funds. We are not in need of money. But, we do need an ocean going boat and men who can sail it. That is what we will need for a specific mission of a very delicate and even criminal nature."

"The fact that you are well provided with cash should greatly facilitate our ability to help you Gentlemen," said Garrison. "We have many friends, but the little cash we have has so many demands on it that we must make do with every resource we can beg. The fact that you are well provided with funds is a Godsend. And as to the criminal nature of your intended mission, I am inclined to think that slavery itself is the most horrible crime against nature itself. Any act that can hasten the end of that intolerable slave institution cannot be a more egregious crime than that."

Samuel went on, "What we need most is information right now, and as I stated some men skilled with a boat, and great skill in keeping quiet," said Samuel. "Do you remember a story that was running in the popular press sometime ago about a man who was the only survivor of a ship that foundered in the South Atlantic about a hundred and fifty miles out to sea from Cape Town? His name was given as Starbuck who is said to have been born on the island of Nantucket? I know him to be the very man who was the first mate to a slave ship's captain named Whitehouse, who brought me to this country as a slave in 1815."

Samuel stopped for a moment gathering his thoughts. He took a drink of water from a glass offered him by Garrison and continued his story.

"I remember him well, because he was the least brutish of the crew who served on that slave ship. He seemed to remove himself from the details of the confining of the Africans aboard and involved himself more in the workings of actually sailing the ship itself. I do not think him to be an abolitionist to be sure, but I knew that he had a distaste for the trade. I could detect this in him. He discouraged the men from bothering the women and made sure that we were well fed and kept as clean as possible. From what I learned from people who arrived on the plantation from Africa later on, even though my ship was a Hellhole, their voyages were much worse. The stories of the horror of the middle passage filled me with more rage than even my own crossing. But Whitehouse is a very different case altogether. He is cold and calculating. His dedication to making a fortune from the slave trade is absolute. He would depopulate all of Africa if he could profit from it. He must be stopped at all costs. Who knows how many thousands of souls he has taken out of Africa and transported into a life of slavery during his long career."

"Why do you want revenge on Starbuck if he were not your chief tormentor then?" asked Garrison.

"It's not Starbuck I want. Starbuck is no saint to be sure. He has no doubt made a substantial sum of money from trading in slaves, but I know in my soul that Whitehouse is the greatest plague of my fellow Africans and that he is still alive on this earth somewhere and still up to his abominable trafficking in human lives for cash. I know that Whitehouse is enjoying a rich life somewhere at the expense of thousands of innocent people ripped from their native lands and families like I was myself. I watched him kill a man with no more concern than he might show snuffing out a candle or killing an insect. I want him to know the pain of the lash, the humiliation of the bondage of slavery, and what it feels like to have a rope placed around his neck and hanged for all of his crimes against my people and me. That, Mr. Garrison, is what I seek. Starbuck can lead us to the man Whitehouse. That is all I want from this Starbuck. What I would like to do is serve Whitehouse as he has served countless others in the Hell of his ships, but my young friend has other ideas."

"What are your thoughts Mr. Charles?" asked Garrison.

"Like Samuel, I do not think this Whitehouse is dead. More than anything in this world, I would like to see him brought to the bar of justice before the whole civilized world in the light of day in a British court. For I do not believe that we can get justice in this country which still supports slavery as an institution enshrined in law. The courts of the United States are primitive and backwards. They would let Whitehouse off with a fine and an admonishment to go forth and sin no more. I want more than that. I want to see Captain Whitehouse punished in a British court of law not only for what he did to Samuel and that poor girl, whose story was just related to you who threw herself into the sea, but for all those lives Whitehouse has ruined, and through that ruin, made profits. He has robbed people of their youth, their lives, and their loved ones, and I am sure that he is still doing so today. To find him, we must find Starbuck and extract from him whatever information he may have. As Samuel has said, we must use him to get to Whitehouse and make an example of him."

"Pompey has excellent reasons for his opinion regarding British justice, and I have been influenced by them. But we must see how the game will be played out. What we chiefly need is a small sea worthy boat and a crew we can trust to effect Starbuck's capture and removal from the island of Nantucket with as little fuss as possible. We do not wish a fight with the locals. I have a good friend with a ship who will meet us in Boston soon with his vessel. He is a friend with very strong abolitionist views. Can you find men and a boat willing to go out to the island to transport the captured Starbuck to our ship? I need people who know the island. I think that we can render Starbuck harmless, without doing him injury in the actual taking of the man," said Samuel.

"I trust that you can do just what you say you can do friends. After all that you have been through, I doubt if there is anything that you cannot do. Come back tomorrow at ten o'clock in the evening. I will have some friends here who will be able to manage what you need. They are always willing to help with the cause," said Garrison.

"We will return tomorrow night just as you say. Thank you sir," said Pompey holding out his hand which Garrison shook with vigor.

Garrison then took Samuel's hand and shook it warmly.

"I thank you for your help William," said Samuel as Garrison showed the men to the door and let them out onto the street.

As Pompey walked away, he turned to Samuel and said, "I thought that I saw a tear in Mr. Garrison's eye."

"That was Pompey," Samuel said, "because you did."

CHAPTER XXXII

Samuel and Pompey dined at the Dunham's Hotel that evening. Even in abolitionist Boston, it was an odd experience for the two men. Not since the visit of Mr. Frederick Douglass had a man of color dined in the great dining room of Dunham's. Polite Boston society took careful sidelong glances at Samuel, but in every other respect, everyone was politely correct. It was a time of change. Of that there could be no doubt. The last year had seen revolutions all over Europe. France was now a republic with a president, Louis Napoleon Bonaparte. He was a man rumored to have imperial ambitions not unlike his uncle. Saxony and other German kingdoms had revolted against their respective monarchs as had the Poles against Czar Nicholas. The Italians, the Hungarians, and Austria were swept away by revolutionary fever. Even the people of the Papal States had evicted Pope Pius IX and had set up a republic. Austria itself now had a brand new emperor only eighteen years of age by the name of Franz Joseph who was as much a reactionary as the uncle that he had replaced on the imperial throne, but at the same time he was also a consummate realist. There was no doubt that the whole western world was gearing up to more democratic change. In the United States, the ancient scourge of slavery was on the minds of all thinking people, and Boston was the city that harbored the most dedicated abolition forces.

Samuel and Pompey could feel this dynamic in the air of the old town that had styled itself "The Hub of The Universe". But Samuel and Pompey had a mission of their own beyond the great struggle of idealists like Garrison. They had no intention of enlisting in "The Cause" as Frederick Douglass or the proper Bostonians, who were strangely incited to the radical concept of racial freedom, would have called it. The United States was about to elect a new president, and it looked as if Zachary Taylor would be the winner of that contest. Taylor had defeated the forces of Santa Anna and Mexico during the late war with its southern neighbor. Though Taylor owned slaves, he had made it quite clear that if elected president, he would oppose any extension of slavery into the new western territories. The question of slavery was the most hotly debated topic in the entire country. Although it seemed to many that it was strange that Samuel was taking his dinner in the dining room of the Dunham Hotel, many insightful people who mattered saw it as a sign of better things to come. This truly was a time when the whole world seemed to be changing. That was nowhere truer than in the City of Boston.

As Samuel finished the last of his roast duck, he looked at Pompey and said, "Do you know that as many as ten thousand people may be on their way to California even as we speak? Perhaps as many as half a million or more fools may follow them looking for gold! Just think of it. These would-be miners of treasure are almost as jammed together on ships as I was on Whitehouse's ship. They all expect to fall all over the gold as they land and become millionaires based on rumors that are less than a month old. It is beyond my belief that people set such store by the stupid stuff that they are willing to kill or be killed for it. I wonder if any of these seekers of treasure think about what happens if they make their way all the way to California and there is nothing for them there? This lust for gold cannot result in anything good. Do you want to know a secret Pompey?"

"What secret can you tell me that would excite more attention than all of the things going on in the world at this very moment?" replied Pompey.

"I am quite serious. Now lean over here. Nobody must hear me. The gods only know what would happen if a reporter of some newspaper would publish this information. I have learned that once a story becomes known, it takes on a life of its own and cannot be stopped. If a thing is told often enough, it becomes the accepted truth does it not Pompey?"

"You are right about that about journalism all over the world at the present time. We do live in a remarkable age when everyone is so hungry for information," replied Pompey.

"Well my friend," whispered Samuel in a most confidential tone, "Back in my country we have vast deposits of gold. We mine small bits of it in secret for ornaments. If the world were ever to find out about our secret, the whole world would beat a trail miles wide through my beautiful country, and our lives as we know our lives to be would be at an end. The white man is foolish for gold."

"I was reading about this thing in *The Boston Transcript* before we came down to dinner," said Pompey. "They are calling it a 'Gold Rush'. It seems that so many ships have made landing at San Francisco that the harbor is beginning to be fairly choked with them. These difficulties are compounded, because most of these vessels have been deserted by their gold crazed crews shortly after making port. Your fears for your country are very well founded."

"I can see that this glut of ships would cause difficulties," Samuel laughed softly. "Can you imagine walking from one side of that huge harbor to the other on deserted ships from all over the world? That would be a sight that I would be tempted to see if I were free to take myself to the West."

"The crews run off to the gold fields to get rich, and I suspect that a few of them might actually strike it rich," said Pompey as quietly as if he were relating a state secret to the king of spies in one of the novels he had read in the Forrester library.

"So what becomes of all those ships in the harbor Mr. Charles? They must become a nuisance after a while," asked Samuel.

"Apparently some of them are dragged up into the town and along the waterfront to be used as warehouses, hotels, and mercantiles. There is a shortage of buildings in the principal place, a city called San Francisco which dominates that huge harbor you spoke of. The abandoned ships become quite useful as a result."

"These are interesting times Pompey, Look at us here. Look at what money can do. Look at the world that gold has opened up for us. I was told this very afternoon by one of our fellow guests, who was very eager to inform me that he was an abolitionist, that he was very pleased to see me here. He then went on to say in the most effusive manner that this establishment that we are favoring by our custom is of, 'The Better Sort'. I replied that his being here must make it so. He puffed up his chest and told me that I was very kind to say so. He then told me that the hotel's proprietor, Dunham himself, has abolitionist sympathies. That is why we have had no difficulties here." Samuel continued, "He said that he would rather dine here with a well-dressed and well-mannered Black man than with an Irishman. Now is that a classic case of damning us with faint praise?"

"I think that this fellow has not really thought out his entire philosophy of equality very well. American democracy is not quite a finished thing it would seem. There are so many contradictions. So many people seem to be so much more equal than others even here in Boston. But I suspect that is generally the condition of most of the world, as is the fear of strangers. Yet this whole country is made up of people from somewhere else with the exception of the Indians who have been pushed further and further west. I wonder if these first Americans are doomed to be pushed into the sea once the Americans cross the Great American Dessert and fill the place up to California?" said Pompey returning to his quiet conversational voice.

"The real difference is that the rest of the world does not profess to believe in human equality at all I suppose. At least if Americans keep saying that they believe this strange thing, maybe someday they really will. But I think most of them today do not embrace that ideal, and quite frankly neither do I. Back in my country, I could kill any of these people around me merely for showing their disrespect for me. Do you know what the word 'Zulu' means? It means 'Heaven's selected people', or sometimes it is interpreted as 'Children of Heaven.' Translating it into English exactly is difficult. But see how well I can adapt to the local standard of what makes up civilization. Even though I am totally superior in every way, I can tolerate dining with these lesser breeds of men all around me."

"Samuel! How very white of you and Christian too. I doubt very much if your attitude can be called democratic," Pompey quipped turning the knife to great advantage.

"Now there is no need to get hostile and call me a pasty white Anglo and a Christian at that! I thought that I was reflecting some of this much so-called celebrated democratic spirit favored in this enlightened city of Boston, or as some of the citizens of this place like to think of themselves so modestly, 'The Hub of the Universe.'" Samuel said a bit less cautiously.

Samuel's smile broadened as he returned the curious looks he was receiving from some of the hotel's patrons who were sneaking sidelong glances at the exotic pair as they dined.

"Samuel, did you see those poor creatures camped all over Boston Common as we rode by there on our way to the hotel this morning?" asked Pompey in a more serious voice.

"They are the much hated Irish we have heard about I suspect," said Samuel.

"Where ever are they going to go? How are those poor people going to live? With the famine in Ireland, and the British government doing nothing to help them, they have become quite hopeless and totally destitute. It is a pity that there is no William Wilberforce to champion them. Do you know that there were hundreds of them on our ship, and we never even saw one of them during the entire crossing? They were never allowed on the deck. I later found out that many of them had actually died during the voyage, and their bodies were dumped into the sea at night so that we would not be disturbed by having to see them being disposed of. Their priests, who were traveling with them, were not even allowed to do a religious service, because they might have been overheard by the first and second class passengers. The Captain was afraid that our being aware of them might have disturbed us. Do you think that is right Samuel?"

"Even Whitehouse and Starbuck brought us onto the deck once a day to take the air while our area was swept somewhat cleaner and the dead were brought out to be tossed to the sharks," said Samuel. "The Irish too are some sort of species of slave it seems. And here on land there are no sharks to swallow their shame."

"Samuel, slaves have a great deal of monetary value. These Irish are regarded as less than human, because they are Catholic and speak an unintelligible tongue. Even people who are in sympathy with our condition have little or no empathy for the Irish, and as I said, unlike slaves these poor people do not even have commercial value. In fact nobody even seems to wish to employ them at starvation wages."

"Maybe the public distaste for the Irish is fanned by the fact that unlike the black man, he is in the public view on the streets and on the commons land. The Black man in his bondage is far away and out of sight on the plantations and in the mines, and the Irishman is living in the open, digging his privy under their delicate noses, and eating his food, such as it is, just a few hundred feet or so from where we are sitting right now. Well, at least they were not brought here in chains as I was and your grandmother too. They actually came here of their own free will as some part of a plan for a better life. If one of these Irish decides to take to the road and seek a job of work in the countryside, he will not be hunted down with dogs and killed or at least beaten because he left his place of confinement. Their children will not be taken from them and sold in the slave market or to dealers who will ship them down the river to work on the rice plantations of the lower Mississippi where they will die after just a few seasons of working fifteen hours a day or of fever or worse. And not only that," said Samuel with a significant look, "They will not be stripped from their parent's arms to be used to settle gambling debts."

"I take your point Samuel. I still want to do something for those poor Irish souls. I think that I saw a Catholic Church on our way to the hotel today. That would be the place to start I think. I think that the church could best help to direct our efforts. After all, these are their own people. The money we have means as little to me as it does to you. It is best that we do something good with at least a small portion of it. I'll ask the waiter how to get to the Catholic Church or better yet, how to reach their bishop."

When the waiter returned to the table with their coffee, Pompey asked him about the location of the nearest Catholic Church. The waiter initially looked displeased, twitched, and sucked in his breath while acting toward Samuel and Pompey with forced civility.

"I believe that the Church known as The Church of the Holy Ghost is located on Tremont Street. The Catholic bishop and priests live nearby I believe. You can ask anyone in the area, and they can direct you I'm sure. They will also most likely tell you whatever you may want to know about the place. Are you gentlemen of the Catholic faith? I am sure that the clerk at the desk is prepared to give our patrons any information they might require regarding church services throughout the city."

"Thank you young man. Very civil of you," said Samuel in his most patronizing manner.

"And in answer to your question, we are not Catholics. But seeing that we are good heathens and Pagans at that, we merely wish to help those poor folks on the Common, as we are sure that any good Christian might also wish to do. So after we go up to our rooms to pray to a half dozen of my African idols, we thought that we'd call on the Catholic Bishop and give him a donation to assist those poor creatures on the commons. That would be so that he could look after his flock a little easier. Now, that would be a true act of Christian kindness which would be most pleasing in the eyes of that Christian God that you most likely believe in would it not?" asked Samuel with a malicious grin.

Samuel's sarcasm was not lost on the waiter who was, at the same time, not inclined to challenge such a large Black gentleman who was also a well paying guest at the hotel where his employer was a well know friend of Mr. Garrison, the noted abolitionist. The waiter merely returned Samuel's smile while simultaneously looking as if he was suffering some gastric discomfort.

"Yes sir," was all the unfortunate waiter could manage without choking.

"Very good boy," said Samuel now enjoying the sweet revenge of thirty-five years of pent up anger as he smiled with ill concealed contempt for the serving man. "Thank you again for your kindness. We will think of you while we enjoy our stroll."

"Take care gentlemen if you stroll too near your Irish friends tonight. There have been some reports of those buggers, pardon the liberty sir, robbing folks after dark. I would be very sorry if you came to harm. And it would not be wise to give them any money sir. It will only encourage them to loiter about and beg for more, and many others may not be as open handed and tolerant as you folks. Besides that, it is well known that the Irish will only use it for drink. Do you know that they have even dug privies on our common, and the women of our city cannot even walk there on a Sunday? It is not safe for any respectable person to go near the place day or night. I tell you sir," said the waiter as he became slightly animated to Samuel's delight, "It has become a disgrace to every decent Bostonian. A year ago, a person could walk through our common in perfect safety day or night, but now, it would be risking your life or worse to attempt it. I am very sure that something will have to be done soon. If the law does nothing it is rumored that the good citizens of this city will take matters into their own hands. There is a man named John Buzzell who is very alert to the dangers posed by these strangers who come over here uninvited in the bellies of ships to make themselves rich by taking our good and decent Protestant women in marriage and turn them all Catholic so that the Pope himself can rule here."

"I was not aware that the Pope ruled in Ireland young man. I thought that Protestant Englishmen ruled there. Am I mistaken in that?"

Noting that Samuel's remarks were drawing the attention of a number of diners, Pompey cut in with, "Where would the poor souls go then if they are forced to move off the commons?"

"I do not know sir. All I do know is that they were not asked to come here in the first place, and in truth, the people of Boston, the American people of Boston, just wish that they would go back to where they came from. But every month, hundreds more of them land, like so much lice, not only in Boston, but in New York, Philadelphia, and many other ports along the whole of the East coast. If you read the papers delivered here to the hotel, one can see nothing else except all this business about gold in California. Well, a lot of us don't think that we should even let them land here in the first place. There is nothing for them here to do for employment. If we don't stop them, they will overrun the city and turn it into a sewer. They might even take all the jobs away from poor American working folks. I am sure that men of quality, like yourselves, can see this and understand how many of us who were born in Boston feel."

"Trust me young man, we can fully understand how you feel," said Samuel with his most sardonic smile.

The waiter walked away from the table, and Samuel turned to Pompey. "I wonder how he likes waiting on a nigger and being forced to be polite to a man sympathetic to the Irish. Well, if I cared enough about what he thought, I might have told him that I was invited to come to this country by some very bad white Christian people who I am very sure were not Catholic Irishmen. I was invited to come to this country to be a slave. No Black man ever came out of Africa by his own desire to be worked to death. We were all invited and transported on those damned crowded little ships. We were crowded together like pigs brought to market. Sometimes even more than half of the human cargoes of damned slave ships died and were thrown to the sharks. But whereas I do not care any more about what he thinks than I care about what a termite or a dung beetle on his hill thinks, I must give him and his stupid thoughts no notice. If I did I would have to kill him you see to preserve my honor. By all the gods Pompey, I am thinking Zulu again."

"Never mind what the dung beetles may think. Let's find our way to the Catholic Bishop and see if we can do some good in this world with our wealth," said Pompey.

Samuel and Pompey left the hotel, and after asking some people on the street for directions, they found their way to the city's principal Catholic Church. Samuel rang the bell at what appeared to be the priest's living quarters. After a few moments, the door was opened by a man in a long black cassock. He looked from one of the strangers standing before him to the other with just a split second's moment of surprise on his face, then smiled thinly, and asked, "Gentlemen is there anything I can do for you at this hour?"

"I do hope so. We wish to see whomever is in charge here about making a donation to your church for a specific cause. We would like to discuss the specific aims of this donation with your superior," answered Pompey.

"That would be the Bishop of Boston, that is Bishop Fitzpatrick sir. Would you be so kind as to follow me to the parlor, and I shall tell His Grace that you are here. Might I have your names sir?" said the priest as they entered the room indicated for the meeting.

"No, we wish to remain unknown for the time being. Our gift will speak for us," responded Pompey.

"Very good sir. Please make yourselves comfortable, and I

will fetch His Grace." With that, the priest bowed and left them in the parlor.

"This is a very strange place," said Samuel as he looked at the hand colored framed prints on the wall of a bearded man and a woman both with very pale skin with thorns ringing their exposed and naked bleeding hearts. Samuel's gaze then went to some statues of different sizes also decorating the room. "Pompey what do you suppose these things are?"

"I take them to be sacred objects of worship of some importance to these religious people," replied Pompey in a very low voice. By the lights of the flickering candles, the whole scene was very eerie.

Pompey pondered, and then he turned to Samuel and said, "I think that these things must be unique to the use of these Catholic people. The Forresters were Christians, but they had no statues of gods like these. I think that they took the Ten Commandments of Moses quite literally when Moses ordered the Jews not to worship graven images. As I recall from Anna's lessons on the scripture back on the plantation, Moses smashed that golden calf which the Jews were worshiping in a huge rage. As I recall, Moses was most certainly opposed to any form of idolatry."

"Do you really think that they worship these pictures and statues?" asked the astounded Samuel.

A soft and gentle laugh suddenly drew Samuel and Pompey's attention. They turned to see a man dressed in the simple black cassock of a humble priest standing in the doorway. About his waist was a purple sash. This was the only change in his costume that distinguished him from the priest who had answered the door. This man returned their surprised gaze with a smile, and then he said with his eyes twinkling with a keen sense of mischief and fun, "Not at all my son. We in the Catholic Church do not worship statues. In fact the worship of such things is expressly forbidden to us. These objects are just to remind us of the saints who watch over us and who have once lived on the earth. Many of these holy men and women gave their lives for the faith so that it would survive to nurture us today. For example these pictures, which you find so curious, are here just to remind us of the suffering of Jesus on the cross and his holy mother Mary who had to suffer his death. Jesus was Mary's son, and she even now intercedes for mankind with her son and God the Father for divine mercy every time we stumble and fall from grace. Oh, forgive the sermon gentlemen. It's an old habit with me to be teaching all the time. I am Bishop John Bernard Fitzpatrick of Boston. Whom do I have the pleasure of addressing?"

"Pardon us sir. We did not wish to intrude on you at such a late hour. I am James Charles, and this is my friend and associate Mr. Samuel James," replied Pompey with a nod of the head, a gesture he had not used since departing from slavery.

"Father Grey told me that you wanted to see me regarding a charitable donation to Holy Mother Church with a mind to some specific use," replied the Bishop.

"Yes sir that would be correct," replied Pompey.

"That is very good of you gentlemen. What form would this donation take, and for what purpose would you like it used? I will help in any way I possibly can," said Bishop Fitzpatrick.

"We would like to give you a thousand dollars as a relief fund to make life easier for the poor Irish on the common's land here in Boston. These poor people are suffering a great deal of privation, and we would like to help them as much as our small donation can. Many of them do not speak English, and they seem to have no means of support. It is important to us that they are afforded every chance to make their way in the world before they are driven to their deaths by starvation and the people of this city in which they enjoy very little sympathy. Some of these poor Irish look as if they have only a little time before they starve to death. We thought that you might be the one individual who might be able to help them if we were to provide you with funds for that purpose. At first, we thought of enlisting the help of Mr. Garrison, but these people are really your people now aren't they?" asked Pompey.

"Thank you young man. I take it that you are neither Irish or Catholic."

"Yes Your Grace. You are correct. We are clearly not as you can judge for yourself," said Samuel with a sort of laugh.

"God welcomes your kindness to strangers," replied the Bishop. "I doubt if he cares that you are anything other than that which you are, and what you are, are two very kind strangers come on a mission of mercy who should enjoy his favor. I am sure that you know that Jesus was a Jew. Remember it was our Lord who said, 'What ever ye have done unto the least of these, ye have done unto me also.' There is no doubt in my mind, and in my heart, that you are pleasing in his eyes, and I thank you from the bottom of my heart for your most profound act of kindness and understanding. This money you propose donating will do a great deal of good. I must also make a confession to you. I am at my wit's end as to what to do about the problems facing these poor people. As you so aptly put it, they are my people. Mr. Garrison is God's own man in his way, and his work is of the greatest importance. But, in truth I must confess that I am glad that you came to me. Mr. Garrison is a very busy man, a very good man, and he does God's work as well. But as you must know, his efforts are spent elsewhere, and that is as it should be."

Pompey and Samuel each produced a leather pouch of gold from inside their overcoats, and placed them side-by-side on the marble top center table.

"May you find this useful to help your people Bishop," said Pompey.

"We are all God's people and his children," smiled Bishop Fitzpatrick. "I know that you gentlemen are not Catholic, but would you accept an old man's blessing in love?"

"We would think that no hardship sir," replied Samuel.

The Bishop made the sign of the cross twice in the air, and recited a benediction in Latin.

As Pompey and Samuel left the bishop's house after some

light refreshments and wine, Samuel said to his friend, "At least we know that there are two just men living in this city."

"I must confess that I found the experience strange. I felt good but uneasy all at the same time among all of those pictures and statues. But you know Samuel, all I could do was think about Anna and what she would have made out of all of that. In all of her life she never saw anything like it."

"I think that she would have liked it well enough Pompey. In fact, I believe that she would have enjoyed the whole thing, because she would have felt the benefit of a good man's blessing there. She would most likely have burst into some hymn or other about crossing over Jordan or something else of the sort."

"Just imagine what the bishop would have made of that Samuel?"

"He would have liked it, and he would have liked her I think. I even think that he might have known that he had met an authentic saint and not just some marble angel."

Pompey had only allowed himself to think about Anna a few times since her funeral. During that long and silent walk back to the hotel, he dared to think things he would not have allowed his mind to entertain before. For the first time, surrounded by the all-encompassing blackness of the night, he felt a tear trickle down his cheek for Anna. In many ways Pompey was still in mourning.

CHAPTER XXXIII

Starbuck revived himself after five hours of sleep. He had drifted some distance, but the sea anchor that he had made out of the old sail and rope had kept the drifting down to a minimum. The sea was calm and the air was warm. Now that his mind was clear, he had resolved on a plan that would bring him back to the island just after nightfall. Starbuck bided his time for the rest of the day as he slowly sailed back to Nantucket. Slowly he worked his way back toward the shore. By the time twilight was upon him, Starbuck was close enough to the beach to land unnoticed not far from the cove where he and his friends had swam as a child. When night fell, he beached Weston's boat.

Starbuck took up a bailing scoop and began seeking out a spot to bury his gold. After looking about for a distinguishing landmark, Starbuck settled for a place near a substantial outcropping of rocks just above the high tide mark. It took him the better part of two hours to dig a hole deep enough to satisfy him. As he dug he felt comforted that the gold would be safe here. Starbuck found the bailing scoop to be an unsatisfactory tool for digging a hole large and deep enough to secure his gold, but this was his only alternative to using his bare hands. After a short rest after more than an hour's work, he deposited his treasure, filled in the hole, and overspread the area with seaweed and rocks. He was satisfied that it all looked very natural.

The only problem now remaining was the actual disposal of the all too well known boat of the late Captain Fuller Weston. Starbuck searched for a cargo of rocks of a manageable size for the boat's last deadly journey. Having worked away at this task for another forty minutes, he next dismasted the craft. He didn't want to leave any physical indicators of the presence of Weston's boat that might invite the curiosity of anyone swimming or boating in the area. Starbuck looked about to see if he had left anything undone. His eyes fell on the new pigskin cases in which the gold had been packed along with a few articles of clothing which were scattered about. Starbuck decided to save the cases and anything else that might be useful to him. All the rest of the debris, that which he considered rubbish, was gathered up to be sunk along with the boat.

Starbuck deposited the cases on the lee side of the outcropping of rocks and covered them with seaweed. He then set off on the last voyage of Weston's unhappy vessel which he suspected knew of much death even beyond the four corpses which had littered its deck over the last few days This shabby little vessel was an unhappy boat by any sane person's definition. Sinking it would be at least an end to its horrible history.

Starbuck had removed his boots and most of his clothing and deposited everything not far from where he had hidden the cases close to the sheltering outcropping of rocks. He did not want to be weighted down by his jacket, shirt, or boots on his swim back to the shore. As Starbuck waded out pushing Weston's boat, he could feel the contrast between the sun-warmed sea, which still held the day's heat, and the night chilled air. For a moment he almost felt like a boy again as the sand oozed up between his toes, and the water swirled about his body as he waded deeper into the ocean.

At last the water was almost chest high. Starbuck stood well over six feet in height and moved with ease through the surf. When he was far enough off shore, he grasped the boat by the gunnels and pulled himself up into the old and largely neglected craft. He then set out on the dismasted craft on its final voyage. He used the tiller to guide the small vessel to a spot he knew well in the channel. Here the water was at least fifty-five feet deep. Starbuck took an ax from the deck chest and pounded away at the planking. It did not take long for the big man to smash a hole in the hull to let in the hungry sea. The boat began to fill rapidly with water. Now the craft would be buried in the deep forever. It would be well out of the way of swimmers and shallow draft vessels a good quarter mile off shore. There were no boats sailing in those waters that drew anything like fifty feet of water.

As he slid over the side of the sinking boat into the still warm ocean, Starbuck felt a sudden sharp pain in his thigh. He had received a nasty tear in his leg from a huge splinter from the edge of the jagged hole he had smashed into the side of the murdered craft. "Damned thing!" he said aloud. The cut was deep, and bled coloring the sea a coppery red near the wound. Starbuck could still move but only with some discomfort. As he got used to the pain, the water felt good on his skin. He had been told from childhood that seawater had curative powers for all sorts of wounds.

Taking note of his course, he struck out for the beach. While swimming with long even strokes, Starbuck rejoiced in his still powerful body and in the fact that he was one of those rare sailors who could actually swim. Swimming was not strange to him. He was, after all, island born, a true web-toed son of Nantucket. Swimming to an island boy was as natural as breathing. Starbuck began entering a strange reverie as his thoughts carried him back to the Nantucket of his youth. Back in his teen years, Starbuck and his friends would run to this very cove, strip off their clothes, and jump into the surf as naked as ever their mothers had born them into this island world. These sons of the rocky and sandy island would strike off out to sea and dive deeply. Then they would burst through the surface of the sea again like dolphins sporting in the sun. Then they would turn in the surf, dive, and spring to the surface again like a pod cavorting in unison. Then they would dive and rise up to the surface once more as if they had been shot from a cannon. They sported in the broiling surf like so many pink porpoises. They excited the eyes and giggles of girls hidden in the dunes and beach grass.

Starbucks, Ridgeways, Edwards, Matthews, Mayhews, Baulches, Coffins, and all the other island boys would sport and swim the whole summer long in this their favorite spot where they were free of chores and their father's supervision and orders to, "Find something useful to do." Their bodies would change from pink to bronze as each clear day changed the pigmentation of their skin. The summers seemed shorter then, and the island girls would also go to the cove, not to swim, but to sneak a peek at the young men from the shelter of the tall beach grass. Here the pretty girls would spy on the young men in all their naked glory. It was a game for all of them. It was delicious and forbidden fun that had gone on for generations. The boys knew about what the girls were up to, and the girls suspected that the boys knew it. But each generation of island youth thought that they had invented this game. They had the innocence to think that their parents and all those who had gone on before had not played at the same thing.

It was a rite of summer and a seasonal ritual going back to the colonial days. The feigned shock, screaming, and laughter and the joy of the girls in the fullness of their reaching for the forbidden fruit of their sexual awakening all blended together to make this the most important show each summer on this isolated island that held little other seasonal novelty.

Starbuck remembered how the island girls would pretend to hide and then sneak a peek at the naked boys year after year. Then when the girls were discovered, how they would scream in all of their assumed innocence as the boys outrageously cavorted showing off their manhood to the girls, who were beside themselves with pleasure. The girls pretended to run away in horror after taking one more long and lingering look at the young men in all their natural glory. They knew that these lads would most likely be their husbands one day before too many years passed. As the island's society was very small, the fact that one of these naked savages would be their life-mate was a foregone conclusion. The boys would dance around and laugh as the girls very slowly ran away. Both the girls and the boys knew that they would be back later in the week to act out this little play all over again. In this moment of eternal truth, both the boys and the girls knew true liberation.

Every girl and every boy knew in their hearts that the game was a ritual to be played out forever. The truth was that almost every adult had lied to themselves and their children about what the truth of human nature was. The truth of human nature was that the girls wanted to see what they proclaimed to be disgusting, and they pretended that they were not supposed to admit to finding the experience at all fascinating and fun, because decent people were supposed to think that male nudity was disgusting. The boys and girls of Nantucket smiled at this, because when one is young, one knows what is really so, because truth is felt deeply where no mere philosophy can profane it. Starbuck's salty bachelor uncle had taken the fifteen year old aside one day after the lad had suffered a long tongue lashing from an old aunt about his cavorting on the beach in the altogether.

"Pay no mind to that Old Biddy son," said the uncle, "She's forgot a real bit of island truth."

"And what truth is that Uncle Bob?" the 'boy Starbuck' had asked.

The old man replied, "Old age gives good advice when it is no longer able to set a bad example."

"That's a good one Uncle Bob. I'll tell the others that one, but how does that apply to Aunt Selina?"

"That one, when she was young, never missed a day in the summertime hiding out in the beach grass looking at us fine young fellows playing in the surf all buck naked. Trust me boy, she and her friends liked watching us real well no matter what balderdash she's spouting today. I think that if she could still see beyond the tip of that very long nose of hers, she'd be sneaking off to the tall grass on the dunes yet to sneak a look at you fellers."

Starbuck had not forgotten this bit of wisdom and smiled to himself. He had never gotten over being fifteen years old after all, and as the memory of those old days came rushing back to him, he was happy in that memory. The truth that the old man, as a boy, had known was that in a few years, that the roles were to be reversed. There would be young marriages of Mayhews, Matthews, Ridgeways, Edwards, and Baulches. But sadly, Starbuck reflected, there would be no Starbucks in this round of weddings to be, except for his brother Lloyd perhaps, who was quite taken with a certain Hannah Richards. And yet the truth of his youth was that these young people would all know each other as they should and end up in love and lying in the grass together. In a short time, they would find themselves in love all over again. This time it would be real and in a warm embrace in their marriage beds. The cycle would continue. That was the natural order of things on this tiny island, and it was as good as Uncle Bob had always held it to be.

Yet for Starbuck, this would not be the story. For he would turn his back on his heritage and run off to sea. He was not alone in making this choice, but he had been away far longer than almost any of his peers. Life on the island was a cycle. Raise sheep, or plant crops in the rocky soil, or run off to sea to follow the whale, or sail off as a sailor on a merchantman, and eventually of course get married to one of those pretty giggling girls who had gone running up from the beach away from the lusty lads of summer.

Starbuck had chosen to become a slaver. Now as he paddled in towards the familiar shore, he began to reflect on his mother and what this good Quaker woman would have thought of her son whom she had loved so well. Starbuck grew gloomier. Gone was that brief sweet bit of reverie, and in his mind's eye, he could see her face and hear her voice saying, "You are going to lose your soul and honor and maybe you'll never come back at all Tristan."

"No more thinking on that for Starbuck," he mouthed to

the air and sea. He shook himself out of his blues, and his gloom was short lived as he returned to his reverie of that last wonderful summer so long ago before he had set sail leaving his youth behind him on that beach in the sun warmed cove. It had been a perfect time and season in that last year of his innocence. Life was so blessedly uncomplicated. How wonderful to live it now all over again in this tiny space of time. Starbuck reflected on the many summers that had come and gone since he had drawn his first breath on Nantucket. It was sad to have missed so much of what his life might have been. This life on the island just when he was becoming a man never seemed more precious than now. For a little time this night, he thought to recapture it, but it was like trying to grasp a moonbeam in a fist. Even though Starbuck had the benefit of hard gathered wealth, the promise of which had seduced him away from Nantucket in the first place, there was still an empty place in his heart. He knew that place should have been filled with the love of a good woman and even children. But he reflected that now he had the wealth he sought, and he was still in the prime of his strength and life. With this Starbuck would have to be satisfied. All these thoughts rushed into his mind as he swam toward that familiar shore he had known so well in his youth. For the first time since returning to the island, surrounded by and immersed in the warm embrace of the sea, he felt something of a real homecoming. Yet all his well wishers were ghosts of only what he could imperfectly recall.

He knew in those days, so long past, that he was not the most loved of boys, nor the most despised. His face was not then a mass of scars. A number of island girls thought him rather good looking both with and without his clothes on. Starbuck smiled at the thought of that. At more than six feet tall, he had been a standout as he towered almost a foot above the other fifteen year old boys on the beach. At sixteen, when he went off a'whaling, he had truly been a strapping lad. Now a sense of real regret came upon Starbuck, and a sense of loss seemed to engulf him. He wished that he had never left the place, and had stayed on

Nantucket like his brother Lloyd to raise sheep and cattle, farm, and do some off shore fishing. Starbuck sadly reflected that even Lloyd had not made time for him since his return.

He now became acutely aware once again of the throbbing pain in his leg where he had received that ragged cut from the jagged splinter as he slid down the side of Weston's old boat into the ocean. It was as if Weston had reached up from his watery grave and inflicted some final measure of revenge on him after all. With his exertions, Starbuck had made a good swim for the distant shore which he reflected was not all that far off now. His leg began to painfully throb once more. Starbuck could also feel himself growing weaker. "Don't panic now you damned fool," he said aloud to himself as he sucked the sea air deeply into his lungs. "We didn't come this far to lose heart now damn your eyes Starbuck! Make for the shore you squid! It's not so far that you can't make it. You can't quit now."

Starbuck rolled onto his back and floated for a while. Once again, a sense of well-being came over him as he rested on his back in the warm sea for a while and built up his resolve and energy for that last dash for the shore. When he glanced at the beach, Starbuck could make out the spot, in his mind's eye, where he had stowed his clothes and red leather cases. Again, his mind drifted back over the decades to that last summer of his youth and joy on the island when the world was so simple and the New York gangs were not seeking his blood. This was the world before he had allowed himself to be seduced into the sordid trade in human life that overtook him. Starbuck now fully realized what he had missed by abandoning the island world. It had taken him thirty-five years to see that this world of Nantucket had been his birthright which he had abandoned. That birthright had existed for him before he had learned that humans were just another commodity to be bought and sold for profit. This former career of slaving was an ugly scar on his soul worse than any physical ugliness on his face. He thought of the four men he had killed during the last forty-eight hours. A dull ache filled his chest.

"Damn it! It was them or me. Could not be helped," he said out loud to the dawn as the first hint of the rising sun began to creep over the horizon.

His reverie was finished now, and any good feelings he had enjoyed shattered into a thousand bits in the reality of the dawn's coming sunlight. Starbuck was now back in that savage world where he was the hunted this time. He had been the hunter of whales and of men, but the painful awareness of himself being the quarry of the New York crowd was now dominating his reality. Those three men from the Five Points at the bottom of the sea were a grime reaffirmation of the truth of his situation. Maybe to sink beneath the waves would be the best way out for him as well. "Damn it Starbuck, you are a survivor," he heard himself saying as he fought off this momentary auto-destructive impulse.

He had once been the hunter of the great whale in his youth. Striking a whale, the very first time, when he had qualified as a harpooner, was the most exciting thing that had ever happened to him. A four and a half hour Nantucket sleigh ride, and lancing the fifty-five foot long giant in his lungs, was the great high point of his youth. "Nothing will ever top that," was the thought that now ran through his mind. He had been right. He remembered at the end of that first whaling voyage that he had expected a greater share of the oil money, but in the end it was only three hundred and seventy dollars less what he had purchased from the slop chest during the three year voyage. After these deductions, his lay was small indeed. Still there were others on that ship who left without a cent of mortal cash and in fact in debt to the slop chest. They left with nothing to show for their three years at sea. In fact, one of the disappointed whalers had borrowed a pistol, walked into the office of a "Shark", the very man who had recruited him for the voyage, and had shot him dead.

Starbuck took the three hundred and sixteen dollars and sixty-three cents, his cleared pay for three years of his life spent on that stinking whaling ship, and went out to a tavern to eat his first meal on dry land in three years. Starbuck remembered that he had reflected that this sum would have been almost a third greater if he did not owe the slop chest for the things he had bought during that voyage. Now that he was finally paid off, he laughed to himself that he had sold three years of his young life so cheaply. That is when he decided that there had to be a more profitable type of employment for a big and experienced lad, like himself, who was Nantucket born at that. Starbuck had concluded at nineteen that his life was worth more than a few cents a day.

It was in another waterfront tavern in Boston that he met the young, dashing, and resourceful Captain Whitehouse. And that is when he had first entered into a conversation on the subject of black ivory. Starbuck then struck a bargain with that sea-going devil. He had decided to go into slaving. Whitehouse had promised him wealth, and wealth is what he had accumulated, and wealth was what Starbuck had deposited in the banks of Boston during his years in the slave trade. Starbuck did not dice, or play at cards, or drink to drunkenness. He had saved his money for more than three decades, and then came the great windfall from that old devil Whitehouse. But, he knew that he had missed something. He had hated most of his life after whaling, and he desperately wanted something fine and decent to round out his days.

Whitehouse had no first name that Starbuck ever knew of, or if he had heard one mentioned, he had not bothered to remember it. In fact, Starbuck had come to think that the name Whitehouse itself was a name that the Captain never properly owned. He remembered that first night in that dark Boston cuddy in that old run down inn by the docks when he had first encountered Whitehouse that there was something about the man that his mother's teachings were militating against from the grave.

He remembered his old *Bible* studies and the story of the Devil taking Jesus to the top of the mountain to show him the world. The Devil had told this holy prophet that this whole earth could be his if Jesus would only fall on his knees and worship him. Unlike young Jesus, Starbuck gave in and embraced the slave trade and all of its rewards. Whitehouse promised the poor whaler that if he threw in his lot with him and went slaving, that he would have more gold than he could ever carry. In this, Whitehouse did not lie. Starbuck was a very rich man. Starbuck knew that he was no Jesus, and he also knew that he had metaphorically kissed the Devil's arse and worshiped him. And in return, he had gotten a lot of gold, but Nantucket was the little world he wanted to rule now. But that ambition, and the world that went with it, was forever closed to him.

Starbuck knew that there were other men in Five Points who would be sent out to look for him when the men he had killed did not return. "Maybe I should have stayed in Brazil with that old Devil Whitehouse when I had the chance," he said softly to the all but faded stars overhead that had almost been totally banished in the light of the coming dawn. "Why do those damned New Yorkers want me?" he asked. Then it came to him. "They must want Whitehouse," was his thought. Then he spoke again to the sea and air as much to keep up his own strength and courage with the sound of a human voice even if it were only his own, "That's it! Those buggers want Whitehouse, and they want me to take them to him. Goddamn him. I'll kill him myself the filthy bugger. Goddamn the man! What has that Devil made of me? Yes they will come again in three or four week's time. I've got to get off this fucking island."

The thoughts in Starbuck's mind became like attacking Furies. For the first time in more years than he could remember, he began to feel truly afraid. As he floated on his back, pangs of hunger began to cut through his consciousness replacing the pain from his wound and the deep pang of his loneliness as his primary source of grief. Then Starbuck became aware of his leg throbbing more intensely. He also knew that he was getting weaker. But in that space of time just before the dawn's full light, he could make out the beach where his clothes and cases were and where his gold was safely buried. His inner compass had not failed him. What he had seen in his mind's eye was a reality. "It is really not so far away now," was the dominant thought racing through his brain. He was again aware that he was bleeding now and was growing weaker, "I can bind my leg and rest in just a few minutes once I've gained the shore," he mumbled to the surf.

Suddenly another memory from long ago intruded into his conscious reality. Slowly it had at first come back to him through the mists of time to the forefront of his mind as he approached the shore. "This is where Quentin Mayhew was lost one morning when he went for an early swim before heading out fishing. Damn it, it was a shark that took him right here on a day just like this, and the poor bugger was only fourteen."

A shiver ran down his spine. It was not spawned by cold, but at the thought of young Mayhew's body, or what was left of it lying on the beach, as white as sun bleached sand, drained of all its blood and color. It was mostly his head, an arm, and part of his torso that the boys had found that night when they went to the cove for their swim. He had been washed up onto the shore with a bunch of kelp and seaweed which had mercifully covered most of poor Quentin's torn parts. The memory of all those generations of sharks which followed the slave ships he had worked on all those years, with their hungry jaws agape waiting for their feedings of dead slaves, filled him with a sudden irrational terror the like of which he had never felt before. Starbuck, in the confusion of his blood loss, hunger, and exhaustion, thought that maybe it was a judgment on him for his misspent life. Now he was fighting both irrational terror and the oncoming of unconsciousness. He gasped for breath as he recalled those high finned demons following the slave ship when the living Black African cargo of the *Catalpa* was thrown overboard into the ocean filled with ravenous sharks. "That was when the British frigate almost captured Whitehouse," he thought. "I wish that they had hanged us both then and there. There is something clean about accepting a well deserved punishment even if it's at the end of a rope."

Starbuck was overwhelmed by the obscene haunting memory of sharks following the ship waiting for their feeding time. The screaming of those poor souls chained to the anchor, seeing the fins and knowing what their fate was going to be, was seared into his brain. This had been so from the time when Whitehouse had ordered the jettisoning of the slave cargo when the English naval sloop was almost upon the *Catalpa*. Starbuck hated the fact that he had done nothing to try to stop the mass murder of the defenseless slaves. "I'm as guilty as that sonofabitch Whitehouse," he sputtered.

Then something rough and rasping rubbed his body as it passed by scraping him. Whatever it was felt as if it were some gigantic and rough steel rasp. Starbuck was on the verge of passing out of consciousness. Then something struck him, and there was a horrible tearing of flesh.

CHAPTER XXXIV

The clock in The Old North Church had just struck midnight as Pompey and Samuel entered the hotel. They collected their keys to their suites and proceeded wordlessly up the wide staircase to their rooms. Mrs. Forrester was finding sleep to be rather elusive, and had decided to take a walk down to the lobby of the Dunham Hotel and back again to use up some of her excess energy. She had been feeling uneasy in this strange northern city, which was famed as a center of everything unfriendly to her native South. "Abolitionist riffraff. Good Lord! A Negro was seen in the dining room tonight! What next in this dreadful place? I don't see why Caroline and her husband insisted on putting me up here instead of at their place. God knows they have room enough. Yankee hospitality is mighty cold just like their damned climate. Even in summer it still feels cold and damp. They don't go in for family guests I guess. It's really shocking when the guest is family!" she muttered to herself as she looked for her shawl.

At last she found it under a throw, which had been draped over the carved black walnut sofa. She looked at the furniture. At least this was something familiar. These things reminded her of her home in Georgia before all of the trouble started and her world was turned upside down. Mrs. Forrester had not had an easy time of it. Caroline and Tilly had set their caps for the two

Yankee gentlemen in Paris, and they had gotten them. "Well, I must have done something right raising those girls. They know how to make their way in this unhappy world well enough. They even seem to like it."

The Yankees had traveled with their whole abolitionist tribe to the French capital on a grand tour. These Brahmin's had fallen madly in love with the southern belles who just happened to be touting themselves as abolitionist converts. Caroline and Tilly had loudly proclaimed the error of their ways, renounced slavery, and embraced the tenets of the abolitionist movement. What could be more attractive to well connected Yankee Congregationalist parsons than souls of slave holding southern women saved from perdition. And what a bonus and a blessing it was that these parsons were also so very very rich.

Mrs. Forrester reflected on her whole tormented life since Mr. Forrester had died. She began talking to herself again in a low voice, "I wish that I could just stop thinking. God, that's all I seem to do lately. Why can't somebody invent a pill that just stops all the tormenting thoughts that go through a body's mind? Revolutions at home, and in France, and now Yankees in the family!"

In fact, the whole tribe of Yankees had fallen madly in love with the Forrester girls who were ever so clever, cheerful, and delightful in their conversation. And why not? After all, had they not embraced the abolitionist cause, and they had such a delightfully outlandish mother who was an endless source of amusement. After a short period of courtship, the girls married their respectable conquests and traveled off with their new relations across Europe safe in the bosom of their newly found good Yankee society. The girls then made the rounds of all the bright spots of Central Europe, returned to Paris to visit with mother, then sailed for Boston to be introduced to that self same Yankee society. Mrs. Forrester had just gotten over that awful shock and the whole impact of the double wedding ceremony, and the loss of Caroline and Tilly when the French Revolution of 1848 burst upon her.

Somehow her personal lady's maid, Violet, rose to this challenge of history like an English field marshal and organized the retreat of Mrs. Forrester from Paris to England. Violet guided her from Paris to Le Havre by coach. They stopped at an inn where they changed horses and met an older man called Smith and his wife. Mrs. Forrester proposed to the Smiths that they all go to London together. Mr. Smith was charming, and he declined the kind invitation. He and his wife then left the inn in a very fast carriage with an escort of several gentlemen who all had a stiff and formal air about them. Violet thought it strange that these dozen men were all well mounted and wore swords and appeared to have a pair of saddle pistols on their horses. When Violet mentioned this peculiar fact to Mrs. Forrester, the lady replied, "Violet dear this is France. Don't all the gentlemen wear swords when they travel?"

Violet replied, "I don't think that they do really as a rule."

Eventually, Mrs. Forrester and Violet made it to London together with a great deal of her baggage. Mrs. Forrester had been amazed to find that this pretty little lady's maid had a will of steel and a grim determination to get things done. She had been her mistress' champion at every turn in the complicated process of getting Mrs. Forrester out of revolutionary France. Mrs. Forrester was also pleased with the fact that Violet spoke excellent French.

Mrs. Forrester felt almost as if she had been deserted by Tilly and Caroline who had long been safely in Massachusetts. As a result, she had embraced Violet as the true daughter of her heart. At first, the two women had made the journey to Le Havre from Paris in three days by private coach with just that brief layover at the inn where they had met the Smiths and their young friends. It was when Violet and Mrs. Forrester were crossing the channel on the mail steamer, that Violet had taken a coin from her purse and had looked at the portrait on it. "Mrs. Forrester, does this image put you in mind of anyone?" asked Violet.

"My word Violet! Isn't that the very image of our Mr. Smith? Can you believe the resemblance?" Mrs. Forrester said.

"I think that Mr. Smith was the king, and those men were his guards. I think that something had been painted out on the carriage.

"Oh Violet. I am sure that you are mistaken. Why would the King of France call himself Mr. Smith? That is such a dead common name don't you think?" asked Mrs. Forrester.

This in and of itself, was a source of wonder to all of those to whom Mrs. Forrester would later relate the tale. After arriving in England, Mrs. Forrester had rejoiced that she had left most of her substantial wealth in Baring's Bank. This institution even had offices in both Boston and Paris. Both offices were still in full operation. What could be better? Tilly and Caroline had written to their mother, in care of the bank of course, saying that she and Violet must come to Boston as soon as passage could be arranged. Bank officer and partner in the firm, Mr. J. Philips Sykes, agreed that this would be the best thing she could consider doing under the circumstances.

Mrs. Forrester's world had always been more than a little unsettled to say the least, but the Revolution of 1848 eclipsed all of her former trials. In fact she took the Revolution, and Louis Napoleon Bonaparte's role in it, as a personal attack on herself. She had traveled fairly well, and seemed alright until she reached London and actually had time to appreciate all she had been through. After that, Mrs. Forrester fell apart.

Mr. Sykes had seen to it that Mrs. Forrester and Violet had been put up in the best hotel London had to offer, The Ritz. The Ritz had been London's best hotel since it had opened its doors in the year of Queen Victoria's coronation, 1837. Assured of this fact by Violet, Mrs. Forrester settled in for what she considered to be a well-deserved collapse into two days of coma like sleep. When she awakened, she said that she was peckish and ate a full English breakfast. She then had asked about lunch. She did not seem quite herself thought Violet.

After a few days of rest, and guided by Violet, the somewhat improved Mrs. Forrester made her way to Barings' Bank and the strong shoulder of the gallant Mr. Sykes. She was now ready to arrange her affairs for her American voyage and reunion with her loving family in Boston. "Make sure that it is a very large ship Mr. Sykes. I don't want it sinking on me. I feel that fate has conspired my ruin. I've suffered quite enough troubles for more than a few lifetimes. My poor nerves really can't stand much more," she said daubing her eyes with a Brussels laced edged handkerchief.

Mr. Sykes was a full partner in the firm, quite full of himself, and puffing like a well-meaning penguin after ingesting a very large fish. In spite of his appearance, he was a hard headed and capable man of business who could mime compassion for all the rich widows whose affairs he managed so well.

"It will be a very large ship, a Cunarder Dear Mrs. Forrester. Let me see here. Yes, here it is right here in *The Shipping News*. It is a newer Cunard vessel, The *Britannia*. It is one of the largest and safest vessels afloat, and I assure you that it will see you safely to Boston my good Mrs. Forrester," he purred like some fat and ingratiating cat. "It will be like floating in a grand hotel with every civilized amenity. I am sure that you will love your crossing my dear Mrs. Forrester."

"I do thank you so Mr. Sykes. I do thank you for all of your kind attention. Indeed I do not know what I would have done without you and my dear Violet. The last two months have been a nightmare. Things have just been moving too fast. The changes in my life are beyond the belief of even fiction. If I could only tell you the half of it. My life was so serene, but with the death of my dear Mr. Forrester," here she unloosed a dam, and she burst into a flood of tears.

Violet comforted her, and gave her some soothing syrup. Slowly Mrs. Forrester seemed to slip into a place of comfort. Within five minutes, she was her old more chirpy self. Mrs. Forrester said, "I hope that you'll excuse me Mr. Sykes. It's just that I've had so many shocks and changes in my life of late. I know that I will not sleep a wink until I reach Boston and have good solid American ground under my feet again even if it is in the North. My dear Violet is my traveling companion and the best of friends any person could wish for. I have discovered that she is ever so well read and can take care of any problem that may come our way. When do you think we can sail Mr. Sykes?"

"As it happens Mrs. Forrester, I have arranged passage for you and Miss Violet one week from this very day from Southampton. I have arranged rooms for you at The Royal Arms, which is the best accommodation that Southampton has to offer. They await your pleasure even now. I assure you ladies that you will be quite comfortable there until the time of embarkation. Here are letters of credit and documents to be presented to our Boston office for any transfer of funds that you may desire. And I must say that I agree with Mrs. Forrester when she says that you are a most remarkable young lady Miss Violet," said Mr. Sykes who smiled in an icy and correctly formal way at someone he knew to be a social inferior.

Violet read this condescension in his voice and manner and returned the smile in kind without speaking a single word. Still the pretty companion of the wealthy widow Forrester blushed under her new and very expensive bonnet in spite of herself. In fact she became rather cross with herself for allowing the unctuous man to cause her to react in such a manner. Sykes interpreted that reaction to his comments incorrectly, but it was of no importance to Violet. Mrs. Forrester arose from her chair to leave, and turned to the helpful bank officer.

"My dear Mr. Sykes, I just want to say that your bank has been everything one could wish for from an institution of this sort under these most distressing circumstances. You have seen to everything so well. All of the best people in Boston shall learn of your gallantry to a poor widow in the deepest of distress. My daughters are married into the leading families of that city, and they will be pleased that their mother has been so well provided for by you and your bank."

"Oh my Dear Mrs. Forrester, tut tut, it was nothing. You were no trouble at all," said Sykes while patting the jeweled Forrester hand and thinking of the many tens of thousands of Forrester pounds sterling on deposit in his bank.

"With that awful Napoleon person coming back to France and chasing out the dear King Louis Philippe! Did I tell you that Violet and I met him while we were fleeing the country. He was such a dear man. Well, it was just terrible! Terrible I tell you! And to think that they had Bonaparte all nicely locked up in that Fortress of Ham for six years, and one fine day, they just let him walk away through the front gates mind you all dressed up like a common working man! Oh Mr. Sykes, you have no idea what I have had to go through with all that trouble with those nasty Frenchmen who can't even keep one small French revolutionary personality locked up and out of harm's way. Now these French are so incompetent in allowing him back to rule! And as such an overly excitable people, the French may be inclined to start chopping off the heads of perfectly respectable people at any moment! The Gallic race is just too much given to the excitement of passions of all sorts. Why, who knows what might have befallen two helpless women such as Violet and myself except for divine providence and the iron will of my Dear Violet."

"Rest assured Mrs. Forrester that this revolution was a rather civilized affair all in all as these things go. I doubt if things will get very much out of hand this time. The French have come a long way since our Mr. Burke observed that the first revolution back in 1789 produced nothing more than a mountain of headless corpses and a dictator," smiled Sykes as he reflected on his own borrowed witticism. And now with a second and third revolution only eighteen years apart, they seem to have made a sort of art of it. The last two revolutionary affairs were not nearly as untidy as the first one back in '89.

"I must confess that I find little comfort in that observation Mr. Sykes. One never knows when the worst elements might revert to some very bad behavior, and we must remember Mr.

Sykes that they are not only backward foreigners, they are French! You never know what they'll be up to. My God man! They eat frogs!"

"That's true enough I suppose Mrs. Forrester, but you should be safe enough in Boston. Three thousand miles of ocean separates you from any real danger from the new French Republic," observed the banker sweetly.

"Oh I do hope that you are right. You do comfort me so Mr. Sykes. Truly that you do."

"Don't fret Dear Mrs. Forrester. Our agents are quite active in the French capital right now. I shall instruct the branch manager of our Paris office to settle your affairs there and transfer your funds to London."

"Oh Mr. Sykes. I did leave some very nice porcelain pieces in my hotel suite and some other pretty things that Violet said were not essential to our survival when we fled. She was quite right of course, I am rebuilding my collection of fine china after…that is, I would like ever so much to have those pieces of Dresden and other things I left in Paris back again. I have lost so much of beauty that I used to take for granted. I don't think that I can suffer any more losses."

"Mrs. Forrester, consider it done. Baring's takes care of our clients' every need. We shall pack everything in straw and send your pretty things on to you in Boston. I would say within two to five months at the latest. And maybe a great deal sooner. I can assure you that there will be no difficulty at all."

"I do thank you Mr. Sykes. Violet and I must return to our hotel now to pack our things."

"I shall see you to your carriage Mrs. Forrester, and I shall meet you at your hotel later with all of your arrangements in hand."

"Mr. Sykes, you do give a body comfort. I just do not even want to know what I would do without you and your bank."

As promised, the voyage in *The Britannia* was a most civilized experience. At first Mrs. Forrester did not want to dine anywhere but in her cabin with Violet. Little by little Violet got her to walk on the deck. During their promenades, Violet engaged friendly passengers in casual conversation introducing Mrs. Forrester at just the right moment. Soon Mrs. Forrester was chirping away just as she had in her drawing room in Georgia. When the voyage came to an end, Mrs. Forrester began a subscription to buy Captain Robert Ware a silver loving cup as a gift from the passengers of the first class to thank him for such a fine crossing. After she had collected invitations to visit half a dozen of the finest homes in the Boston area from her new shipmates, Mrs. Forrester was almost her old self. When she and Violet had disembarked, they found a carriage with Caroline and Tilly waiting for them at the dock along with a van for the luggage and two strong men to take charge of the trunks and chase away the annoying men who try to act as luggage handlers at exorbitant prices. The girls had registered their mother and Violet in the best hotel in Boston, The Dunham.

Now that Mrs. Forrester was in Boston, the city looked a bit provincial. After London and Paris, it seemed smaller and more confining than her plantation. The climate also seemed very damp and raw. "This is the best hotel in Boston?" sniffed Mrs. Forrester as her carriage drew up in front of the Dunham.

Later in her rooms, Mrs. Forrester observed, "Southampton was far better. This place is drafty. Not even a footman to light the fire. I hate hotels. Boston has to be the chilliest place on the whole Atlantic I've ever been in. Of course, this is the farthest North I have ever been in this country. I wish that I could bring myself to wake poor Violet. Poor thing hasn't stopped working since we got here. At least she cares if I'm comfortable or not. She would have been the best of my daughters," spoke Mrs. Forrester into the empty air of the chilly drawing room of her suite. She had been catching herself talking aloud to empty rooms for a while now.

Since her flight from Paris, this was happening more and more. Now Mrs. Forrester was no longer bothered by the habit. She simply accepted it as part of her changing life. She had come to terms with her conversations with herself for exactly what they were, namely a safety valve for venting all of her pent up thoughts to which nobody seemed to want to give a sympathetic ear save Violet. She sometimes thought of her weekly gatherings back on the plantation and of the county ladies who came together to discuss so many things back in the days when her James was the respectable protector of her little world. But that was another time. Now it had been almost seven years past since her life was turned upside down. And then there was that period of time when she had seemed to vanish inside of herself. Those were dark days when she could only guess at what had happened in her world. It still was so shrouded in a dream-like mist of a time that was not really so long ago as it sometimes seemed. But that time was not something she wanted to think about now, or indeed, ever again. Mrs. Forrester had told herself that was a place that was not really safe to go.

She only wanted to escape down the hallway now, and walk down the grand staircase to the lobby away from the little world of these rooms for a few minutes and compose her thoughts so that she could eventually lay down her head and sleep. Her restless nervous energy needed this physical outlet. Mrs. Forrester again fought the urge to wake Violet. She caught herself saying, "That girl had been up almost an entire day and a half. 'What ever would I do without her?"

This little conversation with nobody in particular amused Mrs. Forrester. She often caught herself laughing, as she did now, at her own bon mots as she turned her key and locked the door to her suite and began her nocturnal journey down the wide and dimly gas lit hallway. Mrs. Forrester reflected again on her voyage to Boston and of her enjoyment of it. And then her thoughts returned to Caroline and Tilly.

"No sooner had those wretched girls married those horrid and stuffy abolitionist Yankees, than I had to put up with those awful and insufferable French and their awful revolution and that awful Napoleon person," said Mrs. Forrester softly. These events never seemed far removed from her thoughts no matter how hard she tried to put them out of her consciousness. Before her flight from France, as she and the steady and brave Violet were throwing things together, she had screamed, "How do these wretched people stand to have three revolutions in the span of what could be one person's lifetime? We haven't had but one in seventy years! This place just isn't civilized!"

Now Mrs. Forrester found herself in the corridor leading from her room to the grand staircase leading to the lobby and the plush public rooms still talking to herself. She was in a state in which she could not fully make up her mind to continue to walk down to the reception area of the hotel or not. Violet had been nicely ensconced warm and snug in her bed quite content with the world after her mistress had left the suite. After the chills of England, Violet had felt at home in the dampness of New England. But her warm bed was her most comforting refuge from that sometimes pleasantly familiar but uncomfortable condition. As she gathered her thoughts on awakening, Violet came to the conclusion that she had better get up and investigate what sort of mischief might be going on.

Violet felt strangely protective of Mrs. Forrester who had given her a secure place in the world. After all, Violet had nobody to leave behind in England, and was quite content to be anywhere where she did not have to scrub floors for a living as an under parlor maid which might have been her fate on a good day considering her own past unfortunate domestic experiences. Mrs. Forrester had saved her from all of that. Born into a poor yet respectable clerical family, Violet was then twice orphaned. First, by her parents who died suddenly on the same night on which her brother had been stillborn and then reluctantly by her grandparents through their deaths which were only one year apart.

Thus twice orphaned, Violet had found herself with very few options in life. Her chance of becoming a lady's maid to Mrs. Forrester at such an early age was a good bit of luck. Becoming traveling companion to a wealthy American woman was a dream come true. Violet rather liked the excitement and adventure she had embarked on. And with Mrs. Forrester, there had been no end of excitement either real or in the overly active and excited mind of her employer. Violet had had a great deal of both adventure and excitement. Mrs. Forrester had a natural talent for manufacturing excitement at any hour day or night.

Violet was grateful for the little education her grandmother had given her as well as schooling in good manners. Her grandmother had been raised a respectable middle class girl in Georgetown in British Guiana. As Violet looked about the pretty hotel room, she had never imagined that she could ever be living such a respectable life in such a lovely place with no income, position, or prospects.

What Violet had discovered in America, and on her journey, was that Americans were every bit as class conscious as were her countrymen. The myth of American egalitarianism she had found to be false. She thanked God that she had the courage to go to the agency in London with forged letters and a carefully crafted upper class accent and had dared to apply for the position as a lady's maid. Now here she was, elevated from that position to the position of traveling companion, because she was possessed of real nerve and the imagination of a true survivor.

After hearing Mrs. Forrester moving about in the little drawing room and opening and then closing the door to the suite then returning a bit later and frantically pacing about, Violet had decided to arise, put on her wrapper, and see what was happening. As she put on her wrapper, she thought about what she had seen when she had landed in Boston. She had fallen quite in love with the city, which felt like it had age and an air of settlement much greater than its mere two hundred and twenty year history. As she and Mrs. Forrester had ridden to the hotel, Violet thought how simple life could be if one were very rich. She hadn't minded the voyage at all and was pleased that Mrs. Forrester had overcome her mild mal de mer and had followed her lead in meeting the other first class passengers on the ship. Violet also smiled when she reflected on how different her views of Boston were from Mrs. Forrester's.

America was different from England in as much that England had no slaves in the strictest sense. It was very true that poverty had enslaved whole classes of the English people since The Conquest of 1066. Violet had seen the Irish on Boston Common and had been told about them by almost everyone she had met. Each story seemed as if it were a narration about a different people. There seemed to be no absolute agreement as to what these poor beings were really like. America seemed to have imported everything from old Europe including poverty. Nobody had ever seemed so poor to her as these poor refugees from the famine in Ireland. She felt that no poverty like this had ever been seen here before in America. She also knew that to a large degree, England was the author of this poverty from which these unfortunate Irish expatriates suffered.

As she mulled over these thoughts, Violet considered going into the parlor of the suite then following Mrs. Forrester into the hallway to see if all was well. Violet stopped when she heard the door to the suite finally shut for what she took to be the last time. As she listened, she could discern no sounds of movement at all. She decided to return to her own room to dress and wait for Mrs. Forrester to return to the suite. Ten minutes later, she entered the parlor of the suite to a distinct chill. "I'll make up a fire," she said into the empty chamber. Then she laughed, "I'm talking to myself just like her ladyship. I hope it's not catching."

Violet struck a lucifer taken from the painted and gold leafed tin matchbox and struck it on the brickwork. The kindling caught on fire. A wonderful blaze of life began in the fireplace. Soon a warming roaring fire began to chase every hint of chill from the room. Violet warmed herself before the flames and felt the rich heat on her back. She closed her eyes and tried to pretend that it was years ago and that she was standing in her grandfather's cottage listening to his oral history of her family. It gave her comfort that the heat she was feeling could have come from that cherished hearth three thousand miles away. She glowed in the fact that she was happy and safe again. A few moments later, she heard Mrs. Forrester fussing with the keys in the lock of the door of the suite. Violet arose from her reverie and let her mistress in. Mrs. Forrester breezed through the door after her walk with some late arriving letters in her hand, which she had picked up at the desk in the lobby.

"Why Violet my dear, what a wonderful fire. How ever did you know that a fire is exactly what I wanted? Now that was most considerate of you. I would be hard pressed to think of any comfort you have denied me since we met."

"I'll close the door for you Mrs. Forrester," said Violet. As she was about to close it, two men walked by. One was a tall Black man. He was one of the very few men of color Violet had ever seen. She thought him to be a wonderfully handsome specimen of mankind. She had become aware since she found herself in a more settled position in life and nearing her eighteenth birthday, that she was looking at almost all the men she was meeting in a different way. As she took her eyes off Samuel, she focused on thc other man who was walking with him. He was younger and also tall, and he was handsome and white. This specimen of the race of men did something unexpected. He turned and looked at her, smiled, and gave her a bow. She looked after him unable to speak. She thought him to be the most handsome man she had ever seen in her life.

CHAPTER XXXV

Starbuck turned slightly in his bed. His leg burned as if a hot poker had been inserted into its entire length. His condition had shown a dramatic improvement over the way he was the day before, when the Maycocks found him on the beach writhing in pain and not knowing where or who he was. They got Starbuck back to his house in a barrel wagon, like a cargo of seaweed, pushed by Mr. Maycock. They had loaded him into the wagon, and placed him on a bed of seaweed hoping that the kelp would reduce the shock of being trundled over the rutted paths and unpaved roadway back to the house. The Maycocks had cleaned him up as best they could, and sent for Dr. Graham.

The doctor had attended him as he lay on his bed raving for two days. The horrible wounds on Starbuck's leg caused by the jagged splinter of wood and another caused by contact with something unknown, perhaps some marine animal, had festered. The wounds had begun to smell. A great deal of puss issued from all the wounds and scrapes. Dr. Graham was encouraged by this development. He said that he had done a lot of reading in his English and continental medical journals and discovered that puss was good evidence that the body was fighting the deadly microbes festering in the wounds. There was scientific speculation that puss was made up of dead cells and the harmful elements they had killed in the body.

"I've been reading a lot about these microbes in the *Lancet.* That Brit magazine was the best thing I ever invested in. There's a lot going on over in Europe that our medical fellows over here ought to learn about. By all rights, our Mr. Starbuck here ought to lose that leg, but I think that I can save it, and if I do by God, I'm going to write it up for publication myself I am. It's about time Yankee medicine grew up. Yes sir it is. I studied in Boston at the hospital in the old days. My father before me studied with some doctor until he decided to hang out a shingle on his own way back in Worcester," said the good doctor to the ever patient Maycocks who listened politely to the doctor's homespun wisdom.

"You are a man of skill doctor. Mr. Starbuck is fortunate to have you attend him," said Mrs. Maycock.

"He's not going to feel so fortunate if I have to cut off that leg. He seems to be doing pretty well though I must admit, but I've another old time trick up my sleeve that my father taught me. Now this isn't pretty. If you would rather not look, don't! I'll get about it now."

"There isn't too much that bothers us Doctor," said Mr. Maycock displaying real curiosity.

"Well here it is. This is just what the doctor ordered." With that, the doctor opened a vile of maggots and put them into the festering wounds on Starbuck's leg, and bound them up.

"What in heavens name?" asked Mrs. Maycock.

"Those are maggots right from my very own garbage heap. What those little fellows will do is eat all the festering flesh and prevent gangrene. If he gets gangrene, his leg will turn black, and he'll die of blood poison if it isn't amputated. The maggots are a better alternative. They eat only what has gone bad and will cause what they are calling in Europe 'Infection'. I think, given my druthers, I'd rather have those little fellers feasting on that dead tissue than have my leg lopped off. Those little fellers will eat up all Mr. Starbuck's flesh that is dead and rotted, and the rest will be safe from this infection business. I have read up on infection a great deal. Most of our home raised quacks won't even wash their hands before operating on a feller. They might even be good with a knife and needle, but if they infect their patient, they might as well save all their trouble and just feed the poor bugger opium until he dies. It's a damned good thing that you went out for a stroll along the shore in the morning, or this poor bugger would be dead."

"We've seen that sort of thing back on the mainland doctor. You're right about that infection. My uncle wouldn't let the doctor take his leg, and it turned black as pitch. He died a horrible death raving all the while with fever," said Mrs. Maycock. "My aunt pleaded with him to let the doctor have the leg off, but he said that he came in to the world with two good legs and he planned to go out the same way. Then my aunt told him that the leg was not as good as the one he came in with, and he might as well be rid of the damned thing. She made a lot of sense, but my uncle would have none of it."

During the next several days, the Maycocks took turns nursing Starbuck through his fever and bouts of madness. Starbuck ripped open the hidden vaults of his memory which were holding the black secrets of his life. He exposed his history in fits of incoherent raving sprinkled with moments of something like lucidity. Cold wet compresses, applied to the patient's head, were used to cool the fever. These applications, along with sponge baths and frequent changes of bed linen, helped to keep the fever at bay, which surely would have killed him. On the third day of his treatment, Starbuck's fever broke, and the crisis was over. The big man began to breathe more evenly, and the ranting stopped. By the afternoon of the fourth day, Starbuck came to himself. He blinked his eyes open and looked at the doctor sitting by his bed reading a journal, and felt a searing pain in his leg.

"Where the Hell am I?" he moaned.

"Well, sure as shooting, it's not Heaven, but it isn't Hell either which I'm guessing is pretty good news for you my profane friend.

If half of what you were raving about when you were out of your head is true, then Hell is where you would belong mister," laughed the doctor.

"My leg hurts like the Devil, and just what the Hell was I saying?"

"You were raving about gold, and killing folks, sinking boats, spies from New York, and damning some fellow in the White House. Now you wouldn't be talking about our fine President Polk would you? I can't stand him either, but he's on the way out in less than a year or so anyway. Polk must have offended you something fierce with the way you were going on about him. You must be a Taylor man to be taking Whig politics so seriously."

"What else was I saying mister?"

"You have one wild imagination Brother Starbuck. With an imagination like that, you should go in for writing adventure books. On some of these God-awful winter nights, a book based on your yarns would be damned good company. It would sure warm things up. You ought to sell your stories to *Harpers*. They love things like those wild stories you were telling."

"What the Hell did I say damn it!"

"Calm down. I don't want you bursting any of my fine stitching work. You were talking about hiding your gold under rocks, sinking boats, and hiding the rest of your fortune under a woodpile, and killing a whole passel of folks from New York. Now just how many fortunes might you have Brother? I think you have been reading too much about Captain Kidd and Blackbeard and such. Land's sakes, what a fuss you made. I have heard a lot of stuff and nonsense told to me over the years by people out of their heads with fever, but except for the fact that I thought that you might die on me, I really enjoyed listening to those yarns. Yes sir, you do tell one Hell of a story. You do keep a feller awake you do."

"Who the Hell are you anyway?" asked Starbuck now exhausted from his reawakening into the world of the living and a bit frightened by what he might have confessed to during his awful nightmares.

"I'm Doctor Graham. I saved your damned life, and it wasn't all that easy, and you owe a great debt of gratitude to the Maycocks who found you more half dead than alive on the beach more than four days ago, but they can tell you about that later on. How is the pain?"

"It's horrible doctor. I can't stand it, and my skin feels like its crawling."

"We'll talk about that later. Your heart is as strong as a young ox. I'm going to give you a dose of soothing syrup that will make the pain go away and make you sleep."

Holding a small amount of laudanum in a glass mixed with tea and sugar to Starbuck's lips, the doctor commanded, "Swallow. Come on. Drink this."

Starbuck drained the glass. Then his head fell back onto the pillows, and in a few minutes, he grew groggy then fell to sleep peacefully. This dreamless sleep was to last another day. The doctor returned twice during the next fifteen hours to check the dressing and observe the progress of his maggots until the mortified flesh was eaten away. Then the doctor retired his small friends, cleaned the wound, and skillfully sewed it up again.

"There Mrs. Maycock, have you ever seen so fine a job of stitchery?"

"Doctor, you would be quite a sensation at the quilting bee," laughed the housekeeper.

"Why Mrs. Maycock, I do believe that you are having me on," said the doctor in a mocking tone of injury.

"What instructions do you have for us now doctor," asked Mr. Maycock.

"Well, I'll continue to return twice a day to tend the wound. Give him this soothing syrup as he needs it, but don't give him more than one spoonful less than four hours apart. We don't want to kill him after all the trouble we've taken so far to keep him alive. He's got to be well past fifty by his looks, but he's got the heart of a young ox and maybe the brain to match I'm judging. I cannot imagine the damned fool going in for a swim at that time of the morning where those sharks were spotted only last week. By the look of him, he has lived one Hell of a life. Oh, excuse me Mrs. Maycock for my old bachelor language. Even though I'm married, my language is still that of a bachelor, and I'll be begging your pardon for it Mrs. Maycock. My good lady wife gives me Hell over my habits of speech. She tells me that I'm very unrefined for a doctor. She says it comes from reading too much and not being properly social. I think that we would all be better off if a lot more medical men did a bit of reading and brushed up on their German and French. It wouldn't hurt them none to read some papers out of the University of Heidelberg from time to time either and Edinburgh too. More doctors kill their patients with dirty fingers than any disease ever could. Carbolic soap could save more lives than all the patent medicines down at Lewis' emporium. About my way of talking though, I think that my sweet little wife might be right about that. It's just too damned, begging your pardon, bad that I really don't care much about what people think one way or t'other."

"Think nothing of it doctor. You make me laugh, and laughter is a better cure for what ails a body than even your old maggots. You are a damned good doctor. My sensibilities are not so delicate as all that. I like to hear a man talk like a man sometimes. Mr. Maycock let's go once in a while, and I never minded it. As you say, Mr. Starbuck appears to have led one Hell of a life. What didn't kill him, I think made him stronger," replied the housekeeper.

"Mr. Maycock, you have one wonderful lady there. I wish that my good wife was as liberal minded as yours. She don't hold with my unrefined and unhousebroken bachelor talk at all," said the doctor wistfully as he gave the good woman a slight bow, a wink, and nod of the head in appreciation of her being such a good and understanding sort.

"When will you be back today doctor?" asked the housekeeper.

"I should return by six. I'm going home to get some rest. I suggest that you do the same. He's going to sleep a good deal longer. And that sleeping is what will hurry the healing along. Lord! I hope that nobody else decides to take a midnight swim with the sharks or whatever the Hell it was that got him out there. I don't know how I'll survive if midnight bathing becomes the newest pastime on this blasted island. I don't know but our Mr. Starbuck here has the Devil's own luck, or he even might be the Devil himself to still be alive after all he's been through."

"Mr. Starbuck may not be Old Scratch, but it wouldn't surprise me a bit if he wasn't one of his close relations," intoned Maycock.

CHAPTER XXXVI

Pompey and Samuel found themselves walking down the all but deserted streets of the business district of the old city of Boston. The night was clear and the air was soft with just a hint of chill in it. The two men felt a slight unease as they strode along on their way to Garrison's office. The meeting of the prime movers of the Massachusetts Abolitionist Society was moved back by one night. Garrison had sent word to the Dunham of this fact with one of his own men. A new meeting was to be held for Samuel and Pompey's benefit tonight. Even in this city of greatest support for the abolition of slavery, support for the movement was far from absolute. A great number of working men felt threatened by the prospect of a vast migration of cheap and newly freed Negro laborers moving into the industrialized North. Recent Irish immigrants were also jealous of any threat of competition for any sort of employment at all. Times were not good. Economic stability was a dicey thing even in the best of times. The huge influx of Irish in the cities up and down the Atlantic coast had made the nativist population uneasy. Garrison himself had often considered the problem. Even he had qualms about all of the new immigration. This was a philosophical problem for him armed as he was with his gospel of toleration.

Garrison's offices had been burned out several times and his presses smashed because of his abolitionist sentiments. The support he had enjoyed came mostly from the upper classes, as well as the educated, the academic, and liberal religious community. The city's working poor and the nativists were not at all in sympathy with their African brothers and sisters even though slavery had been outlawed in Massachusetts for more than seventy years. The keenness of competition for unskilled employment was at the base of the problem, yet there was a deeper resentment. The Black man had been in Boston almost from the beginning, long before the advent of the Irish Catholics, who in turn saw themselves pushed out of the labor market by this Black race that they had never seen before in their native Ireland.

And of course there were those who played on that very prejudice and fear to hire white men at a much reduced wage. Even Samuel and Pompey knew that women and children were used and exploited in the same way. It was no secret that Negroes, women and children constituted the most docile manageable labor force that anyone could wish for. Adult white males were, by contrast, much more difficult and fractious. All of this Pompey and Samuel had heard from the lips of Mr. Disraeli himself.

Setting class against class was an old game to these new American industrialists seeking the cheapest possible wage slaves to work in their mills and factories. Disraeli had spoken of Leeds and Manchester and the great problems that labor was having in competition for a living wage in those crowded centers of industrial production. London was the scene of Mr. Dickens' books on the troubles of the city poor as were the novels of Disraeli himself. Was Boston really so very different? Boston looked cleaner to Pompey than did London, but there was a sinister change in the air, and although he did not know the city, he could feel it all the same. All these thoughts went through Pompey's mind as he walked along the streets.

Samuel had his mind on other matters. Unlike Pompey, he was always aware of exactly where he was and what was going on around him. His warrior instinct was alert. His one lapse in this regard had carried a severe punishment of its own, slavery. Samuel had vowed to himself never to make that mistake again. Now as he walked the streets of this strange city, his senses were alert, and he sensed that things were not as they should be. Some secret little voice in his head told him to fall back and walk closer to the walls of the buildings lining the street, pull his dark cloak about him, and stay in the shadows. The big man melted into the night.

Samuel did not alert Pompey as to what he was doing. He was in a perfect position to protect his friend should the need arise. Pompey walked ahead unaware of Samuel's vanishing into the shadows. To the casual eye, Pompey was now prey as he appeared to be ambling along alone. Samuel sensed that somebody was stalking them with the intent of doing some mischief. Now Pompey appeared to be totally alone and vulnerable.

All at once, three young men jumped out of an alley and produced knives and clubs. They tried to form a circle around Pompey, who in turn was surprised to find himself facing three bandits alone. One of them spoke up, "Now yer honor, would yeh be so kind as to be after handing over yer purse so that we poor fellows might be going on our way and leaving yer alone to yer self."

Pompey, standing with his back protected by a brick wall was at least a full head taller than the tallest of these three little Irishmen. They were skinny and dressed in the same rags in which they had left their country months ago. Their boots were broken, and one of the men was barefoot. Pompey slowly stared at the men, smiled, and said, "Do you mean to tell me that you want my money, and that you actually expect me to hand it over to you? Now why would I do that?"

"You are right in what you've been after thinkin' about our intentions sir. That is a fact sir, and we would be right pleased if yer would be after gitting about it before we will be forced to act with some violence on yer sir," said the fellow whom Pompey took to be the leader of the scruffy little band.

All three of the Irishmen were now closing in on him like

wolves around a fat buck. Pompey grasped the handle of his walking stick twisted it and in a flash produced a fine tempered Toledo blade. With one deft move of his thick wrist, he inscribed a perfect arc in the air that grazed one of the men lightly and drove the attackers back in a half circle about ten feet distant from him. The slightly wounded man dropped his club, and the trio regrouped for a halfhearted second try. "You fellows don't seem to know very much about this business do you?" asked Pompey. "As stupid as you are, you really ought to give it up before harm comes to you. I really don't want to kill you, but I will defend myself, and I will kill you should you give me no other choice in the matter. What do you say Samuel? Do you think that these three highwaymen have much of a future in following a life of crime as a profession?"

One of the young and wild red haired Irishmen spat out, "Well mister, I know enough to know that yer are trying to trick me for ye'd not be after talking to none save the air maybe, and I'll not be fooled in that way. Do yer think that we won't kill yer? If yer don't realize that it's desperate men we are, it's a damned fool yer be? We be desperate men we are, and we have others to feed and fend for. Yer won't hire us to do an honest job of work. So robbin's what we've been reduced to. Now don't make this a harder task than it has to be. Just give us the money, and we'll be gone sooner then we come."

Pompey reacted with a few wide and dramatic academic strokes of his blade that sent the men reeling back another fifteen feet without any harm coming to them from his deftly handled weapon. Then Pompey called out in a taunting voice, "Samuel, they think that I'm mad and that you don't exist. What do you make of that? Shall I just kill them one by one and put them out of their misery?"

"I think that they are stupid and have done this sort of thing before. Haven't you lads? You have been very lucky, or you would have all been hanged by now," Samuel roared at them like the Devil incarnate. His huge arm was around the ringleader's neck in an instant and his clasp knife was at the little man's throat. "Now be a good little fellow and tell your friends to throw down their weapons before you get hurt. You fellows look as foolish as I suppose you are, and I am sure, at the same time, that you don't want to die tonight."

"What the bleeding Hell would be the difference if I did I tells yer. We be all but dead in this accursed place now. Yer would be after doing us a good service and even a kindness, so do us in now so we won't have to see our women and kids starve to death and waste away. Just do it quick like for the love of God." The red headed man then said something in an unintelligible tongue to the other two Irish men who then threw down their weapons.

The three little men then stood there waiting for the hand of retribution to fall on their heads. Samuel put away his knife and Pompey fitted his sword back into his cane. Samuel said, "Now boys, tell us your story."

"You be some fashion of rich wild black fellow all dressed up and neat like some kind of a lord. What does the like of yer grand folks care for the ragged arsed likes of us?"

"Just maybe my friend, I care a great deal, and then maybe again I don't. Now how could you know that? Reflect on the fact that we did not kill you as we had every right to do. You attacked us did you not? We could then have tossed your bodies into the river, and we might do it yet," answered Samuel.

"If yer kills us, yer would be after doing me and my companions a kindness just likes I was after saying. Then we could die all at once and not have to watch our wives, and children, and old mothers die by small stages in front of our eyes from the hunger and us not being able to do a thing about it. We are men no longer and can do nothing to save our loved ones from starvation. Is there nothing a'tall but hunger in this damned world? Back in Ireland, we could at least have died in our own ditches, and the fecking English could have covered us up with our own sod, and they could have saved us the needless Hell of crossing the fecking ocean to die in the dirt of Boston with the world looking on wishing that we were never born in the first place. We crossed the God damned ocean puking out our guts while we was hidden away in the hold just a few stinking feet under the swells in their fine first class cabins. We were never allowed topside to be seen by the swells neither. The captain did not want the fine folks and gentry to have to look at the ragged arsed likes of us and spoil their fine time in the sun taking their tea on the deck. Kill us now and have done with it. I just don't care anymore. We're beyond all hope for Christ's sake," shouted the little man almost convulsing between sobs.

"I know that things have not gone well for you. The people here don't want you, but I also know what it's like to be rejected by people who think that they are my betters. I do not intend to let them beat me. You have to pull yourselves together, and make a plan for survival. You must want to live. You have made your way over three thousands of miles of ocean to get here after all. Why don't you tell us your troubles?" asked Samuel.

The little redheaded men looked up at Samuel trying to puzzle out the situation. The little Irishmen looked from Samuel to Pompey with real anger and pain in their eyes. The little red headed man looked almost mad, and driven to distraction by an inner pain which was way beyond the bounds of his human endurance. In a rage he snapped out, "Do yer have any idea a'tall, a'tall of how bad these fecking Brits were to me people. They have so fecking much, and they would rather toss it away than feed a hungry Irish child or give an old Irish body shelter. Do yer have any idea what they would do if yer crops failed and yer could not pay yer rents? They would come down to yer cottage with a pair of great oxen and then some drovers and the landlord's agent himself would be after telling us to get out of the cottage. They would give us but a few minuets only to get our belongings out of the place fer the love of Christ Almighty!"

The little man stopped until he could stop his sobbing, catch his breath, and get his emotions somewhat under control. As Pompey and Samuel stared and waited for him to continue, they felt themselves being drawn into his sorrow. The little man drew himself up to his full five-foot height and began again after batting away a few more tears.

"After we got as many of our belongings as we could out of the cottage, the drovers climbed up onto the roof and tied a great rope about the chimney. They then made the other end of the ropes fast to the great beasts. Then they pulled the house down so that no person could live there ever again. It wasn't that they wanted us out to rent it to somebody else. They never wanted any poor soul to shelter there for evermore. Me people had lived there since before the Battle of the Boyne over a hundred and sixty year or more ago. The blight had taken our crops from us. We had worked like dogs to bring the spuds into being. They had looked to be a fair crop too by the green that was showing above the ground, but the insides of 'em was all black and rotted. Before it was over, we was eating the blackened and rotted things. We was eating the grass itself not long after those poor black spuds was gone. Yer could see hundreds of the dead along the cart lanes, and roads, and in the ditches with the green of the grass all around their mouths. The old women would swallow stones to kill the hunger in their bellies and tell the young ones to eat their very own share of the food, so that the young ones might be lasting at least a bit longer and have a chance to survive maybe. Oh, we dug the tubers when we could find them in fields of abandoned farms. By God, all the spuds was black inside everywhere we went on our way to the sea. Black as coal they was. Me old mother cried with the hunger she did. For there was naught else to eat but stones and grass and sometimes a bit of bread to go on with. But she wouldn't eat what ever we had in the way of real food. She filled her mouth with dirt. She was that hungry, and told us to give what passed for good food that we had to the little ones. In a few days, she died. We buried her tiny wee body in an ancient churchyard. We had nothing except the ditch by the road to huddle in and that was our shelter."

"Was there no help from England at all?" asked Pompey who

could never imagine such privation even in the slave quarters on the poorest plantation in the South.

"Anything from bleeding England? Are yer daft man? Have yer lost yer mind a'tall, a'tall? Those fecking English bastards repealed all the laws that would give us any help. They said it was bad for our character for us to accept charity," replied the little man. "There was nothing I tell yer. We could not fight them. They had all the troops and the fecking guns! They just tore down our fecking homes like I was after tellin' yer, or sometimes they'd be after setting them afire if there was no oxen to do the job of pulling down the place by Holy Jesus! We made our long way to Dublin along with those who had not died by the road. My God, me mother before she went with the stones inside of her belly, and her trying still to keep going with nothing a'tall to sustain herself, said that she would die happy if we promised to eat her when she had gone. She said that she wanted us to have a bit of flesh to go on with. She said that she give us her milk when we was born, and now when she was dying, she wanted to feed us still, and that she wanted us to know that this would be no sin, because she wanted it this way. But we never done it. We buried her in that old churchyard near a grand old stone cross that looked as ancient as Saint Patrick himself. We was after thinking that those who had owned the grand cross and grave site so many hundreds of years back would not take offense if such a fine woman as me dear and sainted mother was sharin' that fine carved stone with them. We took a bit of comfort knowin' that she could lay forever in the sheltering shadow of that holy monument in hallowed Irish ground. Now it was true that more than a few poor folks, near mad with the hunger, ate their dead, but we had not sunk so low as that. No we were not savages yet," with a glance at Samuel, "Begging yeh pardon. I'm that crazed with hunger still. I mean no offense to you sir, and me not knowing your own eating' habits."

Samuel almost laughed at the apology and its suggestion about his own nature. He was used to being exotic, and did not take offense with the little man's remark. The sorrow he felt for this little man waved away any pride.

"We love Ireland misters," the little man went on, "But it ain't ours no more. The fecking English have it now. They have built it up with their fine estates and grand horses and for racin' and hunting and such. They will not be happy until the last of our kind is dead in the ditches or gone west in some other manner of leavin' the whole country open to them to do with it as they want and please." The little man let out a repressed sob then pulled himself together again with all the dignity he could muster. With a forced infusion of pride he said, "We ain't dead yet. No, we not be that at'all, at'all. Mister, you are right about that. I'm sorry that we troubled yer, and if yer let us go, we'll not do such as this again."

"Last night my friend and I went to visit the Catholic Bishop of Boston and gave him a thousand dollars to feed your people," said Pompey," And now I will give you each ten dollars. Make it last, and feed your families. For now that is all we can do. I have seen these Bostonians. They hate you, and if you try robbing them, they will hang you or kill you outright. Give up this business as you said that you would. It won't serve your interest to try robbery to stay alive. It will only provide another excuse to exterminate the lot of you to the last man. What will your women and children do then with you dead and nobody left to protect them? You may not be so badly off as you think. Get out of Boston. There are other towns about who need men to work in the mills and on the farms. Now pick up your weapons, and do not show them to anyone or try this again. You may not be so fortunate in your choice of victims next time."

"Thanks yer honors. I'll tell these two what yer was after sayin'. They speak none but the Irish yer see. We'll be going yer worship, and God bless yer for the kind gentlemen that yer be."

The little red headed man told his two companions what had been said in Gaelic. The eyes of the two ruffians filled with tears. They scrambled to pick up their weapons, hid them in their rags, accepted the money, tugged at their forelocks in gratitude, and made off into the night. They went up the alleyway from which they had come and disappeared.

"The world is too much filled with that sort of thing Samuel," said Pompey sadly.

"At least it was their own idea to come here young Pompey. They traveled here with those who loved them and those who spoke the same language. They have the right to move about and make their way out of Ireland and out of Boston with whatever talents they may have no matter how small those talents might be. There are no chains on them, nor irons about their legs. Still I join with you in your sorrow. They are no lion killing warriors after all. They are just poor farmers who know nothing much about the world. You whites are a sorry lot. Do you know that Master? You white people rule the whole of the damned world, or most of it at least, and are doing a damn poor job of it. You devour each other like wolves," said a somber Samuel.

"Do you think that Samuel? Do you think that I have crossed that line? I hope you are joking, because I live for what you have given me. You have given me back my life. Whatever I have or will become, you have made possible. And I am a Black man Samuel. It's just that I have never suffered like these poor souls thanks to Anna and you, and the old master too I guess, and his ability to cheat at cards."

"Pompey, I need you to be just what you are, and you never disappoint me. Were you less than you are, we would be in Georgia still with no more future than to be with Anna someday in rough pine boxes of our own. You are the Blackest white man I shall ever know," said Samuel with a little laugh.

"Do not make me laugh right now Samuel. I feel that I could cry for those poor people. Life can be a deadly, serious, and very shoddy business. Those poor Irish have a rough road ahead of them."

"I'm not so sure about that. They have grit. It's not well directed now, but I think that once they get the hang of things, they will become Americans just as other white folks from Europe have over the years. But never mind that now young Pompey. Don't forget our mission. We must find this Starbuck fellow, and make him take us to Whitehouse. The day that I punish Whitehouse for stealing my life and the lives of all the others and end his work in the slave trade, that day shall be the day of my real liberation. Only then can I take a wife and father my children. That will be the day that you will decide in what world you will live yourself. You are a young man of great promise, and you will be of even greater wealth. You will make a life wherever you wish to, and that will please me more than even my revenge on this evil man."

"Then we should be away then. Mr. Garrison and his friends will be waiting," replied Pompey.

As Pompey walked among the street to Garrison's office with Samuel, he knew one thing. The Matabele Zulus would never accept him as an equal. They never accepted anyone outside of their nation on anything like a basis of equality. Pompey had no doubt that Samuel had convinced himself that by some alchemy that he could get this pale son of Africa admitted to the Matabele Zulu Nation, but Pompey knew from what he had learned from Samuel's own lips, that his adoption into the Matabele was not even a remote possibility. But he also knew that was a problem to be solved another day.

CHAPTER XXXVII

When Samuel and Pompey arrived at the offices of *The Liberator*, there was only a dim light indicating that anyone was there. Pompey softly knocked at the door. A few seconds later it opened, and Mr. Garrison's man, Harry, simply said, "Come in quickly gentlemen. The others are inside. Please follow me."

The three men moved to the back of the building where a number of well-dressed Bostonians were talking in subdued voices. The gaslights cast a soft glow on the proceedings as the seven men sat in quiet discussion with Garrison. As Samuel and Pompey entered, Garrison arose from his seat and said, "Ah gentlemen, you are here at last."

"Please excuse our being late. We were detained by some of the poor Irish camped on the Common. We settled things without harm coming to them or ourselves," said Pompey.

"There have been some unpleasant incidents involving this riffraff I am afraid to say," said a distinguished looking man of some obvious importance seated at the far end of the table. Pompey and Samuel did not react to this distasteful remark. Pompey reflected that the abolitionists had a compartmentalized view of social problems and society in general. And tonight, he could see how they might view things.

"Excuse me gentlemen," said Garrison, "But I would like to

present Mr. James Charles and Mr. Samuel James. And these gentlemen are Mr. Shaw, Mr. Saltonstall, the Rev. Mr. Beecher, Mr. Lodge, Mr. Cabot, Mr. Smith, and the Rev. Mr. Balcome. We are all here to see what we can do to help you. We are all abolitionists here and dedicated to the total overthrow of the slave system in this country wherever it is to be found."

"Thank you for those kind and reassuring words. It's good to know that such men exist in this world. It seems that there is an awful lot of misery to go around, and it is good to know that there are men of good will about like yourselves who care enough to do something about it. Our delay tonight was both a revelation and unavoidable," said Pompey.

"Pray Mr. Charles, do tell us about your encounter," said the Rev. Mr. Beecher.

Pompey related the story of his encounter with the three Irish immigrants just as it had happened. When he was through with his narrative, Mr. Beecher sadly shook his head and said,

"No good will ever come out of a forced immigration like this. The British Government will have a great deal to answer for either in this life or the next. Not extending Christian help to those poor people in their own country is both inhuman and unchristian. Have any of you read Mr. Dickens' *Oliver Twist*? Now there is a living portrait of English charity for you. I speak of that abomination known as the workhouse. It is true that many of our towns have 'Poor Farms", but they are nothing like workhouses. Workhouses are institutions that degrade human life and robs it of all quality. Thank God gentlemen that we have no such institutionalized poverty in this land except for these poor isolated immigrant pockets in our larger coastal cities! There will come a time that we shall face huge problems of assimilating these unfortunate people as Europe's masses keep on arriving at our gates hungry and desperate. I hope that we do a better job of it than our English cousins."

"That is all well and good Rev. Beecher, but it is not for that business that we are meeting here tonight. I want you to listen to

Mr. James' story first before we begin any sort of discussion," said Garrison." And then I want to assist him with whatever help we can provide. Please Mr. James, do begin."

"Please do tell us your tale," intoned Mr. Lodge.

"I am not about to recite some high flown moral tale gentlemen," said Samuel. "I am going to tell my story straight out. Then I am going to tell you the reasons that I want to lay my hands on a certain man, the very man who stole me out of Africa. He took me from the land of my fathers, when I was only turning sixteen years of age. He must never be allowed to do this dreadful thing again in order to provide slaves for the southern planters of this country or of any other land where this ugly trade is still allowed. This is not a story I will tell you for your amusement or to be written about or spoken of as some high adventure. This is the story of my life from that time when I was taken from my family and homeland up to now. I was a warrior, a prince of the Matabele nation, and a son of Africa. I am not an animal to be beaten, lashed, and mated like a beast of the field. Gentlemen, I am a man, a man who has been most deeply wronged. As I am telling you my story, I want you to try to put yourself in my place. When I tell you of the treatment and outrages that the African women suffered on the slave ship that brought me here, I want you to think of your mothers, and sisters, and your daughters in their place suffering those same outrages. If you can do that, then you will have some small knowledge of what it is to be a slave in the black belly of a stinking slave ship chained to strangers who share your miserable fate with whom you cannot communicate. I want you to feel what it would be like to be beaten, raped, and brought to the most profound depths of human degradation."

All eyes were now on Samuel as he told the story of his capture and of his being taken to Mozambique to the slave factory. They looked at him in awe as he related his biography and Whitehouse's part in it. For one of the first times in their lives, since hearing Frederick Douglass, these white patricians listened to an articulate Black African man relate his own story of personal horror in intimate detail. The saga of his slave abduction, with all of its attendant atrocity, shocked these men to their foundations. They had heard the voice of Frederick Douglass, but Douglass did not have the experience that this Matabele warrior had suffered. For two hours, Samuel stripped his audience of their innocence until they were emotionally drained. These men had looked into Samuel's large black eyes as he held them locked in his gaze for the entire two hours of his narrative as if they were looking into the windows of his most private inner being. They felt his quiet rage welling up inside of themselves until they shook with the fear of their own raging emotions. They sat transfixed right up to the moment when he told them of the murder of James Forrester. It was at this point that Samuel elected to end his story.

Garrison and the Bostonians sat for a minute in almost stunned silence to gather their thoughts and digest what had been told to them. At last Cabot cleared his throat and asked with obvious excitement and unaccustomed emotion not at all natural to him, "Then how did you come to be here?"

"That story involves too many people, many like yourselves, who would be placed in some real danger if I were to answer that question. In the face of these new Fugitive Slave Laws, lately passed by Congress, there are too many dangers in naming one's friends. I would not put any one of them in harm's way any more than I would endanger any one of you fine gentlemen if I were to be asked about your activities. And you cannot be held accountable before the law for what you do not know," replied Samuel.

"Instead of speaking of that," said Pompey," Let us discuss exactly what we need of you gentlemen. If you can help us, that will be good. If you cannot, we will be on our way and will trust to your honor and kindness not to repeat what you have been told here tonight. I will warn you that what we propose to do is clearly against the law, and as unjust as that law may be, it is still the law. If you cannot assist us, we will understand and be on our way as I have stated. What I will tell you now may involve some degree of violence on our part. If you are at all squeamish on this point, I would respectfully ask you to leave now, and tell no one what you have heard this night."

The men looked at each other, and after some hesitation, the Rev. Mr. Beecher stood.

"If my niece Harriet were here, she would want to put on men's clothing and go off with you on your adventure and help you to execute your plans with her own hands. If I can help you with money, I have a little to spare, but given the constraints of my position in the church, I would rather not know what you are up to. In fact, if I did I would compromise my own usefulness to the cause in the particular areas in which I operate. We all do what we can in our own sphere so to speak. So if you will excuse me, I will be off. Good luck with your enterprise, and Godspeed. I know that your cause is right, and I wish that I could do more."

"I will show you out Rev. Beecher. Would you like my people to light you home?" asked Garrison thinking of the possibility of the old man being confronted by some wild Irishman in the dark.

"I would take that as a great kindness Mr. Garrison," the minister replied.

Garrison called out softly, "Tom, Harry, light Mr. Garrison home then return to the office."

The two men nodded assent and escorted Rev. Beecher out into the night. Garrison returned to the room, and faced Samuel and Pompey. "What would you have us do," asked Garrison who did not share Beecher's scruples in the matter of needful action even if those actions were against the law as it stood.

"We will need a boat to sail to Nantucket to get near the shore to take a man off that island who will lead us to Whitehouse. We will also need men to man that craft who know those waters. We have every reason to believe that he is the only man who might know where Whitehouse is. That man is on the island, and as long as Whitehouse lives and is free to operate, there are going to be many thousands of African lives at risk. We do not know what to expect when we arrive on the island, but we are prepared to act in total quiet. We intend to take this man with no trouble with or without his cooperation. We do not wish to harm him now or at all, but we do need his help, because it is essential to the success of our mission. I swear to you he will suffer no undo injury. None of you, or any man who helps us, will be involved as accessories with the actual abduction. We know that what we are doing is a capital crime and that anyone who helps us is putting themselves in mortal danger. We will need no help ashore as I have stated. We will need only the boat and crew for transport. We have engaged a ship for the rest of the business. And that is all it is safe for you to know," said Samuel in a calm flat voice.

"That is all well and good," said Shaw," But where are the funds to come from for this adventure? I think that I can arrange for the men and boat, but we will need some substantial money. I am sure that we can raise the needed money, but it will take a week at least to raise the funds."

"I thank you for your willingness to raise money for us, but ample funds are available to any amount Mr. Shaw," said Samuel with a smile," What we need are dependable men who can keep quiet, and hate slavery. The federal marshals have ears everywhere, and there are some men who would sell their own mothers to the highest bidder to gain a reward."

"May we know who the man on Nantucket is?" asked Saltonstall who had said not a word to this point.

"No sir, you may not, and that is that. I am sorry for it, and I do not wish to impugn your integrity. But for the security of this venture, even the master of my ship will have to be kept in the dark about this man's identity. I would not risk your safety for the world or even the fulfillment of my enterprise. Nobody here will take an active part in the capture, for if my friend and I are caught, nobody else will suffer. In fact, I do not know you officially. This meeting never took place, and none of us are here. We alone can do everything needful in the capture of this man on the island. As far as our being on your craft, our official position will be that the man we seek was drunk when he came aboard and you knew nothing of his true condition. That will give you all cover. Some of you here may be lawyers and understand the principal of plausible deniability," replied Samuel.

"Neatly proposed gentlemen. I think that you know your business, and I believe that we can secure a suitable small boat. I know where there is a good and fast vessel. In fact," said Shaw, "She is my own craft. Now shake my hand and meet your skipper, Captain Shaw, if you want to take me on in your venture as an unwitting accomplice."

"It is our honor to do so," Captain Shaw said Samuel as he and Pompey took Shaw's hand Each man in the room in turn shook hands on the mission.

"It does my heart good to see men of color stand up for themselves and take the initiative in this great struggle. White men can only help. It is for you friend Samuel to take the freedom that is rightly yours and every man's birthright into your own hands. The times are changing, and Massachusetts' reaction to this damnable Fugitive Slave Law is proof of it. There is a bill being discussed around the statehouse now which will outlaw any magistrate or law officer from even attempting to enforce the damned federal Fugitive Slave Law," said Shaw with a sneer. "Of course the law will have no standing, but it will telegraph a signal to the world that Massachusetts and men of good conscience will stand against this national evil of slavery."

"More than that Brother Shaw," added Rev. Balcome, "I understand that this anti-Fugitive Slave Law is going to have some teeth. In fact, it is going to say that anyone assisting in the recapture or returning a slave to captivity will suffer a fine of five thousand dollars or five years in jail or both. And we can impose this law until The Supreme Court tells us that we cannot. And that my friends will take time. The wheels of justice grind very slowly indeed."

"Mr. Webster, the 'God-Like Daniel', has put himself into my bad books with his support of that damned Fugitive Slave

Law at the national level," said Shaw. "And I have told him so. I find that his reasons for favoring that abomination of a law, the excuse of giving into the slave states just to hold this federal union together, is just not reason enough to give in to those damned Cotton Republics of the South. I told Daniel that if war is to come over this question of slavery, let it come. I will commit my life and that of my son, Robert, to such a struggle. It is a holy cause, and the Almighty will bless a crusade for the freedom of the slave and call it sacred."

"That's just about too rich for me," said Saltonstall a bit put off by Shaw's un-Yankee lack of reserve. "But I agree with the idea you express even if you do so a bit too hotly. Daniel is right to fear disunion. I think that Shaw is also right though. There will be a terrible war over this thing someday. My fear is that some European despot will seek an opportunity here to come into the Americas or even make an alliance with the South while we are at the slaughter of our brothers. I am not willing to write Webster off yet even though I do not agree with him on his toleration of slavery to preserve this disunited country. I know that on a purely personal level he detests slavery as much as the rest of us, but he's been too long in Washington. He is now well over seventy. There is no telling how long he can last as a force in the capital."

"I just hope that the Great and General Court acts soon on this proposed law to end cooperation with the federal government on the recapture of slaves," said Rev. Balcome.

"Disunion is a serious business," opined Cabot.

"'Disunion by armed force is treason,' were the only words uttered by General Jackson that I ever agreed with," said Garrison breaking his silence. "Those cotton republics in the South want to go at it and will attempt to quit the union some day. We have the Army, the Navy, the Constitution, and these are the forces that will bring them to heel. We will crush the South like the roaches they are. It is our tradition to defy the power of tyrants, and there can be no worse tyranny than being yoked to the slave republics of the South. Even the slaves themselves will rise up and strike their masters down."

Pompey and Samuel looked at each other. The men in the room were so whipped up in the fullness of the rightness of their holy cause that they no longer seemed aware that their two guests were even there. Samuel looked knowingly at Pompey and slightly shook his head. This message was unmistakable and understood by Pompey. It was a command to be silent and let the force in the room spend itself. Still, such enthusiasm was useful. Pompey knew that he and Samuel had a specific mission. Their view was pragmatic and a bit less grandiose than the hotly expressed more lofty ambitions of Garrison and his friends which were based more on philosophy than the practical realities of the moment.

"Mr. Garrison," said Rev. Balcome, "Do you actually think that the slaves will rise up? How would they even know that a war of liberation would be afoot? How would they achieve unity of purpose? Censorship of materials going into the South is absolute in the post office now. Ever since Jackson's time, no abolitionist literature is even allowed to pass through the mails into the South. Even white people have been flogged and hanged for having it in their possession. Even poor Fred Olmsted had a rather nasty incident in Nashville I heard. If he could not possess such literature in the privacy of his saddlebags, how would Negro slaves get a hold of such news? He was publicly whipped I understand before he was driven out of Tennessee."

"The slaves in the plantation houses know everything that goes on in the white community. The master's contempt for them makes them careless about all sorts of information. Even Fred Douglass has spoken of it and written about that too. The white master's feelings of his own superiority make him stupid, and he underestimates the slaves, which he consistently sees as inferiors. Do not underestimate the power of people who hunger for liberty," said Garrison looking at Samuel and Pompey knowingly.

"You make sense Garrison," said Lodge, "But can we trust

the courts and the government leaders to do the right thing? I think not."

"You raise an interesting question Mr. Lodge. Sometimes I lose faith in the federal system too I suppose. But we must look at what is going on in our own city. Just look at what is going on here in Boston. Here we have judges who are corrupted by the very laws they are paid to uphold. Bribes are built into the laws themselves. For example, take The Fugitive Slave Laws we have on the books now. If a judge renders a verdict saying that the person who is accused of being a fugitive slave is indeed a free person, he is paid five dollars for sitting on the case. Should he decide that the accused party is a fugitive slave to be returned to his master, he is paid ten dollars for fulfilling his office. Now, that is strange justice is it not?"

"An arbitrary rendering of justice breeds a contempt for an unjust law like the ones now being served up to us in the matter of the so-called fugitive slaves. Even Negro Americans, long deprived of all civil rights, will eventually rebel at the grossness of that injustice. Take the case of William and Ellen Craft, who are free Negroes of this city. Not so very long ago, by their own brave deed of stealing themselves from their master, they had escaped bondage. Slave catchers came to Boston to take the Crafts and return them to the state from which they had escaped. Now comes their champion, a man of color who has by his own efforts and hard work made a secure place for himself in this community. On learning that the slave catchers were coming to his house to take his guests, the Crafts, Mr. Hayden, himself a man of color, placed two barrels of gunpowder next to the front entrance of his residence and told the slave catchers that if they attempted to take the Crafts, to whom he had given refuge under his own roof, that he would blow himself and his entire household and the slave catchers all together to kingdom come and let the Lord sort out who was right."

"I know the story," said Balcome. "At that point, the Black Vigilance Committee appeared on the scene armed with all sorts of weapons and drove the slave catchers out of the city. You are right Garrison. The Black men of this country are showing us that they are willing to place their lives and property on the line for freedom. They are a material part of this fight just as Mr. James here is."

"The Black man is feeling the intoxicating air of liberty gentlemen. He is drawing this air with its heady perfume into his lungs," said Cabot quietly, "And that gentlemen will have consequences that will see slavery consigned into the trash bin of history, and the sooner the better".

Mr. Shaw leaned forward and said, "I understand that Jefferson Davis of Mississippi is coming to town to speak at Faneuil Hall to Webster's supporters about the Fugitive Slave Laws. Do you suppose that anyone will want to go to hear one overly gassy windbag speak on behalf of another?"

"There will be those who would venture out to see him I suppose," said Cabot, "But not the best people I think. Why Webster would not tell Davis to stay in Washington is a puzzle to me. I sometimes think that Webster is well past it, and with the passage of his three score and thirteen years, he has lost all pretensions to good sound judgment. I am given to understand that even Congressman Horace Mann, who is from our own state, has turned away from him over the slavery question."

"There will come a day," intoned Garrison, "Not too far remote, when this nation will have to answer for its sins of slavery, and I tell you gentlemen, that day is not far off. Only blood will answer for this crime, which calls out to Heaven for a solution. Each of us in this republic is in our own way a bit guilty of the crime of human slavery either by acts of commission or omission. I thank God almighty that charge will never be lodged against any of us here assembled."

Pompey and Samuel looked at each other unobserved with hooded eyes. They had seen the future, and in their bones they knew what must come in time.

CHAPTER XXXVIII

Mrs. Forrester had turned the key in the lock of the door of her hotel suite as she left for her daily walk down to the front desk. As she was doing this, she suddenly became aware that two other people had also arrived in the hallway and were moving in her direction. This was hardly alarming. After her experience of living in good hotels, she was rather used to the comings and goings of the other well dressed patrons of these places. On the whole, she decided that she now liked hotel life. It could be exciting to meet or just see a refined set of society who habitually moved about such places, and with a nicely appointed suite of rooms, one could always retreat to privacy or entertain as one pleased. One could enjoy so many fine amenities in a really good hotel like The Dunham. She had begun to think that it was not very different from being a first class passenger on a Cunard Line ship. Living in a first class hotel, even in Yankee Boston, was preferable to languishing alone in the finest mansion shunned by all of Georgian society.

She mused about the life she now enjoyed after her lost years in Georgia, and the terror of the French Revolution of '48. With a short passing of time and some reading into the subject, Mrs. Forrester had concluded that compared with the events of 1789, the Revolution of 1848 hadn't been much of a revolution at that. Now she stood in the open door of her suite thinking of the prospect of a voyage back to France on a lovely, large, and comfortable steamer. She wondered how Violet would like that. She even thought that she would like to see Paris again now that President Louis Napoleon Bonaparte had brought order to the nation. Mrs. Forrester now concluded that the new president of France was a great man. She prided herself on always having thought so. At least that was her memory of Louis Napoleon these days. Of course she liked to reminisce about her encounter with Louis Philippe at the inn on her flight to Le Havre. She enjoyed telling her daughter's friends just how gracious the old king had been to her when they were fellow emigres on their way to England. On the whole, Mrs. Forrester was deciding that she rather enjoyed the excitement of the French Revolution of 1848.

Mrs. Forrester was brought back to the reality of the hotel and Boston by the muffled sound of the conversation of the two men she had glimpsed seconds ago. Slowly she turned to them to see if she could recognize them from the lobby or the dining room. They might even be friends of her sons-in-law. She smiled as she thought how well connected dear Mr. Balcome was. She had come to the conclusion that abolitionists could be real gentlemen after all. At least if they were rich enough and were socially well connected. Then one could reasonably accept abolitionists as sons in law.

Then in a moment of disbelief then panic, she suddenly realized that the two well tailored gentlemen were not white men at all. At least one of them was Black. Ill defined fear welled up inside of her as she thought that the one thing she really hated about Boston was how the better classes had taken up the fashion of race mixing in public to show their dedication to the fashionable ideals of abolitionism. That was one aspect of abolitionism as a philosophy that she did not like or even considered embracing. Philosophy was always better in the "idealized abstract" than in reality was her belief. Mrs. Forrester's own experience with Black men in her drawing room had not been reassuring.

She turned away as the men passed her without taking any notice of her at all. Then they appeared to stop outside of their respective rooms to continue their conversation. This time she turned again to look at them more closely in the light of the gas fixtures which were near the stranger's rooms. All of a sudden it dawned on her that she knew these men, both the big well built Black man and the handsome younger man. As this recognition came to her, her knees grew weak as she felt the same sickness in the pit of her stomach that she had felt when she had returned to the world after years of her drug induced absence from reality in Georgia. Mrs. Forrester almost fell as she realized that she was looking at the two demons of her nightmares, in the living flesh, standing not twenty-five feet from where she herself now stood. Her hand moved to her neck where the memory of that missing diamond and ruby brooch provoked the involuntary reflex of her hand. Violet had come to the door by this time, and Mrs. Forrester pushed by her and tumbled through the doorway and onto the settee in the parlor of her suite.

Violet had also been watching the men. Or rather the younger one for very different reasons. She thought him the finest looking man she had ever seen. In the last twenty-four hours, she had seen him not less than three times. She had even contrived to speak to him once as she dropped a letter to the floor, which he then retrieved for her. She loved the way he moved with such effortless grace and the splendid way in which he spoke to her. She thought that she had detected some slight bit of interest returned on his part. That very night of her first real encounter with Pompey she had even dreamed about him. But Mrs. Forrester's dramatic entry into the room had quite distracted her from her romantic reverie for a moment.

"What ever is the matter Mrs. Forrester You look as if you have seen a ghost," said Violet as she shut the door leaving the dark handsome young man talking to his serving man. His image was still fixed in her mind's eye.

"Oh Violet! I have seen a ghost. A pair of them! And they

have rooms just down the hall from our very door!" Mrs. Forester answered in a husky whisper.

"You can't mean that handsome young gentleman and his Negro servant."

"Yes, and that handsome young man is no gentleman. They are no sort of gentlemen!"

"Now Mrs. Forrester, they are ever so nice and have such refined manners. You must be mistaken. Are you sure that you know these men?"

"Oh yes Violet. I know these men far too well I assure you."

"Why ever do they upset you so?"

"That I can never tell you. I can never tell anybody that! How did they find me Violet? How ever did they do that? What do they want of me now? How even did they know that I was here in Boston?"

"Mrs. Forrester, I hardly think that these two men came here to do you harm. Boston is a big city. Many people come here for many reasons. This hotel is famed for its quality. Hundreds or even thousands of people must stop here every year. I do not think that these men mean you any harm at all. In fact, I am sure that they would be just as surprised to see you here as you were surprised to see them."

"Oh I just don't know Violet. I just don't know why so many awful things are happening to me," cried the woman in near hysteria.

"Now I have passed these two gentlemen in the hallway several times, and I have spoken to them. They are very pleasant gentlemen and have very good manners. I don't think that they intend to harm anyone. I am very sure that they don't know you are here. They must know that I am staying in this suite Mrs. Forrester. They have seen me at least half a dozen times coming in and out of it. If they were after you, would they not ask me questions about you? I really am quite sure that they harbor no idea that you are even here or have any evil intentions to do you harm."

"Really Violet? You are not just saying that to put my fears to rest are you?"

"To be perfectly honest with you, I think that they are very busy with some other project just now. They are constantly coming and going with a definite air of purpose about them. They talk to each other almost exclusively, and dare I say, with a total degree of equality considering that one is master and the other obviously servant. I am once again sure that your being here is unknown by them."

"Oh, but are you really sure Violet dearest?" asked Mrs. Forrester almost pleading with her eyes for some reason to believe the reassuring words Violet was speaking her.

"I have met them in the hotel three times to speak to during the last few days. They have nodded to me in the most polite way in passing other times or have said, 'Good Morning Miss,' or, 'Good afternoon Miss' and then went along on their business."

"Oh child you do put my mind at rest. I do hope that you are right."

"Mrs. Forrester, why do you fear these men so? They seem ever so nice and refined."

"They are nothing of the sort. I wish that I could tell you of our history, but I would absolutely die of mortification. I can't bring myself even to think of it. To tell you the truth, I'm not even sure about what they did, but it was a nightmare!"

"Dear Mrs. Forrester, I hope that I do not shock you with this idea I've just had."

"What is it dear child?"

"The next time I see either of these gentlemen in the hotel, I shall engage them in conversation, and I will discover just why they are here in Boston."

"Oh my dearest Violet. You have become almost another daughter to me. I should never have escaped the revolution in France without you. I never could have had the courage to go to England and America without your help."

"Mrs. Forrester, I am sure that we were never in any real

danger in France. I am equally sure that we would have been just fine had we remained at the hotel in Paris. You really credit me too highly."

"No Violet. It might have been that awful business with poor Louis XVI all over again for all that we knew at the time! Those Frenchmen are just so, so......so damned excitable! Yes that's it. That's exactly it. They are excitable! Like raging brutes. Like animals in a zoo. I could not stand the idea of all those heads falling all over the place again. One never knows what those Frenchmen will do. They will behead hundreds of people, and then they will go drink red wine and eat perfectly disgusting things that no true Christian should ever eat like frogs and even garden slugs in garlic! And do you think that it is decent to have three revolutions in the span of one person's lifetime? We have had only one, and that was over seventy years ago. Good Lord! We never chopped off even one person's head never mind tens of thousands! And that revolution of ours was to get rid of the beastly English, and I know that you are English dear, but let's face facts. As a people, you are impossible! Oh, now I am sorry. I really do not wish to insult you or your country. You have been so good to me Violet dear. I'd never say anything to offend you personally. At the time I did not realize that the revolution was going to be so almost civilized. I mean with the French, one never can tell just what will happen."

"Dear, dear Mrs. Forrester, we English are an impossible race of people. Our money alone with its farthings, groats, florins, crowns, pounds, and guineas drives most people to distraction. It is a point of national pride with us to be as impossible as possible, or so it sometimes seems even to me. I take no offense," laughed Violet, "Trust me, I do not take The American Revolution personally. After all, poor old King George III was a bit mad you know, but we are all friends now, and that is all that matters in the end."

"It is sweet of you dear to say that. I agree. It must be so. Oh Violet, I just don't know what to think anymore. I was even thinking about a trip back to France! Can you believe that? Now that I actually know more about it, I want to tour even in the provinces. Isn't that rich? And with those two men lurking about the place, now might be the perfect time to go."

"Mrs. Forrester, I am sure that I am right about those two men, and I am going to make it my business to find out exactly what they are doing here. The very next time I see them, I shall have a conversation with them. I shall find some reason to engage them, and I will discover what they are about here."

"No Violet dear. You have no concept of what awful things they may do. I cannot stand to think of what might happen to you."

"Stuff and nonsense. I can take very good care of myself. I will not have you hiding away here in these rooms in some nameless fear of God only knows what. And now Mrs. Forrester, that is an end to it," said Violet as she reflected that she rather fancied the handsome young man and was in no mood to run off to France before she had really met him.

"Violet," asked Mrs. Forrester looking at the dreamy eyed young girl who seemed to drift away to some secret place in her own mind's eye, "Are you attracted to that young man?"

Violet blushed, smiled, and sweetly said, "Yes. Strangely enough Mrs. Forrester. I rather think I am. I know it's silly, but I find him to be handsome and a rather nice gentleman."

"Violet, I told you that he is not any kind of gentleman. He is a Negro pretending to be what he is not!"

"Now how can you know that Mrs. Forrester?"

"I once owned him! Now I know that I can trust you, and I want you to sit by me. I am going to tell you the whole truth of it, and on all that you hold holy, you must never repeat what you are going to hear to anyone. You may never tell my daughters that you know a thing I am about to tell you. Now to begin with their names are Samuel and Pompey."

CHAPTER XXXIX

Violet sat transfixed as the Forrester Family saga unfolded. The tale covered the time from James Forrester's exposure as a card cheat to the awakening of the Forrester women from their multi-year Cinderella-like sleep.

Violet gasped at the end of it, "So when you awoke from all this, you found that you had either freed or sold all of your slaves? And you have no memory of this at all? Then you discovered that this Samuel had left you very well provided with funds? Now this same Samuel and Pompey are in rooms just a few doors down from this one. It is all very strange. Good heavens Mrs. Forrester. It is no wonder that you are so upset."

"It is all too much really. It is a good thing that I am a strong woman and can stand up under all of this pressure. I wish that I knew what really happened during the time I cannot remember, and then again, I am glad that I do not."

"Don't you find it strange that this Samuel took great care to leave you with so much money when he could have had it all and killed you into the bargain? Most of your property had been well managed and left intact and even improved by your own account. That is all very strange if they meant to do you harm isn't it? By sparing you as he did, has this Samuel not put himself and his friend Pompey at risk now? I really must suspect that there is some redeeming quality in Samuel and his friend. Consider the facts. He did not kill you. He built you a fortune, and he left you alive. Not even the King of France was treated half so well. Then consider what he could have done besides throwing the slaves a ball and costing you a few trinkets and minor indignities."

"Oh, I don't know Violet. Samuel may be the Devil incarnate for all I know. And my God, Pompey was the best of servants. I even thought that he liked us a bit. I don't know what they were playing at. I'm just so frightened here in this northern abolitionist city where nobody cares if we live, or die, or are all killed by our slaves. In fact if the so-called best people here in Boston knew the story of this strange slave revolt, I think that they would all cheer and hold a special gala to celebrate Samuel's dark deed! I am frightened Violet. I think that they want to kill me, and not even my abolitionist daughters will care now that they have become like their husbands."

"Stuff and nonsense Mrs. Forrester. Stuff and nonsense," said Violet tossing her pretty little head, "I am bringing those two in here, and we will get to the bottom of this once and for all. They owe you that, and you will have your due. We will sort this all out right this very minute."

"No Violet dear. We can't have that. The scandal! My sons-in-law! Mr. Balcome and Mr. Cabot! Oh please dear. They are abolitionists. What ever will they think of us? They would never understand all of this. We would be disgraced if any of this sordid story got out. I would be a ruined woman scorned by good society. My daughters would never speak to me again. There is no telling what would happen."

"Mrs. Forrester, think this out reasonably. Why would these two gentlemen, for it is gentlemen that they are playing at being now, why would they be here at all? If they knew that you were here, they would give this hotel a wide berth. They would avoid it at all costs. Trust me. Their being here has nothing to do with you. It is by chance only that they are here at all. They obviously have ample means, and this is the city's best accommodation. That is why they are here I am sure. And the sooner this is confirmed and you know this of your own knowledge the better. I'm off to confront them directly, and I'll return shortly with the both of them. They dare not do anything here I promise you."

In a flash, the little English woman was out of the door and sailing under a full head of steam to Pompey's suite. Mrs. Forrester sat in confusion with the speed of the events overwhelming her. Without thinking about it, she arranged her hair in order to meet the crisis that was to come. She did not know if she should run, hide, or get help. She thought about locking herself in her bedroom or just fainting. But she felt suddenly that fainting would not do. Suddenly, she found herself to be quite angry. After all, she was the offended party. Samuel and Pompey owed her some explanations about their behavior. The more that she thought about it, Mrs. Forrester felt relieved that Violet had gone to fetch the miscreants and put and end to all of this nonsense.

In the meantime, Violet made her way the short distance to Pompey's door. She stood there for a moment only, and then she knocked. A few moments later, Pompey opened the door. He stood there in his shirtsleeves. Otherwise he was quite tidy in his silk waistcoat, cravat, and carpet slippers. Before he could speak, Violet bowed and smiled at him sweetly.

"Sir," she said softly, "Would you be so kind as to follow me along with the dark gentleman from across the hallway back to my rooms? An old friend wants to meet with you. We are just a few rooms down from yours as you may or may not know."

Pompey looked uncertainly. This young woman was very pretty if a bit prim, yet something had drawn him to her at once when he had first met her. He detected something in her manner that was not unfriendly. He smiled at her and said, "I will be most happy to go with you Miss if I may be of help in some way. Please allow me to make myself more presentable." Pompey went back into his room to put on proper boots and a coat. "I think that I will pass muster now Miss," he said with what he wished to be his most disarming smile.

"You will do in a pinch," Violet returned showing no sign that his friendly manner was winning her attention. "Do you think that your servant might join us?"

"I think that I could persuade him to do so," smiled Pompey as he crossed the hall to Samuel's door and knocked.

Samuel opened the door and said, "What is it Pompey?"

Pompey flashed a warning look at Samuel. Samuel got back into his servant's character as soon as he saw the girl, but the slip did not go unnoticed. Violet just stood and smiled at the two men as Pompey continued, "This young lady has someone she would like us to meet. Perhaps an old friend she thinks. Would you be so kind as to put on your coat and come with us?" Samuel looked at the young woman and then back at Pompey. In a very low voice he asked, "Do you think that wise? Do you know anything about her?"

"I know that she is very pretty and seems pleasant enough. I do not think that she means us any harm or intends to tie us up or anything of the sort."

"My friend," whispered Samuel, "She appears to have already begun throwing a rope around you and trussing you up. You are an innocent about women. You may not know it, but you are only prey, and she is such a lovely huntress. Take care my son."

"Are you going to come with me or not?"

"You are such a babe in the woods Pompey. I notice that you don't even have your walking stick. Go back to your room and get it, and then I shall go with you. You do not know who else may be in that suite."

Pompey turned to the young girl. "Could you wait here a moment while my man dresses himself properly? I need to get something from my rooms."

"Please take your time sir. I shall be happy to wait here."

In less than a minute, Violet was leading the two tall men back to her mistress' suite. Samuel and Pompey followed her down the hall. Violet knocked on the door as a warning to Mrs. Forrester that she had returned with the two former slaves. Mrs. Forrester pinched her cheeks in place of using rouge in this unexpected situation and steeled herself for the encounter with all of her fears. She pinched her cheeks again without even thinking of what she was doing and ran her fingers through her hair then patted it into place. She drew herself up to her full height, but suddenly she felt quite small. She shook her head to clear away the cobwebs of thought so that she could focus her wits with more clarity on the situation before her. Mrs. Forrester readied herself to face the men she had not spoken to in two years. She found her voice, which she hoped would not sound too reedy or thin. She sucked air into her lungs and said in a voice of surprising firmness and strength, "Please come in."

Violet opened the door. Pompey and Samuel followed her into the room. As they entered, their gaze fell on the well-groomed woman who stood waiting for them. They were astonished to see their former mistress here in Boston, and they were shocked to see how well her health had been restored to her. Mrs. Forrester looked as if she was about to issue orders on the Forrester plantation just as she would have done five or six years ago. Samuel and Pompey were struck dumb, and stood just staring as Violet closed the door behind them. This made Mrs. Forrester feel oddly strong as the two men looked on in disbelief. "I have nothing to fear," was the thought now racing through Mrs. Forrester's mind. She even smiled.

Pompey and Samuel quickly recovered from their surprise. Samuel stood and bowed from the waist, as did Pompey who then took Mrs. Forrester's hand, as if it were something he had done all of his life, and kissed it in his best continental style. "Mrs. Forrester, I am happy to meet you as requested by Miss Violet here. What service can either myself or Mr. James render you?"

Mrs. Forrester looked at the two men then burst into hysterical laughter. "This is really too ridiculous. Pompey you really are the absolute limit!"

CHAPTER XL

At Mrs. Forrester's invitation, Pompey and Samuel took seats in the deeply upholstered chairs. Pompey looked across the room at Violet who, in turn, was staring at him with an amused look on her face. Pompey thought that she was a pert and pretty little thing with a lot of self possession. Violet was truly a woman of courage to have invited two desperate characters such as Samuel and Pompey into her rooms. After all, they were guilty of the dread crime of being self-stealers. Pompey smiled as he looked at Violet and felt something stirring inside of him that he had never quite felt before. It was a mixture of emotions foreign to his experience. It was true that Pompey knew precious little of women, but he knew that he wanted to know this one a good deal better and to be with her in a loving and intimate way. Violet had touched something deep inside of him that no human had ever reached before. Pompey wanted to absorb her, but now it was all a fancy to be played out in his mind's eye alone. She could never be a reality. Pompey smiled at her, felt a little foolish, and then he turned away with his eyes downcast with the smile still fixed upon his lips. Then he looked up with a bemused expression on his face. He was himself again.

Samuel did not look amused at all. For once in a long time, he felt that he was not the master of the situation. Samuel turned briefly and looked at Pompey. His irritation began to grow as he wondered just what Pompey found so damned amusing about coming face to face with this damned Forrester woman whom they had left in a state of drug induced laudanum euphoria in Georgia. Samuel was thinking quickly and trying to master what he was feeling and to appear, at the same time as if he was feeling nothing at all. In this he was successful. Violet read both of their faces. She had lived a life of some variety of experience herself during the last few years since the death of her grandfather and protector. She had learned to read the subtleties of the world inscribed on the faces of those she met. Then she spoke.

"Now I think that you gentlemen know my friend Mrs. Forrester very well, and I think that neither of you had the slightest idea that Mrs. Forrester was even in Boston until you came into this room a few moments ago did you?"

Pompey bowed his head with deep mock respect, and said, "Forgive me ladies, but I have not given a single thought to the Forrester Family these last few years. It is good to see you Mrs. Forrester. You are looking very well. Trust me, we intend no disrespect, but Mr. James and I have had other matters on our minds, and that is still true even at the present time. I am afraid that the whole Forrester family has been far from our thoughts. I am truly glad to see you well and well provided for. I trust that Miss Caroline and Miss Tilly prosper."

"And just what are those matters that occupy you Pompey? Do share them with us," said Mrs. Forrester. "Where is my money and the possessions that you made off with while I was God only knows where all of that long time?"

Her voice was controlled and flat, and her mouth was arranged in an icy smile. Samuel had been looking at her in a lofty and distant manner. "Mrs. Forrester, we are in Boston in the state of, or should I say the Commonwealth of Massachusetts. There is no slavery here. In fact, the legislature of this place has passed a law, which states that anyone who attempts to enforce the provisions of The Fugitive Slave Law will be imprisoned and fined. It will avail you nothing but scandal for you and your family if you attempt to retake Pompey and myself now. When we left you in Georgia, we left you a very wealthy woman and in possession of a rich property. I left you ten times richer than you were when poor Mr. James was alive. He was my friend, and I saw to the care of his widow and family. I see that you have no problems traveling in style and comfort as befits someone of your class. You have a fine suite of rooms in the finest hotel in Boston. When you consider what might have happened if you had been in the power of some low men, or a Nat Turner, you should be thankful that your fortune and your virtue, and that of your family, remains intact."

"You speak well Samuel. If I were to close my eyes, I would take you for a gentleman. You speak better than any Negro I ever met. But now, how did you manage it? You told me once, but I'm afraid I'm confused in my memory of our conversation on that and many other subjects" asked Mrs. Forrester.

"In my country Mrs. Forrester my father was a chief, a prince under the rulership of the King of the Matabele. I come from a great people. Even the English lived in dread and respect of us. The blood in my veins is royal, and I can learn the wisdom and manners of any sort of people including your own. I was well schooled long before I ever left Africa, or I should say, taken out of Africa, kidnapped and sold into slavery. What have you done?"

"What do you mean by, 'What have I done?' I raised you up against the advice of everyone to be the master of my plantation. I gave you freedom and a part of the profits for running the plantation!"

"So that I could make you richer, so that you could look down on all of those stupid society people that mocked and scorned you and the late master. They were fools that he took advantage of. Yes, that bargain I made with Mr. James before we even met you had worked out very well for the both of us, and all of us should be grateful that it did. Both Mr. James and I have had a great benefit from all that. That benefit now rests with his family, because I honored him and my bargain I struck with him back in 1815. I did not have to do this, but Mrs. Forrester, I am a prince and a man of honor. To do what I had to do for all of us, I had to give you something that would allow me to work my will without interference. I hope that you will forgive me, and I hope that you can see that your present position was vouchsafed by what I did for all of us. Now I suggest that we forget all that has passed and enjoy the fruits of our association. What do you say to that Mrs. Forrester."

Mrs. Forrester took a seat on the settee next to the fire. She looked out of the window on a darkening sky.

"Samuel, I freed you and I guess Pompey too. My memory is vague on a lot of things that happened after Mr. Forrester's death. Now I know why." She turned from the window and looked at the two men with tears in her eyes. "Samuel, why are you and Pompey here in the hotel? Do you wish to harm me?"

Samuel inclined his head and spoke softly, "I was taken from Africa when I was almost sixteen years old. Your husband was on that slave ship. That is when James Forrester and I first met. I do not think that it would be right to tell you more than that. We shared a bond of secrecy you see, and I would not betray it or him even now that he is gone. We were more than master and slave. We were friends. That you must respect. When he and I arrived in America, we slipped away from that slave ship that landed us at New Orleans, and we ran away from the men who stole me from my country, and my parents, and all who loved me Mrs. Forrester. I am a man who can feel loss just as you do, and just like you, I had a home and a very high station in Matabele society. All this was taken from me, and by stealing away from that ship with the Master, we ensured that we would have some sort of a better life. You met James Forrester and me later when things were very good. James Forrester never wanted to let you know these things, and I respect that, but I think that you are owed a little of the truth now that he is gone."

"Then you and Pompey are not here to do me harm?"

"Now why should you think that? We do not hate you personally. You were just in the way of our freedom. You and your family held us in slavery. We could not have that. We only drugged you so that we could keep things pleasant for you and so that we would not have to physically restrain you. We wished you no harm then, and we wish you no harm now."

"I thought you wanted to harm me, because I know what you did back in Georgia," said Mrs. Forrester.

"This is Boston. Pompey and I have our manumission papers, and whatever happened in Georgia does not signify here. Believe me Mrs. Forrester, if you were in danger of coming to harm, as gentlemen Pompey and I would be obliged to defend you, not harm you. I have forgiven you and the family for my slavery, and the only man I want to punish is the man who killed Master Forrester and took me from my home in Africa."

"Mr. Forrester was not murdered Samuel," said Mrs. Forrester sadly, "Poor James fell from his horse. That horrible horse threw him on the night when he was accused, of you know," here she paused a moment then blurted out, "Of cheating at cards by some awful English person at Buckland's."

"Mrs. Forrester, it was that same awful English person who killed Master Forrester," said Samuel.

"Now how can you know a thing like that?" demanded Mrs. Forrester with her voice rising.

"I was there. I could not save Master Forrester. I was unarmed and too far away in the undergrowth of the forest not too far from the road, but I saw him in the light of the moon from where I was hiding by the road. I heard a commotion. And it would not have been good for me to be taken after dark on a road in Georgia by a white man without a plantation pass when another white man had been killed," said Samuel somberly.

Mrs. Forrester sat straight in her chair and cried, "You could do nothing to save dear James? You are a powerful man Samuel. You could do nothing?"

Samuel looked directly into the eyes of Mrs. Forrester and

replied, "It could have gone very badly for me. I was still too far away and unarmed. Had I been any closer at that time and might have picked up a branch to use as a club I might have saved him. But I was just too far away. If some men from Buckland's were returning home full of drink and decided to attempt to make sport of me, they might have killed me, or more likely, I might have had to kill them. Either way, the situation would have been fraught with danger.

When I had wandered away that night after Pompey had come to my cabin and left, my travels took me over the plantation to our road. I heard someone coming. I disappeared into the woods and hid in the undergrowth. Then I saw the man slowly riding down the road. As it happened, it turned out that it was the Master. He was talking to himself a bit, and if you will pardon me for saying so, he was a bit worse for drink."

"Mr. Forrester was not given to excessive drinking Samuel. For God's sake you know that," said Mrs. Forrester sadly.

"Master Forrester was deeply troubled on that last night of his life. You know that for yourself. He rode along on his way home. Then he sort of fell from his horse, but he was not hurt. He sat under a tree and sipped from his brandy flask. That is when he came. That is the Englishman. I could not hear all they said, but they had heated words, and then the Englishman picked up a rock. He slammed it on the side of Master Forrester's head after Mr. James had first mounted his horse then fell off onto the ground again. Then, after killing him, the Englishman laid him down with his head resting on that same bloody rock to make it look as if he had fallen on it and struck his head. Then that man waited, and then he let out a scream as he struck the poor horse. After that, he ran back in the direction of the tavern. That Englishman is the person I seek. He is the reason that I am here. I am going to give this Englishman the justice he deserves for all of his crimes against me, Master James, and the other Africans that he has kidnapped from Africa."

"Who is he, this man who killed my husband?"

"I will tell you someday when he is dead and punished for all the evil things he has done in this world, and more than that I cannot tell you, because you cannot report what you do not know to the authorities. I will not have him warned off by you by accident or anyone else. You will have to trust me Mrs. Forrester. I want that man to answer for his crimes, and I think that you do as well."

"Samuel, I think that I do trust you still. I wish you Godspeed, and you have my thanks and that of my poor James. What you did, I suppose you thought you had to do, and when I awoke into this world after you left, I was so sick and confused that I wanted you dead, but now, in this room after so much that has happened, I can understand things a little better. Maybe I can forgive you and Pompey. In fact until I woke up, I mean really woke up all I wanted to do was run away from Georgia. I will have to admit that after the county gave us up because of Mr. Forrester's cheating scandal, it was a relief to be happy for a while as we were, and after that, it was wonderful to cash out our assets and go away for good and all."

"We didn't expect to see you again Mrs. Forrester either here in Boston or anywhere else. This has been quite a surprise for us as well," said Pompey.

"Violet told me that you intended me no harm. That sweet girl has perfect judgment. You know, I can almost see my poor departed sister-in-law's face and hear her voice telling me that I should have been on to you. I think that she had a sixth sense. I think that would make her a witch. In fact I am very sure that she was a witch, poor creature. Samuel, you are a very smart man. Without you, the place would most likely have gone for taxes. I must confess that you were a much better provider than my poor James. Now you are sure that you can bring this Englishman to book for James' murder?"

"Only if you and Miss Violet do not give the game away. We must really beg you to say nothing of this. Pompey and I have arranged things pretty well, but everything depends on surprise."

"Oh Mr. Samuel and Mr. Pompey," said Violet, "We shall be ever so careful to keep what you have told us in total confidence. Isn't that so Mrs. Forrester."

"Yes Violet. I declare that my life has been no end of excitement these last few years since poor James' untimely demise. Some days, I hated it, and other days I felt excited by it. In a strange way, I suppose that I could almost thank you both for that as well as for the life I have now."

CHAPTER XLI

The people in the hotel dining room had grown so accustomed to seeing Pompey and Samuel sitting at their table that they just nodded politely to them or passed by without taking note of their presence. The two men ordered their meal, chatted quietly, and then they sat reading their papers while enjoying their coffee after their meal was over. There was no conversation now between the two men as they sat each wrapped up in their own thoughts. Pompey's thoughts centered on the pretty English girl whom he knew to be his champion with Mrs. Forrester. Mrs. Forrester, for her part, was quite relieved that there was no plot afoot to further endanger her. All seemed to be going well. Samuel, on the other hand, seemed less at ease. He had not counted on young Pompey becoming infatuated with a pretty English girl. He had even harbored hopes of eventually securing a girl from the Matabele nation as a wife to make Pompey more acceptable to his people. He knew that the Matabele considered themselves the master race of Africa, the Children of Heaven, and the best people of the world. Their acceptance of Pompey would be a very long shot at best. Samuel had thought that Pompey's exceptional talents and a highborn Matabele wife might make Pompey almost acceptable along with an adoption of him by Samuel. Samuel was after all a prince. Yet doubts lingered, and Samuel feared that in the end that his work would come to nothing.

Samuel narrowed his eyes. He had not foreseen the prospect of Pompey crossing the line into the white world with a European wife. But then, he thought, Pompey had never shown any interest in the pretty girls in the slave quarters either. He could have had his pick thought Samuel. But then Samuel had remained celibate, and had encouraged Pompey to remain the same. Samuel was now thinking that lack of encouragement of Pompey to experiment in the slave quarters had been a mistake. Pompey should have been led to the bed of a pretty black girl long ago. Samuel was afraid that he had missed his chance with Pompey who might be now more discriminating in his choice of a love. He might even have banished the idea of an African woman from his mind altogether.

Samuel was not about to mix his royal blood with that of just any woman of no family background from slave quarters where the bloodlines were so polluted by whites and Black men of no distinction. It was not the way of the Matabele. Samuel had always thought Pompey to be someone very special even though he was low born. Samuel had considered the possibility that the boy was following his own lead in this matter of being discriminating in the selection of a proper mate. Now Pompey was a young man. He was feeling what a young man feels who has come to manhood. The possibility now existed that the boy might even choose a white girl to be his wife. This made Samuel uncomfortable. He now began to question the influence he still might have over his gifted prodigy and if that influence was in fact eroding. Samuel had manufactured this grand plan, and he did not want to see it derailed. Still this girl Violet was of no real importance in the total scheme of things, and it would be a small matter to dispose of her should she become an impediment. Maybe there was nothing between them at all. Yes, there was always that possibility.

At last Pompey folded his papers and said, "I think that it's time to return to my rooms Samuel. Will you walk up with me after I sign the check?"

"Yes, it does seem to have been rather a long day," returned Samuel, "I am very tired."

As the two made their way upstairs to the hall, Pompey stopped and said to Samuel, "There is something about that English girl that will not seem to let go of me Samuel. I have a feeling that she is someone very special. I can't seem to get her out of my thoughts. Now that is funny don't you think?"

"She is thin and pale Pompey. There is nothing substantial to her. She is just skin and bones and a hank of hair. Just wait until we get to Africa. To Matabeleland. Now there are beautiful women for a man to contemplate and bed with! They have substance and character as well as beauty. They do not whine and simper like these white girls. They work, and they know how to please a randy man."

"How would you know Samuel? It would have cost you your life to find out," Pompey snickered.

Samuel for the first time felt rage with his friend. Pompey was now the self-assured mature man talking to him like an equal. Samuel forced a smile and covered his feelings. "You know Pompey, I did not play the game, but the gods have given me eyes to see and imagination for the rest. I may have only been a boy half grown when I was taken, but I was not altogether stupid. I gave an ear to my elders when they discussed such matters. Thinking about those women gave me pleasure, as did looking at them frolicking naked in the river. They wanted me too, and I had deep lusting for them. Now I am old enough to have a wife, and in you, I have a fine son already."

"No, you are not stupid my friend," laughed Pompey. "It is funny though. I don't even know why I mentioned it. I doubt if Miss Violet takes any real notice of me at all. Still, I think that there was something there in the way she was looking at me, and I will confess that I felt something for her that I have never felt for anyone else. I almost think that I love her. Now that is silly is it not?"

Samuel did not smile now. He was just the impassive Samuel, seemingly indifferent to the very world, which he seemed to be judging by his look. The world outside of Matabeleland in fact, seemed quite beneath his notice. He felt danger now. Samuel almost snapped, "I saw nothing to indicate that she took notice of you. In fact, I think that you have become quite full of yourself since you have become a white gentleman of this world. Remember that playing at being a white aristocrat was merely a device for allowing us to move about freely Pompey. It is nothing more than that."

"You are right Samuel. I don't even know why I entertain such stupid thoughts. We have a real mission now, and that is all I should be thinking of. Still, I don't know if I want one of your Matabele women. They might be a little too strong for me and have a little too much substance for my taste Samuel. I am not sure that they will have enough of the right sort of intellectual capacity to interest me. Maybe this pale little white girl would suite me better. At least we know that she has courage and spirit. And I like the way she masters ideas. One could talk to her for years and never have a dull interlude."

"Intellectual capacity! What are you thinking boy? Women do not need intellectual capacity. What are you intending to do? Talk to them? Men do not discuss things of importance with mere women. Women do not have the capacity for real conversation. They are all emotion and ragged bits of feeling. They are essentially irrational beings who have to be guided by men. Women exist to breed children and please a man. They cook your food, grow yams and take care of your kraal. They breed sons to care for your cattle. Can that pale thin thing, this Violet, do that? Remember where you are going to spend the rest of your life boy. We are going to Africa to live as free men not as counterfeit white men talking to women."

"Maybe I'm not up to the task of being an African man after

all Samuel. To be Matabele would take more than I have in my, shall we say, confused heritage. Do you think that in the end, the Children of Heaven will only tolerate me because of the respect that they will have for you? I have lived in a house all my life schooling myself to be a western man. Maybe Matabele women will not be to my taste," said Pompey. "And I am sure that I may not be to their taste either," he added.

"Do not judge them young Pompey until you have seen them in the warm night air with their velvet skins shining in the moonlight. They have their own lusty glory, and they will please you I assure you like no other woman on this earth can in a thousand ways beyond your imagination. And should the one you select not satisfy, you can always have another. There is a special power that comes with being an African man who is the adopted son of a prince."

"But won't I be killed if I'm found out not to be thirty-nine if I lay with a woman?" laughed Pompey.

"Nobody knows how old you are you fool."

"I'm twenty-seven or eight. I'm not quite sure which, but I know that I am not thirty-nine. You told me that you had to be thirty-nine to take a wife among the Matabele. I am sure that I might find them very beautiful, but mere beauty has never been enough for me."

"You are many things Pompey, but you are not Matabele. Those rules do not apply to you. Still there is time."

"But is it not the plan that I become a member of the Matabele Nation? And if I become a Matabele, must I not obey the rules?"

"Pompey, we'll discuss this later. You are crossing too many bridges all at once, and you are giving me a headache. Do not be so fast to give your heart away to that English girl who might never want even to see you again. Don't give yourself to any other silly creature either. That is all I am trying to tell you."

Pompey and Samuel had arrived on their floor and proceeded

to move on to their rooms when a voice called to them, "Good evening Pompey and Mr. Samuel."

Pompey turned to see Violet standing there in the hall in a simple velvet dress with a lace collar. He could just see the toes of her polished shoes poking from under her garment. They looked tiny and neat. Her hair was nicely arranged in small ringlets hanging down about her beautiful heart shaped face, and the rest of her chestnut hair was drawn back and gathered behind her lovely little head. She looked like the pretty young Victoria on a bright new six pence. She was perfectly proportioned like one of Caroline Forrester's German china dolls, with just a hint of color on her lips and in her cheeks. She melted him with her beautiful blue eyes, which seemed to laugh with a careless mirth and a hint of mischief. Samuel stood impassively then bowed slightly from the waist. Pompey could have cared less if she could cultivate a yam or do much of anything else requiring brawn. His ideal life mate was not a brawny woman. He was also as sure of her intellectual quality as he was of her beauty. Pompey knew that he wanted to have conversations with this beautiful English girl.

There was something in Samuel's manner that made Pompey ill at ease. That feeling lasted only an instant. When Violet spoke again, she broke the spell with the sweet crispness of her voice. Pompey thought that it was like music. "Mrs. Forrester is not alone. Her daughter Caroline and Caroline's husband are with her. Mrs. Forrester was wondering if you could come into her rooms for a little while now just for a short visit."

"Thank you Miss Violet. Samuel and I would be very pleased to join you."

As he spoke to the girl, he turned a bit red. She smiled at him in such a way that there was no mistaking that his interest was returned. Samuel also noticed this. He was not pleased by this complication in his plans. He needed Pompey's undivided loyalty and attention if his grand scheme was going to work. He wanted this son of his heart to take a Matabele bride.

The pretty little thing turned to her door and then looked

back over her shoulder. She smiled again at Pompey and said, "Mr. Pompey, I do believe that you are blushing. And by the way, as I said, Mrs. Forrester has company. As I said, her daughter, Caroline and her son-in-law are also with us. They are very interested in seeing you. They want to know about Mr. Forrester Samuel. We would not presume to try to tell your tale."

Samuel spoke up with some degree of gravity, "We will be with you in a few minutes Miss Violet. We have one or two things to attend to if you do not mind."

"Of course not Mr. Samuel. Do take your time, but if you could be along in a little while, we would appreciate it. It has been a difficult time for Mrs. Forrester as I am sure that you can understand being the kind souls that you are. I am sure that you also understand that we should not keep her waiting too long." Miss Violet was sweet, but her subtle tone of urgency under all of the pleasantries was unmistakable.

"We will be along shortly," replied Pompey as the two men entered Pompey's rooms then closed the door. "I do not think that we have much to worry about. If worse comes to worse, we have our manumission papers in the hotel safe. We also have funds and new and powerful friends," said Pompey.

Samuel looked a little exasperated then pulled himself together. "Pompey, a Black man is never going to be totally safe in a country that has both slavery and a Fugitive Slave Law. The fact that such laws have been around for generations long before they were enacted on a federal level is in itself an indication of danger. These new laws were only a refinement of what had already existed in different places. I've been reading about them for years. I read about them back in the days of the Nat Turner troubles in the early thirties when I could have been hanged in some parts of the South for knowing how to read. I was not ready to run then. To run away at first would have been easy, but where would I have gone afterwards? I had something of a good arrangement with Forrester. If nothing else, that man knew my worth. Now that the Forresters know everything, they might even want to help us get our hands on Starbuck and Whitehouse. We just have to be careful, and watch out for that sharp little piece, Violet. I can't puzzle out just what she is up to, but she is after something. I don't trust women white, black, or Matabele. They just don't think like us, but at least a Matabele woman knows how to behave herself. A Matabele woman knows her place."

"Why Samuel, have you just come to that wisdom?" laughed Pompey. "Every one of those blessed Forrester women was different. There was a whole education for us there on that plantation just on the subject of women and the many different ways in which their minds worked. Then there is Miss Sally Beers. Now there is a great woman who is possessed of a very good mind."

"Miss Sally is fine. She thinks like a man and always knows her own mind. She's never confused, and she is honorable, but with this lot you never know, and I truly do not know what this Miss Violet is up to Pompey."

"Samuel, I might be crazy, but I really think that she likes me, and I don't think that she likes me like a brother or sister. When I was shaving this morning, I looked into the mirror. I am not so ugly that I would repulse the girl."

"As Anna would say, 'She likes you jus' fine,' but now is not the time for that. We have to see how the land lies here. The Forresters know a lot of what we have been up to, and when we left them back in Georgia, we left them well provided. We might as well go and find out what is going on now." With that, Samuel and Pompey left for the Forrester suite. Samuel knocked on the door, and Violet, still smiling, opened the door.

"Thank you both for coming," she said. "Would you be so kind as to join us?"

The two men nodded and entered. Pompey said, "Thank you Miss Violet. Good evening Mrs. Forrester, and good evening Miss Caroline and Rev. Balcome. I am surprised and pleased to see you here sir."

"Do you and Samuel know my son-in-law Pompey?" asked Mrs. Forrester with some confusion.

"We have had the pleasure of meeting Mr. Balcome," Samuel replied.

"I see," said the slightly confused Mrs. Forrester. "I suspect that it must have been at one of those abolitionist meetings or something of the like."

"Mother, must I constantly remind you that I am every bit as much an abolitionist as my darling husband. Mr. Balcome's courage and faith in this holy cause have shown me the errors of my past. Samuel, Pompey, it is very good to see you again. I hope that we can be friends in spite of the history we share. I now know just how beastly slavery is. Even on our place where you really ran things for father Samuel, and without the whip, was still slavery. I understand how dehumanizing it is to be confined in servitude not of your choosing. If you can forgive me my part in all of that, then we can be friends I think."

"Miss Caroline, I do not remember you unkindly. You treated us well and were good to fine people like Anna," said Samuel.

"I could have done more like protesting against that old harridan, my aunt. She was a vicious and mean old thing. I should have said something. I was too busy with my own selfish pleasures to take any responsibilities. For that I am ashamed Samuel. Under my husband's instruction, I have come to understand the evil of those old days," gushed Miss Caroline while beaming with admiration for the virtuous and all knowing Rev. Mr. Balcome. Caroline continued, "Dear Samuel and dear Pompey, won't you take a seat."

Pompey mastered his feelings of almost giddy pleasure at Caroline's performance. In his mind, he was thinking, "She's really enjoying this, and the slavery in which she holds the good Rev. Balcome is absolute."

"Mother Forrester, Mr. James and Mr. Charles, or as you call them Samuel and Pompey, are the partners of my great work at present, "said Rev. Balcome with quiet dignity.

"Samuel," said Mrs. Forrester, "I think that my daughter and her husband should know how Mr. Forrester met his death at the hands of that horrible man. No matter how painful it is, I want them to hear the whole truth of it now."

"Do you mean to say that my father was murdered," exclaimed Caroline!

"Yes my dear," said Mrs. Forrester, "And Samuel saw the whole thing the night that we thought that your father had fallen from his horse. He didn't want to tell us then, because he knew that the word of a slave would never stand up against a white man in Georgia."

"But mother, we are not in Georgia now! Oh, but what can we do?"

"Nothing right now my dear. Now just listen, and let Samuel tell you what happened," said Mrs. Forrester quietly.

"Very well Mrs. Forrester," said Samuel as he began his narrative.

Everyone sat in rapt attention. All eyes were on Samuel. Within the hour, he had finished the saga. Caroline softly wept on the shoulder of her husband who comforted her with his arms about her. She then brushed the tears from her eyes and was her resolute self again. There was no play-acting in her eyes now, only the steely resolve that was her heritage from her mother. "What are we going to do about this person who seems to have tried his best to ruin us? Oh my dear Samuel, if it wasn't for you, I don't know where we would be now. Do you have a plan?" asked Caroline. "I wish I could rip this Englishman apart with my bare hands for what he did to father!"

"Samuel, may I call you Samuel?" asked the Rev. Balcome, "Is this what you were talking about at Mr. Garrison's? "

"It was, and I am pleased to be called by my American name for the time being," replied the big man.

"I cannot believe that my father was in the slave trade," cried Miss Caroline.

"He wasn't really. It was just the one voyage for him. He was only a sailor, and for all of us that was a lucky thing or we would not be here together in this room right now. And the truth was that he only went on that voyage, because he was trying to escape from some other difficulty I think. We ran away from the ship almost as soon as we arrived in America. Your father, Mr. Forrester, was not more than twenty. And Miss Caroline, I was but sixteen at the time as I told you, I was a warrior prince of the Matabele nation. I was educated by English Christian missionaries, and I can tell you that your father was not a bad man. He never beat a slave in his entire life. He left the running of everything up to me in the fields as you know. His sister was the only bad white person there on the plantation. The rest of you behaved better than any of your neighbors. Believe me when I tell you that on other plantations, like the one on which Pompey was born, that was not the case. Why do you think that Pompey looks like a handsome white man? It is because his grandfather was a white man who raped his slave women. His father was old Col. Selby who owned his mother, and like his father before him, forced himself on the pretty slave women on his place. Master Forrester never forced himself on his slave women."

This was a half-truth, as both he and Mrs. Forrester knew all too well. The truth was that the handsome James Forrester never actually forced himself on anybody. He merely charmed the all too willing women, both Black and white, with his handsome face, gifts, and flattery. He was a charming rogue. Mrs. Forrester knew it well and forgave him his little wanderings for she knew that he loved her best, and she really did not want more children. In her heart, she had gratitude for Samuel keeping this secret, which they shared, and she appreciated him for keeping it from the girls.

Caroline looked at Samuel once again and implored, "This is all so much to learn. Could you tell me once more about my father's role in this slaving thing so that I can really understand what he was all about?"

"I tell you Miss Caroline, your father had never before been on a slave ship in his entire life. He was a very young man, much younger than you are now, and if you will forgive my saying so,

I can tell you that the whole business sickened him. The English Captain saw this as weakness, and for that reason he had it in for your father. He whipped your father several times to humiliate him and set him to cleaning the filth out of the slave pens when on land and at sea. On the ship, we were driven topside every day, and he set your father and other men he did not value highly to cleaning the filth from the slave area under the decks. Your father talked to me, because nobody else would speak to him, and that is when we planned our escape. The rest I think you know. Your father was as good a man as the slave system would allow him to be, and there is no more to be said. Please Miss Caroline, be content with that."

"I am Samuel. And I think that I understand all that happened. I do not think ill of you at all, and I hope that you will harbor no ill will. I have you to thank for many things. I have you to thank for my wonderful husband Samuel, in a strange around about sort of way, as does Tilly for her Mr. Cabot."

"Excuse me my dear," intoned Rev. Balcome, "I really don't understand all I heard."

"It's not important that you do my dear," said Caroline with a sad sweet smile, "Someday, when this is all less painful for me to recall, I'll tell you everything. As you love me, and trust me, and knowing the pain that this brings to me with the remembering of it, I know that you will understand and will not trouble me or yourself with more questions."

"Of course my dear," said the good Rev. Balcome kissing his wife's hand, "How could I be so unfeeling. We shall not mention this again. You have had rather a shock. I do apologize my darling, and in your condition, I must be a beast."

"Your condition dear?" asked Mrs. Forrester.

"Yes mother," replied Caroline, "We, that is I, I mean us, that is to say, Oh Hell mother, we are going to have a baby!"

"Oh my! That is good news!" cried Violet.

"I am so happy for both of you," said Mrs. Forrester while reflecting on the fact that she herself never felt the maternal joy she saw in Caroline's eyes when she was told by her doctor of the impending arrival of each one of her own children, but this was a grandchild and that was quite a different matter altogether along with the fact that she did not have to carry a child for nine months and ruin her figure. "I do hope that you will have a pretty little girl," said the smiling grandmother to be.

"I would love to give my husband a son. I would like to name him either Douglas or James. Sometimes I feel that I was not a loving sister. I sometimes think that I may need forgiveness for that too," said Caroline.

"What ever you wish my love will be fine with me. I do love you so," said Mr. Balcome with a look of utter adoration on his face. Then he came back to himself again. "We must get back to the matter at hand," said the Rev. Mr. Balcome. Turning to the large man the Rev. asked again, "May I truly call you Samuel? "

"Yes you may, because I regard you as a friend," replied Samuel.

"Now Samuel, when are we going to put paid to this Captain?"

"Let us get the boat and men we need, and we will go and see a man on an island. He will guide us to where we must go," said Samuel with a smile that was as cold as any North Atlantic iceberg as his eyes met Violet's.

CHAPTER XLII

The deep blue green waters of the mighty Atlantic are made up of the same essential elements that compose the blood of man. The difference between the two is a question of elemental proportions. And man is drawn to that selfsame sea as if it were a magnet pulling on the essence of his very soul. The sea gives life and sometimes takes it away again. It bears up the ship upon its heaving breast and lets it swim on to its destination. In a fit of temper, the sea may also swallow it whole with its cargo and crew. The great oceans swallow up whole multitudes of mankind without effort or any rational thought process. The great oceanic waters roll on endlessly, and its depths are unplumbed. The lives it has suffered to carry to new lands are without number, and nobody can pretend to count the lives it has consumed and deposited in its depths like so many grains of sand. Starbuck tossed in his bed with a torrid tide of sweat washing over him like the hungry ocean waves closing their sea-wave jaws, fang-like and ravenous, over the hundreds of slaves the salty waters had swallowed up.

Whole ship's full of human life, chained together and twisting frantically to escape certain death, screamed out in the last of their agony in Starbuck's dreams. He could see their bodies, twisting and gyrating in a horrible and obscene dance of death. All these fantastic horrors consumed Starbuck's dreaming as he tried to reach out to save them. But Starbuck could not reach the drowning slave women, children, and men. He could not hold them back from the watery death that engulfed them. He cried out as the sharks swam about the humanity in the water, with jaws busy ripping the living flesh from the bones of these poor Blacks. The sharks just continued roiling up the sea into a bloody foam with their cold eyes like obscene dolls' eyes in Starbuck's tormented reality. He looked into those black eyes which rolled up under their protective membranes as the lethal jaws crushed flesh and bone.

Starbuck called out in his pain, but no sound escaped his lips in that unholy night terror as he saw the slaves going over the side of the *Catalpa* in a never ending chain all linked together and hitched to the ship's anchor chain. Their screams broke his peace, and he too was trapped in the steely vice of his own memory. Hot tears streamed down his scarred cheeks, and he feebly kicked at the bedclothes in his soul-tormented sleep that yielded him no rest. In that dream of death, Starbuck wept at the ship's railing as he saw the endless number of black men, women, and babies swept over the side by the evil force of the relentless gravity of the huge iron weight attached to their iron tether about their ankles. On and on it went without cessation.

"Look at them, "boomed the voice of the Satanic Whitehouse whose face was wreathed in scarlet flames nose to nose with Starbuck. "They look like bloody linked sausages don't they. Look at 'em go, and every one of those black bastards lost over the sides is a hundred and fifty pounds of my mortal money damn your eyes! God damn us all to Hell if even one of those niggers is left dead or alive to be found on this bum boat. That's no Yank ship out there baring down on us Starbuck my lad. That's an honest to God fucking British man o'war. If even one of those slaves is found on this sorry arsed ship when they board us, we'll all swing for it! Do you hear me Starbuck damn your eyes! We'll all swing and drink and dance with the Devil within the hour. If it comes to that, Old Scratch might not be bad company eh Starbuck! Har,

har! Dance with the Devil and none for the rest! Do ye like the tune Starbuck? Eh Starbuck? Do ye like the tune boyo? Dance with the Devil and none for the rest. Isn't that how the tune is piped Starbuck?"

Starbuck bolted upright in his bed as the room filled with sunlight. "Wake up Mr. Starbuck. It's alright Mr. Starbuck. It was only one of your dreams," cooed Mrs. Maycock who was sitting next to the bed busy with her knitting. Slowly Starbuck was coming to himself, and he became aware that he was not at sea with a British man o' war coming down on him while the human cargo of the *Catalpa* was being consigned to the deep. Now he knew that the wetness he felt was not the sea but his own sweat. He felt cold, clammy, and disgusting.

He slowly rolled his head toward Mrs. Maycock. There was still a flickering light from the whale oil lamp on the table between the bed and the chair on which Mrs. Maycock was sitting. He now laid back again on his soggy pillow exhausted from his night's tormented dreaming. Starbuck just lay there thinking back over the years of his mother, sitting by his bedside, when he lay in his cot near death with the scarlet fever that had burned his brain with the intensity of a furnace so many years ago. Starbuck closed his eyes again. He could almost feel the cold compresses his mother had placed on his forehead and the cool well water being poured down his throat by those gentle maternal hands. He almost heard her voice as he lay here with closed eyes, "Tristan, Tristan my son. Wake up sweetheart and try to eat something. Tristan."

A sadness and a profound sense of loss filled him now as he reflected that she too was dead. She had passed away only two weeks after his feeble recovery from that fever. With all of his gold, Starbuck realized that he was a very poor man indeed. He was in a world where not one person loved him.

Slowly Starbuck's mind traveled back from three and a half decades before 1849 and the reality of the world. He blinked his eyes open, and then he closed them, and then he opened them again and looked at the ceiling for a little while as he got used to being back in the world. He became aware of a soft breeze coming in from the two opened windows. He summoned up some strength, and said, "Mrs. Maycock, can I stand and walk? Has the doctor said that was possible?"

"I think that if you try and can manage it, it would do no harm. In fact, the doctor said that you should try to move about as soon as it was clear that you could without falling down."

"I'm wet Mrs. Maycock. I seemed to have sweat a great deal in my sleep."

"That would have been the fever Mr. Starbuck. Now it seems to have broken. I'll fetch Mr. Maycock and we'll get you cleaned up and sorted out. We'll move you into the room next door to a nice clean dry bed with fresh linen so that you can get a proper rest."

"How long have I been out of my head? "

"A week. That is a week since we found you on the beach. You have been in and out again since then. A bad fever will do that to a body sometimes. It wasn't a good idea to be away so long on your little swimming jaunt. You ought not go in for a swim by yourself, and be away for days at a time without telling a body exactly where you are going. When you said that you were planning to be away, we didn't expect it to be quite like that. Look at the mischief you got yourself into. It is a good thing that Mr. Maycock insisted that we set about to find you. We looked for you for days. It is a good thing that we did not give up. You might be there washed up on the beach yet, God knows. But as Mr. Shakespeare said, 'All's well that end's well.' "

"Was there another fellow looking for me? This Shakespeare fellow? "

"Mr. Shakespeare lived a considerable long time ago in England during the time when Good Queen Bess was ruler there. I never heard that he got on a ship and visited these parts. He wrote plays in old-fashioned language almost like my great grandmother spoke. We could never see plays when I was a girl.

My folks were Congregationalists of the old kind and were dead set against the theater. My dear great grandmother was a game one though and very smart. She came all the way from England in the old days long before the Revolution. She had seen plays and such, and she told me the story of them. She was High Church, and her people had nothing against the theater. When I was old enough, she gave me these books with Mr. Shakespeare's plays in them, and we would read them out loud when nobody else was around. She was a wonderful woman. She didn't get on with the other women in the family. She wasn't a strict old time Congregationalist you see. My relations thought that she was too high-toned acting and put on airs you know like some folks do. Actually and as I said, she was High Church. That fact alone was a scandal in my father's family."

"Really Mrs. Maycock. You make me think about things that I haven't thought about in years. I almost feel like I'm a child again when I hear you talk sometimes," said Starbuck.

"Oh, I know that I go on sometimes. I am sorry for that and with you being so unwell and all."

"No please. Go on, and tell me about your great grandmother. I like to hear about people who lived a long time ago. Somehow it gives me comfort hearing such things as that."

"My great grandmother was different from everyone else. She taught me to read way before I ever went to any downstairs school, and she taught me about the places she had seen with her own eyes long before most folks were even born. She seemed to have been ever so many interesting places. She would never tell me how she came to America or what happened to my great grandfather except that he was killed in some battle or other and that she had to raise my grandfather, her only son, by herself. She found a new husband in Boston who ran a public house down near the docks. She had to work hard there until her second husband also died. Then she sold the place and moved to Brewster to a little farm where my grandfather also lived. My grandfather got married, and had my own father. I was raised there too after my father married my mother, and I was born. The farm was small and had to feed a lot of us you see. The ground on the Cape is pretty rocky, and farming those stony acres is a hard life. A hard life makes hard people. My great grandmother and I made a secret little world that we did not let the others know about. So we read plays, acted some out. We did laugh so. We had fun where the others could not see us and come down on us for being frivolous."

"That is the way it was with my own mother's family," smiled Starbuck warming to human contact after his coma like sleep and isolation from the world of his childhood.

"When my great grandmother got so very old, she became like a child, and I looked after her. I tended her, keeping her clean, washing her clothes, and rocking her in a long cradle in front of the fire. The others were content to have it so. It took the burden off of them you see. When she died, I didn't want to stay there any more in that house where the people were so hard and cold. When my great grandmother died, a light in this dark world of my hard and practical family went out of me forever."

"Hard and cold was all I knew except for my mother, and she was taken from me when I was so young. I could not wait to go off to sea and get away from here before the rest made a farmer out of me like they did my brother Lloyd. I think that we are alike, you and me, in some ways," said Starbuck sadly.

"I do declare Mr. Starbuck we may be at that. Mr. Maycock was clerking in the store in the center of the village. We got on very well. He was a good-looking young man then, and he liked poems. We used to walk out together and talk a great deal. I fell in love with him just like in the stories. I decided to marry when I was but sixteen. There were so many of us at home, my father gave us his blessing. My Mr. Maycock is a very fine man who is kind and understanding of me. He loves me just the way I am. Our lives won't make a Shakespeare play, but we get on well enough always working where people need us. We get by the best we can. We tried to run a store once. It didn't work out so well. We gave away too much credit, but that is the way life is. In our way, we are rich enough I think. It makes me blush to say it, but Mr. Maycock and I love each other very much. We never have gone to sleep with a cross word between us during the whole time we have been married more than twenty five years now."

"So it would seem Mrs. Maycock. Your husband is a very lucky man."

"I'll get my husband, and we'll clean you up and get you moved into the next room Mr. Starbuck. I'll make you some lamb's broth and some nice tea, and I'll give you a little of it to see how it goes down."

With that, Mrs. Maycock left the room blushing.

Starbuck looked after her as she left. Suddenly he was aware that this woman was very special. The feelings that returned were not of the kindness of his mother. Instead he began to burn with jealousy of Mr. Maycock who held a domestic prize that Starbuck now wanted.

CHAPTER XLIII

Starbuck fell into a deep sleep after he had been moved into the next bedroom. He had been washed, changed, fed, and put to bed. This time he was given soothing syrup by Mrs. Maycock. The good doctor had left the mixture in her care with special instructions should she feel that it would be needed. Starbuck slept away another day in peace. Whitehouse and the slave ship did not invade his rest this time. He slept the dreamless sleep of the dead until he felt himself stirring and heard the trumpet of the doctor's snoring. Starbuck batted his eyes open.

He turned his head toward the sawmill sound of snoring and saw the island's man of medicine slumped in a chair brought up from the parlor. Here the doctor slept like a sultan against the watered silk tufted upholstery of his throne framed by the polished black walnut. Starbuck smiled wickedly and summoned all of his somewhat restored strength to bellow out one, "Avast there! Who the Hell are ye aboard here? "

The doctor stopped snoring, and awoke with a start. He shook his head, rubbed his face, adjusted his spectacles, looked at his patient, smiled and said, "Well you ain't pretty, but you are pretty much alive there Mr. Starbuck. And that is a proposition I would not have bet even money on almost a week ago. No sir. This is one for the books to be sure. I'd say that I did a first rate job patching you up, I would."

"Well, that's all nice and cheery like I suppose, but could you manage to go down to Mrs. Maycock and tell her that I'd like some soup or broth or something to take the edge off my hunger? And by the way, who the blazes are you?"

"I'm Doc Graham my good fellow. We have met before. You were still foggy in the head at our first encounter, and the soothing syrup has done the rest no doubt. Your memory is still a bit foggy, but you'll live. You and I have been in conversation before. The Maycocks sent for me after they got you home from your little romp in the cove where you were playing and sporting with some manner of savage sea creature, and I cleaned you up and stitched you back together. You swim with some pretty strange company!"

For a second Starbuck was taken aback. He asked himself if somehow Weston's mangy body had washed up in the cove. He then dismissed the thought from his mind.

"What do you mean by that remark Doc? "

"I mean that you were swimming with some kind of shark. I heard that you didn't like island folk's company, but I would not advise that you go off to swim with sharks just the same. He must have been a young and an inexperienced sort of fish, or maybe he just wasn't very hungry. Could be he thought that you were just too old and tough and wouldn't taste too good. Sharks are not known to be fussy that way generally speaking. So if I was you, I guess that I'd feel insulted that he thought of me that sort of way in terms of dinner. And then again, maybe you should just feel pretty lucky that he wasn't hungry after all. You cut yourself up pretty bad too. That's what attracted him. You were bleeding pretty bad. And with your infernal bleeding all over the place, you were like a big piece of chum. It's a good thing that he wasn't swimming in company with some bigger and smarter or hungrier friends, because if he was, we would not be exchanging such nice pleasantries right about now."

"You don't talk like a doctor. You sound like a fisherman or farmer."

"I went to Harvard over in Boston all right, and studied at the big hospitals there. I even read Latin and German because that's what so much of the learning that goes with this business is written in, but I don't care much for the civilization of Boston. Those folks are like so much dead cod. They are cold fish and too goddamned pretentious. I like it out here on the island. I'm damned good at what I do, and people out here are not too easily offended by my manners except for my wife who says that I'm just too goddamned unrefined. The greater part of the folks out here don't care that I like my rum and want to keep to myself when I want to keep to myself except when they need me which seems to be pretty regular."

"So exactly what did you do for me?" questioned Starbuck.

"When the Maycocks sent for me, I came on the run. You were cut up and banged up pretty bad. I cleaned your wounds, which had begun to fester, and put you to bed when I sewed up what I could of you after I cleaned you out. You were pretty lucky to be out of this mortal world of knowing what was going on, or you could never have stood the pain. You were in fact spared a great deal of pain, and you probably would not have liked my little helpers who cleaned out all the mortified flesh around those cuts you got from something sharp ripping at you. But they et it all, and I sewed that gash up too. You had a fever, and how you went on. Now here you are big as life and twice as ugly. I don't like fancy speech, so, there you be."

"Well I'll thank you not to remind me of that 'ugly' bit. And don't ever let anybody tell you that your speech is fancy. Was I raving? Out of my head?"

"Out of your head? That you were matey. But we went over that ground before. I guess that you don't remember that either likely. What a wicked fellow you are if even a tiny bit of what you said when you were out of your head was true. I've heard a lot of folks rave over the last twenty-five years or so when they have fever.

What they do say! They talk about the lives they would lead if they dared to when they were awake. It never ceases to amaze me what folks think about in dark dreams. You were more convincing than most, but you merchant sailor fellows always wished for more exciting lives than the ones you had. It's a good thing that you only dream that stuff and nonsense Mr. Starbuck. If you did half of what you say you did, they would have to hang you fifteen or maybe even twenty times. Killing a bunch of New York boys, and hereabouts at that! That's rich. Just one of you and all of them! I wouldn't give much for them odds. You do go all the way with your fancy now don't you. At least you kept me awake most of the time. You spin some yarns and great whoppers. Where would you lay hands on scads of New Yorkers to kill anyway? If you ever remember any of those yarns, write them down in a book. They will make good reading. That is, they will make good reading if you can get anyone to print them. As I told you before when you were almost back in your right mind, you could try getting your stuff in *Harper's* if you toned it down a bit. By the way, just what were you doing out there on the water and beach?"

"Doc, I have no notion of what you are jawing about at all. I can't remember a damned thing. I don't know where I was or why I was there."

"Well, Cousin Starbuck is that a fact? "

"It's as true as I am laying here. I can remember nothing about how I came to be all stove in and cut up."

"That is not so strange. The mind will play tricks on an old feller like you or me when he's been as banged up like you have been. It's quite normal not to remember anything. You don't recall seeing anything of that old scoundrel Weston do you?"

"Weston? He's the fellow who walks around in rags who's got some kind of old bum boat or other? Don't have any truck with trash like him Doc. Why do you ask?"

"Nothing important. It's just that he's gone missing. It's no great matter. He's not exactly a great loss to the community you might say. He most likely went out fishing and then forgot to come back. Maybe he tossed his anchor overboard and forgot to let go of it. It is the kind of foolish thing that the old reprobate would do most likely. Now most old salts can be classified as characters. In fact I do believe that most of these old coots work at it. Even old scruffy ones have something of a following, but Weston, now he was different. The man had nothing charming about him at all. He's one of those folks that makes a place better by just walking out of it. He is one old character who will not be missed by anyone."

The doctor then got up and wandered off downstairs to get his patient something to eat. Starbuck leaned back against the pillows trying to recall all the things that he had done after sending Captain Weston off on his way into Hell. He relaxed a bit secure in the knowledge that any body filled with stones was not about to come washing up onto the shore, nor was a boat weighted down with all the ballast he had loaded on board Weston's old craft likely to be able to rise and sail again. He was recalling quite a bit. It was more than he'd ever let on. One recollection let to another like flashes of insight. His leg ached a bit at the thought of it, but it was a pain that merely marked a place in his memory that gave Starbuck a strange and twisted sort of comfort. At least nobody was going to waste any effort investigating Weston's departure from the scene.

Starbuck was sure that if anyone thought of Weston at all, that they would just speculate that he had gotten drunk again and that maybe this time he had just run out of luck. So many of these old timers, cast up on the shore after their days at sea were over, had turned to drink and went for that one last bit of sailing. He remembered old Richmond's wife talking about her father-in-law, old Captain Almus. She always said of him that he had sailed off one day with a full cargo of Medford Rum inside of him, and when he tossed the anchor overboard, he had just forgot to let go, and that was the end of the old gent. Reflecting on what the doctor had said about Weston, Starbuck decided that going overboard with an anchor seemed to be a common theme.

That thought made him smile. He reflected that he rather liked Dr. Graham and his salty talk. He liked doctors who sounded like they knew what a person might be feeling. And that did not happen very often.

He laughed to himself about the image of Weston going over the side with the anchor firmly grasped in his boney hands. Starbuck decided that if anyone should speculate about old Weston's strange departure, he would just parade the old story out about Captain Almus. It would produce a laugh, an explanation, and a lofty indifference to the fate of Weston. His smile faded when he thought of the New Yorkers though. They most likely had families in the gangs who might want to know what had become of their kin, and the gang leaders do not like losing money twice to the same rogue. The men of the Five Points would know that he was still on the island if they investigated at all. It was more than likely that they would act again, although he was sure that they could never discover the fate of their three friends. Still everyone was of the opinion that Starbuck had lost his memory, and as the fellow said, a lost memory was just like the old lady's nightie. It just about covered everything.

Then his thoughts turned to the man in Brazil. He was filled with rage as his nightmare revisited him in the bright light of day. If only he could get his murderous big hands on Captain Whitehouse's neck now, he would be well satisfied. If he could only kill Whitehouse and let the New Yorkers know that the Captain himself was dead. Then everything would be alright again. That was a plan that he entertained for a full five minutes before he abandoned it. Starbuck blinked his eyes again and tried to clear his head. One by one he moved his limbs. To his relief, they all seemed to be in working order. The pain seemed to be ebbing away, and the dense fog that had settled over his consciousness seemed to slowly be clearing away as well. Somehow he also felt stronger.

A few minutes later, a knock came at the door. The doctor opened the door and entered as Maycock strode in behind him with some pancakes laced with maple syrup and a great pat of butter melting down the sides of the four-layer stack.

"The excellent Mrs. Maycock is of the opinion that you can consume something more than broth," said the doctor, "And I am inclined to indulge her. If you are not up to the job Mr. Starbuck, I am sure that I could relieve you of the burden of trying."

"That's right good of you doctor, but if that dear lady thinks that I'm up to that task, I would be a real old fool if I were not to try to please her."

"Well if you folks will excuse me," said Maycock, "I have some chores that need doing. If you need anything, ring that bell by your bedside Mr. Starbuck and either my wife or I can hear it and come running." With that Maycock left the room shutting the door.

"That fellow is pretty lucky with a wife like that," said Starbuck slowly with a tone of decided admiration mixed with envy.

"These Maycock folks are really good people believe me," opined the doctor. "If it wasn't for those two finding you on the beach in that secluded cove and taking you back here and putting you to bed and fetching me, you would be dead now and not enjoying my superb company and conversation. Yes sir, deader than the very mackerel I saw being dressed for your next meal down to the kitchen there."

"I guess that I owe you a lot Doc, and that's a fact," said Starbuck between mouthfuls of the delicious pancakes.

"Well I'll tell you what. Since you are all fired up with gratitude, I guess that this is a good time to give you the bill for my fee. I'll just round it off to forty-four dollars and a stack of those flapjacks if Mrs. Maycock is willing."

"I'll give you fifty dollars and all the flapjacks you want. See that billfold on the chest there. Just help yourself. I'll just ring for Mrs. Maycock."

"Thanks for the fifty. I appreciate not being paid off with chickens, eggs, quilts and such sometimes, but don't make that poor soul climb all the way back up here again. I'll go down to the kitchen and put in my order myself. I am happy that the notes that you gave me are on the bank on the island here. I appreciate the fact that I won't have to go home and look them up in the *Thomas Almanac* to see if they are any good," said the doctor as he sauntered out the door of Starbuck's room.

"She is a good soul," sighed Starbuck. As the door closed behind the doctor, Starbuck growled to himself, "That damned fool Maycock is one lucky fellow. Who knows? Maybe I can be lucky too."

CHAPTER XLIV

Samuel and Pompey were relieved to hear of the sighting of Captain Beers' ship off Boston light. It would not dock until nightfall. In the days that passed since the reunion of Mrs. Forrester and her family with Pompey and Samuel, Mr. Balcome had met with the two former Forrester slaves at Garrison's paper not less than three times. Mr. Cabot's vessel had been assured for the trip to Nantucket to collect Starbuck whom it was hoped could link Samuel with Whitehouse at some remote spot on the earth for the purpose of bringing Whitehouse to book for his crimes against the Matabele warrior prince and the peoples of Africa whom he had sold into slavery. Pompey and the rest of the conspirators were all for bringing him to justice in a British court. Whitehouse was after all English by birth and the actual crime had not originated on American soil. Pompey knew that most American courts had failed miserably in the enforcement of the 1807 law which was supposed to have ended the slave trade. Only Great Britain had strictly enforced it uniformly. When an American warship was commanded by a strong abolitionist, things might go a bit differently. But sons of the South also commanded United States men of war.

Samuel was not pleased with this proposed solution, but he agreed in principal to bring Whitehouse to justice in England.

He said that he would go along with the judgment of the rest if Whitehouse was not killed during his capture. At least, that is what he would let them think for the time being. There would always be time for him to exact appropriate justice at a moment of his choosing, and catching Whitehouse was a dicey thing at best. A man could be easily killed in a horrible way in the heat of battle.

Samuel had dreamed of the many ways he could punish Whitehouse. He became almost obsessed with the idea of it. The obsession grew as the days had passed from his first meeting with Garrison. A plan evolved in his mind that he now kept entirely to himself. No humiliation would be too great. No torture was beyond consideration, but in the end, no punishment was horrific enough to satisfy Samuel's huge hunger for revenge except for this exquisite solution on which he had secretly resolved. One night as he had tossed on his bed, it had come to him. This was revenge so sweet that it would last both the hunter and the hunted a lifetime. Samuel lay on his bed and stared at the ceiling of his room in the best hotel in Boston. His mind began to fill in the details of this, his second grand design. The revenge he planned was so sweet in that it could last forever. He almost wished that Whitehouse were younger so that the punishment he had evolved in his darkest thoughts would seem an eternity.

The plan was perfection. Whitehouse's humiliation would be complete, and nobody would get in his way, because he would not actually kill Whitehouse outright. This he had also resolved as a holy promise to all of Whitehouse's victims. Whitehouse would enjoy no quick exit from his torment. Samuel's eyes narrowed even as he thought of it. He sat up on the edge of the bed, and he slipped on his shoes. He would go and tell Pompey just what he had in mind for the slave ship's Captain.

Pompey was the partner of all his grand plans. Pompey was the one human on the planet, Samuel knew in his heart, would never betray him once he had resolved on a plan of action. In all the days since his reunion with the Forresters, all Samuel thought about was how he would deal with the Captain. Now his plan for revenge would be a constant comfort to him. Samuel thought that Pompey too should be allowed to savor the plan, but nobody else was to be admitted into the particulars of his exquisite revenge and punishment. Pompey was after all the son of his heart if not his flesh.

Had he not hidden away a treasure of gold for the day that Pompey could claim it as his own birthright from his adopted father? Pompey's gold too was part of Samuel's master plan. Samuel and Pompey would return to Matebeleland together. Samuel would enforce his will, and Pompey would be accepted as a prince as the adopted son of the great warrior returned to his home. A wedding to a daughter of the Matabele Nation would seal Pompey's adoption. This was the essential element that Samuel hung all his hope on. After this was done, Samuel would enjoy the celebration of joy at his return to his country. He would assume the pride of place in this land of his birth where his true condition would be recognized and he would be exalted in his clan and the Matabele Nation as a hero who had defeated the whole slave system in a magnificent show of real justice. Maybe Samuel could even convince the Matabele king to give him enough men to wipe out all the slaving operations on the Mozambique Coast. The Portuguese could not stop him, and the British would be hard pressed to do so. Any opposition to such a military expedition would be seen as supporting slavery, and the English people would never stand for that. Any prime minister who would adopt that policy would be run out of office by his own party.

Samuel could hear the drums of his wedding day, in his mind's eye. He saw himself wed to a fine young woman of the Matabele nation, who would give him strong and sturdy sons to fill his kraal. His lands would be rich with good grass, and his cattle would be fat, and all would be as it should have been just as if he had never been ripped from his home, and best of all, his son, Pompey, would be by his side. Now Samuel would see if Pompey was in his room.

Pompey had disappeared during parts of each day over the last two weeks. When Samuel had asked where he had been, Pompey would answer that he had gone to the city Library, or to see the Bishop about the Irish, or had just gone for a walk to clear his head. It seemed strange but not implausible for a young man to wander about in a new metropolis. Samuel reasoned that Pompey was a young man eager to learn all he could, and Boston was America's first city in education and culture.

As Samuel started to go to Pompey's room, he thought about the young man's future. Pompey too would have a wife of the Matabele people. The son of his heart would be adopted into the family clan, and he would ask his king on bended knee if Pompey could be exempted from the rule that stated that a man needed to achieve his thirty-ninth birthday to take a wife. Such favors in the old days were rare, but never had a man come back from slavery in America to Matabeleland and with this light skinned son of Africa in tow. Anything might be possible. Samuel was thinking of what names to give Pompey. What great African name would be good enough for this son of his heart? Maybe he would even return in triumph with Whitehouse in chains to be dragged before the throne of the Great King of the People of Heaven at Bulawayo before he exacted his revenge. Samuel knew that his plan for Pompey was very fragile. Anything could run it off track.

As Samuel advanced down the hall a few steps, he heard someone coming up the stairs. He looked up to see that it was Pompey deeply engaged in conversation with Violet who was tightly clinging to Pompey's arm giving him her total attention. Neither she nor Pompey saw Samuel in the hallway. They were totally absorbed in each other.

Samuel was filled with rage with what he now considered to be a betrayal of his trust. Quietly he returned to his room and closed the door. The absorbed young couple never saw him. As his door closed behind him, Samuel found himself standing with his great hands clenching and unclenching. Then he felt a dull pain wrapping itself around his upper body like a constricting serpent slowly beginning to crush his chest. Samuel sat heavily on the edge of his bed. He then reached for his carafe on the table beside his bed and shakily poured himself a glass of water. He slowly drank as the pain in his chest became more acute. He fell back on his pillow and lay there a full hour until the worst of the pain had passed. Samuel had found with rest, the pain had always passed.

Now the pains took longer to dissipate. Samuel tried to calm himself just as he had always done when the pain came. The quiet time was always best. The pain did not come often, but over the last six months it had come when he grew either angry or was terribly upset. Before it came, numbness would invade his right cheek as a warning of the coming storm. This time the numbness had not come.

"I must have time," Samuel softly said. "I have come this far, and I must finish it. That bitch cannot get in my way."

CHAPTER XLV

Whitehouse paced the quarterdeck of his new ship. He was a week out of Rio de Janeiro and beating a course for Cape Town. From there, he was to sail to Mozambique where the Mozambique Company was not too fussy about skirting the laws regarding the slave trade. The trade in Black Ivory was alive and well from the Portuguese colony up through the Sudan. Across the Red Sea, the slave trade also flourished all the way into Arabia. Black Ivory was traded with the same vigor that ever it was. Slaves were traded from the African interior to the East African Coast, and slave ships would fill up their 'tween decks with human cargo and run across the Indian and Pacific oceans and around Cape Horn to escape the British Navy which had concentrated its interdiction forces in the Atlantic. They would then creep up the Atlantic coast of South America to the Empire of Brazil to unload and sell their cargo. The planters in the Brazilian interior would buy the children of Africa to work in the man-killing interior. Rubber was king, and the Rubber Barons must have their slaves to make them rich. The southern United States was also still a fine market as well with healthy black men trading at twice to three times the value of a modest Yankee farm in the North, and healthy women were trading at half as much as the men.

His one regret was that Ajax had not been at his house when

he had returned from his yacht. When Whitehouse had ordered him to pack for a long voyage, Ajax had taken the opportunity to lay his hands on a great deal of money as well as the young and very bright slave boy that he had bought for his own pleasure. Whitehouse had marveled that Ajax could have found a young man even smaller than himself who was obviously intended only for pleasure. Whitehouse had been endlessly amused by this.

Together the two young slaves had made off in the dark of night never to be seen by Whitehouse again. There was no time to contact the civil authorities, nor would Whitehouse have ever done such a thing. Ajax was a smart fellow and knew too much about his most recent master for comfort. In fact, Whitehouse laughed about the matter and hoped that the little fellow could make it to England or even France and enjoy his life. He was the first person in many years for whom Whitehouse had developed a real fondness, but he knew that although his comfort would suffer from Ajax's desertion, he had more pressing worries to fill out the time before him.

Whitehouse decided to make the best of things as he cobbled together his plans for this one last voyage. On this venture, he wanted to take his time and load a cargo of only the finest slave stock that his gold and trading goods could buy. And then he decided that he might sell out his property in Brazil, slaves and all through his lawyer Don Emilio Diez, and live in the sunny south of France after his last enterprise was concluded. He also had to face the reality that he was nearing sixty and he was no longer quite the person he used to be only a year past. He also reflected that this time he might find a pretty little French girl to take Ajax's place who could offer him more variety in his lovemaking.

France was a seductive place to settle in the Captain's mind. President Louis Napoleon had shown himself to be a friend of commerce and the wealthy middle class. Whitehouse intended to live out his life there as a gentleman far away from the threat of capture by the American or more to the point, the British Navy. Such a capture by the Americans would mean the loss of a cargo of unsurpassed riches and a judicial slap on the wrist, but an interception by one of her majesty's ships of war would mean the noose along with all of his commercial losses. This was the last time he would have to risk such a punishment. This was to be his last slaving expedition. This would be the crowning achievement of a brilliant career. He would ship the finest cargo of his life, and he would live like a king for the rest of his days.

"The New York bunch can't be expected to still think me dead," was the thought, which drifted through Whitehouse's mind as he gazed out over that wide expanse of the Atlantic. His ship made eight knots in the relatively light breeze. A full moon overhead seemed to smile back at him as he fancied that it looked on his ship from above with a sort of blessing for his unholy enterprise. Captain Whitehouse was lost in a sort of reverie as he looked now at some place beyond the seascape reflected in the moonlight. He was strangely at peace. Bad dreams never invaded his waking or sleeping hours. Captain Whitehouse was immune to his creations of horror. All he saw in his mind's eye were the splendid beaches of the sunny and warm French Mediterranean coast and the dimly lit shape of a young and pretty country girl whose innocence gave her more beauty than any painted courtesan of the Borgia's'. Amorality carefully cultivated over the years served Whitehouse well. He knew that someday all men died and slept in the earth forever. Long ago he decided that a good man and an evil one slept just the same dreamless never-ending sleep.

He smiled as he thought of all the men he had ever done business with. He reflected that he still lived while most of them were dead. They no longer produced wealth. They no longer had purpose in his or anybody else's life. Captain Whitehouse did not worry about purpose. He only concerned himself with profits and the pleasures that those profits would bring to him. The thousands of suffering souls ripped from their homes and stuffed into his ships that he had commanded did not impact his life. The hundreds of men, women, and children chained together and consigned to the deep as a ship of the Royal Navy bore down on him in the years passed represented only so many red inked entries in some ledger in the Five Points. The screams of the last moments of life of the slaves sacrificed for Whitehouse's safety ended as the sharks tore into the living flesh of these children of Africa. Now they were forever mute in his memory as were the screams of all of the other men he had killed over the last forty years. As his mate came on duty, the ship's bell struck to indicate that midnight had come to that longitude.

"Mr. Wright, I'm going to my cabin. Do not wake me unless the damned ship is sinking."

"Aye, aye sir," replied the mate.

Whitehouse went below and poured himself a tot of brandy. He rolled the amber liquid in his mouth and smacked his lips with its goodness. As he nestled into his cot, it creaked slightly as it hung under his weight from its gimbals. A warm glow of satisfaction passed through his whole being. And he drifted off to a very pleasant rest regretting only that Ajax, or a pretty French girl, was not curled up against his chest.

CHAPTER XLVI

The air was seasonably warm, and Violet was in a fine mood. Her mood was matched by that of Pompey, because this beautiful girl, who was so full of high spirit and intelligence, knew that he had been a slave on the Forrester Plantation and did not care. She herself was unburdened with a family, which would have had to approve of any beaus that she had fancied. For two weeks these young people had come to know each other, and from the beginning each had felt that they had known the other all of their lives. This had been so from the day of their first conversation. Violet and Pompey made time for each other away from the prying eyes of their companions. They learned that they loved the same books, the same poems, and then each other. Their love was immediate and profound. Each wanted the other for a lifetime.

Samuel had felt that something was afoot when Pompey disappeared into the city for hours at a time. Violet and Pompey had truly fused a lifetime into two short weeks. They lived and loved intensely, because they knew that this little space of time was all they had in a life so busy and compressed. They knew that they could not risk the loss of each other for any reason. Each of their lives had conflicting complications, but after discussing the most important relationships in their lives, they decided that the bond that they had forged together was the only one that mattered in the end.

Mrs. Forrester did not know of the fast budding relationship between her handsome former butler and Violet. Pompey reflected that Samuel would have to be told of any new developments in his life sooner or later. Pompey was not looking forward to a confrontation with the man who was almost his father. He knew that Samuel had some master plan for him, but he wanted to be his own man. More than that, he wanted this woman of his own choosing. In his heart, Pompey also knew that he could never live the life Samuel wanted for him. Sometimes he wondered if Samuel could ever return to his old life either. Samuel had also lived more than two thirds of his life in a western culture. Africa had been only a remote dream that had existed in Samuel's head for more than thirty years.

Pompey's world had changed so quickly since this beautiful, intelligent, and brave young woman came into his life like a flash of lightning striking deeply into his psyche. Their first meeting in the hallway and the exchange that followed opened his eyes and imagination to fantastic possibilities and a new world beyond even the heady excitement he had known in the last few years. Then one night Violet had come to his rooms. Here they had talked all night of their respective lives, hopes for the future, and love of life. When the dawn had come, she really did not want to leave him, and for the first time they had kissed as neither of them had ever kissed before. Pompey had told Violet to leave him while they could still master what they were feeling for each other. Violet had returned to the Forrester suite determined to have Pompey for her own. Her trips into the city with Pompey cemented their love.

One day she asked Mrs. Forrester about Pompey, and she was surprised at how much her mistress actually knew about Pompey's coming of age on her Georgian plantation. Violet was astonished at just how aware the woman had been of this little slave boy that her husband had won at a game of cards. It was obvious that the woman, who did not care for her own sons, had been won over by the charm of this little slave boy. Pompey was special. He was attractive in his person, but it was the depth of his mind that had most fascinated Violet whose first love had been her Grandfather Esmond and then his little library of great books.

Violet was so typical of a class of respectable poor privately educated English girls who were caught between being upper middle class and servant class. Their lives of shabby respectability placed these poor but well born girls between classes. Minister's granddaughters, daughters of school masters of the lower ranks, daughters of near-do-wells, and daughters of poor relations of "good families" were most often educated with the daughters of their betters in households who took them in as family charity cases. In the end, most of them became companions of wealthy women, governesses, teachers in girl's academies, or cared for their wealthier relatives. For years they often lived with a succession of gentrified families as a "charge of honor" in a continued state of shabby respectability. Here they grew old and gray. They became silent witnesses to a life they could never share.

This was not the world in which Violet intended to live her life in a shabby respectability. Sometimes there was marriage for such women to respectable men of lesser means. They would wed in such a world with men who were their social counterparts. For these girls, there were poor vicars, some of whom were well over forty or even fifty, and schoolmasters, also of shabby respectability, whose only power was over the cowering little boys whom they taught and on whom their frustration and fury was visited with a cane. Old decrepit men and young and decrepit men with a small living was the usual fate of such poor but respectable girls as Violet if they were allowed to marry at all. Sometimes an older decrepit man might also be wealthy and a prize of sorts. This was especially true if he had no children by a previous marriage, or near relatives of whom he might be fond and leave his estate and his wife as a dependent to be cared for until she died.

The most common alternative for girls and women of Violet's class was a long spinsterhood and a lonely old age as a dependent in a few cold rooms of some country house or in some run down urban boarding establishment of decayed refinement inhabited by pretentious older people who had not the faintest idea of the life they might have had if they had but taken the trouble to do more than pass through life as if it were merely out of habit. Too often young women of the "better sort", who found themselves in reduced circumstances, would end as the companions of self-indulgent older women like Mrs. Forrester. Pompey was a fantastic alternative to all that. Besides that, she found him exciting, fascinating, handsome, and she loved him.

Violet began to make her plans and packed her most essential belongings in a single leather box that she herself could carry without difficulty. She had managed to save more than a hundred pounds sterling in gold coin. This money had come from what her grandfather had left her as well as a substantial part of her wages. More than that, she was ready for a change. This very day she and Pompey had spoken for two hours in his rooms and had decided to marry and go off on their great life adventure together. She was quite ready to storm an island at the side of her husband, pistol or sword in hand, and lay hands on a person she had never met and carry him off in an act of abduction. Together they walked to the Boston City Hall and obtained the license needed. From there, it was a fifteen-minute walk to the episcopal residence of Bishop Fitzpatrick. The good Bishop held Pompey in high regard for the help he had given to the poor Irish on the common. The good bishop had consented to marry the couple.

"But you are not Catholic my son," the kindly Bishop said. "Why do you wish me to perform the marriage ceremony?"

"Neither am I Your Grace," said the smiling Violet melting the older man's heart. He was not immune to her charm. "But my Lord Bishop, Pompey speaks so well of you and your good work here in Boston. I can agree that there is no other man on earth that I would rather wish to be married by than yourself."

With this, the Bishop could not refuse. "What name sir shall I enter into the register," asked the Bishop's secretary.

"Pompey Esmond," replied the groom looking deeply into Violet's eyes in appreciation of her gift to him of her beloved grandfather's name.

"And your name miss?" asked the secretary.

"Miss Violet Hartington," she replied. The Bishop looked surprised, but his secretary would not have recognized the great ducal name.

The two were married in the Bishop's own private chapel with none to see but the Bishop, his secretary, and his coachman who acted as witnesses. After the ceremony, the Bishop ordered wine and cakes to be brought to the parlor. Pompey pressed a donation on the Bishop for the relief of the poor, which the good man accepted. Then it was over. Their walk back to the hotel took on an almost magical tone as Violet and Pompey Esmond moved through the streets without noticing the other people passing them by on the sidewalks. Pompey and Violet passed unnoticed up to Pompey's rooms.

Behind Pompey's door, they spent the next two hours in the deep embrace of wedded bliss. Then they fell asleep in each other's arms. When the dawn splashed them with light they awoke still in an embrace. Their warm skin filled them with delight at each other's touch. They smiled and kissed deeply and tenderly. Their enjoyment of each other was boundless, and they fell again to lovemaking with unalloyed pleasure. They melted into the moment enjoying a freedom and ecstasy that neither had ever known before in their entire lives, and in their passion, neither of them heard Pompey's door open and the soft padding of Samuel's feet on the deep pile of the carpet.

Samuel walked through the parlor of Pompey's suite. He then opened the door of Pompey's bedroom and stared at the sight of the two naked lovers entwined in the utter joy of the moment. They did not see Samuel, nor did they hear him retreat and quietly shut the door on his way out. They only knew each other, in that moment, and the little world they were creating in each other's arms. The rest of the planet and the humanity on it did not exist for them. They were binary stars sharing one orbit as they revolved about each other, reaching for something very deeply they had never known before. They were reborn in love with each pelvic thrust. Their love was now beyond the rational thoughts of their almost academic discussions that had so entranced Pompey from the time they first exchanged words. His rational world could all go to Hell in this moment and time. What he was feeling now was something far more beautiful in all of its dynamic romantic intensity than the greatest ideas ever expressed in spoken words, on paper, or ever revealed in holy writ.

Here in Violet's arms was Heaven, and in her essential reality was his earthly salvation. "Again darling, again," she pleaded as if she were mouthing a holy prayer to the close and eternal gods of love. With one last thrust, Pompey's full measure of love exploded inside of her like a typhoon unleashed on the waters of a mighty ocean. She moaned with her legs locked around Pompey's strong legs in a delight surpassing all the other earthly delights that she had ever known as the mighty surge of Pompey's love filled her like a tide rushing in to grasp the shore. Violet gasped as she achieved the highest plateau of physical and spiritual love in an orgasmic explosion of an earthquake. For each of them it was the first intimate physical lovemaking of their lives. The revelation of the absolute joy of this fulfillment of physical passion was as natural as taking a breath. Pompey and Violet knew that this was always meant to be even from the beginning of time itself. In each other's embrace, they melted into the perfect happiness of their mutual discovery.

Pompey withdrew his manhood from Violet, and he kissed her with a tenderness she could never have hoped to know on this mortal earth. She lay there for a while massaging her excited breasts trying to contemplate all that had happened in the last fifteen hours since their escape from the hotel and the eyes of Samuel and Mrs. Forrester. Pompey leaned back on the pillows not knowing whether to laugh or cry with joy at the great gift that was this woman who was now his life. Pompey and Violet slowly looked at each other. They gently rolled toward each other coming together in the perfect fit of her little body against the hard and well-toned body of her perfect husband. Their arms again entwined, and they became one in making love one last time before they had to return to their former lives for a little while longer. They were resigned to playing out their respective parts until they could slip away to their new life as Mr. And Mrs. Pompey Esmond.

Across the hall, Samuel glowered in his secret fury. His eyes were two red coals. His fury made all of his powerful muscles pulsate with rage. What was that stupid boy thinking? What about the mission? "We are so close, and now he will go in with this stupid complication to ruin it," he growled into the empty air of his room. All manner of thoughts crowded into Samuel's tortured mind. He threw himself onto his bed. He relaxed for a few moments to allow himself to think through the problem of his princeling now gone mad with passion for this white servant of his former mistress. To Samuel, Pompey was throwing himself away on some white woman of no importance who was without clan, cattle, or lofty position in his African world of the Matabele, the very Chosen People of Heaven itself. He hated Violet for stealing Pompey away. No doubt Violet had done this through her feminine powers of seduction of this innocent. Samuel could not understand the horrible betrayal of the adopted son of his soul. And then the pain came on him. Samuel closed his eyes, massaged his chest, and let the pain and tightness abate.

As time ebbed away, the solution to his dilemma came to him. He would make no objection when told of Pompey's liaison. He would assume the mantle of total reason and support for Pompey's union with Violet with a smile. Pompey would then go through with helping him with his calculated revenge on Whitehouse. Then he would tend to the problem of the English girl when the time was right.

Samuel knew that the hungry sea could hold ever so much more than one more small woman in its great maw. Now the pain in his chest melted away altogether. Samuel reached for the water carafe and poured himself a tepid glass of the clear liquid. Then he quietly sipped, lay back on his bed, and composed himself.

CHAPTER XLVII

Violet had returned to the Forrester suite. She could hear no stirrings inside of Mrs. Forrester's room. There would be time for Violet to go to her own room and freshen up and change into a morning dress before Mrs. Forrester awoke. Within fifteen minutes she could finish her toilette and look as if she had slept the whole night through quite peacefully. As she looked at herself in her mirror on the wall of the parlor of the suite, Violet was quite pleased with the person she saw reflected there. She saw Mrs. Pompey Esmond. Pompey had almost decided to take the name Forrester as his own. It was, after all, the often custom of freed slaves to take their master's name. But Violet had said to him, "As my gift to you, let me give you a name that has never been tainted by the stain of slavery. I will give you the name of a vicar who was a friend of William Wilberforce whose ambition was to end slavery in all of the British Empire and then the world. He was my own dear grandfather, and had you known him, you would have found him to be the finest of God's creatures. Pompey had accepted this gift of a free man's identity. Born that day in Bishop Fitzpatrick's parlor were Mr. and Mrs. Pompey Esmond.

"I am as African as my mother made me Violet," said Pompey with all the pride and conviction that Samuel had inculcated in him," And our sons and daughters will also be Africans even if their skins be as white as the snows of England. And there is a chance that their skins may be black."

"I know that dearest, and we shall love them, and give them the best life we can," Violet replied as she smiled at her darkly handsome husband. I shall follow you to Africa if that is what you wish. No matter where my love shall go, I too will go. Isn't that what our marriage vows mean? We are slaves to none but our love for each other, and Pompey, I love you absolutely with my mind, my body, and my soul."

"Then there is no more to be said. I only hope that Samuel will understand all of this," said Pompey now deeply troubled by the prospect of telling his best friend, and the only father he had ever known, that he had taken a white woman as a wife.

"May I tell him myself dearest?" asked Violet.

Pompey stared at her with great discomfort. "Maybe we should tell him together, but we must do this at sea when the moment is right. Samuel's anger is a thing that is both deep and smoldering. His face is a mask. It is always hard to tell what he's really thinking. I must make him love you for what you are beyond color and race first. The white man has taken his life from him. Now we must get it back for him so that he can be whole again. Then he may see you as I do for the wonderful person you are."

When Violet had left with Pompey in the late afternoon on the day of her wedding, Mrs. Forrester was napping. Violet had left a note that she was going out to the shops for a few items and might be rather a long while. This is something that she had done before, and on those occasions when she had returned, she had found Mrs. Forrester asleep in her chair with a novel that she had been reading resting on her knee. This had become a habit with the mistress in the last few months. It was a pattern that her life had fallen into during the time that they had been in America.

Violet went to her room and locked her door. She wanted to be alone for a little while. She looked into the mirror of her dressing table and studied her own image reflected in the mirror with a new interest, because hers was not the face of a middle age lady's companion any longer. She took off her clothes to wash herself, and then it was her intention to change into something fit for that time of day. Then Violet looked into the mirror again to appraise her body that seemed so new and different to her now that she had shared it in communion with her husband Pompey. Her chestnut hair framed her heart shaped face. Her skin was smooth and reflected health and a strong constitution, and she saw that she was ever so seductive. At that thought, she smiled a deliciously less than innocent smile. Her lovely smooth brow and bright blue eyes mirrored the intellectual power she possessed. Her lovely mouth and lips, begging to be kissed, reflected her sensual side. Violet ran her hands over and under her perfectly formed breasts terminating in firm and erect nipples conical and excited in expectation of her next meeting with Pompey. Her figure was slim and curved to show to advantage the firm and lovely body which would be concealed under the dozens of yards of material that would make up the layers of clothing that encased her.

She thought of how much she had liked seeing that mountain of clothing lying on the large chair in Pompey's rooms as she stood before her husband naked and unprofaned by corsets and whalebone stays. She closed her eyes to recall the glories of her wedding night in the arms of the man she loved above all the inhabitants of the earth. This blissful moment of contemplation was broken by the sound of her name called out over and over again. She put on a wrapper and opened the door to see the agitated Mrs. Forrester standing in the parlor of the suite in her chemise and dressing gown.

"Where ever have you been child? I did not see you at all after you went away on to the tradesmen yesterday," said the troubled Mrs. Forrester.

"Oh Mrs. Forrester, you are quite right about this city. I got lost in the tangle of streets. I learned that the popular notion here is that the cows of the first settlers of Boston are responsible for the laying out of the streets of the city. I am sure that this is true.

That fellow who said that the streets of Boston were planned and set out by wandering cows must have known what he was talking about. When I returned from my adventure, you must have been resting in your room. I had such a headache after the afternoon's explorations that I am afraid that I helped myself to some of your soothing syrup and took to my bed. I fell into a deep sleep. I must confess that I did not come to myself until just an hour ago. I slept quite well. I am sorry that I did not wake you to tell you of this, but I was really quite distressed with the headache."

"Poor thing. I quite understand. I suffer so with my own headaches. I know when I take that medicine that I am dead to the world for as much as half the day. You must take only the very smallest amount when the headache comes or you might be dead to the world for the whole of the day. I wanted you to dine with me and Caroline last evening. Dear Mr. Balcome was in one of his tiresome meetings, and Caroline and I were meeting Tilly and Mr. Cabot for dinner here in the hotel. Now I know why there was no answer when I knocked at your door. I know that when I take the soothing syrup, I shall not awaken for at least eight hours of mortal time. You must be famished my dear. Shall I ring for someone to fetch us breakfast?"

"Oh no dear Mrs. Forrester. I think that I would like to go down to the dining room. I want to walk. I will admit that I am really quite peckish."

"I just love your little expressions my dear. They are just so English. But then it is because you are English I suppose. You do brighten things up so. I think that I will dress and join you if that is quite alright. I think that you are having a good effect on me child. You are making the English seem less and less impossible all the time."

"It is very kind of you to say that. I would be delighted with your company Mrs. Forrester. Breakfast is so much more pleasant when one has someone to talk to."

"Oh Violet, I have so much to tell you. We are quitting the city. Caroline and Tilly have arranged the leasing of a beautiful property in the countryside not far from their own country places in a little town called Wrentham. Now isn't that a funny English sounding name? I am told that there is such a place in East Anglia. Now isn't that the limit! It is a nice old place on the shore of a Lake Archer. It seems that it was built by a West Indian planter sometime in the nineties as a refuge from the heat of the American island tropics. It is said that during that awful Reign of Terror business in France that Talleyrand even visited that very planter there and was in residence for weeks in Caroline's house. Can you imagine that? Talleyrand! Right here in Massachusetts. I didn't even know that he existed until Caroline and Tilly told me all about him. His life was quite shocking. I don't even know if a young girl like yourself should even hear about such a wicked man. Would you believe that he began his political life as a bishop of the Catholic Church? It is such a delicious scandal. Then Napoleon made him marry! Can you just imagine that? I'll tell you all about it at breakfast dear. Now I'll dress."

Mrs. Forrester hurried into her room to dress. "She's a bit dotty but very dear in her own way," Violet said to herself. In her heart she thought that she would really miss her.

Samuel knocked on Pompey's door. A few moments later, Pompey opened it for him and Samuel entered and shut the door behind him.

"Where did you go with that English girl yesterday Pompey? And why were you away so long?"

"Why are you asking me this Samuel?"

"Because I saw the two of you on your bed naked and rutting like pigs yesterday."

"I don't think that I like the way you are saying that. You are as my father, and the person whom I have loved and respected above all the men of this earth, but I must ask you only to speak well of Violet. Will you sit and hear what I have to tell you?"

"I think that I must," replied the angry Samuel.

CHAPTER XLVIII

Samuel shut the door to Pompey's room as discreetly as if he were the doorman at a fine hotel. His fury was controlled but at the same time seething just below the surface of his dignified being. He planted himself on a tufted velvet covered black walnut framed chair whose delicacy contrasted with his huge well-muscled body. His face twitched. Yet his eyes focused on Pompey fixing him with a glacial stare. Samuel rubbed the numbness from his right cheek and calmed himself.

"Samuel, I think that I know what you saw. I love Violet, and she loves me. It is as simple as that. She knows that I am an African man and that I will live in Africa with you if you still wish it. She knows and understands this. She has no family or ties to her old world. Violet is very intelligent, and understands your mission. She is willing to help and will leave Mrs. Forrester tonight and ship with us to anywhere we have to go to achieve our ends. Violet respects and has admiration for you Samuel. She wants to be close to you, because she knows how I love and respect you. She wants your friendship and approval."

Samuel looked at Pompey, and in his mind he began to reflect on the thought that he had begun to entertain lately that his dream for Pompey may lack reality. But he could not admit doubt right now. Too much was at stake, and his immediate concern was the capture of Whitehouse. Other problems would have to wait their turn for permanent resolutions.

He gathered his wits and asked, "Do you think it wise to take up with this girl just because you have lust for her? You will need a wife, an African wife, not some foolish white girl who is infatuated with a pretty boy who has black blood in him. It will be difficult as it is to place you in my world because you are so damned white. With a highborn Matabele wife and my support, you might very well be able to enter my clan. I must admit even then it is not certain. What can this woman give you that will be of use in the African world I have proposed to give you? That world is far away from this white world, which sells us, and beats us, and uses us in anyway they want to? Do you think that you are anything special because your speech is fine, or because your manners are those of a white gentleman? Do you think that this white world gives a damn that you can speak French, Portuguese, and Spanish? Do you think that you will be esteemed because you are better read than these stupid sons of cotton planters? You saw the Forrester boys. They were nothing compared to you. They were deemed superior, because they were the sons of a white planter. I shaped you, not just as a tool of my revenge, but as the prince I will make of you in spite of that polluted white blood that flows in your veins not to mention whatever polluted African blood that might be in you as well. It is a very rare thing that any outsider could ever hope to become one of us. With that white girl by your side, any attempt will be impossible. That girl will bring you nothing but trouble."

"Samuel, Violet is my wife. And my white blood or African blood means nothing to her. She is in love with me for myself, for my character, and my love for her, and the fact that I respect her mind. She is the most open of women. She is a love with no room for hate. I can never even contemplate going on without her. She is my world now."

"She is white damn your eyes! Can't you understand anything I have been telling you boy! The Zulu are 'The People of Heaven'.

Can't you understand that in their eyes even you are the most unworthy and bastardized of men. I will have to fight like the Devil for you as it is."

"Violet has done nothing to harm you. Her color does not obsess me. It is her soul, her fire, and her spirit I love. Had she been a black woman with all of those qualities, I would love her with equal ardor. Color means nothing to me when it comes to loving and liking someone. It is the soul of a person that makes them what they are not the pigmentation of their skin. Have we learned nothing if not that? Violet likes and respects you. She loves me. Do not make me choose between the two of you, for if you do, I will have to migrate somewhere with her where we can live our lives as we want. I have not had your horrible experiences. Anna and you protected me from the fate suffered by most of my race. And believe me, I know that I am African, and I have pride in that. My passing for a white man was only to advance your plan. Is that not what you wanted? I am almost sorry for not sharing my feelings for Violet with you before this. I almost feel guilt that I did not share your pain of capture and enslavement. When you tell your story, I sometimes feel as though I was there with you in Africa in the good times and the bad. I love you Samuel as I love no other. You are my father, my friend, and my brother. I am committed to your revenge and the gaining of some measure of happiness for you in what will be the rest of your life. Do not smash all of our dreams over this. Violet has done us no harm and is willing to follow us to the ends of the earth. Now that is love. It is the love I'm blessed to have, and I will not be parted from it. Please see this thing through my eyes."

"Well Pompey, what can I say?" Samuel's voice was flat and devoid of feeling. "You and I will have to make the best of it. Pack your things now. I have settled our accounts with the hotel. Captain Beers is in Boston, and you and your lady must be on the ship by four. We will sail on the tide this evening together in company with Mr. Cabot's boat. By this time tomorrow or the next day, Mr. Starbuck will be our guest."

"You have moved fast Samuel."

"Somebody has to have their finger on things Pompey." Samuel smiled, "Well, let's be friends. If your woman is all you say she is, there should be no difficulty. In fact I shall embrace her as my own daughter."

CHAPTER XLIX

Back in her room in the Forrester suite, there was something troublesome intruding into Violet's thoughts. She really didn't know how to bring up her own long hidden secrets to Pompey. She caught her reflection in the mirror hanging over the mahogany table. She looked at herself again for a few moments, and then she looked away and thought of the secrets long entombed in her heart that had been revealed to her so long ago in a field of daffodils by her grandfather. It now seemed so long past since Violet and her Grandfather Esmond had been summering in a little cottage owned by one of her grandfather's friends John Godwin whom he had known during his days at Oxford. Like her much loved grandfather, Godwin only had wished to be a country vicar back in his own sleepy shire. He had made this wonderful place a little piece of heaven. He had made his cottage available to his old Oxford friend and his grandchild for the summer while he had gone on a grand tour of Europe. The old vicar was off retracing the travels of his own youth.

It was the most natural thing in the world that Violet's grandfather and Godwin had become friends and worshipers of the great Wilberforce. Wilberforce's crusade to end slavery in all of its grotesque forms was their great heart's desire. Their idealism like their faith was a constant reality to them. In this they had never flagged over the years of fighting the good fight until it was won in '33. This common fight had fused their friendship into the strong bond it was. The Rev. Mr. Godwin was her godfather, and now he was her benefactor as well with this gift of his lovely cottage for the use of her grandfather and herself in this special summer of discovery.

As Violet walked through the fields with her tiny hand in the huge and kindly hand of her Grandfather Esmond, she looked up at the blue sky with the clouds floating overhead. The smell of summer and of the fresh earth under their feet in the full noon of the sun warmed day filled her with a joy that she had never felt before in her short twelve years of life. At last they came to a small glade, and her grandfather said, "Let us rest here for a bit child. There are many things that I would like to tell you today about your grandmother and your own parents. These are things you may find difficult to understand, but they are things that you must know. The time has come that I cannot keep these secrets from you any longer in case I am forced to leave you someday sooner than I would care to. You should know your own history child."

"Are these things bad secrets Grandfather? Nobody has ever had very much to say about mother and father. Nobody would even tell me how they came to die. People would always shake their heads and tell me that someday I might understand and forgive them, but that was all any of you would say. As a small child, I found all of this quite confusing, and that somehow or other, I always blamed myself. But now that I am twelve, I am a child no longer, and I must face my life like a young woman."

"I know that my dear, and in no way were you ever at fault. They died for convention and lack of understanding," smiled her grandfather sadly, "But now that Mr. Wilberforce has died and his great life's work is done, it is fitting that you should know about yourself. When I was very young and had just come up from Oxford, I wanted a little adventure in my life before I settled down in some small village to take up a living as a vicar. Looking at me now, I'm sure that you would find that very hard to understand. Nevertheless, I did seek adventure and applied to my bishop to send me out to Jamaica. Permission and support was granted by His Grace, and I sailed off to that exotic island so far away from England that it seemed to smack of an adventure in a place of exciting things like the pirates that I had read so much about in books as a boy. I had been sent out to a small village outside of Georgetown where there was a pretty little church.

That church was whitewashed and looked as if it could have sat in the middle of any pleasant village in the midlands. It was there that I met a beautiful girl who came to the services every Sunday with her family. She was a pert little thing with a lovely heart shaped face and blue eyes. Her hair was the color of dark honey. She wore it in ringlets. I sought to know her, and eventually we met, and we fell in love with one another. This beautiful girl was your own sweet grandmother."

"Was she very beautiful?"

"Yes my darling. She was very beautiful in her face and more importantly, she was beautiful in her soul and heart where beauty really is most important."

"Was her mother also beautiful in the same way grandfather? You used to tell me so," Violet dreamily asked with a faraway look in her eyes.

"Yes she too was also most beautiful even when she was older. She was the daughter of a staff officer to the royal governor himself, and her mother, your great great grandmother, was one of the domestics working in the governor's household."

"So my great grandmother's mother was a servant? The young staff officer and she got married just the same?" Violet half stated and half asked.

"You are a very smart little girl Violet. I am sure that you know that an officer and a gentleman, and a distant cousin to the royal family at that, could never marry a house servant. He most especially could not marry this house servant, even if she were the most beautiful woman on the island, because you see she was also a slave."

"She was a slave, a white slave? How could that be?" asked the wide-eyed Violet.

"My darling, that was just it. She was not white. She was a black slave. She was released from her slavery to hide the disgrace of that unfortunate union with a young officer, which was to result in your grandmother's birth. That poor girl moved back to her own village where her people had come from. They were now freemen. Their master had freed all of his slaves in his will and had bestowed a small settlement on each of them. Your great great grandmother had been sent where she could be with her own kind in their new homes. It was there that your great grandmother was born," replied the old man.

"That was a wicked thing to do to that poor woman leaving her to fend for herself without the father of her baby. What became of her?" asked Violet with her eyes filling with tears.

"Your great great grandmother lived with her people. Then she married a white man with a small piggery on the outside of the town. They sold meat and tallow. In a small way they had a good life. Within her class, a freeman who owns a piggery is a person of consequence."

"What became of the baby?" asked Violet.

"She was a lovely little girl. Her parents educated her and dressed her well. When she was about sixteen or so, she was married to the son of a small plantation owner because she had a small fortune from her father, and the plantation owner was near destitution."

"Was he a free slave too?" asked Violet.

"No my dear. He was a young white man who was so impressed by your great grandmother's beauty that he wed her knowing that her mother was a black woman, but he wanted nothing to do with her people. He wanted to separate himself from all of that business which he found to be so painful. She asserted herself, however, and told him that she insisted on the right to visit her people whenever she chose to do so or there would be no marriage. They separated for a fortnight, but then he came back to her and agreed," replied the old man. "His love for her overcame his prejudice and fear of discovery. She and the planter had a daughter. That daughter was your grandmother."

"Then you came to know my grandmother?" Violet had next asked.

"I was vicar in the little village, and I saw her at services. I extended the hand of friendship to the family and was invited to Sunday dinner at their home. One thing led to another, and in time, we fell in love. We were betrothed, and we eventually married. Your grandmother and I were very much in love with each other. After a few years, she told me of the secret. At first, I was quite taken aback, because I was surprised. Her being part Black meant little to me. A person's color does not matter. It is what's in their heart that does. And in her heart your grandmother was a beauty. As time passed I got used to the idea. I had followed Wilberforce since the 90's, and now I understood better than he about the depths of human relationships and the unimportance of race when it comes to really important things like being in love with just the right person. In time, there came a child. She was your mother born to us there in Jamaica. Her mother, your very own grandmother, looked on her with a beatific smile and named her Rose, then my darling wife, your grandmother, died of complications shortly after childbirth. Darling girl, I wish you could have known her. You would have loved her so much. I was very sad and asked my bishop to return me to England. We, that is to say my beautiful little daughter, who was your very own mother and I, came to Henley where I took up my new living as a vicar of the little church. Oh Violet, your mother grew to be such a beauty. I even had a portrait miniature done of her. I carry it still, and now I would like you to have it to wear close to your heart always."

With that the old man removed the gold-framed miniature portrait from around his neck along with its gold chain and gave it to his granddaughter. Violet took it from him and stared into the face of a young and very pretty woman of about eighteen. She looked up into the face of her Grandfather Esmond and said, "My mother was really very beautiful. This is truly my mother. I think that I remember her a little bit. And there was a handsome man. Was he my father?" Violet had asked open eyed.

The old man had looked sadly down into Violet's little upturned face and said, "Every respectable son of the shire was in pursuit of your mother in those days. Even though she was only the daughter of a poor country vicar with a very poor living indeed, she was seen as a great prize for her grace and learning as well as her beauty. Your mother had real beauty of soul, and this wonderful quality was shown even in her eyes. Then along came your father, the son of a country squire and a baronet, Sir William Hartington. Sir William was the younger son of a marquis who was himself a son of a duke. The young nobleman courted her in a very proper fashion. After a decent period of time, he asked for her hand in marriage. The wedding was a small one. Your father's parents were not well pleased by the match, but your mother and father were quite happy. Then you were born to a great deal of rejoicing, and all was well. In three year's time, your mother was again with child. She was happy in anticipation of the birth. Much fuss was made about the coming event. Even Sir William, your Grandfather Hartington, had paid your mother a visit and had held you on his knee. He loved you at first sight, and he showed some kinder attention to this eventful second birth, which was to come to your mother. This child was very active in your mother's womb. She declared that she knew that it was to be a boy. An old woman came from the village. She was said to be able to tell the sex of a child before birth by swinging a gold ring over the belly of the expectant mother. The old woman came to the house and did this thing with her ring. Then after the swinging of the ring had begun, she suddenly stopped, recoiled in horror and ran from the room. When we caught up to her, all she said was that the child would be a boy and was going to be born healthy.

When she was pressed to say more, she just took the crown from you father's hand and ran off saying that she could not speak of the vision that she had seen. We all laughed of course. For us this whole thing had been but a lark. I was pleased to anticipate a healthy grandchild."

"Are you telling me that I have a brother or sister grandfather? Where have they been all of these years?" asked the wide-eyed Violet. The old man's eyes filled with tears.

"They are dead, all dead. Someday I will tell you about it."

"I want to know now grandfather. I have the right to know what everybody around me seems to know," Violet had replied resolutely. The old man drew himself up for the ordeal.

"You had a brother born to your mother on a dark and stormy night. You see the old woman was right about it being a boy. Your father had paced the floor for an entire day awaiting the birth. Then your brother was born, and he was as black as ebony. Your father went mad. He ordered everyone out of the house including the servants. You were brought to the vicarage by your nurse during your mother's confinement. This was an act of divine providence, and you have remained with me ever since as the treasure of my heart."

"And then what happened grandfather? What became of my father, mother, and brother?" asked the wide-eyed child.

"You had been sent away to stay with me at the vicarage during your mother's lying-in which was a great act of God's mercy as I have just told you. Your poor father went quite mad when he saw that your brother was as black as black could be. Your father had never been told anything of the family history you see. He raved and drank a great deal after he had ordered everyone out of the house, and by midnight, he was filled with a horrible resolve. He went into your mother's room with a brace of pistols and shot both her and the baby dead. Then he reloaded one of his pistols and shot himself. Your grandfather, Sir William, has been supporting us ever since on the condition that the truth of this happening never be told. He never wanted to see you again.

It is the terrible regret of my life that I never told your mother anything of her own history. I am sure that was the cause of all of the trouble she had to endure. I vowed that I would never allow you to live in ignorance of your own past. Now at least you can live your life, knowing what risks you have to face."

Violet reflected on these circumstances as she looked once again into the mirror. She knew in her heart that Pompey would not care if she were a child of mixed race. He might even like it she thought. But for the present, she was content to let the old ghosts lie dormant. "But I must tell him," she said to her reflection in the mirror. "I must tell him someday."

Then her heart was filled once again with longing for her little family, which she never really had a chance to know. It seemed so unfair that her family was snuffed out one dark night over unreasoning hate. She tried to revive the memory of her mother and even the face of the man who had been her father. She reclined on her bed with her head on her pillow sobbing quietly for her mother and the brother she had never known. This loss, that she had felt since she was twelve years old for her mother and brother, seemed to overwhelm her in the moment of her complete joy in Pompey. "How I would have loved him," she whispered into her pillow. "I wish my brother were with me today to share my joy."

Shortly thereafter her grandfather fell into his final illness. On his deathbed, he imparted one last piece of information. He turned to her with the last of his energy and said, "My dearest Violet, remember that your name is Hartington, and you must never forget that. Your father loved you before he went mad. Do not hate him. For in hating him you will hate yourself for the best part of him that is you. Remember that the part of him that is you was loving, and the part of him that was hate is gone. Do not be afraid to love, for love is God's gift to us. I have forgiven him long ago, and now so must you."

Violet pulled herself together. She washed and dressed herself in travelling clothes. Her great adventure would begin this day, and she was Mrs. Pompey Esmond.

CHAPTER L

Starbuck had stared at the ceiling of his room for the last three weeks contemplating the good fortune that his manservant Maycock enjoyed in the possession of his wife. Starbuck had washed and dressed each day with the help of this man's good life-mate. Each day his little walks had expanded in their scope. The doctor had marveled at his progress. Starbuck's mood also grew darker with each passing day as his strength grew greater. He rested in his room a great deal of the time. He lay on his bed frequently with the good lady Mrs. Maycock rocking in the old rocking chair by the side of his bed reading to him. Starbuck did not let on to anyone that to a great degree his strength had returned. When nobody was in his room, he would pace in his carpet slippers. The feelings of unrest mounted in him. His inactivity made him restless. At the first sound of the approach of Mrs. Maycock, Starbuck would jump back onto his bed and assume a position of rest. Then he would close his eyes, and wait until the door gently opened and Mrs. Maycock would enter. Starbuck would then feign awaking with a smile as she entered with a book to read to him.

Mrs. Maycock had been reading Starbuck some of the newer novels available on the island. She had just finished *Dombey and Son* and *David Copperfield.* Starbuck was not too taken with sympathy for the problems of the title character of the second book, nor did he think that Copperfield's life was all that difficult. In the end, didn't Copperfield get both the girls, in turn, and a fine career, as well as the prospect of inheriting the wealth of his great aunt Betsy Trotwood? So what did he have to cry about? Now the good Mrs. Maycock was reading *Ivanhoe* to him. He felt sympathy for the Knight Templar, Briande Bois-Guilbert, who lusted for the daughter of the Jewish moneylender, Isaac of York. Starbuck knew what it was like to lust after a woman that he could not have. He began to fix his sympathies on the character of Rebecca and her rejected Knight lover. This made the joy of hearing the story read aloud greater. It also reminded him of his own mother reading to him at bedtime so long ago and when he was a boy.

During the time that Mrs. Maycock had been caring for him, a transformation had been going on in Starbuck's mind. The transformation had been in his perception of his housekeeper. At first she reminded him of his mother, in an idealized form, then as something more. He began to see wonderful qualities beneath the matronly forty-year-old woman's appearance. Her face became softer and her voice sweeter. He began to wonder what would happen if something happened to Mr. Maycock. Would Mrs. Maycock turn to him for sympathy? The next question to cross his mind was how Mr. Maycock could come to fatal harm. As the days passed, the question became an obsession demanding a solution.

Starbuck became, in fact, the Templar of the Scott novel coveting his servant's wife just as the Templar Knight coveted the moneylender's daughter, the beautiful dark haired beauty Rebecca. A plan to remove the servant from his path grew in Starbuck's mind just as he had evolved the plan to kill Weston and the three New Yorkers. Killing one good man could not be nearly as hard as killing four bad ones he thought. He drifted off into his own inner world, thinking up schemes to rid himself of the husband of the woman he had come to love. Starbuck remembered his *Bible* lessons. He recalled that King David had set his cap for a woman he had seen from his palace window. Then the king contrived to have her husband placed in the forefront of battle. That man was killed, and David got the woman that he had lusted after.

There was a lesson there. Would it be a walk on the headlands perhaps? Here it would look like a fellow, not familiar with the landscape, might wander too near the edge of the headlands cliffs where the earth might give way under his weight. In that case, a man would be pitched down onto the rocks below where he could crush his head against a stone, and that would be an end to it. Such accidents were not out of the ordinary after all. And after all, Maycock was not an islander was he? What would he know of the treacherous nature of its topography? Starbuck knew that he could maneuver the trusting Maycock to walk up on the headlands, and if for some reason Maycock fell as the result of getting too close to the edge, who would be the wiser. Should Maycock survive the fall, a rock applied to his head with some force would have the same effect. Starbuck could then take his time coming back to the house claiming that his condition prevented his swifter return or his saving of the ever-faithful Mr. Maycock. This would give the rising tide a chance to wash away any evidence of his interference with nature should there be a need on his part to assist in the fatal departure of the hapless Mr. Maycock. Starbuck smiled broadly now as his plan gelled inside of his imagination.

"Well Mr. Starbuck, did you enjoy that reading," asked Mrs. Maycock observing the smile on her patient's face.

"I thank you Mrs. Maycock. I am getting more pleasure out of that book than you will ever know. You are too kind, and I appreciate it. In fact, I appreciate all the nice things that you do for me."

"I thank you for that Mr. Starbuck, but I'm afraid that we will have to stop now. I must put supper on. It's good to see you smile after all this time. I don't know when I saw you smile last. You are rather handsome when you smile in a sort of rugged way with your whiskers and nice white teeth. Your smile is really wonderful.

You really don't smile often enough Mr. Starbuck. Oh, just listen to me. Such stuff and nonsense. Please forgive me. I have become such a rattlebrained old woman."

"Not so old I think. Rather pretty in fact."

"Oh Mr. Starbuck! I am ever so glad that you are feeling better. The things you say," said the woman with a laugh, "You do a body good with your sassy talk. Would you like me to read some more to you this evening before bed time?"

"I might at that. Maybe after I take a little walk before nightfall. Would you be so kind as to send Mr. Maycock to see me about it? He can see to it that I don't fall on my foolish but handsome old pigskin of a face should he be free to take my poor old hulk out for a walk."

"Now Mr. Starbuck, you are making fun of a silly old country woman now."

"I told you Mrs. Maycock, not old, and pretty to boot."

"I think that I better send Mr. Maycock up before you turn my foolish head with your devilish pretty talk." Just before she exited the door, she turned to Starbuck once more. "I have to think that there must be at least a dozen pretty women on this island who would want to marry you if you only smiled more and opened yourself up to the idea. You are a real charmer when the feeling takes you in that direction. Wasn't there a lady who used to bring you pies?"

"Oh that one! Mrs. Maycock, perish the thought. My stomach will sour before I can even have my supper if I think about her. She has already been to the parson three times with marrying, besides, I think that she has trapped the deacon in her pastry-baited snare this time around. She will have to be content with him. Besides, I think that it is bad luck to even entertain the thought of making a marriage with a woman who has buried three husbands in one lifetime."

"You are wicked Mr. Starbuck. Still you deserve to be as happy as I am with my dear Mr. Maycock. He may not look like it to the rest of the world, but he is my Ivanhoe in glittering armor.

Oh my, what am I saying now! Please don't tell him I said any such foolish thing. He'll think that I'm daft and gone off to my second childhood. Do keep that handsome smile Mr. Starbuck, and I'll send Mr. Maycock right up to you."

Away she went down the back stairs into the kitchen to fetch Mr. Maycock and see to dinner. Starbuck was not smiling now. Now he knew that if Maycock should be shuffled off this mortal world, in time Mrs. Maycock could very well be his. He determined to rid himself of this in-house rival this very night before he could have a chance to soften in his resolve and change his mind.

Starbuck smiled again. "She thinks me charming and handsome when I smile. If I can win you my love, I'll smile to the end of my days."

CHAPTER LI

It was decided that Captain Beers and his ship would not stay behind in port in Boston after all, but would follow the smaller vessel to Nantucket, which would be manned by Mr. Cabot and the abolitionists who were familiar with these waters. Beers would stand three miles out to sea within sight of the smaller craft, which would work further inshore, and nearer the beach in case of any trouble.

Captain Beers paced the deck with his arms folded behind him and scanned the clear sky ever watchful of changes in the weather. His sails billowed, but he ordered the topsails taken in. Now his ship seemed to labor as she slowed to seven knots. He followed the Yankee schooner very smartly. He liked Cabot's trim little craft, which could operate nicely in a small cove while his ship stood out to deeper waters. He had rounded the Cape, where more than several hundred ships had foundered since old Captain Bartholomew Gosnold first sailed those waters in 1602. Few miles separated that island from the mainland, but that ocean was a barrier that isolated the island culture. To many an islander the mainland might have been as far away as China and almost as exotic. As isolated as the place was, the men of Nantucket had sailed the world both in trade and in the whaling fishery. Yet in many respects those Nantucket men, being isolated from the world in which they traveled on those little ships, in reality never really left home. The majority of these ships were less than a hundred and twenty-five feet long. Wherever they sailed, they brought Nantucket with them. There were often Indians, Africans, Lascars, as well as assorted Europeans mixed in with the ship's crew, but for the most part a whaler's crew was still mostly Nantucketers. They were immune to the culture of the outside world for the most part.

Samuel strolled up to Beers. The sound of his footsteps on the well scrubbed and oiled teak decking alerted the captain to Samuel being behind him. "Well Captain, when do you think that we will make landfall?"

"We should raise the place an hour before sunset, and then we'll work our way offshore. Then you will transfer to the yacht and sail into the cove you showed me on the chart. We'll be riding at anchor before sunset. I doubt if anyone will give us much notice. We are clearly not a whaler, so there's not a dime of mortal island money invested in us to cause undo excitement on shore," replied Captain Beers.

"There was a full moon last night. There should be plenty of light to do our job. Those boys provided by Garrison's people know their business if I'm not mistaken. Look how well they handle their craft. You would hardly think that a refined man like our Rev. Balcome would be such a good deck hand. We can launch a long boat from the Cabot schooner and land quite nicely. Everything should go quite quickly, and we should have no trouble landing and getting our man off the island and stowed aboard ship," said Samuel in anticipation of his meeting with Starbuck.

"That was a strange yarn in the London press about him being rescued at sea. The last man left alive from a foundered merchant ship, and being picked up so soon without so much as a floating plank to mark a sinking. Ships just don't founder without leaving something floating," replied Captain Beers.

"That yarn was spun to bury a man who is not dead Captain

Beers. Captain Whitehouse is still at his filthy slave trading, and Mr. Starbuck is going to take us to him no matter the cost or where on this earth he may be. I will have Whitehouse. I will make him pay for the life he robbed from me and from so many others. I will make him pay for those poor souls he killed. He robbed whole clans of their future. He took my best years from me, because he loved gold. I will find him and give him gold enough to fill his mouth and stop his breath. If it is gold he wants, then it is gold he will have."

"I was surprised to see that your friend Pompey had taken a wife in Boston. Now that was rather sudden. I will say that she is very striking and seems to have more than a bit of fine spirit. In a way she reminds me of my sister."

"That is what youth is like today. Everything for them has got to be now. The young do not know how to bide their time. They grab what they think they want without really thinking too much about the consequences. We'll see how it all shakes out in the end. The only thing that matters now is getting this creature Whitehouse. I have lived for this and have anticipated the exact moment of his being taken most of my life. I cannot be a free man until the stain of his dishonoring of me is washed away with his blood. My people, my ancestors, and my honor cannot be satisfied without this revenge. I cannot rest as a whole man until this special deed is done."

"If I were taken as you were from my home and made a slave, I suppose I would feel as you do. I would want the blood of that man who placed me in bondage and robbed me of my world on my sword point. Exactly what are you going to do with Whitehouse when you capture him?"

"There is an old proverb in my people's tradition. It goes like this, 'Before you sell the lion's skin, it is well to first hunt and kill the lion.' Don't you think it sound advice?"

"I can see why Pompey respects you so and follows you. You have real wisdom Samuel. I'll do all I can to help you in the hunt for the rogue lion."

"That will begin shortly with the hunt and seizure of his jackal."

"Well, we'll be at Nantucket before you know it. Have you got your plan of attack together?"

"It is a simple plan Captain. Pompey and myself will just march up to Starbuck's house. I am sure that when faced with the possibility of having his guts spilled onto his carpet or the alternative of seeking a sea change for the benefit of his continued good health, he will see the wisdom of taking a voyage with us. If he gives me Whitehouse, I shall pay for his return passage in a first class cabin on the finest ship in the neighborhood of the closest port and gold besides. I have no real interest in Starbuck. I never felt that he was more than merely there on the slaver to make money. I may hate him for selling his soul to that Devil Whitehouse in the slave trade, but he was only a part of Whitehouse's evil. I have a score to settle with the Portuguese in Mozambique and the Mashona, but they will have to wait their turn for my justice. Now if you will excuse me Captain Beers, I have business below."

"I just thank God that I was never tempted by the slave trade, and that I had a good sister who provided for me while I was growing up almost an orphan. I was allowed to study navigation, and I found places on good ships. It's not been an easy life, but it's not been slavery either. I've always wanted to be a ship's Captain before I was twenty-five, and I was. It will be a pleasure to help you in any way I can Samuel. Sally thinks well of both you and Pompey. I can say that her opinion of most of the people of Georgia is not so high, and your success means a great deal to her."

Samuel smiled, tipped his hat to the Captain, and went below. Now he had to meet with Pompey to finalize the preparations for their visit to the island. He knew that Miss Sally had her own reasons for wanting Whitehouse to pay for Forrester's death. He stopped for a moment and pondered, wondering what she would think if she knew that Whitehouse had merely beaten him to the punch by killing Forrester almost by accident before he could do the thing himself. Samuel had not hated James Forrester. In fact, he was almost fond of him, but to take over the whole plantation, he had needed Forrester to have that fatal accident. As weak as the master had been, Samuel knew that James Forrester would not stand by and allow him to usurp power on the plantation. On that long ago night of Forrester's murder, Whitehouse's intervention had been a gift in a way. It had saved him from staining his hands with the blood of James Forrester who was almost a friend. He smiled to himself. His hunter's instinct served him well. All he had to do now was deal with Starbuck, capture Whitehouse, and deal, at some point with the inconvenient Violet. That would take real delicacy. Pompey was besotted with her. His reaction to her loss overboard on the first stormy night of the voyage would be one of real pain when it was discovered that the girl had indeed fallen overboard. Nevertheless it had to be done. On this point Samuel was resolved. No mere woman, and a pale thin white one at that, could come between him and the successful completion of his master plan.

Samuel had come a long way since his capture by the Mashona so long ago. He raged inside of his mind again when he thought of it. A Mashona placing hands on a member of the tribe of The Chosen of Heaven, the very Children of Heaven, was the ultimate disgrace. Violet was the only real threat remaining to his enterprise, and he could take care of that when the right set of circumstances presented themselves. In less than a year's time, he would be back with his own people and restored to his proper place of honor. The chest of gold under his berth meant nothing to him, nor did the vast amount of cash he had on deposit in the Bank of England. It was just a tool. Now, there was much to do, and he knew that he better get about it. He knocked on the door of Pompey's stateroom. The door opened, and Samuel looked down and smiled warmly, "Ah Violet my dear, is my good friend Pompey in?"

"Yes Samuel, he is here. Come in. The others are here as well," she replied as she opened the door wider.

"Well gentlemen," the big man said, "We might as well go over our plan one more time. Pompey and I will go into the town and to the Starbuck house. Mr. Cabot and Rev. Balcome, you and your four friends will remain with the long boat ready to take us back to your boat with Starbuck. And that gentlemen is that, until we transfer Starbuck from the yacht to the ship. I am pleased that we have Captain Beers' vessel here not far from shore. The good Captain Beers assured me that his ship could meet us and leave these waters quickly."

"That seems simple enough. I can't tell you how pleased I am that we can do something for the cause and strike a real blow for the abolitionist movement. My wife will be amused by your sudden elopement Violet, if I may still address you familiar, and I cannot wait to see my dear mother-in-law's reaction to it I must confess. I wish that I could have a photograph of her face at the time of my telling her, but I am afraid that she could not hold the pose long enough to get a good exposure. I tell you Pompey, you are a lucky fellow. Violet is a capital girl, and I say well done. Were I not so happily wed myself to my dear Tilly, and with a little one on the way, I would envy you. Such times we live in! It does give one hope for the future," said Reverend Balcome.

"Violet and I thank you for that Mr. Balcome. We did not wish to hurt Mrs. Forrester, but I agree with you, it will give her a start, but then I am sure that the arrival of two grandchildren will be a distraction for her. Mrs. Forrester really is not a bad sort for a member of her class."

"I want you to tell Mrs. Forrester something for me if you would be so kind Mr. Cabot and Mr. Balcome," said Violet. "Tell her that I shall miss her very much, and I know how much I owe her for all of the kindnesses that she has shown me. And I want you to give her this little gold locket. I had my likeness taken in Boston and placed in it. It is a gift for her to remember me by. Tell her that someday I hope that she will come to England in the springtime and stay with my husband and I. Tell her that it would give both of us great pleasure if she would."

"I am really going to get great pleasure from doing you this service. I think that I will try to get a photo-grapher there to make an image of this moment. I am sure that this will soften the blow of your loss to her a bit Violet, with pardon, Mrs. Pompey Esmond," replied Balcome.

"Samuel, if that is all, we had better get about our business on our boat," said Balcome.

"See you topside then," said Cabot cheerfully as he and the others exited the cabin in anticipation of an adventure that involved something other than stocks and bonds. Then he prepared to return to his own vessel with Samuel and Pompey.

Pompey's excitement was obvious as he crossed to Samuel and hugged him. "It will not be long now my dearest friend and father. Then our real adventure begins. I would not be anywhere but here with you now Samuel. These next months truly belong to us, and we will be the sword of justice to bring this son of the Devil to book for his crimes against you and all of our people."

Samuel did not speak as he returned Pompey's embrace and looked over the young man's shoulder to Violet with a smile on his lips that was not reflected in his eyes. This time there was no pain in his chest.

CHAPTER LII

Starbuck looked out over the sea leaning heavily on his cane. The receding sun played on the water. "Red sky at night, sailor's delight. Red sky in the morning, sailor take warning," said Starbuck.

"That is pure truth Mr. Starbuck sir. With such a red sun, the weather is sure to be fine tomorrow. I have never seen it to fail. No sir, never have. When the sun comes up red in the morning, you know that there is going to be a big blow before the day is done."

"I guess that you don't have to be island born to know that, eh Maycock?" laughed Starbuck good-naturedly. Starbuck's laughter was honest in its tone, but his eyes narrowed without a hint of friendship or joy in them. In the growing twilight, Maycock could not really see Starbuck's eyes, nor was he looking for any sign of malice in Starbuck who had treated both himself and his wife so handsomely. Starbuck wandered off the path toward the edge of the cliff overlooking the beach. "Take care there Mr. Starbuck. That edge may give way there. That drop has got to be a good thirty feet or more onto the rocks below."

"I don't plan on taking a leap off the edge onto those barnacle encrusted rocks Maycock. The doc just patched me up, and he would be mad as Hell if I undid all of his fine stitching. Could you see your way clear to come up here and take my arm? I'm feeling just a bit faint all of a sudden." With that he fell, and Maycock rushed up to his side and began to bend over him to help him to his feet.

"I wouldn't do that if I were you," came a voice out of nowhere, "Get away from that old Devil, and do it now!"

Maycock jumped back at the command. The voice came on again.

"Don't you see what he has in his hand? That is a rock in his right hand all ready to smash your foolish and trusting head in no doubt my friend," said Samuel.

"And I'll do it yet you squid. Then I'll take care of you!" shouted Starbuck as he bounded to his feet and struck out at Maycock who stumbled back avoiding what would have been a fatal blow.

Starbuck fell and struggled to get up again. By the time he had regained his feet, Maycock had armed himself with a rail from a fence located by the landward side of the road. Starbuck roared like a bull and charged his servant. Maycock stepped aside in time and fetched him a glancing blow on the head with the rail, which seemed to stun the big man. Pompey and Samuel raced up the dune as fast as the sand would allow them to move. By now, Starbuck was once again on his feet with blood streaming down his face and a sailor's clasp knife opened and in his hand ready to attack Maycock once again. Pompey gained the road and came up on Starbuck from the side.

"Drop the knife Mr. Starbuck, and leave this man alone," ordered Pompey.

"And what are you going to do about it with that cane?" bellowed Starbuck. "I'll gut you like a mullet, and then I'll finish off this cod."

"That cane my friend has its own merits as you will discover Mr. Starbuck. That man must have something that you want very badly. Pray what might it be?" asked Samuel.

"It's none of your damned business, but it won't matter now

that you are all dead men. I want his woman. With him gone, I think that she would have me in time. But, I've got no time for this foolishness."

With that, Starbuck launched himself at Pompey who, in turn, side stepped and turned with his blade in hand dealing Starbuck a blow smartly on his backside which forced the big man to lose his balance and fall onto the clam shell strewn path. In an instant, Pompey was standing over the man with his boot planted in the small of Starbuck's back and with the tip of his sword at the base of the prostrate man's skull. "Let the knife go or you will force me to cut your wind pipe from the back of your neck."

Starbuck hesitated, and Pompey made a shallow token cut to show his resolve. Starbuck dropped his blade, and Pompey turned to Maycock saying, "You, pick up the knife, and take care that he does not try to bite you. He might be mad."

Maycock, holding the rail like a club, gingerly approached Starbuck and swept up the knife. Then he moved back.

"Thank you mister. I don't know what's going on, but I thank you all the same." said Maycock with his voice shaking with rage. "How could you even think of doing this Mr. Starbuck? We have been so good to you. We even saved your life. I just cannot imagine what you were thinking! I don't think that I could tell Mrs. Maycock what you intended. She is that fond of you she is."

"I would guess that this fellow has taken a fancy to your wife and intended to kill you by smashing in your head and tossing you over that cliff onto the rocks below. It would have looked like a convincing accident. I would not be a bit surprised to learn that this fellow has done this sort of thing before. I'm glad that we happened along before you ended up down there on the rocks with the rising tide coming in," said Pompey.

"Not so happy as I am mister," said Maycock as the whole truth of the matter began to dawn on him. "Mister, if you don't mind, I think I must sit for a spell. I really don't feel so good. I just can't think of my wife at the mercy of this man."

"Here have some of this," said Samuel who offered Maycock some brandy from his flask.

"Who are you?" asked Maycock looking at Samuel standing over him.

"I am an old friend of Mr. Starbuck there. I hope you don't mind, but we are going to take him with us on a little trip. He might be gone for as long as a year or forever, that is, if he is less than cooperative."

"Take him and be happy. Will he be coming back anytime sooner than that really?" asked Maycock.

"No, Mr. Starbuck is going to take up residence somewhere far from this place for at least a year. We met your wife Mr. Maycock. She is a fine woman. She deserves a fine home. Now I will make you a gift of Mr. Starbuck's residence for the next year's time. If anyone should ask for him, just say that he has gone to call on old friends in South America and may not be back, because he might decide to retire there and wants you and your wife to stay on and see after the property for him. Will that be a hardship for you and your good wife Mr. Maycock?"

"Not after what he tried to do to us. No sir. I think that he owes us that."

"Can you hold your tongue and tell nobody what has happened here?" asked Samuel.

Looking at Starbuck with rage in his eyes, Maycock replied, "Not even Mrs. Maycock will ever know. I'll have to concoct one Hell of a yarn for her to explain Mr. Starbuck's sudden disappearance, but I've had to spin yarns before. Mr. Starbuck has been up to some strange comings and goings lately. The rest of the island, as far as that goes, won't give a tinker's dam about whether he's here or not. I thank the both of you for my life. Now I think I will be going." Turning after a few steps, Maycock walked back and looked down at Starbuck whose hands were now tied behind his back. "You know Mr. Starbuck, my wife and me really liked you. We thought a great deal of good about you. It is a shame that you turned on me like that. Hell man, I saved your life. It is a real shame. It really is." And with that he walked away never looking back.

"Did Whitehouse do this? Did that filthy bastard do this to me, or is it the New York crowd?" asked Starbuck. "Who the Hell do you fellows work for?"

As Pompey gagged him, he said, "You are a real popular fellow Mr. Starbuck. Why ever do so many people want to see you?"

CHAPTER LIII

Starbuck was hidden in the dunes until well after nightfall. Long after the sun disappeared in the west, Samuel and Pompe lifted the man onto his feet. Samuel growled into Starbuck's ear, "Come along with us real nicely, and you might get to live another day or two."

Unspeaking, the big man nodded. Samuel put a sack over Starbuck's head, and the trio made their way back to the cove where Rev. Balcome, Mr. Cabot, and his crew waited with their boat. Captain Beers had brought his ship up to the smaller vessel under the cover of darkness. Samuel had decided that it would be best to bring Beer's ship closer to shore and deposit Starbuck directly into his cabin on the ship rather than place him on the smaller craft. Samuel thought that transferring the big man from one vessel to the other might not go unnoticed either at sea or in Boston Harbor. Cabot agreed with the sentiment, "I hate to pay for the same real estate twice."

As Pompey and Samuel made their way down to the beach while half carrying and half dragging the unprotesting Starbuck, the big sailor had resigned himself to whatever fate had in store. He decided to wait for things to shake out on their own and then make the best deal he could with whoever had seized him. By making things easier for his captors, he might convince them of a real willingness to cooperate with them. He knew that whoever it was who had him, took him because he must have some information they wanted. Starbuck knew that these well-spoken men were not the New Yorkers unless the people from Five Points had decided to use professional agents to take him. As he was pondering his fate, the hooded Starbuck heard a voice say, "This is the man then?"

In reply, Pompey answered the Captain, "It is he sir."

The Captain nodded to his mate and simply said, "Secure him below." The mate and two seamen took the hooded man below and tossed him onto a bunk in a small cabin and locked the door behind them. Starbuck was left alone, still hooded, and bound on the bunk. For the first time in a very long while, Starbuck felt profound fear. For the first time in a long time, he was in a position of total helplessness where he had no control over his safety. Starbuck's returning strength was of no use to him now. He was now in the grip of panic. Then his reason kicked in. By the force of his will, he calmed himself, and began to assess his situation. Starbuck reasoned that either the Five Points people or Whitehouse wanted him for some reason. As he thought about it during the hours that followed, he could find no reason for Whitehouse to go to so much trouble to get at him. He doubted if his old chief even knew how much he hated him. Then he thought about the New York thugs. He knew that they would have had somebody with them who would have started hammering him right away with both questions and fists. He was convinced that his first thoughts were right. These were not New Yorkers.

Doing things quickly was what they were all about. The Five Points crowd were hardly so refined as to give somebody a nice cabin and clean bunk to rest on. In fact, his olfactory senses informed Starbuck that this was a very clean ship. His nose reported this fact back to him as he assessed just what was around him. He could smell the sea, the lye soap used to holystone the decks, the hemp lines, the canvass, the tar, and all the other smells of a clean well run sailing ship. He could also smell the linseed oil used on the decking. From the smells, he knew that this ship was no slaver, whaling ship, or fishing vessel. From the feel of the ship, he could tell that she was about five hundred tons at least. She was a substantial sea going affair and powered by sail alone. There was no hint of coal or the smell of lubricating oil. Starbuck knew his oils as well as an oenophile knows his wines.

Now that he guessed who had not taken him, he could not reason out who had. He could have kicked himself in the arse for his stupid and ill-considered move on Maycock. He already regretted it. He felt both foolish and guilty. Maycock most likely would have fought to prevent his capture by these strangers out of sheer and unearned loyalty to Starbuck. If only he had not attempted to kill him. Now there would be nobody to raise the hue and cry on Nantucket over his having been taken. Starbuck had been a fool, and now he was at sea. The motion of the ship informed him of this fact. Starbuck also knew from the disciplined silence of the deck and the ship's fast heading out to sea that the Captain was a thoroughgoing professional and ran a good ship with no nonsense tolerated. He now knew that he knew little or nothing at all. Suddenly out of the blue, Starbuck felt real loss. He had never realized just how important it was that somebody in the world had a good opinion of him. On the whole planet the Maycocks were the only individuals who had cared if he had lived or died. Now they were through with him.

Hours passed, and Starbuck dropped off to sleep. The rocking of the ship comforted him, and he decided to just let the situation play itself out. He awoke at seven bells and was for the first time aware of the ship's bell. He heard footsteps first, then the sound of people stopping outside of the cabin door. Then he heard the key turning in the lock and the door swinging open on its hinges. Footsteps came over to the cot. Starbuck began to sweat. He felt the hood coming off of his head and his bonds being loosened. All was a blur. Then as a voice spoke the shapes of the three men standing in the cabin began to take form. "There is a thunder jug under the cot sir," said the voice in the half-light. "There is breakfast on the tray over here and some hot coffee in the pot. There is water in the stand if you should care to wash and shave. We shall return in a bit when you have had time to wash and feed yourself sir."

With that the three men left. Starbuck was dazed. Nothing seemed logical. It was all far too civilized and not at all what happens to men taken by force at night, bound, gagged, and Shanghaied. "This is very bad," he thought. But at the same time it was interesting and maybe something could be gained in the end. Whoever took him wanted something, and that something was something that he alone possessed. Whatever it was, it was the bargaining chip for his life. As he relieved himself in the thunder jug, he thought that he might even be able to squeeze more out of those fellows who held him. Maybe there was something in it for him beyond mere survival. Then another thought occurred to him. Here at last was some real excitement. That might be reward enough. Anything would be better than rotting away on that damn island. He even had quite forgotten Mrs. Maycock.

CHAPTER LIV

Starbuck sat on the edge of the bunk for the rest of the day. He had now been on the ship for two days. The more recent of those days had been spent at dockside while last minute provisions and supplies were loaded aboard.

Starbuck had been fed two meals each day, and from time to time, he was asked if he felt the need to relieve himself. Having taken care of that matter, he had called to the sailors to reenter the cabin. Then he was once more bound and gagged and tied to the bunk. An hour or so later, he became aware of a pilot boat hailing the ship. At the same time, a man in a black broadcloth suit entered with two large sailors who unbound his upper body allowing him to be raised up. The man in the black suit released his gag and said, "I am the ship's doctor. Please swallow this and you will have a fine night's sleep."

Starbuck did as he was instructed without protest. He was lowered back onto a fresh pillow, and he was once again secured to the bunk. A feeling of well being came over him, and he fell into a coma like sleep. While all of this was going on, the ship sailed out of the harbor of the City of Boston. The pilot boat was sent on its way, and a long boat was lowered with Captain Beer's agents in it. They waved goodbye and began their row back into the harbor and on to the Howe's family dock. The ship then got under way sailing due Northeast. The smaller vessel took leave of her bigger companion ship and Cabot then sailed his yacht out of the harbor and back to his private dock below his estate in Marblehead.

"That was an expensive outing," the pilot remarked to the boat's Captain.

"Those folks don't worry about things like money when their pleasure is involved," replied the Captain.

"Ain't one of them fellers Mr. Cabot?" asked a sailor.

"I think that he be," growled the Captain. "Them blue bloods don't worry too much about nothing. Although bigger boats are his love he'll sail anything. Those big bugs sail mostly for prizes and such. Can't figure out what them big bugs is going to win sometimes, but they all take it some damn serious. But the doings of our betters is no concern of ours."

"Maybe they towed some escaped niggers out to a ship offshore somewheres and they got all tuckered out and got a ride back. The quality folks sure go in for saving niggers though don't they?"

"Well ain't that God's work or something?" laughed the pilot.

"I guess that's what the quality folks does to save their souls. God knows, they don't give a damn about the rest of us."

The ship sailed off. Captain Beers gave a wide berth to the Cape and Race Point. "The bones of hundreds of ships are resting down there," said Captain Beers to Samuel, Pompey, and Violet as they stood at the ship's rail as the elegant vessel clipped along at fifteen knots.

"We are quite safe now far from shoal waters," said Captain Beers between puffs of his pipe, which seemed to be an inexhaustible source of delight to him and an intrinsic part of his body almost as if it were molded into his hand like a continuation of that appendage.

"The night is beautiful," said Violet as she put her arm through Pompey's and looked up into his eyes in which she could see the reflected ship's lights.

"I think I'll turn in. Tomorrow might be a long and difficult day," said Samuel in a matter of fact way.

"Good night dear friend Samuel," said Violet as the big man disappeared down the companionway.

Samuel pretended not to hear her as he made his way to his stateroom. His struggle to be civil was a hard one when Violet was present. Yet he knew that he must be ever so civil. He knew that he had to begin to look as if he really liked the girl. She and Pompey must never suspect that he meant her any harm. "Maybe she'll fall overboard on her own," he muttered. Then Samuel shook his head and said softly to himself, "That would be most providential but unlikely."

Samuel tossed on his bunk. He slipped in and out of sleep in the darkness of his cabin. His thoughts migrated back to his youth. He was fifteen and was watching the beautiful ebony maids in the soft waters splashing each other and dreaming of their loves. He smiled as he beheld them. Each was like a flower on the verge of blooming into mature magnificence. The blossoming of their womanhood filled him with pleasure. Suddenly amidst them he saw a face that did not belong there. There was Violet with the sun shining on her alien snow-white bosoms. Samuel was filled with rage. The maids were all looking at Pompey, but Violet was seducing him away from them.

Samuel woke in a lather of sweat. He was enraged. "That damned white girl is ruining all I have planned. When can I get to her alone on this damned ship? She is never alone. I must make an end to her. Yet how? Yet how?"

He tossed again on his bunk as if it were on fire. Samuel's frustration of all of his impossible dreams filled him with a profound sense of despair. Suddenly he found himself saying, "I know it can never happen either with the girl in the picture or not. God damn! What a fool I've been. Pompey is no Matabele."

The pain began in his chest, and he writhed in agony. He struggled to reach for the carafe of water by his bunk. It was tepid, but he drank it. Samuel settled down on his pillow again, and he tried to let all of the pain and hatred drain from him. Slowly the pain abated. Slowly his breathing became less labored. He was exhausted and finally settled back into a dreamless sleep.

The next thing that Samuel heard was the ship's bell striking seven times. The sun's rays shone into his cabin. Once again, he thought of Pompey, and he knew that repatriating him to the home he had longed for would be too much to hope for. He had other things to concern him now like plumbing the depths of Whitehouse's mind through the agency of Starbuck. As he dressed after he had gotten out of his bunk, Samuel wondered just how he would approach questioning Starbuck. Would the man still be loyal to his old chief? He pondered this as he made ready to join the others. Violet receded into the depths of his unconscious mind.

CHAPTER LV

Starbuck became aware that there was a little sunlight in his cabin. He could feel the salt breeze on his face. The portholes were open to admit the bracing sea air. He moved his hands to his face and rubbed his now bearded chin and cheeks until he was awake. Then he looked at his hands and discovered that he had been unbound. Starbuck then looked across the cabin and saw Second Officer Beaton seated at the worktable drinking what he took to be coffee. "Good morning Mr. Starbuck. Have you slept well?" asked Beaton.

Starbuck just grunted in return. His head ached. He just looked at Beaton in his crisp uniform with his clean-shaven face, which made him only more aware of his own filthy and miserable condition. "Would you like to bathe, shave, and change sir? I can have a tub and hot water from the galley brought in to you. The Captain has sent you a change of clothing, and we'll see to the washing and brushing of your own clothes sir."

Amazed by all of this consideration and confused at the same time, Starbuck could only manage a grunt of approval. With that, Beaton went to the door and signaled the two men standing there to carry in a bathtub. Two coppers of heated water were sent for from the galley. Everything was provided for the bath, and then the seamen left Starbuck alone. In an hour's time, the steward returned with a large breakfast, which Starbuck ate with relish. As he was having his second cup of strong black coffee, there came a knock at the cabin door. A few seconds later, Beaton reappeared with two sailors and said, "The two gentlemen who brought you on board wish to speak with you in the saloon. Please be so kind as to follow us Mr. Starbuck."

Starbuck was now much more curious than frightened. Unspeaking, he followed the second officer, and the two sailors followed him in turn to the sunny saloon where he found the Captain, Samuel, and Pompey sitting at a round baize covered table. Samuel stared at Starbuck, then motioned to a chair indicating that he wished him to sit. Pompey began, "Have you any idea why you are here Mr. Starbuck?"

"No, I do not sir." He was determined not to give up any information until he could see the situation clearly and divine exactly what advantages might be gained.

"That is not what you indicated to us before. You mentioned people in New York and a certain Captain Whitehouse. Do not trifle with us Mr. Starbuck you have seen what we can do. You are not safe anywhere. We took you at our leisure. We can torture you and kill you in a hundred different ways each more horrible than the other. You would be wise to cooperate with us. We can set you at liberty with enough money to take you anywhere you want to go when we have what we want. Now doesn't that sound like a good alternative to being tortured and killed?"

"What do you want of me? What do you want to know? And why the Hell am I going to be gone for a year anywhere?"

"Mr. Starbuck, we want to know everything you have done starting with your last voyage with Captain Whitehouse. We know a great many things about you, so leave nothing out," said Samuel as his eyes drilled into the man's very soul.

"You people want information from me, and that is all?" asked Starbuck with surprise.

"We want to know everything you have done and know about in the time period we shall ask you about, and when we know that the information is correct, we can go about setting you at liberty. If you do not tell us everything, or if what you tell us is not correct, the Captain here will deal out the justice that is due a slaver," replied Samuel.

With that, the Captain produced a hempen noose from under the table and dangled it from his fist. "As you see Mr. Starbuck, we are people who really want to know things and will shrink from nothing to get the information we want. Now please be so kind as to begin your story."

Starbuck collected his thoughts, and after considering that he had nothing more to lose, and even his life to prolong or regain, he began his narrative, which lasted about two hours. Pompey took notes, and Samuel listened closely. The Captain listened as he played absentmindedly with the noose. When Starbuck finished, Samuel smiled and said, "You have been busy. Do you think that Whitehouse is still in Rio de Janeiro?"

"I have no reason to think otherwise. Should he not be there, I would be only too happy to help hunt the sonofabitch down. There is nobody on this earth I would rather see dead than Captain Whitehouse. If I can help you to get Whitehouse, I will."

"I find your attitude in this rather odd Mr. Starbuck," said Samuel. "You followed him in the slave trade for more than thirty years."

"I hated that business and kept out of the filthy bits of it as much as I could. I ran the men and the ship after the mate before me made a cat's dinner out of the business. There was nothing clean about that trade, and I do not pretend that I am not a guilty man. I am a greedy one, and I despise myself for it. I betrayed everything I was brought up to respect and hold holy including the teachings of my own mother. Inside of me I am dead already. I cannot lay the whole blame on Whitehouse, but that does not lessen the hate I feel for him which is my own. The nightmares that fill my sleeping hours remind me of the horrors I helped to allow to happen. That is my reward for my greed, and I hate myself for it," replied Starbuck.

"You mean that business with the young slave mother who killed the mate then threw herself overboard? Is that why you became mate, because you could handle the men?" replied Samuel.

"How the Devil could you know anything about that? I never told anybody about that in my whole goddamned life!" snapped Starbuck.

"I was there Mr. Starbuck. I saw everything," said Samuel in a cold flat voice.

"You could not have been! The only people there were the crew and the slaves. You were not there mister. I would have known it."

"There was a man in that crew named Forrester. He was a young man of nineteen or twenty, and Whitehouse had him flogged. Do you recall that?" asked Samuel.

"I do, but how the Devil could you know that?" Starbuck reflected a moment, "You must have been there, but I don't remember any children that would have been your age there. There were a few infants, but they all died. You would have had to have been very young, and a slave at that!"

"I was young. I was a young man of sixteen, a Matabele warrior taken by the Mashona and sold to the Portuguese in Mozambique where I was bought by Whitehouse and loaded onto your ship, a Hellhole! I was brought to America. It was there that Forrester and I made our escape from your ship. Forrester stole Whitehouses' money. It was in New Orleans. That was more than thirty-five years ago. Forrester is dead. Whitehouse caught up with him and killed him. I watched it happen. The man is still as brutal as he ever was. He stole my life Mr. Starbuck, and now I want his. Do you know anything of this?"

"I remember a big buck ran off with Forrester, and I remember that Whitehouse's money was taken," Starbuck began to laugh. "He was furious. That buck was Whitehouse's side deal for himself alone and off the books. That money was all that he had saved over two years. You would have enjoyed his misery. He would have strangled Forrester if he could have laid hands on him. Whitehouse is a bastard. In a way he stole my life as well," said Starbuck reflectively.

"I was a Quaker boy, green as grass from Nantucket. I had no future, my mother was dead, and Whitehouse sold me on the idea of slaving after I had been on a whaler for the better part of three years. I was a large boy for my age and looked older with the beard I had grown. My people were always against the slave trade, being Nantucket Quakers, and having sworn off the trade themselves for the most part. I have no excuse. More than anyone I knew better, but the money was good. The conditions were horrible. When the girl killed the mate, I was glad. The man was a pig, and he enjoyed his work much too well not to mention the benefits he helped himself to. God knows, I never wanted his job. It was all greed. I have no excuse. I've got a lot of gold. Now I don't even want it. When you took me, I was going to kill a man so that I could have his wife. Now don't take me wrong. She is a good woman, which is why I wanted her, but I am no good, nor do I think that there is one redeeming thing in me. Hang me and you will be doing us all a favor."

"What about the man you were about to kill?" asked Pompey.

"He works for me. He saved my life. He's a good man, but he had the woman I wanted most in the world, because she was kind and good to me. I am a very bad fellow no matter how you look at it. Look at what I did to you. Just look at what I was about to do to poor Maycock so that I could court his wife. Hell, I don't even want the damn gold any more. You, big man. I took your youth. Do you want my life? Take it? Do you want my gold? Take all of it. Do whatever you want with it. It means nothing to me. Gold is only a reminder of what a nasty cur my quest of it has made me."

"No, I don't need your white man's slave gold. Give it to my boy Pompey there. He can use it to do some good with it maybe. I am going back to Matabeleland, and I am hoping that it has not changed too much since I have been away, and it is possible that there may be some of my people who will still know me from long ago. They may yet still be alive," said Samuel.

"I don't want that blood gold. I am going with you Samuel just as I promised I would do. Violet has agreed to come as well. We will make the best possible life that we can there in Africa. I hope that you can make this work. If you can, Violet and I will do all we can to cooperate with your hopes. I do not think that we will need Mr. Starbuck's gold," said Pompey.

"Take it," ordered Samuel. "As a white man you can buy the freedom of some young American and Brazilian slaves and give them a chance in life to grow up in that same freedom that you now enjoy. Maybe you can buy a whole ship full of young people and bring them to Africa or somewhere in America where no white man now lives. Maybe they can have farms and communities. Think about it. There is no end to the possibilities if you have enough gold."

"I will think on it Samuel," replied Pompey. "Maybe Mr. Garrison could advise me. You have made me think of good ways to use wealth gotten through evil."

"I will draw you a few maps. My gold is scattered all over my house and island," said Starbuck. "I would like you to share a little with the Maycocks. I owe them a debt."

"I hope that it will buy you some peace," intoned Captain Beers as he absentmindedly played with the noose.

"It will give me more peace than that toy you are playing with. I'm just happy to be on a ship again and one that does not stink of my old life. I hope that when we catch Whitehouse, you will just let me chum up the water with him. Let me cut him up a bit, and toss him in the ocean naked to wait for his high finned friends. They were so fond of him in the old days when he fed dead slaves to them along with an entire living cargo. They followed us no matter what ship he happened to command. They knew that they could count on him for their dinner. And then, if you would be so kind, I'd like to finish up my days as a common seaman on this clean ship of yours Captain Beers sir."

"We will see Mr. Starbuck," said Samuel, "As my people so often say, before we sell the lion's skin, we must first catch the lion."

"If you want to catch this particular lion," said Starbuck, "Perhaps there might be a better place to look than Brazil. I think I know this lion's habits, and I have a very good idea that he is hunting his prey now in Mozambique. I don't think that he is in Rio now. I am sure that he knows that he is being hunted too, and not by you."

CHAPTER LVI

Whitehouse wiped his brow with his large pocket handkerchief. The steam of the tropics was something he had never quite gotten used to in spite of the fact that he had spent so much of his life in those latitudes. As his ship was riding at anchor off the trading factory of a very minor official of the Mozambique Company who also dealt in slaves, he reflected that he would not have to load his cargo for another few weeks. There were still some more captives being brought out to him from the interior. His rejection of eighty percent of the company official's unofficial human offerings had taxed the poor Captain's patience. The slave trader was really beside himself as Whitehouse refused one slave after another without a word of explanation. When he was pushed by the frustrated little man, who was sweating profusely himself under his broad brimmed hat, as to why he had rejected these perfectly good slaves, Whitehouse merely told him, "Sorry, they are just not good enough Old Boy."

The little man almost cried as though he had suffered the worst of personal insults. "But Captain, oh my dear Captain Whitehouse. My father sold you fine slaves from this very place for many years. Our dealings have always been happy ones, fair, and to the satisfaction of all. What is the matter now? These slaves we offer to you are of the finest quality I assure you."

"They are nothing of the sort. Most of them are tired and shopworn material at best. I assure you that the Sudanese must have rejected all of them, and now you are trying to fob them off on me. Get your people into the interior or you will force me to buy from more imaginative dealers who can get me prime stock. Look man! There is not a single bitch there I would take to my bed with a gift of fifty pounds sterling! And the men! Those tired dogs can't get out of their own way. You have starved and beaten these wretches into a state of uselessness. This lot will all be dead after a week at sea. Now what good will that be to me? Bring me fresh stock like the ones I bought from you a fortnight ago. I want big, strong, young, well fed, and healthy brutes. I have told you that I want no women, old men, boys under fourteen years of age or five feet ten inches tall in height, or any grandfathers. I want Zulus if you can force your courage up to get me some more of them. And I want prime material only you stupid sod! Use the slaves that I have already purchased as a guide to the whereabouts of what I desire in merchandise. Is there any part of that statement that you do not understand?"

"Those you bought at first were all Matabele and mostly very young. They were all between fifteen and twenty years of age. Many of them are not quite warriors yet. It is all but impossible to get such captives again. They were caught one at a time. If I dare to capture more of them their king may guess at their fate and decide that they were not all murdered in an ambush by some enemy as I am informed that he thinks now. He could kill the lot of us if he harbored such a notion. He is not like other African kings. He has no fear of white men. In fact, he thinks of us as inferiors. Why do you think that their cost was three times the asking price of the others? They are not like grapes, taken in bunches from some vine. Nor are they taken without huge risk."

"I presumed that the reason I bought them so dearly was because they were the finest stock that I have seen in years. Do you think to sell me an old draft horse just after I have ridden the finest stallion? Don't be daft man and do not even attempt to rationalize an answer to that imponderable question. Your brain might explode. In fact, I am sure that you will do yourself a great injury should you try to be so clever. You will keep and feed those slaves I have contracted to purchase until I am ready to go. They do not all have to be Matabele. They just have to be as good as the Matabele. If you kill or injure any of my cargo, or starve them, you can keep them all, and you'll never see me again. Do you understand me?"

"Yes sir. I think I do. But it will take at least two months to get what you require Captain, that is if we are very lucky."

"Your little problems are of no matter to me. Just do as I wish, and everything will fall into place and you will get your gold. Now I am returning to my ship for a little siesta."

Whitehouse strode across the beach to his boat where six lusty sailors waited to row their Captain back to his fine ship. She was a trim race built clipper of 240 feet length. She was built to carry cargo quickly to its destination in the Far East. She had been built for the tea trade, but she was no stranger to the commerce in opium. In fact, the Captain had thought about entering the tea, silk, porcelain, and opium trade in China right after he delivered his last cargo of slaves to Brazil or the southern states. He knew that he could even sell the ship's ballast of quarried Quincy granite for the paving of the streets of the new British colony at Hong Kong.

Every bit of his beautiful new clipper could be used to make her pay. And San Francisco would pay well for everything in the way of regular trade goods, including barrels of china that would constitute his new ballast. The Captain's plan was that not one prime slave would die during the dread middle passage, and that her cargo would be delivered intact in under a hundred days in his McKay built clipper. Whitehouse had no intention of losing a single dollar of his own investment. As he was rowed back to his ship, Whitehouse reflected on the fact that within one or two year's time he could retire to an estate in the French countryside if he wished and vacation at his townhouse in Rio de Janeiro if it was unsold or if he decided to sell the ship and not go into the China Trade for more than one voyage of the earth's circumnavigation. As he allowed himself to be absorbed by this dream, he took notice of the English merchantman, which had dropped anchor not a mile from where his ship was riding on the placid waters of the Indian Ocean on the previous day. Whitehouse's mate found it strange that this American built ship was flying the Union Jack.

When Whitehouse had gained his deck, his mate had news for him, handed him his glass, and pointed out the ship that was at anchor a mile distant. Whitehouse took the glass and peered at the ship. He shrugged his shoulders and turned to his mate, "Mr. Wright, what do you make of her?"

"I don't make anything of her sir. She's American built. For some reason she is a worry to me. That's all Captain."

"Our good craft is American built, and I used to be British before I decided to become a citizen of the world. What does that signify?" replied Whitehouse. "The Americans build the finest ships under sail, and none is better than Mr. Donald McKay of Boston."

"She just don't seem right with that flag. She does not appear to be armed or have an overly large crew. She might be trading, but I can't guess for what in these waters so far from commercial Portuguese or English trading factories unless it be for slaves."

"You are correct Mr. Wright. There is only one thing she could be here for, and that is for a cargo of slaves. That is the only commodity traded here. I don't mind telling you that I don't like it. The British are having trouble with the Russians right now. And they are also anxious about their allies, the French, not to mention what a cat's dinner The British East India Company is making out of India. Their bloody empire and its problems mean that their fleet is on patrol all over the world, yet they still make time to go after us. The Portuguese are their oldest allies in Europe, but the English are not about to turn a blind eye to the slave trade. I don't want one damned slave on this ship until those people are gone and we are sure that her majesty's ships of war are well occupied elsewhere. Maybe they could chase that American ship with a British flag. Now that Mr. Wright would be a damned funny thing. Keep an eye on her Mr. Wright. She might even be a British Navy ship in mufti."

"You seem to have considered everything sir," replied Wright in his thick burr reflecting his birthplace, Glasgow.

Whitehouse reflected that this Scot was a great improvement over his old mate Starbuck, whose Yankee heritage seemed to have soured his voyages of the last several years. Starbuck was a tough man in a fight, and never backed down from danger or from following an order no matter how troublesome he found it. Whitehouse had counted on Starbuck's tough doggedness when he envisioned the New York gangs taking him from his damned island to discover his fate. He calculated that even if Starbuck survived, that he would never tell the men from Five Points the truth about the supposed loss of their investment in their ship and slaves.

Whitehouse reflected that Starbuck might even have gone down fighting. Whitehouse even wondered how many New Yorkers Starbuck would drag off to Hell before he was dispatched there himself. Starbuck was plagued by his Yankee guilt and Quaker sensibilities. That little matter of Starbuck's emerging scruples had troubled Whitehouse for a long time. Whitehouse was of the belief that there was nothing so bad for business as a man with scruples. He looked at Wright.

What a different sort of fellow he was from Starbuck. He was a confirmed Sodomite, but that made no difference to Whitehouse, and Wright was possessed of no scruples whatsoever. The man was a fine mate, and the crew was afraid of him, his tarred rope's end, and his filthy temper. They jumped at his every command. They knew that the big Scot would open their skulls and throw their body overboard to the sharks should they refer to how he expressed his sexual passions with the young cabin boy he had brought aboard with him. The crew did not wonder that

Whitehouse made no objection. Many of them remembered Ajax and his position as the Captain's favorite.

"Mr. Wright, my former mate, Mr. Starbuck, did not approve of me. Did you know that?"

"Did not approve of you sir?" answered Mr. Wright.

"He was a Quaker who really didn't approve of slavery. He approved of the money it earned him like a good deal of the others of his ilk from New England. They are a strangely conflicted lot these Quakers and Yankees are. Do you have any convictions on the subject?"

"Well sir, all I can say is that if the Brits are in favor of something, you can trust me to be opposed, begging your pardon sir, I am a Scot after all."

"As I told an Irishman some years ago," said Whitehouse, "I have no love for my countrymen, or at least the toffee nosed reformers who cry over the niggers and let their own people starve to death or die in the workhouses. I see my chances and take them when I can make a few bob."

"The English slaughtered my people at Culloden in 1745 including my own great grandfather," growled Wright, "And it still fuels the hatred of we Scots for the British. The bastards slaughtered my people for the three years following the battle. The name of the bloody Duke of Cumberland is still cursed in Scotland to this day. Even after more than a hundred years, many of us live for the day when there are no more Englishmen in Scotland. If they object to the slave trade, I say fuck them all. I doubt if Holy Calvin ever objected to trading in slaves. After all, the Blacks are an accursed race going back to Noah."

"You are a fine man Mr. Wright. When your watch is done and you are relieved, come to my cabin, and we'll drink a toast to Wallace and Robert Burns," laughed Whitehouse.

"Now you're talking Captain. Aye that you are, and might I presume to say sir, ye are a man for that."

"I'll expect you then when Roberts takes the watch after yours is finished. Oh, how is that cabin boy working out? Handy of him to stowaway aboard ship during your last voyage eh what."

"He's a likely lad. With a bit of discipline, he'll be just fine."

"I'm glad to hear that. He's a big lad for his age and strong I'm told."

"That he is sir."

"Well I'm happy to see him getting on. You will join me when Robert's takes the watch. And do fetch along the cabin boy. I might have some duties for him myself."

"Aye sir. That I will. I believe that good fortune should be shared sir."

Whitehouse saluted and went below to his cabin. There was a fine breeze cooling the space. He sat on the edge of his bunk, removed his boots, stretched out, and closed his eyes. In a very short time, Whitehouse was enjoying a fine undisturbed sleep that slowly overtook him.

CHAPTER LVII

Two long boats silently beached themselves in the dark of the night. Twenty-two men armed with pistols and cutlasses pulled the boats ashore without a single word being spoken. The men then bunched together to get their instructions from the Captain and Samuel. Three men were detailed off to stay with the boats, then Samuel, sword in hand, led the party up the beach to the slave trader's stronghold under the cover of darkness. The gate to the compound was open, and two men stood guard leaning on their muskets. They also had swords at their belts, but they were the worse for drink and were almost asleep.

Samuel motioned for his men to stop in the deep shadowed moonless night. The only light provided was the light coming from the slave compound itself. Samuel whispered orders to the Captain and mate who silently unsheathed their swords. Samuel and Pompey moved on unshod feet, and maneuvered themselves behind the guards. Watching each other, they came up behind their respective men, placed a hand over the mouths of their victims and drove their blades up under the rib cages of their victims and up into their hearts. The guards slumped over with their eyes wide open, and they were dead. Pompey silently dragged his man into the brush following Samuel. He paused for a moment then vomited and almost fainted. He had practiced this maneuver with Samuel's instruction dozens of times using two sailors and wooden rules. But this was the real taking of life. It was not the same.

Samuel shook Pompey back to sensibility and whispered in his ear, "Get over it boy, There is going to be a lot of killing tonight. These men would kill you and your whole family in a second if they were ordered to. They would think nothing of it. They would sell you into a life of slavery. These animals should have no more meaning to you than some insect that will sting you if you should not destroy it. So get over this business of being squeamish, or go back to the boat."

"I am sorry Samuel. It's my first time killing a man. It won't happen again," whispered Pompey.

"Wait here. I'm going to have a look around. Be ready for anything. I don't know what peoples they have in the pens. I want to see if I can talk to any of them," said Samuel softly. As he moved off, he suddenly turned and came back. "You did well Pompey. Just stay resolute and all will be well my son."

Pompey nodded. Samuel made his way through the encampment to the slave pens. Samuel was struck by the fact that nothing had changed here. The smell of the place was painfully familiar. After a few minutes had passed, Samuel was very close to the first pen. There was only one guard there. Samuel came up on him in total silence. Samuel's arm came up under the guard's chin in a flash. There was a quick twist and a deadly snap that sounded like a twig breaking under foot, a gasp of air expelled almost soundlessly from the guard's lungs. Then the muffled sound of the guard's lifeless body being lowered to the ground ended the episode. Samuel consigned this body into the shadows of the night. Before tonight, Samuel had not killed a man since the day he was captured by the Mashona. Now all of his old instincts came into play, and it was as if no time had elapsed at all since his blade had thirsted for the blood of his enemy.

A whisper came from the interior of the pen. "Who is it that has killed this man?" Samuel was almost shocked for the first time since coming to New Orleans with Forrester all of those many years ago. For the first time in more than thirty-five years, he was hearing the language of his fathers' spoken. Samuel found his voice and said in Zulu, "I am one who comes from a land far away from which I was taken from this very place. I have come to free you and exact my revenge. Will you help me in this my brothers? All of these foreign men here who have taken our bodies and our lives and sold us into slavery must answer for their crimes against us this very night. I will have their blood for what they have done and will do."

"Indeed they must answer my brother. Some fool has selected us as the best men here to be bought for his slaves. We are all Matabele, and we planned to kill these slave traders or die ourselves on the walk to the beach when we will be taken to his ship. We are the Chosen People of Heaven, and we bow our heads to no man but our King at Bulawayo. If you can free us, we will fight for you once released. We are chained together and cannot move well, but we will fight all the same if we are let out of here. The man who was with this guard may have the key to the pens and our chains. He will be back here very soon. We marked him as the first man we would attack. Without that key we are most hindered," replied the young warrior who was now surrounded by more than half of the men in the slave holding pen who could actually maneuver near.

"I have twenty men with me to assist," said Samuel. "They are all white save one. They are good men and well armed. They are friends to us, and they hate slavery. Take care not to harm them."

"This thing you say I will not question even though the idea of the white man being a friend to us is not within my understanding," replied the warrior.

"I will hide myself until this guard comes. How many men are here guarding the compound?"

"There are at least fifty men altogether who are armed. They are experienced killers. Although they appear to be stupid, do not underestimate them. They are savage animals in their way, and like animals, they act on instinct. Most of them are sleeping in their barracks. Even when they are awake, they still look half asleep. There are no more than eight or ten on guard right now. Most of the other captives are of tribes unused to fierce fighting and are no threat of escape to these traders. So the guards are few in number and very careless. Now my friend, get the key and we will arm ourselves as best we can from the men we kill," said the young Matabele warrior with a smile.

Samuel stole away into the darkness thinking what a stroke of luck it was that the slave catchers had been foolish enough to take Matabele Zulus for slaves. Then these Portuguese had compounded their stupidity by placing the Matabele all together in one pen. "It is fatal foolishness," he said to himself just as he spied his first target. Unlike most of the other Portuguese guards, this was a very large man and powerfully built. Samuel could not afford to make a mistake here. With his sword in his hand, he waited his chance. As the man moved down the path, Samuel waited for the man to move past him, but all of a sudden the man stopped as if suddenly aware that all was not right. He began to turn away from the path and go back the way he came.

Samuel sprang driving his sword into the man's back severing his spine. The man fell without making a sound. All was silence. Samuel found himself on the ground suddenly a bit dizzy with a pain in his chest, and then came another pain running up his arm. Even his teeth began to hurt. He suddenly felt old. He became cold, and his skin began to sweat. His chest began to tighten and a sharp pain again shafted through his massive chest, and he felt as if some giant serpent was crushing him. Then Samuel vomited and passed into unconsciousness.

He was awoken some little time later by the sound of calling voices. It was still dark, but in the East the sky was starting to hint of the coming of light. There was a dullness in Samuel's chest, but his head was clear. Slowly and painfully he made his way back to the slave pens. The warrior was awaiting him. Without speaking,

Samuel passed him the keys he had taken from the big man. In a few moments, he heard the clicks of each lock being opened in turn. There was silence for a moment. Then there was a more significant click as the big lock on the pen door was opened. Within a few moments, tall well-built Black men reeking of filth and stench were surrounding him.

The chief warrior to whom he had been speaking said, "We are ready my friend. We must act now for soon the sun will be up, and the guard will change. I have told my warriors what you have said regarding the white men. We know what these Portuguese look like for we have been here for more than a fortnight. We know most of their faces. Now we will arm ourselves from whatever source we can, and on my signal we will attack."

"Give me time to tell my people what we have done here. I will make sure that they know that the Matabele are with us," said Samuel with his face contorted with pain.

"We will position ourselves to the greatest advantage. Then you will attack making the greatest din my friend. And then we will have a famous victory. Before you go, I would know your name," said the young warrior.

"In the world of the white man, I am known as Samuel, but that is the name of slavery. My name unspoken these thirty-five and more years is Atachawayo. Listen for me. Then attack. It will not be long my brothers."

Samuel made his way back to the sailors and Pompey. As he moved, he became aware of the growing discomfort in his chest. He fell gasping for air, and he almost fainted from the pain. He forced himself to his feet and walked on. At last he saw Pompey who rushed to meet him in the growing light of the coming dawn.

"Help me gasped Samuel almost falling into Pompey's arms."

"Are you wounded Samuel!" Pompey whispered.

"There is no time for that. Now listen to me and do exactly as I tell you. You are to join the Captain and the men. You are to attack the Portuguese slave traders with as much noise as you can manage. I have freed some of the slave captives. They are all Matabele warriors and will attack from the rear when they hear you commence battle. Kill no Black man just the Portuguese or English. My Matabele friends have been instructed not to harm you. Now get me back to our men."

Pompey half carried Samuel as they made their way back to Captain Beers, the second mate, and the sailors. Samuel noticed that some more men had joined the group from the ship. Standing tall among them was Starbuck with a cutlass in one hand and a belaying pin in the other. Noting Pompey and Samuel looking at him, Starbuck sneered in a voice just above a whisper, "What I have needed to set me to rights is to be at sea again and then to crush a few skulls to release my own Devils. My doctor, back on Nantucket, told me that I need exercise. Captain Beers here agrees with me that I ought to get some. There is nothing like a good fight to chase the blues away right boys?"

With that Samuel stood straight and leaned into Starbuck, "I don't give a damn who you kill now or ever, but you will swear to me on the soul of your mother that you will not kill Whitehouse or any Black man. Whitehouse is my property to do with as I please. I have a greater right to that than you do. And do not worry yourself. You may confront him, but you have no idea of what I can do that could even lurk in your deepest imagination. You may watch if you wish, but he is my property alone!"

"Alright, I respect your claim to his life, but if he should get in my way, I lay claim to knock him around a bit," replied Starbuck.

"Tat and nothing more," snapped Samuel with a wince from his titanic pain as he collapsed in a heap.

"Belay all this chatter!" said Captain Beers. "The sun will be up soon, and Samuel, you look like Hell itself. You there, Ryder! Take Mr. James and carry him under the shelter of that tree over there. Get him something soft to make him as comfortable as possible. Give him something to lay on starting with your jumper. Stay with him in case he needs anything. Now jump to it"

"Aye, aye sir," answered the sailor in a whisper as he half lifted Samuel with the help of another sailor and assisted Samuel to the spot under the tree with another tree to brace his back.

The sailor pulled off his jumper to make a pillow for Samuel's head. The big man lay down in great and obvious pain. He looked up at Pompey and the men gathered for the attack.

"You better get in there now. Hide around the central square, and allow the bastards to arise. They will leave their huts at sunrise. There are about fifty of them. They will be groggy from sleep and drink. When most of them are out of their huts, shoot as many as you can. Then cut down the rest. Let the Matabele capture or kill all they wish. Do not release the slaves in the other pens. We know nothing about them, and we do not wish them to come to any harm, but we cannot be burdened with them running about during battle." With that, Samuel passed into unconsciousness. Pompey rushed to him.

"His breathing isn't very good. Sailor, hold a cool wet cloth to his brow and care for him until I return." Looking at Samuel, Pompey growled, "Don't you die damn it. It is not yet your time."

Pompey pulled on his boots, grabbed up his blade and pistol, and moved off with the others into the slave compound. He had been blooded. He was now ready to kill. The men ranged themselves about the edges of the open area screened by the natural growth. The minutes ticked by, and the sun began to rise in the eastern sky. It illuminated the two ships separated by a mile of water as they were at anchor as still as if they were perched on an immense sheet of glass. They looked like two pleasure barges. From the shore one would not guess the grim business in which Whitehouse's beautiful vessel was to be engaged.

The sunrise that followed, in all of its tropical glory, shined on the compound obscuring the real horror enacted there each day. One by one, and then in little groups, the guards began to emerge from their quarters. They did not seem to notice that the night guards were not coming into the center of the compound, as was their habit at the end of their watch. The slave trader himself emerged after a while. He did sense that something was not quite as it should be. The rest of the men merely smelled the food, which had been cooking for breakfast and now was beginning to burn. The slave trader began to look more alert and moved about with some vigor. He alone was exhibiting signs that he was reacting to some unspecified danger.

Observing this, Captain Beers cried out, "Now! Fire damn your eyes!" More than forty shots rang out, and more than two-dozen men fell dead or wounded onto the beaten ground. A war cry went up from the slave quarters, and the Matabele armed with the weapons of the fallen guards, makeshift clubs, and rocks were on the slavers in a flash. Captain Beers' sailors attacked swinging their blades and driving the slavers into a knot of helpless humanity. Here the Matabele were on them. In less than three minutes, it was all over. A few of the Portuguese slavers tried to surrender but were hacked down where they stood. Others attempted flight, but the Matabele, trained to run fifty miles and then fight a battle at the end of a day, were on these hapless men before they could escape. These slavers were killed on the run. Then the air was rent with the cries of victory.

These warriors, who had been stolen from their homes, and then hand selected to be brought together as a prime lot of slaves, vanquished those who would have sold them into slavery in a place half a world away. In spite of their youth, these Matabele proved their legend of being invincible. Pompey felt strangely elated by the fight. The sickness of killing his first man was now forgotten. A warrior spirit had been aroused in him and filled him with a satisfaction only equaled by making love to his woman. Pompey was aroused and felt a swelling in him. He wished that he were then with Violet making love in the heat of the first flush of victory.

Starbuck was no less elated. He had faced off with a Portuguese swordsman of some skill and bested him in a fair fight. After that, it was just slaughter, but Starbuck relished releasing all of his pent up private devils in these busy minutes. He laughed over his vanquished enemies not really caring why he had fought them in the first place. He did not even feel tired from exertion. He felt like a man of thirty again. Pompey came up to him and asked, "You don't happen to speak the language of the Black men who helped us do you?"

"I can manage a little of the Portuguese but not that heathen lingo," Starbuck replied.

"I speak some Portuguese myself," said Pompey. "I'll try to talk to them."

Pompey stood up on a wooden case so that he could be better heard. He spoke in perfectly accented Portuguese. "Greetings friends. I come to free you. Do you understand me?"

The Matabele warrior, who seemed to have assumed the role of leader of the group after Samuel had first spoken to him in the pen and who now stood gazing at Pompey for a moment, broke out into laughter.

"I don't think that they understand your lingo mate," laughed Starbuck along with the rest.

"Why don't you try English Old Boy I don't speak Portuguese very well?" said the leading Matabele warrior. He was speaking the most refined King's English with a crisp patrician accent. This was followed by more laughter from the Matabele and the sailors alike. This laughter broke the spell of unease between the victorious factions of the morning's battle.

"Would you come forward so that we may talk and understand one another," called out Pompey to the warrior who had spoken. The young and tall Matabele stepped from the crowd of warriors and presented himself.

"You astound me sir," said Pompey. You sound just like an English lord."

"Nothing of the sort," replied the man. "I am a perfect mimic. I was schooled by the most pompous of English schoolmasters turned missionary I ever met. When I was a child, I played with the children of our king. When he heard me imitating birds, animals, and the shaman class, he laughed and set me to learning with this Englishman whose sole talent was speaking well. I was to be used to treat with the English in Cape Town as a sort of agent or diplomat at some time in the future you see. I was captured by a huge gang of lesser people when I was out hunting a month ago. I killed many of them, but in the end they took me. I take it that you would like me to act as translator?"

"Would you?" asked Pompey.

"It would be my pleasure. What would you like me to tell my countrymen then?"

"Could you tell them that we are friends, and I wish their help in taking the slave traders on that ship which is commanded by the man who bought you and intended to take you far from your homes over the ocean and sell you into slavery in the Americas?" asked Pompey.

"That would be my singular pleasure," replied the Matabele linguist.

With that, he turned to his people and communicated Pompey's request in his rich baritone. The Matabele listened while he spoke. It was obvious that he commanded much respect among his countrymen. When he concluded with a flourish, Pompey knew just how much the Matabele was a skilled mimic. It was obvious that such pompous linguistic twists were not to be found in the Matabele language. The warriors laughed then roared their approval and danced to celebrate their victory.

"As you can see, my men are in total sympathy with you. They will fight not for you though," said the English talker.

"Why will they not fight?" asked Pompey.

"Have you no understanding of language man? I said that they will not fight for you, but they will fight for themselves. They need no white man to speak for them or to fight for them. We will fight together as your allies on an equal footing. And equality is only extended to you because you have helped free us. Our plan was to attack the slave traders on the way to the ship. No doubt there would have been many losses. Now we are intact. Maybe all of us would have been killed. We knew that the others, now still locked in their pens, would be of no help. They are not like us. They have no discipline. They have learned docility which is a useless virtue. They are, alas, not Matabele. Most of them are of some accursed inferior peoples of no account. My name is Siliva, Englishman."

"But we are all men are we not? I suppose that some of these captives may be other African peoples who are not known to me, but is there no mutual sympathy among all Black men who suffer?" asked Pompey.

"No, young sir, there is not. Some of us are superior. The Zulu, we Matabele, are the Elect Children of Heaven and have no equals on earth. We Matabele work at perfecting ourselves into the perfect warriors. We embrace the reforms of our great King Shaka. Although he is dead for some years now, he set the standard for what we have become, and we will someday be the masters of all Southern Africa. We must keep these subject peoples in their place so that they will not think of rebellion. But you are a white man, and an Englishman. You cannot know these things."

"I am an American born slave. My mother was a Black African. African blood runs in my veins. My cause is to fight against the enslavement of my people. I consider myself to be an African man."

"You are surely no Matabele, but you fight like one of us and are possessed of a good head. I think that I could like you almost as an equal," the scholar laughed as he embraced Pompey. "Where is the older Matabele warrior I spoke to before the fight who wore western dress?"

"You must mean Samuel," replied Pompey.

"He said that his name was Atachawayo," Siliva said.

"That must be his Matabele name. He refused to use it in captivity or ever until now. This man is my friend, and he is like a father to me, and I am as a son to him. Right now I fear for his life."

"He did not look well. May I see him now? Is he close?" asked Siliva.

"Yes, of course you may. It was Samuel who brought us here. He needs to revenge himself on the slave trader who bought all of you of and had you placed together. Freeing you became part of Samuel's plan. For more than thirty-five years, he has been planning for this day, and the gods willing, he'll see it if it can be managed."

"It can be managed. What do I call you? What is your name?"

"I am Pompey. I am afraid that I have no other name but that of a long dead Roman general, which was given to me when I was three years of age, and before that, I had no name at all. That is what it means to be a slave in the white man's world. What is your name again so that I can remember it?"

"I am called Siliva as I have told you. You seem to have little memory, but then you are so bloody white. I hope that I have not misjudged you Pompey. I took you to be intelligent."

CHAPTER LVIII

Samuel lay still under the sheltering tree with his head resting against Seaman Ryder's folded jumper. Pompey came into the clearing with Siliva beside him. Samuel looked up at the pair of them. Some of the old strength had returned to his powerful body, and he raised his hand to greet the pair as they came closer.

"I take it that the fight went well in spite of the fact that I was not there to break my share of heads," Samuel said.

"You were missed dear friend," said Pompey. "This is Siliva. He is the man to whom you spoke last night. He and his warriors made short work of the slavers with a little help from us."

"You are ever so kind Old Boy," said Siliva to Pompey. "You chaps did quite well. We were happy to be given the chance to trounce these villains and have a bit of fun into the bargain," said Siliva who sounded for all the world like an Oxford Don.

"Can this be the Matabele warrior I spoke to last night? If I close my eyes, he sounds like that Gladstone fellow we met at Miss Sally's. Why didn't you tell me that you spoke English?" said Samuel with a cough and a laugh.

"You quite simply didn't ask me Old Boy, and you speak the Matabele dialect so damned well. Quite frankly I had no idea that you spoke English at all. Although your accent is quite as atrocious as this Pompey chap's."

"This is astonishing Pompey," said Samuel who's manner of laughing reminded him that he was in some pain.

By now Captain Beers had returned to the clearing where Samuel lay. He knelt by Samuel's side to get a better look at him. The Captain smiled and shook his head. "My friend, you are in a very bad way. Ryder, take four of the men and go out to the ship for the doctor and bring him here at once. There is no time to lose. "Turning to Samuel, he asked, "Tell me, have you had pains before such as you are suffering now?"

"I have lived with pain. A warrior does not speak of his pain," replied Samuel.

"Lay still and try to rest a bit Samuel," said the Captain quietly.

"Let me speak with Siliva quietly awhile Captain," said Samuel almost in a whisper.

"Very well, but try not to excite yourself." The Captain motioned Siliva to walk over to Samuel to speak to him. "Siliva, talk to him a little while. Try not to let him excite himself if you can manage it."

"You people treat this man with great respect. Who is he in your country that he merits such consideration? Isn't it an unusual thing for white people to treat an African man with such great consideration?"

"Not this man. He is a man of high respectability in any society," replied Captain Beers.

"I see." Siliva went over to Samuel and sat upon the ground next to him. "So Samuel, what great adventure brings you so far from home?"

"This is as close to my home as I have been by my reckoning for thirty-five years. Please speak to me in our own language Siliva. I have not heard it in all this time, and the only place I ever hear it is in my memory and dreams. I have traveled the earth to get back to Africa with these men to bring justice to the man who took me out of Africa and might have done the same with you and more of our people. And for the sake of my poor self, call me by my name, Atachawayo. I am Matabele, and I want to be buried in the soil of my country near the kraal of my father."

"Then let it be so Atachawayo," said Siliva in pure Matabele accented Zulu.

"That is like a cure for me to hear your voice my brother Siliva. Tell me how you came to speak English so well."

"It was the missionaries who taught me to speak English. The man who instructed me was an Oxford fellow with the most outrageous upper crust accent my dear Atachawayo. He must have worked very hard to master it. Even other missionaries commented on his level of ridiculous pretension. He was the son of a country parson, it seems, who had won the patronage of a dotty local lord who saw it as his duty to educate this supposedly gifted boy. The way those missionaries talked about him and made sport of him was most unchristian I assure you. He made us laugh with his pomposity," laughed Siliva.

"It was just the same as for me. How do so many of those fellows make it out here to convert our heathen souls? They all want to sound like those they consider to be their betters in their own land. Maybe that makes them better teachers of English," laughed Samuel. "By the way, do you know my family who gave me the name Atachawayo at my birth?"

"Atachawayo is a great name. My uncle had that name. He was taken from our people many years ago when he was very young. It was said that he was taken by a slave hunting party of Mashona after he had killed a lion. When our people discovered this, they hunted all the Mashona they could find to discover where he had gone or perhaps where he had been taken. Many Mashona were captured and made to talk, and it was then that we discovered that young Atachawayo was sold to the whites in Mozambique and taken away by ship. The People of Heaven took the Mashonas' gold and their weapons away from them and melted them together. Then our people staked the Mashona out on the grass who had taken our Atachawayo to sell to the slave traders. Our people staked them out with their faces to the Heavens from which we came. The Mashona had their mouths forced open, and the liquid gold and steel was poured down their noses and throats so that they could take their wealth from stealing a Matabele man into the next world with them. Atachawayo is the hero of my childhood, and you are that man! You are my uncle and the very last of your royal generation! It was my father and his brothers who exacted this revenge on the Mashona. It was they who related your story around the fires at night. Even our king celebrated your fame. And now you, the famous Atachawayo has come back to set us free."

This revelation had its effect. The life of his family, after Samuel was taken away, had changed. All of the tales told about him as a young warrior had grown in significance, and they were made part of the history of his people. As the older men, who had remembered Atachawayo as a stolen young warrior approaching his sixteenth summer sat about the fires at night, they told their tales of the absent African son. The young ones who were unborn at the time of Samuel's capture listened to the stories told about his stern character and fierce courage in fighting men and killing lions. The young boys had thrilled at the story of his courage in facing the Mashona slave catchers alone and striking fear into them as he felled so many of their number before he was taken. Atachawayo was a man who had cost much to capture. He was held up as the youthful ideal for all Matabele Zulu warriors to follow, except for one thing. The Zulu warrior should not be rash and mistake this rashness for bravery. In that, there could be sorrow and even slavery. That too was told as the lesson to be learned from "The Tale of Atachawayo" as it had become to be called over the last three decades. Samuel smiled as he enjoyed this grudging bit of fame. He was happy that he had not been forgotten by his people.

For the next two hours the two Matabele talked softly and in a language that Pompey had never heard. As he watched Samuel and Siliva in conversation, he wondered why Samuel never taught him his language.

Time passed, and the men fed themselves as well as the slaves who were still in their pens. It was not decided how best to free the non-Matabeles with the least danger to themselves or others. The inter-tribal hatreds of hundreds of years were ingrained into all of these different people. Forced together now only by the circumstances of their capture, they appeared to fear and hate each other even while locked up in their pens. Freeing the captives would be a delicate process. The one thing that all the other captives shared, besides their tribal hatred of each other, was the common fear they all had of the Matabele Zulus who were the most skilled and united warrior people in all of Southern Africa. With the Matabele out of the slave pens and armed, the subject peoples were content to stay in their pens under the protection of these unknown Europeans who have appeared to have killed or captured the Portuguese slavers. That at least they found encouraging even in the midst of their confusion.

At long last, the boat returned from the ship with Ryder and the doctor. Samuel and Siliva had been sitting in quiet communion for two hours since they had exchanged their histories. The doctor went to the prostrate Samuel. Siliva went back to Pompey and the Captain. "I will tell you gentlemen, Samuel, as you call him, is a great man. His life is and has been a legend to our people ever since he was stolen away so long ago. I do not think that he has long to live, and I and my people owe him our freedom. I will do whatever you wish to bring to him this Whitehouse. I think that he will live to exact his revenge. I think that his hate will keep him alive that long. Now I will go and tell my men what I have committed them to do. Your Samuel is so honored among us that there will be nothing that they will not do to please him or you as his agents."

"Samuel is famous in your villages then," said Captain Beers.

Siliva seemed a bit put out and shook his head. "I really don't think that you gentlemen really understand. Samuel has never existed for us here, but Atachawayo is a national hero like

Nelson is for the English you see. We have all been told his story while growing up in our families our whole lives. This great man is my uncle you see. My father was his brother. We will cooperate together. Atachawayo and I have made a plan to make the man Whitehouse come to us. As you may have observed, we are far from presentable. Your people will walk us down to the sea to bathe as if we are still held captive here. If Whitehouse is watching, it will put his mind at rest that all is well here, and we are still being held for him and are being cared for, bathed, and fed. And then he will think a new idea. He will think that his property has been sold to another. To the Captain of this other ship which has arrived not far from his own. This will bring him to you. He will think that the Portuguese have sold his cargo for a higher price. He will be furious. He will not think clearly. He will make mistakes, and we will fetch him up as our captive."

"I think that Whitehouse watches the goings on here from his ship," said Captain Beers.

"I think that this Whitehouse is a careful man most of the time. He knows that a slave that seems docile may cut his throat if given a chance. He may even have heard something of the fight. He must have noticed the movements of your boats during the daylight. If he sees the slaves being washed in the sea, he may think one of two things. First, he might think that the situation here is normal. Second, he might think that the Portuguese might be making a better deal with you for the slaves. In that case, he might come ashore in force to investigate if he is being cheated. After all, he knows who he is dealing with. That means that he will not trust the Portuguese. Yes, I think that this bathing in the sea will draw him out, and we shall be ready for him," said Siliva.

"That is very shrewd thinking," said the Captain. "I think that you are spot on Siliva. After everyone is fed, we will go down to the beach. Will you have any trouble with your people with this plan?"

"Just as your men follow you, these men will follow me

without question if they want to live one moment longer in this mortal world. I am a son of a sub-chief of the Matabele Zulu and kin to the man who should have been our king, Atachawayo. He is the man you know as Samuel. For us there is no Samuel as I have told you. In the absence of a man of higher authority, my word is law here. My people will do as I tell them to do, and they will do it willingly."

CHAPTER LIX

The doctor examined Samuel for some time before walking over to Pompey and the Captain. "I'm afraid Samuel isn't going to make it. From what I can see, he has had a heart attack. He has worked hard all of his life, and his heart has given out. The sweating, the pains in his arms, the pain in his teeth, and the constriction he feels in his chest all indicate that the next episode may be his last. After I had talked to him for a while I found out that this was not his first attack. These began months ago, and they have been getting worse. Frankly, I do not know how the man is still alive."

"But he seemed so strong and well until now. There have been no signs that he was suffering any trouble," said Pompey.

"Samuel is a proud man. His trouble began some time ago. He has been hiding it from all of you. He wanted to finish this business before he rested. Had he taken rest and eaten a light diet even a few years ago, he might have gone on living for many years to come, but now the damage is quite beyond repair I'm afraid. Each attack was a vicious rendering of his heart doing greater and greater damage. We know too little about the human body, but we do know that you can push yourself only so far. We don't know a great deal about the heart. Someday we might be able to cure conditions like Samuel's. All we know is that excessive work, or too much strong drink, and heavy and coarse, or rich food taken in quantity will tend to kill people disposed to apoplexy and related disorders. He must rest and avoid upset if he wants to live even a little time."

"Have you spoken of this to him doctor?" asked Pompey.

"No I have not. We do not think it best to let the patient know these things," said the doctor solemnly.

"You had better tell Samuel everything that you have told me. He will want to know everything so that he can plan his moves. In fact, I must insist that you tell him now," said Pompey.

"I can't do that. I just cannot blurt out the fact to the man that he is going to die!"

"This is not a drawing room in Boston or London. This is Africa, and he is royalty and a warrior of the Matabele nation. You will tell him in detail what is wrong with him, or you will force me to do it without the proper notion of what I am talking about. I don't think that I can say this to you doctor any plainer than that. Samuel is not a mere man. He is a Matabele warrior and a man of great respect and courage. Besides all that do you seriously think that you are going to tell him something that he does not already know? You must show this man respect doctor. Tell him everything. I do not think that I must make this a direct order do I?"

"You are leaving me no choice then. Very well, but I'll do it in my own way. If you will excuse me, I must talk with my patient."

The doctor walked over to Samuel and sat talking to him for ten minutes. Pompey could see Samuel nodding in response to what he was being told. The doctor rose and walked back to the Captain and Pompey.

"He wants to speak to you Pompey. Try not to excite him."

"Should he be moved back to the ship? My wife could look after him until I can come aboard," asked Pompey.

"I'm afraid that moving him would kill him. At least he will last a little longer here. He is content and even happy to die on his native soil. Perhaps we could make him a bit more comfortable."

"I will not talk to him long doctor, but do everything you can for him."

"I will. Now go and speak to him. Try not to upset him. I shall give him something for the pain."

Pompey crossed the clearing to where Ryder had fashioned a shelter over Samuel. The big man motioned Pompey to kneel beside him so that he could whisper to him and not be heard by the others.

"Now hear me Pompey. I cannot last long, and I must have Whitehouse delivered into my hands before I die. If I do not have this man delivered into my hands, I will die dishonored, and Whitehouse will win in the end."

"I cannot tell you how sorry I am Samuel. I feel that the best part of me will go with you into that afterlife to which I will also go someday. You are my father and I shall never forget you. You are the true friend of my heart, and I shall love you until the day I die."

"This is no different than Anna's death. When your heart breaks, there is no fixing it. I do not have time for this sort of foolishness. My nephew and brother in battle, Siliva, tells me that Whitehouse will come here in the late afternoon to see if more Matabele have been captured for him or more likely taken from him. Whitehouse is a very greedy man. This can be used against him. Send the boat back to the ship. Whitehouse has no idea of just how many we are ashore right now. By now, he has seen the warriors at their bath in the sea. Shortly they will be marched back here. Whitehouse will think that they will be in their pens. They will in fact be armed and waiting for Whitehouse and his men. You and Siliva will take them alive, and Siliva and I will dispose of them in our own way. We have a plan that will do the greatest justice. We claim that as our right, and you must not argue that point with me, or," Samuel said smiling, "You will kill me just as if you had struck me down in a fight."

"Samuel, that is not fair," said Pompey sadly.

"I do not wish to be fair. I want my own way, and if this is what I have to do to get it, I will," laughed Samuel. "Now leave me to sleep and rest, and do as I have told you to do."

"I will," said Pompey.

Pompey returned to the Captain and the doctor and related what had passed between Samuel and himself. The three of them agreed to do as Samuel wished, because there was nothing else to be done. The Captain gave orders to his men to range themselves about the clearing with their arms loaded in order to take Whitehouse and his men when they landed. When Siliva and the other Matabele warriors returned from the beach, they were told of the last refinements to the plan. Siliva told his men to arm themselves and wait for his orders before acting.

Captain Beers sent four men back to the ship with casks as if they had been on a detail to get fresh water. And as Siliva suspected, all this activity would be observed by Whitehouse from his quarterdeck.

CHAPTER LX

Whitehouse watched with interest all of the activity ashore. For four hours, something had been going on between the Portuguese slave traders and the British merchants. The watch had alerted Whitehouse when he heard a faint din from the shore. Whitehouse came onto the deck and scanned the beach and the trees, which obscured the slave-trading factory. Nothing more could be seen from the ship. Whitehouse was told of a boat being sent out from the British ship to the shore with some men in it. The lookout confessed that he had not thought too much about it and had not even noted how many men were in the boat. At that point, Whitehouse boxed his ears and knocked him to the deck.

"Look Captain sir, there are niggers coming down to the beach. They seem to be under guard," cried out the mate.

Whitehouse put the glass to his eye and confirmed what his mate had reported. He studied the beach scene for some time then turned to his mate. "Well, I'll be damned! If I did not think that he was dead, or at least on his damned Yankee island, I would swear that the big fellow there was my old mate Starbuck."

With that he threw his head back in laughter then resumed watching the shore. Half an hour later, the slaves were gathered out of the surf and marched back in the direction of the slave camp.

"What the Hell are these damned Portuguese playing at? They don't wash the niggers until they are ready to be transported. Wright, take an armed party of a dozen men over to that damned ship and find out what the Hell they are up to. And be damned quick about it."

"Aye, aye sir," said Wright as he ran to do the Captain's bidding.

Within five minutes, the long boat was over the side and moving in the direction of the English ship. Whitehouse watched as Wright closed the mile distance between the two ships. In a short time, he could see the longboat nearing the Englishman. To his joy he could see one of his men firing a musket and Wright standing with a raised fist and addressing the ship. Then to his unbelieving eyes came the unexpected sight of a brass gun being run out from a deck level gun port followed by a second a few moments later. Then a third of a trio of twenty-four pounders, capable of firing a solid shot more than two miles, was run out.

"The damned ship is armed to the teeth! What the bloody Hell does that mean?" bellowed Whitehouse.

Through his glass, Whitehouse saw Wright take his seat in the longboat again, and then the mate turned the longboat back to the ship. Whitehouse watched as his men made their way back. At last, Wright regained the deck to report to Whitehouse.

"What the Hell was that all about?" demanded the Captain of his mate.

"That ship is an armed private vessel sir," replied the mate.

"Armed against what?" demanded the Captain.

"Somali and any other kind of pirates I was informed just as I was ordered to push off or be sunk. The mate commanding in his captain's absence said that the guns were manned by a former royal marine master gunner and his crew.

"Did he threaten your boat Wright?"

"You might say that sir, and then the ship's mate said that it would be no trouble to dismast our ship seeing that we are so close. He said that I had better push off as his men were anxious for some gunnery practice," Wright replied.

"I take it that the Captain must be ashore with a party of his people. Let us wait awhile and see how things shake out," said Whitehouse as calm as could be. It was obvious that the wheels were turning inside of the darker regions of the Captain's head.

"Mr. Wright. Do you think that this mate now in command of the ship you have just attempted to visit would trade that fine vessel for his beloved Captain?"

"I don't know sir. That is an interesting question," replied the mate.

"Should certain things go right ashore in the next few hours, you may find yourself the master of a prize ship Mr. Wright. We will see. One never knows what might happen. She is a pretty Boston built beauty and should fetch sixty thousand or more in a quick sale I should think."

"Captain, I think that you are a genius."

"Why thank you Mr. Wright. You are a much better mate than Starbuck ever was."

A half hour passed. Then four men could be seen walking down to the English ship's long boat rolling casks. These in turn were loaded onto the boat. The four men then struck out for their ship. "They are taking on water. They are taking on water, and they must be talking to the slave traders." Then the awful truth dawned on him. "These damned Brits are going to steal my slaves! I won't have it. I'll kill the lot of them. The filthy bastards want the world and my property too. I won't have it!"

He turned to his mate, "Mr. Wright, arm the crew to the teeth. We are going ashore."

"How many men sir?" asked the mate.

"All but three. Fill all four of our boats. We'll teach these Portuguese bastards a lesson about loyalty. I'll kill all of those sonsofbitches and take the damn slaves for nothing. What will it matter? After this, I'm done with this rotten trade anyway. And who the Hell is going to care about the fate of a bunch of filthy

Portuguese slave traders. Not even the Portuguese I'll wager. Now get your bloody arses on the boats and be quick about it."

"But what about those twenty four pounders sir?" asked Wright.

"They have no real reason to use them, and they didn't use them before. They may not even be loaded except for the one. Once we are on shore in force, we can take their Captain and friends without much difficulty, and with their Captain as our hostage, there will be no problems with the British gunner, his crew, or his twenty-four pounders. One captive sea Captain trumps any number of brass cannons."

Within fifteen minutes the four boats were loaded with the ship's company armed with muskets and cutlasses. Then Whitehouse made for the shore in force. Whitehouse had a brace of pistols in his belt and his Scots claymore at his side. He loved this weapon, which he wielded with such skill. He loved its eight-pound weight and the fact that he could take a man's head off at one blow. Whitehouse thought that such a graphic act might return the Portuguese trader's loyalty to himself if needs be. Then he mulled the situation over in his mind, and he mumbled to himself, "I think that I'll do it. One of their chappies heads rolling about the ground might be just the thing to bring the rotters to heel quickly. Maybe I'll just do them all and put paid to their treachery. Then my damned profits will be very high indeed. I just might take all the slaves needed to fill two ships. I'm sure that the Britisher's men are not all royal marines."

"What was that Captain sir?" asked one of the rowers.

"Mind your business you insolent rogue, and keep rowing," snapped Whitehouse.

The mile row to the shore consumed the better part of half an hour. The Captain's boat beached first, and the dozen sailors pulled it way up onto the shore. "You, Ryan. You will stay with the boats."

By now, all four of the boats had landed, and a man was

ordered to stay with each. Whitehouse drew the rest of his men in close to him.

"Now listen and listen well. These bastards are going to steal our laves from us. The very slaves that will make each one of you rich. Very, very rich indeed. Are we going to let that happen? "

A chorus of, "No sir," followed.

Whitehouse looked back at the English ship. Nothing appeared to be changed. No movement was to be detected, and no boats put out from her. Whitehouse wondered why. Then he decided not to question his good fortune. "Very well then. Follow me, and do not act except on my orders no matter what may happen," snapped Whitehouse whose blood was up.

This was followed by a scattering of, "Aye, aye sirs." Then off they marched in the direction of the slave compound.

The soft sound of the waves breaking on the beach receded as the men moved inland. They were strung out along the path, which had been so well worn by the soles of thousands of feet over the last four centuries. Africans, Arabs, and Europeans alike had traveled over this path in the trade of Black ivory. The men, women, and children who had walked down to this shore for the last time could not be counted. Tens and hundreds of thousands of souls had marched this way never to see their families or their country again. Some of them had lived hard lives here in Africa, but at least their own life that they had lived on their own term. Those lives, as hard as they might be, were preferable to the slavery that they would come to know all too well. The lust for slaves in the west had brought a profound sorrow to the whole of Africa, but this one trail had seen more sorrow than any other highway in the world over the centuries.

Whitehouse swaggered on leading his men through the oppressive heat of the afternoon. In spite of the wet heat that he despised, Whitehouse felt alive in leading this bold attack on the unprepared Portuguese. He would put paid to those who would sell him out to his hated countrymen. He rested his hand on the hilt of his great sword in anticipation of the battle to come. In his mind he thought, "This afternoon's work will be the talk of Africa and even the world for years to come, but I'll be far away in my villa near the Mediterranean."

Indeed his own thoughts drifted back to France where he would live in the summer and then to Brazil where he would winter should he decide against the idea of going into the China trade. He mused that a pretty woman in each place would suit him well. Not to marry mind, but as housekeepers and someone to be with when the fancy took him. He was sick of having to make do with the cabin boy. Unlike Wright, he was not by nature a true sodomite. Even Ajax was essentially more female than most women. Whitehouse dreamed of this ideal living arrangement as his own captain's paradise on earth. He was fairly sure that this would be the only paradise he would ever know. He kept musing on this as the slave trader's encampment came into view.

Whitehouse and his men stopped. There was a strange and unnatural silence, louder in its presentiment of danger than the biting roar of any twenty-four pounder. Suddenly there was felt an air of danger so chilled that all of humanity seemed dead in spite of the sweltering heat. "Hello the camp," called out Whitehouse."

There was no answer. Whitehouse turned to his mate and said, "Mr. Wright, I do not like this at all. Something has happened here. Something is wrong, very wrong. Be on your guard men. There is some great mischief afoot. See to your arms men!"

The prospect that some of the slaves had overpowered the guards on the way back from the beach crossed Whitehouse's mind. Maybe with this Matabele bunch the Portuguese had bitten off more than they could properly digest. Whitehouse was sure that his men, who were so well armed, could beat off any attack mounted by a party of disorganized slaves.

"Do you think that we ought to go back to the ship Captain?" answered the mate.

"I would agree with that. I think that I may have been tricked, and I am not sure of our position here. Mr. Wright, we shall make for the boats, and get underway. Something is very wrong here," said Whitehouse.

Then boomed a voice all too familiar, "There you are you scurvy cur! Are you ready for what I've got for you?"

All at once Starbuck could be seen in the clearing with a pistol in his left hand and a cutlass in his right.

"What the Devil are you doing here Starbuck?" bellowed Whitehouse.

"Are you surprised sir? Did you think that I'd be in some shallow grave in Five Points now or dumped into the sea by those New York boys? Well I'll tell you this. Four men are in the sea keeping Davy Jones company. Each of those four who were going to do me in. I killed them all in one night, and it wasn't all that difficult to do you see. I just pretended that each one of them was you. Now about your friends. I'm afraid that you'll not be seeing them for a while. They are not feeling too well. In fact, they are all dead. I want you to disarm yourselves. Now!" roared Starbuck. "Throw down your weapons! All of you if you want to live one mortal moment!"

More than half the men obeyed Starbuck's order at once. "Pick up those guns at once you blockheads," cried Whitehouse. "It's your only fucking chance to live you whore's sons. Do you hear me!"

"Shoot the first man who moves," bellowed Starbuck.

"He's only one man you idiots. I don't even know what the daft man is doing here. Pick up your weapons damn your eyes!" ordered Whitehouse again. A sailor stooped to pick up his musket. As he did so, a shot rang out, and the man fell dead shot clean through the head.

"Who is next?" said Starbuck in a flat calm voice that sounded as if he were asking if anyone wanted another piece of pie as he slowly advanced on the party led by Whitehouse. Not a man moved a muscle. "Any man with a weapon in his hands in five seconds will be shot just like this poor bastard," announced Starbuck.

All of Whitehouse's crews' weapons struck the ground at once. Only Whitehouse held onto his claymore.

"What are you doing? He has only a few fellows in the trees there. We can take them! We can kill them all you blockheads! What the Hell is the matter with you Wright! What is the matter with any of you? Pick up your weapons and follow me. If we are meant to die here, sell your lives dearly!" yelled Whitehouse.

"Gentlemen show yourselves to the great Captain Whitehouse and his crew," called out Starbuck. From all sides, Captain Beers and his men emerged along with Siliva and the armed Matabele warriors.

"Gather all their weapons and bind their arms behind their backs," ordered Captain Beers.

"Strip them of their clothes first. See if they like taking the first step of a life's journey into slavery," ordered Siliva. "We will give them a slave's loincloth later. I think that they need to get used to feeling like the lowly human merchandise that they now are."

"Very well," said Beers, "Let it be done."

The Matabele set about the task with delight as the tables were turned. Whitehouse alone stood armed with his naked blade in his hand.

"I'll fight any one of you. I'll fight all of you if you have the stomach for it! I am not afraid to die right here, but I'll take half a dozen of you cur dogs with me by Heaven! And you cowards," Whitehouse yelled to his all but now naked crew, "See how a real man dies. I'll not be any man's fucking slave. Come on then. Who among you is to be first? You Starbuck? You failed at living. Do you want to test me and taste death?"

"I begged for that honor Captain, but it was claimed by another who was far more deserving of the honor than I. I would love to oblige you Whitehouse, in fact I'd give all I have for the pleasure of splitting your head open."

"I'll fight you, you filthy old cur," said Siliva. "I'll fight you to avenge the great Atachawayo."

"No my friends," said Pompey. "You may have him when I am done with him, but since my father Atachawayo is not able to fight this devil himself, it falls to me to take this Whitehouse down."

"I'll shoot you like a dog," called out Whitehouse as he took aim with his pistol and fired.

His bullet flew wide of the mark. As he attempted to draw his other pistol, Siliva threw a rock that slammed into Whitehouse's arm forcing him to release the pistol, which fell harmlessly onto the ground.

"Using a pistol! Now, that is hardly what I call sporting Old Boy," Siliva called out to a confused Whitehouse.

"So be it," roared Whitehouse as he unsheathed his blade and aimed a man-killing blow at Pompey with his claymore.

Pompey parried the stroke with ease just as he parried the next dozen ill delivered blows, which came quickly and with fury but little skill. Each blow however was delivered with slightly diminished strength. For minutes on end Pompey played with Whitehouse easily letting his thrusts and slashes fall harmlessly on his skillfully wielded blade. Pompey allowed Whitehouse to spend his fury until most of his energy was gone. He played with the Captain until it became obvious that Pompey was just amusing himself, and then Pompey attacked with all the cunning of the academic swordsman that he had become.

Whitehouse could scarcely keep his feet. Pompey launched a furious slashing attack that sent Whitehouse reeling back. For minutes, Pompey's blade danced the dance of death. His sword almost sang as he further exhausted the Captain and at last beat him to the ground, disarmed him, and held his blade under Whitehouse's chin. "Well, Captain, who is the yellow cur bastard now?" Pompey taunted with a savage ring in his voice.

"Finish me off you bloody bastard," cried the Captain. "I'm a dead man you nigger loving vermin. Put an end to me for the love of Christ as you are a Christian."

"I am not a Christian, and I'm an African bastard too, and in the end the question of your life or death is not my privilege to decide. Before you meet your God, there is another mortal man who will decide your fate, and it is his mercy that you must beg," said Pompey with a sneer as an evil smile took shape on his lips. Pompey savored the moment of Whitehouse's downfall.

Whitehouse knelt on the ground with his blade by his side. He was broken and could not lift his claymore or indeed himself. "Take his sword Mr. Starbuck, bring it along to the great Atachawayo as a souvenir," said Pompey.

Starbuck jumped forward to do Pompey's bidding. Whitehouse tried to reach up to grasp his old mate's arm. Starbuck brushed him away with a single movement of his hand. Whitehouse managed to choke back a sob of fury. He could only mumble, "You traitor. I made you a rich man."

"No sir," returned Starbuck, "All you did for me was seduce me and steal my life.

CHAPTER LXI

"Pick that man up and bring him along," ordered Pompey indicating the fallen Whitehouse.

Two sailors seized the slaver under the arms and dragged him after Pompey who was striding off to where Samuel was sitting almost enthroned under a canvass awning, which was strung from the trees. On one side of him now sat Siliva like a councilor and on the other side of him was the doctor. Captain Beers, Starbuck, and his mate moved to the side of where Samuel was situated like some high chief surrounded by his generals and advisers.

"Throw him down on his face before Atachawayo, a most high chief of the Matabele Nation so that at last in his miserable life he can show some proper respect for a far superior man," intoned Siliva like a court chamberlain.

The sailors threw Whitehouse down with all the force they could manage. By now, Whitehouse was caked in dirt and sweat, which trickled down his face forming rivulets complete with dozens of tributaries. He struggled to rise, but as he did so, the crack of an ox hide whip was heard over the fallen Captain. Whitehouse's shirt and back was slashed open by the force of its braided coil as it unwound and broke its action on Whitehouse's back leaving a stripe of red raw flesh under the force of its impact.

"Do not lash him except on the orders of Atachawayo. Lashing this dog will only serve to reduce his value in the market, and he is already far past his prime. As it is, we will be fortunate to get anything for the old bloody bugger at all," laughed Siliva.

"What do you take me for you nigger? You simpering baboon!" snarled Whitehouse through his pain and tears of humiliation.

"Baboon? What pray tell is this baboon? Is it the tribe of your mother perchance?" asked Siliva returning Whitehouse's sneer with another. "You sir are in the dust. You are quite grand no longer, and you are, in point of fact, only property to be sold, lashed, or killed as the great Atachawayo may wish. My only concern now is that you are such a shabby specimen that you will bring almost nothing very much when we sell you in the slave markets of the Sudan. The rest of your tribe is a bit better and younger, but they are so ghostly pale. Something must be done about them or they won't bring much money at all in the Sudan where you are all going to market in a week or so. We'll have to feed you up as well as teach you your place, some basic obedience as it were. It is well that we have pens to keep you in is it not? Maybe we'll set some of your fellows to sweeping them out once a day to keep your filth down to a degree we can manage. We don't want you to attract too many flies you see," said Siliva with a wicked laugh that was hollow and without mirth.

"What do you want of me and my men?" cried Whitehouse suddenly reduced to a beaten old man.

"Nothing more or less than you wanted of us. We are going to sell you in the markets of the Sudan to the highest bidders. What happens to you after that is done is of no matter to us. You are only slaves after all. You are base trade goods. You will be quite alone with nothing but your own resources to help preserve you. We just look to profit a bit from your sale. We only follow your own example in this slave business. We do not have your experience in these matters of the slave trade, and we will most likely be cheated, but since we only intend to do this one time as a lark, it really does not matter how much gold this little business venture brings to us. When one stops to think of it what do we care? We would like your professional advice in this venture Whitehouse. After all, you have a long and valued experience in this trade," said Siliva. "What would the fair asking price be of this wretched lot of yours? I am sure that most of these pale white creatures have little value being that they are such poor specimens of men. Maybe we could turn some of you into women. In the Sudan, those among you who have fine yellow hair would bring a fine price if we could snip off a bit here and there and turn you into women. Is that not true Captain Whitehouse?"

Siliva then motioned to his warriors, and Whitehouse's men were marched back into the encampment naked and tied together with a sort of yolk-like device of wood attached to each of their necks, linking them one to another like pale sausages. Whitehouse looked at them attired in nothing but the dust that clung to their sweaty and naked bodies. Suddenly the horrible reality of the situation struck him, and he slumped to the ground. He was now truly a beaten old man.

The big man, who had been identified as Atachawayo, spoke to Whitehouse who was almost prone in the dust before him.

"Look at me Captain Whitehouse. Do you not recognize me?" asked Samuel in a voice that was still commanding in spite of all that had happened to him.

Whitehouse stared at him from where he lay. "Should I know you boy?" he asked mustering all of the cold contempt he could manage.

With that Pompey struck Whitehouse with the side of his blade knocking him back into the dust.

"Speak with respect when addressing royalty, dog!" he bellowed. "Now make apologies or I'll have the skin off you."

And with that he ripped the torn and bloodied shirt from Whitehouse's bloody back. "Beg pardon of the Great Atachawayo now dog or I will have more flesh flayed from your miserable carcass until there is nothing left on your bones for the jackals to feast upon," bellowed Pompey again.

Choking back sobs of rage and frustration, Whitehouse managed to say between gritted teeth, “I beg your pardon.”

“I beg your pardon what?” asked Pompey in an almost sotto voce.

“I beg your pardon sir.”

“Now that is better,” said Siliva sneering at Whitehouse’s distress. “We might be able to get a few shillings more for you now that you have learned a little proper civility.

Most of Whitehouse’s men were quietly sobbing, as they stood there naked and watching their chief’s humiliation as he lay in the dust. Pompey then noticed one big lad, who could not have been more than fourteen years of age, standing there among the older men. He was tall for his age, but appeared to be in shock and his whole body was wracked with quiet sobbing and shaking. Pompey made note of the boy. Samuel’s voice cut through the situation as he summoned all of his strength for the scene that was to come. “Whitehouse, do you know who I am?”

Looking up through his sweat and dirt encrusted eyes at Samuel’s face all Whitehouse could manage was, “I can’t say that I do. Is there some reason that I should know you?”

“Watch your tongue dog. Speak with great respect or I shall cut your tongue from out of your mouth and hang it around your neck. You are addressing a high chief and prince of the Matabele Nation.” With that, Siliva ordered one of his warriors to give Whitehouse another lashing with his whip. “Now dog, answer with sweeter words or stay silent.”

Whitehouse chose the latter. Samuel leaned slightly forward. “Listen to me Whitehouse. Thirty-five years ago, you took me from this very place contrary to the laws of your own country and those of the United States. The United States to which you took me by force had joined Britain in outlawing the slave trade eight years before you stole me out of Africa. You brought me into a state of slavery. You put me on your ship, and took me to America. I saw women and children die under the lash both in Africa and on your bloody ship. I saw the poor bodies of slave women, and children, and those of their dead men thrown to the sharks. When I was taken to New Orleans with a white man you had lashed by the name of James Forrester, I saw a small chance to survive and get back to this very place someday to make you pay for your abduction of me by making a pact with this Forrester to steal myself and some of your gold. When we arrived in New Orleans, Forrester and I ran away from your ship. We made a life for ourselves in Georgia where you tracked him down years later and killed him. You made his death seem as if he had suffered a fall from a horse. Now you will pay for killing him and robbing me of the greater part of my life. You will pay for causing the deaths of many more Africans and for throwing an entire cargo of living beings to the sharks. This man, Starbuck, who has mended his ways and has fought with us this day, is also witness to all that I say. He knows everything that I have said to be true. Is that not so Mr. Starbuck?"

"All that the mighty Atachawayo has told you is true," said Starbuck, "And for what I have done for the larger part of my miserable life, I am truly sorry Atachawayo." Kneeling before Samuel, Starbuck said, "I humbly beg your pardon sir and ask for your forgiveness for all the sins I have committed against your people and yourself."

"Arise Starbuck. You have proven yourself indeed a true friend in the end, and that has saved you from your demons I think, but not you Whitehouse. Nothing can save you. You have no honor, nor do you have compassion or sorrow for those whose lives you have crushed into the dust or sorrow for your own life so miserably spent. You have not begged for anything, even mercy or, at least for my pardon and forgiveness for stealing my life. Don't you think that the least you should do for that crime against me is that you should ask for my pardon?"

"No, nor do I intend to, you jumped up Black bastard! You can rot where you are, and that idiot Forrester was nothing but a low cheat. I curse you both for the living and dead vermin you are," cried Whitehouse.

"You did not heed my warning," said Siliva who was on Whitehouse in a moment. He then called three strong Matabele warriors and told them to force Whitehouse's jaws open. Then Siliva called for tongs expressly on hand in the Portuguese slaver's box of tools for this very purpose. Siliva ordered a warrior to grasp the Captain's tongue with the tongs and pulled the organ from his mouth. Then when this was done, the organ was removed by Siliva with a quick slicing action of his knife. Siliva had made good his threat. Whitehouse was unconscious on the ground.

"Give me a knife and place it in that cooking fire until it is very hot for cauterizing the wound," commanded Siliva. Then he cauterized the wound of the unconscious Whitehouse with the red-hot knife blade stopping any more bleeding from the stump of the tongue. It was obvious that Siliva had done this before. The string Siliva had ordered was found and given to him. Using his knife, he pierced the organ and then hung it about the unconscious Whitehouse's neck. Then, Siliva stuffed the rag into Whitehouse's mouth again. "That will save the bastard from bleeding to death should such a need arise. I will not be cheated of my prize and revenge. Now strip him, and take him to the slave pens with the others." Turning to Samuel, he said, "Please pardon me, but I think that the slaves should know that we keep our promises and that they must be obedient."

Samuel smiled sadly, and in the old language of his young manhood he spoke. "You did well my nephew and brother. Today you were my good right hand. Your father, who was the brother of my flesh would be as proud of you as I. Seeing that you were born so long after I was taken, I am glad that I could give you a brother's protection now from these jackals who would have taken you from your home and people."

"Atachawayo, say my greetings to all the generations spawned of all of our parents when you see them in the afterlife, and tell them how well pleased I am to have had the great privilege to know my brave and good uncle and brother of battle. If I do not see you again in this world, we will meet in the spirit kingdom where we will hunt the lion together. Let me embrace you in love and respect," Siliva returned in Zulu.

The two warriors embraced, and Samuel said in English, "I would speak with you alone Pompey."

Pompey came to his friend and knelt as Whitehouse was dragged away by Siliva's warriors and taken to the pens along with the others of his crew.

"I saw you looking at that young lad among Whitehouse's men. He is too young to know his mind. Do not send him to the Sudan. Take him out of the pens and give him his clothes. He may not even be as old as I was when I was taken by the Mashona. Besides, there must be someone left from that sorry crew to tell the tale of what happens to bad men who steal the lives of innocent people after we are all dead and are no more. There must be someone among the white men to tell this morality tale. Now I am very tired Pompey. I want to rest, maybe to sleep forever with Anna, and my parents, and my brothers. Now that Siliva tells me that my generation is all gone it may be that it is my time to join them. My older nephew is king now, but I ask you to not stay here in Africa. I know now that this is not the land for you or your lady, Violet. The Matabele will never accept you. I have spoken of this to Siliva, and in this he agrees with me," said Samuel softly. "The old ways cannot be set aside. You Pompey can never be one of the Children of Heaven."

"I will do as you say Samuel just as I always have," replied Pompey.

"I must change my mind about your Violet. I can see that she is a very good woman for you. She has real courage, and I am afraid that I have not appreciated her fine qualities, as I should have. Please give her my apologies for my stupidity. I ask you both to forgive me for things you can never know. Take my gold from my cabin and all that which I have in The Bank of England and Starbuck's too. Do good with it. Free your people, and live well. Take your wife, and go to some friendly place far from here. I really think that England is the place for you. America, with her ugly slave institutions and ignorant people who support them is no place for a civilized man to live and have a family. Most of Africa is not too forgiving of your being what you cannot help being either. You are just too damned white my son, and the world is not so loving as you and I. My great plan did not turn out all that well, and I take no pleasure from seeing Whitehouse brought so low after all, but at least Whitehouse can do no more harm. Do you think I should express sorrow for what I have done?"

Pompey did not answer.

Then all of a sudden, Samuel smiled and laughed, "What the Hell Pompey! I lied. Revenge on that bastard is ever so sweet. Now my son, I must sleep. I am so very tired. Soon I shall be truly able to make my way home. Stay with me until I have gone. Let me see if Anna was right. So far I have not seen the River Jordan or chariots of any kind. I do not think that she was right about that bit of geography. And one more thing. When I am gone, you must be guided by Siliva, but remember that I love you my son," Samuel laughed quietly then smiled at Pompey, slowly closed his eyes, and exhaled one last time. And all the rest was silence.

CHAPTER LXII

Many weighty matters had to be worked out during the next several days. Siliva and Samuel had agreed before Samuel's death that he would be buried with all the honors of a great sub-chief of the Matabele. Samuel wished to be taken to a place not far from where his father's kraal stood on his final journey home. As Atachawayo he would be carried by the men he had saved from a slave's life. This place of his final rest would not be many miles from where he had been taken so many years before by the Mashona. As Atachawayo, Samuel's body had been prepared for his long journey home to his beloved Matabeleland. Pompey had said to Siliva, "When shall we depart?"

"There is no 'we' in this departure my friend. No outsider may go where the Matabele now will go to attend to Atachawayo on his last progress home. You are not one of us and can never be Matabele. But of course you have always known this. Atachawayo had said that this was so," said Siliva.

"But Siliva, he was my father. He was the father of my choice and his choice as well." Pompey cried.

"No Pompey. Samuel James was your father, and it is he you mourn. You must bury him as is right, but Atachawayo the warrior of legend is ours. No outsider and no woman may go where we go to do these last rites for this great chief, this man who might even have been our king if he was not stolen away from us," said the stone faced Siliva.

"You really do not understand," said Pompey through his tears.

"Inkaba yakho ipli?" asked Siliva.

"I do not know your meaning," Pompey replied.

"I simply asked you, 'Where is your navel?' Can you answer me?" Siliva asked.

"I know that I cannot answer you in either your language or my own," responded Pompey.

"Then by saying what you have said, you have answered and given the reason that you cannot go with us tomorrow on our far journey. For the answer to that question can only be made by a Matabele who understands that I have asked you where you were born or more exactly where your umbilical cord was buried after you were born. This would tell us of your family and where they fit into things here. This would show us who you are and if you were qualified to attend the rites of so highly favored a man as Atachawayo. You can come and do him honor before he departs. In fact it is expected that many who will not be permitted to go to the burial shall be required to come before the secret ceremonies can be performed. Atachawayo knew that you could not go with him you see. He asked me to tell you why this would be so during our long talk. He said that you would respect him and loved him enough not to make a fuss. Is that the truth then? Did he allude to this himself?" Siliva asked knowing the answer to come.

"Yes. I think that is just what he was telling me at the end. Then that is the way it must be then. I know his voice when you speak his words Siliva. Can you at least tell me about the rituals?" said Pompey with dry eyes now.

"I can do that if you will not ask any questions of me about anything. I shall not tell you some things which are very sacred to us. I should not be even telling you this much, but for the love between you and Atachawayo I will. He will be taken before the rites to a place of honor where even women cannot go. Word will go out to all that are qualified to present themselves to this place of honor so that they can show to the world that they have had no responsibility for the great chief's death. To those who are far distant, spirit messengers will be sent forth to give the news of the great Atachawayo's death. These persons so far away will then send their spirit messengers back with their condolences. Only the gods have to know of this. After this only the true Matabele warriors will take Atachawayo off for a last hunt. We will all of us be together for a last time. After that hunt has concluded, we shall bury Atachawayo with all the honors of his rank. Then we shall plant over his grave an UmLahlankosi tree. The word UmLahlankosi in your language means something like, 'That which buries the chief.' it is a good name for such a tree. This good tree will mark Atachawayo's last resting place for many years."

Siliva paused a moment and looked at Pompey. Pompey returned his look and remained silent. He knew how the Matabele think. He knew that following instructions to the last letter was of paramount importance and showed respect. If silence was demanded, then silence was expected. And silence must be observed. Siliva smiled and nodded his approval then continued.

"This tree Pompey is sometimes also called by the Dutch the Blinkblaar Wag 'n Bietjie. It does not always keep its leaves, but no matter. It will bloom with or without them. In summer the UmLahlankosi will both flower and give fruit. This it will do even when it seems dead. The great chief can give us comfort and advice even if he be dead if one listens to the wind closely. Should the tree be cut down, the accursed hail or lightening will come. If left to itself, the tree will sprout leaves and provide those same leaves and fruit for the giraffe, antelope, cattle, goats, apes, and birds to feast upon. All this wonderful gift of life will benefit from the favors of Atachawayo beyond his death. Even beer can be made from the fruit of the UmLahlankosi. Is it not wondrous and not so sad at all?" asked Siliva offering Pompey a chance to answer this rhetorical question at last.

"Yes this is a very good thing Siliva," replied the young man who had been the spiritual son of Samuel but a stranger to the great warrior Atachawayo.

"Are you now content to have things arranged the way they are?" asked Siliva in a softer voice.

"Yes Siliva. I can see that this is the way things must be. I can see that this is what my father wanted, and it is right," replied Pompey with a sad smile.

Now Pompey had to turn his attention to other things that needed his attention. In many ways the Matabele and the way that they looked on other Africans bothered him deeply. Anna and Caesar had not been Matabele, yet he had loved and even respected them. It bothered him that The Children of Heaven were so dismissive of all other Africans. They were not alone in this however. Tribalism seemed to have swept all of the continent. This made him very sad. When he discussed this fact of African tribalism with Violet, she surprised him and opened his eyes to something that he could not see.

"Pompey open your eyes. What has been going on in Europe, Asia, and America through history. The Egyptians and the Jews? The Pagans and Christians? The Christians and the Jews? The Christians and Mohamedans? Catholics and Protestants? The English and the French? The Irish and English and the Americans? Pompey it has gone on and on everywhere on this planet. It is all evil and flies in the face of the most basic biblical injunction to 'Love one another'. You are right to be dismayed by this. My grandfather taught me to do what I can to make things better when the chance came to me. More than that cannot be done. As we set an example by our actions, we help to change things one life at a time dearest. Your distress does you credit. Do you understand what I am saying?" asked Violet.

"Once again I thank your wonderful grandfather Violet. To do what I can is all that I can reasonably expect of myself or anyone. You have wisdom my dearest, and I love you for it. You give me peace."

Pompey had insisted that the hundreds of slaves, held by the Portuguese slave traders, be released after giving their word, as best as anyone could understand them, that they would all depart for their tribal homelands as quickly as possible. Pompey also insisted that the passage home would be made with haste and in peace without causing harm to any other peoples whose lands would be crossed by the released and newly freed men and women. This was alas but a forlorn hope. The ancient rivalries among the tribes were the absolute reality among these captive people. Too many of the released slaves were mortal enemies and tempting targets for the redress of old or imagined outrages long past.

Each tribe, whose very existence was a living abomination to every other tribe, had this living legacy of ancient hate. Pompey had some trouble convincing Siliva of the wisdom of treating some of the captured people with the same respect that he would show to warriors of his own nation, which he respected. In the end, the Matabele leader agreed to stagger the release of all the captives thus giving each tribe the best chance to set out and return to their homes intact.

In spite of all the best efforts of Pompey and even Siliva, reports later arrived of tribal massacres and even the enslavement of some members of smaller tribes. The weak were forced into subjugation to the larger and more powerful tribesmen among those freed. Too many people never made their way home to their own countries in the distant African North, West and South. The ugly cycle of tribal warfare was forever continued for each new generation. No attempted good will could end that horrible reality of centuries of inter tribal hatred. Hate between tribes was even seen as a true virtue. And friendship between individuals of different tribes was seen as high treason to one's own people. There never could be a basis of understanding amounting to anything like friendship between these African peoples. This unfortunate fact was true all of the way up and down the African Coast and far into the vast continent's interior. It had been like this for thousands of years and would thus continue.

Pompey returned to the ship when he had done all he could to return the captured people to their homes. With a guard led by Siliva himself Pompey had boarded Captain Beer's vessel for the voyage to England. The others of the crew who had assisted with the release of the prisoners in the slave compound returned to the ship with the rescued cabin boy in tow. There was not a person in the whole company who was not anxious to sail away from this unhappy place of enslavement and death.

The Captain directed that the English lad captured at the slave compound be brought to his cabin. Then Captain Beers questioned the lad closely about his life and how he came to be on Whitehouse's ship in the first place. It seems that the boy had been an orphan in London who escaped from a workhouse. When he had escaped from the workhouse, he was starving, and he had hidden himself aboard a ship outbound for an unknown destination. The boy had only sought escape from the Hell of the workhouse, because life there was intolerable. He had been deposited there at the age of two after his mother had vanished back into the streets of the city from which she had come. The boy was told that he was thin and had a very bad cold when he had arrived at the workhouse, and none thought that he would live. But live he did and was given the name Tom Watt by the beadle in charge.

After he escaped the workhouse, Tom had made his way to the London docks clad only in a shirt and some stolen trousers that had been left airing in a clothes yard. His only belt had been a piece of hemp salvaged from some refuse heap. Once he had reached the docks, Tom had climbed aboard a ship in the dark of night. The next day, the ship began a voyage to South America. It seems that he had been discovered four days out, flogged, and made cabin boy on the vessel on which Mr. Wright served as first officer. It also seems that he had become the unwilling intimate companion of the self same Mr. Wright who took his pleasure with him and, in turn, the lad had gone along with him from one disreputable ship to another as a virtual and dependent piece of property. The boy had been brought along with Wright when the mate had sought employment with Whitehouse.

Whitehouse had also been at sea too long, and like some old Roman Senator, he had held to the philosophy that if he were the perpetrator of the act of sex with a male, it was not sodomy. Ajax had even reinforced that philosophy during his short sojourn with the Captain after the death of the unfortunate Mr. Ellis. Tom the workhouse boy had found himself shared by Whitehouse and the mate. This also bound these two men closer together in their own unholy alliance. The only benefit the lad had was that he was now better fed than he had been in the workhouse and had grown taller, heavier, and stronger. It was obvious that the boy's spirit had been broken by a lifetime of ill usage.

Pompey had always really known that he and Violet could have no future in Africa. They were not of Africa and would never be accepted into the life of any African tribe. On their first night aboard ship, they talked long into the night. Blissfully they were unaware of what Samuel had planned for Violet, and the two young people were free to mourn his passing as their great friend with genuine sorrow. After a night of deep discussion, Pompey and Violet decided that it would be best to go to England where no Fugitive Slave Law could threaten Pompey's freedom. Pompey and Violet decided to settle in the Westmorland country in a quiet place not far from Miss Sally Beers. Their gold could insulate them there from the brutal realities of their former lives.

Nothing more was heard of Whitehouse after his being sold along with his crew to the slave traders in the area far to the North, in the Sudan. Siliva expressed the opinion to the others of his tribe that Whitehouse himself, being so old, and a mute at that, could not fetch more than a few shillings at auction. Perhaps he would be refused altogether as suitable merchandise and end up on the streets of Khartoum as a beggar. "The rest of Whitehouse's crew should bring a tidy sum," said Siliva who was anticipating the day when he too would come of age and be allowed to take a wife. This would be a day of great rejoicing.

Siliva found himself on the night of Atachawayo's funeral on top of a hill overlooking Atachawayo's grave. The young warrior looked down in the full light of the moon on the great chief's resting place. There was nobody about to hear him as he looked back to heaven and addressed the moon in all the majesty of its full brightness overhead in the African sky. "Hear me my brother," cried Siliva over the grave of his kinsman. "Hear me for I am your brother of battle. I am Siliva of your own clan and of the Matabele Zulu. Let me tell you mighty Atachawayo how you will extend your life beyond this little piece of earth that gives you rest here under this moon. When I am old enough, I shall take a wife. I shall dance and sway opposite she who will be my bride and who will come to me in joy and into my bed in my wedding Kraal. I shall put my seed into this Matabele woman, and in the greatest of pleasure we shall take with each other we will make a man-child to take your place among us. He shall be the spiritual son of your clan blood. This I do promise you Atachawayo. I promise you that I shall give you life again my brother and uncle in my son. You shall live again in him. I will dance in joy in the moment of your resurrection among your people Atachawayo when my wife gives birth to that life which shall be yours. And I will at the same time do my duty for my clan, king, and country in the life of this man child."

Here Siliva stopped for a time and stared at a star that seemed to flicker distantly in the sky far away from the moon's light. Siliva knew that this blinking point of light was Atachawayo's soul approving of his oath. Again Siliva looked down on Atachawayo's resting place and breathed deeply into his lungs the night cooled African air. Siliva stood erect sucking that air deeply into his lungs again before continuing his prayer to this favorite ancestor. Every part of his being felt a tingling sensation as life seemed to surge through him with a renewed vigor.

Siliva lifted his face again to the flickering star that seemed to hold communion with him. Siliva held his hands up to the star and cried out, "I shall take care Atachawayo not to go hunting alone in the future. This I promise you. I shall also honor you each day my good uncle and brother of battle for the gift of my life. Be witness to my words you stars that I shall honor Atachawayo's memory for all of my life. I shall hold it sacred until the day I draw my last breath for I hold that very gift of breath from him. It was Atachawayo who has saved me from the horrible fate of being a slave in a land far from this place of my people. Atachawayo, you have told me of that brutal life in America where even great chiefs can be beaten and made to do all kinds of low work in exchange for bad food and those beatings from low men who would have power over even a Matabele man and prince. For that great mercy of my salvation you have given me by restoring my life and my freedom, I shall name my firstborn son for you. That life will be yours. And when my son is born, I will lift him high above my head to the heavens for you to see. And I shall say to all of our gods, 'This is my son. He is Atachawayo who lives again in this body! This boy, this Matabele boy is named for the great warrior who has saved me and all of my posterity for all the time to come. He lifted me up in my time of deepest trouble. Yes this is he, Atachawayo in the flesh and spirit together. This is Atachawayo, who now lives again. This man-child is to be a great man of the nation of 'The People Blessed by Heaven.' Behold him you gods and stars! My son is Atachawayo who breathes the free air of Africa. He is the son of Siliva. He will grow into a mighty Matabele warrior! My son Atachawayo will be a brave, mighty, and good man. He will be the greatest of all hunters of lions and defender of The Children of Heaven."

CPSIA information can be obtained at www.ICGtesting.com
Printed in the USA
BVOW020318221111

276686BV00001B/1/P